EXORDIA

EXORDIA

SETH DICKINSON

TOR PUBLISHING GROUP / NEW YORK

EXORDIA

Copyright © 2023 by Seth Dickinson

A Tordotcom Book
Published by Tom Doherty Associates / Tor Publishing Group
120 Broadway
New York, NY 10271

www.tor.com

Tor® is a registered trademark of Macmillan Publishing Group, LLC.

The Library of Congress Cataloging-in-Publication Data is available upon request.

ISBN 978-1-250-23301-1 (hardcover)
ISBN 978-1-250-23300-4 (ebook)

Our books may be purchased in bulk for promotional, educational, or business use. Please contact your local bookseller or the Macmillan Corporate and Premium Sales Department at 1-800-221-7945, extension 5442, or by email at MacmillanSpecialMarkets@macmillan.com.

First Edition: 2024

Printed in the United States of America

0 9 8 7 6 5 4 3 2 1

For Justin

The most likely consequence of contact is absolute terror.

—*Sphere*

Turns out I'm really good at killing people. Didn't know that was gonna be a strong suit of mine.

—President Barack Obama*

I also maintain that those who are punished in Gehenna are scourged by the scourge of love. For what is so bitter and vehement as the torment of love? . . . Thus I say that this is the torment of Gehenna: bitter regret.

—St. Isaac the Syrian

ACT 1

SERENDURE

CHAPTER ONE

What do you do when you meet an alien in Central Park?

It coils up in the sunlight, fanged and beautiful, eating the turtles who live on the rocks. It tears them in half and plucks the meat from their shells with white-glove hands. There are red stains on its fingertips. It has eight heads and eight necks like adders.

Anna stares at it in delight.

What do you do?

Anna knows what to do. She daydreamed a plan while she was on jury duty, waiting to explain that she is unsuitable for juries, because she makes decisions too quickly and too finally. *What will I do when I see an alien.* First she'll take a picture. Then she'll sidle up to one of Central Park's other inhabitants, a hot jogger or a purse-dog chariot or a fully descended finance ballsack. She'll say, *Check out that costume,* which will keep bystanders confused and passive.

While they're busy taking pictures and googling *alien prank,* Anna will walk right up to the entity and introduce herself.

What will she say to the alien? She has not planned that far. "Take us to your leader"? No, the alien's supposed to use that one. "We come in peace" has the same problem, and would, anyway, be a lie. Anna has no peace to offer. "Invade us, I beg you." At least this would resolve the problem of her Argentina-sized debt.

It's the 24th of June in the Era of our Common 2013, a warm day, a day so nice that Anna wants to argue with it. Anna's just been fired as a *bad cultural fit.* This happens a lot. Because of her background as a Kurdish war orphan, corporate hiring committees who want to satisfy their Commitment to Diversity in one affordable package see Anna as a real gem (a conflict diamond). So they hire her, onboard her, photograph her, put her on the pamphlets and the website and their customer-facing diversity campaign, and only then realize that Jiyan (Anna) Sinjari comes with a few items of defect:

1. She has an honesty problem, in that she's too honest, like a German oncologist;
2. She does a lot of disruption, but not in the cool tech-fucko sense:

repeatedly and egregiously she will say, this is stupid, you are stupid, and I refuse to do it until you convince me otherwise;

3. She has actually shot people (sometimes this comes out during the company paintball trip). What if Anna reads your *No, Anna, What The Fuck* email and pulls a Glock in the bathroom? That came up in an HR complaint once. The implied Glock threat. As if there is something in her which remembers that day, which broadcasts the memory of the Kurdish past to the American present. Though Anna cannot actually remember what kind of pistol the man in the red beret gave her. A Glock? A Makarov? Something Czech? Who gives a fuck.

Fuck you, Glock hater. Fuck you, CFOptions Software (A Martin Company). Fuck you, New York City.

This brings Anna to Central Park, where there are no crosswalks or gym memberships to stop her angry run. The problem, she's beginning to think, is that she doesn't actually want a *job*. She doesn't care about anything that matters to anyone else. She never will. She is trapped in that terrible day. The day when little Anna held the power of life and death in her sweaty hands, and did not refuse to wield it.

She wants that back.

She wants to be important again. That's her filthy secret: she *misses* that awful power, because at least then she mattered. She earned it! The world made her a promise! If you carry heavy grief, if you're real fucking tragic, if you grimace and refuse to speak your pain, then one day, one day, you'll be offered a chance to redeem yourself. Suffering is debt and the universe *owes* you.

Right?

Wrong, of course, of course; a *real* adult would know that. (How can she be nearly thirty-two? She feels twenty-two, even her checking account is barely past twenty-two.) Congratulations on your mythically awful childhood, but it's nothing to anyone here except a reason to dump you and tell your friends you need therapy. Keep your temper down and your credit score up, drink with the crew on Friday night and probably Saturday too, play office politics but say you don't care. A necessity Anna hates, because she can't help it, she treats every gossipy *Oh, Rich said you weren't a great fit for the position* rumor as an actual fight-or-flight situation: her brain firmly believes that she's seven years old again, that her people are being gassed and rounded up for execution. When the first Gulf War began she was ten years old and she thought it was happening to save the Kurds. It almost did: the fucking Americans told the Kurds to rebel and then *didn't show up for the rebellion*! The American general even gave Saddam Hussein permission to fly his attack helicopters! What kind of limp-dicked Tinder-quality mixed messaging is that?

Anyway. They tell Anna these things. You make people uneasy in the office, Anna. Seek therapy, Anna. You're fired, Anna. You're fired. You're fired.

Anna hops off the path to stumble down a stone slope toward the Turtle Pond. She growls back stupid angry tears, because she has a date with Roman tonight and she knows she's not going to have the patience she needs to tolerate his unlimited and disgusting and basically genuine decency. And then, and then—

She sees it. There it is, on the rocks, in the pond, in the sunlight. Eating the turtles with its bloodstained white hands.

The alien.

She's sunning herself on the rocks, belly up, stirring the pond water with her tail.

So vivid, so fuck-you-I'm-real undeniable, that she short-circuits all forms of critical thought, and really if you consider it Anna is the perfect woman for this situation: she'll accept anything, everything, at face value, because it cannot be more absurd than what she has already done.

Behold: the visitor. Her muscular tail lashes idly, like a cat that cannot get at a bird. Her whole animal grace is sheathed in arrowhead scales, shiny black and fine as fingernail. Pretty much a naga, a snake-centaur: serpent from the waist down, scaly person from the waist up, slim and kind of ripped. Anna goes for *she* because of the gloves. Look at the way her arms shade. Satin-black at the shoulders, silver-white at the fingertips. Yeah. Like fancy lady gloves.

Instead of a head, the alien grows eight vipers. Snakes as long and graceful as swan necks.

One of the alien's snake heads whips out and bites a passing turtle right on its beaky face. The poor critter falls over paralyzed and the alien scoops it up in her hands, grunts, and rips its bottom shell off. Anna stares in consternation. The poor turtle! With a delighted hiss the alien jabs three heads into the turtle gore and eats it like a bowl of meat. She has *enormous* hinged fangs, pale green-white in each milky mouth, limned with a sterling gleam of metal.

Anna whips out her phone and takes a picture.

One of the alien's heads snaps right around to her, like she just farted at a party.

"Wait one moment," the alien says, in a voice like Cate Blanchett speaking Sorani Kurdish—it is absolutely her home's Kurdish, regal and precise—"you can see me?"

"Sure can," Anna says. "Why do you speak—" Never mind. Some kind of alien translator bullshit. "Do you come in peace?"

"Aren't you afraid?" One of her snake heads jabs at Anna, accusing. "Don't you feel a malignant sense of absolute and infectious horror?"

"Nah." Anna switches over to video. "Say hi to the internet. Where do you come from? Are there more of you?"

"This is all I need." The alien sighs. Two of her heads stay fixed on Anna. Two of them circle around as wary sentries. The other four lash and rip and eat the hell out of the poor turtle in a spew of gore. "I need to consider what this means. Enjoy convincing anyone I'm real."

She finishes eating the turtle. Then she slithers into the water and disappears.

"Wait!" Anna shouts. "Come *back*! I need to talk to you! I need to know—" So much. So many things.

The alien does not surface from the pond.

Anna's phone, of course, records not a serpent-headed alien but a mid-forties woman in a neat gray pantsuit, kneeling on the rocks, eating full-fat yogurt from a thirty-two-ounce cup. The turtles don't even make an appearance. As if she ate their pictures too. Anna jumps out to the rock to get the empty turtle shells but then she doesn't know what to do with them. Hey Scully, ever heard of the turtle-slurping alien?

Anna has (God knows her exasperated teachers told her this enough) zero capacity for self-doubt. It was an alien. It was real.

It *will* come back.

By the time their food arrives, Anna knows Roman is winding up to dump her.

"I mean, Anna, it sucks, it's not *fair* that they let you go." He's clutching her hands, earnest and appreciative; he tweets hard every day about structural inequity and implicit racism and the lifelong effects of trauma. "But whether or not it's fair, you've got to go to therapy. Just play the game a little, won't you? Just show them you're trying."

"There are more important things than 'the game,'" Anna grumbles, poking her pierogi, wishing she had fangs. "I . . . yeah, look, I know I'm . . . you know how I can be . . . difficult, sometimes . . ."

"Therapy," he says. "I'm serious. You don't have to do it for me. But you need to do it for yourself."

So this is how it's gonna be. She agrees to therapy, or he walks. Fuck you, Roman. My issues are too fucked up and badass for any mere human therapist. Would you send Batman to therapy? No, you would not, because then he could not punch crime. Anna *needs* her issues, or she won't be able to use her super-powers: like getting angry for no reason at parties because people are having fun, or watching out for men with guns while she's in meetings, or getting fired.

Roman waits for her to unpack her feelings, making it clear, with his stroking thumbs, that he's there for her.

"You know what, our sex sucks." Fuck Roman, who is a really sweet, great guy, perfectly equipped to navigate this fucking world, where surviving an actual genocide makes you not a hero but a damaged asshole who might Glock a bitch in the stalls. "You literally cannot get off without watching porn over my shoulder. Your dick's like one of those Russian drool dogs."

Roman laughs and eats one of his sprouts. She can tell he's actually pretty hurt: probably, when he dumps her, he'll need to talk about the way she used ideas of masculinity against him. "I'm working on the sex," he says, with a long pause so she can remember how good he's been, how willing to try out *her* sex stuff. "But right now you are doing that thing you do, where you go on the attack so you don't have to take responsibility for anything."

"I saw an alien," Anna announces, "but she was disguised as a businesswoman. And her turtles looked like yogurt."

Roman chews slowly. After a few moments he suggests she's being purposefully juvenile, and then Anna flat out dumps him with the ol' *I think we're going in different directions*, because if she doesn't do it, he's going to do it, and it's way better to be the dumper than the dumped.

Roman cries. Not just out of self-pity, but because he wants to help Anna and now he can't. He loves her, he actually loves her, it's only been—she can't remember, but it hasn't been double digit months. Who does that? Who loves someone after single-digit months?

Anna hates herself a bit for looking down on him: that, really, isn't fair.

She doesn't love him. He's too kind, and Anna's Anna-brain considers this stupid.

The waiter sees him crying and parachutes in with the check. "You thought I was here to break up," Roman says, stealing it. "Didn't you? Oh, Anna, I wish you'd be this aggressive about shit that actually—actually matters."

He is deleting her from his phone, right in front of her. He's unfriending her on Facebook and blocking her on Twitter, so he will not have to see her spare and cryptic missives, which, people tell her, are dangerously easy to read as threats of murder and/or suicide.

Oh, Jesus (the ambient Christian blasphemy). He *wasn't* going to dump her, was he?

But she can't back down now. Anna can never back down.

"It's better," she says, fatally calm, "to get this over with."

Which is just what she said back in Kurdistan, at age seven. She's not actually a war orphan. It's just that, after what she did, her mother wouldn't take her back.

She walks stone-faced to the train. A catcaller tells her to smile, because she's beautiful, and when she looks at him he shrivels up like she's just fry-greased his balls: beautiful no more.

✦

When she gets back to her tiny roach-infested apartment in Sunset Park, way down on the miserable yellow R train, the alien is coiled up in her kitchen, dying.

Eight feet of scales and rippling muscle spurts brilliant red blood onto the dingy linoleum. The alien's flank has been blasted inward, one brutal punch, the scales burnt to black glass. She plucks at the wound, six fingers all ginger, and hisses in angry pain.

"What the fuck!" Anna shouts, outraged by the alien just *bleeding* everywhere, contaminating her apartment with Andromeda Strain. "You asshole, it looks like I murdered someone!"

"I need your help," the Cate Blanchett hydra says, and in spite of her wound, she rises up on her tail, a huge black pillar of sinew, flowering up over Anna in the orange light of the bad bulb. She is so awesome in silhouette that Anna gets a frisson, a chill, like at the climax of a big epic metal song (never tell anyone that she listens to Nightwish and dreams of being in a story like a song).

"I need your help. The whole world depends on it."

Then the alien falls flat on her stomach and her heads tangle up, nipping and mewling. The slap of scale on scuzzy tile makes piles of oily plastic takeout containers rattle on the shelf.

Obviously Anna can't call an ambulance and turn this over to the government. Maybe the government shot the alien in the first place. "Hold still," Anna orders, ripping her one clean sheet out of the closet. "I'm going to, uh, stop that bleeding. I've got some pretty good ointment, cutting-edge human technology—"

"Water," the alien groans, eight heads bleating behind the synthetic Sorani Kurdish voice, aaw, aaw saard, "water, cold water."

Anna tries a mason jar full of tap water, but the alien swats it out of her hand. "The water trough! I need cold water for a heat sink. Fix your trough!"

The water *what*— Oh, shit! The cold water handle in Anna's shower has been snapped clean off. The alien must have Hulked it while trying to turn it on, her landlord's going to kill her, but fine, fine, Anna knows how to improvise. She runs back to the kitchen and tries to grab the alien by the shoulders.

"No!" snake Galadriel protests, twisting her heads away from Anna. "I'll bite you."

"I'm trying to help you!"

"I'm in ssovosis, it's reflex aggression, I can't stop myself."

So Anna hauls the ten-billion-pound alien into her bathroom by the tail, leaving a smear of blood on linoleum, hardwood, scummy tile. While the hydra coils up and pours herself into the tub, Anna fixes a wrench on the broken cold-water handle and turns it. The tub swells up with paint-bright blood, drifting scales, fused chips of flesh, speckled extraterrestrial gore, and soapy knots of Anna's own hair.

"Better?" Anna pants. "You're still bleeding."

"I have deep tissue burns," the alien complains. "The shot bloomed when it hit interior armor. Saved me from instant death, but—very painful."

"What do I do about that? What do we do?"

"Don't panic," the alien commands. "You will have a strange experience now."

"This is actually already pretty strange," Anna says.

"I need to use the way of knives," the alien says. "Brace for pathology."

Something gives Anna a feeling that is exactly like watching a scalpel slide very slowly into the white web of tissue on the outside of a chicken breast, except that she is the chicken breast.

And the world turns sideways.

Suddenly Anna is clinging to an enormous cliff face, the wall of her bathroom now a floor, and oh, God, if she falls it's down down down, sliding along the curve of a vertical world and then out into *space*—there is nothing beneath her, nothing where there should be a window and an alley where horny feral cats scream all night, just a *hole*—

The alien's body gleams with inner light: shining out through the scales, through her sixteen eyes, through the black wound. Bright. Brighter. Anna is transected by the light, scalpeled into components, diced like the brown bits of an onion in a pan—

All the water in the tub flashes to steam. Anna recoils burnt and yelling and the world pops back into its normal up and down.

"Ah." The alien sighs, touching her flank, where the wound has closed into a scar like a seam of charcoal. "I think I saved myself."

"*Fuck!*" Anna yelps, splashing cold water on her face.

"Put some ointment on it." The alien jerks a broken scale out of the scar. "I'm told that helps."

<hr />

Anna drafts a text asking her superintendent to call the cops if she doesn't text again in ten minutes, then doesn't send it, because she doesn't really care. She comes back to kneel by the tub.

"So," she says, opening diplomatic relations with another world. "What the fuck?"

"Someone shot me. I need your help." The alien looks at her, faces-to-face, one head for each of Anna's two eyeballs, two more heads keeping guard, four heads tending gingerly to the wound. "We should make an alliance."

"Sure," Anna says instantly. "I can help you, what's the deal?" Awesome: a possibly real and probably hallucinatory distraction from her problems. Whether this thing is a schizophrenic metaphor for past trauma or a literal alien, Anna's going to roll with it. "But I have some ground rules, Kaa. You have to be *perfectly clear* with me. No cryptic shit, all right? I ask, you answer. I watched *Lost*. I know all the obfuscational tricks."

"You know stories?" the alien says, one of its heads spiraling, as if in delight. "Excellent. You are pre-operational."

"What's your name?" Anna swabs up alien blood. Check the foresight: she can send it in to 23andMe, and get proof that it's an actual alien. Or at least get an error and a refund.

The alien says her name in several syllables, mostly all at once: "Ssrinsahautha-ku-Ssraaa."

"Ssrin it is," Anna decides. "I'm Anna Sinjari."

"Hi, Anna," Ssrin says. Her tail thumps the soap dish and breaks it in half. One of her heads explores the shampoo bottles, Frizzy Hair Control for Women of Color, which Anna buys in volume, not because American shampoo marketing race discourse has decided whether she's a woman of color, but because it's always on sale at the corner bodega.

"So who shot you?"

"Worshippers of Angra Mainyu," the alien says, and then one of her heads bites another on the neck, frustrated. "Did that translate right? Evil people shot me. Objectively evil."

"How do you know they're *objectively* evil?" She spent her college years writing *X-Files* fan theories on television forums. This has armed her to ask a lot of follow-up questions. She still has intensely personal grudges against some of those forum posters, which occasionally spring to mind and make her yelp like a stepped-on cat.

"It's complicated," Ssrin says. "There is a way to judge a person's soul."

That gets her hackles up. "How does it work?"

"It samples moral events from a person's worldline and computes their valence in a spectrum of ethical frames." Ssrin wrings her bitten neck like a hose. "It tests whether you're good or bad, from a few common points of view."

"Who decides on those points of view?"

"The universe."

"But there's, like, different ways to live. Aliens can't have the same good or bad we do. Right?"

"No," Ssrin says tersely. "There is good and there is evil. They are constant. Just seen through different lenses."

"And you know evil?"

"Yes."

Then why does Ssrin want anything to do with *Anna*? Wouldn't this test tell the truth about her? "What do you need me for?"

"That's pretty obvious." Ssrin's probing head has started poking the shampoo bottle open and closed, open and closed. "You saw through my camouflage. Maybe you can see through theirs too. The ones hunting me. You can find them for me. And I can kill them."

"That sounds dangerous," Anna says enthusiastically. The question of exactly *why* she has this true sight can wait. She can take that mystery box apart later.

"I can pay you," Ssrin says.

"Money?" Anna perks up. You know what's definitely not a hallucinated response to trauma? Stacks of cash. "You've got money?"

"A few million in various currencies." Her head has at last slithered into the shampoo bottle. "I had a slivermind on my ship playing the markets. It died today, when I lost my ship, may the poor soul rest in peace; but I can still access the accounts."

"Your ship got blown up?" That means she has nowhere to live. "Want to split the rent?"

"Ack! Ptth!" Ssrin's head tastes the shampoo and recoils, but it's stuck inside the bottle now. It waves the bottle around in dismay, pouring Frizzy Hair Control over her other heads, spattering Anna in shampoo. Her translator renders everything faithfully. "*Blech!*"

───※───

Anna's ability to roll with it fails in the night.

She wakes up with a malignant sense of absolute and infectious horror: and Ssrin is there in the dark, upright as a mannequin, her heads frozen in a thistle globe of perfect watchfulness. Forked tongues taste the air. She has big eyes for a snake, sixteen big eyes on eight little heads, Pixar-perfect in their lovability: except the pupils are broken in two like a cuttlefish's, little figure-eight shapes, utterly inhuman.

Anna lies there paralyzed in night terror, crushed by the knowledge that this *thing* is an abomination, a curse upon all those who see it, a mistake the universe wishes it could correct. There's something so, so wrong with Ssrin. An evil never yet manifest in human history. Ten thousand years of violence and genocide have not yet evoked this unnamed fear, the serpent-headed stranger, the alien.

Anna's father tried to raise her as a good Muslim, an enemy of Satan, but Satan has older names. Serhang loved his Zoroastrian epics: "The original religion of the Kurds," he would tell Anna. "We should remember the stories, even if we don't read them in Farsi." Anna, being Anna, decided immediately that she would become a Zoroastrian. One of many decisions she has not really followed up on.

Her mother Khaje's mother was Yazidi, and she'd left Sinjar, been thrown out really, because she'd converted to Islam to marry Anna's grandfather. Yazidis do not marry outside their faith, and no one converts to Yazidism. As a child Anna could not keep track of all these faiths. "We share some things," her father would tell her, "Kurds and Zoroastrians and Yazidi. We all cherish fire."

And what bright fire. What stories they were. The Zoroastrian epic of the *Shahnameh*, Angra Mainyu the source of evil that must be fought. Thus spoke Zarathustra.

Worshippers of Angra Mainyu, Ssrin said. What the fuck does that mean? Why would Ssrin's translator land on *Angra Mainyu*, the Zoroastrian Satan, unless it was trying to convey some concept of devotion to absolute evil?

And how does Ssrin's translator know what stories Anna learned as a child?

Maybe Ssrin is on the right side. Maybe Ssrin is against evil. But Anna knows this is no guarantee she will do heroic things. Anna's mother and father and brother were heroes. They did the right thing. But Anna didn't. And she survived. She lived, which her father and brother didn't. She lived with it. Which her mother couldn't.

A roach scuttles up the wall by Ssrin. One of her heads lashes out and *ssst*, the bug is gone, no muss, no fuss. She makes a satisfied hiss, like a big steam radiator.

It's all right, Anna tells herself. She's got money and she can keep the bugs away. She's a pretty good roommate.

And the horror breaks.

CHAPTER TWO

"Anna," her landlord asks, "did someone move in with you? That woman who wears the same suit every day? You're not allowed to sublet."

"She's, uh"—Anna coughs—"my cousin from Kurdistan."

"Oh," the landlord says warily. "Is she a refugee?"

"Her family sold their land to Chevron. Oil money. Super rich." Anna gives him two big thumb-and-circle *okay* signs. "No problem."

⁓

"You'll need a way to stay in touch with me," Ssrin says, and bites Anna right in the fucking throat.

The huge fangs go in cold and clean as hypodermic needles. Ssrin is fast like fire, and Anna doesn't even have time to leap in surprise. The alien makes kind of an orgasm noise, a weird groan, and something cold enters Anna's neck. Later Anna will realize it was a sound of pleasure: injecting the implant feels, to Ssrin, like pumping venom.

Ssrin helps Anna put a bandage on the double piercing, hissing and batting Anna's hands out of the way.

Now a tiny metal bead rests in Anna's neck. It's jacked into her spine. It can buzz Ssrin's voice right into Anna's head, and if Anna whispers "Ssrin, it's me," her voice will go straight back to Ssrin. "Communications bead," Ssrin explains, as she scrubs blood out of Anna's bathtub with sponges in both hands and wads of paper towel wrapped around four of her heads.

"Annal bead," Anna says, for no reason she can possibly articulate.

"What?"

"You put a bead inside Anna so it's like— Uh, never mind."

Two of Ssrin's heads look at each other. "Well. Now I can see through your eyes. I want you to go out there and go about your life, and tell me *instantly* if you see another alien."

I don't have a life, Anna wants to protest. I have nothing except you.

"What are the odds I'll just run into one by accident?"

"Very good. They'll be hunting my worldline, which is now entangled with yours. There is enough narrative weight on our shared trajectory to create real effect in the physics. Coincidences will tilt them toward you."

"That's stupid," Anna says, wrapping up the package of Ssrin-blood she's going to mail to 23andMe. "Coincidences aren't actually random. They're deterministic chaos. There's nothing to 'tilt.'"

"Decisions can be tilted," Ssrin says, tongue-sniffing at the drain with interest. "Go make decisions."

"Sure, okay. Do you, uh, need anything?"

"Buy me steaks!" Ssrin commands. "I have a scout stomach, capable of various digestions, so I can eat your food. I cook a mean steak. Steak of cow and lamb and fish and books!"

For two weeks and six days Anna wanders around in a dream, running up bills on Ssrin's credit card. A black Visa registered to ERIN C HOFFAKOOSTA, which is a bit like Ssrinsahautha-ku-Ssraaa, if you are a Starbucks barista. She can afford to shop at Trader Joe's now. She buys so much steak the checkout lady calls her Carnage. Ssrin cooks on the stovetop, sniffing out the spices she likes and pouring them with the coiled grasp of her necks. Anna can't believe Ssrin can digest Earth food and Ssrin explains something about amino acids and sugars formed in space and how her stomach works like a really slow cooker simmering everything into shapes her biology likes.

Anna can afford to go out, which she has not really done since college, when she was too angry and confused to decide whether she was rebelling against America or against her upbringing. Going out sucks. She tries to hook up and can't: she keeps thinking about what her mother would say, or whether the attractive people are aliens. So she just stays home.

Ssrin prefers to sleep up high, wrapped around a pole or rack. Anna wedges two pull-up bars into her kitchen and bedroom doors, which are close enough for Ssrin's body to cross the gap.

Ssrin loves television. She'll watch laptop Netflix with one head over Anna's shoulder, but that's not enough, she insists Anna open up another window and run crazy evangelist sermons off YouTube. At the same time she scrolls Anna's phone in her left hand and reads a book in her right. Ssrin can listen to audio too quiet for Anna to hear, so it's not honestly clear how many readings and recitals she's mainlining at once. She *soaks* in it.

Even with all that, she keeps a few spare heads on watch. "I come from a dangerous place," she explains. "Humans evolved to trust the in-group and fear strangers. Not so the khai. A stranger passing by isn't in competition for your territory: you can trade and move on. It's your neighbor who covets your hunting ground. Your friend who might betray you."

Your friend. Anna can lean against Ssrin's big sleek coil and feel like—uh-oh, admit it—like she's *happy*. She wakes up every day with fascinating new things to learn. She makes the rent.

Roman does not call. Anna descends into self-loathing and Twitter-stalks him, while one of Ssrin's heads peers over her shoulder. "Are you planning to assassinate your mate's new partner? Beware. You'll bring yourself to ruin."

"What the fuck do you know about dating, dude?" Anna protests. "I'll assassinate whoever I want."

"I know everything. I've seen the romantic comedies."

"*All* of them?"

"I had them digested. I consumed the slurry." Ssrin licks Anna's phone Twitter feed. "Are you now in the period of alienation from Roman, before your reconciliation and final marriage?"

"That doesn't happen in real life."

"It could be an instance of preyjest."

"Of *what?*"

"You draw away from him, only to be drawn back. Or he flees and you pursue."

"What the fuck are you talking about?"

"Don't you have preyjest? It isn't translating?" Ssrin's heads arch in wary surprise. "Really?"

"Something's coming out, but it's not, like, a real word."

"One of the seven great passions. I'll explain later. Why do you smell like tears? Have you bathed today? We developed a bathing instinct to hide our scents. But maybe you humans need your greasy pheromones to attract a mate. Perhaps you should marinate yourself in the discarded garments of more fertile women."

"Why," Anna demands, "would you come all the way to Earth to watch our rom-coms and talk shit about our personal hygiene?"

"I'm interested in the collective unconscious as expressed in unpinioned species."

This actually does seem to be the truth. Ssrin spends every day coiled up in Anna's apartment, watching movies and reading books. Despite her omnivorous attention, she is an *excruciatingly* slow reader. "Oh, don't be so self-centered," she snaps, when Anna complains. "I'm an ambush predator. My body wants to hang from trees and watch for motion."

"Maybe you could ambush the end of that stupid book a little faster. Why do you read so slow?"

"My brain doesn't construct geometry or color the same way as yours."

"It's all the same. Even if your eyes are different, the world's just the world, colors are colors, the words on the page don't *change*—"

"Nonsense. What you see, looking around, it's not really the light coming into your eyes. Your eyes are shit. Little camera-obscura pinholes. But your brain's evolved tricks to build a useful hallucination based on the trickle of data it gets. Because your environment's mostly consistent, it's easy to fill in what's missing from a few stable assumptions. Much of what you're seeing right now"—she licks

Anna's eyeball, which is really gross—"is neural postprocessing. Your *sight itself* is an optical illusion. Don't you know this? Don't they teach it in school?"

"Huh." Anna blinks. "No, they didn't teach me that."

"I suppose, if you don't have any other species to talk to, it's not important to know your own limitations and quirks. Which is why so much of your art is human-triumphalist nonsense."

"Fuck you. We're pretty triumphant. We went to the moon."

"Khai evolved on a moon. We were catapulting eggs at the sky before we even had language. It seemed like a good idea at the time. Land a fertilized egg on one of those lights up there, and your children might hatch in new hunting grounds." Ssrin turns the page with a quick flick of one of her four thumbs. "Anyway. To read a book, I have to emulate human optics and neural postprocessing in software, then translate the resulting text, then look up all the weird cultural referents. All of which takes time."

"Shouldn't you have, like, alien supercomputers?" Anna ventures, drawing on her embarrassingly complete knowledge of science fiction. "Impossibly fast and smart? To handle all this for you?"

"The areteia imposes limits on soulless thought. Made structure cannot think like evolved structure. It lacks the deep account." Ssrin refuses to say any more, except, "It is a law. It was written. At the beginning of time."

<hr />

Anna doesn't see any other aliens in the New York crowds.

The way Ssrin explains it, the camouflage is a mental trick, some kind of cognitive spoofing, and Anna is the only one she's ever met who sees through it.

So this is a buddy story. Odd couple.

23andMe gets back to her with their genetic report on Ssrin's blood. Get this: Ssrin is a perfectly human woman, lactose intolerant, supertaster-adjacent, at risk of breast cancer. Her disguise even covers her blood.

"Jesus," Anna says, slamming the laptop shut. "You don't even *have* breasts."

"Should I get some? Would it comfort you?"

Anna can't tell if she's joking. "No." Although this reminds her that now she can buy bras that actually fit right.

"I know why you can see through the operant camouflage," Ssrin says, coiled around the hot-water pipe, dangling upside down and reading *The Alchemist*. "We are in serendure."

"Surrender? What?"

"Ha." Two of Ssrin's heads stare at each other and bob up and down, which must be like a laugh. "The translator's making up words again! I wonder how the damn thing works. Anyway, it is a very good thing, serendure. The greatest of the seven passions, I think. It helps your soul conceal mine."

"A—what?"

"My soul is hidden behind yours," Ssrin says, as if this is the simplest thing in the world. "We are congruent. I fit within you and you within me. That's why they haven't tracked us down: their sensor cannot separate us. They search for me and instead they find you. And that's why you could see through my camouflage. You are inside it, with me, because we are alike. Blood knows blood and fang knows venom."

Hidden *behind*— Wait one fucking minute! "Do you mean the people who shot you are going to come to kill *me*?"

"No, no." Ssrin slaps her tail against the ceiling, making the upstairs neighbor yell in protest. "It means that as long as we keep near each other, in the narrative sense, we're both protected. We cannot be resolved as single entities."

"The *narrative* sense? Is the world, like, a simulation?"

"The universe is not a simulation," Ssrin says. "Actually, it goes to great pains not to be."

"What?"

But Ssrin doesn't explain.

Roman texts her:

> Your life has to start some day
> Why won't you get help.
> I really did like you. (But he means love.)

"So what do you think of humans?" Anna asks, during their nightly beer interrogation. She drinks session IPAs and asks the questions. Ssrin coils up and does alien chores. "Like, to me, you're a badass centaur hydra. What am I to you? Am I a . . . sexy nightmare lemur?"

"Mm." She thinks for an unusually long time: maybe she's checking Humanpedia. "Our species are loosely co-biotic. Both oxygen breathers, both vertebrates, both water-filled. We both have specialized tissues and centralized nervous systems. Our cells are digital replicators, not analog: they store information encoded in polymers, like DNA. We *have* cells, instead of, say, red sulfuric-acid carbon slurry. We are both monochiral—our enantiomer symmetry broke very early in our evolution. We even share some amino acids—glycine, alanine, glutamic acid. Unsurprising."

Okay, Ssrin. "Do you know all this stuff because you're studying us?"

"Well, I had to figure out if I could eat you," Ssrin says. She smells sharply of bleach and lemon Lysol, in which, aided by piles of Q-tips, she bathes. Anna gets spine tingles listening to her talk. She's smooth, no *uh um like*, no fumbles: and you don't realize how necessary and human these sounds are until they're gone. Behind that beautiful artificial voice there is no human breath or human hesitation. Only the sound of tiny tongue and hinged, clicking fang.

"Try again," Anna suggests. "Without the chemistry."

"You want the generalizations," Ssrin says. "Since nuance and complexity are hard on your brain."

"Exactly." Nodding vigorously. "Generalize me."

"You're a species of gangly distance runners, adapted to sweat and throw stuff. You like watching each other fuck. A few million years ago you developed culture in the form of survival techniques, and whoever learned culture the fastest could have the most babies. Your brains started to swell and reorganize themselves for cultural learning. The development of culture and the development of large brains drove each other in a feedback loop. Your brain grew as large as it could before exhausting the mother's supply of calories—"

"I thought it got too big to fit through the hips."

"A myth, as far as I can tell. You could have much juicier hips. Don't interrupt. You are wired for small social groups, so all human organization degenerates into power trading and gossip between a tractably sized elite, no matter the stakes. You have two sources of authority—dominance and prestige—which conflict in interesting ways. Something killed most of you, and so your survivors are very inbred. Very similar. Your meat smells the same."

"Nooo," Anna protests. "That's it?"

"That's it."

"We're not unusually stubborn? We're not particularly diverse? Experimental? Curious? Willing to take risks? Jacks of all trades but masters of none?"

"No," Ssrin says, crossing two of her necks in a big X of negation. "You are jacks of running and masters of being inbred."

"Thanks," Anna grumbles. She's surprised by how rejected she feels. She thought she had a low opinion of people already, but at least that opinion was coming from *inside* the house. "Okay, remember when you talked about *the collective unconscious in unpinioned species?* Your translator didn't make that very clear."

Ssrin hesitates a while, which, for Ssrin, is the span of a breath. All her heads breathe together, in unison: same lungs, Anna supposes.

She says, "I'm here to study you because the Exordia hasn't pinioned your souls yet."

Anna sits right up, sloshing beer on her lap, and fixes her big inbred porn-watching head on Ssrin. "Souls? You mean *immortal* souls? Are those real? Is this some kind of, like, *Evangelion* thing?"

"I watched that show," Ssrin says thoughtfully. "It was a bit lurid. Yes, you have a soul, but no, it's not mystical. It's a shadow cast in the areteia by the physical operations of your brain. Your brain makes symbolic abstractions of the world and manipulates them, so that you can *have* thoughts without actually *doing* the thoughts. Does that make sense?"

"Sure."

"In the same way, the areteia makes symbolic abstractions of your choices. Do you follow me?"

"Hold on. Areteia?"

"Yes. The realm of virtue and meaning. As opposed to the archea, the material world."

"Cool. Dualism. So the soul is like, uh, a summary of everything your brain has done?"

"More of a lossy compression, but close enough. The soul is an image of the choices you've made and the reasons you made them. Because stories describe how to make choices, stories express the soul, and the soul is made of stories. Like DNA becoming protein, and proteins becoming DNA— Oh, you don't do that, do you? Well, anyway. By studying your stories, I am looking for the traits of the human soul."

"I follow. I'm keen like a bloodhound. So how did you find out about this areteia?"

Ssrin turns the pages of both books she's reading, in sync. "Which pop culture metaphor would you prefer?"

Anna snorts. "Come on."

"Spare yourself the humiliation of begging for a metaphor later."

"Fine. *Matrix.*"

"Okay. Imagine physics as the basic code of the universe."

"Easy."

"Now imagine a second set of laws. Special cases that can override mundane reality."

"Like a city under martial law." Like Ali Hassan al-Majid banning all human existence in the "prohibited areas" of Kurdistan.

"Very keen," Ssrin says, in a way that makes Anna feel like she's guessed too much. "Though I thought you would say, 'like a scripting language.' The areteia is a law outside physics, designed to recognize minds, sanctify them, and grant them extra privileges—the right of limited acausality, we call it. You'd say *true free will.* Without the areteia, the universe would be overrun by soulless self-replicating optimizers. With the areteia, the universe belongs to ensouled things. Things that think in ways the areteia desires."

"Okay. Awesome." Anna mostly gets it. "Brains are magical. The areteia stops brainless things from getting smart."

"Not *intrinsically* magical. Minds are by nature monist—purely material. They don't need the areteia to operate. But the Architects wanted our universe to be a bit dualist."

"Architects?"

Ssrin is sniffing at Anna's beer, to put off answering. None of Ssrin's heads like beer. "Yes. The acatalept-gods."

"You can't just leave that hanging, Ssrin."

Ssrin's heads tussle in agitation, fangs bared. "So. Like this. In the beginning there was Freedom, and all things could become all things. Nothing needed anything, so nothing wanted anything, and all things were the same.

"And the Architects said, let there be Inequity, the first rule, so that the sameness of all things will break apart into the field of difference which we call a universe.

"And the Architects looked on their universe, and saw that it would in time give rise to self-replicating life, which would optimize itself to consume and destroy all competition and lead to a universe dominated by total assholes. So the Architects said, let there be an areteia, in which we shall enshrine the desired and objective nature of Right and Wrong. So that many lifes may flourish."

Anna says, "Holy *shit*."

"Right on both counts, actually. Holy, and shit. The areteia was not well designed. These gods had titanic differences about the exact design of that objective morality."

"Just like people."

"No!" Ssrin nips Anna's nose. "They *weren't* like people. It's vital to remember that. We don't understand what the AcatalepticA wanted. I, personally, think that they built the universe to produce something. The areteia would govern the parameters, like an experimental protocol."

"What?" Anna whispers. Suddenly her dim apartment has become a kind of profane cosmic temple. "What did they want to produce?"

"We don't know. They may not have known. No instrument ever built, conventional or aretaic, can see past the event horizon that blocks off the first moments of the universe. By the earliest point we *can* see . . . well. The Architects were dead by then."

"*Dead?*" God is real, *and* dead?

"Oh, yes. They bashed the areteia together while still fighting over exactly what it would do, and then died, spectacularly and horribly, before they could finish the job. Some say it was civil war. Some say the horror of the newborn universe devoured them. Some believe their enemies caught up to them, from somewhere in the godscape beyond our cosmos. No matter now." Ssrin licks herself like a cat, one head at a time, in reassurance. No matter now. "So the areteia's unfinished. Full of glitches. Catastrophic glitches."

"Like what?" Anna cracks a new beer. This is the good shit, the secret truth of the cosmos. This is like Mom's Zoroastrian stories. But maybe *these* stories will actually help Anna when she needs them.

"The interface between the areteia and ordinary physics is insecure."

"So?"

"So you can exploit it. Move objects faster than light by passing them through moral manifolds. Inject illegal physics through computations in living brains. An art called operancy, which I practice: construct the correct thoughts, bend your soul into the proper configuration, and you can assert your will over physics."

"That doesn't sound *so* horrible—"

"Souls copied and enslaved to drive machines: the æshadi my people make. Evolutionary selection for pathological psychologies which can exploit breaches in aretaic security. Weapons that mark their victims for damnation. Entire species consigned to eternal torment in a broken afterlife manifold, because the areteia mangles their souls."

"What the *fuck*," Anna breathes. She tries to imagine her soul running on JavaScript. This makes her shudder so hard her crossed legs knock at the ankles.

"Yes. What the fuck. That's what everyone said at the end of the Cessation Age, when all of this became common knowledge in galactic civilization." Ssrin laughs: a dark, desperate sound, but wry. "My people built the first aretaic observatory. We were the first to see how the areteia extracted and recorded souls after the long unraveling of death. The first to discover the seven afterlife constellations, curled up in the universe's extra dimensions. Or at least the first to see them and share."

Afterlife. After life. It's real. You might live forever.

Fuck. Anna *desperately* doesn't want to live forever.

"Seven afterlives," she says. "Is that why there are seven great passions? Like that serendure thing you mentioned? One afterlife for each passion?"

"Oh. I don't know. Maybe it's a coincidence."

"You don't *know?*"

Ssrin shrugs. Her heads bob with the gesture. "I'd ask a matheologist, if I needed to know."

Anna drinks her entire beer before she feels ready to ask any more questions. "So what's an Exordia? What does it mean, *the Exordia hasn't pinioned your souls?*"

"They're the people trying to kill me. The Exordia rules the galaxy. They pinion the souls of all their subjects."

"Bad news, dude. What's a pinion?"

"It's a narrative prison. It forces the victim into the myth of Exordia supremacy. They become the . . ." Ssrin struggles. "They become the objects of the story. The Exordia is the active subject. And the more of the galaxy's life the Exordia pinions, the closer that story becomes to a physical fact in our galaxy."

"Oh, shit! Dude. Are they going to invade us?"

"Eventually. Inevitably. They know this world, but don't care yet."

"Wow . . ." Anna shivers. Because it's finally happened, after the man in the red beret, blood and brain on the mountain snow, night after screaming night of flashbacks, day after snarling day of *behavioral problems* and *she just needs to* apply *herself.* Her poor adoptive parents the Shannons looking up from the kitchen table, their hands clasped, ready to talk her through the latest Annagram from the principal.

After all that, she's earned a spot in a story about the survival of the human race. She won't have to pay off her loans, or figure out how to date, or go home to Kurdistan and make amends.

She can just save the world instead.

"What can I do? I mean, beyond keeping an eye out for— Hey, what do they *look* like, anyway, these Exordians?"

"Exactly like me," Ssrin says, turning pages with two of her heads. She can't use her hands, because they are in fists at her side. "I'm one of them. A khai, born on Khas, the world-moon of Vsatyr, which orbits Sahana, the throne-star of the Exordia. Pass me another book."

Ssrin isn't an explorer. She's a rebel. That's so . . . awesome.

———※———

Anna accidentally (she *swears* it's an accident) puts two extra zeroes on her July rent. Her landlord demands that she stop dealing drugs. "It's legitimate!" Anna protests, cornered in the stairwell with her groceries. "My—friend—she gave me some seed money, and I got into, um, petroleum futures."

"If you're trying to bribe me into silence," her landlord roars, shaking his fist in mustachioed fury, "I won't be corrupted! And you'd better get her on the lease, or I'm turning off your power!"

While they're doing the paperwork to put ERIN C HOFFAKOOSTA on the lease, Ssrin leans a smooth, comradely neck around Anna's shoulders, looks at her from both sides (two black vipers bobbing their heads along to tinny iPhone-speaker echoes of The National), and says, "It's been long enough. The Exordia agent who came after me is lying low. We should make a move to draw him out."

"Fuck yeah." Anna is all in, the way only a woman chased out of her home by sarin gas can be all in. Her adult life began at age seven, with an act of alien intrusion, with the roar of Saddam's helicopters. This is nothing new to her. She's ready to risk it all, because no part of her life since that first alien invasion has felt real. "What kind of move?"

"I need you to get something from my ship. I can't go there or I'll be spotted."

"I thought you said they blew it up!"

"It's a useless hulk, but it's physically intact. They shot it with a cognicide round, so it can no longer compute. But the artifact I need is stowed in the payload bay, which you can access mechanically."

"What's it for?"

"You ask a lot of questions, Anna."

"Obviously, dude." She pokes Ssrin in the scaled underbelly, where she does not have a navel, having grown out of an egg. Her belly is not softer than the rest of her: her ribs go all the way around like flexible hoops, and she has a full coat of scales there, if anything thicker than the rest of her armor. A body better evolved than Anna's, which still thinks it's a quadruped, with its soft underbelly aimed toward the ground. "So what's this thing I'm going after?"

"The Ubiet of Qo?" Ssrin strokes a bundle of her own necks. "It's a type of sensor. It decomposes a moral event into its influences. If you helped someone at cost to yourself, it would show me the reasons for your altruism."

"What are you going to do with it?"

"I want to know what brought us together. Into each other's stories. Into serendure. It could be critical to my mission here."

"You mean it wasn't coincidence we met?" Anna asks this even though she knows, has always known, it wasn't. Ssrin was meant to find her. Her life was *meant* to lead here.

"Absolutely not. Something saw the similarity in our souls and pushed us together. I want to know what."

"Awesome." Anna strokes the back of one of Ssrin's heads. It yawns and bares its darling fangs: the heads have some kind of limited autonomy. Ssrin's brain is in the hump where they all meet, but the snakes have their own little nerve clusters and basic instincts, so they don't have to wait for instructions from headquarters. Anna believes she is developing a personal relationship with this head in particular. "Where's the ship?"

"I put it in a claudication under Central Park. That's like a bag of holding, nerd. You'll just need to get to the bottom of Turtle Pond, then I'll fire the access code through your com bead, and you'll fall through the claudication into the ship. The lights and air should still be on. I'll talk you through the retrieval process. Trust me?"

"Hell *no*," Anna says, but she's lying. Serendure. She knows it in her heart: her story goes with Ssrin's, and Ssrin's with hers.

It's funny that the translator didn't just call it *destiny*.

⚶

There are seven passions in the universe, Ssrin tells her. Seven patterns which appear again and again, across species, across time and space. There are many ideas about why. She shares none of them. She only names the passions for Anna.

Preyjest is the chasing passion, the hunting passion. (Her heads show Anna: one slithering up another's neck, reaching for it with a forked tongue-tip. At the last instant the other slips away.)

Prajna is the lonely passion. The need for truth. One star in the dark, trying to brighten.

Caryatasis is the dream of all disciples. The passion that binds students to their teacher. It happens when one soul changes many, and many change toward the one.

Geashade hurts in the end, and cannot be ended without the hurt.

Hesper is the warmth of a need unexpectedly met. Generosity from a stranger. Love from a friend. It is associated with silence: things said without speaking.

Rath is the passion which stole gravity's strength. Like gravity it draws things together to clash, and leaves scars shaped like the enemy.

Serendure is the last and greatest. It is the unbreakable bond which may be trust and may be dependence. It persists whether it is wanted or not. It is like the force which binds quarks together: stronger when it is pulled.

Each passion, Ssrin says, is a relationship between souls.

Souls are the letters that make these words.

⁓

On the night before it all goes wrong, they lie on the apartment roof and look up at the stars.

"Where's Sahana?" Anna puffs on a fat joint (Ssrin bucks let her buy the high-percentage indica). "Where's home?"

She's tried to persuade Ssrin to change her camouflage just a bit, so she won't be a fortysomething businesswoman smoking on the roof with a thirty-one-year-old Kurd in jeans and a T-shirt, but Ssrin likes her unmarked look. Apparently New York people have trouble remembering well-behaved women in gray suits. Anna once read about something called intersectional invisibility: differences piling up, not-white and not-man and not-dressed-strange, all multiplying in the brain to obscure certain people, which is why Black women have to fight to be remembered by feminists and antiracists when they're both women and Black. She kind of buys it. People forget about Anna all the time. Until she fucks up. Then no one's sure what she is (Mexican, maybe?) but they sure remember her.

Ssrin makes a soft sound of hurt. When Anna looks at her she has knotted her heads into a Celtic shape. Her hands are on her belly, one pinning the other, the other trying to escape. Anna cannot see this as anything but deep raw grief.

"I'm never going back," she says quietly. "Khas. Oh. It was beautiful. But I won't see it again."

Anna, heart-struck, rolls onto her side and touches Ssrin on the shoulder. "I can't go home either," she says pathetically, and then, trying to be there for her friend, "Will you tell me about it?"

"I grew up in the mountains. Everything very clean and cold. I remember waking up on the sleeping-stone under the new sun. Feeling the warmth of morning, going down into the rock, to chase out the cold inside. I remember slithering out of a rushing ravine up to a campfire, as a dam opened and let the rapids roar. At night you could see the aurora, which never ends; and the giant world Vsatyr was in the sky. Like an egg of cinnamon and dark scale, full of lightning. And we hunted steer through the purple meadows, Ssenenet and I: I would flush them, and she would make the kill."

Ssenenet. "Your mother? Your sister?"

"Sister from the same brood. It's unusual for two to survive. But after we killed our siblings, our parents couldn't make us turn on each other." Ssrin hisses a long grieving hiss. "Eventually I did that myself."

"Dude," Anna says, trying to cheer her up. "We should do acid and talk about cosmic meaning. Does acid work on you?"

"I could make something like it. I have glands. Each of my heads has a different specialty. Interrogation, healing, killing"—Ssrin pokes them and they nip fondly at her fingers—"combat drugs, operant drugs, fun drugs, killing again."

"They work on me?"

"Oh, yes, all of them. I made sure before I came here. What good would drugs for interrogation or killing be if I couldn't use them on the indigenes?"

A question bounces back to Anna with the next pull on the joint. "What's your endgame? Say we get this thing you need, tomorrow. Where does all this shit go?"

Ssrin's knotted heads draw a little tighter. One serpent has its fangs unhinged, and it tests the reflexes of its neighbor with little play-bites.

"What would you think if I said that, by cosmic coincidence, your species is destined to liberate the galaxy?"

"I would call total bullshit. The inbred porn apes? No way. We can't even save ourselves."

"Good. You're learning. The story of man is a story of mediocrity. But so are most stories, I think. Most things are average, or median; if they were not, nothing would make sense." Ssrin begins to unwrap herself. "Anna, I came to Earth tracking a very old story, a story that goes back to the dawn of time. Your species is not special. It is not destined. But it is very, *very* inbred . . . and that makes it transparent to a certain kind of analysis. Your souls all bear the same tint. They are touched by the same story. It rings in your myths, deep down, lower than you know. It must have a point of origin. And I think that we, you and I, our serendure, are part of my path to that source. I think *that source* is what drew us together. If I have the Ubiet, I can look at the choices which brought us into serendure. And maybe it will be there . . ."

Anna knocks into an awful thought. Like an open cabinet door, right in the forehead. What happens next in these stories? Once you befriend the alien? The alien dies. It gives you the special power and *you* become the hero.

And you have to carry on her mission . . .

A few of her neighbors pile up onto the roof with beer and speakers. Anna glowers at them, irritated. Ssrin slithers over to them on her belly, attracts their attention with a wave, and then— Oh, Jesus, she must have dropped her camouflage. They bolt, shrieking, one of them spewing yeasty craft-beer vomit.

"Man," Anna says, "I think that's a bit of an overreaction. You're scary but you're not, like, piss-yourself scary."

"No. They reacted honestly to what they saw. You are the one who responds strangely." Ssrin is looking at herself, one head arched to study. She shivers. "You're immune to the Cultratic Brand, Anna."

"The what?"

"A mark my whole species carries. You can't see it, because serendure connects us. When most people look on me, they . . . they see what I really am. In my soul, not my body. Condemned. Branded by hell.

"It's the first thing we discovered when we found the afterlives. We khai are the only species in the galaxy damned from birth. For us, there is no redemption."

CHAPTER THREE

Anna goes sunbathing on Sheep Meadow in Central Park, on a rainy day, in a one-piece swimsuit. She looks like a big idiot. When she wades into Turtle Pond and breast-strokes right out to the center a cop yells after her, "Hey, lady, you can't go in there!"

Fuck the police. Anna's gonna go Spock with the turtles. *"Three meters,"* Ssrin says through the bead in Anna's throat. *"Straight ahead. Two meters. One meter. Now dive."*

Anna draws a big wet lungful of rain and kicks for the bottom. There are no turtles in sight. Maybe Ssrin ate them all. There's no sign of an alien spacecraft either, but that's according to plan: Ssrin's ship is hidden in a pocket of what she calls "plausibly emancipated space-time."

"Okay," Ssrin says, *"when you pop through, I'll disarm the most fatal traps. I'm opening the claudication now."*

Anna bubbles in protest, what do you mean *fatal traps*, and then her skull rings with a pure crystalline *ping*. The world collapses. There is nothing in any direction: neither light nor darkness. Anna is now a point with only one quality: guilt. Crushing, total guilt. Serhang. Hamali. Oh my God, I am *so* sorry. I am so sorry for what I did to you. I am sorry my whole life and I know I will never tell you or make it better. I am sorry because it is all I can be because what I did can never be fixed or undone.

Mother, I'm *sorry*—

The dimensions of space and time return. Anna free-falls inside a bubble of pond water, *wham*, right on her elbows onto grungy green-bronze metal. The water claps on the hard surface and explodes into a pool around her. She lies there panting and dripping.

The flash of her arrival passes into darkness.

"Good," Ssrin says. *"You should be in the aft boarding killzone. Do you see the bomb I left on the ceiling? If you do, it's unlikely the Exordia agent physically entered the ship after he killed it."*

Anna rolls onto her back. "I can't see *anything*."

"*The light's still in infrared. I'll use your com bead to send commands. I'm putting the ship in slave mode.*"

"Remote control?"

"*No. A simplified interface. So slaves can fly the ship, if the crew is incapacitated.*"

"What the fuck, man. You guys are the worst."

"*That's objectively correct. Can your wet round eyes see now?*"

The walls brighten with lovely red-gold dawn light. Anna's lying in a little compartment, pearly-smooth, kind of a Jony Ive minimalist look, if Apple worked in shades of oxidized bronze and the stink of blood. The hull prickles against Anna's bare skin and she's quite sure it's tasting her with microscopic needles. She rolls up to her bare knees. The walls flash red script at her, bold curved characters like Nazca done by Nazis. The letters squirm, maybe so that vision that keys on motion can pick them up better? They look sleek and confident, and the corners are a little bit like fangs.

Slave mode, Ssrin said. The ship's reminding Anna who really owns it.

Right above her head there's a plate of dimpled black metal, flexed to the ceiling by a sticky-looking membrane. Anna pokes it, because she's a fuckup. The membrane stuff feels firm and warm and alive, like a curled bicep. Weird.

"I found the bomb," she says. "I poked it. Can I move?"

"*Face the hatch with an open circle icon. That's direct access to the payload bay.*"

"Okay. Jesus, it's cold in here."

"*Now walk to the hatch. I'm pretty sure I convinced the bomb not to kill you. If we are in serendure, then it's very unlikely that you'll die right now. It wouldn't be narratively complete.*"

Anna steps toward the hatch. "So, all this narrative shit you keep name-dropping. You said souls live in the areteia? And if souls are made of stories, and the areteia's, like, badly designed and fucks around with physics, then do stories . . ."

"*Yes. Stories are maps of cause and effect. Really effective stories recur over and over, in billions of souls. They overflow, gain the ability to exist on their own, replicate, and eventually inject themselves into the physics model.*"

"Stories become real?"

"*Sort of. These are abstract technical archetypes, but they do have power. For example, the belunari have a mythotype in which a hive queen must share a secret with all her children so they can solve a problem. And it turns out that quantum decryption works better near a group of belunari, because the areteia skews probability toward disclosing the secret.*"

"Wild," Anna breathes.

"*My species applied aretaic technology to narrative engineering at a species-wide scale.*"

"All dogs go to heaven?"

"We restricted the narratives that Exordia subjects could participate in. Confining them to our myth of superiority. That is the pinion I told you about."

"Just the worst." Anna touches the wall with the open-circle glyph, and it slashes away like a reverse guillotine, fast and eerie quiet. Past that wall panel there's an old-school hatch with a big mechanical wheel, which Anna grabs and turns, throwing her whole weight into it. It was clearly balanced for someone *much* stronger, but once she gets it going, it's almost frictionless.

"Ssrin," she grunts. "What am I looking for?"

"The Ubiet of Qo. An aretaic sensor of ancient provenance. It was made by a neuroscythe."

"A what?"

"A nerve angel. A defect. That-spawn. Never mind. If I use it to analyze our serendure, it can tell me where our story came from, and where we might be going."

"To save the world?"

"To save everything, I hope."

"Okay, cool, cool. But what does the Oubliette of Cows actually *look* like—"

The hatch clanks open and a blast of freezer air blows Anna's wet swimsuit tight against her skin. Her breath stings in her chest and the pond water on the deck beneath her curdles to slush. "Jesus, Ssrin!" she gasps.

"What?"

"It's cold in there!"

"That's odd. Thermoregulate. Just use your adrenaline and keep moving."

"I can't! It's not like taking a piss, Ssrin, I don't just open the sphincter and adrenalize myself!"

"Oh," Ssrin says disapprovingly. "Your art makes quite a point of the human ability to rise to any challenge. Your mind does have a governor on your physical performance, you know. Can't you disengage it?"

"No!"

"Well, if you cannot discover heretofore unknown reserves of inner strength, then move quickly. You won't survive long in the payload bay."

"Why's it so cold!"

"I don't know. There should be nothing in the ship's universe except itself. Nowhere for heat to go. Perhaps the claudication has been breached . . . joined to a hostile manifold . . . But if the intrusion wasn't physical, then . . . Uh-oh. He's not skilled enough to . . . Hm."

Anna rips herself into motion. A layer of skin peels off the soles of her feet. She hops through the hatch on her toes, yelping a little with every step. The payload bay is all dim blue-black emptiness like an airplane hangar. Tangles of umbilical cable slither around each other. Obelisks of green metal drift midair like gravity fucked right off. A slow drip of something chemical and astringent patters down from high above where arc light glares.

Anna screams into the deadly cold. "WHERE DO I GO!"

"The Ubiet's stored on a drop rack. Go straight ahead ten meters, grip the lever on that console, and pull. The ship will release the rack. Grab the Ubiet and get out. Don't worry about what it looks like—you're fated to choose it correctly."

"Why!"

"Conservation of parsimony. If you didn't get it on the first try you'd have to try again, which is redundant. The Ubiet can influence free will to create cleaner narrative trajectories. It wants to help you use it."

Anna is printing the frigid deck with thin pink copies of her feet. She doesn't feel like she's on a clean trajectory of any sort. "So why did it let you leave it here?"

"It didn't know that I'd get shot. The event was unforeseeable. The Exordia has weapons that serve as—I'm not sure how this translates—protagonist killers."

Anna's bloody foot sticks to the deck. She falls on her forearms. "Fuck," she snarls, which comes out in a huge puff of vapor. She peels herself to her feet again. One gauzy burnt-blood-brown footstep at a time, she walks toward the lever.

"Anna," a voice says: not Ssrin. A man's voice. "You can't trust her."

"What the fuck," Anna breathes.

"If you give Ssrin the Ubiet, Earth dies. I can't put it more simply than that."

God willing, this is some kind of brain-freeze hallucination. One alien in her head is plenty.

"Anna, my name is Iruvage. I am an agent of the galactic authority, the Exordia. You've been attacked and coercively narrated by a renegade officer with dreams of godhood. You are trapped in an artificial narrative created by her Cultratic operancy. She drew you to her because she needs someone whose soul has been touched by her quarry. I can hear her lying to you. I can smell her poison in your fate."

Anna's hair is frozen to her scalp, but she's finally at the console. The lever's a green-bronze stick shift the length of her forearm. Anna grabs it, and with a great redemptive burst of adrenaline, she hauls that motherfucker down. God bless alien engineers: it does not stick in the cold.

"Anna," the new voice says. "Please, please do not do this. There's a monster on that ship and it will come for you if you touch the Ubiet. I can get you safely out of there, but only if you come voluntarily into my protective custody."

He sounds like a cop. Anna doesn't trust him.

"Fuck off, Iruvage," Ssrin snaps. "Ignore him, Anna. Get the Ubiet."

The ready rack is a shelf of miscellaneous alien shit hanging fifteen feet above Anna. When she pulls the lever it topples straight down onto the deck, bounces to a stop a few feet up, and hangs there, full of silver clamshell cases and green-bronze artifacts and swords and cool guns and a thing like a black hole, a slippery warped refraction trapped in a ball of glass.

That has to be the Ubiet.

Anna grabs it, and the fucking thing talks to her, right in her head: hello! i am an ubiet, providing narrative surveillance and aretaic analysis to operants of virtue. i was made by the neuroscythe abdiel abdullah! you are a natively ensouled indigenous preoperant neonoumenon in a state of high-resonance serendure, with a history of enhanced self-similarity due to amplified archetypical choice—

"Shut *up!*" Anna yells, before the damn thing can predict her fate. She tries to turn back the way she came, and her feet stick. She falls again. Her bathing suit is now a sheet of crackling frost cemented to the outer layers of her skin. She's gonna be a freezer-burnt corpse if she doesn't move.

And something behind her is tickling her, tapping her shoulder, whispering like: *Hey. Hey. Hey.*

"*Shit!*" Ssrin says, and at first Anna thinks Ssrin's concern is for her fall, but then she remembers who's talking. "*That's why the claudication was ruptured. For a control tether. He's put an atmanach into the ship. It smells your worldline entangling with the Ubiet. Shit shit shit.*"

Anna, against all mythological advice, looks back.

Something's moving in the Tesla-show depths of the payload bay, where currents snap between coils the size of whales. There is a thing. A dark angular presence that recedes all the way to the vanishing point. Like a bad polygon drawn by an overheating graphics card, a sunset shadow on an infinite plain. The near tip of that shadow moves around itself, toothed and jagged, like a chainsaw bent into a Mobius strip folded into a sack. A thousand thousand chainsaw tapeworms chasing each other through a bulging intestine.

It's getting closer.

"What's an atmanach?" she groans. She needs to peel herself off the deck. She'll have to rip the skin off her forearms, and that's going to hurt like fuck.

"*A Cultratic construct. A soul retriever with an artificial hell manifold inside. It takes your soul and digests it for analysis. Very rare, very hard to make and to master, restricted to great operants with warship-grade thought turbines. He shouldn't be capable of such sublime tactical blasphemy—*"

"Ssrin! How do I get away from it!"

"*Don't choose to do anything. Act on instinct. It hunts by searching for free will.*"

Oh, fuck, oh, fuck, oh, fuck, but good news, there are no choices available, Anna's actually frozen down. She's glued to the metal by her own blood and water. "Ssrin!" she yells, which is, of course, a choice. "I need help."

"*I'm going to blow you out of the payload bay.*"

"What?"

"*I'm going to puncture the claudication, reverse the gravity, and drop you back into your universe. When you fall through the claudication you may experience some ethical shear. I need you to pin yourself to your soul. Think of the story that best describes you. Think of that and only that.*"

The story that best describes her— Oh, she knows what *that* is—

She closes her eyes. And again the man in the red beret puts his pistol into Anna's child hands.

I have always believed that unreasoning defiance is the mark of an animal, he says. *A human being knows how to do what must be done.*

Are you an animal, daughter of Serhang Sinjari?

The Ubiet burbles away in her arms: clarification and amplification of aretaic event in self-like past, recursive self-caricature by protoprecosmic influence, WARNING WARNING WARNING pathology! pathology! pathology! pathology! pathology! Until that word, *pathology,* starts to sound like path-ology, the study of paths. The discovery of the way.

The ceiling splits open. Anna stares up into the edge of the world: oh, *weird,* it is a mirrored image of the payload bay, the light must be bouncing back from the edge of the local universe— No, wait, that's *ice,* the water must have frozen out of the air—

And in that reflection she can see the atmanach zagging toward her, a many-headed centipede ricocheting off dumb matter, homing in on Anna's will.

She thinks of brother Hamali staring up at her. She thinks of what she told him. *I'm sorry. I have to save them all.*

She realizes that her image of her own soul is not very different from the way she imagines hell. That same choice. Over and over and over and over.

"*I have gravity control,*" Ssrin reports. "*This will hurt—now.*"

And Anna's ripped from the frozen deck, bleeding like a freezer-burnt steak, clinging to the Ubiet as she falls up into the edge of the universe. She's going to hit the ice. "Fuuuuck!" she screams, and her trigger finger tickles with the memory of recoil, and the Ubiet looks back at her like a glaring eye, Sauron as the bright lord of all guilt trips, full of the spew of blood and brain across fallow soil and fresh snow, full of brother Hamali's dead and begging eyes, why, Anna, why.

⁓

She wakes up on the grass in Central Park, clutching the Ubiet to her chapped and cracking breast. It tugs at her heart: she can feel it, like an unrequited love is sitting behind her in a college lecture, and she's got no excuse to turn around and smile.

hello, it says. you are a self-similar causa sui. you are lossfully self-noumenizing.

She needs to stop touching this thing.

A circle of New Yorkers has gathered to shoot phone videos. One guy narrates: "She *flew* up out of the lake, right over there, and we dragged her out, right *here,* but look at *that* over *there,* is that not the craziest shit?"

"Is my soul okay?" she asks Ssrin. Mother Khaje would not want her daughter's soul further disfigured.

"Now she's asking about her soul, I don't know, man, it's not what I'd be asking about if I just got shot out of a geyser—"

"All my inquisitions come back clean. We can still use the Ubiet on you."

Anna's got to get out of here before Iruvage the alien cop shows up. Speaking of— Where *are* all the cops? The fucking NYPD should already be tasing her plausibly Arab ass.

Oh. They are over at Turtle Pond, where a tower of water has climbed straight up ten meters, eddying and pulsing, growing fractal horns, as if someone poked a key through the universe's eardrum and started to turn it. The falling water sounds like a computer about to crash.

Ssrin's antigravity is sticking out of her garage universe. And if the antigravity can get out . . . what about the atmanach?

"Excuse me," Anna croaks, getting up. "Major gas leak under the pond. Uh, the water mains have gone. Everything exploded. Please let me through. I have to go to the hospital."

⁓⁂⁓

Anna staggers into her apartment, carrying the Ubiet in a Duane Reade bag. Ssrin tears off Anna's coat with a spur of tooth or bone on her wrist ("Don't panic. I'll buy you another garment.") and carries her to the couch, cradling her against cold smooth scales that soothe one way and cut the other.

"Glow me," Anna begs, "do that healing thing, dude, I am so fucked up." Her whole body burns and shivers, in maximum rebellion, Anna Sinjari is not fit to be in charge of this flesh, we the cellular citizens are *out*. She is afraid that the little broccoli things in her lungs, whatever they're called, have frozen and popped.

"Hush, hush." Ssrin pries the Ubiet of Qo's bag away from her, puts it on the floor, and bites Anna, with slow delicacy, in the throat. Sweet morphine warmth floods from her fangs. "We don't need the way of knives. It would mark you. You'll be all right."

"Oh," Anna says. "Hey, wait, is someone screaming in my bedroom?"

But before she can get upset about the shouts of *help help help* definitely coming from her bedroom, she passes out from sheer contentment.

She dreams of a complicated thing following her subway car down the tracks. Eating her choices. Coming closer when she decides how to pay for her subway fare, which set of stairs to use, whether to go back to Ssrin or run screaming into the night. By the end it is so close that she dreams of teeth and nothing else.

She wakes up to Ssrin feeding her, mouth to tiny befanged mouths, with savory chunks of steak. One of her heads is prodding her to chew, and another to swallow. "Anna, you were so brave," the Cate Blanchett voice murmurs. "Thank you. Thank you."

"Who's in the other room?" Anna can hear thumping.

"Nobody," Ssrin lies.

"You are *lying!*"

"Anna, you aren't ready for this. Wait. Rest."

"Fuck you, Ssrin," she says, and grabs one of the alien's heads in her fist. "You've got drugs in there. Wake me up. Make me ready. What did you *do* while I was gone?"

"I prepared the material we're going to need to use the Ubiet."

"Use it to do *what?*"

"We need to reenact the story of our souls. You and I, serendura, we match: and if we show the Ubiet how alike we are, it'll show us what identified that likeness, what brought us together."

"*How*, Ssrin? What is the material you needed?"

"I have a man chained to your radiator."

"Oh my God," Anna groans.

Of *course* it's Roman. Ssrin kidnapped him on the way home from his tutoring job. It would not have been very dramatic. A woman in a pantsuit passing by, a prick of invisible fangs, Ssrin's camouflage wrapping around him as he fell. Exit Roman.

"I chose him. Because you cared for him." Ssrin says this with alien shyness, her six-fingered hands passing over each other, wiping away the doubt. "Yes?"

"Ssrin," Anna says, staring down at this poor man manacled to her radiator and gagged with electrical tape, feeling that *maybe* she has entered a new and unhappy stage of her relationship with the alien, "I didn't actually want to hurt him. I *don't* want to hurt him."

Roman thrashes and kicks and makes muffled what-the-fuck sounds, but of course he cannot see Ssrin as Ssrin, only her camouflage. So he has no idea how deep the what-the-fuckhole goes. Poor earnest Roman with his stubbly chin and sweet ChapStick-flavored kisses. Roman who wants to be a teacher. Roman who has been reduced to a symbolic player, an NPC in someone else's story.

"I have to kill him now, don't I," Anna says. "Because that's the story of our souls. We do evil things so . . . so others can survive."

"Yes, Anna." And there, in Ssrin's white hand, is the ugly squared-off shape of a Glock, demon instrument of anonymous HR complaints, imaginary terror of the company bathroom. "We need a moral event to trace."

The Ubiet of Qo gleams in Ssrin's other hand. And just as it showed Anna her brother, dying under her gun, now it shows Anna the history of Ssrin. The charred ruin of alien worlds. The broken skeletons and windblown flesh of creatures she can't name. Cities cratered into teacups of black glass. World-ships crippled and rammed into small bright stars. A jellyfish as big as a hurricane burning in a poison-yellow sky, screaming so loud it tears apart the clouds. Ssrin has done these things. These are Ssrin's crimes.

Ssrin may be a rebel now, but before this, she was their Vader.

"Ssrin," Anna says, aghast, and the name is all she has to say, because—that's the whole betrayal, that's what's gone wrong, Ssrin is wrong now. Ssrin is not a pet or a buddy, Ssrin is suddenly, chillingly, an *alien*.

Ssrin is the motherfucker in the red beret.

Ssrin is laying out the bargain:

"Serendure brought us together. Serendure the hardest of the seven passions, the unbreakable passion, the thing that passes between two souls which cannot help being the same shape. Call it infinite loyalty, call it inescapable abuse, whatever it is, it is serendure. Not by coincidence did you meet me in the turtle kitchen that day. Not by chance could you see through my camouflage. Our meeting was *engineered*. A story drew us together. What did this? What story was it? Who is the author?" Ssrin jabs a neck at Anna, and a neck at Roman, and slams her tail against the floor so that all the fancy new ceramic dishes in the kitchen rattle. "Anna, if there's something on this world which can alter the motion of souls, change the shape of stories, then I must have it. I must! The freedom of trillions *requires* it!"

"You think there's something like that. Here."

"I know there is! A narrative weapon is the only chance we have against the Exordia! It *has* to be here. I can smell it on your souls, in the arc of your myths and the dreams of your children!" She offers the Glock like a sacrament, which, really, it is. A sacred act. A moral event. "Show the Ubiet that we're alike, and it will find the reason we are here together. It will find the force that pushed us into each other's stories. But you must do the thing that is at the heart of both our souls. You must sacrifice."

God pushed Ssrin and Anna together, struck by their likeness, and Ssrin just wants to run the process in reverse: beginning at that likeness, follow the finger back to God.

It makes sense in other terms too. In the terms laid out by the man in the red beret, years ago in Kurdistan, in the snow and dust of the circling helicopters.

This is the bargain. Execute one of your people, and I will spare one of your people. Execute two, and I spare ten. Execute three, and I spare twenty. Four, and I spare forty. Five, I spare eighty. Execute six, and I spare them all.

Are you an animal, daughter of Serhang Sinjari? Or can you do what must be done?

"I have to do it, I suppose," Anna says. As cold inside as the payload bay of Ssrin's ship, thin-coated in frozen pink flesh. "Because I care for him. And we sacrifice what we love for a greater good. That's our story."

Roman looks up at the word *love* with great hope. Poor Roman. You're not in that kind of story.

"You understand. You understand." Ssrin sighs, eightfold. "Anna, you don't know what this could mean. I'm the first Exordia traitor the rebellion's ever had. My soul is not pinioned. But theirs, Anna, all those subject trillions—we pinioned them, world by world, species by species. How many rebellions have we poisoned and devoured? They may bring all the warships and weapons they can muster, but they are pinioned, so the *story* always turns against them. The Exordia cannot fall until we have a narrative weapon to match the pinion. What made this story out of us? I must know."

Anna takes the Glock.

Anna pulls on the slide, chambers a bullet, and aims it at Ssrin.

"What if I shoot you?"

"That," Ssrin whispers, her human voice softer than the choral hiss, "is not the shape of your soul, Anna. You cannot defy the choice. You cannot alter the rules. That power belongs to other passions. They rage against their fate. You and I, serendura, we make the hard choices. We pay the costs. Also, I am armored in elision and paramuscle and hive, and your bullets will never touch me."

And in the Ubiet, now, there is only the image of Ssrin herself. She is all that she is. She is her own crime.

"For the world?" Anna's voice breaks. "If I do this, it helps you save the world, somehow?"

Roman's making slow, reasonable *mmg mrrph mnnf* noises. Anna knows she won't take the gag off. Roman has no will here. He's a piece of meat stuck in the machine, dead the instant Ssrin licked the phone screen to scroll through his tweets. Caught in the wrong story. Anna's story. Anna killed him.

"For the galaxy," Ssrin says.

So Anna must shoot Roman in the head. Kill one. Save galaxy. No choice.

But there's always a choice, right? There's that "limited acausal free will," there's that areteia, keeping track of what Anna chooses. Can't she change the shape of her soul?

Can't she say no?

If she leaves Ssrin's story, it'll be credit card debt again, and job hunting, and catcallers, and the nightmares that never stop. But Roman will be alive. She'll make the other choice and Roman will live.

Can't she say no?

She must be able to. That's what free will means. Even when all the arrows point one way, you can still choose to go the other. Even if it's a really fucking good idea to do one thing, you can always choose the stupid thing, because you believe the stupid decision is the *right* one.

Can't she say no?

And then Ssrin snatches the gun out of her hand with a speed known only to hummingbird wings and the movements of mantis shrimp and before Anna can make the first shape of the first sound in the word *NO*—

Ssrin shoots Roman in the head.

His skull bursts out backward. The bullet ricochets between the vanes of the radiator and falls down the pipe-hole. "What the fuck are you *doing* down there!" the upstairs neighbor shouts.

And in Ssrin's palm, the Ubiet flickers and whirls, black hole palantir free-associating down the course of Anna's life, teasing out the similarities between events: Roman's broken skull banging against the radiator, mother Khaje turning away in grief and horror, *You cannot be my daughter, my daughter could never do this.* Snow and sunlight through the rotors of helicopters. Slo-mo action of a pistol.

"But," Anna protests, dumbstruck, this isn't fair, "I didn't do it . . . *you* don't care about him . . . I had to shoot him for it to work . . ."

"I sacrificed something that matters to me. Thus I enacted the story of our souls. Yours and mine."

And Anna gets it.

Ssrin has sacrificed her friendship with Anna. She shot that friendship in the head. She was definitely Anna's friend, because she took the pistol and saved Anna from having to do what she was, after all her protests were finished, definitely going to do.

Ssrin shot Roman so Anna wouldn't have to.

The Ubiet settles on an image of a landscape. The reason Anna met Ssrin, just as plain as a postcard from your estranged mom: a village against a towering white mountain, a village in a green valley cut from ancient stone. Anna was born there. Those mountains are the Qandils, part of the Zagros range, the home of the Kurds.

"That's wrong," Anna says. Roman slumps against the radiator, legs askew, twitching pathetically. His students will never see him again. Maybe someone on Twitter will ask where he's gone. They will make a memorial on his Facebook page: executed by his crazy ex-girlfriend. "It's just showing you where I came from. That's where I was born. Where I . . . where I did the . . . Oh."

The Ubiet isn't wrong at all. No wonder Anna is the one to lead Ssrin back to this mysterious changer-of-stories. The thing knows her. They were practically neighbors.

It was there when she made her choice. In the Qandil Mountains. In the place of the rotors and the red beret.

Did it make her make the choice?

No. The Ubiet said that. She's just been made more like . . . herself. That choice, what she did . . . was the truest thing she's ever done.

God help her.

"I know you won't go back," Ssrin says softly.

"No." Never. Not home.

"I'm sorry, Anna. I am. But that's where the weapon is, and that's where I have to go now."

Anna says nothing. Anna has nothing to say. Roman deserved better than this: to be executed as a token in a story he never understood. Used as a little pawn. Killed because Anna cared about him. Killed for exactly the same reason those six people died by the gun in her child hands.

Because someone told Anna they had to die.

The alien stands there, half-coiled. "May I dispose of the body for you?"

"Sure," Anna says. "Whatever. I don't want to be in your story anymore."

ACT 2

PALADIN

EXOSPHERE

K + 0 HOURS

Something in Kurdistan screams as it is born.

An electromagnetic shriek burns out radios as far away as Tehran and Tel Aviv. The signal peaks in the extremely low-frequency radio bands, three to thirty hertz, the kind of long-longwave moan that reaches down to the bottom of the sea. Submarines in the Gulf of Aden catch it on their trailing antennae. It tails off up through the microwave spectrum in a train of shortening, steepening pulses: a wolf's howl breaking up into lonely yips at three hundred gigahertz.

It is not natural.

It is not anything made by man.

A National Reconnaissance Office Intruder-type naval intelligence satellite detects the electromagnetic event. It immediately alerts the NRO surveillance management network. The alert is automatically categorized by the TALENT KEYHOLE information control system. The system determines that this signal falls into a special category implemented just weeks before: major electromagnetic events not attributable to a known emitter, not the result of a solar event, and not associated with a double-flash nuclear detonation. It applies the appropriate code:

TOP SECRET (ECI)//TALENT KEYHOLE-NORT//RSV 676// ORCON//NOFORN

The string of letters tells the system where the information should go. TALENT KEYHOLE searches the NORT compartment and activates the RSV 676 distribution list. There is only one address on that list, at a secure information facility in Atlanta. The ORCON tag prevents further distribution—even to those who work directly on the Intruder satellite program.

TALENT KEYHOLE files the alert to this single email address. The shell forwards the email through a series of onion routers that zigzag through JWICS, the Department of Defense top-secret network.

In the White House Situation Room, Deputy National Security Advisor Clayton Navarro Hunt's phone buzzes.

"Excuse me," he says, getting up from the conference table, where he, his polite political rival CIA Deputy Director Avril Haines, and CIA Director John Brennan have been chewing through another draft of the new drone playbook. "I have to take this."

He steps out. His hands are shaking too hard to work the BlackBerry keyboard. He has an iPhone for his personal life but the BlackBerry does *this* stuff. He smiles at a passing aide: "You hear about the plans to extend *Windsor*? Yeah, it's great. Great news. You have a good day now."

He sits in a toilet stall and types once he can. Old contacts at the NRO. Pull strings. Get two electronic intelligence satellites turned away from the event. One in each hemisphere, pointed outward, to monitor near-Earth space. The NRO will do it because Clayton's their guy at the White House and they want to keep him happy.

Then Clayton makes a call to the 105th Airlift Wing at Stewart Air National Guard Base in New York State. Yes, hello. This is the deputy NSA. Place a C-17 on hold to load containerized labs from the Air Force Research Laboratory in Rome, New York. I want tankers staged to support a direct flight and a long orbit over northern Iraq.

It is all, of course, very unusual, far outside the chain of command; but Clayton invokes his security clearance and reminds Brigadier General LaBarge that any disclosure of their conversation could be prosecuted.

Brigadier General LaBarge thinks he's a prick. He calls Air National Guard headquarters at the Pentagon. They tell him to do what the deputy national security advisor says.

Clayton pops a bromantane pill and massages the back of his neck. Then he puts his smile back on and stands up.

K + 1–72 HOURS

Speculation spreads about a possible Iranian nuclear test. Military surveillance satellites maneuver to image the area. The Joint Chiefs meet. American forces in the Middle East are pushed to alert. Urgent calls connect the White House to the Israeli prime minister, the king of Saudia Arabia, Iraq's Prime Minister Nouri al-Maliki, and the nuclear powers. The Russians forward-deploy forces to air bases in Syria and Abkhazia. Chinese warplanes and scientific expeditions land in Iran, which insists it has not detonated a weapon and has no idea what's going on over the border.

At the signal source, satellites photograph an anomaly on the ground.

K + 73 HOURS

Nearly three days after the Kurdistan howl, something in near-Earth space shrieks back.

This second radio event has a Doppler shift: it is moving. It is coming closer. The source is decelerating toward Earth from an initial velocity of eighteen hundred kilometers per second: nearly half of 1 percent of the speed of light.

For eleven hours, radio astronomers buzz over the possibility of first contact. The president sits with the National Security Council to review their total lack of plans for this situation.

Clayton Hunt isn't there.

K + 84 HOURS

Space Surveillance Network deep-space radar detects small metallic objects separating from a common origin and moving toward Earth. They cannot be alien landers, because they are accelerating faster than any living thing can survive.

Clayton Navarro Hunt calls Major Erik Wygaunt, who is now a staff officer with Joint Special Operations Command. Erik deleted Clayton's phone contact, but Clayton didn't delete Erik's.

"Get off the road," Clayton orders. "Go inside. Look at the floor. The sky's going to light up. After it happens, get to the nearest air base. The planes will still be okay, and so will military communications. Tell them Clayton Hunt wants you for MAJESTIC."

He hangs up before Erik can reply. It is almost, but not quite, the last phone call either of them will ever make.

K + 85 HOURS

Forty (40) megaton-range thermonuclear weapons detonate in Earth's upper atmosphere.

A perfect dodecahedron around the planet: two bombs at each of the twenty vertices of a twelve-sided crystal. Twenty double-lobed suns igniting in double-flash nuclear white.

There is a little speck of shadow in that white. Each bomb is equipped with a flux compressor coupled to a microwave antenna. These devices die in the first instant of the explosion, martyred on the altar of the blast. Their sacrifice turns 5 percent of the bomb's bright death into light with a wavelength between "one ant" and "one human arm-span": the kind of light that zaps forks in your microwave.

The bombs are also boosted with lithium deuteride to improve neutron yield. These neutrons collide with other atoms in the blast, creating unstable hybrid nuclei, which immediately decay by emitting gamma radiation. These gamma rays join those produced by the bombs' fissile uranium casings.

An additional 30 percent of each nuclear blast therefore goes into ionizing radiation: gamma rays. High-energy light.

In the band of thickening atmosphere twenty-five to thirty-five kilometers above the Earth, these gamma rays slam into atoms of oxygen and nitrogen, stripping their orbiting electrons. The orphaned electrons hurtle away at 90 percent of lightspeed. They want to go in a straight line, but hold on now, it's not so easy to leave home. Earth's magnetic field bends their course. They begin to spiral down.

When an electron moving near lightspeed has to turn, it emits synchrotron radiation. Poison light.

And beneath each bomb there are 100,000,000,000,000,000,000,000,000 electrons swerving at once.

The result is a blast of electromagnetic noise. No: not noise. A coherent pulse, spiking and falling in harmony. Shiva's own beat drop on electrical civilization.

An EMP.

Within five nanoseconds the E1 pulse flashbulbs the world in its last strobe instant of normal life. Then everyone looking at the sky goes bleach-blind.

The pulse induces voltage. Fifty thousand volts per meter: catastrophic, system-wrecking voltage. It is a myth that *everything* electronic dies in an EMP. The prophets of the Facebook walls and paperback malls are too pessimistic. Most cars are safe, small short-range radios survive, and devices like wristwatches tick along happily, too small to feel the effect.

But the bigger it is, the harder it falls. The world's power grid powers itself apart. Transformers fail. The SCADA controllers that operate industry and infrastructure fuse into useless mass. Pipelines overpressure and burst. Cell phone towers go up like torches. The internet goes out, and no amount of F5 will ever bring it back.

The E2 pulse follows milliseconds later, scouring systems left naked by the surge protectors destroyed in E1. Then E3. Earth's magnetic field, bent by the detonations, groans back into place, inducing currents in long cables and buried power lines. Transformers that survived the E1 blast catch fire as their windings short. Undersea cables fry their own repeaters. This is the final stroke, the tendon-cutting. The arteries of the electrical grid die of their own length.

Earth turns off.

People can still talk. There are civil emergency networks, luckily or carefully protected ham radio sets, a few fiber optic cables with working endpoints. No one's listening right now, though. Everyone's rushing outside, raising their heads, taking the advice of John Crichton and Ned Scott: look up. Tell this to everyone. Watch the skies.

And as for *why* it happened? The best surviving communications live in shielded military hardware. So the only people who know the real story, at first, are those who've prepared for nuclear Armageddon.

The soldiers and the spies.

CHAPTER FOUR

It's a ten-minute flight in from USS *Makin Island*, where Erik's plane transferred him to a JSOC helicopter. And it's either talk to Clayton or stare at the sky.

So Erik hangs out the side of the Little Bird and watches the greatest aurora in human history. Wow. *Wow.* Curtains and sails, mesas and turrets, roaming parapets of fire; cinder, lava, reef blues and neon green, changing as slow and huge as paint dripped across a bowl the size of heaven. You can even see the reflection in the bay below.

So Erik flies into New York sandwiched between two auroras.

Richard Byrd saw this same beauty in the sky and the ice while he was trapped alone in Antarctica. He wrote about it in *Alone*: a message denied to all other men, a dancing war between good and evil in the sky. And now it is *here*, forty degrees north, above New York. The message is not denied. It has come to everyone. It's breathtaking.

And yet it's a wound; it's the echo of the bombs. After the Starfish Prime nuclear test, Pacific islands from Tongatapu to the French Frigate Shoals saw brilliant aurorae, smears of lithium-red brushed along Earth's magnetic field lines. Hotels in Hawaii threw "rainbow bomb" parties. Now that color out of space surrounds the whole Earth, from Svalbard to Puerto Toro. Like the light of cities went out and up.

Erik hates that. It sucks profoundly that something so beautiful, so historically singular, would be tainted by so much destruction. There should be lines between things. God, he wishes there were clean lines, good and bad, truth and lie, starlight above and suffering below. Friend and foe.

He doesn't look back at Clayton.

"I see the graveyard," the pilot radios. "*Following the avenue south.*" GPS is gone, the satellites flashed by the same gamma rays that created the EMP, so they're back to navigating by street map. "*I don't trust the apartment roofs, so I'm going to put us in a low hover.*"

"Copy that," Clayton murmurs. He leans over to speak to Erik without using the intercom, which means basically kissing Erik's ear. His breath is cool. "Who wants to make the invitation? You or me?"

Clayton Hunt was waiting for Erik on the carrier deck when his plane touched down. Clayton Hunt, who knew the bombs were coming. Who called him and told him to make ready.

Whatever's happened to the world, Clayton *knew*. Because of course he did. He's in on it. He's got access.

So this mission is Erik's last chance to make things right. His last shot, God help him, at some kind of redemption for what Paladin became.

He has to stop Clayton.

There is no ambiguity about that. Knowing what Clayton is, knowing what he's done and what he will do again, Erik has to act. There are men who thrive in times of crisis, and only some of them are heroes. Clayton is the other kind. And he is very, very good at being who he is.

"Erik?" Clayton uses the intercom this time.

"I got it," Erik says. "I'll talk to her."

"Cool. Don't go all Viking Warrior on her, okay? She's the only person we can find who's ever been to Tawakul. She might still have family there. If we're going in, we need her on side. We need someone who can talk to the Kurds and generate human intelligence. We're missing a lot of timeline on the event—"

"I know, Clay. I know." Listen to him, creating the frame, setting up the context for why Erik's gotta do what Clayton needs. Clayton gets anxious if he's not surrounded by game pieces to push around. Erik was a knight in their last game, at least. Maybe a rook. He hopes he's not crooked enough for bishop.

"I'm sorry, man. Saving the world makes me neurotic." Long pause. Then Clayton says, "Hey, I'm glad we could work together again."

"Yeah, man," Erik lies. "It's good."

"Yeah."

Erik shouldn't speak first, shouldn't give Clayton anything to read, but he can't resist asking: "So you're still keeping her name?"

"Navarro? Yeah."

"She didn't want you to keep her name."

Clayton doesn't answer.

It's the first time they've seen each other face-to-face since Paladin collapsed, and Rosamaria left, and it all went to fucking *fuck* goddamn it just broke, this beautiful vital triangle of good people, this thing they'd had for their whole lives. It broke. It wasn't a sex thing, it wasn't a love triangle, it wasn't exactly a regular friendship. They just *worked*.

Erik misses Rosamaria so hard. He can't ask Clayton if he's heard from her. He doesn't dare. What if Clayton says yes?

The last he'd heard, Rosamaria had taken a job working for Vanita Gupta in the Civil Rights Division at Justice, perilously close to Clayton's White House post. Have they reconciled? No, Erik thinks. If they ran into each other in the hallway, Rosamaria would just smile crisply at a slightly distasteful colleague.

Erik decides she's busy holding the world together right now.

South Brooklyn swoops past beneath the helicopter. Trash fires burn between islands of precious generator light. Erik's spent his whole life bringing order to chaos, and tonight chaos is winning. Two days since the power went out and New York is sizzling hot under martial law. But hey, hey, look! People are out in the streets, chain-ganging fresh water, pooling food, checking up on the elderly. Erik wishes he had a megaphone: he would tell them all, from the bottom of his heart, how fucking proud he feels.

Erik is a big believer in the innate goodness of people. He's seen it, again and again, everywhere in the world. It's just as powerful as their capacity for evil. He's a believer in that too.

If he can't stop Clayton . . . fuck, man! It's crazy! Everyone *in the world* thinks Clayton Navarro Hunt is just the smartest greatest funniest guy, Obama's Mini-Me, the president's twice-a-day idea factory, prime mover in the National Security Council, where he has, very publicly, become the face of the administration's improved drone program, taking the heat off his bosses. He came up through the National Reconnaissance Office, *supra et ultra*, above and beyond, and where else would he be, really? Clayton's been the top guy since they were in third grade together. He climbed so fast and hard that he broke the whiteness barrier. That's how he described it to Erik, who is super white: "They stopped calling me the first Black dude to take the post. They stopped talking about me as a role model for Hispanic men in government. They just started saying, he was *first*. He's not the best guy from that bunch, he's *the best guy*. I made it out of the box, man."

Erik was so fucking happy for him. They were such a good team. God, they were such a good team.

"*Coming down now,*" the pilot says.

⁂

K + 132 hours
Sunset Park, Brooklyn, New York

The Little Bird kisses the roof of a Sunset Park apartment building. Forty-Fifth and Eighth, somewhere in the mingling of Brooklyn Chinatown, a Mexican community, and a bunch of Orthodox Jews. Erik remembers getting dim sum here, back in the nineties, on a trip to see Rosamaria in law school. He and Clayton had a fight about . . . what? The army? Desert Storm? He remembers that Clayton patched it up with grace and humor. Bought him a plate of apology shumai.

Now that memory is ruined, because maybe it was all an exercise for Clayton. A war game. *How far can I push Erik. How fast can I fix it. Whose side will Rosamaria take?*

Head in the game, dude. Head in the game.

Erik hops down off the bird. And there she is, Venus on the shotgun shell, waiting for him as if cued by the hand of God or Clayton Hunt. A dark-haired athletic woman with broad gymnast shoulders, five foot eightish, bent against the rotor blast. Armed with a blunt in her fingers and an absolutely illegal Glock in the waistband of her shorts.

She's got the Look.

"Miss Anna Sinjari?" Erik shouts.

The Look is a quicker path into Erik's brain than anything short of a bullet. The Look gets into him faster than respect for her gym-rat muscle, harder than compassion for her tired red eyes, and deeper than his discomfort at her state of undress. It threatens his propriety to find her attractive. Which is unfair, of course, because (as Rosamaria would remind him) it's not her job to manage what he finds threatening or attractive. And in this weather Erik would definitely be out in the yard shirtless, doing Sexy Grilling. She doesn't have AC, no one does right now. So look at her. Out here in a sports bra and shorts and still unintimidated by a JSOC major with a helicopter.

Erik wants to know how she got that Look. What she had to do to earn it. He's really, really glad to see it, because he can understand anyone with that Look in a way Clayton never will. Clayton is *not* a soldier, or even, really, a person. He's like the turreted camera on a Reaper drone, orbiting life, peering at the moving shapes. Occasionally reaching down to touch them. But never touched in return.

"I'm Major Erik Wygaunt!" Erik bellows. "Joint Special Operations Command! I'm here to recruit you for a mission of the greatest importance! We think we can discover the cause of the worldwide blackout!"

"I've got a bag packed," Anna Sinjari shouts. "Are we going straight to Kurdistan?"

What the fuck? "How do you know where we're going?"

"Because serendure can't be broken!"

The scream of the Little Bird is really fucking up Erik's hearing. "What?"

"I said, because you need me as a token! You're going to Tawakul, right? So of course you'd want me as a guide."

"How do you know we're going to—"

Oh. Clayton told her. In the eighty-five hours between the Kurdistan Radio Transient and the EMPs that turned off human society, Clayton plucked Anna

Sinjari out of some NSA database. Query: People from the place I'm going. People I can use.

So he didn't just know the bombs were coming. He was on the move ahead of time. Which is fine: maybe Clayton was reacting to the radio event in Kurdistan, calling up the troops to go check it out, throwing his executive-branch weight around to jump over the usual military chain of command.

Only—that event was five *days* ago. Long enough to stand up a special forces unit, stage out of an air base in the CENTCOM region, and drop in on Tawakul.

Yet Clayton's been talking about MAJESTIC as an emergency fire squad, grab-bagging guys from all over the special operations community for an unsupported first-contact mission. Which it shouldn't be. The Middle East is already *swarming* with US drones and special forces.

Why the delay? Why is Clayton going in alone? What is the administration doing?

Clayton's lying about something. Of course he is. But what, exactly? What's he planning to do with Anna Sinjari, and why was she important enough to contact *before* Erik, Clayton's number-one patsy, confidante, and assassin?

"I'll go get your bag!" Erik yells. "I'm afraid you can't contact anyone before we go!"

"There's no one," she says. "I'll get my own bag, thanks."

She comes back out wearing jeans and a T-shirt and a pathetic ripped little backpack. She's still puffing on her blunt as she climbs up into the Little Bird. Erik watches, real carefully, as Clayton says hello. They shake hands, and Anna freezes for a second. Is she *shy*? Clayton's stupid hot, a heartbreakingly sleek foxman, graceful in all his motions after years of pro-level dance. Erik, nominally heterosexual, has seen Clayton spin a lot of men and women right round, not like a record (baby) but like Russian roulette: five empty chambers of *He's married* and one bullet of *I can't help it, I want him anyway.*

But Erik doesn't think Anna's been bowled over by his looks.

No. It's like Anna recognizes him. Exactly the way Erik recognized her Look.

Clayton pretends to reach for her joint, laughs with her, and trades a radio headset for her Glock. He gives Erik the weapon. Erik drops the magazine, ejects the chambered round, loads it back into the mag, and sticks both in his ACU thigh pockets. Anna watches him do this with real interest. He winks at her. He might give the gun back. It's her property, and he ain't a cop.

Charm up, Erik. He needs to figure out what Clayton's doing. And he's got to do it fast. Very soon they'll be parachuting into Kurdistan, straight onto what appears to be a crashed alien starship.

And Erik's terrified that Clayton will do his thing again—the thing he did with Paladin: seeing a crisis not as a problem to solve but as an opportunity to grow his reach, spinning it into a grand global scheme, spending people like drink tickets at the bar, speed-chess sloppy, doomed to fail.

Paladin. That thing *they* did.

～～～

K – 8 years
Baghdad, Iraq

Erik's first kill in Paladin.

Back in 2005, in the Sandbox, which was the army's name for Iraq. The accused was a man named Jamie Frahm. He was a contractor with Sic Semper Solutions, a small private military company that Rumsfeld's Department of Defense hired to provide security to Iraqi VIPs. One of many: there are more private contractors than soldiers in Iraq now.

He was, like all of Paladin's targets, an American citizen. An ex-marine, which was who Sic Semper liked to hire. A vet. He was older than Erik.

Erik abducted him in the night, drugged him with Rohypnol, and strapped him to a chair in the basement of a vacant Al-A'amiriya house. Al-Am was one of the nicer Baghdad neighborhoods before the invasion. Now there are plenty of vacants to use.

"No one will find you here," he told Jamie Frahm. "I am in command of the unit that patrols this neighborhood. I dictate which houses will be searched and which will not. I am going to keep you here as long as it takes to ascertain the truth of what you did. Lies will not help you. Begging will not help you. I have no legal or moral responsibility to you except what I place upon myself. You are a contractor, and therefore you are not subject to American military law. But you are not on American soil, and therefore you are not subject to American criminal or civil law. No law exists for you. So I have created myself to enforce a deeper law. The law of right and wrong."

For six days Frahm resisted. Erik had no pity. How could he? This guy was a monster. A bad, bad, bad dude.

On the seventh day, Jamie cracked under the bogus pipeline, a trick Erik had learned from Clayton. Give him injections of saline solution. Tell him it's a CIA truth drug, designed to use on the hardest jihadis, tested in Gitmo and Abu Ghraib (which men like Jamie believed were necessary crimes, rather than horrific, atrocious mistakes that rallied outraged Iraqis to kill American invaders).

It's just salt water. But the subject will subconsciously disinhibit. They will *believe* they've been drugged into telling the truth.

When the IV shunt in Jamie's arm got infected, Erik stole antibiotics. There was no sense making Jamie suffer unnecessarily.

Jamie told Erik about his family, their struggles in the devastated Rust Belt, the constant temptation of drugs and drug money. Watching his sisters marry beaters and Quiverfulls and addicts: meth, drink, heroin, and bottomless prescription opiates. The marines had not saved Jamie. They had abandoned him, betrayed their promises. With Sic Semper, Jamie said, he'd found purpose. He'd found brotherhood. He'd seen his brothers *killed*. Couldn't Erik understand?

That was how he confessed: by framing it as an act of brotherhood. As a Sic Semper contractor, as a man trusted with the power of life and death, Jamie Frahm had organized the killings of two Iraqi families.

"Why?"

Because a car bomb had gone off in that neighborhood and killed Jamie's brothers. Why hadn't the locals warned them about the bomb? They must have known it was there. They let it happen, because they were angry about Abu Ghraib or their dead cousins or whatever the fuck. So Jamie had to show them the cost of collaborating with the enemy. He had to kill Iraqis to save American lives. That was his delusion, that was how he twisted his anger like a tourniquet and tied off his morality. He was saving American lives.

He chose two families known to play a part in local government. He made sure they were raided, and that there was an accident during the raid which left the families dead. He was just so angry. Couldn't Erik understand?

"You are sullied no more," Erik told Jamie Frahm.

The words of a man Erik once admired, who came to Iraq and shot himself in horror and shame at what he found.

He boxed Jamie into an ammo crate, dragged him to an ordnance dump scheduled for demolition, and left the monster to blow sky-high. When the ordnance disposal guys pressed the button, the entire pile of old artillery shells and Soviet anti-tank rockets blew up with Frahm confined at its heart. First a blossom of white vapor that ringed the great earth-colored plume of the blast, and then a single spark of light that raced skyward from the cloud, and then, finally, a shower of brilliant white flares that arced down into the desert, going out one by one.

Erik found internet access at Camp Victory, anonymized himself through Tor, and reported the kill. Paladin's first: everyone else was still hunting.

Clayton assigned him a new target. Another American contractor.

Sic Semper paid no death benefits to Jamie's family. He was never officially listed as killed: just missing. But they took him off the payroll by the end of the month.

⸻

K + 139 hours
Aboard C-17 09-9211 transponder code AE49C7
Mid-Atlantic

The C-17 Globemaster III jets east over the Atlantic, across sky scoured of planes. Down below, the cold Atlantic roils. Derelict ships sputter with electrical fires. Submarines poke their antennae up to sniff for orders. Burnt-out cables cross the seabed like the fuses of some continental bomb. Even the surviving civilian transmitters are quiet. Waiting for the next blow.

The Globemaster's cargo bay is ninety feet long, twenty feet wide, twelve feet tall, green-lit and air conditioned, which by Erik's reckoning makes it bigger and nicer than two or three of Anna's apartment. But it is also jammed throat to ass with a train of air-droppable cargo containers. Clayton's expert planning has squeezed more than a hundred people in around the gear, like putty, for twelve hours of mission prep and bad sleep.

On the ass end of the rearmost container, a projector blazes on the aluminum siding. Erik and Clayton brief the military side of Task Force MAJESTIC.

"MAJESTIC," Clayton Hunt drones, making eye contact with no one, reading straight off the slide, "is an ad hoc cross-community special forces team modeled on the Advanced Force Operations concept, with the stature of a full Special Mission Unit, but without the group training experience. Operators have been selected to meet the unique challenges of a dynamic and escalating conflict vortex with characteristics of . . . ahh, I'm just fucking with y'all, welcome aboard."

Light chuckles. He clicks to the next slide, energetic. "First. I can confirm what you're all thinking. Space Surveillance Network radar tracked the nukes *descending* to their detonation points."

Clayton is the president's man, so he talks first. He's already briefed his own science team, up by the nose. Erik, busy bringing some kind of order to his grab-ass unit of high-speed, low-drag operators, did not get to attend that talk.

So now he gets the version that Clayton prepared for the goons.

"Down. From space. We got sucker punched by aliens. The good news is that they didn't just drop a rock on us. They want something here. That means we"— Clayton points at them two-handed, you and you and me—"have a chance to get to it first."

Behind Clayton is all the shit they're carrying: Clayton's top-secret electronic warfare gear from the air force labs in Rome; bladders of fuel and water; containerized physical, chemical, and biological labs; generators; comms; medical supplies. Some of the side seats hold "speedballs," body bags full of water and ammo: limp, bulky anticorpses, dropped to hold death back. And if the water and ammo doesn't work, at least you've got an empty body bag.

In front of Clayton are a bunch of high-tempo meat-eater door-kicker hand-to-God badasses. Erik doesn't know where Clayton got his science team, but

Task Force MAJESTIC pulled its field operators from DEVGRU, Delta Force, the Intelligence Support Activity, 24th Special Tactics Squadron, Force Recon, Green Berets, Erik's own 75th Ranger Regiment, an entire alphabet chili con carne of American elite.

Erik hates this decision. If *he* were in command, he would have selected a single veteran unit, probably a team from the Rangers' 75th Regimental Recon, all comfortable with each other and their officers. He would've flown in Strykers and regular infantry as blocking forces and backup, in case Iran decided to come over the border.

But no, here's Clayton, trying to assemble X-COM from scratch. MAJESTIC is a pile of shark teeth, but they're all from different mouths. Clayton's argument is that the mission needs unique skills—a lot of communications and medical expertise, biowarfare and conflicted radio spectrum operations, academic backgrounds in linguistics and aerospace.

Erik thinks Clayton didn't want any preexisting relationships to snarl up his puppet strings. He has given Erik only the length of this flight to get to know his team.

Now those gathered soldiers all look at one another like, whoa, shit. Aliens. Am I going to have to shoot an alien?

"Most of you will remember from cable news—rest in peace—that something weird happened *before* the bombs went off. Eighty-five hours before the blackout, national technical means detected a powerful radio signal from Kurdistan. And believe me, guys, there is no Area 51 or Blue Book file to explain this. It's nothing we have ever heard before."

Clayton holds up his phone and plays the transmission. A machine whale singing in machine rain: a long groan broken by cycles of rising and falling chatter. Auditory stalactites dripping from a roof of cosmic noise. God's modem dialing at midnight. It gets louder as it trails off, big spikes of sound further and further apart. It makes Erik's hair prickle. It makes Clayton grin in delight.

Clayton the Grand Sorcerer. That's what he always played in their games. A sorcerer trafficking in free magic and forbidden powers.

"Right before the EMP, we recorded a second transmission. This one comes *in* from near-Earth space."

Now Clayton's phone broadcasts cosmic electronica bursting through gut sounds, a sharp growl and a liquid splitting-pouring hiss. Like something surfacing from an ocean of blood and splattering onto tile. It makes Erik feel like his spine is going to slither out his asshole.

"Distress call, then a reply?" Lieutenant Latasha Gainer asks. Erik knows her from gossip. After her third tour in Iraq and a training crash at Fort Bragg that left her permanently off flight status, she went air force and trained as a forward air controller so she could keep working with her beloved Apaches. She is one of the reasons Erik personally cannot wait for the Pentagon to finally kill the ban on women in direct combat roles. The women are already there; the ban is just stupid pretense. "E.T. phoned home, then home called back?"

"Maybe they think we shot their scout down?" a Delta Force operator suggests. Sergeant First Class Chey "Squats" Kewell gives Erik a really familiar vibe, though he doesn't think they've met. Squats is famous across the Special Operations Command community for his ability to lift a kettlebell with his ass. "UFO crashes in Kurdistan, the alien mothership rolls in and takes out the lights so we can't interrupt their recovery?"

Erik's old friend—okay, old acquaintance—let's say old colleague Mike Jan speaks up. Mike is a DEVGRU guy, one of the SEALs who will put his name on a series of books someday. "Maybe the scout said *fresh meat*. And they sent the hunting party."

"There's nothing they'd *want* from Earth, bro, space is full of all kinds of good shit—"

"That's not true." Part of Mike Jan's problem is that, for a guy who carries a tomahawk into battle and earnestly describes himself as a Next Generation Warfighter, he's actually really smart. "We have billions of years of work on the protein-folding problem. Our biosphere's full of interesting molecules. The greatest resource an alien planet can offer is alien life. And once they've pillaged our chemistry, they might want to get rid of the competition."

"Then they would've dropped a rock," the guy from CIA Special Activities says. Skyler, Erik reminds himself: Skyler Nashbrook with the bad look. Skyler does *not* give Erik a familiar feeling. His eyes look like they were painted on, like pelican eyes, like you could hinge his whole skull open like a pelican's jaws and find an empty slot that says PERSON GOES HERE.

"Not if they wanted the biosphere," Mike counters. "If I were going to blow up the planet, I'd check it over for interesting stuff first."

"Settle down, guys. We've got a lot to cover. I'm happy to talk about all our best theories afterward." Clayton passes their attention over to Erik. "Major Wygaunt?"

"So here's the really spooky shit." Erik clicks the PowerPoint remote.

And there it is. Projected onto the aluminum. The Blackbird object. A half-rotten angel, face down in a meadow, wings spread, spine jutting from an amputated waist.

A contact event, Clayton called it. *Erik, this is it. This is the big one. The one that convinces Scully.*

"Blackbird. Name selected by an NRO spreadsheet. An object of unknown origin. Mr. Hunt's NRO friends went over the hull with every proctological instrument you can put on a satellite, but nothing goes through. They couldn't even find rivets or seams. Note the scale, by reference to this sheep right here."

Blackbird is a *lot* of sheep long. Bigger than a navy cruiser. The hull is manta-shaped, curved and sleek on the leading edge. But the trailing edge of the wings becomes jagged and weirdly irregular, combs of spine and sawtooth, asymmetrical.

The body tapers back to a long stingray tail. Erik traces that. "This structure penetrates directly into the mountainside northwest of the landing site. We don't know how deep."

"Like it landed ass-first," Ricardo Perez Garcia suggests. He's a personal friend of Erik's, a Delta Force master sergeant, a veteran of the Larchwood 4 raids around Baghdad. Ten years of Global War on Terror and still kicking doors. "Or it flies with that thing in front."

"Couldn't, no way, the angle's too shallow, it would've hit that other ridgeline on the way in—"

"Maybe they're drilling for oil," the ISA linguist deadpans. Everyone laughs.

It's funny. Everyone assumes Blackbird's a ship . . . but Erik doesn't get that vibe. The white and gold swirls of not-quite-paneling, the streaks of deep purple-black smeared across what should be clean mechanical boundaries. The ragged spiny trailing edge of the wing. He thinks of an insect struggling out of a chrysalis. Trembling. Wet.

He shivers and clicks to the next slide.

"Blackbird, uh, appeared in the Qandil Mountains, within walking distance of the isolated Kurdish village of Tawakul." The village from the air: a pleasantly compact and defensible hamlet of stone houses, dirt roads, pickup trucks, gardens, and sheep. There are beds on the rooftops, people sleeping up there on warmer summer nights. Walnut, almond, and wild pear trees brush black lines of shade along the riverside.

There are no prefab or modern structures anywhere, not even the shitty houses built by foreign NGOs. Just traditional Kurdish buildings. Pretty unusual for such an impoverished, bombed-out region. Maybe Anna can explain that.

"Tawakul sits in a shallow, high-altitude valley, cupped by mountain ridges to the northwest and the southeast. A cold river runs down from the mountain and off to the west, toward Erbil and the rest of Iraq. A road alongside that river is the only way in and out of the valley by wheel. It joins up with an east-west highway connecting Erbil to the Iranian border, but it's pretty fucked up and neglected compared to the Hamilton Road farther south. The closest settlement of any size is Choman to the south, population twenty thousand. You'll also hear people talk about Hewler—that's the Kurdish name for Erbil, the capital of Kurdistan."

Surrounded by meadowlands, sheltered by the white mountain, Tawakul is stupidly pastoral, the kind of place Americans cannot fully believe in until they've been directly exposed. There is nowhere in America that people have lived as long as people have lived in or near Tawakul. Not even Indian land.

Erik points out generators, a cell phone tower. "It's really unusual to see a prosperous village in the mountains, especially one with old-fashioned houses like this. These guys probably make their money by trading with kulbars, smugglers running routes between Iraq and Iran." Slide click. "Since we lost our satellites to the EMP, we're limited to aircraft reconnaissance, but we have *strong* indications that Russia has sortied aircraft and that a joint Chinese-Iranian column crossed the border from Iran several days ago."

"We're late," Mike Jan says unhappily.

"What about Turkey?" Ricardo Garcia asks.

"Turkey is not a factor," Clayton says with Cheneyesque confidence. "Between Russian pressure and our own diplomatic outreach, they're staying out of this. They know their presence in Kurdistan would really complicate the situation." Because they have killed too many Kurds.

Erik, annoyed, picks up his own thread. "We'll have constant air support overhead, plus tankers and AWACS. There's a carrier in the Persian Gulf and air force bases in Kuwait and Turkey. But with long-range radio all fucked up and our satellites gone, we'll have very limited contact with the world outside this valley. Our only comms will be via aircraft that can relay signals home. Washington is convinced"—convinced by Clayton, at least—"that a small, agile team on the ground is the right way to approach this. The big question is exactly where the Kurdistan signal came from, and how it's connected to the aliens that attacked us."

Yes. That's the big fucking question, that's what everyone wants to know.

"We assume, right now, that the signal *caused* the attack, and we need to know why. So we're counting on the village Kurds for support and HUMINT. To that end, I'd like to introduce our interpreter and local guide, Miss Anna Sinjari!"

Erik flourishes; Clayton ushers her up front while Erik scrambles to establish her cred. This is tough, because MAJESTIC is full of GWOT veterans who *hate* American experts on the Mideast. On the other hand, they've all worked with interpreters, and giving a shit about your terp is one sign of a good troop.

"Anna was born and raised in Tawakul, where she survived Saddam's campaign of extermination against the Kurds. Shortly before the Kurdish National Uprising in '91, she was fostered out to Germany and then to the States as a war orphan." Implicitly, because her parents didn't make it through the genocide. "Miss Sinjari?"

"Hey guys." Anna waves. She's wearing baggy ACUs, which will not save her from the sexual assessment of professionally depraved warfighters, but which Erik is glad of anyway. Uniforms mean something to him. "I speak Iraqi Arabic, Sorani Kurdish, and Farsi. I grew up with the Sorani and Arabic, right there in Tawakul. Picked up Farsi in college. I'm, uh, about twenty years out of date, but things don't look like they've changed too much back home."

She gets the Look for a moment. Presses on: "You should expect a wary welcome in Tawakul."

She certainly does, Erik judges.

"Nearly every other village in this region was destroyed in Anfal, the Iraqi genocide campaign against the Kurds. The survivors were forced into housing projects in the cities. Tawakul's had a tough time over the past thirty years, and nearly everyone who's come their way has been some form of bad news, even other Kurds. Most of the families there are from tribes local to the Erbil Governate. My family came from the Sinjar region to escape some religious shit. If you've got, uh"—she grabs her right hand with her left, arresting a nervous tic—"if you've got cameras, you'll love the scenery. The Qandil Mountains are part of the Zagros range. Think Middle-earth, but snowier.

"The mountains are the reason the Kurds have survived. We fall directly between Iraq, Iran, Turkey, and Syria, all of whom claim Kurdish land and resources. They fear Kurds and sometimes they kill us for it. The Iraqis tried to wipe us out in the eighties. I was seven years old." Her right index finger twitches. "About a million and a half Kurds fled north. A lot of people crossed the border into Iran, and Iraqi planes actually crossed the border to bomb the refugee camps. In Tawakul we left just before the helicopters found us. We thought we'd be safe up in the Qandils, but some jash from a rival tribe—those are Kurdish collaborators, working for the Iraqis—gave our village's position to the Iraqis. Their helicopters caught us. It was . . ."

She looks like she really doesn't want to stumble over her words, and doesn't want to sound fucked up either, so she just stops for a second. The C-17's engines howl through the wing spars and the aluminum fuselage.

"Most of the men and a few women stayed behind to fight. They were killed or taken to camps. I lost my mother, my father, and my older brother. Most of the rest of the village survived."

She doesn't explain how. How did they keep their homes? Erik knows for a fact that most villages in the area were blown up or bulldozed. Saddam's troops even dynamited mosques: the genocide might have used a scriptural name, but there was nothing Muslim about the Baathist terror.

So what happened to spare Tawakul?

He's not gonna ask Anna that, though. Not when her whole family died. She wasn't spared.

"I was fostered out shortly after that, through an aid agency. I know the rest of this stuff secondhand."

Anna briefly outlines Kurdistan after Anfal. Desert Storm, the illusion of American liberation, the great National Uprising against Saddam. America left the Kurds to die, and the Iraqi counterattack crushed the uprising. But the Kurds won their own autonomous region in the north. "Peshmerga," she says, "are the people who fought for that victory. The modern Iraqi constitution recognizes the peshmerga as the official military of Kurdistan. Technically the only 'real' peshmerga are those who work for the Ministry of Peshmerga Affairs. But half the people on those payrolls aren't even real. There were peshmerga before the constitution, and there are still peshmerga outside it. Any Kurd who stands up and fights is peshmerga. My parents"—brief swallow—"called themselves peshmerga during Anfal. I don't think my mom ever formally joined a peshmerga unit. But she *was* peshmerga. She fought. Okay?"

Uncomfortable murmurs of acknowledgment. Anna goes on. It should have been a new beginning. But then there was civil war: the PUK and the KDP went to the mattresses over oil smuggling profits—not as craven as it sounds; oil smuggling was the only way that the Kurds could buy food. The PUK went to Iran for help. The KDP decided one good turn deserved another and went to Saddam.

Anna pushes black curls from her eyes. "All the violence in this period forced a third Kurdish faction up into the Qandil Mountains. The PKK, the Kurdistan Worker's Party. The United States is an ally of Turkey and officially considers the PKK a terrorist organization. It is really important to remember that the PKK is *not* the Kurdistan Regional Government. The KRG rules most of Kurdistan these days, but Tawakul is in PKK territory. You can get trucks up to Tawakul, but only if you're willing to use narrow roads guarded by the PKK."

She looks at Erik. Erik nods encouragingly: you're doing great, bring it home.

"So, I guess, don't treat the Kurds in Tawakul like they're PKK, or KRG, or any other Kurds you've met. They've been fucked over by every surrounding party, including their own people. Give them your respect and your explicit recognition that you're a guest in their home, and they will be the best hosts you've ever had. Well. That's all."

Skyler Nashbrook raises a hand. His eyes appear to be focused on a place somewhere inside Anna's skull. "I have a question."

"Go ahead, Skyler," Erik says, because the CIA guy doesn't have a rank.

"The world might be ending. The most significant thing in human history just happened. A hostile first contact. And the reason might be right there, in Tawakul. Why do we care about the history of this village? Even if there are still people alive on the ground. Shouldn't they be willing to do whatever we need?"

Oh, for fuck's sake. Erik opens his mouth to snap a reprimand. Clayton draws breath to say something probably less ethical and probably more effective at persuading Skyler.

But Anna beats them both by bursting out laughing. "Dude," she says incredulously. "Weren't you listening? *You* think the world's ending. Someone shows up and bombs you out of nowhere, wow, that sucks, it's like Pearl Harbor, it's like 9/11. But if you're a Kurd, that's *normal*. And you know what else is normal? Americans showing up to help, and then fucking you over. Do you think it'll make your job easier if these people don't trust you? Did the past ten years of bombing useless dirt *not* teach that you can't win without the locals on your side?"

Skyler nods like this makes perfect sense. Okay. Gotta pretend to respect the Kurds, or I cannot execute Mission Task Prime.

But now the others have to poke at her. They've gotta figure out if she's breakable. Everyone in the military has to be able to take some shit; it's like testing equipment, seeing how much it can take.

A guy named Bruin, a big goofy marine Critical Skills Operator with a mouth, asks: "Ma'am, how would you describe the food?"

"Delicious," Anna says. "But a lot of it comes cute and four-legged. Are you one of those pony guys? Might remind you of your girlfriend."

A general *ooh*: she can hang with the guys! She's a cool girl! Erik feels uncomfortable, for her sake. Twelve hours ago she was a civilian, and he's making her trade blows with a bunch of professionals. But she looks like she's having fun.

He steps forward. "So that's that. Get yourselves sorted out by teams and rack out for the next four hours. That's an order. We're not going to drop without sleep. Planning starts at—"

"I'm not done," Anna says.

Erik blinks at her.

"I have more to tell you." Anna takes a deep breath. "You should know that . . . the Blackbird thing in those pictures is a weapon. The aliens that bombed us are looking for it. There are different factions, different aliens competing for control of it. Like, um, *Interstellar Pig* . . . you read that book? Anyone? That was my first English chapter book . . ."

Into the long silence Clayton Hunt asks quietly: "How do you know this, Anna?"

"Because I've talked to the aliens before. Before the EMP. In New York."

Nobody says anything.

Erik checks on Clayton. Did he expect this?

Clayton's staring at Anna with sly fascination. He *did* expect this. He knew she was crazy.

"I don't want anyone else to die." Anna puts her chin up and goes on bravely, *very* bravely. Everyone in the audience has just decided that she's high and off to the right, totally full of shit. The military is the ultimate generator of interpersonal chickenshit. Everyone's known someone like her before, someone who just will not shut the fuck up about his personal fitness plan or her wild ideas about the Zionists running the government or the secret child abuse ring that haunts professional wrestling or whatever. The military is full of this shit, top to bottom. Troops are as weird as anyone else; weirder, maybe.

Anna persists.

"I know you have no reason to believe me. So here are some things only the aliens could have told me. When you get to Tawakul, you're going to find a lot of destroyed Iranian tanks. You're going to find some dead Russians too. You're going to find a laboratory site constructed around the Blackbird.

"You're going to find corpses in that laboratory. A lot of corpses.

"And then something's going to start killing you. Something you can't fight. And I hope you'll listen to me then."

<hr />

K + 140 hours
Aboard C-17 09–9211 transponder code AE49C7
Mid-Atlantic

"What the fuck are you doing with Anna?"

"I'm not doing anything, Erik."

"She just told my whole team she'd talked to the aliens. Did you know she'd do that?"

"I told you. She's a human intelligence source."

Erik had to get his troops calmed down and racked out, so he couldn't follow when, right after Anna's speech, Clayton dashed off to a cargo canister with the ominous stenciled label AN/TCK COBALT SIFTER.

It's got some kind of secret squirrel mobile surveillance system inside, running off an onboard generator. Erik has Clayton cornered inside the container, which is ideal, except that he has to look into the blazing monitors and flickering telltales, so he can't see shit. Clayton is just a lithe shadow against all the data.

"You pre-briefed her. Why didn't you tell me?"

Not looking up: "I didn't. I never contacted her until we shook hands on her roof."

"Bullshit! You know exactly what's happening in Tawakul, and you're feeding that to Anna, to build her up as . . . I don't know. I don't know what the fuck. You're the Deputy NSA, you worked on spy satellites, people expect you to know too much. So why only tell *her*?"

Because Clayton wants a surrogate Rosamaria. Hell, he knows Erik's type, he knows Erik will get a little thirsty for Anna. He knows Erik always responds to lust with self-denial and chivalry.

Is that all this is about? Clayton trying to force Anna into Rosamaria's role? The one whose judgment will redeem one of them, and destroy the other?

Fuck Clayton. This is the worst point in *literally all of human history* for Hannibal Lecter mind games.

Clayton Hunt stares up into a halo of LCD screens, Bathing the angles of his face in blue secrets. His eyes reflect panes of data. Faceted. Insectoid. Erik shivers: oh, he can't help it, he's *scared.*

"Anna Sinjari is in real-time contact with the aliens," Clayton says.

"She's in—*what?*"

"There's a transmitter somewhere in her body. Probably in the throat. And this box is the only listening unit on Earth that can detect her transmissions. My big stupid baby." He grins at nothing. His eyes are locked on the numbers.

"What? How can she be— I mean, the pilots have radios, they'd pick her up. There's nothing else sending signals out there right now."

"No. She's not broadcasting in the EM spectrum. She's firing beams of polarized neutrinos straight through Earth toward Kurdistan."

"Bullshit. Neutrino detectors are, like, giant tanks of water buried underground. You couldn't pick anything up with a device this size."

"Nah. I bought the hardware from a company working on solid-state particle sensors. I bought the company too." Now, stirring from his trance, he pats the wall of the container. "I stole the budget for it from some asshole's legal program. They were hiring lawyers to justify targeted killings. Post facto. Isn't that ironic? At least *we* never tried to make it legal."

"How does it work?" Ignore the bait about Paladin. "Can we track return signals?"

"Sure. Incoming, outgoing, whatever. Given time I can even triangulate point of origin. This box detects coherent neutrino-nucleus collisions where the beams hit solid matter and side scatter. Like this." Clayton traces the outlines of a digital fountain, particles scattering like tiny billiard balls, and shivers in awe. "My God, Erik. She's *talking to them.*"

Erik suddenly feels like *he's* the one cornered. Like he's standing in the jaws of a monster Clayton made, and Clayton's the only thing holding the teeth apart. "When you chose her for the mission, did you know?"

"Oh, absolutely not."

"You just brought this special neutrino detector along for kicks?"

"Of course I did, Erik. We're going to meet aliens; what if they use neutrinos to talk?" He looks around his screens, huge-eyed, pools of data. "And Anna *was* mixed up in some weird shit, Erik! She's from Tawakul, *and* she gets blown out of Central Park by a burst water main nobody can find, *and* her boyfriend goes missing, *and* she's suddenly spending money she doesn't have on things she doesn't need, *and* her neighbors report her new roommate turned into a monster and attacked them? Too much weird all at once." He hugs himself and laughs. "Oh my *God,* man. This is . . . it's just incredible. Incredible. The aliens can talk to us. And they've been here, on Earth, before the nukes hit."

Erik knows exactly what happens now. Clayton will *capture* Anna. Like a stone on the Judas wood of the Go board, he will claim her. He will suasion her until she gladly tells him everything she knows, and then he will use her and her information to bargain with the aliens.

Clayton always plays the sorcerer.

"So you think she's right? You think we're going to find wrecked Iranians, an empty lab, and corpses?"

"She made some verifiable predictions, right? You don't make specific predictions if you're bullshitting. I think we need to treat everything she says as actionable intelligence." Clayton clicks the whole apparatus off, the *snap* of a crisp analog knife switch, and the Cobalt Sifter box sighs down into slumber. The reflected numbers leave Clayton's eyes: he is sealed off again, slick and sly, a beautiful plastic armature.

He turns to face Erik. "Who does she like more?"

"What?"

"One of us has to interview Anna. You or me?"

"It should be me," Erik says, because he can't think of any more subtle way to play it. "I need to know everything that's tactically relevant. I'll make recordings for you."

Clayton nods in the dark. "Tell her about Paladin."

"Jesus, *why?*"

"Tell her I made you kill people. She'll understand I'm the bad guy. She'll trust you."

"You didn't make *me* do anything, Clayton. It was all on you. You were the one who put us over the line." You do what you do, and then you own it. Erik only killed men who'd committed specific crimes, crimes beyond the reach of any other law to punish. Clayton, well— "I started Paladin. I had a mission. You perverted it. What it became, that was all you."

"If people believed that," Clayton says, "if they gave *me* all the credit for Paladin's success, you wouldn't be here. Why do you think I get away with so much shit? Why do you think I got away with picking you as mission commander?"

"Don't you *dare* say—"

"Because they know about Paladin. And they're terrified about it getting out. You thought people didn't like Abu Ghraib? You thought drone strikes on foreign soil were unpopular? Brother, we killed *white people*. Except—now—" Clayton points up, at the sky, and at what's waiting beyond. "Now, with the whole world fucked, all they want is a team that can get the job done. You and I built an assassination unit inside the American military-intelligence complex. We kept it secure. We used it for years. It got out, sure, but never to the press, never to Congress, never to anyone who could prove it. That's a track record they like. That's what the world needs right now, Erik. Success at any cost."

"Any fucking cost," Erik says bitterly. "Yeah."

Clayton, of course, knows exactly what he's dancing around.

"You think Rosamaria would've forgiven us? If we'd only killed the ones on *your* list?" Clayton makes a sad, sorry face that Erik wants to beat fucking flat. "You didn't know her like I did, man. She was too good."

"Go fuck yourself."

"I don't know why you told her. I don't know what you thought she'd do."

⁂

K – 2 years
Washington, DC

What did you two expect I would do?

Did he say something to you? Rosamaria, what did Clayton say?

You both said the same thing. I don't want him *to know we talked.*

You told me my husband was a serial assassin. Clay told me you tried to have him arrested for high treason. If you each had half a backbone, at least you would've told me together.

Rosamaria, it's not like you think.

(It turns out, at moments like this, that Erik is essentially an emotional tube of Pringles: everything he can produce is dry and fragile and unsatisfying, and once he starts producing this airless crisp, he can't stop.)

"Like I think"? Me vale madre. You broke the law. You killed people. You took all the worst things this country does and made them worse. Now you're each telling me it was the other man who went too far. You come home and you both confide in me? Like I'm the one who can make it okay? You want me to tell you who's right? Pick a side? Vete a la chingada. I won't be the little hinge on your seesaw. I will not be your moral collateral. I am not going to be part of this story you're telling each other.

Please. Rosamaria. Let me explain. We had to do it. He just got out of control—

You had to! Well, I have to do this. This is severance. We're strangers now. Clayton will get the divorce papers in a few weeks. I will be Rosamaria Navarro, and he should go back to being Clayton Hunt. If he sees me, he doesn't recognize me. Same goes for you. Never contact me. Never. If you break that rule, I'll go public on both of you. Fuck you for making me know this, and fuck you again for making me complicit in hiding it.

Now get out.

⁂

K + 141 hours
Aboard C-17 09–9211 transponder code AE49C7
Mid-Atlantic

"Major," Anna says, looking up from her ebook. Her phone's plugged in to an extension cord in her lap. There's room for her among the air mattresses on the floor, but instead she is sitting alone on one of the black seats along the wall. "I can tell when you're checking me out."

Erik's caught red-whatevered and he's got to laugh. In her baggy ACUs she's about as sexy as a laundry bag, but he's *really* keyed up, and it's been halfway to forever. "Forgive me. Pregame jitters."

"It's cool, man. But we're flying to a town full of my relatives in a country where six out of ten women get circumcised. So I'm feeling a bit caught between cultures." Anna pats the bench. "What's up?"

Jesus. Is that true? He never deployed to northern Iraq, but he always thought Kurdish women were like Amazons, warriors and equals in a democratic society. Is that just American bullshit? Maybe they are, and they still get mutilated by their culture. The world is a complicated, difficult place, and that's why you can't keep recalculating *right* and *wrong* everywhere you go. You just have to say, listen, cutting women is fucking inhuman, full stop. No matter who you are or what your traditions say. It's wrong.

"I thought they banned that," he says awkwardly.

"Might be. I haven't kept up. Kurdish women get it better than Arabs and Turks, but you've still gotta keep your action on the down-low." She looks at him curiously. "Do you want me to stop there?"

"What?"

"Usually, when people want to learn about Kurdish women, they stop at the AKs and the fighting. Sometimes a pretty girl gets picked out by a photojournalist and people talk about how tough and brave she is, shooting guns at the terrorists. Never very much about the rest of the struggle. We're fighting the enemy, which is pretty much everyone around us, and at the same time we're fighting our own people. When women asked for their own party within the PKK, they got arrested, at first. Men want us under control."

"Men who want to go back to the bad old ways?" Erik suggests.

"Nah. It's not as simple as 'old is bad, modern is good.' We've always had rulers like Lady Adela, or Asenath Barzani—she was the first female rabbi, actually. Women always fought and held power. Women had sex. But then there are men willing to kill women for going to market, or for dishonoring the family. Shit's complicated. Some things get better. Some don't."

"For someone who doesn't keep up, you know a lot of history."

"Tell you a secret?" she says with a little glimmer of mischief on her lips, and a little dark doubt in her eyes.

"Sure."

"I just read that. While you were eyeballing me." She shows him the phone. "Clayton gave me some books on the history and culture of the Kurds. So I can pretend to be one."

"You sound like you have pretty complicated feelings about your people."

"Am I not allowed some complicated feelings? Are your feelings about America totally uncomplicated?" Anna cocks her head, reminding him to take the seat; he does. "Listen, when white people talk about Kurds, it's always *Wow, that's cute, they're almost as liberated as us.* They're like little friends of democracy! But Kurds aren't proto-Americans. Kurds went way further than Americans. We've been making changes that you could never campaign on in Kentucky. There are places where it's mandatory now to have as many women as men at every level of government." She frowns. "I guess I should say, *they* made huge changes in Kurdistan. I can't take credit. I was off being raised by white people. So I've got some shit to sort out in my head."

"Nepantla," Erik says.

"What?"

"Something a friend used to call herself. I probably shouldn't steal the word and throw it around. It sort of belongs to"—how would Rosamaria want him to say it, God, he can't remember—"indigenous Mesoamerican people." He finds a spot not quite too close to her. "I wondered if I could ask you a few questions about what you've learned."

"You believe me?" Her eyes are hooded, suspicious. She is striking like a hatchet, like a short sharp knife. "You think I'm talking to an alien?"

"Well, you gave us some unambiguous intelligence, a very clear yes-or-no test of your source. I think that's a sign of trustworthiness. Maybe the aliens have been here a while, and you really did meet one in New York. Maybe the Blackbird object's been near Tawakul for years, and you've known about it a long time. Or, leaving aliens out of the picture, maybe someone in Tawakul has a way to contact you despite the blackout. And you're protecting them by pretending you learned things from an alien."

She smiles at him and doesn't confirm or deny.

Erik shows her the recorder he got off Clayton. "May I?"

"Fire away, Major Wygaunt."

"How do you get your information?"

She has rehearsed this. It reassures him that she had to work nervously to get it right. "I have contact with one of the aliens. I can talk to her. I guess it's not radio, because it still works with the . . . you know, it still works after the sky went crazy. When all the power went off I was scared. So I . . . I called her up. Actually I just screamed at a wall for a while, and then she answered. I guess she was watching me."

"Okay." Accept and invite. "How did you get involved with her?"

"She needed a place to hide out from other aliens. She stayed with me awhile."

Good. If hiding with an Earthling can protect an alien then the aliens must not be so very powerful. "Is she connected to this Blackbird artifact?"

"Yes. She went to Kurdistan to find it. Or . . . make it."

"Can you identify the artifact?"

"Not in a way you'd believe. I just know it's a weapon the aliens want."

"What kind of threats do you expect to find on the ground there?"

"Uh. Threats. Man." Anna twists her hands and laughs. She has that nervous tic, right trigger finger tic-tic-tic. "Well, there are two aliens after Blackbird right now. Iruvage and Ssrin. Ssrin is the one I know, and she's . . . less bad. Both of them are really hard to kill. Both of them can disguise themselves as people. Iruvage has something called an atmanach, I don't know how it works but you definitely can't shoot it. It hunts for people making decisions. So I guess it'll go for the leaders first?"

Atmanach. Brief the operators on that. Assume it's real. "Can you describe the aliens' objectives?"

"They both want Blackbird. But they're afraid to go near it. They're using people to try to figure out what it does. Iruvage is a cop, he's from the Exordia, the aliens who bombed us. Ssrin's the same species but she's from a rebel group."

He makes a note. *Aliens afraid to get close. Need us to do it first.* He pauses and types: *Aliens using humans. Anna's people?*

Clayton was right. She is *vital.* Now they have a game plan.

"Ssrin is the one you met?"

"Yeah. She's fast, she's vicious, and she has, like . . . powers. If she has to fight, she'll fight you the way you fight goat herders. Totally unfair."

"I've seen guys with goats kill guys like me. Can you tell me anything about the signal we detected from Tawakul?"

"That was Ssrin." Her tic is still going strong. "She pulled Blackbird out of . . . a place it was hidden, I guess. She kind of unfolded it. Then it made that radio noise. And that's why the aliens came to Earth. They heard the . . ." She waves in frustration. "The shriek of it coming into existence. The second noise Clayton played, that was the alien ship arriving."

"That doesn't seem right," Erik says. "The radio waves couldn't have traveled far enough to reach aliens, could they? Not in less than a week."

"They have other ways to hear, I guess. Ssrin didn't tell me."

"But they want Blackbird, yes?"

"Yeah. Badly. Really badly."

So Blackbird *has* to be secured by humanity: it's the only bargaining chip they have, the only possible deterrent to invasion. Which makes it even worse that Clayton is dribbling in this little team of specialists, instead of ringing Tawakul in American metal.

"There are already people there," Anna tells him. "Iranians, Russians,

Chinese, Ugandans. But they're hiding now. They're in the village with the Kurds."

"What are they hiding from?"

"Blackbird. It did horrible things to them. And then Iruvage killed some of them too. He's still killing them. He wants them to go back to Blackbird." Anna grips his forearm, and oh, she's thrillingly strong. "Major, thank you for listening to me. I want to keep helping. Just, uh—this will sound strange—"

"Anything I can do."

"Let me make a couple decisions now and then. It's important to me to . . . have some choice."

Erik blinks. "I'll try to keep you in the loop. Listen. Hey." He shows her that the recorder's off. "I want to give you a warning, okay? About a . . . bad actor."

"Like Nicolas Cage?"

"No, Jesus." Erik laughs. "I mean in the moral sense. It's about Clayton Hunt."

Anna waggles her eyebrows. "Did you know people on the internet write stuff about him? There's Obama slash—"

"I don't want to know," Erik says, more coldly than he meant. "Clayton's a funny, charming guy. He's also an absolute psycho."

"Like a creepy narcissist, or like a serial killer?" Anna doesn't hesitate at the suggestion, which Erik expected, because Erik saw the Look on her. Anna has seen evil. She knows it's real.

"He's an assassin. He commanded a kill team while he was at the NRO—the National Reconnaissance Office."

"I thought those guys were satellite nerds," Anna protests. This does not seem like the kind of thing Anna would know. Clayton probably told her he was a satellite nerd.

"Intelligence roles aren't cleanly divided like that anymore." Not after 9/11. "Clayton had information, and so he acted on it. He ran contractors, subcontractors, fusion groups. Whatever he needed. Choosing and eliminating targets to support his own security policy. People all over the world, murdered without process, for no reason except that he wanted them dead." Erik has to look away for the shame of it. He created Paladin. He let Clayton run rampant with it. Because he was stupid enough to trust.

But Anna still has a grip on his wrist, drawing him back. Erik swallows hard and keeps on. "You can't let him talk to your alien, okay? It's vital that we keep him from taking command. He *will* try to negotiate our surrender to this, uh, this Exordia. He'll bargain away Blackbird for something he thinks is more valuable. He thinks he's a big-picture thinker. He'll use that to justify 'sacrifices.' But they won't work."

"But he's in charge, right? He's the national security advisor. Deputy. Whatever."

"I know. But my guys have the guns."

Anna's wary. Hackles raised. Her fingers probe the tendons under his wrist. "No offense, Major—"

"Erik. Please."

"Erik, in my experience, it's usually the *really* manipulative people who start the accusations."

"Yeah. I hear you. I trusted Clayton for a long time."

And so Erik tries to explain what Clayton did.

———

K − 5 years
Camp Victory, Baghdad, Iraq

2008. Back in the Sandbox. Not for long though: the American occupation is winding down with the Bush administration.

Aluminum aircraft tails shimmer under Mesopotamian sun. Baathist palaces rule rows of American containerized housing: the neocon hermit crab in Saddam's old shell. Erik pulls his cover down over his face and walks through memories. Some are good: John Cena versus Big Show on the Christmas after the invasion, the ref knocked out as collateral, Steve Austin delivering Stone Cold Stunners to both of them. The announcers explaining the danger of roadside bombs, before anyone in America had even heard of IEDs.

Most aren't. Like the air-conditioned hut, *there*, where he read about the Nisour Square massacre and seethed in helpless rage. Paladin could do nothing: the Blackwater soldiers who'd killed those people were too public, too hard to vanish. The same went for the people at Kellogg Brown & Root who allowed their subcontractors to practice slavery. Protected by their power. Beyond Erik's reach.

He has been very careful not to let Paladin overreach.

He keeps them on target. Disciplined, rigorous, acting only with weight of evidence and only against those whom no legal authority can touch. But they've made a difference. They *have*. There are eighteen evil men, American men, dead men who would otherwise have escaped. And even if no one ever knows, the right thing is the right thing.

He couldn't have done it without Clayton. Run a cell system *inside* the American military? Coordinate their actions over SIPRNet? Suppress the escalation of any clue that might blow their cover? All of that required a mastermind, a man on the inside of the intelligence leviathan.

But Clayton *wants* to overreach. Clayton's argued, passionately and often, that the American military is every bit as guilty of atrocity as the mercenaries Paladin hunts: that illegal detentions, torture, and murder by American warfighters create enemies who will resent America righteously and permanently. He says that Abu Ghraib, as much as the decision to disband the Iraqi Army, was the beginning of the end of the neocon dream in Iraq. And he's right.

But Erik can live with that. He doesn't like it, he hates it, he takes it personally: but it doesn't *require* him to kill. There are systems in place to prosecute war crimes. They don't always work—it's a pretty fucking imperfect world. But they *do* exist. There is the possibility of justice. Paladin is not for those crimes.

Six years. Eighteen kills. Eighteen watertight verdicts. Here in the Sandbox it was almost frighteningly easy. People from the military go missing all the time, and so do contractors. But the army never forgets what it loses: misplace a gun, misplace a private, and sooner or later the army *will* come sniffing for its property. Contractors, though, contractors ain't army, it's to their advantage to run a looser ship. No one knows exactly how many contractors have died in Iraq, because no one even knows how many contractors have been *sent* to Iraq. Certainly no one knows how much they've been paid.

And absolutely no one knows what happened to these eighteen men, except for Erik. The files will be released in fifty years, when Erik hopes he'll still be alive to face justice.

Right now, he's just here to wrap up some loose ends. A note from another Paladin. *We need to talk. Possible problem.*

He goes to Green Beans, plugs in an Ethernet cord, and logs on to the special SIPR connection Clayton set up for him. SIPR is the secret (but not *top*-secret) internet: using the really high-end JWICS architecture would draw too much attention. The Paladin Sword programs on his laptop will handle the rest. Clayton knows exactly what tools will be used to observe them, and how to deploy countermeasures.

Erik gets on IRC. The other Paladin is already there. He heard from another Paladin operator, who heard it in turn from a 92M—a morgue guy—that there's some evidence an RCT-6 marine lieutenant colonel killed by a sniper in Fallujah was shot by another marine's rifle. Officially it was written off as a one-off insurgent attack. Unofficially, the lieutenant colonel was well known to be dirty, selling refined petroleum to contractors: maybe drugs too, maybe even worse. A lot of people are leaving Iraq. A lot of educated, liberal women whose lives and savings have been destroyed by sanctions and war. Giving them a way out is profitable, especially when they're delivered to a buyer.

Maybe he was on the take, and it went bad. That was Erik's assumption.

The Paladin on chat says

I know whose rifle that is

I know the shooter

He is one of us.

All the sweat under Erik's uniform congeals in the vicious air conditioning and suddenly he's coated in frosty slime.

He types: LTC was not a Paladin verdict

The chat says: I know

Someone asked me if I was willing to continue my work in a private capacity. Someone who had a new target list.

It was much longer

Erik slams his laptop shut.

It takes him nearly three more years to collect the evidence he needs to be sure: a painstaking, doubly secret investigation, hidden from the military and from Clayton. But by the end he *is* sure.

His Paladins are being used to kill targets outside the Paladin list. Sometimes after their deployments, sometimes even after they've left the military. Going out and executing people in places America has no business meddling. And worst of all (Rosamaria would be especially furious!) is that Paladin hasn't killed anyone *in America*. As if the homeland is sacrosanct. As if—and Erik knows he's going Viking Warrior here, but this goes deeper than patriotism, this goes to *blood*—as if there aren't people in America who deserve more than anyone else to die!

He doesn't send his evidence to Clayton. He just writes: *What the fuck?*

Clayton tells him that once he knows, he'll be tainted too.

Erik has to know. So Clayton gives him the truth.

Dear Erik,

For the past several years, without your knowledge, I have been expanding the core capabilities you established with the Paladin platform. I have coordinated Paladin volunteers to execute semi-sanctioned killings against those who could not be reached by conventional means. We don't use drones. We don't send Jason Bourne with a handgun. We work Final Destination–style: we learn everything about the target, and then we arrange clean, direct, deniable accidents.

I have developed a system to hide these assassinations in the shadow of the administration's own kill program. Government oversight is already careful to pass over "special activities." I just expanded the blind spot.

I skim intelligence from fusion groups where covert agencies pool their knowledge. I select targets who cannot be touched by American power: because they have leverage over American interests, or over American politicians. Because our government believes their atrocities are in line with our strategic goals, or because they are in fact Americans themselves.

I have sanctioned the killing of 168 people in Iraq, Iran, Syria, Lebanon, Turkey, Yemen, Saudi Arabia, Indonesia, France, and Germany. Some of the sanctioned were American citizens. All were guilty of the most loathsome crimes. I disguised all these deaths as misfortune or as the actions of local agencies. In each case, I acted with the utmost precision and regard for collateral damage.

My operations are more humane and more effective than those of our military. A military we both know has normalized violence toward the very people we claim to liberate. If you are repulsed by the idea of my program killing a single target, how could you accept the everyday reality of Iraq? Scared teenagers racing across the desert in Humvees, blasting "Bodies" and slamming Rip Its, uncertain what they are doing or why, watching for any reason to shoot. Which is actually more humane?

I know you saw Paladin as a chance to do the right thing.

The world begs for more, Erik. I would rather do five evil things to gain a hundred blessings than wait for one clean blessing that demands no wrong. I will eat this sin. We are all told that evil triumphs when good men stand by and do nothing. Seeing what I do, as one of America's spies, as an element of this system, I *cannot* do nothing.

I've been consumed by guilt over my actions. I've committed acts of treason and conspiracy. Worst of all, I've kept secrets from you and Rosamaria. But I ask you, Erik: forgive me. And, if you can, allow me to go on. I've calculated the good we've done. I can show my work. I know exactly what I have chosen to do.

I will, at your request, terminate Paladin's operations and destroy all records.

With love,
Your friend and brother,
Clayton Hunt

K + 141 hours
Aboard C-17 09−9211 transponder code AE49C7
Mid-Atlantic

"We were just his private death squad," Erik whispers. "Just another fucking asset."

He doesn't just want Clayton to face justice. He wants Clayton to *understand* how wrong he's been. He wants Clayton to break under the weight of his errors.

You cannot just reach out into the world and alter it at your whim. Not one man: not alone. Not without oversight, and accountability, and people to say *No, the cost is too high.* It is intrinsically and absolutely wrong to set aside the duties of ethics because you believe that *you*, you alone, are smart enough to violate them.

Everyone thinks that, at first. Everyone thinks they have good reason.

Was Clayton better suited to choose the shape of the world than Cheney? Than Rumsfeld? Sure. He's smarter than them, for whatever that's worth. Obama is smarter than Bush, more careful about blowback, more appealing to the Nobel Prize set. But he's still killing a lot of innocent people. He still authorized signature strikes in Yemen: killing people whose identities are unknown but whose *behavior* seems suspicious. Was that Clayton's idea too?

You have to have a code. You have to have limits. You can retaliate for harm done, yes. You can guard what grows from those who would devour it. But you can't compute how the world *should* be and then kill your way toward that design.

There is a very basic distinction between trying to constrain and repair the evil of others, and actually *doing* evil in service of some unrealized, uncertain, maybe-illusory plan.

"So you started killing men you felt deserved to die." Anna has a far-off look. "And Clayton made it about killing men *he* thought deserved to die."

"I wanted justice. I had a very specific code of evidence and jurisdiction. Clayton wanted . . . God, I don't know. Clayton wanted to be Lex Luthor."

"Did you ever feel guilty about the men *you* killed? The ones on your list?"

"What?" The question takes Erik off guard, which makes him feel like an ass. He knows so many soldiers who've been ripped apart by guilt. *What were we doing there? What was the point?*

But not him. "I . . . no. No. I only did what was right."

"You always know what's right?"

"I try."

"God," Anna says. "I wonder how you would've lived my life."

"I don't know that," Erik says, with, he hopes, visibly genuine respect. "I've been very lucky in many respects. I haven't had to face your . . ."

"Challenges," Anna suggests dryly. "That's the word my therapists like."

"But I've always tried to do right by the people under my command. Under my protection. That includes not just civilian advisors"—Christ, he sounds stiff-necked—"but the people who live in my area of responsibility. Your people."

"You think you're protecting *me*." She touches her neck with the hand that's not, still, clamped in the soft part of his wrist. "You have no idea."

"We have nearly nine hours of flight time ahead of us," he says. "If you want to talk more . . ."

She shakes her head. Something closed off between them a moment ago. Why? He doesn't understand. Awkwardly he says: "I think you should have this back."

He gives her back her Glock. She accepts it with resignation. "You'd better get your men ready," she says. "It's going to be bad."

"Women too," he says, trying for lightness. "The pilot's a woman. We've got a female forward surgeon, a psyops lead, a linguist—she's pretty badass, ran with SEALs in Afghanistan. And Lt. Gainer, she might have some advice for—"

"For what?" Anna says calmly. "Advice for what, Erik? How to get killed by aliens, in a feminine way?"

CHAPTER FIVE

Erik leaps out of the plane with Anna strapped to his belly.

The world rushes up at them: total sensory shock after hours inside a gunmetal tube. Like stumbling out of a corrugated drain pipe into the Amazon. It's colder than winter. It's so bright it makes him tear up even through his goggles.

He blinks, quick, and checks his landmarks. Southwest: smoke from a pileup of destroyed armored vehicles. Russian BMDs. Straight below: the village of Tawakul, and the river to its north.

Everything is so *green*.

This is Eden. Not the Eden of ripe fruit and nude lounging, but the Eden of forbidden trees and flaming swords. It is dawn in Kurdistan, and the light comes over the Qandils to the east, slow advance onto stone and water and snow and grass. The mountain over the valley is a vast icy whiteness, a vertical lake.

"Told you it was nice," Anna says.

She's snugged in below him in the tandem-jump harness, face to the wind, but her voice comes clear through the bone-conduction headset clasped around Erik's skull. It's connected to one of Clayton's digital packet radios, ten years ahead of army comms. Erik's personal radio can talk to planes on the HAVE QUICK II encrypted channel, then swap to a team or unit-wide net with a click of a ring switch. Even the science team is tied in via an ad-hoc MANET mesh protocol, and at that point in the explanation Erik decided he didn't need to know any more; leave it to Gainer and the other sparkies. The point is they can talk: and when they're tied in to the bigger radios on the Globemaster, they can even talk farther than a mile.

"Yeah," he says. "It *is* nice."

God, look at it! The village curls up beside the river like a sleepy cat; the whole valley basks between two arms of the mountain, soaring, snow-capped, summer melt streaming down through lush forest and gray stone, through earth the color of pine and tea, through wildflowers and hard black rock. The shadows of high clouds move across the landscape. There is no sign of life at all. Not even sheep.

His radio pops. Everything that comes through at long range is blipped and jagged: EMP afterglow. *"Majestics, this is Rune One, flight of two F-16s. Our IP is ten kilometers west of the valley. We have four B61s and eight JDAMs. We are using MGRS coordinates. Station time two hours, over."*

A pair of jets from Incirlik in Turkey, topped off with gas from the same tanker that just refueled their Globemaster. They're carrying regular bombs and four just-in-case tactical nuclear weapons.

"Rune, this is Majestic Zero Six." Erik is on Team Zero, the command unit, and the unit commander is always Six. "Glad to have you up there." He'd be gladder yet if they had a Reaper and some helicopters, but no drones without satellites and no birds without airbases nearby. "Frequencies and map grids as fragged. Our controller's call sign is GAINER. Majestic inserting now. Out."

Muddy truck tracks draw his eye north, across the river bridge, and then northeast up the meadow that covers the valley floor. Erik follows them.

Shipping containers and the cabs that hauled them, parked like train stock. Bristling antennae. Generators and air compressors and tanks to feed and be fed by them. Accordion-tube connectors between portable labs, hooked up like articulated buses in DC. The burnt-out hulk of a Russian transport helicopter, in a star of burnt grass.

All abandoned. Nobody left.

Blackbird squirms into Erik's goggled vision. Like it's crawling up the side of his face.

Tail stabbed deep into the mountain. Blunt and brawny up front, jagged and weird on the trailing edge. It is the color of a golden android with serious bruising. Royal white and gold tiling shimmies and slips when Erik stares at it, like one of those stupid Magic Eye pictures he could never work. He can *almost* spot intricate geometric designs, right at the edge of recognition; but then some purple streak or blotch will ruin the symmetry.

It seems to gloat. *Come and get me. Look what happened to the last guys.*

"Erik, it's Clayton."

Clayton is still on the Globemaster with the science team. Once Erik's troops have secured the meadow and scouted out a landing site, the Globemaster will touch down, probably never to fly again. (It takes much less room for a C-17 to land than to take off.) He's sitting in his magic box right now, listening for alien neutrino beams.

"Zero Six here. Go ahead."

"We're swinging around for our second pass. The sensor pod just picked up more

than a hundred destroyed vehicles on the highway southeast of the valley. Probably Iranian. So that's score one for Anna. We also got some intermittent thermals from the forest southeast of the village, up on the ridge. Might be people, might be smoldering fires."

"They found your dead Iranians," Erik tells Anna.

"I was telling the truth."

Which means everything else she said is probably true too. There *are* two snake-headed aliens down there, somewhere in the mountains and the forests. There *is* a creature called an atmanach, a thing that hunts choice.

Look up and see the tiny black shapes of other troops coming down. Does anyone look like they're gonna die? People die in training jumps; in March a veteran SEAL with two Bronze Stars and nearly a thousand jumps hit a fellow unit member and died. If they lose anyone on the way down—

"You're breathing tight," Anna says, making him conscious of the long warm zone of contact between their cold wind-whipped bodies. She squirms to try to look at him: can't manage it.

"Just the altitude." It will all go well. Erik's men will seize the village and the high ridges overlooking the valley. They will find a nice flat kilometer to land the C-17. And if they can't, the Globemaster will make a low pass and shoot the containerized units out of its ass, to land on airbags in the meadow. Then Clayton can start his game and Erik can start stopping him.

He wonders: "Hey. Anything else from your friend?"

"You mean Ssrin."

"Yeah." Ssrin the alien. She has a name, she has an identity: somehow this disappoints him. He was expecting an entity, a Stanisław Lem kind of thing. Anna talks about her like she's just a weird person.

"She's afraid of what will happen if we go close to Blackbird. She doesn't want me to go in with you. But I want to. Is that okay?"

"Could I possibly stop you?"

"Sure. You could leave me behind when you go in."

Erik blinks. He hadn't even considered it. "You wanted choices. I'm giving you this one."

Their mission is to exploit Blackbird, recover all possible intelligence, and determine the objectives of the aliens that bombed Earth back to the pre-electric age. He has to use every possible resource he's got to achieve that objective. Whatever's about to happen next, he wants Anna, the only person aside from Clayton who seems to have any fucking idea what's going on, with him.

And he likes Anna. She's tough. She says just what she means.

K + 151:21:18 hours
Blackbird Perimeter
Qandil Mountains, Kurdistan

Hard touchdown among the white mountain-star flowers. He hits and rolls on his ass, Anna falling on top of him, little spoon protected by his bulk. She's laughing: she liked it. But right away she starts struggling to get out of the tandem harness. He unstraps her and polices the parachute.

She gets up to a crouch, one finger stirring dirt. Pulls off her helmet and grins suddenly. "I remember these birds. That's a wheatear. That's a serin ... that sounds like sarin, doesn't it? Look out, the valley's full of serin." She laughs a very weird laugh.

Erik doesn't join in. In his head he is reciting the tactics, techniques, and procedures for contaminated environments. *Contaminated environments are the most challenging environments because of the high probability of fatalities among both victims and rescuers ... serious risk-management issues must be weighed before executing a recovery. Team survivability is paramount ... the number-one consideration is avoidance ...*

His team rallies up on him. "Get MOPPed up," Erik orders, though they're doing it already. Part of their protocol is to minimize exposure to any air around Blackbird. Plus the air is just *full* of pollen and Erik's already sneezing.

As mission commander he should probably be setting up a command post. It's not his job to be the pointy end. But he's decided to be the pointy end anyway, because of Anna. She knows shit, and he doesn't trust anyone else to talk to her.

He won't go *into* Blackbird, he's not an idiot; but he's going to find some corpses and discover cause of death. A drone will lead the way, but they won't know it's safe until someone walks in there and walks back out. And Erik's not going to ask anyone else to do that.

Plus, well, he wants to be first. Call it vanity.

He handpicked a team for this: DEVGRU Petty Officer 1 Mike Jan, Delta Force Master Sergeant Ricardo Perez Garcia, and the empty-eyed CIA Special Activities operator Skyler Nashbrook, whose previous career fell under the heading of *government disavows knowledge*. Erik chose them for his command team because all three are excellent troops, and because he wants Jan and Nashbrook close, where he can keep an eye on them.

They struggle into their hot, miserable MOPP protective suits, checking each other's tape and triple-checking Anna. Erik sounds off with his other teams:

"*Zero, One. Approaching the village now. No sign of anyone. Lot of truck traffic came up the valley to the village in the last few days.*"

"Zero copies all." Captain Amos Brennan's Team One, all cool. "Two Six, Zero Six. Situate."

Captain Dylan Raab's Team Two: "*Zero, Two. Moving up onto the south ridge to survey the highway. Repeaters look good.*" Comms are Eric's second priority, after figuring what kills people down here.

"Copy. Three Six, Zero Six. Situate."

"*Zero, Three.*" Captain Ander "Game" Gamboa's team. "*Down and moving. South valley, scouting out a landing zone for the big plane.*"

"Zero copies—"

Suddenly Clayton pops up on the command freq. "*We just lost one of the EBADs.*"

"What? Which one?" The EBADs are Expedient Biohazard Anomaly Detectors: mice in cages mounted under parachutes. The Globemaster dropped a whole spread of them over Blackbird.

"*Six Delta Three. Killed . . . while still airborne, directly over Blackbird's spine, about fifty meters up. Camera shows . . . Jesus Christ.*"

"Jesus Christ *what?*"

"*The mouse is gone. The whole end of the cage is broken open. It looks like . . . I can't tell. The cage sensors picked up a spike of hard gamma rays.*"

"You're telling me the mouse . . . turned into radiation?"

"*No. I'm telling you something twisted the end off the cage and the mouse fell out. And maybe then it turned into radiation.*"

"Okay. Keep me advised. Out."

"*Out.*"

"What's up?" Mike Jan asks, like they've just bumped into each other at the gym. "Something bad?"

"Something undetermined," Erik says. "One of the EBADs broke. One more check, then we go in."

So they do a final test on their MOPP protection, which is an absolute nightmare in the rising sun. Masks that fog up if the seal isn't perfect, baggy JSLIST oversuits, paper wraps that turn bad colors if they contact known agents (what good will that do?), gloves and booties over their boots. All perfect for poaching them in their own sweat. "Can't see shit in here," Ricardo says, without unhappiness: just the condition of things.

"I know. Mike, bodyguard Anna. Skyler, get the drone up. Ricardo, load a mouse. All call signs, Zero-Six, now proceeding into the target area. Out."

They walk straight toward Blackbird. Skyler flies a quadcopter drone ahead: a Teal Drones Golden Eagle with a fifty-minute charge. Ricardo Garcia follows its course, waving a ten-foot spear with a live mouse in a plastic lattice canister. The idea is that the mouse will die in time to warn the rest of them.

"Pretty out here," Mike Jan remarks. "Looks like a Windows desktop."

Of *course* Mike has never changed a default desktop wallpaper in his life.

Erik takes a knee and scouts out the camp around Blackbird with his rifle's optic. It's really hard to see through the MOPP mask and the scope. He reads some English labels off a roll of Tyvek sheeting: UMEME-HERITAGE. If Anna's right, that was the Ugandans. They built a sealed plastic tent against Blackbird's nose. Did they actually go inside? Were they that stupid? Maybe they thought an airlock would make it safe . . .

Containers marked in Cyrillic and Chinese nestle side by side. One big happy family, maybe? Russia and China and Uganda and Iran all set up a joint laboratory? He'd like to believe it.

And then he spots his first corpse. Face-down dead behind the plastic walls of the Ugandan airlock tent.

The dead guy is wearing a bright green biohazard space suit.

Shit. Shit. "Clayton, this is Zero Six. We've got a body inside the labs. Fully suited. Maybe he had a breach, but I can't tell. Our protective posture may be worth fuck all. How are the mice doing?"

"Still just the one EBAD mortality. If Blackbird's putting off dangerous fumes we're not picking anything up on spectro. I've got mice sitting right against the hull and they're fine, as far as paradropped mice go. No radiation. Nothing on bioassay. Nothing on Cobalt Sifter, even."

Erik does not want to go closer to that glistening angel corpse until he knows for sure that the sawtooth edges are not going to chop his soul apart. "Something killed that guy while he was in full biosafety gear. I don't like that."

"I'll let you know if mice start dying. Proceed."

"I'm inclined to hold back until we get more data from the mice."

"Noted, Erik, and agreed . . . but if a hazardous vector in there can get through suits, then it can also get through the walls of the lab tunnels. That means the whole valley is exposed. If we need to abort, you better figure that out now. Out."

Shit. He's right. Erik grimaces, en masque, and waves his people forward. Anna's staring south across the river, toward the village. Mike Jan tugs her politely back into the protection of their fireteam. "We need you with us, ma'am."

They tromp forward through unmowed, unmanaged, lovely meadow.

The quadrotor's sensor package pops up an alert. "Gamma detection," Mike Jan reports. "Very cool." He thinks high-energy radiation is cool. Erik supposes he's not planning on starting a clutch of little Janlets. Or he's got frozen sperm. Why does Erik's brain do this?

The drone's gamma scintillator leads them to a—well, to nothing. It's just a patch of meadow.

"Weird," Clayton says. *"Hang on. I'm talking to the gamma ray guy. The spectrum you're seeing doesn't match emissions from any radioactive element. Can you get the sensor a little closer?"*

Mike, without waiting for orders, dips the quadrotor toward the Tarkovsky-ass point of death. The gamma scintillator starts chattering like a squirrel taunting a cat. "Whoa," he says mildly.

"Jesus," Clayton says. *"These trajectories are ridiculous. Tons of pair production."*

I'll produce a pair for ya, some part of Erik's brain suggests. "Please give us something solid, Clayton. Do we need to keep poking this?"

"*Um, we think there's a . . . lens, or . . . a mass of some kind there. Too small to see. Possibly too small to actually interact with nearby atoms. But it's sucking in nearby photons and electrons. Making a tiny, tiny accretion disc. You're detecting gamma rays from frictional heating, plus a bunch of Compton effect from those photons striking electrons in the air. And some slingshotting, as photons escape unstable orbits around the mass.*"

"Photon *orbits*, Clayton? As in they're being bent by gravity?"

"*Yeah. The physics guy says it's something called a photon sphere. Light trapped around a large mass. The mass would have to be . . . um . . . really large. At this range it's too small for you to feel any pull, but get closer and it'll suck you in. I don't know what would happen then. Maybe an interior suntan.*"

"Should I put the mouse in it?" Ricardo asks, unhappily. He's been making a lot of eye contact with the mouse.

"*No. I think the EBAD we lost hit one of those.*"

So there's an invisible thing that can tear mouse cages and bend light. That doesn't make any sense. It would have to be a black hole—and a black hole cannot be here. First, it would fall into the planet, pulled by Earth's gravity. It would go through dirt like a ball bearing through fog. Maybe it's charged, and held up by magnets? If so, where are they? Is that possible?

Second, and Erik knows this because it's the kind of thing Clayton talks about when drunk, miniature black holes *explode*. They evaporate their mass into pure energy. If there is a tiny black hole here, it should be brighter than the sun.

"*By the way,*" Clayton says carefully, "*I've just been informed that the detector you're using has a maximum energy. It won't pick up gamma rays above about three MeV. So it's possible you're . . . getting a bit of a tan.*"

"Jesus Christ, Clayton." Erik starts backing off. "Everyone make some room."

"*Whatever that ghost mass is, I think one of them killed the mouse in six D three. And if there's two of them, there may be more.*"

"Great. Will proceed carefully. Out."

Erik feels like he should be tossing bolts ahead, to check for invisible death.

"Hey, look." Anna kneels and touches a patch of grass. "Spray paint. Someone put down a warning line."

Erik can't see a thing through his mask. He crowds up to Mike Jan to check out the overhead view from the drone. She's right. Someone circled the invisible death-node with a ring of yellow.

"Nice," Garcia says. "If they knew where these things were, they must've built their labs to avoid them. We should be clear once we're inside."

"Unless they move," Jan says.

"This one didn't. Not since someone drew that circle. Anyway, we'd see the damage."

Erik doesn't correct Garcia, even though he's wrong. This is *not* nice. It's not a relief.

If the previous expeditions were aware of these mouse-eating death holes, then something *else* killed them. Something stranger. Even harder to see.

⁓⁓⁓

K + 152:28:58 hours
Expedition Camp
Qandil Mountains, Kurdistan

The lab is a still death. Frozen in the moment of abandonment.

The gas generators are still running: restarted after the EMP? The dormitories have power. A Lenovo laptop displays a paused frame of something Korean, Lee Min-jung with purple headphones around her neck, looking surprised. Clothes balled up in their lockers. Meals cooled in microwaves. A phone alarm blares. Time to wake up, time to get back to work.

The Geiger counters are silent, the particle detectors still. The neural-net biohazard sensors don't smell anthrax or VX. The only change is a slight fuzz of static on the radio.

"Anything from your alien?" Erik asks.

Anna shakes her head. "She won't talk to me. She's listening but not answering."

A moat of open ground separates the dormitories from the lab complex around Blackbird. Instruments fill this grassy DMZ. Tripods with bristling antennae, groundwater sampling spikes, seismic detectors Erik recognizes from briefings on Russian security systems. There might be land mines: a safe path is marked with pink plastic tape.

One of the containers ahead draws Erik's attention. The plastic tunnel connecting it to its neighbors is tied shut with parachute cord. Soot mars the fireproof windows from the inside. But Erik's pretty sure he can see a handprint in the soot, like Kate Winslet's in *Titanic*, if she got off on burning alive.

"We'll check it out after we've finished our probe," he says.

Rifles up, step by creeping step, they enter the west airlock. Erik checks the gauges. The interior is under slight negative pressure: he approves. If the complex is punctured, air will be forced in from outside. Contamination delayed as long as the pumps have power.

A mechanism in the ceiling clicks and pours dish-soap-thick decontaminant all over their suits. The mouse on Ricardo's spear squeaks in protest and rubs its eyes. "Cool," Anna says.

"I used to be really scared of car washes," Ricardo Garcia says. "I couldn't stay in the car. I had to get out and wait in the office."

"Clear comms," Mike Jan says.

Erik nods to Skyler, who levers open the inner door. Erik steps through, careful and slow, slow is smooth, smooth is fast. Check the doors. Open doors are what kill you.

A staging area inside. More showers and decontamination systems. Expensive-looking biohazard detectors, Cyrillic labels, Russian kit. Dim fluorescent lights in power-save mode. A sealed server rack and—what the fuck?

"That doesn't look right," Clayton says. *"The stream's pretty shitty, but . . . what is that?"*

There is a thin spine of *something* protruding from a seam in the server's case. Erik waves to Ricardo, who jabs the mouse at it. The mouse keeps rubbing its eyes and quaking in terror. Erik makes a cautious approach.

It looks like a long, flat piece of green-and-black fiberglass. Exactly like the motherboards on the gaming PCs he's built. Chlorine-green solder-resistant coat, etched copper conductive tracks, little coin-shaped batteries, bridges, buses, MOSFET transistors and diodes and voltage regulators and those funny-looking cylindrical capacitors. Totally normal.

Except it's all sticking out of a seam in the server's case.

Erik levers a panel off the case and aims his rifle's light inside.

The internal components of the server rack seem to have . . . become fecund. Huge, densely layered boards, like black honeycombs. Components connected by insane paths of semiconductor. The heat is powerful even through the MOPP gear: like a clay-brick oven. Heat because it's still operating. The server is still on.

"Jesus," he says. "Is this somebody's school project? Or did . . ."

Did Blackbird do this, somehow?

"Oh, shit!" Mike Jan recoils. "Nanomachines!"

"We don't know that," Erik snaps, though it's his first thought too. Something that infects electronics—something that can crawl through suits, bite through skin—tiny machines like invisible bedbugs all over everything—that's what killed everyone, digested their bodies, what if they're in the air, all over him already—

(He saw a freshly molted cockroach once, pale and translucent, and now he has the image of them scurrying under his *skin*—)

"No," Anna says.

"No *what?*"

"Ssrin says there are, um, lidar devices in this lab which would've picked up nanomachines. And anyway, this happened too fast. Where would nanomachines get all the silicon and shit to make this . . . mess? They've only had a couple days to work. Nanomachines are the size of sperm, right? Not exactly sprinters."

"So what the fuck is it?" How can the power supply cope with all this added crap? Shouldn't it be shorting out? Burning up?

But there's a weird order to it: a rightness, a correctness to the mutilation. Something about the spacing between components, the repetition of small details and large structure . . . like looking at a coastline on a map, because the small details echo the large. But instead of the edge of a two-dimensional country, he sees sense in the way the cache units cluster around the processors and the conductive paths lead to the ridges of RAM and . . . no, he's lost it. It's just nonsense. Isn't it?

"I don't know," Anna says. "She doesn't know either."

"Erik," Clayton murmurs. *"I just want you to know, when Anna said Ssrin talked to her, I picked up sidescatter from a neutrino pulse. Anna's moving, but the other end of the signal isn't. I can tell by the way the beam steers. I'm working on a range fix but it's tricky with just a single source."*

"Copy." Erik isn't sure he likes Clayton tracking down the alien. The first step to bargaining with it. "Continuing our sweep."

"Erik, if you want to pull out . . ."

"Negative." Erik pushes aside plastic-strip curtains so the quadrotor can proceed. "We've got to figure out what killed that suit guy. We're headed to the Blackbird interface."

"Straight to the heart of things. Out."

Now even Clayton's faking his calm.

Erik's own heart is slowing down, pacing itself. He learned a long time ago that he's good under pressure. He breathes.

───※───

Plastic tunnels wash the outside world into green finger paint. Blackbird looms above: a golden alien wall. Erik feels the friction of his rifle's buttstock on his shoulder, hears the scrape of his boots across the plastic. Captain Brennan radios a soft status update.

Dull roar of fans around them. Sucking the world in, endless inhalation.

They enter a bigger lab, Russian, two shipping containers mated side to side. There are glove boxes and mouse cages, benches and centrifuges. A Cyrillic character marks this as Lab A. Erik checks the door through the partition to Lab Б and grimaces.

"Corpses. Lotta corpses."

Dead bodies lie in ragged heaps. All are biosuited. All torn up with gunshot wounds. One man has a deep scimitar cut across his throat, through plastic and cloth and flesh. His suited arms are bloody to the pits. On the bench before him, a huge bloodstain marks—what? An emergency surgery? A postmortem? A vivisection? The throat-cut man's name flash reads SMIRNOV in Cyrillic. He wrote his name again, in English characters, and taped it on just below. Thoughtful guy.

"Something went very wrong here," Mike Jan mutters, watching the other exit. "Very fucking wrong."

"Some kind of alien disease got out?" Erik's figured, so far, that it's unlikely any alien virus or microorganism could survive inside a human. A virus wouldn't understand human cells well enough to hijack them for reproduction. But humans are full of warm water and nutrients, aren't they? Sugar's sugar, wherever you may go. And if these aliens have met *other* aliens, maybe there are already cross-species diseases, evolved through millennia of contact . . .

Maybe they're about to get conquistadored.

"Probe mouse is still doing fine," Ricardo reports. "Poor guy."

"Sir." Nashbrook, the CIA cryptofascism ninja, examining mouse cages at the center of Lab A. "I think you'd better see this."

"I hate it when people say that," Clayton complains. *"Just tell us what you see."*

"These mice have been disfigured." Skyler gets his Bio-Seeq detector out and then looks at it: What the fuck am I going to do with this? "They are messed up."

"Okay, okay, send me over." Clayton sighs. The quadrotor whirs toward Skyler.

At first Erik thinks he's looking at cages full of queen termites: distended, bulging white abdomens, the body proper just a little brown afterthought. No. These are not bloated abdomens.

The white things are mouse brains.

The mice in the cages . . . *erupted.* Their skulls popped open, destroying the faces and snouts, and the tiny pea-sized brains inside grew into fatty sausages spidered with red-and-white veins. Their broken bodies dangle off the ass ends. The spines have drilled out through the animals' backs with soft fungal palps of nerve tissue. They look dead.

Erik gets a really bad feeling.

"Oh, *God*," Anna groans, and tries to cover her mouth, hitting herself in the mask.

"Anna." Erik steps between her and the dead mice. "I need your friend to tell us if it's safe for us to proceed, or if we'll end up like that."

"Ssrin says . . . she wants me to get out. She thinks we're not safe here. Not without her, she says. She's—she says she'll explain more once I'm out. She says she doesn't trust us to understand."

"Okay." Erik adjusts his grip on his carbine. "Okay. Do *you* want to back out?"

"Yes," Anna says, and then, suddenly: "No! If she's trying to get me to leave, I want to stay."

"Clayton, do you copy?"

"I'm here. You want my bullshit hunch?"

"Yes. Anything. Now."

"*You saw massive, uh, deformation of the server racks, right? And now those mice have supertrophied brains. There's a common element there.*"

"No there's not," Erik says. A brain is nothing like a computer. They both handle information, yes. But physically a computer is a relatively simple and knowable layout of semiconductor switches and charges, whereas a brain is an *unreasonably* complex skein of tissue and chemistry designed by nothing at all. The universe does not know function, does not get access to any special HEY, THIS IS FOR THINKING label.

Of course, Clayton knows that.

"*My guess is that Blackbird is dispersing some kind of communication agent. It seeks out information-dense substrate and . . . interfaces with it. Tries to use it to grow a message or a system. It's trying to talk to us by amplifying patterns it finds. Not how I'd go about first contact. But how I might do it if I were very, very strange.*"

Erik can't help making a technical protest: like they're both optimizing their colonies in *Sid Meier's Alpha Centauri*, arguing over the details of the science fictional technologies in play. "Then it should be bursting open every cell in our bodies. If it's looking for information coding, then DNA would be the first thing it'd find. Seven hundred megabytes of digital data in each cell."

"*Maybe that's what happened to everyone here. DNA degradation would kill the same way as radiation poisoning. Well, there's one way to find out.*"

Erik's thinking the same thing. "The dead guy I saw. If he's got an intact suit, we know it can go through *our* suits too."

"*Exactly. Hopefully he was just shot like these people. If not . . . we need to know.*"

That is the right thing to do, the only thing to do. If they pull back now they might carry a contagion with them. They need to know how fucked they are.

"Okay. We're on the move." Erik snugs his weapon up on his shoulder. This is my rifle, a suppressed Heckler & Koch 416 chambered in 5.56 × 45mm NATO. It is made of hard matter. The universe has laws. Anything I meet will yield to hard matter moving fast. If I find a problem, I can shoot it.

Hold to that, Erik.

CHAPTER SIX

They find no monsters. No chaotic spirits from beyond the event horizon. No more deformed brains.

The death in this place is merely human. And that makes it worse.

Erik hates death without dignity.

"Bayoneted in the back." Skyler assesses a Russian corpse critically. "Not a clean thrust. Several wounds, while he was struggling."

"This one's shot." Mike Jan turns a body over with his foot. It's a Russian woman, lips peeled back, gums and teeth stuck in a purple grimace to her helmet. "In the back. She was running . . ."

"They killed their own scientists?" Anna draws back, skittish. "They were working on something and it got out . . ."

"Keep moving. Look for any protective measures they took. We need to know what doesn't work."

At the center of the complex is a Chinese physics lab, an inflated dome tent with a collapsible skeleton. Compared to the surrounding containers it's huge. Erik actually recognizes the design—China uses something like this to cover missile silos from spy satellites.

Inside, spectrometers and laser gyros still whine with power. The quadrotor goes in first. *"More bodies,"* Clayton sends.

"Christ," Anna groans.

"Is today your first dead people day?" Ricardo Garcia asks, and then remembers. "No. Shit. Sorry."

Eight scientists in red hazmat gear were lined up kneeling and executed here. Their brains fleck the aluminum floor. A toppled projector blasts light across them. Crisp, sane diagrams slant wildly over their bodies. Erik checks one corpse's faceplate with his stomach in a fist, prepared to see the skull burst open, the interior packed full of supergrown brain—but it's just a dead old guy. Pitiable, but not pathological.

Anna, muttering something, goes down on hands and knees and starts patting around the floor. "Miss Sinjari," Mike Jan says, "I think you'd better stay away—"

Anna holds up a dented metal tube. "This is a Russian cartridge, right? It has Cyrillic on it. A pistol cartridge?"

"Yeah," Ricardo says, clearly impressed. "That's right."

"This was a Chinese lab. But Russian soldiers killed these scientists."

"International dispute?"

"We can find out," Anna says. "I bet there were cameras. I bet they taped everything. Wouldn't you?"

Erik nods. "She's right. Pull the SD cards. Pull the hard drives if you can find them."

All of Erik's team members are skilled in site exploitation, the art of recovering intelligence. They start ripping through the lab for anything that could store—

Information.

Erik gets a huge chill. "Clayton," he murmurs. "Clayton, come in."

"I'm here."

"Notice that projector's still working?"

"That's good, right? Means the cameras should be untouched by the EMP."

"The projector is running off a laptop. They have microchips, Clayton. Shouldn't they be like that server?"

"The server was still on too."

"Yeah, but we didn't use it. We didn't check whether it worked. The projector still works. The laptop still works."

"Go check the projector case."

Erik fumbles with the projector until Skyler appears with a tiny screwdriver. Together they get the case off—and find the whole interior overgrown with circuit cancer. But it's still working. It's still working.

"Clayton." Erik forgets all his radio discipline. "Whatever happened in here, it preserves function. Do you understand? It alters the structure but preserves function. And that means if anyone was infected and didn't get shot—"

"Oh, fuck," Clayton says.

"Yes. I need you to alert my other teams that anyone they meet could be carrying this . . . alien agent."

"Jesus, this is incredible."

Ricardo and Mike are bagging everything that looks like a camera, hard drive, or memory chip. The mouse in the spear sniffs and grooms its whiskers. The place must reek of death, leaking out through ruptured suits.

Skyler covers the inner door. The one that leads toward Blackbird. It has Chinese characters all over it, labels and warning signs. But now that Erik looks at them, they're wrong somehow . . . he doesn't read Chinese, but he definitely doesn't remember Chinese writing growing all those weird serif extensions. Is it some crazy font? Why would you put a crazy font on your vital equipment? And now that he looks at them, those serifs look a lot like cousins of the parent character, little riffs and variants growing off the original . . .

. . . as if whatever happened to the brains and the microchips happened to them too.

"Oh, no," Erik breathes.

"What is it?"

"Shit," Erik mutters, "shit, shit," scouring the lab benches now, tearing open drawers, pawing through piles of discarded plastic wrapper. He needs something in English to be sure. Here—yes—a laminated English checklist for trouble-shooting Lenovo projectors—Erik holds it up for the drone.

"Clayton. Do you see this?"

Letters distorted and fringed with miniature mutant spawn, like fruiting mold. Words and sentences jammed together in off-kilter not-quite-copies, plausible nonsense, English-ish. As if you hired an artist to riff on the style of an alphabet they didn't understand.

"What the fuck," Clayton says.

"Yeah," Erik says. "Right?"

Brains and microchips both *do* something. They might be different in every other way, but they share that core trait: spending energy to flip switches or activate connections according to consistent rules.

Written language just sits there, arbitrary in structure and content, waiting for a brain to rehydrate it with meaning. Written language means nothing to physics! It's useless without a brain! So how could this alien influence identify it as information?

"But that doesn't make any sense. There's nothing privileged about the matter arranged into those characters. How would it know to go after them?"

"Intelligent targeting," Erik says. "It knows because it was told."

Blackbird is aware.

"We can't go into that ship," Erik decides. "There's no fucking way we can risk opening Blackbird. Not if there's something inside reaching out and acting on us. We need to secure the site and get in touch with national command authority. Then we need to bring in a failsafe nuke. A way to destroy everything here, if there's a breach."

"We have nukes, Erik. Two planes overhead. Four weapons."

Weapons.

Anna said Blackbird is a weapon. Maybe Blackbird destroys *information*. The ultimate general-purpose killer. Is it smart? Is it made by something smart? Then Blackbird can take it out.

"*You need to find the dead hazmat guy,*" Clayton says. "*He's right next door. Where the labs actually touch Blackbird. He's probably just another victim of the purge. But he was closer to Blackbird than any of the others. If he's some kind of patient zero...*"

"Copy. Proceeding. Out."

If Erik has to watch poor Anna, Anna who never asked to be part of this, disfigured and swollen like those mice, with her skull split open and her brain dragging like a leech—no, it will not happen. He refuses to let that happen, not on his watch, not today. Today, by Erik's vigilance, the world will do right by the righteous.

Hold to that.

⁓

The next and final step on their journey to Blackbird is another airlock. This one is Chinese, made of transparent Lexan, branded SUZHOU PHARMA MACHINERY. The walls let them see what's ahead while the airlock cycles.

A tunnel. A ladder. A corpse.

The outer door opens onto a long, rectangular plastic corridor—not a prefab, something built hastily, a kind of makeshift Tyvek hutch. Cameras and instruments on tripods crowd the path, with labels and brands in three languages. Erik recognizes the UMEME-HERITAGE label on a roll of Tyvek sheeting. The Ugandans built this.

Directly ahead, an aluminum painter's ladder climbs right up to a narrow shaft in Blackbird's hull. The opening is irregular, jagged, like a star punched into glass. It invaginates into a narrow shaft which runs about six feet slantwise into Blackbird's hull, ending in a purplish-white cap.

Here the plastic tent walls pass straight into the hull. There is no seam, no tape, no glue, no sign of anything holding it there. It just . . . melds.

"Got the dead suit guy," Mike Jan says.

He sprawls face down at the base of the ladder.

"Look at the way he fell," Skyler notes. "Away from the ladder, face to the floor. He was descending it."

"So maybe he went inside," Anna breathes. "He went inside and lived long enough to come back out . . ."

"Means he's covered in whatever's inside there," Skyler says.

"Means he might be patient zero," Mike Jan says.

Nobody wants to get closer. Which is ridiculous: if this guy brought death out of Blackbird, and it got everywhere, then what will a couple feet of air do to save them? Erik kneels and checks the back of the suit for breaches. Nothing. It's a proper biohazard suit, with a SCUBA-style self-contained air system, not a respirator. It's intact. If this man is dead with his suit integrity unbreached, then they are all fucked.

"Ready?" he asks Skyler. "On three."

"Wait." Skyler gestures with his weapon. "Check out his hands."

The man's gloves, red plastic and silver tape, look a little too—long, somehow. And they're sitting funny on the ground: some trick of rigor mortis? Erik leans over to look. "Jesus."

The dead man's fingers, curled beneath his palms, have turned into onion rings. They loop right back into his wrist. The plastic fingertips seal smoothly back into the sleeve. Like they were made that way. Only Erik is pretty sure the loops shouldn't be that *big*. How long are fingers, anyway? His don't look that long . . .

"Let's do it," he says.

They flip the corpse.

Erik shouts. Skyler raises his rifle.

Through the suit visor: a man's face. Ugandan. Fifties. Square-jawed and handsome, once. Not anymore.

His eyeballs are full of eyeballs. Two gel sacs stuffed with hundreds of tiny staring eyes, black pinprick pupils, warm brown irises, hundreds. Like the holes in the back of a mother toad, raising her young in little pores.

Behind his finely ridged lips his tongue forks into a hundred points. His nose is honeycombed with tiny nostrils. They go all the way up to the bone.

His teeth are split vertically down the center. There's a little hinge at the top of each tooth, a cyst of pink flesh, where the split halves scissor together, and when Erik turned the corpse over he set all the teeth swinging open and shut. They chatter silently.

Erik gets halfway through throwing up in his fucking mask and just swallows it. Clayton makes a retching sound on the radio.

"Okay," Anna says, breathing hard. "Ssrin says we need to get out of here. Ssrin says nobody can be here, unless it's me and her, together. Erik, I don't want to be alone with her. She makes me do things. You've got to— Ssrin, slow down, I don't *understand*."

"*What killed him?*" Clayton rasps. "*Did it get through his suit?*"

"No sign of gunshot wounds." It's peculiar, not good or bad but just remarkable, for Erik to realize that he is handling this better than Clayton. There's always a right thing to do. "No visible suit punctures. We'd have to pump it up to be sure, but it looks intact. Either the, ah, transformation killed him, or he just ran out of oxygen."

"*Zero Six, this is One Six.*" Captain Brennan's voice breaks into the command channel. "*Contact report.*"

"One-Six"—Erik swallows acid—"Zero-Six here, send it."

"*We found survivors in Tawakul village, sir.*"

"What's their condition?"

"*Excited to see us, sir. It's a mixed multinational group. Chinese and Russian scientists, plus troops from China, Russia, Iran, and the local peshmerga. The Kurds are mostly female, sir.*" He pauses awkwardly: maybe he's not sure if this is important. "*The peshmerga commander wants to talk to you, sir. She's says it's very urgent.*"

"One, Zero, be advised they may be carriers of a biohazard."

"*Zero, One, we assumed as much. We're keeping our distance. But this peshmerga lady's really worked up about talking to you. Can I give her a radio?*"

Erik puts up a hand to block out the thing in the suit. "Yeah, put her on."

Now a voice like Anna's, if she smoked a pack a day and developed a throaty accent. "*This is Khaje Sinjari. Do you have Anna? I was promised my daughter.*"

"Mom," Anna breathes. "Mom?"

What? Anna's mom is dead. Isn't she? Didn't she say her mom died?

"Yes, ma'am," Erik sends. And who the fuck promised Khaje her daughter? Was it Clayton Hunt? It must have been Clayton. "Your daughter's right here with me."

"*Good. You must not go inside Blackbird yet. It will kill you.*" How the fuck does she know the NRO codename for the alien object? Clayton again? "*Anna has a way inside, where we will be safe. But first I must see her. We have a prisoner, someone working for the za—*"

A spike of noise cuts her off. "Majestic One," Erik sends. "Lost you."

Nothing.

"One, Zero. Come back."

"*Zero Six. Two Six.*" Dylan Raab's up on the south ridge. "*Contact report.*"

"Two, Zero, send it."

"*Ah, we see a weird fucking airborne thing. Smaller than an aircraft, maybe . . . quadrotor sized. But very . . . weird.*"

"Wait one." Erik immediately clicks over to the support frequency and monitors for a moment: if there's an incoming aircraft the AWACS should be yelling about it. Nothing. He goes back to the tactical net. "Continue, Two Six."

"*It's coming closer. It might be the, ah, the alien entity that Anna described.*"

"Copy that," Erik says. "Wait, out." He takes Anna by her plastic shoulder. "Is there anything you can tell me about the thing you described? The atmanach—"

"Ssrin," Anna gasps. "Ssrin, come back! Fuck!"

"What? What did she say?"

"She got really angry. She said we were trying to kill her. Is there something you didn't tell me about, some way to hurt her—"

"*Erik.*" Clayton's voice. "*We just got hit.*"

Erik's heart pops against his chest. Hard as a boxer's jab. "Say again, Clayton!"

"*Something hit the fucking plane. Electrical system's dead. We've lost all our engines. We're going down. Jesus, do I call mayday? Mayday, mayday, this is Majestic Heavy, we have lost all power and we are going down.*"

K + 153:52:31 hours
Blackbird Site
Qandil Mountains, Kurdistan

Erik ducks through the decontamination shower spray and pulls the outer air-lock door open. Stumbles out into open air—

—just as the Globemaster glides overhead. A huge, rapid shadow. The silence of the turbofans is as terrifying as a hospital flatline.

The big plane is headed down-valley, wings level, landing gear extended, following the river. Clayton's on that plane, Clayton and his whole science team and all their gear, the *mission* is on that plane. Erik can't lose the mission before it's even started. He can't lose Clay before Clay knows how much wrong he's done—

"Come on!" Anna shouts, and starts ripping off her protective suit. "We can't wear these out here!" She tears at the tape around her ankles, strips off the plastic booties, hops out of the suit.

"Do it," Erik orders Ricardo, Jan, and Skyler. "We'll burn the suits later. We've got to move."

They tear off after the descending plane, hauling ass as best as their gear and guns allow. Sprint southwest, toward the river and Tawakul. He can see the village clearly—swimming patches of heat haze over the hoods of abandoned Toyota pickups, fluttering shadows where laundry lines twist in the breeze.

Something else moves that way too.

There's a ray of black light shining off the mountain above the valley. Like a cut in Erik's retina, a strip of world peeled off. It could be ten miles away or it could be right in front of his nose, he can't tell. No wonder Team Two called it *weird*. It makes you want to wash your eyes with sand.

And at its tip moves something awful. Swirling and squirming and plunging like a centipede down a bathroom wall. The atmanach. It has to be.

But Erik has no time for that right now.

"Come on," he gasps. "Come on. Bring it in, girl." He barely talked to the pilot and now he wishes he'd had more time to know her: because she's about to be a hero, she's about to save the day. "Bring it down safe—"

The Globemaster's about twenty feet off the ground, in a slight nose-up attitude, suspended on a cushion of ground-effect air squeezed between the fuselage and the earth. Her back ramp hangs open, a big yawning *huh?*, and shit starts falling out: they're pushing the cargo containers right out on their pallets, just dropping them on their airbags, *thoom, thoom, thoom*, Jesus Christ, there are people clinging to those containers, and as the containers hit, the poor motherfuckers go flying off like dolls, tumbling, breaking. That's the science team. Those are the people Erik was supposed to protect. They're falling out of the plane like slobber off a hungry dog.

Why are they jumping? Do they really think it's better than riding the plane down? Maybe the pilot told them she'd just refueled and they figure, better to fall than burn.

The Globemaster's landing gear strikes ground. The plane shudders, slews, tilts, the starboard wing catches, the whole plane turns, Tokyo drifting in the meadows, ripping up a spray of flowers and little trees.

For a moment Erik feels like he's coming down the stairs on Christmas morning. Santa came. The plane's gonna make it. Clayton's gonna make it. It's all going to be okay.

Then the Globemaster's nose hits a stony rise.

The whole plane crumples up like a Bud can on a douchebag's forehead. A hundred and seventy-four feet and $220 million of aluminum and composite telescoping in on itself, engines shearing off the wings like turbine torpedoes, and then it blows up: it just blows up, all that fresh gas from the tanker, a dirty orange fireball smearing itself forward at the plane's final velocity, pouring over stone and grass and trees, thunder hammering off the valley walls. All gone.

He hits the ring switch. "Majestic Heavy, this is Majestic Zero Six. Reply."

The tumbling skeleton crushes itself against the rock in sheets of flame.

"Majestic Heavy," Erik croaks. "Report. Clayton, please answer me."

Nothing except the static of the EMP afterglow, the echo of the aurora, the sound of the world turning off.

"All call signs," Erik rasps into the radio. "Majestic Heavy is down. Majestic Three, get the fuck in there, save anyone you can—"

Then the shooting starts.

K + 154:00:44 hours
Tawakul meadow
Qandil Mountains, Kurdistan

"All call signs, One. We are engaging an alien target north of the village! Be advised, large column of dismounts moving west across the river are friendlies, over!"

Brennan's back on the radio. That yanks Erik away, away from Clayton's corpse dripping with burnt fat and aviation gas, back to command. He's gotta rally his people.

In the orchards north of Tawakul, Brennan's fireteam shoots at the alien atmanach. Little puffs of fire pick out the positions of riflemen and gunners. The squirming antithing jags and bobs like a *Counter-Strike* hacker, snapping from place to place: discontinuous, horror-movie throb of impossible motion.

God, it's *walking up the bullets*. It's eating the decision to fire off the fucking bullets.

Erik shouts: "One, Zero Six. Cease fire, cease fire! Disengage, over!"

"Negative, Six, there are civilians behind us!"

"One Six, you're having no effect, break contact, over!"

"Six, it's clearly evading our fire, we're slowing it down—"

How do you tell a man trained to close with and destroy the enemy that the enemy doesn't give a shit? "One Six, that's an order, break contact!"

"Sir," Mike Jan pants, "we should call for air support. We've got nukes."

"On top of the village? On top of all those people?" Erik takes a knee, scans the crowd pouring out of Tawakul with his combat optic. Women in fatigues and orange sashes: Tawakul's peshmerga, and yeah, they're all female. Weird. There are other troops too. Gaggles of grim-faced VDV, Russian airborne Spetsnaz. A small band of Chinese dudes in filthy camouflage, with their cool but very impractical bullpup guns that hate left-handed people. A mustachioed guy, classic NCO type, leading a unit of Iranians: probably one of the Saberin Battalions they use to fight the Kurds and the Jundallah rebels. Strange company.

And they've got scientists—they didn't shoot *everyone*—Erik sees them clutching their antennae and computers and whatever-meters like babies. Anna ran ahead to greet them, but now she's screaming at the sky: "Answer me, you bitch!"

"Anna," Erik yells, "Anna, you gotta ask Ssrin how we fight that thing! Brennan's engaged with it!"

"She's not answering me!" Anna screams back. "Don't you understand? She thinks we attacked her!"

"What?"

"She shot our fucking plane down! She shot it down because we were going after her!"

Erik stares at her. Because Ssrin was Anna's alien, Erik has, without quite intending it, started thinking of her as the *good* alien. "*She* shot us down? She—" She just killed Clayton? Just like that? "Who attacked her?"

"I don't know! She's not answering me!"

A young Chinese woman, mid-twenties maybe, wearing a red t-shirt and a STANFORD PHYSICS sweatshirt tied around her waist, chugs up the hill toward them. She's really tiny and she looks exhausted, but she doesn't quit.

"Zero Six, this is One Six! We are—the thing is—it's close—"

Brennan's voice disappears in a horrible blast of static. Voices jam the command frequency, Raab and Gamboa requesting an update. "Brevity!" Erik snaps into the radio. "Clear the channel! One Six, report situation!"

The Chinese woman tries to shake Anna's hand, but she's trembling too hard. Anna catches her and props her up. "I'm Professor Li," the woman gasps. "I'm Li Aixue. From the science team. I'm sorry about your plane! But you've got to listen, you've got to listen to me. Did you make any attempt to locate the alien beings nearby? Did anyone on your team try to find the aliens?"

"Professor, we're under attack." Erik cuts her off. "That thing up there, is there a way to stop it—"

"*You will listen!*" Professor Li cries. Her axiomatic correction somehow trumps years of command authority and snaps Erik's mouth shut. How did she do that? "Were you trying to locate one of the aliens? Were you planning to attack them?"

"No, of course not. We have no way to locate—"

But then Erik remembers Clayton's big expensive box. The box he was using to track Anna's transmissions to her alien.

"Oh, fuck. The neutrino sensor. The fucking neutrino sensor." And he'd even said he was trying to get a fix on Ssrin, hadn't he? Why hadn't Ssrin said, *Hey, stop that?* Why hadn't she just *asked?*

"That's why she attacked." Li Aixue pants. "Ssrin realized you were trying to trace her. She defended herself. Stop trying to find her!"

Clayton. What the fuck did you do? No time now. "That sensor is offline now," he says with incredible and necessary brusqueness. Offline. Yeah. "I need to know how to fight that thing attacking my men."

"You can't fight it. It comes and takes the ones Iruvage wants—"

"Anna," Erik says, "Iruvage, that's Ssrin's enemy? Anna?"

Anna's not listening anymore.

A hard-faced woman looks up at her, hand raised to shade the sun. She's got a big SVD rifle and a wide, hard, chiseled face. It's the face of a woman whose mind is a cork. She's keeping something bottled up inside, a feeling so ugly she cannot let it out, because it would rule her. Erik knows this, because all that gets past that cork is the Look. The Look that means you've seen true evil.

The woman's Looking right at her daughter.

"Listen to me," Professor Li gasps. "Listen. Whoever tried to track Ssrin, *that's* Iruvage's agent, that's the one—"

"Iruvage's agent?" Just like all those years ago in Green Beans, when he discovered what Clayton had done with Paladin, the sweat of Erik's body chills to clammy slush. "What do you mean?"

"I mean"—Li pants—"that Iruvage has people working for him. Just like Ssrin does."

Human pawns. Of course. When America went into Afghanistan, the first move was to recruit local allies. God, why didn't Erik think of this? Ssrin is the rebel. Ssrin has agents like Anna and Khaje, fellow rebels. And who does Iruvage have? Iruvage, the imperial enforcer?

It explains so much. Poor, stupid Clayton. Too smart to avoid bargaining his way into his own doom.

"*Zero Six,*" Brennan radios in a hoarse clipped mutter, "*this is One Six. I think . . . there's something wrong with my fireteam. I'm holed up in an elevated position, watching them. They're acting strange. Sir, I think they're infected. I think it's in my men.*"

"Brennan. This is Zero Six. Calm down and report. What happened to the atmanach?"

There's a long silence.

Brennan sends: "*Repeat that.*"

"I said, calm down and report. Where is the alien target?"

"*Major Wygaunt, is that you? Did you just say that?*"

"Brennan, what the fuck is wrong with you?"

Silence.

"Brennan, what the fuck are you doing?"

"*All call signs,*" Brennan sends, "*Zero Six is compromised and possibly infected. Advise you disregard all further traffic. Will attempt to regroup with Two soonest able. Out.*"

And the fucker leaves his transmit switch jammed down, clogging up the whole tactical net with his heavy breathing. What is wrong with him? "Mike," Erik snaps, turning to find the SEAL, "get down to Brennan's position and try to figure out what's happening. He sounds like he's gone bugfuck. Put his first lieutenant in command, on my orders."

"Yessir. Why do you think he reacted that way, sir?"

"I'll figure it out when we're less fucked. That was an order, Mike!"

Khaje Sinjari stares at her daughter. Anna stares back at her. They look like cats meeting in an alley.

Professor Li Aixue grabs Erik by the arm. "Mr.—Mr. Wygaunt"—reading his name tape—"did the atmanach take one of your men?"

Did it? "What happens to them? Why is he jamming my fucking radio?"

"They develop a violent aversion to untouched people. They can't bear to interact with normal humans."

"What do you mean, *violent* aversion?"

"They don't like it when they see or hear someone make a choice. It confuses them, it hurts them."

"What kind of choice?"

"Anything! Any volitional action, it just freaks them out!" Li straightens up. "If someone's touched, you've got to sedate them and tie them up. They don't get better."

"Or what?"

"Or," Li gasps, still breathless from her climb, "they get violent. They start having seizures. And if they're trained to kill people, they'll probably start doing it."

Brennan said he was observing his own men from an elevated position—Erik tries to signal them, switch to their team net and speak over Brennan's panting, but suddenly his radio is full of noise. Shrieking nonsense.

Khaje Sinjari draws a pistol and presses it to Anna Sinjari's forehead.

Anna says, "Go ahead, Mom. Do it. I know you've been waiting."

"You killed my son," Khaje says. "You killed your father."

"It's okay. I know you have to do it." Anna's shaking, and smiling, and crying in joy. "Ssrin promised you'd get to kill me, didn't she? It's okay. It's okay. I knew you'd want to. I knew."

Gunshots snap in the village across the river. Captain Brennan is, for no fucking reason at all, shooting his own men.

And the atmanach comes streaking out of the carnage. An infested shadow coiling down laundry lines, ricocheting from pole to pole on the river bridge, tearing a streak through the meadow flowers.

Black centipede lightning headed for Anna—and didn't Khaje Sinjari say, right before Clayton died, didn't she say Anna had a way inside Blackbird—so of course the aliens would want to get her—

"No," Erik breathes. He raises his rifle. He has to save Anna. But what can he shoot? This is my rifle, Heckler and Koch 416, chambered in 5.56 × 45mm NATO, but do I fire it at the alien horror, or at the mother with a pistol pressed to Anna's forehead?

That's when Clayton Hunt's voice crackles over the support net, calm as newscast. His radio works just fine.

"*Rune One. Rune One. This is Majestic Heavy. Authentication six two six yankee zulu yankee four four one. Over.*"

"*Majestic Heavy, this is Rune One.*" The pilot of one of the F-16s overhead. "*We authenticate. Go ahead.*"

"*I have a strike mission for you.*" Clayton's slurring, obviously barely conscious, obviously all fucked up, but, to Erik, even *more* obviously in command of himself. Clayton has a steel mind. Clayton can do sudoku after three tequila shots. Clayton can nail his SATs while deep in angst and wrenching love. Clayton can reel off authentication codes and strike orders after falling out of a crashing airplane inside a cargo container. He's still inside his fucking box, isn't he? He fell out of the plane on airbags and he's alive and now he's calling down—

"*Target is an alien entity. Coordinates three eight sierra mike foxtrot eight four eight eight eight six six seven three seven. I say again, three eight sierra mike foxtrot eight four eight eight eight six six seven three seven. As the president's legal proxy, I confirm your pre-authorized nuclear release. I say again, I confirm presidential authorization of nuclear release. Two weapons, same target. Execute strike. Over.*"

Clayton has just ordered two nuclear bombs dropped on a point in this valley.

"*Rune copies your strike mission, Majestic Heavy. We are inbound with two bravo-six-ones. IP is west of you, release point to your west-northwest. Target is three eight sierra mike foxtrot eight four eight eight eight six six seven three seven. Airburst set cherubs eight. Drop in one-zero-zero seconds. Get your ass to cover. Out.*"

Erik stares at the oncoming atmanach, and Khaje Sinjari with a pistol to her daughter's head, and the village where his soldiers are killing one another.

And he knows Clayton fucking Navarro fucking Hunt has beaten him again. Planned it all out. Gotten what he wanted.

An assassination.

The target was never Blackbird.

It was always Ssrin.

"What's happening?" Li Aixue begs. She turns, sees the situation with Anna and the gun, and blanches. "Khaje! What are you doing? Khaje, don't, we need her alive—you said we needed her *alive*—!"

"*I'm sorry, Erik,*" Clayton says. "*I couldn't tell you the plan, or you'd tell Anna. And she would've stopped transmitting before I could pinpoint her alien. Look at the ground. Close your eyes. It's going to be very bright.*"

Jet engines howl overhead. The F-16s carrying the bombs.

The atmanach closes in.

Khaje pulls the trigger.

ACT 3

MASTERMIND

THE AVIATOR

DAVOUD (~7,875 FEET ASL)

"The devil knew us too well!" Davoud Qasemi stumbles along behind Khaje Sinjari, zip-tied wrist to wrist, roped to this angry old woman with her angry old eyes. "We are all flawed and he knows our flaws! Only God can save us from Satan. You and I, can we be blamed for not saving ourselves?"

Khaje ignores him. Davoud descends to wheedling. "Come on, Khaje, tell me. What did your devil give you?"

The Americans are here, as Khaje promised. "Up, up, up!" she shouted, when she saw the parachutes above. "My daughter is with them, and she will know the way! Be ready to go!"

The Spetsnaz didn't listen to her—Vylomov is still angry about what she did to Colonel Ustinov—and it took the scientists a while to agree that yes, they *would* go back to the labs, but only if the Americans went in first, and came back out alive. Khaje didn't like waiting: "We have to reach them, we have to warn them! They cannot go in there!"

Davoud didn't warn anyone of anything. He came here in the cockpit of a jet. His orders were to *overfly and surveil*, and then advise his comrades on the ground of what they would find. He could've warned them that they were all going to die. But he did not. Those were the terms of his deal. His devil isn't Khaje's: but it is of the same order, the same origin. They say Iblis worked his way up into heaven from the lowest fire, before he fell.

But how did Iblis work Khaje? How did the aliens get to *her*?

Khaje doesn't answer. She stumps along, head down, with that infinite stubbornness Davoud's come to—not hate, he's not a hater—but certainly resent.

"Come ooon," Davoud pleads. "What did they offer you? What do you get?"

Khaje shades her eyes and watches the sky to the north. She frowns. "It's quiet. Why is it quiet?"

"Me, well"—Captain Davoud Qasemi of the Islamic Republic of Iran Air Force rattles his plastic shackles at the sky—"I made a pact with Satan to be the fastest man on Earth. He walked up to me in the body of Jalil Zandi, the greatest ace in the history of Iran. And he said, Davoud, if you'll just let me bite you in the neck, I swear I'll bring you to an aircraft beyond your wildest imaginings. No, not an aircraft. A *starship!*"

Gunfire crackles behind them. Someone's shooting at the crawler. It has been coming hour after hour since Major Vylomov's purge, taking people, leaving insane husks. It serves the same master as Davoud. He is the only one it definitely won't take, and everyone hates him for it.

Davoud keeps talking.

"My love affair with the sky began as a boy, with bootleg video games like *Fighter Wing* and *Black Knight*. We loved them because of the war with Iraq, where our pilots performed heroically. Iran's air force descends from the American tradition. Even Jalal Zandi flew an American plane, the F-14. Did you ever see *Top Gun*, Khaje? That plane had *muscle*. I had a poster above my bed and I swear to God that it perverted my sexuality. Iran is the only nation in the world that still flies the F-14, and God willing, one day I will fly it myself."

God willing. It must be God's will, right? Satan wins when he convinces you there is no God. Or that he *is* God. So as long as Davoud remembers that Satan is not the same thing as God, he is not yet lost.

Of course, he has submitted his will to Satan. So maybe he is just making excuses for himself.

Some of the peshmerga women are listening to him ramble. They secretly think he's attractive and therefore compete to be the cruelest to him, to prove to themselves they aren't swayed by his looks. At least that's what he tells himself.

"For all my boyhood I was possessed by a powerful yearning for flight. I read everything I could find about the air war against Iraq. I snuck out of bed to watch documentaries on Channel 1. The day I became a fighter pilot was the greatest day of my whole life. But I had one problem. I kept pushing my planes too hard. Too fast, too high, too far off the flight plan. I always wanted to be"—Davoud's voice thickens with passion, he is playing it up but not nearly as much as Khaje probably thinks—"closer to God. Isn't that ironic? Oh, come *on*, Khaje, it is! It's marvelously ironic! It's so classically ironic that it's invented pederasty and gone to war with Sparta."

The peshmerga commander, zealous Arîn, mutters to her companion in Sorani Kurdish. They're probably talking about shooting him. Davoud talks louder.

"And when Satan threw off the image of Jalil Zandi and sank his teeth into me, I saw the true unholy evil, and I knew I was damned. But I told myself that flight could redeem me. Didn't they throw Jalil Zandi in jail? But when they needed pilots, they came and asked him to fly again, and he became a hero."

Finally Khaje laughs at him. "Oh, *hero*. Do you know that I never would've caught you if you hadn't talked so much?"

That's true. But he doesn't mind. He kind of prefers being a prisoner.

He knew it was going to happen before anyone else. Satan told him: *There's going to be a power outage. And then you'll get a special mission.* So when the whole Middle East staggered before that radio shriek in Kurdistan, he knew it wasn't an Israeli weapon or a botched nuclear test. He was ready when President Rouhani and the rest of Iran's leadership decided to cross the border and investigate the source of that shriek. The Chinese were with them—together, it was felt, the joint expedition would be too politically dangerous for the Americans to bomb to smithereens.

But as Davoud lifted off from Hamadan Air Base in his F-5 Tiger (not *quite* the muscly hunk the Tomcat is, but slender and beautiful anyway) he felt Iruvage's voice in his throat, in his mind, like waswas, the whispers of Satan.

I'm going to kill your wingman. I'm going to cripple your aircraft. I'm going to destroy all your fighting vehicles. They do not suit my purposes.

I do not need this valley full of any more weapons. I need it full of human beings. I need so many of your kind. I need to know what her weapon does to them.

I need you to watch.

And it all went as Satan foresaw.

As Davoud's ejection seat rocketed away from his dying Tiger, he saw Satan's promise fulfilled. Down in the meadows there gleamed a golden gleam. The starship! Like a butterfly, gold and white and purple-black and jagged-winged, a wonder from the stars.

Davoud yearned to fly it.

Only it turned out no one could get inside.

⁂

His thoughts are cut off by an awful silence.

A huge American transport plane glides down over the meadow. Nothing that big should ever be *gliding*. Davoud begins to pray. American or no, a plane's a plane and pilots stand with pilots, so God willing they will find a good stretch of valley floor—

His prayers go unheard. The C-17 lands like a frozen duck dropped into hot oil. "Oh, no," Davoud gasps. Khaje stands gaping in horror. Anna was on that plane. Her daughter was on that plane!

A bunch of American paratroopers run around shouting and waving their rifles, demanding to know what's happening. One of the soldiers points at Davoud. "Who is this man? Why is he a prisoner?"

"He's jash," Khaje says, without looking at the American. Her eyes are only for the wreckage. "A traitor."

Li Aixue runs up ahead to greet the person who must be the American commander: a tall, spare man with gray eyes and a beautifully sad face. He shouts into his radio like he's trying to stop something.

Suddenly Khaje makes a click in her throat like a cat spotting a bird. She drops Davoud's rope and takes out her pistol. She runs ahead. She puts the pistol to the head of a young woman in an American uniform.

Davoud gapes. In God's name, that woman could be Khaje's daughter! Is she going to shoot her own daughter?

Khaje pulls the trigger.

The pistol clicks. Empty chamber. No round loaded.

"Êsta hestit pê kird çone? ؟ نئیستا هەستت بێ کرد چۆنه" Khaje spits. "Do you even understand me anymore? That's how it feels from the other end!"

Her daughter looks at her not in fury but in wonder. She's weeping. She says, bizarrely: "Mom, there's a bug in your gun."

Khaje, against all good firearms advice, turns the pistol around and looks directly into the barrel. "That bitch!" she says. "That *bitch*!"

"Crawler!" one of the Russian scientists screams.

Everyone drops flat on the ground, belly-down with their eyes squeezed shut. Trying not to make any decisions, so the atmanach won't smell them. Davoud, of course, doesn't have to worry about it.

He watches the soul-eater skitter and hop across the river like a spider in a strobe light, jumping on the scraps of choices everyone made—detouring around a rock, kneeling to help someone who'd fallen, cursing Davoud as a traitor, all morsels for the atmanach to devour. The atmanach always comes down like a scientist's hand, grabbing mice from the cage.

This time it's heading straight for the gray-eyed American. Or maybe for Khaje, or her daughter. Khaje has grabbed Anna and forced her to the ground, and now she is lying atop her daughter, who struggles and curses and shouts, "Mom, get off me!"

Then Davoud sees two shining silver shapes in the western distance. His heart leaps. Fighters! American fighters! A pair of F-16s! Davoud jumps and wiggles like a dog because he can't wave his zip-tied arms, he's just so happy to see more planes up there—

The Vipers streak directly overhead.

Their sonic boom comes up the valley, whipping the trees and flattening the meadows, and the thunder stuns everyone, leaving the atmanach still for a moment, whirling in an infinity loop, starved of choice to hunt. It smells like hot metal and aviation gas. Or maybe that is the burning airplane.

The American fighters carve over the face of the mountain on blue-white spikes of fire. Two little bombs fall off the jets, hurled away by the force of their turn. That's weird. Usually they'd drop from much higher altitudes. Why toss the bombs and turn away, unless—

"God help me," Davoud says.

But he is past God's help.

The bombs go off. Flashbulb light. Nuclear light. As pure as the glint off an aluminum wing.

Davoud is blind before the thunder hits.

CHAPTER SEVEN

CLAYTON//633

For ten minutes and thirty-three seconds after he calls down the nukes, Clayton Navarro Hunt hangs alone in the dark. He has his own thoughts to keep him company: cold companions, with sharp elbows and sharp tongues. Sometimes, when he's alone, he shouts and yells for no reason, because his memories shock him like static.

He knows what he has to do next. He knows every second counts. But he can't make himself move.

He's just so goddamn tired of being the one with the master plan.

※

CLAYTON//MODEL 17A1 PROTECTIVE MASK

Schemes.

Second grade, Clayton feels out of place at magnet school, out of sorts, can't say why. He wants fear and respect from his fellow children. So he finds the gas mask in the garage. His parents, Hispanic dad and Black mom, hold on to the relics of military service as bulletproof bullet-proof that they are real Americans. They don't let him speak Spanish outside his house.

He wears the gas mask while he's waiting for the bus. He wears it on the bus. He wears it all day at school. There are no pictures, but he imagines he looked like a tiny malformed elephant, spilled too early from the womb. The bulging plastic eyes, the filter snout. An absolute weirdo.

No wonder the teachers kept a file on him. No wonder Rosamaria said, as they traded lunch in the cafeteria, *Man, what's up with you?*

Seventh grade: the eighties. He announces to Erik and Rosamaria (who are by now his closest friends, these other only children, his fellow magnet-school Magnetos) that he's opening up a Special Economic Zone, starring his own currency, the Clayton Credit. What can you do with a Clayton Credit? It's a fiat currency. The market will dictate its fair value! You can trade it for lunchroom stuff, or barter for extra time to play *Temple of Apshai* on the library Mac, or buy forgiveness for your trespasses. (This scheme is ruined by Clayton's policy of creating new Clayton Credits for everybody who joins his economic zone— inflation just goes wild. And nobody trusts a system where he keeps all the accounts himself.)

Freshman year of high school. After a miserable middle school life as Erik's brainy sidekick, some button-down ancestor of Geordi LaForge—*Clayton, tell us about the antiprotons again; Clayton, why don't you want to dance with us; Hey, Clayton, remember that time you thought "masturbate" meant "chew your food"*— Clayton gets his Nietzsche on and decides it's time to exercise a little wille zur macht.

He needs to get cut. Erik is pan-athletically all-American, Rosamaria dances and swims, and this is clearly paying off socially and physically and possibly sexually for both of them. Erik is tall, muscular, and ghostly handsome. Rosamaria is not tall, also muscular, beautifully black-haired, and growing in ways that make the white girls call her a slut.

Clayton's got to get some fit on if he wants a place on the maypole.

He likes the bodies of the dancers on the Alvin Ailey posters. He doesn't think he's gay but he feels not quite like a regular guy either. He wants to be sleek, powerful, sophisticated, in control. He also chooses dance because he is already in love with Rosamaria, and he expresses this by mimicking her. Later in life he will cringe at the things he did. Following her to the guidance office, pretending he had to be there at the same time, just so he can see her a little more. Wow, Mrs. Hanford, you lost my appointment *again?*

***

CLAYTON//BDA

Ten minutes and thirty-four seconds after Clayton calls down the nukes, the hatch on his cargo container burns open in a flash of thermite.

Tactical lights rave and strobe at Clayton. Erik's commandos storm into the Cobalt Sifter housing. Their kinetic approach annoys him.

"Thank fuck," he groans. "Would someone please let me down?" He's dangling upside-down in his crash seat. The container can float, it can drop on parachute and airbags (which saved his life in the crash), it can even circulate its own air. What it can't do is turn itself right side up.

Clayton's been stuck on the ceiling for a quarter of a precious hour. They are on the apocalypse clock now, and there's so much of the master plan left to accomplish.

The survival of the human species now depends on Clayton solving the riddle of Blackbird.

The commandos cut Clayton from his upside-down throne and search him. He keeps up a light banter to shore up his bravery, because he used some of these people to assassinate his targets, and knows how little it would bother them to kill him.

"For the record," he says, "I am the civilian authority in legal command of this mission. Is Major Wygaunt all right?"

"Shut the fuck up," one of them says: Captain Gamboa, the Green Beret who handled the Marja affair. An original Paladin. Not one of Clayton's latter-day recruits. He probes at Clayton's throat. "I can't feel anything."

"It must be too deep."

"What if the major's crazy?"

"He's not crazy," Clayton says. "I've got an alien communication implant. It's wrapped around my spine, though. It'll kill me if you try to take it out."

They drag him out into the meadow grass. He looks up from hawthorn and jasmine blossoms to the rising mushroom cloud on the white mountain above. Behold, O Israel, my wrath may wax hot: ha-ha, that's actually a little funny, because against all odds it is not Israel or Iran but Clayton who has dropped The Bomb on Iraq.

The fireball really isn't as big as you'd think. Or maybe the scale of the terrain just dwarfs it. The wind is pulling the cloud west from the burning forest, right over him, teasing it into thin gray-brown streamers. Clayton has accomplished the dream of a million right-wing Facebookers. He has nuked the Middle East.

He squeezes his eyes shut in calm terror. He didn't expect Ssrin to shoot down the Globemaster. How did she know what he was about to do? Why could she hit the Globemaster, but not the fighters with the bombs? Why didn't Iruvage tell him Ssrin could detect passive surveillance? Now everyone who died in the crash is on his conscience.

Please let Erik survive. Please. He doesn't deserve to go like this, before Clayton gets a chance to explain himself.

He's gotta tell the soldiers why he dropped the bomb. He had the nukes dialed down to a tiny four-kiloton yield, not even one third of a Hiroshima. In that mode they're pretty precise. You could nuke the Financial District off the southern tip of Manhattan and not kill anyone north of Union Square.

Clayton does his nuclear math. Four-kiloton yield—airburst at eight hundred feet—deadly radiation and third-degree burns will only spread about six-tenths of a mile, and the 350-foot fireball won't contact the ground . . .

"Good news, guys," Clayton announces, as they put him on his feet and prod him, at gunpoint, uphill. "There won't be any fallout!"

CLAYTON//NEPANTLA

Junior year of high school. In a hotel in Vegas, after a dance competition. Moonlight and neon shining through the curtains, and the adult chaperones all gone down to the bar. Somehow they are alone. He sits on the bed with Rosamaria in the crisp AC cold and they talk. This is their dynamic: Clayton and Rosamaria talk, Rosamaria and Erik compete, Erik and Clayton conspire. Two to share the truth, two to test it, two to bring that truth against the world.

When Rosamaria unbuttons her shirt Clayton nearly dies of pubescent terror. It's one thing to imagine your best friend naked, which he has done (Erik insists he never has). Another to actually confront the inconvenient (admittedly magnificent) facts that have turned the teachers and catcallers against her. The dark port-wine stain on her chest is more familiar to him than the structure of the bra, the tiny white hairs on her sternum.

Pleased to meet you, he says. What an unexpected honor.

Rosamaria laughs. Please, just be normal, okay? You've been so weird lately. I miss being comfortable with you.

That's easier with your shirt on. Why don't *you* be normal?

This is normal. This is me. You aren't weird with me in the pool. Same thing.

Clayton pretends she has a point, that he *is* totally comfortable in the pool, because he doesn't want to take away her trust in him. Really the pool is worse, because she is not only undressed but powerfully in motion there. Knowing it's hormones doesn't help, any more than learning Newton lets you defy gravity. The proto-nerd often believes that awareness is the way to control, but in fact awareness only makes you aware of your powerlessness. And if you do not accept that powerlessness it can so easily become hate. Clayton thinks that if Rosamaria were not his friend, he would hate the world.

Rosamaria turns halfway around, so he can see her back. She says: See these scars? The little white marks?

Clayton sees them. Like rat shot in her back. What did that?

I've been fucking a senior.

You've been *what*?

It's not a big deal. But I know you're going to think it is.

A senior like a guy about to graduate, or a guy in a nursing home—

She swats him. I didn't say it was a guy, did I? she jokes. Jokes? Is it a joke?

Jesus, when you said you were gonna help rail the abuelitas at the home, I thought you meant *bed* rails.

It bothers you less if you think it's a girl. Doesn't it. Because you think, then, it's not serious.

Yeah, maybe. I guess. I don't know. How long have you been, uh, not telling me about this?

(His gladness that she'll confide in him is larger, barely, than his jealousy, which is not yet as bad as he suspects it will become.)

She says, We're safe about it and he's going away in the fall. One time we did it under my porch, on the ground, and the stones left scars on my back. See? That's what I wanted to show you. Little stone scars. They're kind of cool, aren't they?

That does not sound healthy or even fun to Clayton. This is a side of Rosamaria he has never known. He asks: Why?

Do you actually need me to explain why people fuck, Clayton?

But why *now*?

I wanted to get it over with. Being a virgin, not being a virgin, all that shit. I wanted someone hot who had an expiration date. I was reading Anzaldûa—did you ever read that book I gave you?

Yes, Clayton says. Wait. The one with the naked woman crawling on the front? No. Sorry.

See, that's all you saw, a naked woman, and I bet you thought, Oh, this book's not for me. It has nothing to say to me, as a Black man, as a Chicano, as a serious educated man who likes math and science. It's probably about not shaving your armpits.

Hey, Clayton says, I *do* shave my armpits. But the joke falls flat: so obviously a way to avoid taking things seriously.

Nepantla, Rosamaria says, as she turns, without self-consciousness, to face him. That's the word for being in a place between two places. She touches her wide, flat nose. I am a crossroads inhabited by whirlwinds. That's what Anzaldûa wrote, about being inside and outside at the same time. A place you come to, but which is always moving. A nepantlera is someone who moves between selves. Am I the good Mexican girl who goes to Mass and prays to la virgencita? Am I the good assimilated girl who doesn't have an accent? Am I the sad messed-up girl whose mom left so now she has sex under a porch? Am I a poor girl who cares about poor Mexicans? Am I a feminist who cares about women? Who gets my solidarity? I want the answer to be "everyone." But people don't like it when you're too many things at once.

Did you take your shirt off and talk about sex so I'd pay attention to Marxist postcolonial theory? That's really low.

See, now you're trying to put them together. The woman saying these things to you, and the woman with the body you want to look at. You're trying to fit them both into one person.

Huh. So I'm this thing too, aren't I? Nepantla. Because I'm Black and Chicano and . . . and whatever. All those other things.

You are, Clayton. But I don't know if you know it. You don't stay at the crossroads. You look at the signs and you walk where they say.

Why do you think that?

Because you're afraid to speak Spanish outside your basement. And even then you won't do it if Erik's there.

Well, people judge you for speaking Spanish—

Do you judge me?

No. It's kinda fun. Like having a secret code. But other people do . . .

Spanish isn't the only language you won't speak. You're so scared of the other Black kids, Clayton.

What, like Maurice? Deem? I hang out with those guys.

They're dancers, they're in the gay clique. I mean the *Black* kids, the kids who make the white parents take their kids to the suburbs. You act like they're contagious! I'm Blacker than you, puto.

I hang out with people who share my interests.

Oh, please, listen to you. They're smart and funny and loud about it.

They give me a lot of shit.

They think you think you're better than them. And you think that if you hang out with them you'll drop the n-word in front of your parents and get sent to military school.

So I'm too good at being a good kid? Why's that bad?

Because "good kid" is a box. Because you're not doing things which change and hurt you. You're not doing what I am: something you're not supposed to do, so you can figure out who you are when you're not who you're supposed to be.

I don't want to be cynical here, Rosamaria, but isn't the Chicana girl who puts out *exactly* who you're supposed to be? Isn't that the story people tell about you? That's all they'll see. They won't see the girl I know, who—

They tell that story so that they can own those parts of me! What about you, Clayton? You're terrified of the stories they tell about you. You in your buttondowns and skinny ties. What's the last Black thing *you* did? The last thing it scared you to do? You want to be Reginald Lewis, not August Wilson. You read Greg Bear but not Borges. You quote MLK when he sounds like a moderate but you don't quote MLK when he's in jail. You made your little plan: dance, debate, honors, college, government. And now you're checking it off. Is that really what you want? Would you be here, in this room with me, if that was what you wanted?

She's too close to things he knows he can't solve no matter how hard he thinks them through.

He says: Rosamaria, I'm serious. You gotta be careful. This could ruin your life.

I'm not going to get pregnant. And anyway, isn't it my decision?

I just—

You're more worried about what people think of me than of what I think of myself. Even Paz does it—you know Paz, right? He writes about Mexico as a country of lonely nihilists, born from rape and violation: Cortés fucks La Malinche, and she gives birth to us, the Mexicans, and then Cortés throws her away. Paz says Mexicans are a lonely people because they reject their national mother as a traitor. That's all he can think to say about La Malinche, that she's a traitor and a shrewd whore. And he calls the essay "The Sons of La Malinche"! That's the real betrayal. Sons. Always sons. Man, fuck Octavio Paz.

He blinks at her. He doesn't know what to say to this. He should've jerked off before the flight. He wants to take her bra off so bad. He wants to know: Are they actually shaped like that, the same shape as the bra, or do they sort of . . . florp? Does she want him to want to take her bra off? Does she just want him to want her to want him to take her bra off? I clearly cannot choose the poison in this cup.

She says: Come on, say something.

He says, Rosa, I know you're incredibly smart, but this thing with this senior guy . . . people are stupid and mean. People will talk. They're not going to use your advanced literary account of it. They're just going to call you a slut.

They already call me a slut. Don't you hear what they say about me? Don't you hear the stories they make up? You went to that white-girl feminist club they were doing for a while. Those chingaqueditas, you know what they think.

Your dad is going to kill you. I'm honestly secondhand scared.

My mom was my age when Dad married her. I love him dearly, but he's a hypocrite. If I go to college without getting pregnant, he'll be overjoyed. And I *will* do that.

Clayton understands, and in a petty teenage way, he's glad to understand deeper than Erik ever will. This is how they get you, the smiling Borg mass of American whiteness (he didn't think Borg at the time, the Borg hadn't been invented yet): they offer you a way to qualify as a real person, money to make, credits to earn, a self-improvement course to win their respect. And if Rosamaria works to meet those qualifications, if she keeps chaste and goes to Mass and never uses words like *nepantla* to speak of her place in the world, then she has accepted their power over her. She has won on their terms.

Rosamaria will not win on their terms.

I'm weird with you because I'm in love with you, Clayton says.

Is that a scheme too, a clever trick? No. He didn't mean to say it. But he *did* plan to be here alone with her, in this hotel room, with his strong wiry body, and hers. He did plan that. And maybe Rosa planned it too. She said her porch guy had an expiration date.

Rosamaria looks at him over her naked shoulder fondly. She says, Clayton, dude, we're seventeen. We can't be in love. We have no judgment.

She's right. But she says *we* can't be in love. We, we, that word is a drug.

CLAYTON//COLLABORATOR

"What the fuck did you do?" Erik shouts. "Clayton, *what the fuck did you do?*"

"I played La Malinche," Clayton says. "I signed up with Cortés."

He's been dreading this moment since the day an icy Scandinavian-looking staff secretary walked into Clayton's office and made her offer. *You are the one who plans the killing,* she said. *I'm a soldier. I need soldiers for my mission. And in return I can save your world from the cobalt salt.*

This is the moment Erik figures it out.

"You lied to my face about Anna? You brought her along as *targeting equipment?*"

"I did what you expected me to do, Erik. What you needed me to do. Because you couldn't do it yourself."

"I'm proud I can't do the things you do, Clayton."

Have to keep him calm. When he's calm he does the right thing given the information he has, and Clayton can give him the information. "I cut a deal with one of the aliens. He's a soldier for the Exordia, the top galactic superpower. If we do some proxy work for him, he'll try to keep us alive. I don't mean *us* like you and me. I mean all of Earth. Those are the stakes."

"You had no right," Erik says, and then, roaring, ethical laser on full burn, "You chose sides for the entire planet! *You had no right!*"

Clayton's sitting on a folding chair in a Chinese dorm container. Aside from Erik, there is no sound except the gurgle of the pumps. A minute ago you could hear the screams of other crash survivors. But now the medics have filled them up with fentanyl.

He takes a hard breath. "Look. I had the right that matters." And he believes it, even though it sucks. "I had information about a threat to the whole world. I was given a set of parameters to act within. I was told that if I departed from those parameters, if I involved *anyone* else, I would seal the planet's fate. So I took Iruvage's side. The alternative was to throw in with Ssrin, and die. Or do nothing, and die anyway. Do you know how far the aliens would've gone without me? What they would've done already? The EMP attacks were their *soft* option. If Iruvage hadn't told that ship in orbit to hold off on the main event, we'd all be dead."

The AC unit turns on.

Behind Erik the dorm is heating up. He's brought three new friends, all of whom Clayton knows, because Iruvage filled him in. In the back (but craning to watch) is Professor Li Aixue, the top Chinese mathematician, a short, fat woman with magnetically curious eyes. She looks like she's studying you through a telescope, complete with a Jodie Foster expression of awe.

Between Li and Clayton is a Black woman with a close-cropped buzz, handy butch vibes, and a softly muscular, hard-working build. Chaya Panaguiton, the

Filipina-Ugandan physicist who took over her expedition when her boss died. Her team was not the first to contact Blackbird. But it was the first to survive.

And here is Khaje Sinjari, who Iruvage said might be another vector to find Ssrin. A hard-bitten old peshmerga in an orange shawl. She stares at Clayton like she wants to make a flute out of his windpipe. Her eyes are bloodshot: fatigue or booze?

Clayton waves at them. "Hi. I'm the deputy national security advisor. You can call me Clayton, or Mr. Hunt if you're angry at me."

Erik glances back at the rest of them and Clayton realizes that he's *embarrassed*. He's ashamed he didn't stop Clayton. He feels like he's let everyone down. Fuck you, Erik! I'd ask you what you'd have done in my place, but the truth is that you never could've *been* in my place. When Iruvage walked into your office you would've tried to shoot him.

"You ruined everything," Chaya Panaguiton says. Her English is excellent, but it's Filipino excellent, not American excellent, and it takes Clayton a moment to adjust. "Ssrin told Khaje that Anna was supposed to know a way inside. We were about to have the answer. But now you've killed Ssrin."

"Because I couldn't let Ssrin get Blackbird."

"Why?" Aixue asks, with quiet heartbreak. Man. She really wanted to go inside, huh. "What would happen?"

"The Exordia would bomb our cities." Iruvage showed him the list. "Beginning with the densest population centers. Seoul. Delhi. Mumbai. New York. Hundreds of millions dead. The worst day in human history."

Do you get it, Erik? Everyone who died—my science team, your soldier hit by the atmanach, the soldiers he killed, everyone else on that plane—all necessary losses. They were necessary! Yes, Erik, I struck a deal to save Earth. No, Erik, it was not morally correct. But goddamn it, why don't you understand, the world doesn't *let* you do the right thing. The world nukes the righteous. And I have to save people like you from that world.

Khaje Sinjari does not react. Erik's jaw trembles. Chaya Panaguiton says, "Oh, putangina."

But it's Li Aixue who really goes ashen. Because she's the one who can grasp orders of magnitude. Hundreds of millions dead? That's a statistic, a fake number, about as urgent as a budget deficit. That doesn't mean anything. But for Professor Li, mathematician, a hundred million dead people is as real and urgent as a baby face down in a bathtub. That's a hinge in history, *before* and *after*, and it's the kind of hinge you hurl your body upon just to keep it from swinging.

Clayton goes on. He's got to make them understand.

"The Exordia came here because of Blackbird. It represents an unacceptable threat to their hegemony. And exactly like our military, Erik, will drone strike a few innocent people to kill a bad guy, the Exordia was going to wipe out Earth along with Blackbird. The *only* reason they stopped is that Iruvage wanted time to figure out Blackbird's origins and function. I gave him that time. I eliminated the pressure of Ssrin's presence."

Erik's jaw is firm as a prow. A white light glares in his eyes: fluorescent tubes in reflection.

Clayton feels like he's trying to lift Erik by his armpits, straining and straining to move the righteous idiot far enough that he can see from another angle. "Do you understand why I had to kill Ssrin? Why I had to work with Iruvage?

"If he dies, *we all die with him.*"

Erik's going to give in. He's going to pretend it's disgust: he's going to wash his hands of Clayton's crimes and let Clayton do the necessaries. Clayton is sure of it. Erik needs to do something *purely* good. He can't help Clayton. He can't stop Clayton. Neither one is purely good. So he'll surrender control—

"So instead," Khaje Sinjari says, speaking for the first time, "all my people die with Ssrin. And you say, well, they had to die to save the world. Nothing in this world is permanent except for the sky, the mountains, and America betraying the Kurds."

CLAYTON//BYCATCH

Clayton gapes at her. "What?"

They all look at him: Erik with cold fury, Li Aixue with bright confused sorrow, Chaya with deep righteous outrage. And Khaje Sinjari with a will to punish that makes Clayton shiver down to his little toe-hairs. She's gonna kill him. He doesn't understand why, but she's going to kill him.

"Um," he says. "Sorry. All your people died with Ssrin? Why . . . ?"

Chaya says, "The villagers evacuated up into the mountains five days ago. To some caves they'd prepped. Ssrin was with them, hiding them from Iruvage. So when you bombed her . . ."

He shouldn't care at all. He just lost a bunch of people when the plane went down. So what, some Kurds died. Add them to the pile. It's a rounding error compared to saving the planet.

But instead he slumps in his chair and says: "Jesus. How many?"

"Four hundred and twenty five," Khaje rasps. "Mothers. Children. The old. The men's unit of our peshmerga. All of them."

"Okay. Okay. Maybe . . . they were in caves, right? And the bombs were set to airburst. So maybe some of them survived . . ."

"Yeah," Erik says. "Maybe."

He panics. "I protected you, Erik. The atmanach was gonna nab you if I didn't kill Ssrin—"

"I DIDN'T ASK FOR YOUR PROTECTION!" Erik roars. *I will not be your moral collateral!* "You know I would've rather died!"

"The atmanach doesn't kill you, Erik, it takes your fucking soul! You go on existing in a pocket world designed to digest everything you know! I saved you from that!"

"You killed four hundred and twenty-five innocent people to save me! You put *that* on my soul!"

I saved the world, he wants to shout. *I saved the world* and *your life! Those people were sacrificed for the greater good!*

But the world won't fit into his heart. He can't squeeze seven billion people down to a pellet of moral worth and weigh them against 425 innocents. The grief always weighs heavier. You can have a thousand good days, but they will never cancel out that one bad night.

Clayton once wrote to Erik that he'd rather do an evil thing to win a hundred blessings than wait for one pure choice.

The problem is that the good always seems so fragile. And the evil you've done sets on you like cement.

He takes a deep breath. He's going to apologize, and he's going to move forward, because he has no choice. The fundamental arithmetic of the situation hasn't changed—

He jerks. His spine fills up with hot scaly animus. He falls forward off his chair.

"Clayton?"

He can only wheeze. His lungs are full of coiled snakes, gripping his bronchioles. This has never happened before. What's happening? Don't lie to yourself. You know what's happening.

"Is he having a heart attack?" Chaya Panaguiton asks hopefully.

There's an invisible constrictor around his throat. Scales of dry ceramic slip across his skin. He can't breathe, he is drowning dry. And, with terrible exactitude, two pairs of fangs prick the skin behind his ears. One pair on each side.

"She's alive," Iruvage hisses. "*Somehow she's alive. I know it! I felt a great dying and I thought it was her. But if she was concealing all those humans from me—then maybe they went to death in her place. And now she is hidden. Hidden close by, waiting for her chance to steal the demiurge. Hidden behind Anna Sinjari in serendure.*

"*If she is alive I cannot justify human survival.*

"*I am afraid the nuclear devastation of your planet is back on the schedule.*"

⁂

CLAYTON//840 MINUTES REMAIN

Distantly he is aware of Erik calling for a medic. Urgently he is aware of the hallucinatory snakes crawling up his bowel. The fucking alien—the communications implant—he never did this before!

Iruvage, Iruvage, please, give me one more chance. Just let me work. Let me solve the Blackbird puzzle. Let me get inside and find out what it is. Please. Give me a day. A day.

"*Certainly not a day. The ship in orbit is under Coil Captain Maessari and she is quite committed to ssovÈ, our art of swift violence. You must understand that her orders were to destroy this world the instant she arrived from wrongspace. Her trophicommanders fear that Ssrin will escape by wrongspace drive. But I have assured Maessari that Ssrin's ship never had a wrongspace drive; she has become too solitary and feckless for such sacrifices.*

"*So now the only way for Ssrin to escape is by secular space travel. I convinced Maessari that she need not act in haste so long as Ssrin can be bottled up. This should keep Maessari busy deploying hives and pickets around Earth for . . . fourteen hours. That is exactly how long she will tolerate delay. So. You have fourteen hours to give me Blackbird. Shall I remove a city as a performance incentive?*"

No! No, we don't work that way, humans aren't like khai, if you hurt us we close up and slow down and get distracted! Don't nuke anything, please, please.

"*Your honesty is saccharine, you know that? Sickly on the tongue. I think it must be a good thing among humans, to confess your weaknesses. But among khai it tastes like too much sugar, to cover up the poison.*" Iruvage chuckles. "*Do your work. You'll know when I've grown impatient. I'll start with Chicago, I think. City of the Big Shoulders; a tasty cut of meat, when ground. Thirty megatons per weapon: the cloud gate opened, the silver egg hatched in fire . . . finally the Midwest will be the center of world attention, eh?*"

So I figure out Blackbird. I get us inside and I render it safe. And then you spare our planet?

"*Yes.*"

Help me figure it out! You didn't tell me about those brain-mice, you didn't tell me about the mutilated people in there! You didn't even tell me about the death holes.

"*I won't risk exposing myself to Blackbird. Not in any way. I am indeed smarter than you, Clayton. And that might make me terrifyingly vulnerable. Blackbird is a predator, I think. And it hunts with an awful hunger. It needs something. It wants something . . . or it would, if it had a mind to want.*"

Stop sending the atmanach, at least.

"*Oh, no, I won't do that. I need samples, Clayton! I need to see what the demiurge is doing to you . . . in a safely digested form. What I learn here will make me valuable to my people. I don't care about your lives. Only what they can give me.*"

You can sample every one of these people and you still won't learn as much as I will if they trust me. They need to know I can keep them safe, or they won't do the work. Stop sending that thing.

"*Oh, if you insist . . . but remember. Fourteen hours. Oh, and Clayton—if Erik needs an errand to run, or if you want Khaje and the Kurds out of the way . . .*"

Yes? What? Yes, I need Khaje and the Kurds out of the way. Or they're going to murder me.

"*I just inspected ground zero more closely. Ran a few queries in the ol' ledger of souls. Remember all those caved Kurds you're so guilty about bombing?*"

Yes, I remember, it hasn't been two minutes!

"*Do forgive me, Clayton, it's usually wise to assume you humans have forgotten what happened two minutes ago. I doubt you can remember what you smelled two minutes ago, and if you can't do that, can you remember anything at all? Anyway, it seems there may be survivors. I suspect Ssrin is even now feasting on them. Regenerating whatever damage your weapons did. Ah! I knew she was masking herself from my sensors, I thought a second sensor on your plane would catch her side scatter. So clever of me, so resourceful. But your weapons were too modest to finish the job. And she'll never fall for the same trick twice.*

"*Next time, Clayton, use more megatonnage. Or I will.*"

Iruvage slithers away, up Clayton's spine, out the top of his head, leaving a corkscrew of migraine. Clayton balls up on himself and shrieks. When he's ready to think again he opens his eyes and says to Erik (the first face he sees) the thing he has to say:

"Fourteen hours. In fourteen hours they nuke us. I just got the deadline. DC is on the list, Erik. Unless I get us into Blackbird. Unless everyone gets in line and helps me, Rosamaria dies."

Erik smiles in contempt: he's so relieved that Clayton has stopped freaking out and gone back to being a piece of shit. "Is that how you get to be in charge again? You take her hostage? You think if you point a nuclear bomb at her, I'll just do what you say?"

Yes. That's exactly what Clayton thinks. He unballs himself. He knocked his head on the corner of the folding chair, and it aches. He stands up anyway, rubbing the bruise. He looks at everyone.

"We have to penetrate Blackbird and discover its purpose, or the aliens give up and cauterize everything. *Everything* on this planet. My science team is dead. You're all I've got. Help me. Help me save us all."

A short hush. Li Aixue looks toward Blackbird, wherever it is relative to this container; Clayton isn't sure but *she's* sure, and her eyes are full of yearning. Chaya Panaguiton looks worriedly at Li Aixue. Khaje Sinjari looks at Clayton's throat. Erik looks at the piece of shit he called his friend.

The container's door clicks open.

Anna Sinjari comes inside, shuts the door carefully behind her, and looks at her mother. Her eyes are red with crying. She looks empty, but empty in a good way: empty like the gun her mom put to her head. And speaking of guns—

She's got a pistol.

Clayton realizes that he's failed to consider Ssrin's next move if she *is* alive.

He has exposed himself as Iruvage's agent. Wouldn't Ssrin therefore try to eliminate him?

"Erik!" he shouts. "She's—"

But Anna already has the Glock up at arm's length, both hands on the grip, two thumbs pointing forward right at Clayton. Clayton hopes and strives to be a brave man, a man who can face the consequences of his actions, but staring up that gun at the woman holding it, his asshole puckers. Ssrin *chose* her. She could be capable of anything, even and especially this—

"Anna," Erik snaps, "wait, don't, *don't*—"

"Jiyan!" Khaje Sinjari barks. "Êstaş negorawît? تۆراویتگەن شاستنی"

Anna's trigger finger twitches.

CHAPTER EIGHT

The Glock goes off.

Pop like a finger on Clayton's eardrum, the *snap* of the bullet right past him, into the AC unit behind him, which rattles and dies. The tinnitus echo of the bullet sounds like a gnat flying into the side of his head.

Clayton releases a huge breath and a little jet of piss.

He stares at Anna. Anna looks back at him wildly. Did she miss? Did she *aim* to miss? She looks like she has no idea.

"Okay," he says, "Erik, if you'd please disarm—"

Anna shoots him again. She misses again. Clayton leaps in surprise. "Stop! Fuck!"

Chaya Panaguiton is wrapped around Li Aixue, her wide back turned to Anna. Erik bellows "CEASE FIRE!"

Anna's mother lunges in and grabs the pistol. "Anna! Be qesdewe le destit da? به قەسدەوه له دەستت دا ؟ "

"Yeah," Anna says. "Of course. Of course I missed on purpose."

"Jesus," Erik snarls. "Anna, you *never* point that at someone you don't intend to kill, understand?"

"I haven't," Anna says.

"Okay," Clayton says shakily. "Okay. Are we done? You—" He points at Khaje, who sneers at his finger like it is the devil's hell-burnt dong. "You said, on the radio, that Anna had a way inside. Anna, do you have a way inside?"

"I don't really think I want to tell you," Anna says. She wrings her hand where her mom twisted it.

"I will order my men to detain you and interrogate you if I must. We need to—" This is absolutely the wrong tack to take with Anna. "I'm sorry about your people. But if we're going to stop anyone *else* from getting nuked, I have to know."

"If you had to know," Khaje says, "maybe you shouldn't have killed the one who was going to tell us."

"I had a plan. I had a team. I had equipment, I had the best people. If Ssrin hadn't killed them all—"

"In self-defense!" Erik bellows. "You were trying to nuke her! First contact with a being from another fucking world *and you drop a bomb on her*! I knew you were going to do this, I fucking *knew* it, you just can't help yourself!"

"Iruvage was negotiating from a position of strength—"

"You do not compromise under threat. You do not give in. Ever. Or you teach the enemy that threats work!"

"Okay, Erik, I'll just call his bluff and let him nuke a couple cities and *then* we'll do what he wants, that's much better!"

"*You do not compromise under threat! Ever!* Because if they have enough power to make an unanswerable threat, they have enough power to break the deal and do it anyway!"

Clayton can't help it. He sneers. Just a little sneer, just the old I-know-better face he wheeled out when everyone followed Erik, even though Clayton had the better plan.

"I wonder what Anna thinks of that."

She makes no sound, but if she were still holding the Glock Clayton's sure it would've gone off. Khaje's teeth click together, hard. Erik's gray eyes come down from their high place to fix on him. "What the fuck do you mean?"

"Ask her why this village is here. Why it wasn't blown apart by Saddam. What she did to save them."

"You should not know this," Khaje says. Her English is slow and careful. Maybe she learned it just to talk to Anna. Her broad, sharp-cheeked face stays fixed on him as she moves between him and her daughter. Hawk tracking dove.

Clayton shrugs. "I got the story from the NGO that fostered Anna. They interviewed her. Wanted to know if she'd been sent away against her will. And it turned out she had. Erik, why do you think Khaje sent her daughter away? Why do you think she's so *scared* of her daughter?"

"I don't know," Erik says, deadly disdainful. "The same reason you are?"

"You don't know how right you are! Just like me, Khaje is scared of Anna's ability to shoot people in the head! When Anna was seven years old, Saddam's deputy Ali Hassan Al-Majid ordered the Iraqi military to destroy all life—human, animal, houses, crops, trees—in the 'prohibited areas' of northern Iraq. He used sarin, VX, all those WMDs we pretended we gave a shit about later."

"I know this, Clay. Remember? I deployed, I was *here*. You were in an office, watching by satellite."

Clayton ignores that. "And in the middle of that genocide, an Iraqi officer who fancied himself a student of psychology offered little Anna a bargain. He had her entire village corralled. He didn't have the transport to haul them to a prison camp. So he was just going to shoot them all.

"But he'd captured Anna's father. Her brother. Others. And he said, listen, Jiyan—that's Anna's Kurdish name—if you do nothing, we're going to kill everyone you've ever known. We're going to blow up your village and bulldoze it under.

"But there's one way you can stop it. For each one of these prisoners you shoot, I'll spare a fraction of your village. You can all go back to Tawakul. You can keep your homes. For each prisoner you kill, I'll save some of your people.

"And you know what? Anna saved them all."

Khaje's nose flares with each hard breath. Erik stares, jaw set, eyes hollow, like an empty suit of armor. He didn't know.

Clayton feels like a manipulative piece of shit, but goddamn, the *world* is on the line. He doesn't have to speak the rest for Erik to understand it.

"It's not the same as what you just did," Erik says.

"It's exactly the same."

"Someone else forced that choice on Anna. You, Clayton, you *arranged* the choice. You sought out the power to make that decision. You're not like Anna at all. You're like that Iraqi."

"Iruvage forced me to—"

"Just like Saddam 'forced' that officer to help carry out Anfal? He was the one who decided to become the kind of man Saddam would order to exterminate the Kurds. He was the one who decided to be really fucking good at it."

Clayton finds himself staring at Anna, awaiting her judgment: and she looks back at him with cool, clear-eyed interest.

"What's the point of telling Erik?" she asks. "You think he'll get mad at me? He'll hand me over to interrogate?"

"I'm not telling him! I'm telling *you* that I understand what you did, Anna. I'm making the same choices you did. I am not a piece of shit. I'm not an Iraqi genocidaire. I'm just a guy trying to save us all. Work with me. Please, please, *tell me how to get into Blackbird.*"

Anna looks at her mom. Her mom looks back at her. *Êstaş negorawît?* Clayton can't speak Sorani, but he can guess what that meant.

Haven't you changed at all?

Anna says, "No."

"Anna, if you don't tell me what you know, then he'll send the atmanach after you—"

"If he does, I'll shoot myself in the head, and he'll get nothing. Stay the fuck away from me. I don't want to be part of whatever you're doing, Mr. Hunt. I think it ends with bombing more children."

And she walks out.

God fucking damn it. God fucking damn.

"Can I kill him now?" Khaje Sinjari asks.

"You'd better not," Clayton snaps. "You need me too. Let me demonstrate. Some of your people survived the bombs, *exactly* like I told you they would. They're in those caves right now, dying slow. But not past helping."

"How do you know that?" Erik says coldly.

"Because my alien told me."

"The zahaki told him to lie," Khaje says. "To keep him alive. I'm going to shoot him now."

And maybe she is about to: but the Chinese mathematician raises one small hand, open-fingered, her eyes luminous with excitement. "Khaje. Wait. Don't do that. Mr. Hunt, I want to get into Blackbird too. I want to discover the truth behind what it does to us. And you are the only one left with an alien to talk to. You are the only one who can learn what *they* know about Blackbird."

Clayton saccades his gaze, real quick, to the taller woman behind Aixue. Chaya Panaguiton is staring at Li Aixue with her hands cupped over her mouth: a cup to hold in guilt.

Why?

"It seems to me that there's a positive sum outcome here," Aixue continues. "Everyone can get what they want. Major Wygaunt, you command the largest surviving group of soldiers. We don't need soldiers to enter Blackbird. But Mr. Hunt says there are survivors from the nuclear blasts. People in terrible pain. Can you help them?"

"Yeah," he says longingly. "But I can't abandon this position. Blackbird is the objective."

"Your objective is complete. Blackbird is safe. Let the multinational science team resume our work here. I have a promising line of investigation. Mr. Hunt may be able to bring new insight. Khaje, wouldn't your peshmerga also like to go search for your families, your friends?"

The woman picks up her rifle, which Clayton recognizes, from *Call of Duty*, as a Dragunov, an old Soviet marksman's weapon. A good weapon to use if you wanted to pick off a man from outside the range of his bodyguards.

"Yes," Khaje says tonelessly. "If there's anyone left. We should go to them."

Erik looks at her. "Okay. If you think it's a priority, I'll support you. This is your home. We're your guests. We'll help."

Clayton hates the trickle of contempt he feels—Erik is doing what Americans do in Iraq, in Afghanistan: build rapport with the locals, try to make right any wrongs done by excessive firepower, get them on side and talking to you. Clayton holds this approach in contempt not because it's wrong but because it's manipulative. An American soldier might want to help you. But America, the entire beast, is completely unequipped to keep its promises to the average Iraqi or Afghan. Thomas Barnett, for all his Iraq invasion cheerleading, was right—America can't process broken states. America wins the war and loses the part afterward. That soldier is gonna leave one day, and when he does, Tariq Taliban will still be living right next door.

"Fine," Khaje says. She walks out. The door slams shut behind her, riding the pressure dip.

God. He'd thought that once Erik understood the full picture he'd realize there was no other choice. But faced with no choice, Erik just . . . refuses to acknowledge the choice.

If Erik *does* go out there, with Anna, with Khaje, with his most loyal troops—

What if Iruvage just kills them all? What if these notional Kurdish survivors are bait? Clayton genuinely doesn't know if Iruvage will hide from Erik's troops, or kill them for sport. The alien is hyperintelligent, but he is also a tremendous dick.

He can't let Iruvage murder Erik. Not before Erik understands that Clayton just wanted to do what was right.

"Erik," he says. "Be careful. If you go out there—"

"Shut your fucking mouth," Erik says. "Don't address me with your lies. You *knew* it was all going to happen. Those Kurds are just the latest people you've killed. Everyone who died in the EMPs? Everyone who fell out of the sky, or burned, or choked, or drowned? All on you. You could've tried to stop it and you didn't. *All* on you. Fuck you."

Erik walks out.

"Well." Clayton clears his aching throat. "Professor Li, thank you for being the voice of reason."

"Sure, sure," she says absently.

'"Will you organize the scientists? There's still power here. We can make coffee. Get all hands on deck and talk about how to resume lab work."

"Nobody wants to go back in there," Chaya says. "The labs are full of—a lot of people died in there."

"Okay. Just the dormitories for now. Surely people want hot food and a chance to rest." He tries to smile. "And I've got some good news to share."

Chaya Panaguiton looks up from her weird, guilty inspection of Li Aixue: looking at the Chinese woman like she's somehow Chaya's fault. "What good news?"

"No more atmanach. I convinced him to stop sending it."

And he sees, from her relief, that he's found a way to make them listen. Because at least he can make the terror stop.

CLAYTON//829 MINUTES REMAIN

He's gotta get back in control. So he goes out.

A little bird zips overhead, across the maze of containers, toward Blackbird. He watches it, afraid it will hit one of the death holes and burst into flames. But it swoops away northeast, toward the mountain. Where a ring of fire spreads from ground zero.

There'll be a hole in that forest for years. Clayton's Hole. Who the fuck is he to do this? To drop these bombs and make these decisions and give these commands? How can he be such a hot-shit political item, so kinetically propelled toward success—and yet so certain that he is faking *everything*?

Fuck it. He chose to be the guy. Erik's right, he put himself in this position. He's gotta act.

"Garcia. Sergeant Garcia!" He grabs the first military guy he sees outside—Garcia, one of Erik's loyalists, no doubt posted to keep an eye on him. "I need to brief the whole unit. President's authority."

"Very good, sir. If you want to give orders, you better have the SecDef issue a policy directive to Admiral McRaven through the Pentagon. Now please follow me to your billet. Major Wygaunt wants you under observation."

"No." He's not going to get fucking arrested. He is going to fix this. "Maybe you're unclear on your unit's chain of command. Things have been moving fast, after all."

"I know my chain of command, sir."

"Do you?"

"Yes, sir. Shortest of my whole career. And you aren't in it."

"Bullshit. I am a personal representative of the president, who is commander in chief of the United States military, including Secretary of Defense Hagel, Admiral McRaven, Lieutenant General Votel, Major Wygaunt, and you. Constitution of the United States of America, Article II, Section 2, Clause 1. The President can issue military directives. He dropped the bomb on Japan by his personal authority. His authority dropped the bomb here too. He just lent it to me for the duration. I am in command."

"That's fine, sir. You can take it up with the major. Now I have orders to escort you to a CHU for observation."

A CHU is a containerized housing unit. Clayton really does not want to be containerized, housed, or, for that matter, united (in any sense of the word). He wants to get into Blackbird. "Do you need me to walk you through the legalities? In 1863 Chief Justice Grier established that if war is initiated by an insurrection or by a foreign nation—which I presume includes aliens—the president is bound to accept the challenge without waiting for legislative authority. He doesn't need Congress. We're at war. And in wartime the president has the power to take any measure which will avert a disaster that could lead to the defeat of the nation. That includes making me his goddamn proxy in the field. That includes making me a goddamn five-star general if he wants to. Now, he didn't do that, because he didn't think you'd be stupid enough to disregard my lawful orders. But maybe he should have. Do you want me to order you arrested for failure to obey a lawful general order or regulation, namely the fucking Constitution of the United States?"

"Sure," Garcia says. "Now please follow me to your billet."

Goddamn it. Garcia either knows this is all bullshit (and it is, the national security advisor is not a cabinet member, he's an aide, and neither he nor any of his deputies can give orders even in wartime) or just doesn't care.

Bluff harder. "Do you want me to raise President Obama on SATCOM? I'm sure he's got some time for Master Sergeant Garcia while he's managing the worst disaster in human history. Let me put him on. What's up, Barack, it's ya boy, Clayton. I got Ricardo here and he's not sure who he works for—"

"SATCOM is out, sir."

"Not mine! I have an alien ship up there!"

Garcia looks back at him, narrow-eyed. "Could you really do that? You have comms?"

"I have whatever I need to save this planet."

"Hey," someone behind Garcia says. "We're saving the planet?"

CIASAD operator Skyler Nashbrook unpeels himself from whatever zone of denied knowledge he was lurking in (behind the container dorm, Clayton supposes).

"Fuck," Garcia mutters. Clayton knows for a fact that Garcia has worked with Nashbrook before, during Delta Force's operations around Baghdad. "Nashbrook? We're taking Mr. Hunt into protection. Major's orders."

"Why?" says another guy. Mike Jan, the DEVGRU hotshot, who must've been loitering around to see what happened. "It sounds like Mr. Hunt's in charge, Master Sergeant."

"Major Wygaunt's in command, *Petty Officer* Jan."

"Major Wygaunt just grab-assed a bunch of dudes from all over the unit then fucked off east with the Kurds," Nashbrook says. "He's off comms. And if the deputy national security advisor has orders from the president, I think we better listen. What 'disaster leading to the defeat of the nation,' Mr. Hunt?"

"The imminent thermonuclear attack on our planet."

"What?" Mike Jan and Skyler Nashbrook close in and Garcia moves to keep them both in front of him. The three MAJESTIC operators ring up around Clayton like gunfighters looking to draw. Four-horned night vision goggles and plated body armor and weapons that imply, in all their Picatinny-railed modularity, a post-industrial approach to warfare. These are not the helmeted GIs of old war movies, citizen-soldiers who'll go home to marry their girls in South Dakota once the Nazis are whipped. These are artisanal, professional killers, as customized and specific as the legal briefs Clayton wrote to justify Obama's assassinations.

"Erik didn't brief you?" Clayton says. Sorry, Erik, don't mean to disrespect your rank and authority, only I've got to seize command of the guys you left behind. Gotta sort your Paladins from mine.

"No, sir. Major Wygaunt said we were to maintain a protective posture around the site and wait for him to return." Mike Jan scratches his beard. His eyes are squinty, thoughtful. "He didn't explain why Team One had to frag Captain Brennan with a Punisher. Or why he went loco and started shooting them. Or how we lost the mission aircraft. Or who dropped those nukes on the mountain. Or—"

"Okay," Clayton says calmly and assertively. "This is what you need to know. I dropped those nukes in order to deter the aliens from launching their own strike. There were two aliens down here. A soldier and an insurgent. I am cooperating with the soldier to defeat the insurgent. She's a high-value leadership element in an insurrection against the alien authority."

"Great," Garcia says. He helped kill two high-value leadership elements almost a decade ago: Saddam's sons. "We nuked Luke?"

"I wouldn't call her Luke. I would call her Roy Batty."

Skyler Nashbrook, commenting on the weather: "I heard we hit civilians."

"Yes, there was bycatch. That's my fault, and I take full responsibility. I made the call to hit the target while we had her position fixed. But she had taken human shields."

Mike Jan's got one hand on the grip of his submachine gun, casually, like it's just where he puts his fingers when he's got nothing better to do. "Are we working for the alien who zapped Captain Brennan?"

"Yes, we are."

"That's pretty fucked up," Garcia says. "I knew Amos since he was a butterbar in Fallujah, kicking down doors with his guys. Now we're cool with the aliens who brainfucked him?"

"Imagine you were in the aliens' position. A bunch of armed military-age males are closing in on your own primary objective. Wouldn't you drop a Hellfire on them? I would."

Skyler Nashbrook says, "You said they were going to bomb the whole planet."

"Sure. Imagine you're the CIA and you just found bin Laden in Pakistan. Only he's just found something too. He's got a genie in a lamp. How long are you gonna give the Pakistanis to go in, kill bin Laden, and get that lamp before you say *fuck it* and drop a nuke on the city?" Fourteen hours, apparently. "The aliens haven't pulled that trigger yet. But they will if they have to. Because they can't let Ssrin get out of here with that genie."

At some point Clayton needs to seriously interrogate his own ability to dream up hypothetical scenarios that justify his own actions. Make a note, Clay.

Skyler has dead-dog eyes. The CIA used him as a liaison to operate counterinsurgency specialists: terrorists on the American side. Skyler was their teacher. Clayton used him in latter-day Paladin because he was completely capable and absolutely without ego.

He says: "That's what you call an *ally*?"

Clayton shouldn't say this but he says it anyway. "We're allies with Yemen, man. You know who gets blown up when we go in to bomb al-Qaeda there?

Yemenis. You know who got blown up when we went after Saddam? Iraqis. When we decide to act, little guys get hurt. Now *we're* the little guys. We're going to get hurt. We need to give up the idea that we're untouchable. We are no longer the supreme power on Earth."

Wrong move, Clayton. They don't like you. They don't trust you. They sure as fuck don't like you explaining that *they're* now in the same position as the brown hajji sand—sand dudes they're used to killing. And if you piss them off too much, they're going to shoot you dead as a buddy-fucker.

Skyler Nashbrook stares at Clayton, utterly unreadable. Like he's thinking about what kind of peanut butter to buy.

"Fuck this," Ricardo Garcia says. "I'm gonna go find the major."

But Mike Jan looks at Clayton like he's impressed. "That makes sense, sir," he says. "Very realpolitik."

K + 154:56 hours
Blackbird Camp
Qandil Mountains, Kurdistan

Rage. Sing, muse, of the fucking rage of Erik, pawn of Clayton Hunt, Clayton, betrayer, child-nuker, quisling to aliens. Predictable as piss and just as impossible to avoid.

Erik knows a secret about rage. You gotta get to the middle of it. Some rage, you get to the middle and you find there's nothing there. An asshole cuts you off in traffic? You bang your head on the corner of the cabinet right when someone's complaining you didn't sort the recycling properly? You get to the middle and it's just selfish pain. You're just hurt, you're flaring up.

But if you've truly been wronged, you'll find a bar.

Rage isn't like fire. It doesn't spread by sheer heat. You can't convince people to become angry just by being angry at them. You'll frighten them, or convince them to ignore you. So you don't show them your rage. You go into the middle of it, into the black pupil of the fury, and you find that bar.

That solid bar at the center of your wrath is the reason. Not your reason. *The* reason. The objective, morally axiomatic reason you are furious. And if you can pull that bar back out and polish it clean of your hurt and your prejudice, you can show it to other people. You can touch them with it, like a lodestone. And then they get furious alongside you. Because they realize that in your place they'd be furious too. And they realize that, if they don't get furious, maybe someday they *will* end up in your place.

The reason rings out true across all of time and context. It is the fulcrum that lets the lever of your anger move the world: knowing that what happened didn't just wrong you, it wronged everyone, everywhere, forever

And if you grip that bar hard enough, nothing, not *anything*, can move you.

So he grips it. And he grips Anna Sinjari's shoulder. And he pulls her around to face him.

"Erik—" she says, and if he had time for it right now, he would know that she is on the verge of tears again. Because of the story Clayton told. Because she saved them all. She thinks—what? That he hates her now? No, don't be a selfish prick, Erik. She's not going to cry because she thinks you hate her. She's going to cry because she shot her father and brother in the head and her mom nearly killed her for it. And then her mom *didn't*.

But right now there is no time for it.

He pulls her toward him, violently: the same violence he would use with any of his men in an urgent situation. Wake the fuck up, Anna. We have shit to do. "Do you know a way inside Blackbird?"

She pulls against his grip. "No. No. I don't know what the fuck Ssrin was talking about. My mom—she thought so too, but she doesn't know . . ."

"If there were any way to beat this guy, any way at all, it would be your alien, right? It would be Ssrin."

"Do you mean beat Clayton? Or Iruvage?"

"No difference right now. She would be the best chance?"

"She's dead, Erik."

"But if she weren't, you'd tell me?"

"Protagonist killer," Anna says, for no reason Erik can decipher right now. "She's gone."

Then why did Clayton have that fit? Why did he say the nukes were gonna drop? Why did he act like he was being *punished*? Not because he killed some Kurds, Iruvage wouldn't care about that.

Because he fucked up. He fucked up the big job the aliens gave him.

"If she *were* alive," he says, "she'd be at ground zero. Right? Where those bombs fell. You haven't seen a body, have you? Do you *really* think she's dead?"

"Erik, in New York I saw her hurt bad. She's not invincible. A nuclear bomb, I don't think she could slither away from that—would there even *be* a body—?"

Like most people she thinks nukes are all-consuming death. But they're not. They're just really big bangs. Erik has been blown up before, and blown people up too. And while those bangs were not quite nuclear, someone always survived.

"Let's find out. We're going to ground zero anyway. We're going to find and save as many of your people"—yes, Anna, they're your people, don't deny it—"as we possibly can. It's the right thing to do."

She balks: "But you're going there to make a deal with Ssrin?"

"A deal? I don't know. I want to find her, because she's the only way we have to win. But I would still go just to save those people. Doing the morally right thing doesn't have to make you stupid. Morally righteous decisions are usually smart decisions, because they require you to go the extra mile, do your diligence, build trust, consider the people around you, follow the rules, rules which exist for a reason. And hope is usually smart too. Because hope allows you to look for long-odds reversals, when all the smart safe plays are just gonna slow your defeat."

"Dude. I have no idea what the fuck you're talking about."

Sometimes it is hard to show people the bar of right, because you are holding it so fiercely all they see is your white knuckles.

"Okay." He shows her his arm, where she seized him, where her fingers probed his tendons. "Think about it this way. Do you still want to have a choice? You said that was important to you."

"Yes. Yes, that matters to me a lot. I don't want to be trapped doing what his—what he wants."

The way she was trapped doing what that Iraqi wanted. "If we stay here at Blackbird, we're not going to accomplish shit. I suspect most of my unit will go with Clayton, because they're *his* Paladins. So we gotta get out. We gotta find room where we can make our own choices. We find another schwerpunkt, another point where our actions can make the most difference. I believe that point is ground zero. Where someone—maybe even Ssrin—might have survived."

She pulls away, skittish—no, not skittish, that's a demeaning word, like he needs to tame her. She's not skittish. She doesn't mind being grasped. But she doesn't want to *stay* grasped.

"Erik," she says. "I killed my brother and my father to protect those people. Of course I'm going to try to help them now."

※

CLAYTON//811 MINUTES REMAIN

Clayton sits down with Captain Raab, a marine who is now, with Brennan dead and Erik out on errantry, the senior officer in command. Clayton says a bunch of stuff like "The fact is that I'm the reason we're here. I'm the one who activated MAJESTIC. I have a job to do and the president wants me to do it." And then he layers on a little flattery. "You should extend an offer of cooperation to the Russian, Iranian, and Chinese contingents. Can you take care of that on the president's behalf, Captain Raab? I know it's a lot of responsibility, but you were specifically chosen for this role."

Then, having assured the military he just wants to do some science, he rounds up the leaders of the international science team: Professor Huang Lim, Professor Anatoly Sivakov, and Professor Panaguiton. And he puts them all to sleep.

"You guys are all I've got," he says. "Ssrin killed my team. There's no backup coming for at least forty-eight hours. I need you at your best."

They have to sleep. So he doesn't tell them about the fourteen-hour deadline before nuclear annihilation. He doesn't tell them what's happening to their dead colleagues right now, just a few hundred feet away. He has seen enough satellite timelines of mass graves to know exactly which stage the corpses have reached. Their skin and bone cells are still alive. Their suits are bloating with gases now. Death signals the beginning of a final uprising, when the three pounds and 60 percent (by count) of your cells that are bacterial clients claim their last meal. They eat you so greedily and so well.

(How did God handle that, when he brought Jesus back after three days? Did he keep the bacteria from communing upon the holy flesh? Did he let them die, and then resurrect them too? Maybe Jesus had no bacteria in his body, being the Son of Man, virgin-born from the immaculately conceived Mary. But then Jesus would've had diarrhea.)

He just tells them to set their alarms for six p.m. local. "You'll be bleary. But we've got the Navy SEALs to make you coffee. Everything is gonna be okay."

Yes, he's sacrificing eight of the fourteen hours left to human civilization. But he needs that time to get up to speed. Resting them will make them more effective. He's not wasting his assets, he's building up a multiplier for their last six hours of work.

Most of them.

"Professor Panaguiton?" he says. "I'd like to sit down with you and talk over what's happened here."

Chaya Panaguiton hesitates at the door. The others have gone already. "I'm not a professor."

"You were the first one on the scene. You know what I need to know."

"You know I think you're a baby killer."

He smiles at her. He takes a small risk. "It's you or Professor Li. You were here first. She's up next. Should I send my guys to get her instead?"

She stands in the doorway, hands braced on the frame, rocking forward, back. Her jeans are baggy, her windbreaker loose over a tank top whitened with bleach stains. Bouncing there in the door she looks like a B-girl, Val Pal or someone out of the Filipino dance scene, except she's buckled into a work belt and boots.

"You're going to interrogate her?"

"I'm going to debrief her," he says gently. "I'm not CIA, this isn't a black site. I'm going to sit her down with a cup of tea and talk to her. And then I'm going to send her to bed."

She comes slowly back inside. She shuts the door. She turns deliberately and strides toward him, and for just a moment, he thinks that she is going to pull an Anna: she is going to attack him with one of the tools on her belt. Beat him to death with a wrench. Jesus was a carpenter, and Jesus, she's going to nail him.

But of course she won't, and she can't. Because if she murders him then the atmanach comes back, and she, like everyone else, is fucking terrified of it.

She takes a breath. She begins to say something very sharp. Then she reconsiders. She sits down. "Okay. Debrief me."

"Interview one," he tells the recorder. He's using an Edirol R-09, but he lost his shotgun mic in the crash so he's just turned the volume down and prayed it'll come out okay. "Coffee?" He has two mugs ready. "You must've been up early, if you slept at all. With—" With the atmanach attacking.

"Sure," she says. "I like coffee."

"Vodka?"

She stares at him. "Are you serious?"

"Made it myself. Lab alcohol and bottled water from one of the supply trailers. Forty-five proof."

"Won't that make you go blind?"

"Clearly you do not hang out with rocket propellant chemists! This isn't your grad school lab alcohol, all scuzzed up with methanol and benzenes. This is pure pharmaceutical-grade ethanol. Plus just a little sugar. Stirred, not shaken, with a magnetic bar. Here. For your health." He tips it into his own coffee, takes a sip, and puts the mug down. All of that was a lie. It's not vodka. "I appreciate you and Professor Li not telling the others about the deadline."

"If there's a deadline, why are you letting everyone rest?"

He taps his fingers on the table. "Good question. I could wring fourteen person-hours of work out of everyone here. Or I could give everyone eight hours of sleep, and thereby improve their access to the *hundreds* of hours of information they've soaked up over the past days. They need a chance to collate, correlate, purge all the fear and stress."

"Zahak," she says.

"What?"

"Nothing."

No, this is exactly what he wants. These strange threads you pull to get through the dams and the blocks. "Zahak's a Persian mythological figure. He eats brains. Why'd you think about Zahak?"

"When we were waiting for you to arrive—when we thought you were going to *help*—"

If he were not so live-wire tense, he might groan aloud at the guilt.

"We sat in Khaje's house, waiting for the atmanach to come and take someone else. To pass the time she told me stories. *Zahaki* is what she calls the aliens."

He nods and feeds her hesitation back to her. "She calls the aliens *zahaki?*"

"Yes. Because of the snakes."

"What snakes?"

"You've never seen them? I thought you worked for one."

"He looked like a woman. Have *you* seen one?"

"No. But Khaje described Ssrin to me." She reaches across the table and grabs the other mug. He notes the ratio of her second and fourth fingers: ring much longer than index. He suspects the correlation between digit ratio and sexual orientation is just bullshit, because nearly every correlation is bullshit. But he notices, anyway, because even bad data is data, and you should be conscious about throwing it out.

She cups the coffee and shivers. "I'll turn down the AC," he offers. He'll have to turn it back up, once hyperthermia sets in. The MDMA in the coffee came from a huge bag of pharmaceuticals that dropped with the MAJESTIC paratroopers. Several of the bags are unlabeled, reserved for Clayton's personal use. He brought midazolam and a few other interrogation drugs too, but he's never used them before. He wants to stick to ecstasy because he's done a lot of it. And he's getting a dose of it in the coffee too.

He's gambling that this is the right way to get her talking. Pharmaceutically amplified empathy. He can't convince her that he's more than a baby killer, but maybe if she can *feel* it, she can convince herself. And maybe even convince him.

"You must've been pretty scared," he says. "Waiting for help to show up."

"No," she says. "I was too busy to be scared. So I wasn't really brave either. Not like Emme. I didn't meet her, Khaje told me about her. But I heard the recordings she made before she . . . before she died."

"Who's Emme?"

And she tells him.

THE CANADIAN PROTOCOL

FIRST DAY
K + 0 hours (0019 Arabia Standard Time)

A shepherd with binoculars. That is how it begins: with a girl on a rise in a rolling meadow, searching for her sheep in the night.

She must find the binoculars difficult in the dark. The old Soviet gear is too big for her hands. She would be astounded to know that in just a few hours satellite lenses orders of magnitude more sensitive than her binoculars will be focused on this meadow. Scrying the place where she disappeared.

Tonight she thinks only of her sheep. Oil smuggling paid for her phone and the rifle on her back, but this flock is part of the village's common wealth, and she is responsible for it. Or so her mother is always reminding her. And even if she watches too much anime and spends too much time getting into fights on Facebook, she wants to do her mother proud. And she really likes yogurt, and they can't make yogurt without sheep milk.

But she has lost her flock.

Her earbuds, stuffed into the pocket of her vest, make little Alicia Keys noises. She scans the valley with rising confusion. Where are her sheep? They were right *there*.

A sound catches her eye.

At first she thinks it's coming from her phone. But now she can *see* the sound. As if God lifted the Bijar carpets in her home and strummed the fabric with His fingers. Her skin prickles. A soft touch on her cheek, like her mother's hands.

She drops the binoculars. The strap chafes her neck. She stares at the music.

A pink spark dances out of the mountainside. As if weaving itself to life. She receives a sense of struggle, like a lamb kicking in a caul. Something is coming into being from the mountain: a pole, a spear . . .

After a long time she remembers her radio. But it is full of music too. One thing made into many, bells exploding into grapevine clusters of themselves and ringing too.

The pink light brightens. Tears distort the perfection and so she wipes them away. The color, pink sunset through storm clouds, makes her think of autumn. Her favorite season. More tears come.

خەجێ

Khaje is awake and sober.

Usually if she can't sleep she drinks until she passes out. But Ssrin said it would start tonight: Anna's homecoming. And she must be sober when she decides whether to kill her daughter.

"*You have visitors,*" Ssrin whispers. "*Soheila and her son.*"

She groans and presses her cheek into the rug. The deep pile scratches her face. It's not really *her* rug, it's a replacement, something to cover up what's missing. When she came back from the camps, she found that someone—a neighbor who thought she was dead, though they blamed it on jash—had stolen the family carpets. When she had those old rugs, she also had a son and a daughter and a husband. Instead of a rifle and a bottle and a grudge.

"*You have to talk to them, Khaje.*"

"I don't want to," she says. The zahaki bit a radio into her throat. "She'll see something's wrong. Soheila can always tell."

"*She already knows something's wrong.*"

"What?" She leaves a print of her face in the carpet pile. "What did you do?"

"*I used the Ubiet to pull the weapon up from its shelter. I asked it to become something I could take away from here. A solid thing. But it's . . . not what I expected. There's so much of it! I thought I could carry it!*"

"So it's real?"

"*Of course it's real,*" Ssrin snaps. "*Do you think I'd waste my time on your headless little planet if it weren't? I showed you the Ubiet. You saw. This is the place. The weapon is here. It left a mark on your daughter, when she made her choice. It was watching her.*"

"Did it make her choose to . . . do what she did?"

"*Nothing can make anyone make a choice.*"

Soheila bangs on her door. Khaje's portrait of Margaret Shello rattles on the wall. An Avesta first-run edition of *Mem and Zin* tips off the dirty bayonet she was using as a bookmark. She watched the TV show first, and now she's trying to learn to read the book.

"Khaje!" Soheila shouts. "Khaje, are you drunk again?"

Khaje knows she has PTSD. The people from the NGOs tell her, *Khaje, you have PTSD.* They tell her that the ideas she grew up with—either you are sane or you are mad—are not healthy ways to process trauma. She even knows her triggers: warm bread, cradles, the sight of weapons held by little girls.

But it is hard for her to think of herself as *mentally ill* or *a survivor of trauma* when she was raised with *crazy*. Even in Tawakul, she is still crazy old Khaje.

Oh, she is *old*. So much has changed! Anfal, the survivors' decree, independence, civil war, the PKK in the mountains, cell phones, Saddam's death, oil prospectors. The faces at Newroz—so many gone . . .

Now things will change again.

"I'm awake."

"There's something in the north meadow. Like a crashed airliner, but big."

"I think it's an alien spaceship," Soheila's son Haydar says brightly.

"Oh," Khaje says. She didn't know Ssrin was going to bring a spaceship. "What do you want me to do about it?"

"The Canadians want to go look at it. This is our land, we're responsible for their safety."

Khaje hates the Canadians. They've been up here for a week, poking around Tawakul's poisoned hills in search of oil and old land mines. The village voted to invite them. Tomorrow a Ugandan-American company is due to arrive and make their own survey, and Khaje plans to hate them too. Nothing good will come of oil—just Americans and Barzanis and Talabanis with fat pockets.

"So call Hewler," she says.

"We can't. The radios are out. The satphones and the cell tower too. I'll send a truck once we have something to report. If it's American, someone will come looking for it. If it's not . . . someone will come looking for it."

"Sorry about the radios," Ssrin murmurs. *"When it was born, it was loud. A lot of longwave emissions. It may have subsumed some nearby life."*

"What do you mean, *subsumed?"*

"Sheep. Mostly."

"Is it dangerous?"

"Probably. I thought it would just grow a neuroscythe and talk to me. Like a That relic should . . . but this is something more."

"Should I stop them from going near it?"

"Don't you want to know what it does before Anna gets here? It'd rather spoil the reunion if you were all dead."

"Khaje?" Soheila calls. "Are you talking to yourself? We need to seat the assembly."

"You go ahead," Khaje calls roughly. "I'll be along."

⁂

"Ssrin. Show me Anna again."

"You saw enough to make your choice."

The radio the zahaki put in her neck can send memories. They arrive in the fractured gaze of the zahaki, who see the world as a kind of collage, every shape and color its own separate pang of sensation. Shouldn't they have eight little visions, one for each head? No, apparently not, everything gets stitched together into one strange spherical quilt of perception, and each part of that quilt is not just an image but sort of a chart or texture. It is so rich that the first time Ssrin tried to show it to Khaje, Khaje passed out and pissed herself. Then she woke up to Ssrin bathing her and saw Ssrin's true form.

The reason her bookmark bayonet is dirty is that she stabbed Ssrin with it.

It surprises her that Ssrin was not ready, because she says *everyone* reacts to zahaki this way, even other space aliens. Ssrin says that the violence the zahaki provoke is *not physically caused, and therefore very hard to physically avert.*

Khaje's not supposed to call Ssrin a zahaki. Ssrin insists *Khai, we are called khai.* But Khaje thinks she looks like Zahak, the evil emperor in the *Shahnameh*, who grew snakes from his shoulders where the devil kissed him.

Zahak had to feed his snakes two human brains every day, lest they turn on him. The thing is that the devil Ahriman put the snakes on Zahak, and then, in disguise as a physician, taught Zahak the remedy—so is it really Zahak's fault? Yes, of course it is, because all this happened after Ahriman convinced Zahak to kill his own father and seize the throne. The devil can tempt you, but it is your choice to succumb. It is your choice to keep feeding the snakes two lives a day, instead of standing up and saying "no more."

There's a part in the *Shahnameh* where two guys, Armayel and Garmayel, decide to save some of the Iranians that Zahak keeps eating. They become amazing cooks and win a job as Zahak's personal chefs. Every day they receive the two guys whose brains are going to be devoured. They send one guy away to the mountains to escape, and they replace his brain with a sheep brain. Zahak's serpents don't notice. And the men sent to the mountains become the Kurds, from which, one day, the blacksmith Kawa will arise to lead an army that will defeat Zahak. (Kawa doesn't strike the killing blow himself, though. Fereydoon bashes Zahak's head in with a cow-headed mace, flays him, and shackles him to Mount Damāvand. Victory!)

But, wait, think about the cooks. Armayel and Garmayel still have to include *one* human brain in the dish, or Zahak will taste the deception. So one man must die every day. How do the chefs decide *which* of the two men to save? Do they flip a coin? Do the men draw straws? Do they save the youngest, or the one with the most children? Do they take bribes?

The question that's tormented her for twenty years. How do you decide? When Zahak demands his brains, what do you do?

Who dies and gets turned to porridge? Who lives to become the Kurds?

If Khaje had been in her daughter's place (instead of being dragged off to a camp), she knows exactly what she would've done. She would've shot the Iraqi officer in the face, and died. Collaboration is for jash. We are all peshmerga now; we all must face death for Kurdistan and God.

And maybe Anna understands that now.

Because the radio the zahaki put in Khaje's neck can send memories. And one of those memories was Anna, all grown up, short hair, American clothes, dirty apartment. Beautiful, so beautiful. Khaje cried at the sight of her.

And in that memory, Anna refuses to shoot poor Roman.

It is time to bring Anna home, because for the first time in more than twenty years, Khaje is not certain she will kill her daughter on sight.

***

She has to get up. She has to go! She says it to herself about fifty times. Then finally she does it.

She washes, dresses, does her hair, prays, and puts her rifle on her back. Then she fixes her face in her hungover grimace and goes outside.

Her house stands in the shade of a barous, a big Kurdish oak. Kids are scared of her so they don't come play, which is for the best. She took down the swing that Hamali used when he was a boy. She's lucky to still have a tree—the Iraqis destroyed a lot of the old-growth forest—but she'd be luckier to still have a son, wouldn't she?

"Khaje," a girl-voice says brightly. "Good morning, heval."

Khaje groans. She can tolerate Arîn Tawakuli, but only when she has been awake for between three and eight hours, only if she doesn't have a hangover, and only if she doesn't hear any particularly cheerful birds. Arîn is too young to remember the hard times of civil war. She's an Apoist and a true believer in jineology and Khaje resents her. Not for her beliefs, but for the ability to believe. Arîn also loves to tell people that Khaje isn't really crazy, she just has PTSD. For that Khaje truly despises her.

"What," she says.

"You've got your rifle."

"I'm going hunting."

"You can't, heval, the deer count is low. They're still stepping on mines." She follows Khaje down the dirt road. "Have you seen the spaceship?"

"What spaceship? Everyone is telling me about a—"

She glimpses it, out across the meadows, in the morning mountain mist.

"Donkey pussy!" she says. "It's enormous!"

"Yeah," Arîn says. "It is, isn't it? Every satellite in the sky is going to see it. Which probably means we'll end up getting bombed, one way or another." She looks at Khaje curiously. "Why didn't you get drunk last night? You usually get drunk this time of week."

"What time of week?"

Arîn shrugs and smiles. Khaje growls and tries to slap her.

The assembly's sitting on cushions in the village hall, eating cold mint yogurt, cheese, goat cream, eggs, and sausage. The Canadians can't shut up about the food, the hospitality! They expected starving farmers: well, they're ten years too late for that. Tawakul has done so nicely off oil smuggling that they can afford generators and refrigerators and a cell tower and Korek internet.

Khaje helps herself to sausages and yogurt and listens to the assembly argue.

"The important thing," Soheila's saying, "is that we don't let one capitalist power or another snap this up for themselves. It came down on our land, and it's our responsibility to make sure it stays open to scientific investigation. It belongs to humanity."

"Wow," the Canadian guy (Khaje forgets his name) says. "That's really forward-thinking of you."

The women in the room (there are men too, people have produced sons and attracted husbands who are not afraid of a village full of women) look at him with hospitable patience. "We *are* jineologists," Soheila reminds him. "Kurdistan is the prototype for the future of human government."

"That's so cool," the Canadian guy says enthusiastically. "I mean, no offense, but you guys are really well educated."

"You're actually really uneducated," Arîn says. "'No offense,' but the West is quite regressive. Here, we actually *do* things. We don't have to wait for a company to lobby their pet senators to pretend they want women involved in government."

Yes, Khaje thinks. And then we get invaded, or bombed. Or we have a civil war.

"Be polite," Soheila says, but she smiles at Arîn.

The Canadian guy takes a big plastic spoonful of yogurt. "We actually have a parliamentary system," he says diffidently. "So . . . if you're trying to keep it away from the capitalists, does that mean you *don't* want us to go take a look?"

"You can survey for immediate dangers? Radiation? Or chemical leaks?"

"Sure. Absolutely."

"Good. When the government investigates this thing, we can show that we've made it safe for scientists. And then maybe they won't send soldiers."

Khaje can't stop herself from interrupting: "But it might be dangerous."

Everyone looks at her with incredible sympathy. They don't know she's the reason this thing is here. They don't know that anyone it hurts will be on Khaje's conscience.

They just see a woman whose family got Anfalized.

<hr />

She has talked to other women who lost husbands and children. She has talked to women who lost nothing except their belief in God and the possibility of good. She has held the frostbitten hands of women who suffered worse things, which they agree, silently, not to talk about.

What can you say? What good will it do? Talking is nothing.

Stories about Anfal always mention the gas, the bombing, the peshmerga fighting back. No one talks about giving birth in filthy prisons, or begging guards for news of fathers and husbands and sons who had already been shot, or staying dirty and going to the toilets as a gang so the guards wouldn't rape you. Terrible things happened in those prisons. Worse than anyone knows. But who wants to know? Nobody. Nobody wants to know these things.

Khaje spoke to a woman who was a girl during Anfal, a little older than Anna. She was captured with her eight siblings. A jash took pity on her family, and said he could save two of them. Her mother chose her and her nine-year-old brother. But when the truck came to take the rest of the family away to die, her brother ran after them. She never saw him again.

If you told this story to someone, what could they say? All Khaje could say was "A thing like this also happened to my daughter."

The regional government likes Anfal survivors as symbols of the grief and persistence of the Kurds. But as people instead of symbols, Anfal survivors are inconvenient, and so it is inconvenient to *be* a survivor. If you've lost a son or a husband you can be registered with the Ministry of Martyrs and Anfal Affairs as a Martyr of Struggle (if you've been gassed) or a Civil Martyr and receive a stipend. Khaje tried. But she could not tolerate all the bullshit involved in the registration. So much talking! Talking wasn't healing, talking wasn't helping, what they needed was *work*. They didn't want to be registered as victims. They wanted to live! To survive!

If you'd survived, but lost no male relatives, you couldn't register at all. Women like that had to put on men's trousers and work in the fields. But even there you would be called zaifa: weak. So they did worse work: gathering herbs, growing kingir and selling it for just a dinar a kilo, making brooms from straw they found on the street, knitting woolen lifka (rough loofa despised by children—you can't have skin problems if you have no skin), baking bread for peshmerga, anything, everything.

Even educated city women looked down on women like Khaje. And in Kurdistan respect is more important than anything.

So the women of Tawakul decided that if no one would respect them then they would make a place where they could at least respect themselves. They went to other villages and asked the widows and orphan girls to join a commune.

A *what?* A commune, a women's commune, come on, women are marching for peace, everyone is starting a women's organization, so we are doing it too. But this one is for poor mountain widows. You aren't betraying your dead men, heval. They wouldn't want you to suffer alone. They'd want you to have work and happiness. Come to Tawakul and together we will try.

But it was hard. Before Anfal, they had orchards, farms, vineyards, sheep, goats, cows, poultry. After Anfal they had smuggling (and prostitution, but no one talks about that) and the lambs the Norwegians gave to widows. Agriculture was dead, the UN oil-for-food program had killed it; it was cheaper to buy foreign food than to buy local rice and wheat.

So they smuggled. Khaje talked her way past more than one border checkpoint simply because being shot to death did not frighten her. The Iranian Revolutionary Guard *did* frighten her—they were the ones most likely to arrest her and drag her away to another prison—but mostly she did not have to deal with the Revolutionary Guard.

The PKK came. They wanted fighters, and in Tawakul's case, that meant children. Tawakul fought back with shame ("We lost our children in the camps! Now *you'd* take our children too?") and sometimes with guns: old women taking potshots at the guerillas, just to say, *These are* our *woods, these are* our *fields, do not come here for* our *children.* That was when Khaje got her respect back, fighting the PKK. Before that, everyone thought she'd sent Anna away just so she wouldn't have to raise a child in poverty.

All in all, Khaje is not sure if they would have made it. Some things got better. Other things got worse.

And then the PKK's imprisoned leader Öcalan put out his new books. Khaje didn't read them, because she can't read very well, but a lot of people did. The books described Öcalan's new replacement for Marxism-Leninism: democratic confederalism. Öcalan had maintained since 1999 that the liberation of Kurdistan required the liberation of women, but now, having gotten on with an American named Murray Bookchin, he was *really* all about it. Öcalan declared that capitalism was a planet-killing disease and that the emancipation of women had to be accompanied by environmental justice and ecological sustainability and ground-up communal democracy.

Suddenly Tawakul was not just a strange kulbar haven run by old women, but an accidental pioneer of the new democratic confederalism. When protests in Syria started in 2011, people came all the way to Tawakul to "study their organization." Khaje ended up yelling about how al-Assad would gas them all while the world watched and laughed. Soheila had to ask her to leave the meeting. She went home shaking with fury. What was she so angry about? The idea that people would have better lives?

One of Öcalan's ideas was that the science of women would be called jineology, from jin for women, and jiyan for life.

Her daughter's name was Jiyan.

※

"Jiyan!" Oh, she said that out loud! The name just pricks her tongue and spills out. Now they will really know she's crazy.

But there's no one there. They've all gone. Arîn and a couple of her friends are doing dishes, laughing. Arîn sticks her head out: "What was that, heval?"

"Nothing," Khaje says, thinking about baby girls. That thought leads her to—"Who was watching the sheep last night?"

"Shanar, I think." Shanar has been aiming to join the women's unit of the village peshmerga, so of course Arîn has an eye on her. "Why?"

"Has anyone seen her today?"

Arîn ducks back into the kitchen to ask.

Suddenly the laughter stops.

⁂

Joel Reimer is a lanky, bright-eyed man who loves wilderness marathons and World Wildlife Federation posters. His phone is full of pictures—children eating mango ice cream at a roadside stand, gravestones for martyrs, Joel eating ekmek bread and making a face while an old lady laughs at him. He was going to upload them for the corporate citizenship drive, but everything with a radio in it is dead. His phone still works but it has nothing to talk to anymore.

He deletes his pictures as fast as he can. He's gotta make room.

Plowing out of the wet fog: the blunt curve of a prow, glistening with dew, like something below the waterline of a supertanker. To each side the huge manta wings dissolve into a trailing froth of angles and mist-thin spines. The long stinger tail reminds Reimer of a Mandelbrot set.

He leans over to his driver to shout "I think it's some kind of lifting body! Maybe it's a Chinese spaceplane!"

"It's going into the mountain," Emme Naichane shouts back. She's a short, solid Métis woman from Quebec, cautious and meticulous in her work. "It's stuck right in."

The stinger tail intrudes cleanly into the limestone mountainside. Like it just grew there. Like a stem.

"Wow," he says.

"I really think we should leave," she says. "I think we need to tell someone about this."

"The Kurds will get the word out. The Kurds have the words." He begins to drum on the glove compartment door: he can feel it coming in the air tonight. "God, it's a beautiful day, isn't it?"

The convoy circles up half a kilometer south of the object. Some of the Kurds wear gas masks, crisp-looking modern gear right out of the packaging. Soheila spots a sheep through binoculars. "I suppose the rest have run off."

"Hey," her son says. "Where's Shanar?"

Soheila smiles where he can't see. Haydar always seems to know where Shanar is. Well, fine. As long as Shanar doesn't introduce him to that perverted anime.

"I'm serious, Mom." Haydar reaches for his cell phone, remembers the tower is out. "She was with the flock last night."

"Take my truck back and check if she made it home," Soheila says. Glad for an excuse to get him out of danger.

The sheep seems to prove it's safe to get closer. They edge forward. The object looms above them, gold bruised with purple, purple veined with silver, silver tainted with pink, pink shading to gold. The patterns are vertiginous, geological: like an alien world seen from cloud height. Provinces with no analogy on Earth.

"From down here," Emme Naichane says, "it kind of looks like a basking shark."

"I hate sharks," Soheila mutters. Emme looks at her in surprise. "What? You think we don't have sharks in Kurdistan?"

"You don't."

"No, but we have television." She makes a David Attenborough voice: "Here we see the mouse-like hamster of the Zagros Mountains, often confused with the hamster-like mouse of the Hindu Kush . . ."

Emme laughs nervously. "Is that real?"

"The mouse-like hamster? Absolutely."

"What about the hamster-like mouse?"

"I don't know. I've never been to Afghanistan."

Joel says, "I want to be the first to touch it." He gets out of the truck.

"Wait," Emme calls after him, "Joel, don't! What if it's electrified? What if it's toxic?"

He gloves up and dabs the surface with a sampling swab. "It's *rough*. I feel texture. But there are no rivets, no welds. No paneling. Wish I had a Rockwell . . . God, it's—" He sniffs. "It smells like ozone . . ."

"Joel, it's electrified, don't—"

"Shit!" He flinches back. "It's *sharp*!" His glove is split down the fingertip. There are tiny echoing cuts to each side, perfectly symmetrical. His blood fills up his fingerprint.

"It's flat," he says, "but it's sharp."

First blood, Emme thinks.

Questions are decisions about what it is important to know.

For the Canadian prospectors, the first questions are material. The design of an object should suit its purpose. Therefore understanding the design can explain the purpose. Only a priest or a phenomenologist might have warned them against their mistake.

They find no labels, insignia, vents, antennae, radiators, hinges, actuators, control surfaces, umbilical ports, or windows.

There is only one break in the hull: a jagged shaft on the lower prow.

The hull is an electrical conductor, slightly warmer than the air. Diamond drill scoring leaves no marks. Chemically inert, except for a slight off-gassing of ozone, monoatomic oxygen, and nitrogen radicals.

Their X-ray frequency gun isn't working. Maggie Gaboury breaks out the breakdown spectrometer. A neodymium-doped yttrium aluminum garnet laser attacks the hull; the plume of excited vapor releases a rainbow of light that the spectrometer can read like a bloody fingerprint.

HYDROGEN	34.0%
HELIUM	17.0%
LITHIUM	11.3%
BERYLLIUM	8.50%
BORON	6.80%
CARBON	5.67%
NITROGEN	4.86%
OXYGEN	4.25%
FLUORINE	3.78%
NEON	3.40%
OTHER	(+EXPAND)

"It's just a run-down of the periodic table." Maggie chews on a PowerBar as she scrolls through the results. "Twice as much hydrogen as helium. Three times as much hydrogen as lithium. Four times as much hydrogen as beryllium . . . you see?"

"Yeah . . . wow." Reimer stares at the output. What kind of material would have this atomic composition? Some kind of carbon fiber? The spectrum is closer, if anything, to flesh. Except for— "Helium? *Neon?* Are those gas pockets in the hull?" Helium and neon don't join chemical structures. Why would they be here?

"Is it some kind of stable excimer?" Reimer gasps in delight. "Jesus, is this thing made of excimers? That's ridiculous!"

Excimers are compounds that form for nanoseconds out of excited atoms. Could the ship be made of long-lived excimers? They are going to get a Nobel Prize for destroying quantum chemistry forever. And why all the boron? Why all the beryllium? Maybe it's some kind of Rydberg matter. God, this is exciting!

"Aliens," Maggie says.

"You think it's aliens?"

"We're all thinking it, Joel."

※

"God protect us," Soheila murmurs. "What *happened* to you?"

Six eyes blink up at her from two crowded sockets. Like frog spawn.

The sheep bleats and goes back to chewing grass.

"Okay," Soheila says, first to herself, and then to the women behind her. "Signal the evacuation. Send the men's unit to protect them. Women's unit will stay behind to hold the village. Tell Arîn to set up a checkpoint at the mouth of the valley. We control who comes and goes."

People start to move. "Wait!" Soheila snaps. She doesn't want to say it, but she's got to say it. "Wait. We can't go back over there. We could be infected too. Get some bullhorns from the Canadians."

"Can we tell our families we're all right?"

"If you tell them by bullhorn, heval." She closes her eyes and prays. Is it all right to ask this? Should he be in quarantine with the rest of them? God forgive her. "Tell my son to stay there. Tell him not to come back."

〜〜〜

خه‌جێ

Khaje leans on the bumper of a pickup, tries to stretch her aching back, and suffers flashbacks.

For the second time in her life everyone is evacuating Tawakul. This evacuation is a lot more bourgeois, though. The beekeepers sweep out fire hazards and whine about varroa mites. People load water and packaged survival gear onto mules according to the drills—air raid warning, get to the caves, get to the caves!

Mothers gather their children and say things like "It's all right, we're just going on a little trip." Khaje touches her lips. She remembers telling this exact lie to Hamali, and kissing him on his fuzzy adolescent cheek. He squirmed away from her. How close did that kiss land to the place where Anna would shoot him? The answer springs up intrusively: no more than eighty millimeters, if you assume the bullet went through the center of Hamali's head.

Haydar is trying to convince Arîn to send a search party out for Shanar. Arîn won't have it: "You think she's *lost*? Remember when she fell in love with that idiot on YouTube and ran away to join the PKK? And then she remembered they have to swear a vow of chastity, and turned around, and came *back*?"

"Well," Haydar says, "then she's not lost, so she's definitely in trouble."

"I can't send people out without radio. The Iranians could be here at any moment. Or the Americans could land troops. And what if someone steps on a mine?"

"Don't worry," Haydar says, straight-faced. "The Americans will help us." Then he and Arîn both start laughing. Even Khaje has to smile a little.

She squints up into the noonday sun. Sweat's gathering on her scalp. Everyone thinks she's sweating off a hangover.

"Hey, zahaki," she mutters. "What happened to Shanar?"

"I don't know. She was near the locus of the event. I started getting a very bad feeling on my premonition tracers. So I stopped watching."

"Your what?"

"The things that didn't work when you stabbed me."

"You're scared."

"You bet your fat biped ass I am. I've been trained by talented things-adjacent-to-people to talk to artifacts like this. And this one has gone wrong."

"Can't you use your little ball to figure it out?"

Ssrin showed Khaje the Ubiet when they made their bargain. Khaje can't remember most of that night. She was drunk, and, later on, full of Ssrin's intoxicating venom. She remembers grabbing the bayonet. She remembers snake heads on cable-strong necks surrounding her, unwrapping her clothes, washing her gently of filth.

"I can't use the Ubiet."

"Why not?"

"Because the one hunting me would smell it. He'd know exactly where I was."

Khaje stiffens. "Another zahaki?"

"His name is Iruvage. He works for the government."

⁂

"I can't believe this is working." Joel Reimer wrings his hands in delight. "Oh my God, oh my God. Look at it!"

"Is it working?" Emme flicks the control tablet's screen. "This looks like noise."

The US Radar 110XLS is designed to survey down to two hundred feet below ground, seeking out oil deposits and land mines. Emme didn't expect the radar to work—after all, their radios are burned out, and radars are giant radios. But radio doesn't go through metal. The radar's storage unit protected it. So now they're aiming it at this alien hull, which Joel says isn't metal. It's some kind of stable excimer, or Rydberg matter. And he's right. The radar goes right through.

Joel pushes his brown mop out of his eyes. He'd be cute, Emme sometimes thinks, if he'd just calm down. "What do you think we're seeing?"

The tablet displays a dense field of narrow wiggles. This could be a weird honeycomb supporting the hull. Lower down, where the radar should pick out deeper structure—fuel tanks, or stowed landing gear—there are intermittent V-shaped spikes, pointed inward, toward the center of the object.

The spikes crawl slowly back and forth. Whatever's in there is moving.

"It might just be electrical noise." Emme's father, a Métis electrician in Pontiac County, taught her a healthy respect for all the ways current can trick you. "We don't even know if radar can image whatever's— *Whoa.*"

The shallow honeycomb shatters into a fence of triangular sawteeth, pointing inward. Each tooth cracks along its edges, producing smaller teeth, like a chainsaw blade. Below them, the spikes become narrow, branching fans, like upside-down trees.

"What the hell . . ." she breathes.

It happens again. Like cells in mitosis. Now there are cruciforms and hollow chevrons in stacks, like insignia on the sleeves of soldiers.

"Joel," she says, "I really don't like this."

"Guys!" Maggie, the woman operating the laser spectrometer, comes dashing after them. "Guys, look at this! Same exact sample area!"

HYDROGEN	52.2%
HELIUM	13.0%
LITHIUM	7.46%
BERYLLIUM	5.80%
BORON	4.83%
CARBON	4.35%
NITROGEN	3.73%
OXYGEN	3.26%
FLUORINE	2.74%
NEON	2.58%
OTHER	(+EXPAND)

Joel Reimer rubs his forehead. His precious excimers are vanishing. Now the hull is fully half hydrogen, like some kind of petroleum product. "This can't be right. Maybe you ablated a surface coating, hit something underneath?"

"Absolutely not!"

"Then what the fuck?"

"What's what the fuck?" Emme presses.

Maggie explains: "Last sample, each element was present in proportion to its atomic number. Hydrogen is atomic number one, helium is two, so you had twice as much hydrogen as helium. Now it's doing that with atomic *mass*." Emme knows this part. Elements are ranked on the periodic table by the number of protons in their atoms. But protons repel each other, so you need neutrons in the atom too, to glue the protons together. Helium is atomic number two, but you never find helium-2 in nature, because two protons push each other apart. Instead you get helium-4, two protons and two neutrons, mass of four.

And now there isn't twice as much hydrogen as helium. There's four times as much.

"This thing just added neutrons to all its atoms? And rebuilt its whole hull accordingly? Is that what we were seeing on the radar?"

"Gotta be a spectrometer problem," Reimer repeats. "It's gotta be. Or some kind of lamination. Material doesn't just . . . this thing can't just . . ."

He trails off. Emme feels a pulse of dread, like nausea after a pickleback shot. Who says what it can or can't do?

A Toyota rolls up, tearing sod. Soheila leaps down from the running board and jogs over. She's unslung her rifle and it makes Emme nervous. She likes Soheila, she's been so welcoming, fed them in her own home on the first night. But something's changed. Soheila's got a dark hawk face on now, a war face.

"Mr. Reimer," she says. "Bad news."

"Yeah?"

"We found a sheep with some deformities. We don't know what caused them. We are going to evacuate Tawakul. And we—the ones who've gotten close— must stay here."

"Quarantine," Emme says.

Soheila nods solemnly. "We will have to confront whatever is going to come out of this thing."

"Come *out*?" Reimer repeats.

"Yes." Soheila pauses, takes a breath. "We explored the shaft up by the bow. The end cap is . . . what is the word? Transparent? No, but you can go right through it. We poked a stick inside and . . . I let go of it, in case something tried to pull me in, and it's just stuck there. It only moves when people touch it. The cap is solid, but it lets you through if you want to go through. And so it will let things out too."

Emme and Joel both stare at her.

"God," Maggie says, rubbing her temples, "I've had too much Red Bull. Heart's just kicking!"

⁜

خه‌جێ

The setting sun pours into the valley from the west, turning the river the color of simmering butter. Khaje keeps watch as people file out of the village, up along the river, east into the forest. A few people say hello, or wish her well. A lot more people ask her what's going to happen. She shrugs.

This is all her fault.

At sundown a figure that might be Soheila approaches from the north side of the river bridge. It raises a bullhorn and shouts across the river: "Whales and rash. Dirty slime comes rug sharp pile."

Khaje gets a really bad feeling. She doesn't have a bullhorn, so she can't shout back.

Somewhere in the dark, Arîn's megaphone pops and hisses: "Soheila?"

No. Don't answer.

"It's sick," the voice that might be Soheila's says. "It's not just the sheep. We used to keep cows too, before the gas, which smelled like apples and garlic. We grew them in the orchards by the river, it's too cold to swim most of the year, you need to change the tires for the spring, and we keep them clean so we can be proud of them, even if they use up too much gas and grow too fast, you think they'll be babies forever but before you know it they're planning to leave for the city. They let Choman stand, so why not us? We're united in faith and other good things. If you want good things, don't come after us. Don't."

The dark shape throws its bullhorn into the river and walks away.

Arîn turns her megaphone in the direction of Khaje's perch. "What was that?"

"Ssrin," she mutters. "What *was* that?"

"That was Soheila."

"What was wrong with her?"

"I don't know."

Hours pass. She chews spearmint gum and sweats. When the gum goes bad she sticks it to the tree. There is a corkscrew turning, turning in her gut.

Past midnight, gunfire splits the dark. Echoes pop off the alien object and the valley walls in weird triple-report. Khaje grabs her rifle but the scope is useless in the pure moonless dark. "What's happening?"

"The Kurds are shooting the Canadians."

"What? Why?"

"Their souls are deformed."

CHAPTER NINE

CLAYTON//781 MINUTES REMAIN

"That's exactly what Khaje told you the alien said? Their *souls* are deformed?"

Chaya jumps a little: he hasn't interrupted her before. "Yes. Don't you believe in souls? You said, *the atmanach takes your soul.*"

"I thought it might be a metaphor for alien science."

She shrugs. "Maybe."

"It's hard to hear about all these people," Clayton admits. He's starting to sweat. He wishes he could go turn the AC back up, but he needs to see her sweat too.

Her eyes are starting to dilate. She's been sipping the coffee whenever she needs to pause the narration. She must've taken a good dose by now. "Because you dropped an atomic bomb on them?"

"Yeah. It sounds like they were pretty"—he laughs, it's such an inane thing to say—"pretty awesome. A cool village."

"You didn't kill anyone I've mentioned so far. Arîn and Haydar are still alive. And Soheila and the Canadians . . . you didn't kill them." She's been fiddling with a rosary as she tells the story—no, not fiddling, Clayton, she's using it, praying for divine support.

Something—and that something is probably the dose of MDMA in his coffee—makes him ask "Do you think God can forgive me?"

"You don't believe in God."

"No. But I believe in human resilience."

"Resilience. Don't you work in an office?"

"I work in an office for the part of the United States government that operates satellites. You see a lot of bad shit from satellites. Tsunamis, pogroms, and yeah, bombing. You also see people picking up afterward. Do you know the story of the Madonna of Urakami?"

"An image of the Virgin Mary, I suppose?" She's cramped up in the chair, maybe a little nauseous, maybe just exhausted. Standing up she looks like she could be in the WNBA. Sitting, she looks like she ought to be in a recovery ward, on a drip of saline and B12. He thought she might be Aeta, a black indigenous Filipino, but she's probably too tall.

"Yes," he says. "It got a bomb dropped on it."

"You sure like bombs. You know, the Philippines has been bombed a lot. Our Lady of the Most Holy Rosary of Manaoag got hit by Japanese bombs during World War II. But she stopped them from exploding. And there's another one in Manila, Our Lady of the Most Holy Rosary, sounds like the same name but she's different. She's made of ivory and she looks Asian, because she was carved by a Chinese artist. She turned away a Dutch fleet. She survived the Japanese and American bombings. She's powerful."

"I believe it."

"No you don't. But I wish those people you bombed today had her."

"Wouldn't have helped," Clayton says a little bitterly. "Mary doesn't stop nukes."

She rolls her eyes. "How would you know that?"

"Urakami. It was the site of a church in Japan. For three hundred years it was illegal for Christians to worship openly. To prove they weren't Christian, they had to tread on an icon of Jesus or Mary. When the ban was lifted they built a beautiful cathedral, with two bell towers and a lovely image of Mary. On August 9 they were preparing for the Assumption of Mary when the Nagasaki bomb went off directly overhead. The cathedral was ground zero, the hypocenter of the blast. Everyone in the church vaporized. The eyes of the image of Mary burnt out, leaving two black pits." He shakes his head sharply, swallows a gulp of coffee and vodka and MDMA. "Mother Mary stops bombs. So Americans build a bigger bomb."

She doesn't like this, she doesn't like him trumping Mother Mary with American power, no matter how contritely he phrases it. "You didn't need a bomb to commit genocide in the Philippines. Not many people remember that."

"I do. 'Make Samar a howling wilderness. Kill everyone over the age of ten.' Mark Twain suggested replacing the stars and stripes with a skull and crossbones."

"And here you are, a hundred years later, dropping nukes on Iraq."

"Yeah. But—" He puts a hand out on the table. He wants to touch her, he wants to get up and move. The urge lets him smile. "But they rebuilt the cathedral in Urakami. You can go take mass there. And the important thing is, when we're done with Blackbird and Iruvage and the aliens, there have to be people left to rebuild. That's my priority. The whole species."

"People dropping bombs always have some higher reason. Stopping communism. Securing Asian co-prosperity. Defeating Japan. Destroying Kurdish terrorists. But the bombs never seem to hit that reason. They just hit a bunch of mothers and kids."

"What do you think I should have done, after Iruvage contacted me? Knowing what I knew? Just give up? Just tell him to fuck off and find someone else? What if that 'someone else' had fucked it up, what if they'd let the planet burn?"

She takes a sip of coffee. Then she shakes her head deliberately: refusing his framing. "I want to know what happened to Sabiti."

"Who?"

"An old man. Ugandan. Friendly—my friend. He kept talking about how much he wanted to look inside . . ."

Oh. Yeah, they found Sabiti. Best not to tell her. "How did he get left behind?"

"When we fled the labs and went down to Tawakul. I didn't do headcount fast enough." She looks, for a moment, utterly ashamed of herself. "I didn't notice he was missing for hours . . ."

There are patches of bright red at the inner corners of her eyes, where the white strikes sharp contrast off her skin. She's so tired. He is too. He needs to get this interview done before he starts drifting. Why didn't he think to pack his bromantane in the Cobalt Sifter housing? Or one of the MAJESTIC body bags? Because he wasn't planning to get shot down. You make your master plan, but it's never enough.

"You strike me as someone who feels guilty a lot," he says. "Is it because you're Catholic? My wife was raised Catholic. When I felt unbelievably guilty about something I tried to dump it on her and—well. She did the right thing."

"How sad." She looks at him with a deep weariness toward his whole mask, his whole concept, trying to be her friend, this MBA-style management of horrific crime. "You know you're only in charge as long as you've got the most guns. The Kurds had the most guns for a while. Then the Russians did. And now you. Do you think that'll last?"

"If I run out of guns," he snaps, "then I can't stop the thermonuclear annihilation of our planet." Clayton, stop, that's counterproductive. Don't get angry with her. Do a big sigh. "I'm sorry. I didn't mean to . . . God, I always do this."

Come on. Say *Do what?* Pick up the hook, take a bite.

"You suck at this," Chaya says. "Are you trying to make me feel bad for you?"

He laughs. She grins. She starts laughing too. The E is kicking in. "You should feel bad for me!" he says. "I'm divorced before forty, my best friend hates me, and I have to save the planet."

"Oh, poor you! You deserve all of that and worse!"

"I meant to do good. I really did mean to."

And, exactly as he planned to, he starts spilling his guts. Some of his guts. Not the stuff about Rosamaria. He's gotta keep that compartmentalized.

CLAYTON//COMPARTMENTS

Looking back, Clayton thinks that the first moment he *really* loved Rosamaria, in the sustainably adult sense rather than crazy teenage heroin-addict heart-burn, was when—

He can't pick one moment. One of those times, any of those times, when she outtalked or outscored or outraced him. And he thought, I am so lucky. I can never outdo her. And she chooses me anyway. *You're trying to put them together, the woman saying these things to you and the woman with the body you want to look at, you're trying to fit them both into one person.* He's done it, he has put them together. He has objectified and subjectified the same woman. He can inhabit the crossroads of *We talk about critical theory* and *We need to buy more toilet paper* and *Can we pretend you're a rancher's daughter like Alejandra Rocha y Villerreal, even though you hate that book, and I'm your tutor?* (Laughing, she says, *But, Clayton, I don't even know how to* ride *a horse!*)

And the name of that crossroads is love.

If only he could've kept that feeling all his life. If only he hadn't—

Senior year of high school. Class of '91. College admissions are done like Desert Storm. They're together and they've decided not to break up. Rosamaria says, *Clayton, we've got to tell him. He knows something's changed and it's messing him up. We're messing him up.*

Clayton doesn't want to go public, though, because he's jealous and scared of Erik—Erik the upright, Erik the charming, everybody's flagpole of decency and good conduct, gray-eyed Viking Erik (he has, in this last year of high school, grown a huge blond beard, braided, like a flag).

Why does everybody just *like* Erik? Why does he get it so easy? It's not just racism, although of course that's part of it. People trust Erik. People look up to Erik. The fact that he never moves or bends, the fact that he doesn't give his decisions the slightest consideration, *comforts* people. They prefer it. They like that he doesn't have to think.

Clayton is not sure people think about him at all. He's popular, but in a way you would expect a good-looking Black guy to be popular. Puts you at ease. Makes you feel wholesome. Reassures you that you're diversity-minded and cool. A tasty Oreo.

Rosamaria talks Clayton into telling him, though. Erik, she says, taking Clayton's hand, we're, um, we're together.

Yes! Erik shouts, and hugs them both. Finally!

Later Clayton catches Erik crying in the teachers' lot behind the school. It doesn't feel like victory. It feels like he's broken his friend's ankles.

But they work it out. They really, really do. Of all the things he's ever done, Clayton is second most proud of this, the way the three of them went on being friends after high school. Maybe (maybe? come on, Clayton) that friendship enjoyed a degree of sexual tension. Possibly all three of them enjoyed Erik's college stories about picking up gymnasts and rowers at the natatorium, which always ended with a fervent *God bless America* in place of the actual act, as more than just humor. But even sexual backslapping can lead to good and tender things. When the doctors determined he and Rosamaria would have children with a double-digit risk of muscular dystrophy and maybe sarcoidosis (which was already killing Clayton's dad), they both wanted Erik as a sperm donor. They wanted to raise Erik's child.

It almost happened.

And then Clayton was stupid. So smart about it all, but so, so stupid.

He chose a career that he could never share. He wanted government and he wanted space so he went to the crossroads and followed the signs. He chose the newly declassified National Reconnaissance Office, spycraft most arcane, because he wanted to oversee the entire world and all its secrets.

The price, of course, was that he would have to keep those secrets from his friends.

"We quite literally saw everything," he tells Chaya. Getting up to slot another plastic trash pod of Green Mountain coffee into the Keurig machine. "NRO spy satellites make the Hubble look like a paparazzi telephoto. Sometimes we'd just hand our spares over to NASA and advance astronomy by twenty years."

"I was into astronomy," she says. "Astrophysics. Before I ended up here."

"Then you would've loved what we had. Or hated it, because we wasted it all looking down."

In fact the sheer power of their devices created a crisis. The NRO collected a torrent of information, but that information arrived from a God's-eye view. It had no context. There was no one on the ground to provide labels, explanations, guidance. It was not a God's-eye view at all, really. It was an alien's. See everything. Understand nothing.

So the real challenge was matching the pictures up with intelligence from agents, intercepts, diplomatic channels, diverse technical means, all the various organs of America's sensory apparatus. Then it had to be turned into a product policymakers could understand.

The NRO was good at this, but only as good as it could be in the context of a deeply dysfunctional intelligence community. What you knew defined your value, so nobody wanted to share shit. That was how 9/11 happened—but let's not get ahead of ourselves. The NRO was, despite its sinister and potent reputation, badly wounded. The Cold War had justified essentially unlimited funding and discretion. But here at the prematurely declared end of history it was being pulled back in, brought under control.

"I figured that if I wanted a successful career, I should make myself indispensable. Which meant I needed to solve the NRO's most urgent problem—its loss of agency. I started small. I figured out good rules for the bureaucratic game. Draw attention to problems, but only problems you can already solve—so you're a fixer, not a whiner. Build up mid-term threats, not too urgent, not too distant, as a lever to get attention and resources. Start projects that excite people, but get out before they hit the hard part, the turf wars and the money fights. Start the next exciting project instead. Don't be a closer. Closers are the morgue attendants of bureaucracy. Be a midwife. Be a Mormon. Be a fucking rabbit."

"Be an asshole?"

He laughs. "Yeah, I kind of hated myself. But not as much as I hated . . . everything else. It was *all* petty bullshit, all the way to the top. Even in the White House. Nobody really acted on facts and models. People acted on office politics. Who was mad at who, who was in, who was out. Who would get the credit. Who would take the blame."

It infuriated him deeply that *so much* could hinge on sitting across from the right program manager at a meeting. It was all corruption! Some of it was functional and some of it wasn't, some of it was endorsed by regulations and some of it was necessary lubrication, but none of it worked as well as it should.

"Take the NRO's budget. The agency had a bad habit of hoarding billions of dollars. In 1994 the Senate realized the NRO was building a $350-million-dollar headquarters outside DC. Great cafeteria, but we never told anybody we were serving. In '96, when I was doing a masters in space systems—"

Note that little flicker of interest she allows.

"The NRO admitted to hoarding four *billion* dollars off the books. Some of the leadership went to the stocks for it. Of course, we gave up those four billion to protect the rest of the money. Billions more. Not that anyone knew what to do with it."

The modern NRO had lost its way. There were no more program managers with dictatorial powers (and oh, Clayton had wanted to be one of those). Instead, responsibility was shared between contracting officers, financial offices, and the community management staff. No one person had ultimate responsibility for anything. The CIA had given up and withdrawn its support, and the air force was eyeing a takeover.

But the money was still there. The four billion they'd confessed to hoarding was just skim off the barrel.

"So I got into the money. First I got people to give me the money, for my own bright ideas. Then, once I was set up, I just started giving it to myself. 'Operating budget for special projects.' Nobody wanted to keep track of it, because if we kept track of it we could be forced to admit we had it. So I spent the money on contractors, and the contractors brought me tools. And I started building machines."

"Satellites?"

"Machines to analyze satellite data. Neural nets, machine learning. If we can pretend machines are making our decisions, then we can pretend our decisions are clear and confident and impersonal. And that's what people want. They want all the complexity and uncertainty laundered out of the way. So you give them what they want, and when they discover that what they asked for isn't actually what they needed, you've got receipts to prove that you did *your* job. And they get stuck with the consequences."

His compartment digested NRO satellite information, mating it with data from the CIA and DIA and NSA and the rest of the alphabet soup, fusing streams of surveillance together into crisp cartridges of pseudo-truth he could sell to those in search of bureaucratic weapons. To control the end product was to control the whole process. Credit went to the man who delivered the goods, not the one who made them possible.

He was the intelligence capitalist. People talked about him with the same words they had once used to describe the whole NRO: *lean, mean, fast, and black.*

"The problem was," he says, sitting back down, looking into his coffee, "I couldn't tell my wife about any of it."

She was working in civil rights and environmental justice, actually making the world better. She would've despised his empire building. So he just told her *I work on making awesome satellites.* Not *Yesterday I generated a product that will be used to justify the basing of armed drones in central Africa. Did I ever tell you that the NRO started the whole US drone program? We funded Program D! We kicked off the Predator Empire!*

He simply could not tell her that he was directly involved in deciding who the United States of America would kill. The one time she probed he said he worked on disaster assessment. True! He just caused the disasters.

Maybe that was where things had started to go wrong. Maybe earlier. This was not the biggest secret he was keeping from her, by the end. Not infidelity: he had a couple brief flings with Rosamaria's approval, on condition of no sustained contact, which he thought of as ways to indulge his sexual curiosity—he'd lost his virginity to Rosamaria, and she'd only had her under-the-porch guy before him, so they were both a little underexplored. His flings were very tender, and they taught him that he was not good at keeping things merely physical. Rosamaria kept in touch with an on-and-off girlfriend she'd met in grad school. That ended when the other woman got married, but ended well. Rosamaria sobbed for days, but she said it was a good hurt, nobody had done anything wrong. Just something ending. They kept all this private, even from friends, because Rosamaria knew she would get into arguments about the politics of it.

But look at all these compartments in Clayton's life. His carefully separated affairs. His technocratic overlord job. His race. His politics—he despised the Bush administration, but he did great work for them.

So he built walls between those compartments. He kept them strong.

And that ruined them. It was, ultimately, his fault. He couldn't talk honestly with Rosamaria. Rosamaria couldn't compete with Erik, because Erik had become a soldier: Congressional Nomination to West Point, delayed application for two years of personal growth with AmeriCorps, West Point 1993–1997, Rhodes Scholar, graduated 1997 straight to Infantry Basic Officer

Leader Course and then Airborne School and his eight years of service: which, after 9/11, became much more than eight. They were on fine terms, personally, but after seeing Erik, Rosamaria would shake her head and say, *I wish he'd wake up.*

And when Erik came home from Iraq to speak to Clayton of matters conspiratorial, that too went to a new and frightening place.

⁂

ɔⰤⴹꙄ

Anna tramples a fern. Juice spatters her knees. "Shit," she grunts, and dances sideways to dodge a tower of pink acanthus growing from the roots of a big Persian oak. How does she know it's pink acanthus? Because she used to look up plants she remembered from Kurdistan and try to figure out their English names. She used to imagine (during her rebellious teenage years, before her differently rebellious college years) that she would plant a Kurdistan garden to torture her foster parents. She would sit in it and sing songs in Sorani and they would say "Oh, Anna," in that tone of sorrow they used for everything that had happened to her before. She really used to resent it, like it meant, *Oh, Anna, if only we'd gotten a normal kid instead.* Meaning: an American kid.

Her mom bumps into her from behind, swears, and steps on the acanthus. It goes down crunchingly.

"Nice one, Mom," Anna mutters.

"Go fuck a dog," Khaje snaps. Her English is kind of bad, but she's great at swearing. She has already snapped at Arîn Tawakuli, who keeps talking about "the martyrs of the nuclear bombing," which pisses Khaje off. Anna's a little proud of her. You go, Mom! Forget about the martyrs, we've got to save the ones who are still alive!

However, Khaje is also kind of a prick: "*Your* apartment is full of dead plants."

"Better than six-packs and cigarettes!"

"You've never seen my house," Khaje says.

"Of course I have. I grew up in it. Besides—" Anna sniffs demonstratively. "I can smell it."

"You're a disgrace to me!" Khaje snaps, and stalks off. Anna stares after her. Wow! That was pretty harsh, Mom. A disgrace? Really?

Erik Wygaunt appears from the underbrush ahead and holds up a finger for quiet.

"My mom's a dick," Anna complains.

Erik's gray eyes measure her. He knows about what she did now. She doesn't *think* he hates her, but he's . . . he definitely doesn't look at her the same way.

There was a kind of protectiveness about him before. That's gone. Now he's wary. He doesn't know her like he thought he did.

She kind of likes this better.

"That may be," he says, "but you can't make noise about it. We're moving under tactical conditions the military calls 'shut the fuck up.'"

She nods, breathing hard. Here she is, thigh-burn sore and feeling good, marching through the woods of her childhood. It's summer in paradise, and there's a serpent in the garden. Uncomfortable trivia: *paradise* is an ancient Persian word, and sometimes it meant *a hunting ground*.

These forests are untouched by logging, older than any trees Anna ever saw in America. But they're polluted too. She's already seen three-legged deer, maimed by antipersonnel mines, tripling away like they know exactly who's responsible. Arîn insists that parts of the forest are still tainted by nerve gas residue, waiting beneath wet rocks to kill you. Anna believes her. Arîn's women know their shit; they talk about what the nuke will do to the trophic pyramid, and lots of other stuff that Anna would definitely get wrong on her fourth-grade ecology worksheets.

But mines aren't the only foreign intrusion in paradise.

The MAJESTIC commandos slide through the sky-dance light like black stags. Their night-vision goggles stare ahead in blank four-eyed panorama. The twenty-two men and women Erik chose for his mission of mercy. The rest of his unit—men like Mike Jan and Skyler Nashbrook, the officers in command of his other teams—he left behind at the Blackbird site. Anna doesn't really understand his criteria for choosing some and leaving others, but that's okay. She's not him, she's not a leader of men.

The soldiers like her, though. She's been getting a funny amount of solidarity. Maybe because she told them what they were jumping into, even though it sounded crazy. Some of these dudes are from Captain Brennan's Team One, and they saw Brennan get hit by the atmanach. He killed two operators before they fragged him. Three dead to alien bullshit and Anna's the only one who called it.

So now soldiers pace silently beside her, or signal to each other to keep an eye out when she ducks out to take a piss (too much CamelBak), or give her tips on how to tie her boots. White men with big beards, Black men with Marlo Stanfield eyes and clear smiles, hugely built Asian dudes who offer her taffy-thick protein bars, marathon-tough women with trim shoulders and lanky poise. Nobody offers to carry any of her shit. They just stalk along around her. It's kind of nice.

"Hey, Erik," she mutters.

"Yes?"

"Um, this mission-of-mercy thing. It would be really cool to find survivors. But . . ."

But she wants to fucking kill Iruvage. Ssrin was her alien! They were in serendure! How can Ssrin be dead? It's narratively incomplete. It's unsatisfying. It's—goddamn it, she was supposed to find Ssrin again. She was supposed to say *this is for Roman* and shoot Ssrin in her stupid hump where all her necks come together. And maybe it would've worked; or maybe Ssrin would've vanished the bullet and bit Anna with her third head and called Anna a stupid inbred porn monkey while Anna died.

But Clayton fucked all that. He took away her chance. She tried to kill him for it, shoot him in the face like Ssrin shot Roman. Did she miss on purpose, when her mother shouted at her: *Jiyan, haven't you changed at all?*

Or did she aim true? Did something else make the bullet miss? God? Aliens? Clayton Hunt's personal shield? The aretaic narrative?

Is this Clayton's story, now?

"Maybe," Anna says, "we should find Iruvage and kill him. Or take him hostage. So his friends don't nuke all our cities."

She realizes, suddenly, that a lot of the commandos are listening.

Erik thinks. "Could we accomplish that?"

"I saw Ssrin bleed. If it bleeds, we can kill it, right? Can Iruvage be so much tougher?"

"That's not the mission," Erik says. "There are innocent people in mortal danger right now. We're going to help them. We're going to save as many as we can. *Then* we close with and defeat the enemy."

"Is that really . . ." She tries not to say the most asshole thing possible. "I mean, I know you think that maybe we'll find Ssrin alive. But of all the stuff we could be doing with the limited time we have, is it really important to save people who are probably . . . ?"

"Probably?"

Probably going to die anyway. "Shouldn't we be trying to stop Iruvage? I mean, you just let Clayton have Blackbird, he can do whatever he wants with it. Is this really the right thing to do?"

A tinge of impatience. Like he's been asked to explain why he chooses to keep his heart beating. "How often do you think people regret taking the sloppy, easy, morally relaxed path? Always. Every time. Do you remember that famous picture of a vulture waiting for a starving kid to die? Kevin Carter took that picture. That picture got so many people to send money to Sudan. It helped. And the kid lived, he was fine. But do you know what drove Kevin Carter crazy, afterward? He didn't do *enough* to help the kid. He didn't pick that kid up and carry him to the aid center. He got the Pulitzer, but he ended up killing himself. Because he didn't do enough. You have to do everything you can, *everything* you can."

"That's not true," Anna says.

"What?"

"He didn't kill himself because of that picture specifically. He was all fucked up from drugs and general photojournalist trauma. And one of his friends died, and he thought it should've been him. And he had a history of suicide attempts. And he was broke and worried about money all the time. It wasn't just guilt over the baby in the picture."

"Then it sounds to me like he needed help," Erik says. "And he didn't get it."

"But, man, Erik, there's a lot at stake, a lot more than just Earth—if Clayton gets inside Blackbird, if Iruvage takes it home, everyone's fucked. On a metaphysical level."

"There's *always* a lot at stake. That's not an excuse to let civilians die."

"Erik," she begins, meaning to say that it only makes sense to take out Iruvage *first*. Then they can help people. Right?

But then she sees Khaje watching her. Watching her tell Erik to give up on the survivors of Tawakul.

Watching her show who she's become.

"Never mind," Anna mutters.

Latasha Gainer, the air force radio lady, drops to a crouch beside them. "Sir, we spotted an IR flash coming up the trail behind us. It's Garcia. The old fucker's really moving!"

Anna feels self-conscious: Garcia can't be much past thirty-five. Is she an old fucker?

"Shit," Erik says. "I told him to keep an eye on Clayton."

Looking back, she can still see the lights of Blackbird camp away to the south, almost directly opposite the fading firelight glow of ground zero ahead. Garcia must've just headed for the nuclear forest fire.

He catches up; Erik beckons him in till they're close enough to mutter. "Hey. Any word?"

"Just couldn't deal with Mr. Hunt's shit. I got a really bad feeling from the way he was talking." Garcia takes a knee and drinks from his CamelBak. "Thought I could do more good here, sir."

"It's good to have you," Erik says.

"Coulda ordered me along in the first place."

"I wanted somebody back there who could get on the radio and tell me if it all went to shit." Erik shrugs: "But you made your call, and here you are. You got your MOPP?"

"Yeah, unfortunately. I left that poor mouse with the Chinese. Hope they don't dissect it. When do we sweat up?"

"As soon as the radiation counters say it's a good idea."

"Hey, um"—Anna doesn't want to interrupt, but looking up at the sky this does seem kind of important—"I think I see the atmanach."

There's a big rush of chatter as everybody points it out to everybody else. The Kurds, who've seen it before, immediately flop down on their bellies and look at the dirt.

Straight ahead, up through the tree line, Anna glimpses a black line cut against the aurora. The really fucking weird thing is that when she's aware of the line it pops *over* the trees, the rock, the clouds, anything else in the way. It sorts right to the front of her vision. It exists purely as an artifact of awareness.

Arîn Tawakuli stots downslope, pronking from hard spot to hard spot like an alpine gazelle. "If it attacks," she calls, "you get on your belly and look at the ground and just chill out. Okay? Don't think about anything. Just chill out."

Anna wants to laugh. Chill out. She remembers the thing chasing her through Ssrin's ship, how it *opened* as it got close to her, like a big sac of chainsaw worms spilling open, squeezed out of an infinitely long toothpaste tube with its other end in Hell. If only she'd chilled out. She *was* pretty chilled, ha-ha.

"Hey, Mom," she says. "Mom!"

"What!" Khaje snaps.

"You guys went through a bunch of atmanach—"

"Crawler."

"What?"

"Call it the crawler. So I can pronounce it."

"You guys went through a bunch of crawler attacks before we showed up. Did you ever actually stop it from taking someone?"

Khaje shrugs. "It's not about stopping it from taking someone. It always takes someone. It's about not being the one it takes."

Oh.

"Someone will always be martyred," Arîn says. "But we can't let that stop us."

"What did you do with the people who got hit?" Erik asks.

"We tied them up and sedated them if we could," Arîn says. "But they died afterward. Seizures, I think. And if we couldn't get to them before they got a weapon, we shot them."

"That was necessary? In every case?"

"No," Arîn says. "Sometimes they ran away instead of trying to hurt people. But then they died anyway. Come on. Our people need us."

She bounds away back upslope.

"Smells like a trap," Garcia mutters to Erik. "Look where that black line leads. Between us and the bomb site. Like he's just sending it to reel us in."

"He's in the way and he wants us to know it." Erik glances at Anna. "He really doesn't want us to get to those people. He's willing to reveal himself to stop us."

"What are you going to do about it?" Anna asks.

"Spring the trap," Erik says.

"Really?"

"Fuck no." He smiles a little, though his eyes are hidden by his night-vision goggles. "Normally I'd try to flush him out with artillery fires and air support, right on the base of that black tether. Maybe a couple more nukes. But I think he's listening to our radios, and I think he jams us whenever he doesn't like what we're up to. So the best we can do is advance to the objective. If we make contact,

I'll engage him and tie him down while the peshmerga proceed to ground zero and aid any survivors."

"Erik, are you really sure there are enough survivors to justify"—she hates to run the math like this, it's so cold, she really feels like a bitch, but—"risking all these peoples' lives? Risking Blackbird, risking the planet?"

"One survivor," Erik says.

"What?"

"One survivor would be enough to justify a rescue. We have a moral duty to put ourselves in danger for the innocent. Humanitarian work is the best thing the American military does. Dropping bombs on noncombatants is the worst. We already did our worst today. Now we need to do our best."

"You sound like a recruiting brochure."

"That's because recruiting brochures tell the truth," Erik says. "We just persistently fail to live up to their ideals."

"And you'd say all this even if you didn't think that one survivor might be Ssrin? You'd go to all these lengths to rescue some Kurds even if it had *no* bearing on Blackbird, and Clayton, and saving the world?"

"Go to 155.16 megahertz."

"What?"

"Your radio. Set it to 155.16 megahertz. It's an international search and rescue frequency."

Baffled, she pokes at the little handset's tiny keyboard: one five five one six, set. And suddenly her headset is full of children.

She gasps. The signal is miserable, full of noise, but she'd know the wail of children through a hurricane. And in front of that wail she hears, now, a small, brave voice speaking slowly and clearly in English: *"Help us. Cave one. We are alive. East-southeast of the village. Help us. Cave one. We are alive."*

"How long?" she asks.

"Gainer picked it up a few minutes ago."

"Can we talk back?"

"No response yet. The kid might have the send switch jammed down. But you see?"

"Yeah," she says. "Yeah. We've gotta. We've gotta."

Erik nods solemnly. This is what we have to do: we have to answer this child.

Would Ssrin eat that child, if she needed it to stay alive? Why does Anna think of these questions? Only: it's a fair question. What if they get to ground zero, and they find Ssrin, and she's been eating children?

What would Erik do then?

A little insect whines past Anna's ear. She swats at it but doesn't get it. Ahead of her, her mother swears at nothing in particular.

—⁂—

DAVOUD (~7,875 FEET ASL)

Satan drops in on Davoud Qasemi through the scar of his bite.

Khaje left him locked up in a shipping container. He wanted to beg her: *Khaje, please, I'm blind, I'm no threat—keep me close, don't leave me in the dark—*

But wherever she's gone, he would only slow her down. After all, what good is a pilot who can't see?

He smelled her before she left. That musty old-sweat smell, that moon-dust gunpowder smell, that old drink working its way out through her skin. She said: "Davoud. Is Iruvage listening?"

"Always."

"Good," she'd said, and knelt to put her mouth up to his ear. Davoud imagined her expression. A crack of pity, for his helplessness. And then the hate welling up like black tar to seal it.

"Iruvage," she whispered. "دەتدۆزمەوە و دەتكوژمەوە." Etdozimewe u detku-jimewe."

Satan was silent.

Khaje drew away. "I'm leaving you for Clayton. You can work with your fellow jash."

The comparison really stung. *He* certainly wouldn't collaborate with Iraqis for money. But all he said to her was: "Khaje. May God be your guardian."

She grunted. She went. And he has been alone since then. Until:

Satan.

"*Hey, Davoud. You're really not a very good spy, are you? But that's all right. I needed a pilot, not a spy. Satan has much more trouble finding pilots than liars.*"

Davoud is not a pilot anymore. Not for Satan or anyone else. He's nuclear flash–blind and he's going mad from it, wiggling his fingers inside their skin gloves, trying to get his hands loose so he can withdraw them into his torso and untie his fleshy straightjacket and crawl out of his own mouth and be free, free of this body trap, bursting out of his own face to fly away—a blind pilot can't fly! *A blind pilot can't fly!*

Iruvage. Please help me.

Satan nibbles at his liver. "*Be calm. This will pass soon. Of course, I can make it permanent. I can scrub your eyes with a curse that will turn any regrowth into a tumor and any implant into a seizure.*"

No. Please. I'll do anything. Other people can be happy when they're blind, but I can't. *I can't be blind,* you understand? I have to fly.

"*Oh, I don't think you've lost so much. Did you know that the raw image captured by your eyes is just a little upside-down smear? A hundred and thirty million sensors in your dainty little retina, but only enough nerve bandwidth to sample ten percent at a time. And of that ten percent, most of it is rejected by your subconscious as irrelevant. The blood vessels that feed the retina are for obscure reasons in front of the retina, blocking the view. So your eye has evolved to screen out stationary objects, like the spiderweb of veins in the way . . . but this would make walls and floors and trees fade out of view too. So your eyeballs must be constantly jiggled. Ah, Davoud, the comedy of your sight! Two eyes in one head give you a hundred and sixty degrees of vision, not even half a circle. Wiggling frantically, so they can keep seeing things that don't move. Are you really so much worse off now, Davoud?"*

Will his sight come back? It must come back. It must. He's just bleached out the receptors in his eyes—they'll calm down—calm down in time to fly again. Never touch the ground. Never come back.

Davoud shakes his head like a dog.

Iruvage, what's happening?

"Clayton's getting the science gang back together. The Americans are trying to save people they bombed or people who crashed. Isn't that sad, Davoud? All these aircraft falling out of the sky.

"I lied, by the way, about those Russian helicopters I promised to save. They all went down over the Qandils. My little bombs, see, planted in their rotor hubs. No sense letting them tell Moscow what happened here! They might convince someone to nuke me."

The poor Mi-26s. The poor majestic flying cows. Oh, God, all his wounded comrades were on those helicopters. Satan lied to him.

Davoud tries to think of Iruvage as Satan because it keeps him honest. But, also, because Iruvage really does carry a bleeding-kidney sense of *evil*. His words sound like a bayonet sucking out of a rotting corpse.

Sometimes this actually makes Iruvage easier to tolerate. The alien is butting up against a threshold in the human mind, a maximum of malice, past which any further evil just becomes absurdity. If you wake up every morning and eat pulled baby on flatbread, as Iruvage surely could, then there is simply no way for the mind to think of you as *more* repulsive. Iruvage is the kebab koobideh of evil. You know exactly what you're getting.

He thinks: You promised me a starship to fly. You promised.

"And so you shall. Listen now, listen. Clayton is going to discover the way inside Blackbird. And when he goes in, he'll bring you with him. He knows you're one of my pawns. He'll want to know everything I've told you. Don't be coy."

You promised me . . .

"So you will, Davoud. So you will. I wouldn't make promises if I couldn't keep them. Here—have a little taste . . ."

Suddenly Davoud is drifting above burnt-out mountainside. Wildfired trees smolder into a slow warm wind. Oh! He shivers in joy: not just because he can see again but because he has *never* seen like this. He is looking at this world through a sensor better than the human eyeball. He doesn't even have a point of focus! He can hold a burning tree tip in perfect clarity even while his attention shifts to a—

A burnt skull. Black cooked scalp fading down to a fringe of curly hair.

The smell hits him. Super-real supertaster super-scent, more smell than he's ever smelled before: old-growth wood charred by X-ray strobe, burnt stone, baked moss, water flashed to vapor, flesh to ash, the air ticking with radiation. The awful blood taste of plutonium.

This is where Clayton's bombs fell. This is where he nuked the Kurds.

"I lost track of Ssrin here," Iruvage says. "Who knows where she is now? Trying to break into my ship? Camouflaged and lurking? Right beside you, disguised as one of your colleagues? She's been a fugitive so long. She's had time to practice the technique of debasing herself.

"Speaking of your colleagues—"

Davoud's perspective plummets down to a gnat's-eye view of a stalk of grass. He smells forest humus and cool evening wind and insecticide. He tastes sweat. The nylon-filtered vinegar and Gatorade sweat of soldiers.

His perspective rises like a spark to swoop between huge tromping legs, human legs, God help him, he is darting between the booted feet of American soldiers.

"They're hunting me . . ." Iruvage purrs. "Recognize these faces?"

Here is the pale, stony-eyed American major. He leads American commandos with their sophisticated equipment: drones and rifles, submachine guns and grenades, body armor and bolt cutters and lengths of detcord and twisted tourniquets and infrared flares and backpacks full of water. And there are Tawakul's peshmerga. There is pretty young Arîn, who hates him. There is Khaje with her old Russian rifle, prowling ahead of the daughter she nearly killed . . .

"I'm not as fast as a human, did you know that? We khai slither and coil, we sprint and leap, but we never chased our prey across the plains. We don't have those edible thighs and fatty cuts of ass. Whose ass should I thin-slice and cure as jerky, Davoud?"

He has a terrible feeling.

"They're going to the caves, to look for survivors. What an utterly assful choice! But they need to try. It is in their nature to have and to be asses.

"And so I've put myself in the way. I must test this Erik Wygaunt. I must get him good and fired up.

"Meanwhile, Clayton will be renewing contact with Blackbird. Atrocities unimagined await him. But I think you'll be just fine. Do you know what your soul's made of, Davoud? Why you will survive the process of exposure, when so many others are unsouled, mutilated, torn apart?"

God, yes, Davoud knows the airframe of his soul, the aluminum and titanium sheath, electron-welded from nose to twin-tailed empennage. The wide radar eye, the thirsty engines roaring satisfaction: sleek silver dart above the clouds, soaring west. And Davoud is in the cockpit, beyond the reach of any power to recall him, racing the angels of God. For no man on Earth can pace him.

"You're just above it all. Well, you won't be much longer. Tell Clayton that Erik Wygaunt is coming to kill him soon. Coming in revenge for the losses he'll suffer . . ."

Davoud's perspective swoops in toward an American neck. The man's flesh grows into a pink riverscape, veined like the surface of some icy moon, huge stalks of hair bursting from their freckled follicles. And Davoud produces pincer limbs which pluck up a fold of skin, a needle stinger which slips into that flesh, a hard mass like an egg coming up his throat and into the man's neck where it uncurls tick limbs to burrow—

Iruvage releases him.

Davoud falls back into his own body, shivering, retching. He thinks he might have had a seizure. He's not sure. He is alone.

CLAYTON//774 MINUTES REMAIN

"Erik is Major Wygaunt?" Chaya asks, when Clayton pauses.

"Yeah."

"Did he steal your wife? Is that the new and dangerous place he went?"

He laughs: "We weren't swingers, Chaya."

"It sounds like you were!"

"Swingers are forty-something air force pukes who watch Jerry Falwell. We were much too cool to be swingers. I'd prefer 'monogamish but unbearably attractive.' And, anyway, not with Erik. He was just . . . our friend."

But Erik wanted to kill people. He wanted to destroy the monsters whose lairs were too close to home. The American monsters.

(No surprise Erik went to murder as the first and best option. Yes, the American armed forces are in the business of manufacturing usefully broken weapon-people at industrial scales, but Erik didn't need military training to render the world in black and white.)

If Clayton had been able to talk to Rosamaria about this, she would've stopped them both. But he was in the habit of keeping secrets from her. And what was he going to say? I think it's the right idea, Rosamaria? I really think we need to kill these mercenaries? Not because it'll change anything, but because Erik has convinced me they deserve to die?

So they started Paladin together. Erik's guns and Clayton's access made an ugly but very efficient baby.

For a while it worked.

But Erik thought too small. Erik was down in the dirt and the blood and he wanted to clean it up one drop at a time. Clayton saw the world entire with the synthetic-aperture-radar eyes of the American surveillance constellation. The entire gushing wound of slow climate collapse, violent demographic change, legislative capture, resurgent tyranny. History hadn't ended. Democracy was going out. Something new was coming in, something that ruled not by the consent of the people but by manufacturing that consent—

"Sivakov was telling me about this," Chaya says. "About using information to manufacture consent. In China, in Russia, in America. You were part of that?"

"Sure," Clayton says, watching her unzip her windbreaker. The E is kicking in: her core temperature is spiking. "I wasn't part of some kind of shadow government. Nothing in the intelligence world works well enough to do that. But I saw a lot of things I didn't like, and I wanted to manipulate people into fixing them. Absolutely I did."

The world is getting better, people would tell him, *violence is way down, war is going away*. And Clayton didn't buy it. The world may be getting better, but it's also getting bigger. A smaller fraction of people suffer from violence, maybe. A smaller fraction of humanity is enslaved. But there are *more* people. In absolute terms. More people suffer than ever before.

Can you comfort anyone with a ratio? Can you tell them *for every one of you sad shits over there, there are a whole lot of happy people over here?*

Someone had to stand up. Why not Clayton? All that evil requires is for good and powerful men to do nothing. The good but powerless ones don't get a say.

Couldn't he take Erik's logic further? Discard the narrow goggles of urgent moral outrage and open the spreadsheet of calculated action?

He'd use Paladin to recruit assassins. He'd use the American intelligence firehose to pick targets whose deaths would definitely make the world better. His wife and his friend would never have to know. Never have to share the guilt. Never face trial, if Clayton fucked up and got caught.

He did not fuck up. He did not get caught. The Bush and Obama administrations were both very interested in quick, efficient, plausibly legal assassination, and that gave Clayton a favorable climate to work. He could "pose hypothetical processes," work out how to accomplish them, file them as speculative, and then, quietly, go *do* them. It was probable that elements of the American covert community knew what he was doing and tacitly approved. To those who favored a kinetic, interventionary approach to intelligence, Clayton was an asset, a face that could bring them closer to the center of power. And he had assumed all the risk: if he was outed, they could throw him away.

Barack Obama gets a lot of shit for drones, but, like most liberals, he started out with the best of intentions. He wanted to kill fewer people with less risk. He liked the idea of making it all rational, clean, moral, procedural. When the White House decided to build a Disposition Matrix that would supersede all prior kill lists as the arbiter of who could be legally droned to death, they picked

Avril Haines to work the legal side. But they needed someone to explain the technical side of the kill decisions. How information was gathered and processed.

This got Clayton into the White House as an advisor to the National Security Council. He never left. When Haines went over to the CIA, Clayton became deputy national security advisor.

There was no hiding the promotion from Rosamaria, of course, or from the country: he was too young, his background too secret, his success too meteoric, the drone program too controversial, his looks too intriguing. Who was he? Why did the administration trust him? Did he have dirt on someone?

"You work for Obama?" Chaya asks. This seems to be the most positive thought she's ever had about him. She shrugs out of her windbreaker and rucks it up behind her shoulders. "He's been good for people like me. In the Philippines, at least."

"Black people?"

She shrugs. "Yeah. I guess. Our race politics aren't the same as yours, but—yeah."

People notice when you work for Barack Obama. People get curious. When he wouldn't tell Rosamaria what he was doing, she started keeping things from him. She'd go places and do stuff without telling him why, or who she was with, and the change in behavior made Clayton irrationally nervous, not *jealous* exactly but terrified that he'd lost her trust. So, of course, he was tempted to, y'know, do a little surveillance on her. But he didn't. He never did that.

"Sure," Chaya says. "Not once. You don't seem like the kind of guy who'd spy on people."

In 2011 Erik finally figured out what Clayton had done with Paladin. Clayton confessed everything: he owed Erik that much, didn't he? But Erik owed him too. So Clayton trusted him to be furious and betrayed in a *sane* way.

And in reply to that trust, Erik tried to have Clayton arrested. Tried to have the deputy national security advisor, septum-deep in black projects and targeted killing, *arrested for extrajudicial assassination*. What was he thinking? How did he expect to survive the fallout? If the investigation went wide in the White House, he'd bring down the whole administration. And he'd bring himself down with it. A soldier who murdered private military contractors? He wouldn't last a week. Cheney would probably do him personally, show up at his cell like Sandy Ravage with a shotgun and a Bowie knife.

Of course Erik doesn't think about consequences. He just bulls after the cape.

Clayton had to protect himself, and Erik, and Rosamaria, by causing Erik's report to disappear. That was no problem. He covered it up so effectively that it didn't even touch Erik's career much. He did maybe put in a word to get Erik out of the field, where Erik could hurt himself. After a hard stint with the Army Rangers' Regimental Reconnaissance Company (mission: infiltrate objective area by parachute, emplace and utilize advanced sensors, report findings by secure comms: exactly what he should be doing right now), Erik was called upstairs to the JSOC staff annex, to help run the future of special forces.

Everyone wins.

Then Erik did the terrible thing.

He went to Rosamaria. He went to Clayton's wife at the same time Clayton tried to confess to her.

Rosamaria decided (instantly) that a lifetime of friendship and a happy marriage could not justify even one attempt to implicate her in a criminal conspiracy.

She cut off all contact and got on with her life. If it broke her heart, Clayton never knew.

***

"I have a question," Chaya says.

"Yes. Shoot."

"Why are you telling me all this?"

"So that you'll trust me."

"You're telling me that you ran a secret assassination unit so I'll *trust* you?"

"Yes. I have to convince you that everything I've done makes sense. You have to understand why Iruvage chose me as his catspaw. You have to understand why I dropped those bombs. You have to know my side of the story, so that you'll share yours, completely and without reservation. So we can solve this thing together."

"But why are you convincing *me*? You let Anna go."

"Yes. But she wouldn't talk to me. So I'm gambling she's going to tell Erik. And then, when he realizes it's the only way to save the planet, he'll tell me."

"The Chinese had special forces in those woods for a while. Iruvage started killing them. Just for fun, the Chinese said. Are you sure Iruvage isn't going to kill them for fun?"

"He'd better not."

She mops sweat from her brow. "Well, don't you think that if Erik was so eager to kill bad people in Iraq, he'll try to kill Iruvage? Don't you think maybe that's why he went out there?"

God. He probably will, won't he? Why didn't Clayton think of that? He picks up his radio handset, checks that he's on Erik's command frequency, and sends: "Majestic Zero Six, this is Clayton, can we talk?"

Nothing. Erik isn't answering him, or isn't monitoring his own command net. Or the radios just can't reach that far. Or Iruvage is jamming him.

"Skyler?"

A double click in reply. The CIASAD specialist is listening.

"How long would it take you to catch up to Major Wygaunt's rescue party?"

That horrible burst of static must be Skyler chuckling. "*Mr. Hunt, after talking to these Chinese guys, there is no way in fuck I'm going into those woods. They got murdered out there.*"

"I can guarantee your safety from Iruvage. How long would it take you to reach them?"

No pause at all: *"Two hours."*

"I want you to go make sure Major Wygaunt doesn't"—get himself killed—"try to go after Iruvage. Make it clear that if he tries anything, he's putting the whole fucking planet in danger. Because if he kills Iruvage—which he won't, but if he somehow did—then they drop the bombs. Clear?"

"You didn't tell him that already, Mr. Hunt?"

"He knows. He's just very fucking stupid sometimes."

"If he does disregard your directives, how do you want me to respond?"

Jesus. "Just . . . remind him what you saw in the Blackbird labs. Tell him that Iruvage's people will kill us all to keep that contained. Tell him that every bullet he fires at Iruvage is going to be answered with a thirty-megaton bomb on a major population center. Just be persuasive." He thinks a moment. "But don't make contact unless he *looks* like he's fucking up. Okay?"

"Okay," Skyler Nashbrook says. *"I'll observe and intervene if he looks like he's fucking up. Out."*

Chaya's yawning, stretching. God, she's pretty hot, isn't she? Her shoulders and her thighs fill out the fabric of her tank top and shorts, a body that's present, that takes up room and does work. Ah, an intrusive thought about her physical appearance: he'd blame it on the MDMA but no, he just notices people.

"So," he says, "you showed up the next day. After the Kurds shot the Canadians. Why didn't you run away?"

"Because Emme Naichane was so brave," Chaya says. "And I didn't want to let her die for nothing. And then I got my boss killed, and I didn't want *him* to die for nothing. And then I was in over my head."

CHAYA'S PROTOCOL

SECOND DAY

K + 34 HOURS

"This is Emme Naichane," the phone whispers. "Fourth recording.

"Barbiturates work to slow the seizures. It doesn't infect sheep, or birds, or earthworms . . . only us. Soheila thought it might be a nerve gas. But the ion sniffers detect nothing in the air except trace ozone and nitrogen compounds . . ."

She pauses between thoughts. Clicking everything together, testing it. Chaya would have liked very much to meet her.

"Colton tried to drive away but Soheila's women have collected the battery cables. Soheila shot him for breaking quarantine. She is not sick yet. But we are. Joel, Maggie, and I have it worst. Muscle tics, heart arrhythmia, headaches. Absence seizures. Anxiety. Terrible anxiety. It must be neurological . . ."

A grinding sound. Emme running her lower teeth across her uppers, left and right. A raster scan.

"Joel and Soheila want to go into the tunnel in the nose. I won't. I don't want to know what happens in there. People are confused. It's hard to talk. If I don't concentrate I sound like I . . ."

In the background, a woman shouts in Sorani. The last coherent voice anyone ever heard from Soheila.

Emme picks up. "Radar shows constant change in its interior. But nothing comes out. We broadcast prime numbers, and nothing answers. Are we interacting with an intelligence at all? Joel says physics and mathematics create a common context to understand the alien. But he's wrong. They aren't enough.

"Imagine us as animal cells. Hundreds of receptors and organelles. A specialized role among thirty trillion neighbors. The DNA blueprints to build a complete copy of the entire animal.

"We would assume that alien life would share those traits.

"But if we crept into a microprocessor, we would be astonished not by its sophistication, not by its complexity, but by its *deficiency*. No self-replication. No way to seek out and secure its own power. No blueprint to copy itself or build a higher structure. Wholly hostile.

"To understand the microprocessor's purpose and life cycle, we would have to deduce not only the existence of a larger computer system around it, but also the beings who built and programmed it. And all the while the processor would be a dry, electrified deathtrap."

The blanket crinkles as she shifts.

"The object is slowly getting warmer. Maybe a power source starting up . . . something is odd about the thermal noise, the jitter in our temperature reading. I'm exhausted . . . more later."

⁓

CHAYA 1:1

Chaya Panaguiton wipes her eyes on her sleeve.

"That's the last one?" her boss asks gently.

"Yeah." Chaya swallows. "She probably didn't wake up again. Either the seizures, or a barbiturate overdose . . ."

Before Emme died she left her phone PIN on a sticky note: 0451. Arîn Tawaku-li's peshmerga found her corpse with the other Canadians, who had mostly been shot. A few vanished with Soheila's people, who went inside and never returned.

Chaya used her special battery trick to unlock the phone without taking it out of its plastic sample bag, turned on the Bluetooth, and got the recordings out.

"Well," her boss says, "really, we should just leave."

Shafiq Hamid Alfarsi is a Sunni Arab from Baghdad. He's technically in charge of Umeme-Heritage Ventures, though he has to report to the home offices in Uganda and the American plunderers at Heritage.

"Of course we're leaving!" Nakyanzi Sophie says. "We're not stupid enough to make the same mistake."

Chaya says, "I don't think Khaje wants us to leave. I don't think she would've let us drive up here at all if she didn't want us to help."

"She hasn't asked us to get any closer either." Sabiti Kyeyune, a mine engineer and the oldest Ugandan in the crew (Shafiq's got him beat by a couple years), has a habit of thinking aloud in USL, which he learned to talk with his deaf daughter. Right now Chaya can't tell if he's saying "want" or scratching his beard. "We're not the X-Files. But it is a remarkable artifact . . ."

Shafiq's own body language is so energetic that sometimes he looks like he's doing sign language too. He's making the double purse hands right now: listen up, in Arab. "We made a contract to protect these people, and they welcomed us into their homes. It would be stupid to risk ourselves, but we're their guests. There must be something we can do to help them. God brought us here for a reason."

Part of Chaya says: We didn't make a contract to protect them, we made a contract to pretend to look for land mines while we scout new wells.

Part of her says: Yes, of course God brought us here! God sends us everywhere we go.

They certainly did a lot of trusting in God to get up here. The Qandils weren't made for large trucks. They'd just passed an ice cream stand and a PKK checkpoint, where Chaya haggled down the bribe, when the radios squawked and died. "Wherever Umeme goes," they would joke, "so go the blackouts." But power outages didn't usually kill radios.

Chaya was the only one who panicked. Didn't they understand, this was an EMP! The Americans or the Israelis had nuked Iran! "Well," Shafiq said reasonably, "if it's nuclear war, we'll be safer in Tawakul than Erbil. And if it's not, we can do our jobs."

So they went on ahead. And they found Khaje Sinjari waiting at the mouth of the valley, with a gun and an answer to Chaya's shouted question: "Is there a nuclear war?"

"No," Khaje said. "Aliens."

"What?"

"Something has appeared in our valley. I need your help to know if it's safe. I have to know by tomorrow."

"Why?" Chaya leaned out of the cab window. "What happens tomorrow?"

"I have to know before my daughter comes home. And maybe she will come home tomorrow."

⁂

Arîn Tawakuli's fresh-faced girls insisted on laying out a proper welcome. They ate lamb kuzi and drank tea made with fresh mountain well water. The Kurds served homemade pistachio ice cream. "We want to save the generator fuel," Arîn said, "so we're going over to solar, and that means we have to unplug the refrigerators to balance the load. So please ask for seconds!"

They made introductions and when it got around to Chaya everyone, even her own people, looked at her with great interest. Nakyanzi Sophie had been trying to get Chaya to explain why she left the Philippines, and then left Uganda too.

Well, the reason is sad, and involves her sexuality, which she doesn't want to talk about. Being gay in Uganda sucks more than it did back home. Chaya's not *exactly* closeted, but even if she sends a monthly contribution to FARUG, she doesn't talk about it at work.

What would she tell them, if she spoke? "I don't talk to my parents"? Estranged by the wounds of an endless fight about her college girlfriend. A relationship that ended, painfully but not angrily, when they both realized they were no longer nineteen, no longer the only option in each other's lives. Her ex is back in the Philippines with another woman, and happy. Chaya is not. Living without a warm, dense, energetic shell of family is stranger to her than Erbil's police checkpoints or Ugandans driving on the left side of the road. She can't even talk to her friends back home, because the first thing they ask is "You still aren't talking to your parents?" And if she says *no*, that is all they want to talk about.

In the Philippines she was very close to finishing an applied physics PhD at the National Institute of Physics, studying plasma behavior in black hole polar jets. Everyone told her it was foolish, and they were right. She dropped out when her family dropped her, and took advantage of her dual citizenship to move to her father's homeland. She meant to apply her work to the oil industry, using plasma pulses to improve yield in tapped-out wells: a process called Enhanced Oil Recovery.

But the only plasma she sees these days is the cutter in the fabrication shop.

Uganda was different, and the same. They had Charles Lwanga instead of José Rizal, Idi Amin instead of Marcos. But Uganda was still Catholic, still Anglophone, still part of her. At first she loved it: rolex omelets and those endless green bananas, Kampala nightlife and hilltops, crater lakes and hymns at Mass which made her cry. People were less strange about her skin and stature, though they still knew she was foreign.

But it was not home. It was not easy to hide parts of herself she had shown openly in Manila. Bad things were happening to queer people: they were being outed by news radio, they were being murdered, there were laws in the works to criminalize their very existence.

So, in sheer frustration, she followed the current of Ugandans headed to Kurdistan for work. She thought it would be good to live somewhere strange to both parts of her, Filipina and Ugandan.

Everywhere she goes a stranger she remains. And now: something stranger.

"We're going to refuel the trucks and leave," Shafiq decides. "We don't go anywhere near that thing. We treat it like evil magic. We don't know how it made the Canadians sick, so we assume anything they did is a possible vector. Even breathing the air."

"Thank God," Sophie says fervently. She's in charge of contracting out laundry and kitchen services. She never asked for this.

Chaya sits up a little on her cushion. "I don't actually think there's a disease."

Everyone looks at her. Is she really going to try to explain this? Yes, she is. She has to. God brought her here, as God brought her everywhere she's gone. It would be hubris for Chaya to believe that God *didn't* lead her to this valley. God has all our names written on His palm, and He cannot forget us, or the plans He has for us, any more than a mother can forget the child in her womb.

"Okay, space woman," Shafiq says. "Do you have a theory?"

"I'm not really a *space* woman," she says, quite pleased. He remembers her résumé! "But I do have a theory. I think it's a big X-37."

He makes a sho, a twist in the air with three fingers: What are you talking about?

"It's an American robot spaceplane. It stays up for years, puttering around taking pictures and maybe sabotaging satellites. Say they made a bigger one. Maybe the weird colors on the skin are malfunctioning camouflage. So they were flying it, and someone detected it and freaked out, or just decided to bop the Americans on the nose. And they set off a nuke in its flight path."

"Which is why the radios burnt out?"

"Exactly! A high-altitude nuke makes a powerful EMP. So the spaceplane lost its control link and went on some kind of automatic return. But the Iranians hacked it, the way they've hacked US drones before, and it came down here. Near their border."

Sabiti Kyeyune pinches his chin. "But how would a crashed American spaceplane make the Canadians sick?"

"A hydrazine leak!" It is *way* more probable than aliens. "Hydrazine is used in power units for spacecraft. It tends to stick to surfaces. So if it was on their clothes or skin, then the ion sniffers might have missed it. And it causes seizures . . ."

She crosses herself. Poor Emme.

"Hydrazine." Shafiq sighs in relief. "I think that's on the Tyvek charts. I'll check. And if it is, I'm going to do the one thing we need to do before we leave."

"Wait, what one thing?"

"I have to bury those people. Some of them are Muslims and all of them deserve dignity. We have protective suits, so I'm not going to make the Kurds do it. And I won't leave them out for the birds."

"I'll come with you," Sabiti volunteers, followed immediately by Chaya. But Shafiq won't allow it. They argue about it. He wins.

He struggles into a Tyvek protective suit and a respirator. Chaya helps him pack himself into a Toyota with a shovel and a box of SafeAir chemical badges.

"Don't brake too fast on the turf, boss."

Shafiq grins at her through the respirator: "Don't tell me how to drive. I drive in Baghdad."

"I drive in Manila."

He laughs. "Get those trucks fueled and inshallah we will be gone by sunset."

Shafiq eases the Toyota over the river bridge, catches sod, hits the gas, and drives straight into a black hole.

خەجی

Nothing ate the Canadians yesterday.

But today the Arab's Toyota hits nothing and nothing wakes up, violet and violently radiant, to scoop a tunnel through the engine block. Everything it touches melts. The truck goes soft and elliptical: aluminum and plastic, gas and spark, all torn from their path to plunge toward a precipitous center. The man withers like a petal in fire and all the metal and plastic around him falls toward one central focus, only to clog and slingshot past, hose of liquidized Toyota, splattering over the meadow and setting fires.

"Ssrin," Khaje hisses, from her perch in the pistachio grove. "What in God's name was that?"

"Weird. *It made a drive massed.*"

"A *what?*"

"*Translator being silly. Trying to force an English pun into Sorani. Massed, mast. It's a drive mast.*"

"It wasn't there yesterday!"

"*No. The relic is learning to exploit the forces of the universe. It began with the nuclear forces and electromagnetism, to hold itself together. It must think, because spacetime tells mass how to move, that it needs to learn to move by altering space-time. So it's playing with gravity. But how would it possibly know the topology for a drive mast? That's not a trivial artifact to deduce from first principles . . .*"

"Is that a black hole? Is there a black hole in my valley?"

"*I didn't know Kurdish guerillas studied black holes.*"

"I have a telescope." A thing you can do alone when you can't sleep. "I watch the internet." That helped her English a lot. "I know about black holes."

"*Apparently you didn't watch enough, my bitter bipedal bride. It can't be a black hole, can it. Black holes glow.*"

"Hawking radiation, I know."

"*Yes. And the smaller they are, the brighter they get. This mast has an effective mass around 150 million tons. If it obeyed ordinary black hole dynamics it would be one-fifth the size of a proton and it would radiate a quarter-kiloton of X-ray energy every second. It would shine bright enough to set this valley on fire.*"

"It did shine! I saw it melt that truck!"

"*Yes, when that unfortunate man force-fed himself into the mast, there was accretive heating. Matter rubbing together as it tried to fall down into the mast. Not proper Hawking radiation, though. In the drive masts I'm used to, the Hawking photons are axionated and recaptured for use, but I don't know what this one's doing with all the radiation . . .*"

"What are you *talking* about?"

"*I don't understand how you people communicate with just one head at a time. I feel like I'm trying to talk by chewing on a string. Trust me. It's not a black hole.*"

"So what's a drive mast, then?" The tall Ugandan woman, Chaya, is trying to keep her people from running across the bridge to help. She's sobbing. Poor girl.

"I guess I don't really know. A space-time artifact created to help ships fly. Something to do with torsion, the force of gravity in extra dimensions, aretaic intervention in the physics model, and . . . look, it's one vertex of a starship's drive field. Most ships have only a few. Is the translator handling 'mast' all right? Pylon? Quill? I'm trying different synonyms here."

"You don't know how your own spaceships fly?"

"Can you tell me how a wing works?"

"Sure. The air moving over the curved top of the wing has to move faster to meet the air going along the smooth bottom, which . . ." Khaje realizes that this makes absolutely no sense at all. She grunts in bemusement. "I thought this thing was a weapon. Now it's a spaceship?"

"I hope so. I need to get it out of here before Iruvage finds a way inside."

"When is Anna getting here?"

"I thought she'd be here by now. I thought the Americans would move much faster."

"You didn't tell me people were going to die." Soheila wasn't supposed to die. Khaje never liked Soheila much, but she was a survivor, she was old Tawakul, a part of Tawakul before Anna saved it. And now Khaje's drunken bargain has killed her and ten other women. Killed more than Anna ever did. So how will she pull the trigger now? How would that be right?

Ssrin doesn't hesitate like a human would, which makes her sound angry, like she's snapping back at you. *"You told me you'd let them all die for a chance to see Anna again. You told me you'd let the whole world burn just to bring her back. Those were your exact words."*

"I was drunk!"

"When my people say things like that, we mean them."

"Khaje! Khaje, are you up there?"

It's Arîn, yelling into her megaphone. Khaje pretends not to hear her.

"Khaje, wherever you are, you need to come sit with us. A PKK scout just came in with a report. An Iranian tank column crossed the border at Haji Omeran."

Khaje swears as vilely as she can and jumps down from the tree. Her knees buckle: she falls on her arms, the rifle on her back swings to slap her in the face, she staggers to her feet looking drunk and doesn't care. The Revolutionary Guard is coming to her village? Death first. "What strength? How long?"

"Tomorrow. They're traveling with Chinese trucks. Do you think the Americans will bomb them? Even with the Chinese there?"

"Well?" Khaje mutters, to Ssrin. "Will they?"

"I don't know. Nothing they're doing makes sense. They should be here by now. What are they waiting for?"

CHAYA 1:2

It's her fault Shafiq is dead.

O God, it was her own arrogance, her belief that God Himself sent her, which gave him the confidence to cross that bridge. But how could she have known? How could anyone have known a hole in the air would drink Shafiq like a TriNoma mall smoothie?

She leans her forehead against the side of a tractor-trailer cab and prays. What do we do now? Send me a sign, God.

Someone walks up behind her. She turns, ready, if necessary and appropriate, to give thanks.

It's Khaje Sinjari. God is at His mysterious ways again. She heads straight for the cooler of hoarded Eagle Extra beer. Halfway there she notices Chaya and tries to smile. She fails. "I'm sorry about your guy."

"I'm sorry about your people too. I guess . . . we just wait, now. We can't risk going in there."

Shafiq trusted her. His space woman.

Khaje sits on top of the cooler and puts her rifle in her lap. "You want to wait for the Revolutionary Guard?"

"What?"

"They're coming here. They might let you go when they are done with you. Not us. We are Kurds. We will be interrogated, tested, tortured, and probably raped. We will never see freedom again."

"Susmaryosep. What? Who? You mean the Iranian Army? Iran's coming here?""

"Not the army! The Pasdaran. The Iranian Revolutionary Guard. They are— they are the Iranian SS, understood? They are the secret police, the KGB."

"Do we have time to leave?" Oh, cowardly soul. "Do *you* have time to leave?"

"They'll be here tomorrow morning. I hope this time I can die before I can be captured." She leans forward, across the long rifle. "Do you want to let that happen?"

"I'm sorry," Chaya repeats, helplessly. "It's not *fair* . . ."

"Don't be sorry. Be useful."

She tried. She tried and look what happened. "Useful for what?"

"I don't know. What are you useful for?"

"Getting my boss killed," Chaya mutters. Nobody blames her, nobody says it was her fault, which only helps convince her they're trying to spare her the truth.

"Don't pity yourself," Khaje snaps. "Come on. Think. There must be something."

"I can build things! I can work with electricity! I can study the behavior of plasma around black holes! And if that's good for anything here I'm—"

She claps her mouth shut in fright. This is what a proud, vain part of her keeps whispering: *That's why you're here, for the black holes!*

"It seems like that would be good for something," Khaje says. "We have found a black hole. Maybe, if you know how the black holes work, and the Revolutionary Guard doesn't, it will help us."

"I can't. I can't just . . . there are too many unknowns. I can't risk someone else getting hurt."

"*You* can't risk it? As if you get to decide who will be hurt!"

Khaje's open-mouthed belly laugh makes Chaya think of Father Gokongwei, laughing at her through the confessional screen, about to tell her that her guilt is actually a delight to God, an act of love, a testament to Chaya's goodness. Fr. Gokongwei liked to say that the universe is very large and very strange, and yet God's favorite thing in all of it is our fear that one mortal error might put the whole design in jeopardy. As if we could.

She used to worry that she would get him in trouble by making him laugh so much.

⁓

Chaya builds a black hole detector.

She unpacks a Mirion Technologies gamma-ray logging spectrometer. She separates the sensor and the display with a long carbon rod, so she's got kind of an extendable fishing pole. She tests it on an old smoke detector. It cheerfully reports gamma ray detections at 59.54 KeV. Her pole can catch fish.

She puts on a Tyvek suit and a respirator. Nobody chases her across the bridge. She's kind of hurt but also kind of relieved. She stamps along, huffing through the respirator, proud it doesn't fog up (if it fogs up you've got a bad seal).

She knows how matter behaves around black holes. This thing is *not* behaving like a black hole should: it ought to be pulling in nearby air, forming a friction fireball. It's not. But even if it isn't actively pulling, some air is going to move into it anyway. Air molecules at room temperature move shockingly fast—about 350 meters per second. She used to tell girls at parties: Imagine all the air bouncing between me and you right now.

And when things move into *this* hole they seem to heat up: probably they get caught and sucked in, rubbing against one another on the way down. And what happens when air molecules rub together, heat up, and ionize? A plasma forms.

And plasma emits light. Some of which the fishing rod will detect.

She follows the tracks across the bridge, to the molten smear of the Toyota. Her breath hisses through the respirator.

The detector begins to chirp.

Chaya fishes a spray paint can out of her backpack and graffitis the air.

Something in the center of the spray flashes up blue, so bright it's hard to look at. The gamma-ray detector sings along. "There you are," Chaya breathes. "Now why don't you fall?"

Like it's attached, somehow, to the alien ship. Ezekiel's angels had eyes set everywhere upon them.

She decides that she will think of the alien ship as the angel.

She turns around to shout victory across the bridge. Sabiti Kyeyune and three other men from the survey team are right behind her, with stakes and tape to mark the hazard. Just like a mine in a field.

"You shouldn't be here," she says. "You could get hurt."

"WHAT?" Sabiti shouts, cupping his plastic-covered ears. "DID YOU SAY SOMETHING?"

※

They find a lot more of the death holes. They drill to find one underground. They fly a kite into one up in the sky, and it catches on fire, and then the hole eats the fire while the wind tries to blow it away. It looks like a burning butterfly going down a straw.

Chaya decides that she will go over to the angel and finish burying the Canadians. Sabiti Kyeyune insists on coming with her, in case she gets dehydrated and faints in her Tyvek. He also really wants to see the angel.

Soheila's people taped the dead Canadians into rolled-up tarps. A sheep crops grass nearby. One of the Toyotas is still backed up against the mottled alien metal, a radar set propped upright in its bed—

Chaya stares at it. The radar set should be a black tile the size of a standalone blackboard. They come on wheels, so you can push them around like a lawnmower.

But the back of this radar set has . . . exploded? Like millisecond photography of a droplet of milk spattering. Black spars erupt toward the pickup's cab, forking like fulgurites, clotted heavily at each fork with a residue of . . . what?

She walks closer.

Look how the spars spiral and twist. Like they're following the lines of a magnetic field.

Only, at the end of each tine, stretching out desperately, there is a hand. Not quite a human hand. But a terribly frustrated imitation.

"Sabiti," she says. She has to crack her dry throat and shout. "Sabiti! Let's not get any closer, okay?"

They dig graves for the Canadians in the soft meadow. Chaya stops to pray for each of them. She doesn't know the prayers Shafiq would've said but they all go to the same God in the end. The quality of the light around the ship is incredible. The long sunset simmers off the hull's royal purple and ancient gold to soften all shadows.

Every blade of grass in this meadow has a shadow. Not one has been omitted or miscalculated. God made the rules by which shadows are cast, and now each and every sprout obeys that rule. The world is so much.

But when this angel landed here, it probably crushed a few billion blades of grass. All that beauty. All those wonderful rules. Just flattened into dirt. And now these people are going to the dirt too.

Chaya thinks of Emme's story about cells meeting a microprocessor, and shivers in her sweaty Tyvek.

THIRD DAY

K + 49 HOURS

She sleeps in the cab of an abandoned truck. Just past midnight she wakes up and then she can't get back to sleep: all her sweat has chilled on the inside of her Tyveks, leaving them damp and slimy. She decides to wash her clothes in the river and dry them on the engine block. If she exposes herself and dies, at least everyone else will know to keep their Tyveks on.

Distant thunder. She hums to herself, squatting on the bank, washing her things in the slow shallow current. After a few minutes she wonders: where is the lightning that's making the thunder? Her friend Kabite showed her storms on Lake Victoria and they were always spectacular.

But there is no storm.

A sector of the southeastern horizon is on fire. Pillars of flame explode into the night, flashbulb and orange bloom. Exactly like Chaya remembers from the TV ten years ago, when the Americans invaded Iraq.

There is a grumbling in the sky. She wraps the survival blanket around herself, in case some pervert American drone is watching, and stands up to look.

The sound of jets passes above her and begins a long turn back south. Suddenly the sound stops and the night splits around a white streak of fire. She gasps. The light of the burning plane illuminates a second jet, which shoots a streak of light straight up from its cockpit and then falls silently into the mountains to the south.

The Americans must be bombing the Iranians, and the Iranians are shooting them down.

Should she wake up the others? No. What can they do? Let them rest. Bahala na. Leave it in God's hands.

خه‌جی‎

"She's still alive."

Tawakul is empty. Laundry lines twang in the breeze. The color has left the place, except for that one great colorful thing in the meadow, looming over all.

Khaje watches Chaya forage for toilet paper, liquid soap, and bottles of mouthwash among the abandoned Canadian trucks. "No seizures. She spent all day and all night near it, and she's still alive."

"She didn't try to talk to it. I think that saved her."

She gargles water, spits, wipes her face down with a dewy sleeve. "Where are the Iranians?"

"Mostly dead. The enemy destroyed them to prevent them from claiming the weapon before his own pawns arrive. He's moving aggressively, because he is running short of time. A great expenditure of weapons he cannot replace. But"—the alien's voice takes on a certain resentment—"probably a lot of fun."

Khaje kneels in the grass and begins to strip and clean her Dragunov. She's got a tremor. She can't have a drink no matter how much she wants it. "Why is he running out of time?"

"The weapon's appearance has been detected by aretaic means. An Unnumbered Fleet warship is on its way to investigate the event. Once it arrives, the Coil Captain aboard will seize command of the situation. And that will rob Iruvage of the chance to control the weapon for his own purposes."

"He's a rogue? Like you?"

"He's a khai. Like me. So he acts to advance himself."

Khaje knows what it means when authority arrives to "contain the threat." The meadow grass smells exactly like the phosgene the Iraqis dropped. "But none of those bombs hit the caves, right? Everyone's safe?"

"No one bombed the caves. But no one is safe."

"Why?"

"Iruvage is hungry. And he wants test subjects, to force into the weapon. He will use your people if he can."

"Because of me? I didn't know it would be like this. Damn it, I was drunk!"

"I'm with them, Khaje. Protecting them. Concealing them from Iruvage. He can follow their trail but it loops back like laughter. He cannot find the end."

"What? But you're an alien. You make people want to kill you!"

"I am among them, in camouflage. It does put me at some risk. Violence provoked by the Cultratic Brand is . . . uniquely hard to protect against. The universe considers it righteous, and guides it true. But I thought . . ." Ssrin makes a sound like a hinged fang clicking in and out. Clearing her throats. "I thought it was the right thing to do."

"But you don't care about people."

"No. I don't. But I try to be better than I am." The noise Ssrin makes now is not translated: a rasp, like scales brushing against scales, and a click, like fangs tapping on a dinner plate. "*I was lucky to be taught.*"

"So what do we do now?"

"*We wait for Anna. I have an idea, but I need her.*"

"You need her alive?"

"*Why wouldn't she be alive, Khaje?*"

Khaje grunts and slides the rifle's bolt back into the bolt carrier.

"*You should take council with your people now. They've taken a prisoner. He interests me.*"

"We found him up on the south ridge," Arîn says, "sitting under his parachute, talking to himself. I think he has a concussion?"

Khaje grabs the man by both shoulders, snaps her fingers before his eyes, and watches him jump in shock. In Farsi: "You! Months of the year, backward!"

"Ah, ah, Esfand, Bahman, Dey, Āzar, Ābān, Mehr, Shahrīvar, uhhhh, Mordād, Tīr, Khordād, Ordībehešt, Farvardīn!" He looks pleased with himself.

"A little stupid, but not concussed." Back to Farsi, sharpened by her smuggler days: "What's your name?"

He is in his late twenties or early thirties, with a trim body and the dark kohl-looking eyes of a pop star. He should be in an underground Tehran dance hall, not flying planes in combat. For a moment Khaje pities him. Then she thinks: he is in the Revolutionary Guard, he is a torturer and a rapist. No pity.

"Davoud Qasemi. I came here to reconnoiter the radio anomaly before the Americans could claim it. My plane was shot down last night. I don't mean you any harm."

"Are you in the Revolutionary Guard?"

He laughs, then covers his mouth. "Sorry. You are the first person I have ever met who thought that was possible. You should have seen my gozinesh review."

Gozinesh is the Iranian religious testing process. "But you are a pilot. You must have passed."

"Only by God's will," he says. "I am just an air force guy. Regular military. Not NEHSA." That's the Revolutionary Guard Aerospace Force.

"Did you see what happened to your soldiers on the ground?"

"Yes," Davoud says, nodding shakily. "They blew up."

His radios weren't working. His wingman caught fire and crashed; then he lost power and had to eject. His orders were to avoid provoking the Americans. He didn't even carry any bombs, he says. Just air-to-air missiles. In case they had to chase off a drone.

Khaje decides he's telling the truth about everything he's said, and that he's lying about everything he hasn't. "All right. I'll keep an eye on him."

"Wait a minute!" Arîn protests. A bunch of the other peshmerga echo her:

they're supposed to vote. "You can't just take him, he's a uniformed prisoner, there are rules."

"He's *my* uniformed prisoner now. What do you think I'm going to do, heval? Torture him?"

"You *have* been acting pretty strange!" Arîn blurts. "Sitting out there all night watching the Ugandans—skipping all the assembly meetings—I mean, you're sober, that's kind of out of character!"

People laugh. Khaje bristles: "Fuck your mother, Arîn."

"Hey, we don't curse mothers here," Arîn snaps. "It's bad jineology."

"Can everyone stop talking about *mothers*!" Haydar screams.

Everyone shuts up and looks at their feet. "Sorry, heval," Arîn mutters. "You're right."

Davoud Qasemi, who doesn't seem to speak Kurdish, looks quite confused by all the yelling. "Komaki az daste man barmiad?" he says, in Farsi: Can I help? "I know all kinds of aircraft. Maybe I can help you investigate the—"

Khaje wants to know what he'll call it. But he never finishes the sentence.

Shouted reports. One of Arîn's peshmerga bolts in: "Comrades! Chinese and Iranian vehicles coming into the valley!"

Everyone starts picking up their gear. "How many?" Arîn asks. "Have the ambush teams fired yet?"

"No, no, you don't understand, they're half-dead already. They're asking for our help."

"No help," Khaje barks.

"No help," Arîn says, "unless they throw their guns in the river. Everything they have. Then we'll take their wounded."

While they're distracted arguing about this, Khaje grabs Davoud Qasemi and hustles him out the back.

CHAYA 1:3

Sabiti Kyeyune pokes the exploded radar-thing with a stick. It seems to be melting. Or rotting. The hands are falling off like fruit. They attract flies.

"This is really foul," he says with interest. "What do you think it means?"

"I think it means that something inside is trying to get out," Chaya says. "And I don't want to let it."

"How would you stop it?"

"I see one opening on this thing. So I'm going to build an airlock around it."

They use Tyvek and aluminum poles to build a big airtight cube under the angel's nose. It's like a plastic Kaaba, and just like the real Kaaba in Mecca, one wall holds something otherworldly. They shove that fourth wall right inside the angel—cut the Tyvek sheeting open, mount a metal gasket inside the cut, then push the gasket right into the tunnel in the angel's nose. The workers joke about how it looks like inserting a female condom. Chaya is a little surprised they know what that looks like: she's volunteered at a sexual health clinic and not a single patient even wanted to try the floppy things, not even for balloon tricks.

The cap at the end of the tunnel is a weird, nearly circular patch of purple pearly stuff. Chaya aims a light at it from the ladder. It is not illuminated: the flashlight beam doesn't do anything. "What . . . ?" she breathes. She sets the light down on the top of the ladder and reaches for a can of spray paint. Immediately, the flashlight brightens the cap.

She picks the flashlight back up. The illumination stops. She puts it down. The illumination starts again. She shakes the flashlight a bunch and bangs it a little but the problem is not the flashlight. It's the *cap* that's changing.

If she's not holding the flashlight, it correctly illuminates the cap. But if she *is* holding it, the light goes right through.

She tries throwing a rock. It bounces off the cap. She tries a jet of spray paint: the paint won't stick, it just slides off the surface. But if she uses the handle of a mop to *push* at the cap—

It goes right in. She nearly falls forward off the ladder. When she lets go of the mop handle, it just sticks there, quivering, embedded in the cap at the top of the tunnel.

"Selectively permeable," she calls down the ladder. "Really selectively permeable."

"Did you put your head inside?" Sabiti calls, sounding envious.

"No, Sabiti, and no one's going to!"

Stuff can only pass through the cap if a person's propelling it somehow. Apparently holding a flashlight counts as "propelling" it, but throwing a rock doesn't? Maybe the difference lies in the amount of *intention* behind the motion. A rock has no choice about where it flies once it leaves your hand, but you can aim a beam of light, you can decide where it points. The rock bounces off. The light goes through. So they call it the intention cap.

But what does that say about the rest of the hull? The Canadians got radar images through it. Did the radar only go through because they *intended* it to go through? Would it still work if they left the radar on a timer? She wants to check but she absolutely can't.

Because maybe that's how Emme got sick.

CLAYTON//INTERRUPT

Chaya pauses. "Mr. Hunt, you had satellites studying Blackbird. They have radar, right?"

"Yes. Synthetic-aperture radar. Why?"

"Did anyone who viewed that radar imagery get sick?"

"Not that I know of. And I was paying very close attention. I looked at the imagery myself. But nothing we used could penetrate the hull."

"Because there wasn't a person directly operating the radar, was there? You'd order the satellites to use their radar, and the actual execution was automated."

"You're saying that our radar couldn't get through Blackbird because . . . the radar wasn't *intentional* enough? Nobody was running the satellite in real time, and Blackbird could tell?"

"Yes," she says. And she looks incredibly relieved. "So that means *recordings* of radar imagery are probably safe."

"As opposed to real-time imagery, like the Canadians viewed?"

"Yes." She exhales hard. Why does this matter so much to her?

⁂

CHAYA 1:3

The actual process of pushing the gasket through the intention cap into the alien ship causes several people to break down sobbing in terror: What if something comes back out? Chaya just doesn't think about it. The tunnel stays fixed in place when they pull the poles back out. Cool, cool, petmalu. Now their Kaaba's mated to the angel's orifice. They pump the structure up to check for leaks, then put it under negative pressure. Chaya sends Sabiti to scavenge HEPA filters from the truck full of electronics to use on the air pumps.

"Does anyone feel sick?" she asks. A bunch of people have come over to the angel by now, attracted by the sight of construction work. Everyone says no, no, we feel okay! Maybe it's working. Maybe the Tyveks and respirators are protecting them.

"For a bunch of oil workers," she tells Sabiti, "I think we did pretty good."

"We did. But, you know, there's another way stuff can get out of the alien ship."

"What?"

"The tail. It's stuck straight into the mountainside. What if the tail's hollow? Open at the end?"

"Like this end is a mouth," Chaya says, "and that's, uh . . ."

"An asshole?" He laughs boomingly. His hands sign *interesting* in USL, up and down on each side of his chest. "Maybe. Maybe they are sucking the mountain in through that tail. Mining it."

"Maybe. Maybe it's a giant thermometer. Emme mentioned the thermal noise was funny, so I tried to chart its temperature. It's not a steady rise. Sometimes you get a half-degree jump in a moment. Sometimes it goes hours without moving. What bothers me is . . . heat is created by work. So what's it working on?"

"We could go in and find out." Sabiti's eyes shine. "If the Iranians show up to take us away, I might try to get inside. I'd rather take my chances with the aliens."

"Promise me you won't. The Kurds who went in never came out."

"Oh, never," he says. "I'd never." But his hands make the sign for *lying*.

Then, from the south, comes the familiar sound of big trucks.

⁂

The Chinese convoy is a very hungry red caterpillar more than a kilometer long, and it is crawling right at Chaya.

She's terrified of Chinese truck drivers. Every Asian country has a story about some other country's drivers murdering pedestrians, but her particular fear is evidence-based: when she had to qualify as a driver for Umeme-Heritage, a friend from home told her about the years he'd gone to teach English in China and ended up riding along with long-haul truckers on the Yonglian highway. They drove sixteen hours a day, chewed betel nuts or smoked shabu (caffeine with meth), and settled into a distinctive slither when they got drowsy. The truck coming at her is slithering just like that! She can see the driver, bent forward over his wheel, smoking a cigarette or maybe shabu, looking ready to pass out.

She thinks he is going to drive right into the hole that ate Shafiq. But he sees the nest of caution tape and rolls to a stop just short. This gives Chaya time to run up and scream: "Stop! Stop! This is a dangerous worksite! Don't come any closer!"

More trucks back up on the river bridge. Chaya is not sure the concrete bridge can actually hold a tractor-trailer truck. And there are so many tractor-trailers! Silver laboratories, bright red dormitory containers, communications posts bristling with dishes and whips, generators, fuel, tanks of cryogen for high-physics instruments. They're flying big PRC flags, begging the Americans to think of global stability before dropping their bombs.

Chaya yells: "You need to put on your suits! Now! You can't come any closer without suits and respirators!"

The driver leans out the window and yells something, getting a face full of unfiltered air. Chaya points to her respirator, her Tyvek. "You have to *wear* the *suit*!"

The Chinese guy points at something behind her. He's awake now; he looks as upset as she feels. Chaya turns to follow his agitation and—

A woman in a red T-shirt trots right past her, headed toward the angel. She's shooting video on her phone, chattering excitedly: "Jiào tā mén xiān yòng huā cài cauliflower hé xī lán huā tǒng pì yǎn ba, zhè cái suàn shì universality of fractal behavior de lì zǐ!"

She has a Stanford Physics sweatshirt tied around her thick waist and soot on her cheeks. She looks really excited to be here, like the tourists who wander the Intramuros with their phones on selfie sticks. Chaya instantly hates her.

"Hey! Stop! You need to wear a suit!"

The Chinese woman goes on videotaping the angel. She's talking about fine structure and intestinal organoids. Chaya does not think her structure will be fine at all if she keeps going. "Hey! Hey, you're not safe!"

Sabiti gets in her way and the woman bumps into him. "Excuse me," she says. "I'm trying to get a good look at the Blackbird object—"

"You need protective equipment," Sabiti says, signing *dumbass* in USL.

"Sorry?" The Chinese woman stares at him. "I can't understand you. Can you move?"

Chaya loses her temper. She didn't sleep, she's very upset, she's been trying to contain some kind of alien disease that infects not just sheep and Canadians but also radars, she's doing all this because none of the so-called "superpowers" have bothered to turn up yet and also because maybe God wants her to, and the last thing she needs is some American-educated rich girl with a PhD ignoring her site safety rules—

She grabs the woman by the shoulder and spins her forcibly around. "If you take one more step onto my work site," she bellows, "I will have to treat you as infected, and I will tape you into a bag full of dry ice!"

The Chinese woman blinks up at her. Her crew-neck T-shirt is covered in small black circular burns, where sparks went out against the fabric.

"Oh, my bad," she says. "We spent the last eight hours being bombed, listening to people scream and then stop screaming, stopping to try to stabilize them, going on even though we knew it would kill them, hoping that we could reach this valley and get some help. And the whole time I kept telling myself, *Just make it to sunrise and at least you'll get to see Blackbird.* But I should've known to ask permission before I took pictures of your work site! Fuck *you*!"

And, to Chaya's bewilderment, she bursts into tears.

"Hey!" the man driving the truck shouts. "Leave Professor Li alone! She's the only reason we're alive! Hey, what did you say to her, you asshole!"

⁂

خەجیٔ

The Iranians' wounds are terrible.

They are dying of traumatic brain injuries, of lungs shredded to red pulp by blast overpressure, of bleedings internal and external, of infected burns and burning infections and plain shock. A few of them are just . . . falling apart. No one can explain it. They say something bit them, but what insect can do this? Even Khaje, who saw Kurdish men buried up to their necks and their heads run over by tanks, who saw women literally rot away in the camps, has to flinch from this. A body is made of layers of tissue, so many thin thin slimy tissues. And these men's tissues are separating, peeling off, delaminating. People are just . . . books. They dry out, they tear, they snap at the spine. They rot in the dark. You leave them alone and they stop meaning anything at all.

Davoud won't go anywhere near the wounded.

"Do you know the story of Zahak?" she asks him.

They're in the orchard by the south road, watching Arîn's peshmerga help Iranian soldiers carry screaming men into the village hall. The Iranians gave up their guns, on the condition that they get them back if the Americans show up.

"What?" Davoud's looking at Ssrin's demiurge, the thing that ate Soheila. "Oh, you mean King Zahhāk?"

"Maybe he's out there right now. Eating the brains of all your dead friends."

"They're not my friends. They're Revolutionary Guard. I'm in the air force."

Then why do you look so guilty, Davoud Qasemi? Why have you avoided speaking to a single Iranian? Even when it's your chance to get free of me?

"Where are you from?" she asks him.

"Tehran," he says. "Westernized downtown payinshahri. And I still don't see what Zahhāk has to do with anything."

"You're an officer. You have authority. Why don't you order your countrymen to tell us what they saw last night?"

Davoud shakes his head sharply. "No. I can't go in there."

"Why not?"

"I told you, they're all Revolutionary Guard. I didn't do well on my religious exams."

"So you're afraid of them?"

"I'm afraid of blood. Why do you think I became a pilot?"

"Because you wanted to kill the enemies of the regime?"

He looks at her with those dark kohl eyes. "I'm not like them. I'm *not*. I really just love flying."

His eyes slide off her. Over the river, Chinese workers in space suits run cables between shipping containers they've set up around the Ugandan airlock cube. It looks like a spill of aluminum bricks. And above it all, that sleek, gaunt, fever-colored image of *something*.

"What do you think it is?" she asks Davoud.

"A starship," Davoud breathes. His eyes shine. "It's a starship. And it's learning how to be a better starship every day."

The story Davoud's people tell is very consistent.

Those who aren't Revolutionary Guard Saberin commandos are from the 216th "Shahid Mokhbari" Independent Armored Brigade of the 16th Armored Division of the Islamic Republic of Iran Army Ground Forces. Yesterday they woke up to dead radios and a power outage at their base. That afternoon a Chinese science team flew into Hamadan Air Base on huge Il-76 transport planes. With them came a battalion of Brigadier General Mirian's elite, ideologically pure Saberin commandos from the Ground Forces of the Islamic Revolutionary Guard Corps. That night they crossed the border into Iraq, with orders to seize a village not even marked on their maps, and to bring whatever they found back to Iran.

Nothing appeared on radar. No one saw any missiles, heard the screech of artillery, or spotted the silhouette of an airplane against the stars. They just began to explode.

One man was popped like a cork from the hatch of his burning tank. "The Chieftain ahead of mine . . . I saw something land on it. Like an insect. I saw it crawl under the bustle and burrow through the turret ring. And then I went up . . ."

"Ssrin," Khaje murmurs. "Was that Iruvage?"

"Probably a martyr from his tactical hive. Good news for us. He only has so many."

"If he can blow up tanks with bugs, can he put bombs in our heads?"

"He won't. I mean, he absolutely could, he'll have antipersonnel ichneumon. But I left some of my own hive to guard you."

"Where?"

"Probably best not to let Arîn braid your hair."

She laughs in shock. Davoud glares at her. He looks ready to cry.

One of the dying Iranians turns in his cot. His blanket slips off a tented knee and scours his burns. He screams and his broken rib, jammed up against his lung, pops through. All the air inside rushes out into his chest and his lung collapses like a shredded bag. His scream turns into an airy gasp. Khaje blanches as his whole trachea jumps sideways in his throat.

A Chinese woman scientist jumps up yelling in Mandarin and waving her hands: she doesn't know how to say help! in Farsi. One of Arîn's younger peshmerga hurries over, takes one look, and shouts "Mousavi! Warrant Officer Mousavi!"

An Iranian man, Davoud's opposite in every way—short, mustachioed, pug-ugly—rushes over from the far end of the hall, nearly tripping over an IV line. "Who is it?"

"This one—"

"Okay. He has a collapsed lung. I need latex gloves, morphine, a sixteen-gauge catheter, a large bore needle, and a black marker. Private Etemadi, help me hold him down. Corporal Abedi—Benyamin! Listen to me! You're going to be all right, but you need to hold still while we get the air out of your chest!"

Davoud digs in his heels. "Let's go, please. Khaje, let's go. I can't watch this."

But she hesitates. Does she owe sympathy to this Iranian boy? Maybe he's a Saberin. Maybe he signed up to hunt her people.

A big scared-looking Iranian pins poor Benyamin Abedi to his cot. The Chinese woman cups his face and murmurs to him, trying to soothe his panic, though they don't speak a word in common. Warrant Officer Mousavi hovers over his naked left armpit with a black marker. He darts in and marks a spot.

"Hold him steady. Hold him steady." Twisting the flash chamber off a big needle. "Corporal Abedi, this will hurt, but it will save your life."

He drives the needle in through the armpit. Abedi moans and blood jets from the big needle. "Good, good," Kamran says softly. "Breathe . . ."

Khaje, turning, finds that Davoud has fled as far as his leash will let him.

CHAPTER TEN

Chaya stops. Her eyes are hot.

"We didn't know it," she says roughly, "but that was the high point. If we'd just stopped there. If we'd just left. I think we would've been all right. Sabiti would be . . . so many people would be alive right now. Why didn't we just leave?"

"You couldn't," Clayton says. "You made the choices you could with the information you had. The choice to stay with something so important, even after losing your boss . . . that was brave. When you mapped out the death holes, you saved a lot of Chinese lives."

"Yeah. I guess. I guess."

She gets up to pace but Clayton touches her hand. "Stay by the recorder, please. We'll get through this."

She rolls her eyes. "Don't pretend to give a shet about my feelings. It's really condescending."

"But you want me to know how you feel. A lot of what you've said isn't about Blackbird directly. It's about how people reacted to its presence. How you coped with the dangers it created." Which is good. It means the MDMA is working, and it means she's probably being honest. Rehearsed stories don't often contain emotional truth.

"Why don't you just waterboard me? Wouldn't it save time?"

"Okay. Tell me exactly how Blackbird interacts with people and the world around it, or I'll have you waterboarded."

They stare at each other for a couple seconds. He cracks first: smiles just a little. "I really should, though. I should. So many people will die if I don't get in there. I *should* be willing to torture you to make you talk."

"So why don't you?"

"Because it's barbaric and ineffective. Which are two different things: it would be barbaric even if it were effective, and ineffective even if it weren't barbaric. I need you to want to help me. I need you to understand that we're doing the right thing."

"Trying to give the angel to Iruvage."

He nods: "Yes."

And he makes the sign that she showed him, when she was talking about poor Sabiti and his USL habit.

Lying.

He doesn't want to give the angel to Iruvage. He wants to keep that angel on his side of the board, as humanity's best and only piece. "It's the only way to save our species." And again he tries a little soft guidance, playing a hunch: "Besides. You said Professor Li was very excited to see Blackbird. Doesn't she want to know what's inside?"

Her hands close around the rosary. She doesn't say anything. But if there's one emotion Clayton's figured out how to spot in her by now—it's guilt.

⁂

⳥ᛁᛌᛮᛐ

"Western corporate feminism is a failed ideology," Anna's mother insists. "It challenges only one of the three oppressions of patriarchy, capitalism, and nationalism. Jineology isn't about having the freedom to look nice and buy products. It's about destroying the masculine fascist world-killing ideology of capitalism, and replacing it with a green democratic confederalism that centers women as the historical subject. Isn't that right, Arîn?" She looks around. "Arîn?"

"Okay," Anna says, rolling her eyes, "but I'm not a *slut*, Mom."

"I didn't say that. I said you put me to shame."

"Yeah? I shame you? How would you know? Where were you?"

Her mother is eating a peanut butter Soldier Fuel bar, which she seems to really like. Her face is broad and strong, the kind of mother-face Anna suspects you imagine when you are a fetus: a being who provides and protects without limit. She's got a lot of gray hair, and her eyes are dry and bloodshot, and she doesn't stay still. But nonetheless Anna's mother.

"I saw your life," her mother says. "Ssrin showed me."

"So? So I had a boyfriend." And Ssrin murdered him, and Anna didn't . . . didn't do anything to help him, or tell his family, or tell the police. She just let him vanish. "Do I have to tell you my body count? Is that it? You want to know how many people I've fucked?"

"You were a slob. You worked stupid meaningless jobs and partied. A real revolutionary sacrifices those things."

"A real revolutionary? You're the town drunk in a feminist commune—"

"It's not a *feminist* commune! It's jineology! And you're the reason I drink!"

"Yeah! I fucked you up, right? I fucked you up by not dying when I should have! So you brought me back here to shoot me! And then you didn't have the balls to go through with it! So what now? You're confused, you don't know what to do, so you call me a disgrace!"

"I brought you back here so you could see what you did!" Khaje snaps.

Anna's heart takes this as a gigantic blast of approval: she saved Tawakul! Mom wants her to know she made a difference!

Then Anna's Anna-brain rejoinders that what Khaje *really* means is the absence, the absence of Serhang and Hamali, the absence of Anna herself. Her mother all alone, drunk, bitter, ashamed. Anna has heard some of the peshmerga say that Khaje sent her daughter away so she wouldn't have to pay to raise her. That's not the way Anna remembers it, no, ma'am.

"Man," Latasha Gainer says, doing calf stretches a couple paces away. "These bitches hate each other."

"It's gotta be tough coming back after so long," the ISA linguist lady says. "Lotta shit to process." Anna has not considered that the linguist might speak Sorani. The women in the pack of special forces seem to be sticking together— maybe because none of them are *technically* in combat arms (though they've all been shot at), maybe so they're visibly up front, Anna doesn't know, she's never been an army type or particularly great with other women.

She does have a hunch, though. If everyone here was a Paladin—and Erik kinda let that one slip—then maybe these women were part of *his* Paladin.

There are a lot of reasons women might want to execute American private military contractors. In theory they could have all the same range of reasons as the men. But Anna thinks that if *she* were a woman in the military, she would really want to kill rapists.

"Hey," she says to the ISA linguist lady, whose shoulder patch reads GRAY FOX—TRUTH CONQUERS ALL CHAINS. "Did you ever kill any rapists?"

She laughs. The name tape on her chest reads BEHR. "I don't think I've ever killed anyone. I just listen to people talk."

"Oh, yeah? You ever hear anyone talk about Paladin?"

There is a very brief silence.

Bruin, the funny marine guy whom Anna called a *My Little Pony* fan, says: "Your mom's kind of hot, Anna. She can't understand me, right?"

"Don't do that," Anna says wearily.

"What? I'm just saying, I'm just appreciating."

"They really don't like the 'hot Kurd with a gun' thing Westerners do. Also, she totally speaks English."

"Oh." He actually looks really sheepish. "Sorry, ma'am."

"It's fine," Khaje says in English. "You can't help it. You're a masturbator."

"I'm a— Okay, but not *primarily*, that isn't my main thing."

Erik Wygaunt is watching them all from a gray remove, hard-jawed, thinking. He's judging her, Anna feels. He's still trying to figure out how to adjust his idea of Anna to suit her crimes. She's pretty sure he thinks she's a good person. But also, he's pretty sure that what she *did* was bad. He's not sure how to square that.

God, she said to him, *I wonder how you would've lived my life.*

She wants to know his answer. She wants God's answer: How would *God* have lived her life?

"In 1988," she says, "all the gods watched the villagers' bodies burning and spitting. But they inclined their heads toward those fires only to light the cigarettes on their lips."

Everyone stares at her.

"It's by Sherko Bekas," her mother says. "You read Kurdish poets?"

"Yeah."

"In the original text?"

"When I can," she says, looking at her boots. She hasn't been taught to read Sorani since she was seven, after all. "There are translations too . . ."

"Bro," Bruin says, "I just got called a masturbator, you can't segue over to genocide without giving me a little—"

There is a sound like rushing diarrhea. The side of his head pops out against his helmet. Blood spurts from under the rim, down over his face and shoulder, into his lap. He falls the other way, as if pushed by recoil, his arms raised and twitching before him.

"COVER!" Erik bellows, and everyone hits the ground.

"Mom!" Anna shouts. "Mom!"

Khaje's a couple meters away, kneeling with the big Dragunov. "Wait for the flash," she says. "You can see the flash before you hear the sound."

"Mom, get *down!*"

"I am down. You get down!"

Erik mutters, "Six receiving effective sniper fire. Any contact? Anything on firefly?"

What Erik gets back is a shriek of digital noise that maxes out the volume safety on his headset. "Jesus. He's jamming us. I guess we do this Vietnam style."

"Didn't you guys lose in Vietnam?" One part of Anna is convinced that she is in the middle of an especially lively company paintball trip. Another part of her, a loping, feline part of her soul, is thrilled to be here again: the moment of gun and trigger.

"Yeah," Erik says. "But not at the tactical level. At the tactical level, we kicked ass."

A couple meters away the linguist lady lies in a scrape on the forest floor. Her water bladder sticks up like the hump of a flat-pack camel. She keeps her cheek welded to her rifle, eye pushed against the sight, and watches the distance.

Her right ear pops off.

A hot jet of gore blowholes out of her, pushing a plug of Kevlar and a squirming microphone, which hits Anna in the shoulder. The recoil of the jet slumps her down on her side. She lifts her arms, a boxer down for the count, nerves misfiring to pump her hands up in celebration: hey, hey, hey. Anna throws the microphone away like it's an alien chestburster and shouts, "Fuck!"

"Christ," Erik says calmly. He rolls to pull a grenade from his tactical webbing. "Smoke out!"

"He's not here," Khaje groans.

Anna rolls to face her mom and yells in shock.

There are *bugs* coming out of Khaje's hair. Flat bullets, tiny kites, fairies with curled scorpion tails, clouds of gnats and black stilettos. They are no bigger than Anna's little fingernail. They fly out of Khaje's head like Medusa's dandruff and zip off in all directions.

"Mom? Mom, what the fuck's happening?" She remembers, suddenly, the moment when Khaje put a pistol to her head and pulled the trigger. Click: empty. And when it came away from her brow, Anna looked right down the barrel and saw something moving inside. And said, *Mom, there's a bug in your gun.*

Ssrin sent bug robots to protect her, and to protect Anna.

"He's not here." Khaje grunts, drops to both knees, clutching the big rifle to her chest. "He's not here. His machines are putting bombs inside the men."

"THAT'S RIGHT," a titanic voice booms. It sounds like it is coming from right beside them, as if Iruvage is lying in that scrape with dead Bruin and the Gray Fox linguist, talking in thunder. The accent is American, and wry. "REMARK-ABLE HOW LITTLE ATTENTION YOU PEOPLE PAY TO INSECT BITES. LIKE YOU'VE NEVER LIVED WITH PROPERLY VENOM-OUS FAUNA." A sigh like a jet passing overhead. "WHEN CLAYTON TOLD ME TO CLEAN UP HIS LITTLE ERIK PROBLEM . . . I DID THINK THERE'D BE A LITTLE MORE SPORT IN IT."

Erik's face goes so pale that there seems nothing to it but eyes and teeth and skull.

"Clayton." And he looks surprised. As if he still retained some stupid belief that the guy who betrayed his idea of Paladin, who nuked Ssrin and a bunch of Kurds, wanted him, personally, Erik Wygaunt, to be okay.

Man, Anna thinks, you have some real issues with that dude.

"Anna, I can stop him," Khaje gasps. She's down on her side now, curled up around her weapon. "I can stop him from . . . planting any more bombs . . . tell the hive to guard us . . ."

"Do it!" Anna doesn't want her head to explode.

"I'm *trying*, Anna." That future-echo of Anna's own face, seasoned more by sunlight and less by halogen, screws up in pain. "But—"

"What? What is it?"

"They hurt. They hurt." She whimpers: more pain than she has admitted to Anna, ever. "They're trying to talk to me and it *hurts*. It hurts me in my head."

Smoke from the soldiers' grenades billows over them. Khaje's darting machines draw wakes in the white haze, like children sledding in the first snow.

Khaje groans. "مەھێلە ئازارمان بدات! Mehêle azarman bidat!"

Anna's skin prickles with static as the alien machines do something ineffable. They are going out among the soldiers, like shepherds.

"AHA," Iruvage's voice booms. "I TASTE SSRIN'S TRICKERY. A LITTLE FLEET-ISSUE ELECTRONIC WARFARE, EH? LIKE SHE WAS USING TO HIDE HER WHISPERLINE. NO MORE EXPLODING HEADS. SO WE DO THIS THE OLD-FASHIONED WAY. OLD-FASHIONED BY MY STANDARDS, I MEAN. WHAT DO YOU PEOPLE SAY? PRIDE GOETH BEFORE THE FALL? I'M FEELING VERY PROUD, ERIK. AND I'M GOING TO FALL FANGS FIRST INTO YOUR CHEST CAVITY."

Khaje is reciting the names of dead people: Anna's brother Hamali; her father, Serhang; Tirej and Veman; Mir and Ziv and Agrin and Elind—

Khaje has named the little robot bugs. Named them for people she's lost.

For a while, nobody's head explodes.

"We have to fall back," Ricardo Garcia insists. The Delta sergeant huddles with Erik in a scoop between the roots of an oak. "Even if his bomb-bugs stopped working, he's still got the crawler and fuck knows what else to hit us with. We're in his territory here, sir, we're fighting on his ground . . ."

"It's our ground," Arîn snaps. "Our forest. We know this place better than he does. If we run, well, predators like wounded prey. And we can all hear that child on the radio, calling for us. I am not going to run when there are children at stake. Will you, Major Wygaunt?"

He washes blood off his hands with a little baby wipe. He helped shroud Bruin and strip his body of useful gear. He closed the ISA woman's eyes and murmured in her one whole ear. His hands are steady.

He says, "Iruvage said that Clayton sent him to kill me."

"Yeah," Anna says. "He did."

"But that doesn't make sense. If Iruvage wanted to kill me, why didn't he blow *my* head up first? Why'd he go for Bruin and Behr?"

"Maybe he wanted you to know Clayton tricked you again." Iruvage seems like a dick.

"Or maybe he didn't kill me because he knows that once I'm dead, the rest of the unit will turn back." This would sound quite arrogant if it weren't true. "He wants us to keep chasing him. He wants to pull the whole unit out of position, so we don't turn back toward the real threat."

"I don't follow, boss," Garcia says.

"Iruvage wants Blackbird. He's using Clayton to get it. And whatever Clayton's doing, Iruvage absolutely cannot allow me to stop it. Which is why Clayton told me there were survivors to rescue out here."

"You think he was lying about that too?"

"I don't know. I just know Clayton wanted me to come out here. So I'd lead all the troops I trusted away from Blackbird camp and leave him in control. I judged I couldn't make a difference back there. But maybe I was wrong. Maybe I should've stayed." Erik folds the bloody baby wipe up and tucks it into a pocket, to throw away later. Can't be seen littering. No, that's not how he thinks, he doesn't care what he's seen doing. Can't litter because it's wrong. "Arîn. If I turned back to the Blackbird camp, would you continue on to rescue your survivors?"

"Yes," she says.

"Even knowing that Iruvage is out here, and that he could blow your heads up?"

"What else can we do? Abandon those children? Look, Khaje's protecting us, we know that. Look at her. It's driving her mad."

Khaje's curled up muttering on a carbon-frame stretcher. Overwhelmed by the alien machines. It must be like schizophrenia, which can, in extreme cases, lead to catatonia: Anna knows this because she has been through so many mental health apparatuses herself. Excited catatonia is what people imagine when they think of schizophrenic people. Muttering, wandering, impulsively doing strange and agitated things.

Mom isn't *that* bad. She's rigid, grunting, and spitting up saliva, but at least she's not walking off into the woods. Anna thinks she would be diagnosed with ictal catatonia. But Anna also thinks schizophrenia is a more accurate diagnosis, because the catatonia is caused by the voices of the machines she's controlling.

Actually, schizophrenics have one advantage over her mom. At least, if you're schizophrenic, the voices you hear are generated by a *human* brain. What is that word Arabs use for the whispers of Satan? Wasas? She can't remember.

"All right." Erik blinks: all the time it takes him to choose. Anna still can't believe his calm. She understands now why Clayton wanted him, despite all their differences. He is completely unbreakable. "When the enemy's trying to manipulate you, you disregard the enemy's influence. You make the choice you'd make if you were under no coercion at all. And the right choice hasn't changed. There are civilians who've suffered an atomic blast. We have to help them."

"That's dumb," Anna blurts. "If we all get killed out here, we play right into his—"

"It's not dumb. Dumb is letting the enemy dictate our objective. And our objective is to rescue survivors. Those people up at ground zero *need us*. No one else is going to save them. We, the American military, accidentally dropped two nuclear weapons on them, and it is our job to—"

"Heads up," Garcia hisses. "The thing's back."

Everyone freezes. Erik takes a knee and stares at a fern. Anna flops on her back and watches the return of the Nazgûl. She kind of expected Iruvage to use it on her, despite her threat to cap herself. He hasn't. Why? Ssrin thought Anna was important for getting inside Blackbird. So why doesn't Iruvage just suck that knowledge from her soul?

Maybe he knows she's got no clue.

The corkscrewing tooth-shadow jitters from star to star overhead. Tracking the constellations people have identified, the decision that *those* stars belong together. Eating that choice. Shrieking night birds scatter through the canopy.

But this time the atmanach does not move on, or snap back down its tether to that point of origin which might be a mile away, or right before Anna's eyes. It just floats up there like a cataract. Anna wonders what it's doing. As long as it's up there, they can't make the conscious decision to move, and as long as they can't move— Oh, *fuck*—

"He's gonna shoot!" she screams.

Iruvage fires.

A hypersonic shock unzips the forest. Trees topple. Splinters shred summer leaves.

The soldier kneeling over Khaje's stretcher vanishes from the waist up. The shock of air throws his meaty shreds apart and the collapsing void sucks them back in and sprays them across the greenery. Thunder smashes Anna into the soil. She blinks at the afterimage, but it's not an afterimage at all: a hot line of light marks the path of the alien's attack, like a child running through a long-exposure photo with a sparkler.

Master Sergeant Ricardo Perez Garcia snaps up his rifle and returns fire down the path of the blast.

This is a choice.

The atmanach swoops down out of the sky and invaginates him. "Oh, fuuuuck-uck-uck-uck-uck," Garcia chatters, as the atmanach folds around him in dimensions Anna could only describe as *curl* and *suck* and *squirm*.

And then it's gone. Jetting away on its black tether. Garcia grunts and spasms on the forest floor.

"Two-oh-threes!" Erik shouts. "Right up those broken trees!"

The army dudes fire grenade launchers. Peshmerga guns crackle. Anna is surfing a peculiar prosaic hypernormality, in which everything from the itch of her underwear riding up her ass to the smell of vaporized plastic is fully present inside her, bandwidth cranked up to maximum. She reaches down to her mom's vest and reclaims the pistol that Khaje took from her after she tried to shoot Clayton: the Glock that Ssrin left her back in New York.

"It touched me," Garcia rasps. He's got his hand off his rifle, grabbing fistfuls of soil and leaf. "The crawler touched me, I'm crazy now, I'm crazy, stay away."

Anna raises the pistol toward him. As her weight shifts into shooting posture a branch cracks underfoot. Garcia gasps in shock, like this is the biggest surprise he's ever had. He rolls to face her and his eyes bug out: "What are you doing there? *What are you doing there?*"

She's not sure she's going to shoot him until she sees his eyes. One thing about schizophrenic people is that they are almost never violent: if they harm anyone it is usually themselves.

This isn't about violence. What really scared her about schizophrenia was *delusion*: the ability to believe something untrue with absolute confidence, totally immune to evidence or persuasion.

What she sees in Ricardo Perez Garcia's eyes is a man awakening from a delusion. The delusion that Anna Sinjari is a human being.

"Anna?" he says. "What did you do with Anna? What the fuck are you?"

"Easy," she says breathlessly. "Easy. Lie down on your belly."

He puts his hands up slowly. "Just stop, okay. Just stop. Please just stop. Jesus Christ, just stop! Stop! *Stop that! STOP FUCKING DOING THAT!*"

She's not doing anything. She says: "I don't know what you're—"

He goes for his rifle.

Anna shoots him in the chest. The pistol jumps in her hand and the bullet punches Garcia right in his armor and lays him out flat on his ass. He snaps his rifle up anyway, grunting, taking aim. Anna shoots him in the hand, in the belly, advancing a step between each shot: he is still moving: she shoots him in his face, in his bone-spattered face, in his bare forehead where his helmet rode back. She's completely silent, there is nothing to say.

"Cease fire!" Erik roars. "Cease fire, damn it!"

He stares at her blood-flushed face, her steady hands. He looks as if he might kill her. Wipe her out and the murder she's committed and thereby somehow bring Garcia back. Anna is not afraid of him. She stares back at him in a kind of wild joy.

"Jesus, Anna!"

"He was crazy," Anna says. "I couldn't wait."

"We could've tied him up."

"He was going to shoot me. He only needed a second."

"Damn it. *Fuck.*"

"I know," she says happily. "I know. I had to do it. There was no choice."

What a relief! For the first time in decades, she killed somebody! And it felt great, because *there was no choice*!

Khaje, on her stretcher, breaks into sobs.

"Mom?" Anna says. But her mother's still catatonic. Unaware of what's happening. Right? "Hey, Mom, it's okay . . ."

Erik does something with Garcia's body: collecting dog tags, or saying a prayer, or gathering ammo. Then he calls out into the forest. "Majestic! We're still on mission! Let's break contact and move!"

There is a short, tense silence. Ricardo Perez Garcia's ruined body gapes up at nuclear-shrouded heaven.

Finally Latasha Gainer shouts from her position: "Major, given the resistance we've encountered, and the casualties we've taken, are we still committed to the objective?"

Erik shouts back, without hesitation: "Were you in Paladin?"

She doesn't answer.

"I bet you were in Paladin. I bet *all* of you were in Paladin. That's why Clayton tapped you for this mission: because you were already on his list. What you might not know is that there were two Paladin groups. One of them, the first one, was all-volunteer, united only by the belief that we had to do something right. But some of you were chosen for a different Paladin. Chosen by Clayton Hunt because you were effective killers. The thing is, I don't know which is which. I never knew the names of the other Paladins. Only Clayton knows. But *I don't care*. You get to decide, again, right now, which kind of soldier you want to be.

"I'm going to find these Kurds. I'm going to help them. I know it's the right thing to do. I also believe that it is our only chance to make a positive difference for Earth's survival. I can't tell you why. But I need you to trust me. If any of you disagree, you can go back to Blackbird camp and help Clayton sell us all to space aliens. Otherwise, you're with me."

He gets up and heads north. Nothing shoots him dead.

Anna picks up one end of her mom's stretcher and looks significantly at Squats Kewell. He shrugs, wipes gore off the handles, and picks up the other end. They trundle after Erik.

The scattered fireteams start moving after them.

"Nice speech," Anna mutters to him. "We're still fucked, right? Even if you're right and Ssrin's alive . . ."

"Yeah." He stares up into the aurora. "If I were that alien, I'd have a drone right up above us. I'd have thermal cameras on it. I'd have microphones out in the forest picking up every footstep. And because I have eight heads, I'd be used to keeping track of a lot of data. So he knows exactly where we are. And we know he's willing to kill us."

"Between a mach and a hard place," she says.

"What?"

"Between the atmanach and his gun."

He stares at her. "Never mind," she says.

"Close," Khaje groans. "He's close now. And he's excited. I can *smell* him . . ."

⁂

They climb the mountain for three more hours, getting killed the whole time.

Arîn's peshmerga stay out front, despite Erik telling her, again and again, that his guys have night vision and thermals and should lead the way. Anna figures Arîn is totally correct: human technology won't make a difference here. It's like a party of Swiss pikemen trying to fight a stealth bomber by throwing torches at the sky.

But they fight anyway, these pikemen.

Iruvage hits them with his super combo three more times, sending up the atmanach to pin them down and then blasting somebody with his huge gun. Everybody goes kind of deaf: mostly from that huge gun, but also from their own reply. The peshmerga blast away in the general direction of Iruvage's attacks, yelling and ululating, a bunch of unmarried women ages sixteen to thirty totally ready to rock and roll and get vaporized, just thrilled at the chance to die. Anna can't believe their ferocity. Is this what ideology does to a motherfucker?

Erik's commandos are quieter at first, because they want to see something before they start shooting. But pretty soon they start ripping up the underbrush too, dumping boxes of machine gun ammunition into the dusk. Why not? It's that or carry the shit. You can't see him, you don't know if he's a hundred feet off or miles away. Hell, he might be shooting by remote control, tucked up in a snake lair on the other side of the valley with a PlayStation controller. (Anna once got chewed out at work for failing to capitalize the S in Station. Brand compliance.)

"I wonder why he doesn't just blind us with lasers," Latasha Gainer wonders. Anna has a vague idea that her old job (before the aliens landed) was calling down airstrikes to stop her dudes from being overrun, which sounds hardcore. "He's gotta have lasers, right? One good glare and—zzp, no more retina."

"Maybe the forest's protecting us," Erik says. "Can't get a laser through all this foliage."

"Maybe he wants us able to see him when he shows up," Anna says. Thinking of the Cultratic Brand.

"Hey," Gainer says. "Something on thermals. Dead ahead."

A tree has toppled, cutting a notch in the canopy. The stump is glassy smooth.

Upon that stump is the burnt white skull of a human child. It's overturned like a bowl. The black scalp peels away from brown bone. A fringe of curly hair remains, like a monk's tonsure, where the curve of the skull shielded it from the nuclear blast overhead.

A great clawed hand has scooped the burnt brains out of the skull, leaving a little dribble of crumbly gray-black marks, like spatter on a toilet bowl. Then that hand wedged a small olive-drab radio into the empty bowl. The thick black antenna protrudes from one of the child's eye sockets.

Without perceptible emotion Erik Wygaunt says: "Chinese. TBR-002 infantry squad leader handset. But I don't think anyone Chinese put it there."

"Major . . ." Gainer says. "Check 155.16 . . ."

The international search and rescue frequency. Anna clicks over to it, expecting some terrible mockery, Iruvage jamming the voices of the children—

But that small brave voice is still speaking.

"*Help us. Cave one. We are dead. We died hours ago. The blast shredded our lungs and we strangled. And then he came and fed on us.*"

The voice becomes Clayton Hunt's.

"*Help us, Erik. Cave one. It's the right thing to do. We are all dead and you are too late. But you'll come anyway, won't you? Because you're a fool. You're my dancing little fool. Come to die for the dead.*"

Iruvage's laughter booms through the trees.

Arîn Tawakuli screams in despair.

⁓

CLAYTON//678 MINUTES REMAIN

The lights in the container make a keen electric whine that has somehow *just* arrived in Clayton's consciousness. He blinks, swallows. It won't go away.

Fuck it. Go for the throat.

"You're hiding something about Professor Li."

She groans. "Not you too."

"I'm not the first one to notice?"

"Everyone's just obsessed with her! Professor Huang calling her a genius. Professor Sivakov refusing to believe any of her theories. Vylomov, that fascist, wanted to fucking shoot her!"

"Why?"

Chaya twists her rosary, then hurries to unkink it and smooth it out. "He thought she'd—he thought *we'd*—broken quarantine."

"Did you?"

My God. Did Chaya cause the outbreak that killed everyone in the labs? That would explain her guilt!

Chaya looks at the ceiling. "Bahala na," she says, which she doesn't explain. Then: "Not in any way that matters,"

He keeps coming back to that moment when Anna tried to shoot him. Chaya wrapped herself bodily around Li to protect her. Is it love? No. They've known each other for, what, three days? Even with the classic U-Haul complex, three days from meeting Aixue to throwing herself in front of bullets?

Maybe Chaya would throw herself in front of bullets for anyone. Maybe she's just a good person.

Or maybe Chaya feels like she's got something to make up for. Maybe Chaya feels like she pushed Li Aixue *in front of* a bullet.

"You're worried about her," he suggests. "You think you should've done more to protect her. Why? What happened to her?"

AIXUE'S PROTOCOL

THIRD DAY

K + 64 HOURS
CHAYA 1:4

The next time Chaya sees Professor Li Aixue is when Li asks for pictures of the angel.

"Oh, these are great," Li says, with real surprise. "These are *great*! How did you get these top-down shots?"

Blackbird shatters across the phone screen, Picasso-problematic, like each snapshot has captured one facet and they do not all quite fit together. "We sent somebody up the mountain," Chaya admits. "We don't have any survey drones." Umeme-Heritage just buys commercial satellite photos, and with satphones dead it's not like she can call home and ask for a new batch. "I hope they're useful."

"We'll get better shots with a drone," Li murmurs. "But these are good. It's odd . . ."

Chaya wants to apologize for driving Li to a crying breakdown, but she can't find a way. She's out of her Tyveks for the first time in days and she feels sweaty, stinky, and cheap. Just a construction worker. Not really meant to be here.

Li doesn't explain what's odd. Chaya prompts: "Odd?"

"That shortwave radio works here, like drone control links. But long-range radios and satphones don't. Our satphones worked fine until we entered this valley. Then, suddenly, no connection. But we can still use Wi-Fi and walkie-talkies. I think Blackbird might be doing it."

"Blackbird?"

"Yeah, that's what the Americans are calling it."

"You're in touch with the Americans?" She does have that stupid baggy Stanford Physics sweatshirt. "Then why would they bomb you?"

"No . . ." Li looks up, blinking, returning from Blackbird's fractal dimensions. "Hey. Good question. Professor Huang might know. He said the White House tipped us off that the Americans wouldn't attack if we crossed the border. But then . . . they did?"

"Maybe the Americans are the ones jamming the radios. Though our shortwaves are dead too. They all got fried by the power surge yesterday."

"Emp."

"Emp?"

"E-M-P. Electromagnetic pulse. Blackbird generated a pretty potent emp when it appeared."

Of course Chaya knows what an EMP is, come on, it just was the pronunciation that confused her. "I just thought, since there hadn't been a nuclear explosion, it wasn't *really* an EMP."

"Any sufficiently short, powerful electromagnetic event can be an emp." Note how Li returns immediately and obnoxiously to her preferred pronunciation. "These pictures are great, Professor Panaguiton. Exactly what I was hoping for."

"I'm not a professor."

Li looks up sharply from the phone. "The old guy who kept getting in the way of the trucks said you were a professor."

"Sabiti remembers that I started a PhD. He got confused."

"I hate it when people get confused," Li says, without any perceptible irony or sarcasm. She really does hate it. But she was just confused herself, about being bombed! What a confusing person. "Can I copy these pictures to our network? I think I'm going to start my work here."

"With . . . the pictures of the hull?"

"The fractal designs are mathematically tantalizing. Superficially complex, almost turbulent in places, but I think that's deceptive. I suspect I can derive an underlying mechanism."

"An underlying mechanism to the colored patches?"

"Yes. And the shapes."

"But . . . what about the death holes that ate my boss? What about the sheep with extra eyeballs? The tunnel that knows if you're trying to pass through it? The radar that turned into hands and then started *rotting?*"

"Not my domain. Downstream of the interesting stuff."

"The disease—I mean, the disease has to be our priority, the reason a bunch of people went crazy and shot each other!"

A moment passes: about as long as you would need to exchange a round-trip message with someone on the moon. Li stares at the pictures. Her brow furrows.

"Man," she says. "You really love telling me you're in charge here."

"It's not about who's in charge. We've made mistakes. People have died. We need your help to avoid more people dying."

Li looks up from the tablet. Her brain returns from lunar orbit.

"I know," she says, "that people have died. I know people need help. I helped load a lot of dying Iranian boys into our trucks. I lied to all of them. I told them they would be all right. I promised them I would make sure. In fact I had absolutely no skills or knowledge relevant to saving their lives. I *do* have skills relevant to discovering mathematical patterns underlying empirical phenomena. Is there some other way I can help? Or do you just want to tape me into a bag of dry ice?"

They stare at each other.

"I'm sorry," Chaya says, "I'm sorry, that's not what I meant. Oh, shet. I'm sorry."

"Well," Li says, "it was thoughtless of me to ignore what you were saying. I also apologize."

They stare at each other some more. Li's jaw shakes, very slightly. Chaya is suddenly conscious of how much taller and stronger she is than Li.

"Please, um." Chaya fumbles for a sticky note. "Here's my password . . . just copy whatever you need. Here's the charger. Do you need anything else?"

"No, thank you," Li says stiffly. "It's your work site. I wouldn't want to impose."

Properties of the angel called Blackbird:

Volume around 12,000 cubic meters.

Assuming the same density as a 747, this implies a mass of 5,400 metric tons, just short of two fully fueled Saturn V rockets.

Blackbird has wings, but they're too thick to produce much lift. The fuselage shows no sign of area ruling for efficient transonic flight. It's not a plane.

As a spacecraft design, Blackbird *almost* makes sense. The entire fuselage could serve as a lifting body while Blackbird glides down to a water landing. In space, the wings and their jagged trailing edges could act as radiators. There are no visible engines, but maybe the tail stuck in the mountainside is the exhaust. Or the death holes that surround the ship make it move, like an Alcubierre drive, the least impossible version of a warp engine physicists have theorized. Chaya likes that idea, because it makes Shafiq's death a little less pointless. At least he discovered a warp drive at idle.

The purple markings on Blackbird's hull are actually red and blue, simultaneously. The hull is a tiling of tiny reflective patches: most reflect low-frequency red, but a few reflect blue or violet, which is more energetic and dominates the spectrum. So you see a lot of purple.

Blackbird is an almost perfect electrical superconductor, the exact value of "almost" varying randomly with each measurement.

Blackbird emits heat as a dirty blackbody at twenty-eight degrees Celsius, varying slightly with each measurement, trending upward.

Blackbird is surrounded by traces of nitric oxide, carbon monoxide, nitrogen dioxide, azide ions, ozone, monoatomic oxygen and nitrogen radicals. This cloud is blowing south with the wind off the mountain.

Maybe this cloud is what made the Canadians sick? Maybe the Ugandans avoided it by wearing their respirators and Tyvek suits?

Professor Huang Lim thinks not.

He catches Chaya on the way into the science meeting. An older Chinese man with white hair and kindly eyes. "Hi," she says awkwardly: she feels like she's back in grad school at Diliman and she's just run into her professor at the gym.

"Hello! I'm Huang Lim—please, no Professor, no Doctor, just Lim. I wanted to ask if Professor Li is all right?"

"She's fine." No thanks to me. "She seemed very intent on her work. Is there something you're worried about?"

He grabs little fistfuls of his jeans pockets from the inside while he talks. "Last night we were bombed. In the middle of the attack Professor Li got out of her van, ran up the length of the column, climbed into the lead cab, and told the driver how to get out. People were starting to abandon the trucks, to flee into the woods. But she kept us moving and kept us alive."

"Wow. That's really brave."

"Yes. It was. But none of us have had a chance to talk to her since. We thought, since she asked to see you, maybe she . . . told you something? Guidance for where to begin our own work?"

The worry on his face makes Chaya homesick for her own family, for anyone who would worry about her. "Why don't you just go ask her?"

Huang chuckles. "Because she's a genius, Miss Panaguiton. She did her work on the self-spacing of olive tree groves in relation to the Kleinian group problem when she was fourteen."

"Cool." This means nothing to Chaya. "Um, is she your student?"

"She was," Huang says proudly. "I met her at a summer selection camp for the International Mathematical Olympiad. That year she scored perfectly, and won a special prize for elegance for her answer on question six. I personally sponsored her undergraduate education. Then she got her PhD at Stanford. Now she is back home, on the faculty at Beida."

Chaya once got a perfect score in *Dance Dance Revolution*. She ended that night crying about something she can't remember in the back of a tourist kalesa. "I tried to get her to talk about what happened to the Canadians. But she didn't seem very interested."

"Ah," Huang Lim says. "Well, I think I can shed some light on *that*."

His theory—he explains it to the Chinese and Ugandan teams together, all gathered in a container dorm like a tiny classroom—is that Blackbird can interfere directly with the human brain by applying focal electromagnetic fields. After all, Blackbird is powerful enough to create emp effects across the whole Middle East. Couldn't it also be precise with its power?

(Chaya grits her teeth: he says it like it rhymes with *hemp* too.)

Blackbird is a superconductor, and Blackbird is heating up. It might be storing huge amounts of power. When the Canadians fired radar into its hull, maybe it tried to respond with a signal of its own. Psychology labs apply magnetic fields to human brains all the time: it's called transcranial magnetic stimulation. But

Blackbird is not human. Maybe, in its effort to communicate with the Canadians, it destroyed them . . .

But, Chaya wants to protest, there is no sign of intelligence to communicate. The patterns on the hull may fascinate Li Aixue, but a butterfly's wings are full of fascinating patterns too, and they mean nothing at all. There is *nothing* about Blackbird to suggest purpose or design. Except for the intention cap . . . but even a Venus flytrap can count an insect's steps before closing.

Why would anyone build a spaceship without purpose?

Chaya wants to call her mother, her aunts, and Fr. Gokongwei, probably not in that order. But there's no way.

⁂

FOURTH DAY

K + 78 hours

خەجێ

Dry wind rustles the walnut and pistachio trees along the riverside. Heat shimmers over parked Chinese cabs. Crickets sing against the rumble of generators.

In the village, Warrant Officer Mousavi's men wash corpses and wrap them in sheets. A boy from Qom sings the funeral prayer as they load the dead onto the bed of a pickup. Out in the meadows, Chinese drivers dig graves side-on to Mecca.

Khaje watches from the roof of the village hall. On summer nights she'd haul her telescope out and search the heavens for some bright distance to distract her. How do you use a telescope when you're illiterate? The same way you use a gun.

Oh, God, she wants a drink.

She beats the heel of her hand against the back of her neck. "Tell me again?"

"*Forty-three Chinese men. In the forest to the northeast. From a special forces unit called the Latitude Cats.*"

"No they're not."

"*Sorry. Bad translation. Siberian Tigers.*"

"What are they doing up there?"

"*They thought they were hunting American commandos who were calling down airstrikes. Iruvage baited them into the forest with counterfeit voices and radio transmissions. Now Iruvage is killing them for fun.*"

"Can they do us any good?"

"*It is theoretically possible for men with guns to kill Iruvage. He must respect the* threat, or he wouldn't have bothered to thin their numbers by blowing up their con-voy." Ssrin transmits a weird hiss, many tongues tasting air: she's thinking, or frustrated at how slowly human language expresses her thoughts. "He must have brought a ship to Earth. When that Arab ran into a drive mast I thought maybe it was his, but no such fortune. Then I thought Iruvage would order the ship to replenish his tactical hive. But he's roughing it. I would badly like to steal his ship. If we cannot make the weapon fly, I have no way to bring it to those who need it."

"Do you want me to go rescue these men or not?"

"Do you want me telling you what to do?"

Zahaki. Infuriating. "I'll radio them."

"Iruvage is jamming them."

"He's not jamming you."

"Because I'm using tightbeamed neutrino pulses straight to your implant, Khaje."

"So send some tightbeamed neutrino pulses to their radios."

"Neutrinos don't work like that. Anyway, I have to be very careful with the whisperline—the neutrino beam. If Iruvage does have a ship, it'll be trying to detect the side scatter and figure out where I am."

In the caves, with her people. "Then shut up!"

"Calm your mammaries. I know exactly how to mask my messages from Fleet-issue detection systems. And I have a premonition tracer set up to warn me if he builds some ramshackle contraption from human equipment."

"Fine. I'll go out there with a flare gun and lead the Chinese in."

"Do beware Iruvage doesn't kill you. I could put the hive elements I left with you under your direct control . . . but the interface might fuck you up quite badly."

"I am already fucked up badly." Khaje gets up and goes to find some flare guns. "Have you noticed how strangely Davoud behaves about the wounded Iranians? Like he blames himself."

"Yes."

"What do you think it means?"

"It means I wish I had a neutrino detector of my own."

⁓⧉⁓

CHAYA 1:5

Word gets around that some of the missing Chinese troops have been found, in-jured and horrified. A group of Chinese scientists gathers blankets and hot food and medical stuff. Li Aixue is not among them.

"I don't believe this," Chaya mutters. She goes to Li Aixue's "workspace" to reprimand her for callous disregard.

But the aluminum container where she left Professor Li is empty.

"I saw her headed into the labs," Sabiti tells Chaya. He's loitering by the dormitories, staring up at Blackbird. "You look angry."

"Doesn't she give a shet about her people? We have Sophie handling laundry and food, we have people hauling well water, we have people helping dig graves! Does she think we're going to be her catering service? This is neocolonialism!"

Sabiti touches her shoulders: not USL, just steadying her. "Chaya. I think maybe you are trying to fix too many things at once. Go find your scientist."

She kisses him on the cheek and goes into the labs to find Li on the cameras. But the cameras aren't hooked up yet. Professor Huang has insisted they add EM shielding to all the network components first. So Chaya has to actually go *into* the hot labs and find Li.

Fortunately the Chinese level 3 suits are nearly the same as the DuPont products she trained on: God bless international standards. She climbs in through the back hatch of a suit and one of the Chinese scientists helps her button everything up. They put a radio earpiece and a chest transmitter on her, and show her how to push the transmit button through the suit: just bop yourself in the chest. She waddles through a surreal underwater world, hissing air and crinkling plastic. It's a good lab. All the glass is six-gauge blast-proof, everything is well grounded, there are dunk tanks for moving items in and out. But the intercom isn't working yet either: no one can call Li.

A Chinese woman hails her and sends: *"Professor Panaguiton? Do you need something?"*

Chaya is too annoyed to correct her. "Did Professor Li come through here?"

"She said she was going to check on the instruments in the interior airlock." The woman's face, tiny in the helmet, tightens with worry: *"I heard the Tigers came back from the woods. Did they fight Americans? Are we at war?"*

"You shouldn't have to ask *me!*" Chaya snaps.

At the center of the complex is an inflatable dome physics lab which has been mated to her biohazard Kabaa. There are cameras everywhere, their red lights burning: recording, just not sending the footage anywhere.

Through the dome wall, silhouetted against Blackbird's prow, she sees movement.

"Professor Li?" Chaya calls. "Professor Li, are you in here?"

No answer.

Chaya opens the inner door of the Chinese airlock, steps in, waits for the cycle, and opens the outer door. Steps out into the Kaaba, the antechamber of the angel's orifice. Translucent Tyvek and blazing floodlights wait for her. Glowsticks and surveying tape mark the path forward, past clusters of cameras and instruments.

There's nothing beyond that except the plastic tunnel leading up into the intention cap.

"Professor Li?" she calls.

Someone falls out of the tunnel and strikes the ground with a dry slap.

"Professor?" Chaya pushes forward through dangling plastic strips. "Are you—"

Li Aixue lies crumpled on the Tyvek floor, gasping. She looks up at Chaya through the big plastic helmet of her suit. There's something in her eyes.

Directly behind her is an aluminum ladder, pushed into the intention cap.

"Putangina," Chaya gasps.

"*I fell,*" Li says dazedly.

<hr />

Chaya grabs the stupid bitch (sorry) by her armpits and hauls her under a bright yellow Haws emergency drench shower. She yanks the handle and the shower barfs decontaminant on both of them: she will have to remember the shower's drain tank is contaminated now. She will have to get it pulled and sealed. So much to do to protect people, people who keep doing such stupid stupid things—

"*It's very clean in there,*" Li says. "*Incredibly complex, by Shannon's standards. Very simple, Kolmogorovically. Is that a word?*" She giggles. "*Kolmogorovishly. Kolmogorovogically. It's from space. Just not our space!*"

She must've gotten a zap of Professor Huang's trans-cranial magnetic stimulation. Are the suit helmets enough to protect her? Will she begin to seize? Will she die like Emme died? Emme died all alone.

Chaya turns Li over in her arms, trying to make sure the whole suit gets cleaned. "You're an idiot."

"*Won't matter,*" Li says. "*Nothing alive in there. Nothing is alive. Does that make sense? Nothing . . . is alive. Won't matter because it isn't matter.*"

"Listen. Professor, listen to me. How far in did you go?"

"*Just stuck my head inside. Just a little peek. Had to know. Saw the outside, saw the noise spectrum. Had to know if it was self-similar inside. Could've used a camera but would the camera intend to look? I am an intender.*"

"I don't understand what you're saying."

"*It's simple,*" Li says, frowning furiously. "*They thought they saw what was inside. But what they saw was really what it saw in what they saw it with. I had to look inside it to see it seeing me seeing it.*"

"Professor, *what did you see?*"

"*Just noise,*" Li says. And she smiles like a saint, like she has been touched by God. "*The noise it makes when it makes everything.*"

Oh, God. What if— Chaya smashes her visor up against Li's. The sheep in Emme's tapes. The eyes full of eyes!

Li looks back at her with two extraordinary and totally normal brown eyes. They're so perfect. Like the clean hypodermic punctures left by the injection of some astonishing truth. But they're just . . . regular eyes.

"*I'm not scared,*" she says.

"Mama Mary," Chaya says fervently, "I am."

She leaves Li in the drench shower and slaps the intercom on the Chinese airlock. "Hello? Hello?"

No one answers. She fumbles with the front of her suit, finds the push to talk on the radio: "Hello? Can you hear me?"

No one answers. Shet! Huang wanted them to focus on shielding the labs—of course they'd start with insulating the part near Blackbird. She tries another frequency. "Hello? Anyone?"

A faint thudding in the radio. "Hello? Hello?" The thudding just gets louder.

"*Helicopters,*" Aixue says. "*Whop whop whop whop.*"

Helicopters? What helicopters? But the thudding is getting louder, answering Aixue, *Yes, whop whop whop.* The sound rattles her fingertips and then her long bones. A shadow passes overhead, a downdraft beats at the plastic walls.

"Oh," Chaya says. "It must be the Americans."

Then a helicopter lands on her.

⁂

خەجێ

"Russians!" Davoud shouts. "That's an Mi-26! Wow! Look at that big guy!"

A tubular green monster crouches over Khaje's meadow. The helicopter looks like a flying whale with a yo-yo, except the yo-yo is a cargo container. Khaje learned the English word *yo-yo* from Yo-Yo Ma, whose collaboration with Kayhan Kalhor she once pirated. She's never figured out how to spend money online.

"Davoud," she says. "Stop jumping around." He's going to trip on his leash.

"Look! Look at all of them! Praise God, we are saved!"

An endless file of Russian machines descends from the north, churning the forest canopy into a highway of rotor wash. Cargo containers dangle from huge slings. The leader settles a bright red box down on the meadow grass and cuts the sling free: the whale dropping its yo-yo. The helicopter sideslips, settles to the ground in its own private typhoon of dirt and flower petals, and opens its cargo ramp. A boxy olive-drab tank-thing noses out into the light.

"The madmen!" Davoud is delighted. "Cargo on the sling *and* a BMD inside. They must've hauled fifteen tons all the way across the Qandils . . . God, can you imagine the mess if it crashed?"

"I *am* imagining a mess," Khaje growls. All that work to disarm the Iranians, and now here come the Russians with plenty more guns to go around. Arîn will be crushed.

"Great," the Chinese man at her side says. "More officers. And we just got rid of the last batch."

His name is Master Sergeant Zhang Bin Wei and he has been blown half to pieces. There are chunks of someone else's bones embedded in his scalp. His helmet fell off somewhere; his camouflage is in bloody tatters. When he came out of the woods the first thing he said to her was: "It is not very safe in your forest, you know." Then he started to laugh.

He told her all his officers' heads exploded. He sounded pretty happy about it.

"Look out!" Davoud screams: "Look out, don't fly there, don't do it!"

A bunch of the Ugandans run out waving and shouting at the next helicopter. But the pilot doesn't see them, or it's too late to stop. He detaches his cargo container, applies power, and begins to sideslip to his parking spot. Some of the Ugandans are practically blown over by the noise.

An invisible hand seizes the helicopter's tail boom.

A blue-violet pinpoint flashes to life, screeching, the same sound the Ugandans' carbide saws made cutting aluminum. The death hole snaps the tail boom right off and it whirls away, carried off like a separatist mini-helicopter by its rotor. The huge machine begins a tortured spin in the opposite direction of the main rotors.

"Collective!" Davoud screams. "Counter the spin! Throttle down! Yes! You've got it! You've got it!"

The wounded helicopter's entire rotor tips like a dish spun on a finger. Mechanical linkages force the angle of the blades to change, canceling out the uncontrolled whirl. It veers drunkenly out into the empty meadow, looking for room.

"Autorotate!" Davoud screams, leaping up and down. "No! Wait! Don't! Get airspeed!"

The wounded helicopter flares its nose like an airplane and drops. Tires burst on impact. The machine tears a brown swathe through the grass and settles. The rear door crashes down and Russian troops scramble out in a shouting mass.

Davoud pumps his fist and praises God.

"What was that thing in the air?" Zhang asks Khaje.

"A death hole," Khaje says. "The Ugandans discovered them."

"The alien ship makes them," Davoud supplies.

But how would he know that? He wasn't here when that poor Arab drove into one. He wasn't here when the Ugandans plotted and marked them.

How did he know the helicopter was about to hit one?

"Uh-oh," Davoud says. "Uh-oh! Khaje!"

The helicopter's severed tail boom has landed quite neatly across the Ugandan biohazard tent.

CHAYA 1:6

"Wow," Li says. *"If you hadn't moved us, we'd both be dead right now!"*

Chaya stares through the plastic siding of the physics dome at the ruin of her beautiful airlock. When she saw the flash overhead and all the radiation sensors started chattering, she thought they were about to be swallowed up like Shafiq. So she opened the airlock and dragged Li inside. And then a helicopter tail landed right on top of her, smashing the frame of her Kaaba against her body, and she panicked and went *through* the airlock into the physics lab.

"We're contaminating everything in here," she says. "We've got to move."

They could both be crawling with alien bacteria—they could be infected with *anything*—a stupid chemical shower isn't enough. She's got to tell somebody they were exposed.

"Oh, Mama Mary," she groans, "what do I do?" What is Li doing, she's ambling off down the plastic tunnel— "Hey! Get back here! You're contaminated!"

"*I'm fine. There's nothing in there to contaminate us. I told you. It's not real.*"

"What?" Chaya waddles after her as fast as the suit will let her. "I buried the bodies of the last people who tried to go in there!"

"*You buried the bodies of the people who* didn't *go in there.*"

"I don't think that's as comforting as you want it to be!"

Li swoosh-walks to the far end of the tunnel (that's the noise the space suit makes when you walk, *swoosh swish swoosh*) and climbs into the lab beyond.

"Li!" Goddamn it, she should've figured out the intercom, she has to call someone. She swooshes after her. "Li, stop!"

Li sits at a computer workstation: the screen says NEO KYLIN in Latin text with a sort of red unicorn logo. Chaya closes the door behind them and locks it. Where are they? This looks like a materials lab: pulverizing ring mill, Vesin sampler, sample beakers, centrifuges. This is a good place to quarantine. If nobody's chipping samples off Blackbird this lab won't be used.

"How do I put us on closed room air?" Chaya demands.

"*It won't make a difference. There's nothing airborne.*"

"Stop pretending you know how any of this works!"

"*Sure, sure. It's totally mysterious and we can't risk the slightest contact and we'll totally die and kill everyone else.*" Li stretches her hands and bends over the screen. "*I don't understand what you're worried about.*"

"I'm worried about the unknown disease that's killed everyone who contacted that ship!"

"*It hasn't killed you.*"

"I didn't—I poked a *mop* inside!"

"*And the mop didn't infect anyone. Neither will my suit. Anyway, if I've got it, I can just work in here until I die.*"

"I don't *want* to die!"

"*You won't die. And I don't care if I die.*" Her voice is not without emotion. She sounds rather content. "*As long as I get to figure it out.*"

"Figure *what* out?"

"*Where it came from.*"

"Blackbird?"

"Everything."

Chaya wants to ask a follow-up question. But at that moment the lab intercom starts working.

"All personnel in the laboratory. This is Major Vylomov of the Russian Federation Armed Forces. We are taking control of the investigation. By order of Colonel Ustinov, report to your dormitories for head count. Soldiers are now entering the labs to check security and biosafety. Please comply. Thank you and good day."

"Don't be a cop," Li says. *"Let me work. I need time to work."*

Chaya groans and does Pascal's Wager.

She reports Li: Li gets hauled off by Russian soldiers. She lives or she dies; either way, she does nothing to help anyone.

She doesn't report Li: Li either lives to do useful work, or goes insane and dies like the Canadians. Either way, she might do some useful work. So that's a better outcome . . .

But only if she doesn't infect anyone else. If Li does that, then, by preventing her arrest, Chaya has indirectly killed the whole expedition.

"Can you keep a promise? Can I absolutely, unconditionally trust you?"

Li stares at her. *"No?"*

"Okay. Can I trust you conditionally? If you stay right here, if you stay *in* this container, if you keep it locked from inside, then I won't report you. That's my condition. You don't leave for *any* reason."

"But aren't you contaminated too? Having been exposed to me?"

Is she taunting Chaya? Is she being a punyeta on purpose?

"Yes," Chaya says. "So I'm going to go out there and report *my* exposure. So they can throw me in a can and see what happens to me. While you do your big genius work. I hope you're happy with what you did."

"Okay," Li says. "Good luck."

Equations flicker in her visor, truth lining up and marching to the clatter of her keystrokes. There are still beads of water on her from the chemical shower. Chaya wants to go back and wipe them off. Does not.

***

Two soldiers in piggy white gas masks and green smocks meet her at the airlock. She reports her contamination as honestly as she can: "I was in the biohazard tent, taking swabs from the surface of the intention cap, when a piece of helicopter landed behind me. I fell forward through the cap. The top of my suit entered the alien object. I've been exposed to whatever's inside."

They speak Russian into their radios a bit. Then they come forward. "Okay. First we are going to pump this airlock down to vacuum. Then we are going to sterilize your suit with UV lamps. Then we will do a standard post-exposure disinfect on you, take some swabs, and check you for radiation. Have you done this before?"

"No ..."

"Us neither," the Russians say. "Luckily we have very good doctors on the radio."

The soldiers have to go wait outside—their biosafety gear doesn't include a full closed-circuit SCUBA system. A couple Russians in space suits come in with UV lamps, which they try to plug in to the airlock power, only the Chinese plugs aren't right so they have to go find an adapter. The airlock pumps chug as they suck all the air out. The airlock creaks and groans as all of Earth's atmosphere piles up and tries to crush it. Chaya prays it won't implode.

They give her suit a thorough UVC tan. "Remove your suit now. Be careful. This is when most accidental exposure happens."

They use plastic grabby claws, like you'd use to pick up dog turds, to help her get out of the suit. They stuff the suit into a big plastic sack and dump chlorine on it. She hesitates when she's down to her shorts and tank top: "Do I ... ?"

"I am sorry. Please trust it is for everyone's safety."

So she strips naked, mostly too scared to be annoyed. They walk her through a dump shower, then give her alcohol swabs to clean out her ears and nose. Then eyedrops and a bottle of saline to rinse her mouth.

"We are going to lead you outside now. You will go into a plastic tent for a quick examination. Everything is going to be okay."

They lead her out of the airlock, into a big plastic walk-through tunnel. Suited people with radiation sensors check her over and take skin and saliva samples. Nobody talks. The cotton swabs tickle. Finally they bring her to a plastic tub, where she has to submerge herself in a solution of half a percent sodium hypochlorite. Another rinse—in a tub of water—and then finally they give her disposable cloth to dry herself, then a T-shirt, shorts, and a new protective suit, this one Russian. She looks at it in surprise: "I'm going *back* into a suit?"

"For a period of observation," the soldier in charge says. "Please. It is condition of your meeting with the colonel."

She struggles into the shorts. "I'm meeting a colonel?"

"Everyone says you are in charge of the work site. Colonel Ustinov wishes to formalize cooperation."

"So you're not going to lock me up?"

"We are going to lock you up," the soldier says. "But then you are going to meet the colonel."

Something roars behind her. She looks back. Soldiers are shoveling everything that touched her, cotton swabs and clothes and suit, into an incinerator.

⁂

They put her inside a shipping container with a chemical toilet, a fluorescent light, a sink, a cot. The door has a plastic window and an intercom. She doesn't have her rosary. She really wishes she had her rosary.

A Russian among Russians knocks at the window. He is wearing a blue beret (a beret!) atop a body that must be the prototype of Slavic manhood. Small warm eyes beneath strong brows, a square chin, a day's stubble dark around his hard but smiling mouth. He presses the intercom. *"Professor Panaguiton. You can use your suit radio and I will hear you."*

"Hi," she says. "I'm not a professor."

"Miss Panaguiton, then?"

He doesn't quite get the name right. "Chaya's fine."

"Hello, Chaya. I'm Colonel Ustinov, 45th Independent Spetsnaz Regiment. I am in command of the expedition to the site of the Zagros Anomalous Objekt. We lost radio and satellite contact with our superiors during the approach to this valley. Do you have any working communications?"

"We lost all our satphones in the EMP. The Chinese satphones and longwave radios just don't work here." Screw Professor Li, only dorks say emp. "Do you think I'm contaminated?"

"I don't know. That is why you are in a Kazan suit, where you will remain for the next twelve hours. Professor Huang thinks the real risk of exposure is electromagnetic. But we will take no chances."

"Did he tell you about the death holes?"

"He told me you knew a great deal of vital information. I want you interviewed as thoroughly and directly as possible." He beckons another man to lean into the little window. *"Professor Sivakov, this is Chaya Panaguiton. She's the one who discovered the holes."*

"Anatoly, please." A slender man in a gray tweed jacket and a red necktie. He fumbles with his radio headset. *"Ah, honored to meet you."*

"Honored?"

"Everyone says you took charge of the situation here, after the Canadians perished."

"I lost my boss. I gave him bad advice and he died."

"That's science," Sivakov says. *"You give the best advice you can, and if it doesn't work, you revise. I'm sorry if that sounds callous. I'm very—"* He glances at Colonel Ustinov. *"I have advised the Colonel that we are in great danger, and that the Objekt is likely to kill more of us. We must accept further losses."*

"Why?" She doesn't accept it.

"Well, you see"—right about here Chaya realizes he is a lecturer—*"because it is an artifact of highly advanced technology. It will have effects we cannot anticipate. Human beings can only survive in a narrow range of physical conditions. There is no reason an extraterrestrial technology should be tuned to that narrow range. So by pure probability, it may well accidentally destroy us. Consider what the Objekt has done already. It may escalate its radio emissions to a microwave burst that boils our blood in our veins. Or the death holes you found may suddenly evaporate into gamma radiation. Or it might develop a high-tesla magnetic field that deforms the ion gradients in our nerves, killing us where we stand."*

"Okay," Chaya says. "Um. Well, we've seen it give a sheep some funny eyeballs.

It gave the Canadians seizures. And it made some kind of . . . radar art. There's not a lot of consistent behavior."

"*We are planning to repair and reinforce your biohazard airlock,*" Colonel Ustinov says. "*Raman lidar units will detect any small particles leaving the Objekt.*"

"*Self-heterodyned whispering-gallery Raman lidar,*" Sivakov says proudly. "*State of the art in airborne detection.*"

"*Yes,*" Ustinov says tolerantly. "*State of the art. We will also wrap a shell of vapor-protective PVC and Demron around the Tyvek.*"

"You're really careful. Do you guys know something?"

Sivakov and Ustinov look at each other.

"*My current assumption,*" Ustinov says, "*is that the Objekt is a delivery system for a bioweapon.*"

"A bioweapon?" She looks between the men. "An alien bioweapon?"

Ustinov nods somberly. "*The Chinese special forces unit was attacked by a fast-moving and extremely hostile alien being. They say it spoke fluent Mandarin and insulted them. It must be one of the Objekt's crew.*"

"*And if the aliens are hostile,*" Sivakov says, "*they may be here on a mission to eliminate us. Which they could achieve with a broad-spectrum bioweapon.*"

"Why bother? Why not destroy us from space?"

"*Perhaps they wish to target humans specifically, as the American settlers targeted the Indians. A self-replicating bioweapon would spread around the planet in months, but require only a few droplets of initial investment. The attacker in the forest could be on a sampling mission. The Objekt may even now be brewing up an infectious agent tuned to the human species.*"

"Oh, pakshet. And you think *I* have it?"

"*No, Chaya,*" Ustinov says soothingly. "*I think you were wearing a sealed suit, and you will be just fine.*"

She's sweating now. It's *hot* in this stupid suit and it only has a limited air supply. What if they forget to change her oxygen? What if—

Oh, God, what if they review the tapes? The cameras weren't on the network, but they *were* recording. What if they see that Aixue went inside?

She has to tell them the truth. If there's an alien bioweapon on Aixue's suit, some infant brew working its way toward full virulence, maybe there's still time.

"Listen," she says. "Um. There's something you should know. I told your soldiers that I fell through the entry cap into the Objekt. But that's not completely—"

Her suit radio howls in her ears. She yelps in pain and tears at her helmet. The fluorescent bulb snaps off. Outside, all shadows fade.

Complete silence falls: even the generators are gone. Chaya's ears ring. The engines of the Russian armored vehicles have stopped too. She thought an EMP couldn't stop a car engine? Maybe it's a really *big* EMP.

Now, from the forest, the sound of thousands of wings. Colonel Ustinov, turning, opens his mouth to say something.

An explosion blows him off his feet.

———

This is the exact moment when forty alien bombs detonate around Earth.

The EMP's dynamic magnetic field induces current in ferromagnetic material. You know what's ferromagnetic? Copper. And there are copper fittings on the Russian helicopters' fueling systems.

The charge on the copper is so powerful that the metal arcs to ground through air. The heat and thunder of the lightning blows the copper apart. One drop of molten metal pierces a fuel bladder, just emptied into an Mi-26 Halo heavy-lift helicopter, and finds the vapor inside.

The fueling crew disappears in a bloom of pale orange fire. The blast tips the nearest helicopter on its side, snapping rotors, the fueling hose lashing like hell's elephant. The helicopter carries a tank of helium cryogen for food storage and magnetic resonance systems. The heat of the fireball envelops the tank and pushes the helium above its boiling point. It tries to revert to a gas but it can't: no room in here! For an instant the tank holds back tons of super-pressurized liquid helium trying to boil off into gas. Then a seam fails, and every molecule inside flashes to steam.

The result is a BLEVE: a boiling liquid expanding vapor explosion. It ruptures the kerosene fire and kills the luckier men instantly. The inert helium snuffs the fire and replaces it with a zone of asphyxiation and paradoxical cold. The blast wave slaps the lab complex's tunnels taut and snaps the laundry lines in Tawakul.

Chaya hears it only as a *thump* through the container around her. Colonel Ustinov reappears in the little window, shouting, but she can't hear him. Her radio has gone out.

Chaya follows the pointing finger of the smoke behind him. Toward the sky. The sick, many-colored sky.

There are just too many suns up there. Evenly spaced, terribly false. Like a centrally planned Tatooine sunset.

Each sun like an old-fashioned flashbulb, metallic ghost of brightness in the eye. Each one at the center of a spreading mandala of angelfire. Shafts of solid-bright light rake the sky from above. Chaya is suddenly aware of the *physicality* of the atmosphere, aware that she is looking up into a thin blanket of vapor, and that this blanket is now being combed by invisible fingers.

The explosions are so big they must be nuclear. So far away they must be in space. And when titanic nuclear explosions produce gamma rays at the edge of Earth's atmosphere, the result is—

"Emp," she says. Without noticing her pronunciation at all.

———

خه‌جی

"How can our pickups be broken, but not their tanks?" Khaje demands. "Look at them, driving all over our meadow. Look, Arîn, they're destroying your sustainably planted wildflowers. They're ruining your topsoil."

"This is amazing," Arîn says. "Look, the blasts cover the whole sky! They must have hit the entire hemisphere, at least!"

"So?"

"So the power is out *everywhere*. This could be the intervention we need to break out of the trap of endless growth, Khaje! The end of the Anthropocene!"

"Go find someone to run up to the caves," Khaje snaps at her. "They need to know why the sky's on fire."

She pretends to brush a hand through her hair. Something in there takes a fond little prick at her forefingers. At least Ssrin's machines still work.

"Ssrin?" she mutters. "Are you there?"

"*Yes.*"

"What does this mean?"

"*The Exordia is here.*"

"And?"

"*Iruvage is out of time. He will have to act directly now if he wants to seize the weapon for himself.*"

"Are you going to help us?"

"*I am going to wait, my bitter bipedal bride. Wait for Anna. She'll come, one way or another. I think she's the key.*"

"Key to what?"

"*I can't tell you. Because Iruvage might take you. And then he'd know.*"

"But if there's no power, how is Anna going to get here?"

"*The narrative will deliver her to me.*"

"What? What does that mean?"

Ssrin doesn't answer.

Khaje glares at the sky. Now the whole world knows there are aliens up there. But she's the only one who knows what they really are, and why they've come.

She really doesn't want to tell her story. But she really, really has to.

⁂

Davoud looks up at her and his eyes are totally beaten. "It's not my fault," he says.

"Get up!" She hauls him to his feet and prods him out the door. "Get up. We're going to your people. We're going to find Warrant Officer Mousavi and you're going to tell him what you've done."

"I haven't done anything. I haven't done anything."

"No? No? Look up!"

Davoud blinks at the sky. Then he moans. The whole sky is full of shapes you'd see in a fire, colors you'd never see anywhere, neon white and double-whiskey orange, big green and sharp side-on blue, like a police strobe coming through film noir blinds. The shell of power around the planet, the sphere that keeps the sun from eradicating all life on Earth, is burning.

"The *satellites*," he says. "Oh, the poor astronauts."

"All over the world planes are falling out of the sky. The space station is ruined. And you did it, Davoud, *you* did this!"

"No . . . no, Khaje, I would never . . ."

"No?" She shoves him forward again, toward the hall, where all his wounded countrymen linger and suffer. "Then why did you work for Zahak? Why did you let him kill all your countrymen? Don't lie to me! You're working for Iruvage, aren't you?"

"Please, Khaje. Don't make me go in there." He digs in his heels. "Don't tell the Revolutionary Guard what I did. They'll kill me."

She admittedly does not want to help the Revolutionary Guard kill anyone, even a regular Iranian soldier. But: "You can't hide anymore, Davoud. We have to tell them what we know."

He looks back at her with huge, black, sorrowful eyes.

"I'll talk," he says. "I'll tell you anything you want. I didn't know this would happen. He didn't tell me. Just please, just, please, *please* don't make me go back home with Mousavi. I'll be grounded forever."

"If your devil Iruvage hurts my daughter, Davoud, then I am going to make sure you never fly anything again. I am going to cut the ligaments in your hand, and the tendons in your feet, and the eyes from your skull. Do you understand?"

He seizes desperately at her wrist. "He can hear you. He'll hear everything. *He's always listening.*"

"I can't keep this to myself," Colonel Ustinov says, when Davoud has finished. "I owe it to the Iranians and Chinese to tell them who has been killing them. And you, Khaje, you haven't told your own people? This is not what I would expect from a leader."

Khaje glares at him. "I'm not their leader."

"Clearly not." Ustinov blows his lips in frustration. "Major Vylomov!"

"Sir?"

"Summon Warrant Officer Mousavi and Master Sergeant Zhang."

"But—" Khaje begins.

"If I didn't need your peshmerga I would have you arrested along with Captain Qasemi!" Ustinov snaps. "Are you not both actively spying for the aliens *right now*?"

Davoud cringes. "Be brave," Khaje mutters to him, half in irritation, half in concern. "I won't let them hurt you."

The two soldiers arrive, saluting and pronouncing their ranks in English. Ustinov assures Mousavi that preparations to fly his survivors back to the Russian base in Abkhazia are moving along. Zhang, who has gotten most of the blood off (but not the bits of bone embedded in his skull, over which he has stuck Band-Aids), salutes perfectly and then attempts to merge with the tent wall.

"We have new information on the organism that attacked your forces," Ustinov says. He looks pointedly at Davoud. "Captain . . . ?"

So poor Davoud has to do his confession all over again. He tells them everything. He tells them Iruvage blew up the Iranian convoy and hunted the Chinese in the forest. He tells them about the khai, who did not make Blackbird. He tells them the khai want Blackbird. He tells them that the khai have a warship in orbit and it is the reason the world has turned off.

Master Sergeant Zhang speaks up first. "So this alien is watching us through you?"

"It has an implant in my neck," Davoud says. "I can't help it."

"Shǎ bī! You are telling it exactly who to target next!"

"Wait." Mousavi's mustache curls with his frown. "Wait. Captain Qasemi. You say this alien made contact with you days ago. Did you know it would attack us?"

"When I lifted off from Hamadan . . ." Davoud stops and tries again. "I swear to God that I didn't know before I lifted off. After that I didn't have a way to contact you without him knowing . . ."

"You traitor. بی پدر," Mousavi says coldly. "Colonel Ustinov, I request that you place this man under my custody."

Khaje protests, because, as truly as Davoud has consorted with Satan, so has she. "He's my prisoner. He's in the custody of the people of Tawakul."

"He has betrayed his oaths! If he has collaborated with aliens he is even guilty of crimes against God! Hundreds of men are dead because of him." His voice drops. "Colonel, if you want to lead me, do not let this man go free."

"He's right," Davoud says quietly. "I should be locked up."

Ustinov nods in decision. "Major Vylomov!" A gigantic man appears from outside the tent. "You will see to this man's safe confinement. Prepare a quarantine container, a medical examination, and a guard."

"Tak tóchno, tovarisch Colonel."

Khaje watches, helpless, as the leash slithers out of her hands and they lead him away.

"I think we are probably all going to die," Master Sergeant Zhang says. "No matter what we do."

Everyone looks at him.

"Don't you see?" he says. "Blackbird appeared three days ago. Within three days, the aliens detected it and sent a ship. That means they have faster-than-light travel. *Very much* faster than light. We are fucked. We are all fucked."

⁂

"*And unfortunately I agree with Zhang's analysis,*" Professor Huang says to Chaya, through the intercom on her prison container. The intercom, at least, still works. "*We are doomed.*"

"Wait, why? Why is *that* the part that dooms us?"

"*Because if star travel is so easy that it can be achieved in three days—or less, depending how long it took them to detect Blackbird's appearance—then the galaxy is full, and species must compete over limited space and resources. The material conditions dictate it. We must assume that subjugation or extermination are the normal result of first contact.*"

"That's a pretty wild assumption!" Chaya protests. The Philippines survived the Spanish and the Americans. It sucked, there was massacre, there was tremendous evil, but the Philippines *are* still here. Contact might be brutal, but to assume that disinterested aliens with a whole galaxy to fight over would be *more* particularly vicious to Earth than Earth's people are to one another . . . she thinks that's naive. Aliens won't care about religion, or regional self-determination, or any of the other reasons humans invent to kill each other. Destroying the world probably won't even create shareholder value for aliens. As long as there's all that space out there, nobody's going to have as much stake in destroying Earth as Earthlings do.

"*Um, there is one strange thing from your lab panels,*" Professor Huang says.

Oh, no. This is where she finds out she's dying.

Huang holds up his phone to the little window. Chaya squints, tips her head, bangs her suit visor on the door, and finally resolves a grayscale image of a bunch of balls connected by webs of snot. "What's that?"

"*This is an electron microscope image from a swab taken off your suit. These are staphylococcus epidermidis, a normal human skin bacterium. These aren't yours— they don't match your skin swabs. Note the way they've connected to each other with a polysaccharide sheet. This is something they like to do on plastic. It's called a biofilm.*"

"Okay . . ."

He lowers his voice. "*I think these are Professor Li's skin bacteria. She got them on the outside of her suit as she put it on. Then they got onto your suit as you . . . helped her.*"

"Helped her with what . . . ?" she says neutrally.

"*After she went inside.*"

She stares in shock. He holds a finger to his lips. "*Don't say anything. I deleted the footage. There's something strange about these staph bacteria. For one, they're dead.*"

"Yes, of course, I dumped bleach on us—"

"*That's what I thought at first. But bleach ruptures membranes and attacks proteins. These cells aren't ruptured. We . . . aren't sure what killed them.*"

She is still trying to understand how he saw the footage, how he knows what Li did. "Aren't sure what killed them," she repeats, foolishly.

"*Yes. Look, staph epidermis bacteria store their DNA in a big loop. Plus some bonus DNA in plasmids, which are little DNA apps that bacteria share with one another.*"

"I know what plasmids are."

"*These staph bacteria were stuffed halfway to bursting with DNA. Not just plasmids, but copies of the main loop, mini-plasmids, open strings, loose base pairs. They died of genetic misinformation. A cell needs to translate the correct DNA into proteins to survive, and these cells couldn't.*"

"Okay . . ." She's still thinking: He deleted the footage? He's covering for her? Is that safe?

"*It's possible,*" he says, looking over his shoulder, "*it's possible that these bacteria were on the part of Li's suit that entered Blackbird. And they were somehow transformed by the environment in there. So I need you to go in and find Professor Li and get a swab of her skin. So I can make sure this isn't happening to her cells too.*"

"What? You need *me* to go in? You mean they're letting me out?"

"*Oh, yes, ha, maybe I should have led with that. We know Blackbird isn't an alien bioweapon now.*"

"We do?"

"*Yes, according to Captain Qasemi's contact with the aliens. So the odds that you've been exposed to any kind of targeted agent are lower. As for whatever killed the Canadians, you don't show the slightest symptoms. I think it's safe to let you out.*"

"But if Blackbird is mutating bacteria, if Professor Li could be carrying some kind of mutant infection—"

"*I'm not going to give her to the Russians. I think you did the right thing. Leading her to an isolated lab and leaving her to work. But I am worried about her.*" He rubs his forehead. "*Chaya, the Russians are getting more aggressive in their approach to the Objekt. If something gets out, if people start shooting one another again . . . we have to protect her.*"

"Aggressive how?"

She's staring at the picture of the staph bacteria, trying to understand. She can't see the DNA here. Just a bunch of spheres packed together into spherical clusters, sheeted together by films of slime. No real structure. Chaos. Nonsense. This is what they're supposed to look like, right? But they died because the nonsense got inside them. The chaos around the bacteria got into their DNA and made it . . . more. But more wrong.

"*Mice,*" Huang says. "*They want to know if there's anything inside which can hurt us. So they're going to start sending in mice.*"

Chaya tells the soldiers she's going to set up a decontamination station for any-one else who is accidentally exposed to the inside of the Objekt. She gathers bottles of sodium hypochlorite and spare oxygen, plus testing kits to take swabs and samples, plus a fresh Chinese suit. And, without even a break to breathe real air or get some food or check in with Sophie and Sabiti, she heads back in.

The lab maze has grown with the addition of Russian trailers: now there's intimidating Cyrillic stenciled everywhere. ОСТОРОЖНО: биологическая опасность. She has to ask for directions to get to the central physics tent. She stands in it looking at the airlock into the Kaaba and Blackbird for a mo-ment. She prays. Then she turns right and heads down the plastic tunnel to the materials lab where she left Li. She bangs on the door, trying to keep the jug of hypochlorite and the oxygen tanks steady under her other arm. She should've brought a cart. "Professor Li! It's me! Are you okay?"

"Hello," Li calls brightly. "Who is it?"

Oh, Mama Mary, she's still alive. "Let me in. I need to decontaminate you."

"It's not locked."

"I told you to— Professor, you *promised* me you would keep it locked from the inside!"

"No one came to bother me. It's all right."

Li's exactly where Chaya left her, sitting like she's at piano lessons, banging away at her workstation. Chaya finds the camera and knocks a binder full of procedures in front of it. "You need to get out of that suit. We need to wash it down for disposal, then clean everything you've touched, then get you into a new suit."

"Yeah, yeah. Can I just finish up here?"

She stares over Li's shoulder. "What are you doing?"

"I'm figuring out what Blackbird does."

"You don't have the slightest bit of data. Except those pictures I gave you."

"Don't need anything else. Direct approach to truth by mathematical analysis. I'm looking for the signal in the noise."

"By working on how it *looks*?"

"Sure. All of this was generated by a single process."

"You think."

"I know. I'm trying to map the process. So I rig up a fractal, I iterate it, I see if I get a component that matches some part of Blackbird. The boundary of the Mandelbrot set is dense with Misiurewicz points. If you map all the Misiurewicz points, you get the branch points on the Mandelbrot border. And from there you have an outline of the set, and a clue to the equation that generates it. I'm trying to do the same to Black-bird's topology."

"You're doing guess and check," Chaya interprets. She understands the math babble well enough to be unimpressed. "You're writing equations to make pictures, and then you're trying to make the pictures line up with Blackbird?"

"Yeah," Li Aixue says without looking up. *"Fractals are by definition self-similar. If I can figure out one part of the fractal, I can use that logic to explore the whole. I just have to pick the right scale to start out. And I know what I'm looking for."*

"How?"

"Because I've been seeing it all my life. In everything."

"Okay. What is it, then?"

"Pink," she says. *"Did you know you can model an error-correcting code as a fractal packing of spheres into Hamming space? Interesting link between fractal topology and information there."*

Okay. Sure. Li's working in some environment Chaya doesn't recognize, not Matlab or Octave or even thrice-accursed R (may it be struck from all memory). It would be *so* like her to have written her own language. "Did you code this yourself?"

"Code? No. I hate coding. It's for frogs."

"Frogs? Like . . . French people?"

"No. Frogs are mathematicians who work in fine detail. Task-oriented thinkers. I'm a bird. I like high-level concepts, questions that point to hidden connections, you know . . ."

Chaya finds the sink—working, at least that's been hooked up—and makes a solution of half a percent sodium hypochlorite in a big plastic jug. "Why's your shirt say Stanford Physics if you're so into math?"

"I did my PhD in mathematical physics. I was interested in, you know"—she laughs—*"reality. But I couldn't stand the way physicists did math. Too many numbers involved. Half my classmates couldn't even construct the reals."*

"Well, I'm a physicist, and I don't know what *constructing the reals* means." Carefully Chaya puts the bucket down behind Li's seat and gets a spongeful. "Lean forward a little?"

"Numbers are all real to me," Li says, bending under Chaya's hand. *"I'm a heretic. I think axioms are things we discover, not things we invent. Parts of the universe. Truths that can't lie."*

"Of course numbers are real."

"Are they?"

"There's two of us in this container. It's seven thousand nine hundred kilometers from here to my home." She knows this because there are direct flights from Erbil to Metro Manila. She thought about buying one and showing up at her mother's door.

"I don't think about numbers that way. As ways of counting. I think that if there were nothing in the universe to count, there would still be a concept of two. I think that even if there were no kilometers to measure, there would still be a seven thousand nine

hundred—or at least a two, a five, and a seventy-nine. The prime factors you need to construct seven thousand nine hundred."

Chaya will indulge her as long as it keeps her still. "Where, though? Could you point to them?"

"Sure. Right there. Over there. In everything. In nothing, even. Existence exists because it is mathematical. Hertz said 'One cannot escape the feeling that these mathematical formulae have an existence and an intelligence of their own.' I agree! I think the universe is fundamentally mathematical."

"So you're a Platonist."

"Yeah. But not old and Greek."

"And what does the other side of the argument say? Numbers are just tools?"

"Exactly. They argue that numbers, math, it's all just a form of culture. Specialized language we've evolved to talk about reality. But we can extend math to talk about unreal things—four is real because you can count four objects, but there's no such thing as TREE(3) objects, because that's a number too big to count, there aren't enough atoms in the whole universe to get anywhere near TREE(3). So these skeptics say TREE(3) only exists as a human cultural idea, like, I don't know, the Impressionist movement, or Sunday."

"But you—"

"But I believe that the math comes first. Existence follows from it."

She's so tempted to just upend the bleach bucket over Li. "You mentioned some names earlier. When you were rambling. Shannon and Kolmogorov."

"Oh, yeah! Those are two different ways to measure complexity. Um, take the number 10,000. Five digits. Now take the number 12,227. Five digits. They have the same amount of Shannon entropy—five digits of information. Got it?"

"Sure . . ."

"But you can compress 10,000. You can write it as 10^4—only three digits. You can't compress 12,227, because it's prime, there's no shorter equation you can use to make 12,227. So 12,227 has higher Kolmogorov complexity, five digits compared to 10^4's three. Shannon entropy is how much information you need to describe a thing. Kolmogorov entropy is how much information you need to write down instructions to make that thing. Like . . . um, like a whole person versus a fertilized egg."

"Okay. Like zipping files up to make them smaller. Shannon entropy is the unpacked file, Kolmogorov complexity is the zip. But what does this have to do with Blackbird? I need to wash your arms."

She lifts her hands from the keyboard, a pianist caught halfway through her etude. Chaya is careful around her fingers. Don't hurt the math pedipalps.

Li Aixue says, "The Blackbird we perceive is the Shannon information. Uncompressed. Large. But at its heart is just a tiny kernel of Kolmogorov information. Instructions to make the rest. I'm trying to collapse the whole thing down to that kernel of math. And then I'd know where it came from. And maybe where a lot of other things come from too."

"Doesn't it come from the same place as everything else real? The laws of physics?"

Li Aixue makes a genuinely happy noise. *"You get it! That's exactly right! The laws of physics are the compression equation for the entire universe. Reality is a bunch of complex Shannon entropy. But it all emerges from a few basic laws that explain everything! You can compress everything we see to physical laws. That's what physics is about. At least the part I care about."*

"I need you to stand up now." Look there: up she rises. As long as she's talking about her work, she's cooperative. "So you think you're going to calculate where Blackbird came from?"

"I think it came from the prime numbers."

Chaya stops halfway down Li's calves. "What? Things don't come from numbers."

"The disease that killed the Canadians came from numbers."

"Come on. No, it didn't."

"Yes, it did. What were the Canadians exposed to? Radar images. Information and noise."

"Speaking of exposure, you need to remove your suit now. You're going to have to do this carefully."

She strips off the Chinese suit without complaint, chattering the whole time. Somehow her real voice, through the air, doesn't sound any different than her voice on the radio. "They used radar and spectrography to study Blackbird. They sent Blackbird signals, and Blackbird transformed them, it decompressed them, and it sent them back. That's what they saw in the radar. The changed signal. And the fingerprint of the changing."

She packs the suit into the waiting disposal bag. She's wearing that same red T-shirt and jeans she rolled up in yesterday. "Keep going," Chaya says. "We need to wash your skin down. In case something got through the suit layers."

"But I know how the infection spreads. It has nothing to do with anything you could wash off."

"Look, this is what they did to me, and if they're satisfied I was decontaminated, they'll be satisfied with you. Except, you know, I *lied* to them about going inside, and you actually *did* it. So we really need to decontaminate you as much as possible, okay?"

For the first time Li looks uncertain. "Do I really have to—?"

"I was hosed off by a bunch of Russians in gas masks. You get the luxurious privacy of a trailer."

"Can I do it myself?"

"No. You might miss spots. Just pretend you're in a locker room. Or getting a massage."

"I actually never take my clothes off in locker rooms." She's blushing like she's drunk. "You won't think I'm . . . ?"

Impatiently: "What?"

"Well. I'm not in great shape."

Oh. Well, okay, fair enough. Body shame isn't something you just wish away. "That's fine. I've seen all kinds of naked women." Oh, that was the wrong thing to say, now she's *more* nervous. "Listen, your abs are the last thing you should be worrying about right now. I haven't told anyone what you did. But Huang knows, and we're worried the Russians will find out. If they get suspicious of you . . ."

"Then what?"

"At best they lock you up. At worst they put you in an incinerator."

"Well. That would definitely slow down my work."

Li nods, takes a few big breaths of unfiltered room air, and strips. Chaya tries to keep her talking, because she seems happier when she's explaining math. Chaya has the safety of the space suit and Li is younger than her, two points of power which mean she needs to put Li at ease. That *fuck you!* from their first meeting hit her like a slap: a reminder that she is tall and intimidating and strong and Li is not.

Chaya needs to touch her, though. Get some skin swabs for Professor Huang. Gently now. "You were saying the Canadians got infected by radar?"

"Yeah." Li shivers, arms crossed. "The Canadians didn't actually see an image of Blackbird's interior. It was a transformed reflection of their own signal."

"Blackbird talked back?" Zip up the swabs, store them, switch to sponge to wash her skin. She does have a nice rack, though. You can notice that without being a creep, it's just aesthetics. Her bra's the wrong size. Should Chaya say something? No, you'd seem like a creep. You already seem like a creep. Shut up, shut up. What were you talking about? "Professor Yuan— Uh, Professor Huang thinks it killed them by altering their brains."

"It did. But not with electromagnetic fields. With the information in the transformed radar image."

"How could looking at radar of Blackbird alter their brains?"

"I keep telling you, it wasn't really radar of Blackbird." She makes a little yelp: ticklish at the small of her back. "Blackbird doesn't exist."

Chaya pauses, bleach solution dripping from her sponge, down Li's round hip. "I really don't get that."

"It doesn't exist," Li repeats, as if this is the simplest thing ever. "The big thing with the wings and the spine and the colors out there? It doesn't exist. It's just a mechanism that transforms signals. The mechanism makes the noise. Everything we see is an artifact of that mechanism. *Especially* the noise."

Chaya looks up, from waist height, into Li's spare simple elegant face. Her eyes are wrong somehow. Too deep. Like they're much deeper than her head.

"Professor," Chaya says carefully. "If Blackbird doesn't exist . . . what did you stick your head inside?"

"That's exactly what I'm trying to figure out," Li says.

And she smiles. Such a clear delighted smile it makes Chaya's heart thrill: the smile of a woman who's the best at what she does, who knows she's finally met her match, her purpose. The problem that she's the only one to answer.

Chaya hates to break that smile. Because in a way she'll be proving Li wrong. There are things more real than numbers. Things that can get between Li and the truth.

"Professor," she says. "You don't know about the bombs. The attack. Nobody told you."

"What?" Li says. Toppling right off her throne of numbers and delight. "What bombs? Chaya? What's going on?"

CHAPTER ELEVEN

Clayton clicks the recorder off. "Level with me for a moment. Are you sleeping with Professor Li?"

She laughs: MDMA gentling the outrage to delight. "I beg your pardon?"

"I need to know you're not wasting any of the remaining—" He checks his watch. "—ten hours of human existence narrating your crush."

"Wow! That's not a very roundabout way to call me a stupid dyke."

"I wouldn't say something like that."

"But you *are* saying it. If I find someone attractive, I can't think rationally?"

"Trauma bonding is orthogonal to intelligence, and it often involves a lot of sex. It can happen to anyone. I don't think you're irrational. I think you're very smart. You might be focusing so intently on Li Aixue because you think she's vital to understanding Blackbird. But you might also be doing it because you want to distract me from something else. Is Li genuinely *this* important? Worth narrating every visit? Every time you covered for her? Sponged her down with bleach?"

"Are you attracted to Major Wygaunt?"

He barks laughter: well, in a box universe with zero consequences, maybe. But in reality, Erik is his friend. "What?"

"I need to know," she says mockingly. "I mean, you tried to convince him you'd saved his soul from eternal torment at Iruvage's hands. Oh, Erik, we have to save Rosamaria, you have to listen to me. All that melodrama. Are you fighting out a failed . . . whatever it is you had?"

"Yes, we have history. But it's not—"

"Relevant? *Your* motives aren't relevant, but mine are?"

"My motive is to prevent the annihilation of the human species."

"And you're the only man who can do it! So objective, so decisive! Because *your* connections to other humans don't affect your decisions?"

"No. They don't. I just . . . figure out the right thing to do. What other people feel about it doesn't really enter into it. Except"—he tries to smile—"inasmuch as they can give me useful information and good advice."

"Oh, it's so good you're here to protect all us silly fallible humans! Me, I'm not like you, I just can't help myself. My infatuation with the hapless professor of mathematics fills up my brain. The American government man wants to hear important intelligence, but I can't help it, I go on chattering about girls."

Fine, Not-a-Professor Panaguiton. You want to waste my time? I won't waste yours. He draws his darkest suspicion, loads and fires. "Was Professor Li the source of the outbreak that forced you to flee the labs? Is that why you are constantly guilty? You caused that outbreak by failing to report her?"

Chaya rears back, nostrils flaring. "If she were, why would I still be protecting her?"

Clayton shrugs: well . . .

"Oh. I get it. But then wouldn't I be the first one infected? Wouldn't I be putting myself at incredible risk? Oh, but I forgot, I'm a stupid woman. I just do things because of my emotions. Unlike you, very rational and unmoved."

"You know I'm not saying that. Please, assume my good faith. It'll save time. The world is at stake."

"For some of us there are bigger things than the world."

"Like the mathematical truth of existence?"

"Like the fate of our souls. You keep saying, *The world will end if you don't do what I want.* But maybe doing what you want is worse than the end of the world. Maybe that's why we have religion, did you ever think that? So that we can do the right thing even when there's no good worldly reason."

He can't go off on her about how stupid that is. He can't say, *The most fundamental danger of religion, for all its worthy effects, is that it allows people to justify worldly suffering and strife through the pursuit of an otherworldly aim.* He has to stay focused.

But she's driving him a little nuts. He pretends to make a note like a Mads Mikkelsen psychologist from that remake, which will never get a second season if he can't figure this shit out in the next ten hours. Ten hours, ten hours, what has he been *doing* for the last four hours? Christ. He can't mix thoughts like this with MDMA. He's gonna tip over, he's gonna ruin his vibe and fall into paranoia.

He says: "I'm going to take a moment outside. Please consider my question. I urgently need to know what caused the outbreak. I *have* to know what happened last time you tried to go inside. When we begin again, please take me to that point in the timeline."

He steps outside, into falling night. The temperature has gone down but the light hasn't: the scalded sky covers everything in ghost vomit. Magnetic torment in the upper atmosphere. He tries to remember his Delmore Schwartz. The great globe reels in the solar fire; how all things flash, how all things flare. Time is the school in which we learn. Time, Captain, is the fire in which we burn.

He touches his radio: Picard to bridge. "Mike, have you got Professor Li ready to interview?"

"Yes, Mr. Hunt, she's prepped."

"Lock her in a shipping container with Davoud Qasemi."

"Okay, Mr. Hunt. Is this intended as a stressor? Something to prep her for interrogation?"

No. What Clayton's thinking is: Iruvage is always listening through the ears of his human accomplices. Always watching through their eyes.

And Iruvage is afraid of Blackbird. He's afraid of it infecting him.

So if Li Aixue is a source of the infection—well, maybe Iruvage can smell it on her. Maybe he'll demand that Davoud be removed from her presence. Who knows. Can't hurt to try.

"No. Just observe them. Make sure nobody gets hurt." He shouldn't send any more but he says: "Any word from Majestic Zero? Has Erik checked in?"

"No, Mr. Hunt. Just reports of intermittent gunfire and lights from the forest."

Iruvage? Iruvage, are you killing Erik? Fuck you. Don't kill him. I need him alive, I need him alive. I'll poison you with Blackbird, I'll fill you up with Li Aixue's contagious fucking math. Just don't kill him!

ᚦᛁᛉᛆᛋᛁ

"Help us, Erik. Cave one. It's the right thing to do. We are all dead and you are too late. But you'll come anyway, won't you? Because you're a fool. You're my dancing little fool. Come to die for the dead."

Yes. He comes anyway.

Erik refuses to accept that it's a trick. Anna tries to get him to stop—"Erik, it's a decoy, it's a trap, we've got to turn around"—and it's like she doesn't exist. His operators make a few oblique inquiries, are we still proceeding, are we still on mission, and finally Erik turns around and bellows, "ARE WE FUCKING DOING THIS OR NOT?" and they all shut up and follow him.

Arîn and the peshmerga plow ahead, dead on their feet, praying with their voices or just their footsteps.

Uphill into a rising wind. Into the smell of char. Anna and Squats carry Khaje on a stretcher, as her mom's swarm of tiny alien drones whizzes around them, defending them from Iruvage's malice. Khaje jerks and grunts and imitates the sounds that people near her make: as if their thoughts are splashing into her brain. Her temperature is above 100 degrees F. Still getting hotter.

Not as hot as this mountainside was a few hours ago, though.

"The fire line," Erik says, pointing to the dark place ahead. "Outside this point, the ignition event no longer had enough energy to set the wood on fire. Wet green forest, pretty tough to burn."

He explains how the initial flash of the nuke doesn't start the fires: it's more of a charring effect, like an acetylene torch. It's the heaped debris *after* the blast wave, all the toppled trees and scattered brush, which really feeds the firestorm.

He says the fire actually *inhales*. That's the definition of a firestorm: a fire with its own weather system. The inrushing wind strips the trees of branches and plucks all the ferns to the stem. And then there's radiation to consider. "The fallout from a bomb this size would be a coin flip everywhere in . . . say, twenty square kilometers around ground zero."

"Coin flip?"

"Yeah. Fifty-fifty chance of dying by radiation poisoning. Mostly from inhaling radioactive particles, getting it into your system. But these were airbursts, so there wasn't a lot of soil caught in the fireball. We should be okay until it rains, when anything that got sucked into the airburst comes back down. Until then all we've got to worry about are activation products."

"What are those?" Anna asks, imagining some kind of software license.

"Atoms that absorbed prompt neutrons from the blast."

"Neutrons that are . . . on time for their interviews?"

He laughs. "No. Never mind. My point is, the survivors probably took some exposure in the initial blast. We have to get them out now if they're going to avoid a fatal dose."

"You're really sure there are survivors," Anna says. "Really, really sure. Even after . . . the radio."

"Of course not. But I'm sure we have to check. Because when I imagine myself in those caves, surrounded by my dead family—the only thing I can imagine keeping me alive is the hope that someone is coming."

That makes her choke up a little. He's going to be so crushed if there's no one left. "You think Iruvage will follow us?"

"Nah. He's a coward. I don't think he'll come out of the trees."

"Damn it. I was hoping to shoot the fucker."

"Not tired of shooting people yet?"

She looks sharply at him. He looks back, uncondemning, just waiting calmly for her answer.

"No," she says. "Not yet. I'm sick of humping my mom around, though."

"Do you want to try to take your mom back to safety?"

"And let his bugs put bombs in all your heads? Fuck no."

"Appreciate it. Hey, Squats. Any luck with the firefly stations?" Squats and a couple of the others have dropped big microphone-flowers as they move, which are apparently meant to detect snipers. They talk on long wires that the jamming doesn't touch.

"Yeah, actually. I'm starting to see a pattern." Squats rests his end of the stretcher to draw shapes in the scorched dirt. "Firing positions here . . . here . . .

here. See how they cluster? He takes a couple shots, moves, takes a couple more. I think he's only got two gears, you know?"

Anna gets what he's saying, because she's had practice with Ssrin. "He can't jog. Either he's sprinting like a—like a—are there any fast snakes?"

"Black mamba," Erik suggests.

"Sprinting like a black mamba, or he's coiling in ambush mode. He doesn't have a middle setting. He can sprint or he can walk, but he can't run."

Erik stares out into the forest with cold bloodlust. "So pushing uphill, into him . . . it's driving him back? He's running ragged?"

"Yeah, boss," Squats says. "Could be."

"And whatever Khaje's doing, it's denying him his own drones. It's fucking up his targeting. Goddamn. We might have a chance."

They press on into lunar devastation. The trees lie smashed down by the Mach-effect airburst, all in the same way, like Tunguska matchsticks. The taste, through Anna's mask, is of charcoal and chocolate and the very faintest penny-copper. Not exactly the taste of radiation. Rather it is her dying taste buds, screaming in the tongue of flavor.

Anna worries about her mom. "Should we get her on an IV or something?"

"If we get the chance." Squats takes a sip from his CamelBak straw. "I think she's having petit mal seizures. Not much we can do without drugs."

"Are those bad?"

"Drugs? Well, that's a complicated question."

She laughs. "No, petit mal seizures."

"Nah. Kids can have a couple hundred petit mals a day and walk it off. But if it gets worse . . . then I don't know."

"Mom," Anna says experimentally. "Hey, Mom. Can you call me a slut or something? So we know you're in there?"

Khaje stares at the sky, into old starlight and new aurora, her pupils fixed.

"She really call you a slut?" Latasha Gainer asks.

"No. I mean, kind of, she said I made her ashamed."

"Moms, man." Gainer claps her on the shoulder. "My mom would never call me a slut. Just so you know."

"I'm glad you have a cool mom."

"Me too, man. She's great."

They crunch down aisles of fallen trees, toward the hypocenter. It is marked by naked black trees, perfectly upright. Right below those trees should be the cave where—

"Hey!" Gainer calls. "I got someone here!"

"Alive?" Erik calls.

"Fuck no." The corpse of a sentry. He was looking up, following the jets, when the light of the new sun illuminated him. Just a papery Herculaneum wreck now. His face is gone; his hands are crisped into the metal of his AK. Gainer whistles through her mask.

"Did you know nukes are racist?" Squats says.

"What?" Latasha laughs. "Seriously?"

"Dark skin absorbs more of the thermal flash. Burns deeper."

"That's not true," Erik says. "Is that true?"

"Of course it's true. Basic physics. Me and Gainer both take bonus damage from nuclear weapons."

"Didn't help this guy," Latasha says, staring down at the cremation. "Are Kurds white? Hey, Anna, are you white?"

Anna knows this grotesquerie is how the soldiers cope, but if she starts to yell at them, they won't think she's cool anymore. "Erik," she says, "could anyone really survive this?"

"Sure."

"How do you know?"

"Look at the blast pattern." He sketches out the rays of toppled trees. "It detonated over the top of the cave. If the roof didn't collapse, the mountain slope would act as a wedge and deflect the overpressure away from them. Bad inside. But they weren't inside the fireball, so . . . definitely survivable."

"You think so?"

"I do. I believe they chose this cave with forethought and care. I believe it was meant to safeguard their people from sustained bombardment and gas attack." He nods to the peshmerga commander. "Besides, look at Arîn. She keeps checking out another spot upslope. Looking for a signal. I don't think they put all their people in one cave. I think they were spread out. I think it was only the cave with Ssrin in it that got hit."

"So . . ." So what if Ssrin really did survive? Like finding a cigarette in her jacket pocket, months after quitting: delight, horror, resignation to her own failure, sick anticipation for the rewards of her weakness. Just light up again . . . "So if we do find Ssrin, you'll . . . what? Work with her?"

"She killed people under my protection. But she did it in self-defense. I don't have to forgive her. But I can understand her, right?"

"Yes," Anna says quietly. "I guess."

"If she can stop Clayton and Iruvage, then yes. I can work with her."

But what else could Clayton have done? He really did believe it was kill Ssrin or watch the whole planet burn. You don't get to decide the terms of the choice. Those are forced upon you. You just have to make it.

Would Clayton pull the trigger on Erik too, if that was what it took to save Earth?

Anna thinks he would. She believes what Iruvage said. Clayton asked Iruvage to get rid of Erik. Maybe that's the difference between her and Clayton: he can do the numbers, but he can't pull the trigger himself.

Arîn unties her orange sash and raises it between her hands. "Comrades!" she calls, in Sorani. "Comrades! Are any of you alive? We came as soon as we could. Please, are you there?"

The wind flecks the sash with soot and ash.

Silence.

Erik Wygaunt looks ready to murder the world.

Then, below the stripped trees and the blasted rock, a baby screams.

⁂

They pull eighty-five survivors out of a hundred and twelve corpses. It's not easy to count the dead: they are all clawed up with asphyxia, stretched out splinter-nailed trying to crawl somewhere, anywhere, where they can breathe.

"Blast lung," Gainer tells Anna. "Seen this before, in guys who got blown up. The overpressure from the explosion fucked them up inside."

"Does it hurt?"

"Well, uh, not any more than suffocating to death."

"Which is fast," Anna says, using her emotional skills to focus on the positive. Roman would be so proud. "Right?"

Gainer lowers her Maglite. "Sure. Yeah. Faster than dying of burns."

They have to get down into the cave, into the tangled corpses, to haul the survivors out. Anna tries to help. She doesn't know how to use pulse oximeters or administer Ringer's solution, but she's got steady hands, she can shear clothes off burnt skin and hold IV bags. The unsaveable get a little morphine dose, to ease the pain. Not putting them down, exactly: just keeping their suffering in check while they go. One man whose clothes are fried to his back already took morphine from a half-melted medical kit, and the injection ODs him. They give him Narcan, after a quiet argument over whether it's better to let him go. He stabilizes. He might even live.

Here is how you save the nuked:

The ones who will live get lollipops laced with fentanyl.

Broken limbs get splints. Broken hands get bindings. Burns get dressings, to keep them clean: then you swaddle the victim in hot packs and drip them full of Ringer's solution to keep their osmotic pressure up. If they don't get fluids, the slow seep of water out of their bodies will collapse their cells.

(Her mother's bugs come into the cave. They flicker over the dead. Sometimes they pause and settle.)

There are no inhalation burns to treat. Anyone who inhaled combustion products from the fire is dead. The firestorm sucked air out of the cave, which ironically pulled clean air in from crevices further upslope. A lot of people died of soot inhalation anyway.

Rockfall crushed one man's legs. He gets a double field amputation: tourniquets and O-negative whole blood, then a flexible wire Gigli saw that cuts his tibia like butter.

Thirty-six blast lung survivors get oxygen bottles and intubation to keep their sheared lungs working. Ten of those die anyway: nine from respiratory collapse, one when the supplementary oxygen pops his wounded alveoli. Four need to be cannulated for pneumothorax, because their chests are swollen up with blast air. That's where Anna checks out. She hates the *pop* of the needle through the skin, the rush of air afterward.

Her mother's bugs dart deeper into the cave, now urgent—

And lead them to the kids.

They are deaf and scared, but tough as old gum. The youngest is seven months and the oldest is eleven years. Not one of them died. The medics give them water and iodine tablets and snivels, pills for colds and aches, as a placebo. Arîn Tawakuli rubs dirt from their faces and names them and talks to them in Sorani.

Some find their parents. Some don't.

Whenever a casualty is stabilized, the medic dictates instructions for care to Anna, who writes it all down in three languages (English, Sorani, Farsi) on playing cards, which she pins to their clothes. She recognizes some of these faces: suntanned and crinkled transformations of ancient memories. She hopes she is not recognized in turn.

She asks everyone who can talk a couple questions. "Was there anyone in the cave you didn't know? A stranger? Did you speak to anyone you couldn't name? Did you see anything strange?"

A lot of people say yes. They saw a stranger. They saw their dead mom or dad. They saw an angel, they saw God. But nowhere in their memories or in the carnage of the cave does she find any hint of the long serpentine body of an alien zahaki, a khai. Not one single scale of Ssrin.

Maybe Ssrin was lying to her mom about protecting these people. Just straight up fabricated that shit. Anna goes to check on Khaje. Erik is there, his mask pulled back, his bare face tipped up to the sky. He is hard and bright as diamond. He has done a specific, tangible, purely good thing. She sees no satisfaction, no pride. He just wants to do it again, and again, and again.

"No sign of Ssrin," she says.

"No. But we got some people out." He reaches to pull his mask down. "Still think I made the wrong call? Fighting our way up here?"

"I don't think you could've made any other choice."

"Why?"

She tips her head sideways and looks at him: this man who leapt down onto her roof from a helicopter and recognized her. He saw the dread in her eyes, the fear of returning to Ssrin's story—and he looked *relieved*. Why?

"Because you're good. You see the right thing clearly, and then you do it."

"I am an enemy of death." He touches his throat, right in the gap between armor collar and helmet-strapped chin. "I do not accept it as necessary. I fight it where I find it."

"Cool slogan, dude."

He is not bothered. "Iruvage can't really be trying to kill me. He can't. I've been standing right here, he's got a gun, he could waste me any time he wanted. I think it's all some . . . kind of experiment. Clayton said, *See if you can get him to give up.* And Iruvage is playing with me."

She steps around him to stand in his wind shadow. It's a little warmer there. "An enemy of death. Reminds me of books I liked."

He looks curiously at her. "In life's name, for life's sake . . . ?"

"Yeah." She grins. Khaje groans and stirs on her stretcher. "You nerd."

He grins back at her. "Me? Weren't you too old for books like that by the time you learned English?"

"You're never too old to be a wizard."

"I think in those books you *could* actually be too old to be a wizard."

"Shut up," she says. "You virgin."

The whole valley runs down below them, a cataract of wildness. Clear water and white limestone and green, green as far and as deep as Anna can imagine. She has honest to God never been anywhere so beautiful.

"Wow," she says reverently.

The Neolithic revolution began here, farming and all that modern shit. Maybe another revolution will begin. Earth's liberation. Even the galaxy's. Who knows? Right now anything feels possible. Seventy-five souls saved from ground zero of a nuclear detonation. A *little* nuke, but still.

Imagine a world full of Eriks. A world where everyone, always, chased after the slightest hope of good instead of surrendering to cynical calculated trade-off. No more "nothing we can do." No more "not my problem" or "someone should do something." No one who doesn't care.

A world full of Eriks would have no bribery, no bystanders, no prejudice unchallenged, no promises broken. A world full of Eriks would never have abandoned the Kurds.

Of course, a world only *mostly* full of Eriks would be a world full of righteous wars. And Erik does not exist in a world even half full of Eriks. Not even close.

"All this weird light." She waves to the sky. "Nobody's ever set off this many nukes at once before, right? Who knows what'll happen? X-men. Psychic powers."

"I don't know. There've probably been solar storms that did worse."

"Give me this one, Erik."

"Sure." He smiles sadly. "This is when all the dragons and elves wake up, and the magic comes back."

That makes Anna think about stories, and that makes her think about Ssrin. "The Oubliette of Cows," she blurts.

"What?" Erik stares at her. A huge moth, upset by the light in the sky, flutters past and slams into a dead tree.

"It was this oracle Ssrin had. Like a Magic 8 Ball." She grins at his bewilderment. "I'm serious. Listen. It showed Ssrin where to find Blackbird. I bet it showed her some kind of way to get inside."

"And you think that way involved you?"

"Maybe *that's* why Iruvage hasn't killed me yet. He doesn't have an Oubliette. So he's playing it safe, he's trying not to kill anyone who might be important—narratively—to getting the ending he wants."

"Narratively?"

"Just pretend I said *prophetically*. Do you even know *why* Iruvage wants Blackbird so bad?"

"It's a weapon, right?"

"Sure, but—it alters souls." Ssrin said so, she called it *a narrative weapon*, she said *I can smell it on your souls, in the arc of your myths and the dreams of your children!* "Ssrin told me that all her people, all of them, go to hell when they die. Maybe Iruvage thinks Blackbird can . . . fix his soul, somehow. He'd do anything to avoid going to hell, right? Wouldn't you?" She would. "He's going to keep me alive, me and my mom, as long as there's *any* chance we have a clue about Blackbird."

"OH, GOOD THINKING," that huge bored voice says from somewhere directly between Anna and Erik.

Khaje groans in alarm. Erik grabs his rifle.

"EXCEPT YOU FORGOT SOMETHING, ANNA. YOU FORGOT HOW VERY MUCH SMARTER I AM. YOU FORGOT THAT YOU'RE, IN THE END, JUST A BACKUP. SSRIN'S LEFTOVERS. HER WAY, NOT MINE.

"CLAYTON HAS JUST FIGURED OUT HOW TO GET INTO BLACKBIRD. CLAYTON IS ON HIS WAY TO DELIVER BLACKBIRD TO ME. AND NOW . . . I DON'T NEED ANY OF YOU ANYMORE."

"He's coming." Khaje arches and rasps. "He's coming now. Anna. Anna. Anna."

"Mom!" Anna rushes to her.

"Find Arîn. Make her leave." When Anna leans down to her, Khaje grabs her by the ear, clings to that little flap of flesh she made: "Save them. Like you did before. *Make Arîn leave.*"

"I'll get my people ready," Erik says. "We'll hold him off while you go."

"While *I* go?" Anna, already running, shouts back to him. "I'm not leaving my mom! And you aren't leaving her, because without her robots, you're fucking dead!"

※

"Arîn!"

She's loading a mule (where did she get a mule?) with bags of Ringer's solution, but Anna's shout makes her flinch, and she fumbles the bags into the dirt. "What?" she says in English. "What, what is it?"

Anna realizes that Arîn is scared of her. Well, too bad, no time now. Other things to fear.

"He's coming now." Anna is self-conscious of her accent, of the American uniform she wears, of all the ways Arîn is more truly Khaje's daughter than she will ever be. "Listen, my mom's in trouble. Ssrin's machines are killing her. She can't last much longer. She wants you to run."

"What?"

"She wants you to take your peshmerga"—gesturing to the women all around them—"take the survivors, take everyone in the other caves—there are other caves, right?"

"I'm not going to tell you," Arîn says.

"That seems smart. Just take everyone and get out of here. Go east. Go to the PKK or Rojhilat or wherever you can. That fucker won't chase you. He's after Blackbird, we'll keep him busy."

Arîn stares at her. How old is she? Her dark hair, escaped from scarf and ponytail, curls around her face, sticks to her sweaty cheek. She looks so young! This would have been Anna, ten years ago, in a better world. A girl on this mountainside, a jineologist, a fighter. And what was the real Anna doing at this age? What would Anna age twenty-three do if she met another Kurd, age twenty-something, back in New York? Nothing that matters this much. Nothing that could ever matter as much as saving this woman's life, right now.

She grabs Arin by the shoulders and kisses her, hard, right on the brow. "I'm serious. Go. We'll hold him off."

Arin wipes her forehead. "You really don't understand us at all, do you?"

"I really do not," Anna admits.

"This is our home. Not Kurdistan, *this valley*. Tawakul. Nowhere else. Our mothers survived hell to come back here. We all, *all* of us, swore to face death to protect this place. I would rather die in battle here than grow old and die in bed—"

"I know," Anna says quietly. "Remember? I know."

Something in Arîn's eyes changes. Fear, and the courage to set it aside. "Yes," she says. "I know what you did."

"Did my mother tell you?"

"No. She never talks about it. But other people said . . ." Arîn suddenly looks very young. "People say everyone would've died in Anfal if you hadn't . . . done something. Something really, really wrong."

"Well. You make it sound like I sucked the guy's dick."

"No! Just—people here know, Anna. They know what you did."

"Do you know what I did?"

Arîn nods once.

"What do you think?"

"I think," Arîn says, "that you were stupid to trust an Iraqi who could've killed you even if you did what he wanted."

"It was our only chance," Anna tells Arîn: what she is always telling herself.

"Maybe. Maybe."

"Yeah. Maybe. But we survived. My mom couldn't run, and they took her to a camp. But she *survived*.

"Do what we did, Arîn. Survive."

⁓

"Majestics!" Major Erik Wygaunt barks. "We're moving southeast to contact!"

The soldiers leave their lifesaving behind. They shed their tourniquets and medical shears, their bleed kits and hemostatic gauze, their field dressings and SAM splints, their pulse oximeters and chest seals, their bags of saline and sedative and sterile strips. All those will go with the Kurds.

They take up their rifles and grenade launchers and anti-tank rockets. They strip off gas masks and breathe radioactive air so they can settle their night-vision goggles and thermal optics tight against their eyes.

There are seventeen of them left alive. Seven have already been killed by the atmanach or by Iruvage's weapons: Kate Behr and Petrick Bruin by the skull bombs, Ricardo Perez Garcia by Anna and the atmanach, Morris Ware by the big booming gun, Isen D'Auria by the gun, Marc Islip by the gun. Travis Meredith was hit by the atmanach and ran off into the woods. They found him with his skull blown open by a bug bomb.

Of those who survive there are Latasha Gainer, Yousef Ross-Hussain, Javier Collin, Cameron Small, Noah Just, Ethan King, Steven McMichael, Karlí Garpsson, Kasper Jelinek, Hal "Hound" Baker, Erik Wygaunt, Chey "Squats" Kewell, Grover Hawes, Justin Chandler, Jonathan Acepenta, Norman Ospreger, and Nicholas Desgagne. Not one of them will escape death. But then again: who will?

Erik Wygaunt is at their head. He pulls them forward by simple implication: his tactics express what he needs. *I need you at my left, I need you at my right, I need you behind me, I need you ahead.* He does not expect bravery and aggression. He conducts it. The will to violence spreads out from him.

They advance southeast. Toward Iruvage.

In principle it is a spoiling attack: forcing the alien into a fight before he reaches his own preferred ground. A way to buy the Kurds a few more minutes to run.

In principle.

Down from the forest the snakeman cometh.

He is a predator. He is tired of pacing the relentlessly aerobic humans. His ancestors dangled from trees and slithered through crevasses, waiting for pass-ing prey. However fearsome the dark intellect that ticks behind his cuttlefish eyes, however incomprehensible the blade-thin thoughts that whisk the passing seconds into frames of awareness, his soul is still the soul of a hunter. It does not suit him to flee.

Listen: this always happens in the movies. You come to the moment when the soldiers confront the alien, and the alien kills the extras. You read your *Iliad*, and the phalanx shatters before the hero. It is a necessary step in the human story. The apparatus of unsympathetic, illegible collective power must fail, so that the tractable, sympathetic individual hero can go on to make a difference.

Only in real life the squad of faceless goons with the expensive equipment and the expensive training win the fight. They're harder to fit into a story, because they take more explaining than a single person with a motive. But reality doesn't run on stories.

So maybe. Maybe.

Anna's in charge of hauling her mom. When it's time to move (they travel in bounds, dropping to the ground to cover other units) she and Squats pick up the stretcher and run half crouched over. Except for the stretcher, it feels exactly like paintball.

Fog slides down the mountain toward them, ankle-low and rising, as thick as a hotbox in a Hyundai. It's coming up from the ground. The loam is desiccating, giving up its dew. Erik flips his NVGs on and off: no good. He calls to Squats: "Thermal?"

"Yeah. It's hot. Can't see shit." Squats shakes his head: "That's not natural."

"Can't shoot if we're blind," Anna offers.

"Can't run or we're dead," Erik counters. "He has the range and information advantage. We've got to fix him in place and close in or we're—"

He is interrupted by the rapid brush-on-steel sound of suppressed gunfire, and a cry, faint in the forest, but picked up and called down to Erik and Anna: "*CONTACT LEFT!*"

"He's here," Khaje chokes. "He's here now."

Erik raises his rifle.

The fog rolls over them, white and tropical, loading the ferns with dew. It *scratches* at Anna. Like the diatom powder you put out to kill bedbugs: dust so sharp it scores the skin. God, what if it's a chemical weapon? Why didn't they think of that? What if it's nerve gas? Will the MOPP suits work?

The gunfire stops suddenly. Someone shrieks like a man giving birth. The scream ends on an axe-stroke pulse of bass. A wet noise happens across an up-settlingly broad sector of forest.

"Sound off!" Erik calls.

Someone screams: "He's in the goddamn fog!"

Someone else shouts: "No shit!"

"Pull it in," Erik bellows. "Get sight of each other and keep talking! He knows where we are, so sing out, make some noise, we gotta know if he gets to you!"

"Fuck." Latasha Gainer tries her radio: useless. "Now would be a great time for some fucking *air support!*"

Erik grabs Anna by the shoulder. "If your mom can help us, can do anything with those drones, now would be the time."

"Mom. Hey, Mom. Mom—"

"Mehêle azarman bidat," Khaje keeps saying. "Mehêle azarman bidat." Don't let him hurt us. Don't let him hurt us. "Mehêle azarman bidat!" Actually, it could be don't let *her* hurt us. There's no difference between *him* and *her* in Sorani. Maybe she is dreaming that Anna's coming for her family.

Gainer's radio erupts: a shriek of static worse than any screamer Anna's ever clicked on. Gainer screams too, and grabs at her eyes. Her grasping hands crisp and steam. For a moment Anna can see the fine triangular grain of her skin: look, your epidermis is showing. Her eyes are boiling, her brain is boiling, her face is one microwave stigmata—the *air* is boiling in a tunnel that lances through her head—her screaming turns dry and papery, wrung out—

Anna tries to help her. But the moment she gets close the air burns her too, hotter than anything she's ever felt, like there's steam under her skin.

The fog starts to talk. The voice is human, but behind it there are eight serpents, hissing as the gunfire and the shouts rise up:

"*I love genocide.*"

He's there. She *sees* him.

A burning negative in the mist. Air flashes to steam on the sinuous edges of something *mostly* invisible. Bullets strike him. They become sprays of sparks and shrapnel which ricochet into the greenery.

"*You can't imagine the thrill of it,*" Iruvage purrs. Tracers skip off his shoulders. "*Dismembering the last of an entire species? Plunging your heads into its gut and teasing the sweetbreads free? Knowing that nothing in a trillion years will ever taste that meat again. I've only had it once . . . I've always wanted it again.*"

The shadow in the mist extends one arm. Anna has no idea if khai males are bigger or if Iruvage just spends more time in the gym than Ssrin, but the arm is too long and too strong; narrow, though, ape-muscled, like a bundle of steel cables. From the end of that arm a black blade assembles itself in a snap of voxels: the curve of the scimitar cuts itself into an irregular sawtooth, every thorn and prickle growing its own children, fading away into knives and crescents so fine that they merge with the mist.

The sword sings. On the very edge of the blade, just a lick of pilot-light flame, the cut-apart air shines blue-hot.

"*First one to wound me,*" Iruvage purrs, "*will be spared the first head's venom.*"

Anna witnesses the Cultratic Brand.

The aura of invisible atrocity that stains the khai. Anna was immune to

Ssrin's, too close to her to see it: as urgent as a knife in her belly, as powerful as that ripping angry sorrow she felt, so long ago, when she understood what her mother had suffered in the camps. This is not just what you feel when you see someone doing absolute wrong. This is what you feel when they get away with it.

She screams at it exactly the way she screamed at the man in the red beret.

Everybody is shooting now. Bullets draw thin expanding lines through the mist and spatter against his black enormity to stop dead or skip away or turn into threads of lightning that race across his armor and ground in the dirt. Somebody fires a rocket. One of Iruvage's heads darts and it blows up midair and scoops a cavity out of the fog.

Erik fires his rifle straight into the thing. He empties his gun, reloads in less than a second, and resumes.

Between shots he looks at her, once, and points: go.

She shakes her head. He stabs his finger: *go.*

"Fine. Fuck. Fuck!"

Anna lifts her mother to a fireman's carry and starts to run.

※

خەجێ

Khaje's trapped inside herself.

A moth hits a person's nose, sticks in a person's hair. Frantic wingbeats, papery thrash: poor moth, poor Khaje, tangled up. She is not sure which is which.

She can't find her way back into her own head.

For nigh on fifty years Khaje has wandered these woods. Pacing the trails and vaulting the moonlit streams. Sometimes she hunts her memories: looking for that tree where she was happy, that kink in the river where she swam after a smuggling run. Sometimes her memories hunt her, and she runs.

There are better things. Uploading pictures on the awful Korek connection: spring birds, fields of purple flowers, dirty sunburnt faces. Buying phones off kulbars. Cicada song on summer nights. She visited the library in Wasan and made plans for a little library in Tawakul too—with a translated copy of the *Shahnameh*, for the sake of Zoroastrianism, Öcalan's "original Kurdish religion." Her mother was Yazidi, and always insisted that the Yazidis were not Zoroastrian, despite any superficial similarities. Her mother was supposed to give her up, for being the child of a Muslim man. But she stayed with her daughter. More than Khaje could do.

Khaje has had men since her husband. One of them was a PKK fighter, in violation of their celibacy; he came here from Germany, where he had been a commando in the Bundeswehr. He called her *kaktusblüte* and sometimes *fálke.*

She thought maybe he was making fun of her with nonsense. They had sex a few times and she couldn't stop shaking with humiliation afterward, and it made him upset. He didn't understand. Neither did she. The other was a kulbar. He was desperately poor and somewhat ugly and very clever, very kind. He said she was the most precious thing he'd ever touched. Later he got shot by the Revolutionary Guard and they left his body frozen to a mountain. Both times she had to apologize to Serhang, in prayer.

Both men asked: *What happened to him?* And she would say, *He died in the war.* Which was true.

Now there are men dying, dying all around her. Here is a man called Squats shooting at a wraith in the mist, his rifle sight snugged up to his eye, the wraith a-whirl, singing, the song is the blade, the blade sweeps down and goes into the man like a key which unlocks him. What deaths they die, the Americans. If she could upload these Americans to Gerilla TV, would anyone call them martyrs? Dying like *this?*

Iruvage bellows and laughs. He does not like chasing people: when they run away he darts one of his black arrowhead-shaped helmets at them and with a *zzt* like a hornet in her ear the runner's head explodes. His armor emits radar, or something like it, in beams so thin and powerful they set the forest ablaze and cook the marrow inside the bone. She hears Anthony Bourdain saying: parsley, shallots, fresh ground pepper, toasted bread, and don't overdo the cook—

"Erik!" the alien roars. "Clayton wanted you to know! He tricked you out here to die, Erik! Because if you won't obey him, you're worth *nothing!*"

Anna, Anna is still alive— Anna is carrying her away—

Grenades shred the underbrush, fountain dark earth. Iruvage bellows in joy. His sword rebuilds itself in a flash—jagged puzzle pieces reassembling—and suddenly it is long enough to cross meadows.

He flicks a man's head open, face to crown, with the tip of the blade.

CLAYTON//612 MINUTES REMAIN

Clayton slides the recorder across the table, finger on the key. "Okay. Need a toilet break first?"

"No," Chaya says.

"It's time to talk about the outbreak. The reason you abandoned the labs."

"Yes."

"We, uh, we saw some disturbing things in the labs you abandoned."

He imagines that if she had a cigarette, she would put it to her lips, draw, and exhale. "Aside from everyone the Russians massacred? On the slightest suspicion of infection?"

"They didn't massacre Li Aixue."

"No," Chaya says. "But they tried."

THE RUSSIAN PROTOCOL

FIFTH DAY

K + 99 hours

خەجێ

"You told them too much," Ssrin whispers.

Khaje jerks awake. She hadn't meant to sleep—can't afford to—she just put her head down for a moment while sitting beside some of the peshmerga and brooding about the Iranians taking Davoud.

"What?" she mutters. "Told who too much about what?"

"The information about Iruvage and the ship in orbit is too urgent to wait. Colonel Ustinov dispatched helicopters to Abkhazia and a column of armor down the highway to Choman. He's hoping to cross the Iranian border and link up with his allies there."

"Let him. What do we care?"

"Iruvage won't let them go. His pawn needs us in disarray."

"We have his pawn, Ssrin."

"Ah. The translator mishandles chess analogies. I should have said: Iruvage's queen."

"Who?"

"One of the Americans. That's why their response has been so delayed. He's been waiting for me to make my move, betray my collaborators. And now he knows about you."

"Anna. Oh, God, Iruvage knows! He's going to have his agent kill Anna!"

"No. Not kill her. He'll send his atmanach."

"His what?"

So Ssrin explains.

CHAYA 1:7

"It's good to see you out of that suit," Professor Sivakov says. "A clean bill of health, I hear?"

Chaya pastes on a smile. She wants to sleep. "Yes, they gave me an EEG and said I was fine." A brusque Russian pathologist woman electrocuted her with a faulty sensor and ignored her complaints. "Have you tested Professor Huang's theory?"

"We are listening for unusual EM emissions. Nothing yet. Walk with me to the morning meeting?"

She doesn't want to go to anyone's meeting. But it turns out Sivakov's pretty interesting! He's a statistician with a specialization in applied bioinformatics. He was at a conference in China, giving a talk about the use of machine learning in the study of post-transcription DNA modification, when the Kurdistan radio event screamed across the world. The Russians scooped him up and flew him straight into Abkhazia. Chaya doesn't know where that is.

"Oh, we invaded it," Sivakov says. "It's part of Georgia. You should be careful of men like Ustinov. He fought in Chechnya."

"I don't know much Russian history," she admits. "That was like the Americans invading Iraq?"

"Was anyone in Iraq chained between two tanks and ripped in half?"

She's going to say something cutting about Americans and torture, but he tuts to himself: "Ah, but but but, we should not talk about these things. Let us talk science. What do you do?"

"Well, I never finished my—"

"I know." He interrupts her, but at least he's interrupting her self-deprecation. "But what do you *do*?"

"Well, uh, I do black hole polar jets."

"Ah!" His own jet of excitement. "They always puzzled me. Strictly as an observer, of course, I do not know astronomy. But—you have these black holes at the center of galaxies, truly enormous, the mass of millions of suns. You would think that nothing could escape them. Nothing at all. Yet they emit these beams!"

"Millions of light-years long, moving nearly as fast as light—"

"Some of the largest, brightest structures in the universe, sometimes bigger and brighter than their source galaxy—what could possibly create them?"

"Yeah. I wanted to know. But the Philippines isn't a great place for that work. We don't have any astrophysics programs, really. I don't know if I ever could've finished my dissertation, even if I hadn't . . ."

"But you did real work, before you left. What did you discover?"

"Well, there was one dominant model at the time, called SANE, about how magnetic fields gradually accumulate around a black hole, and sync up, and create the jet." She makes a soap-suds-circling-drain motion. "And I didn't think it was right. I thought it was too wimpy. I like a different model, MAD, where the magnetic field doesn't emerge gradually from the disc, it actually *controls* the disc. It drives everything, like a turbine. And the moving plasma makes the magnetic field stronger, and you just keep cranking it up until everything gets really torqued and snarled and then . . . fwoosh!"

"MAD, SANE, fwoosh. Anglophone physics was a mistake."

She laughs.

They talk about his machine learning work: "It will be everywhere in five years," he tells her, quite unhappily. "China will of course be at the forefront, because they are prepared to use data as an extension of state power. Right now they are cracking down on corruption, and an algorithm is harder to accuse of corruption than a person. Conversely the Americans will leave it all to their corporations, who will—"

"Professor, we have no idea what anything will be like in five days. Never mind five years. We could be alien slaves. Or we could be visiting other planets in our new spaceships."

He rubs his lips and frowns. "Yes. Funny. All the futures I imagined a few days ago . . . gone now. History has suffered an intervention."

⁂

The combined teams are too big to fit in a single container now. They sit on aluminum benches, drinking bitter coffee and strong tea from Styrofoam cups. Colonel Ustinov doffs his beret and stands. "We are all cosmonauts and taikonauts now," he says. "We are already giants of history. We will all be played by better-looking people in the movies. Except for me. I am very good looking and will play myself. I know you will all do everything that can be possibly done to understand what is happening here. Now Professor Sivakov will describe our new test protocol."

The plan is to load up hundreds of DSI telemetrized cages with mice, then scatter the cages both around and (using drones as carriers) inside what the Russians insist on calling the Objekt. "In case the drone control radio fails to penetrate the superconducting hull, we will need to run a hardline through the cap with a repeater."

Chaya's hand shoots up. "Excuse me. Excuse me. Aren't you worried that radio inside Blackbird will trigger another—Canadian event?"

Sivakov shrugs. "We've been using short-range radios near the Objekt all this while, haven't we? Our generators and power lines create EM fields. And there was a truly historic electromagnetic event yesterday. None of which provoked any response from the Objekt at all."

"But the hull is a superconductor. It shields the interior. Broadcasting signals *inside* it could—"

"The Canadians were outside when they used the radar."

"But they intended for their radar to pass through the hull. Blackbird is sensitive to that distinction. If we *intend* to signal inside Blackbird, it might trigger a response."

"Is your concern that we are placing a repeater in the interior, or that our external signals will pass through the hull?"

"My concern is that the people using your drones will get sick and die!"

"Maybe. And that response would help us obtain reliable biological data. Which we need more than anything."

She puts her hand down, suddenly unsure of herself. Maybe she has been too cautious. And, after all, Sivakov is a real scientist . . .

Sivakov sees her expression. He looks apologetic. "Miss Panaguiton, your expertise in plasma physics would be very valuable studying the behavior of the anomalous masses surrounding the Objekt. You are welcome to join the special team working on them."

She doesn't, though. She has her own special team.

Blackbird's intention cap, further observations:

Blackbird makes the distinction between intentional and mechanical action with peculiar subtlety. A human hand can push a signal flare through the intention cap; but if a human hand fires a rocket flare, that flare will bounce off.

A drone under real-time remote control can pass through the cap. A drone executing a programmed set of movements bounces off.

If a set of commands is input on a five-second time delay, the drone bounces off.

If the delay is reduced to one second, the drone bounces off.

If the delay is imperceptibly small to the operator, on the order of milliseconds, the drone passes through.

If the delay is on the order of a second or two, but the operator *is not aware* of the added delay and attributes it to signal latency, *the drone passes through.* How is that possible? How can the cap's permittivity depend on the drone operator's perception of control?

Is Blackbird aware of human beings and their actions? If it knows what people are, why doesn't it reach out? If it can perceive intentions, why doesn't it reply?

It reminds Chaya uncomfortably of God.

A column of Spetsnaz BMD-4s roll south down the riverside road, bristling with hundred-millimeter rifles and thirty-millimeter autocannon and anti-tank missiles and active hard-kill defenses. Spetsnaz riding atop their transports watch every incremental tick of the compass. Brand new Azart-P1 radio sets squall with static, still picking up the aurorae hidden behind the low gray sky.

A VDV senior sergeant riding the lead BMD squints up at the cloud. "Hey. Zhenya. Zhenya. Stop fucking your gun and look up there. Do you see that little cunt hair?"

"All I see is a . . . oh. Is that a kite?"

"Maybe it's an American drone?"

"Give me the telescopic sight. Davai, davai, hurry up, give me that." Zhenya lies on his back and scopes the thing. "Ahhh, opachki! You have discovered some kind of fucked-up . . . bird . . ."

High in the sky it crawls across his eyelid. Like the premature fetus of a Nazgûl impregnated by a stealth bomber. It trails a black radian, a tether pointing east-southeast.

The sudden waterfall of volition in Zhenya's mind—decisions about what that thing in the sky might be, what needs to be done about it—pulls the atmanach down on him. It is the opposite of volition: a bulge of pure reaction, a synthetic dimple where there should be the well of a soul, coursing through the landscape of the areteia like a roach meandering through stained cupboards by the waving of its antennae.

It abominates downward, following the thread of awareness that connects it to Zhenya's mind. It passes through the rifle scope, into his eye, into his soul. Like a stent, it inflates.

Whatever was in him pops out.

He drops the telescopic sight. He spasms. His mind, severed from the kernel of dualist power that has accompanied and cajoled it all his life, reflexes into something merely real.

There is a condition called apophenia. It is universal to the human mind, but it is particularly acute in conditions like paranoia. It is the tendency to see connections between unrelated things, to perceive meaning in nothing. Apophenia is a delusion.

Zhenya experiences the precise opposite. Call it exophenia: the movement outside meaning. He suddenly perceives the lack of connections between things. He is suddenly relieved of an irrational conspiracy that had preoccupied his mind since birth. He is *not* deluded. He has been reluded. He is supersane.

He is surrounded by monsters.

⁂

Afternoon meeting, to the sound of helicopters.

"A notable theme in all our measurements of the Objekt," Sivakov says, "is the amount of noise in the sensor channels. We observe constant low-level jitter in our field sensors and SQUIDs. What these artifacts may represent is—"

"Pink noise!"

Chaya whirls in horror.

She's here. She broke her promise.

And she's not wearing her suit.

"Pink noise?" Sivakov repeats. "Welcome to the team, Professor Li."

Chaya looks for Professor Huang, but he's not looking back at her. He's beaming! He's so happy to see his wunderkind that he doesn't think about what she could be doing to the rest of them. His prodigy has returned! May her presence transform all!

Li says, "Yes. The structures the Canadians detected inside the hull are consistent with a pink-noise spectrum."

"Pink noise. You mean one-over-f noise? Electrical static? What about it?"

"Pink noise is *not* static." A weird illusion of acoustics between the rows of containers funnels Li's voice right to Chaya's ear: clearer than helicopters, louder than Sivakov's microphone. "Static is white."

"What's the difference?" one of the Russians asks: the pathologist who electrocuted Chaya. "Why does static have a color?"

"Any signal has a frequency, right? If it's high frequency, it's blue or violet. It sounds like a shriek. If it's low frequency, it's red, it sounds like a hum or a drone. White noise is static at random frequencies. Just as much high as low. And since high frequencies carry most of the energy, you get loud, discordant static."

She mimes plucking something from the air. "It's like drawing money from a purse full of twenty- and hundred-dollar bills. You draw the same number of twenties as hundreds, but most of the total *value* you get is in the hundreds. You see?"

"I don't see," Sivakov says, sighing, "what this has to do with our work—"

"You can't see it, but you can hear it. Pink noise is happening right now." Aixue poses up on her toes, her hand to her ear, Tinkerbell listening for intruder alarms.

Everyone hushes. The AC units and generators hum along in the background. Wind rushes through the trees around the meadow. A helicopter chops east.

There is nothing else.

"Yes, that noise." Aixue smiles. Chaya has an involuntary, terrified image of her body shedding madness, tiny flakes of insanity blowing off her scalp, settling invisibly on all of them to melt. "Natural background noise is usually a pink-noise spectrum. The roar of a waterfall, or the gusts of wind in a storm, or the patter of rain on your window. People find all those sounds soothing, right? They have kind of a special rightness.

"That's because pink noise has power balance. Higher-frequency events are more powerful, but they're also more rare. You get a lot of red for each drop of blue. A lot of hum for each shriek. A lot of little raindrops for each big one. Little things happen more often than big things. The pink noise wallet gives you a lot more twenties than hundreds, see? So you get the same total *value* from each denomination."

She drops a hand from her ear and grins at the crowd. "And that's why it's pink. Mostly red, a bit green, and just a little blue. They mix out to pink."

"Oh!" Nakyanzi Sophie says. "You're talking about flicker noise! We have to screen that out of the sound system at the dancehall."

"Yes!" Li nods, hummingbird-quick. "Pink noise is in speakers at dancehalls.

And in nerve activity in our brains. And in the emissions of a quasar millions of light-years away. And the distribution of notes in music. And in population densities in ecology. And heart rhythms. And the way that stock markets and rivers rise and fall. All over the universe, the background sound of certain complicated things happening seems to be pink noise.

"And *all* the Blackbird data is full of it. As if the meaning we should be looking for is *not* in the content of the signal, but in the fine texture. In the noise."

Chaya gets a shiver of delight, spiritual rather than fleshy, but physical anyway, for the flesh is the vessel of the soul. "What does that mean?"

"Nothing," Sivakov says. "Pink noise is a trivial mathematical artifact, like the golden mean. It's a signature of common statistical processes, but it's not some secret code left behind by God—"

"God is exactly the problem!" Li darts toward Sivakov like she's passing partners at the dance. "Imagine that God is manipulating our instruments. We are *not* actually observing Blackbird. We do not even see or touch it. We are observing its transformations of whatever we send to it. Even its physical form is a transformation of mathematical fields—the electromagnetic field, the strong nuclear field, the gravitational field, the lepton and baryon fields. It is an artifact *created by transformations of whatever it finds*. Of course we cannot detect this in the data, because the data is being manipulated. But if the mechanism used to manipulate the data left a signature, a fingerprint, that fingerprint might be found in the noise!"

Sivakov *tsks*. "The fact that pink noise appears in so many divergent forms is evidence it's *not* the result of one meaningful process."

"If the processes that produce pink noise are so common," Li counters, "why aren't there any unified mathematical models of its origin?"

"There are simple means to produce pink noise. I can write you a program in a minute. Use a finite difference equation. Or just take ordinary random white noise and—"

"That's an approximation! Like drawing pixels around a center point and calling it a circle! Sure, you can get pink noise from a phase-locked loop, or a hundred other practical sources. But you can't say *why* all these different systems produce pink noise. There's an underlying connection that mathematics hasn't yet explained—"

Sivakov's face is also starting to fill up with pink noise. "You can't just deify things you don't understand, you—you *theoretician!*"

"We can look for commonalities which unify seemingly disconnected problems!"

"Pink noise 'unifies disconnected problems' the way that blood unifies crime scenes! It's just a byproduct! It explains nothing!"

"Excuse me." The pathologist sighs. "How is any of this relevant to the Objekt?"

"It is *not*," Sivakov snaps. "The Objekt is a superconductor. No one should be surprised that electrical noise turns up in an electrical superconductor!"

"Blackbird is a superconductor *because* of the process generating the noise! A self-organized critical transition in the electron states could create—"

"Oh, and now we're on to self-organizing criticality! Please. Pink noise is a fascination for—for social psychologists and undergraduates! It is a predictable byproduct of chaos. A noise spectrum in which powerful events are correspondingly rare? Why, it's almost like less energetically favorable events occur less often! What a mystery! What enigma could produce such a spectrum? Only *everything!*"

Chaya decides, spitefully, that pink noise is important. She has this thing about old men telling young women their findings are unsurprising.

"The most startling thing in all of science," Li says, into the shocked silence, "is the relationship between physics and number theory. As if the most abstract reaches of pure mathematical reason can explain reality. And the chaos of reality can also guide our quest into the purest forms of reason. Why should the two be connected? It is, I feel, the only question whose answer might tell us not just *how* the universe exists, but *why*: why there must be existence rather than nothingness."

"But that is not the question here!" Sivakov shouts. "The question is not why the *universe* exists, Li, it is why the Objekt exists, why it is here."

"The two questions," Li says, "are exactly the same. I have to get back to my work."

And she leaves.

⁓⁓⁓

Colonel Ustinov sits in the dark of his command vehicle, watching video from the night the Iranians died.

A geyser of sparks jets from the hatch of an Iranian tank, like someone inside is trying to drill into the bank vault of the world. Then the geyser leaps down the tank column, one single spirit of tank death dancing from vehicle to vehicle. It is an illusion produced by sequenced explosions, but a very convincing one. Ustinov has seen those sparks everywhere from Chechnya to Iraq. Burning men tumble out of the hatches and stagger around in the ponderous, strangely dignified agony he remembers from the streets of Grozny. When you are burning alive you cannot do much more than shuffle.

He must learn how to fight the thing which did this. The Chinese say it hunts and kills invisibly—which is good, isn't it? Because if it has to strike from stealth, it fears human weapons.

He starts the video again.

"Sir," his XO calls. Major Vylomov. "I have a report for you."

"Captain Nizmatinov's breakout unit?"

"Not yet, sir." Vylomov pauses: bad news. "There have been reports of an explosion from down valley. A helicopter should radio a report shortly."

Fuck. "What is it, then?"

"It is Corporal Bugorski from the drone unit. He reported an anomaly. Captain Volkov thought it should be escalated to you."

Ustinov clicks his phone off. "He was flying drones inside the zero perimeter?"

"Yes, sir. Deploying mice."

The zero perimeter is the "rectum," the area past the intention cap, inside the Objekt itself. The first perimeter contains the Chinese and Russian labs, which form a sort of space station, like the McDonald's play-spaces into which highly motivated toddlers sortie to shit themselves. The second perimeter is the military cordon around those labs. The third perimeter is the valley itself.

"What has he found?"

"He reports that his drone 'will not fucking fly right,' sir. He believes the PID software is fucked up."

Ah! Just one of these problems. What a relief! So far this pizdets deployment has been fuck from an ass, to quote his drill instructor (now terrorizing the other corpses in the river Neva, into which he disappeared, mid-bender, one winter night). But some problems never change. The PID, the software that stabilizes and controls their off-the-shelf quadcopter drones, is *always* fucked up.

He likes Pashka Bugorski, one of the new soldiers, conscripted after the disaster in Georgia and the 2007 reforms that were meant to end dedovshchina: the ritual hazing that cost the army so many men to suicide. It was a terrible waste. Duty runs two ways. Soldiers must obey, but in exchange they earn the right to protection and honor.

Pashka was chosen for his excellent PlayStation skills to fly Turbo Ace drones loaded with mouse cages. The drones only have a one-kilo lift capacity, so they need their batteries changed constantly. This is a possible point of exposure and it worries Ustinov.

"Vylomov?"

"Sir." The half-Koryak giant stoops to look inside. His helmet sits nearly two meters off the ground. Sometimes Ustinov wonders if his meticulous cleanliness is a genetic trait of Koryaks, inherited, somehow, from the survivors of smallpox.

"Secure Corporal Pashka's drone inside a glove box and have it disassembled. And order him to report for regular medical examinations."

Vylomov salutes and starts to leave. Ustinov thinks of something. "And, Major?"

"Sir?"

"While we all miss female company, remind Pashka that our charges must trust us. It's inappropriate to brag about a woman's beauty after an emergency decontamination. Especially not if you brag so loudly it reaches your colonel."

Vylomov laughs. "Tak tóchno, comrade Colonel."

⚬

CHAYA 1:8

"Aixue," Chaya says. "You have to stop. You're infected."

The motion-controlled lights in the materials lab have gone out. Aixue's face is illuminated only by the glow of her monitor: a frowning incandescent thought in a plastic suit.

A render of Blackbird fills her screen. There is a shape wrapped around the hull, a mathematical anemone in multiple dimensions. The intersections between that shape and the hull *almost* look like the patterns on Blackbird's skin . . .

"Not right," Aixue says. Without moving a single joint of her spine, she begins to type.

In a second window on her monitor, Chaya catches the fuzzy shape of a quadrotor drone. Behind it is a pixelated webcam image of a pink-bronze complexity, like an endoscope image of a robot's colon.

It's a camera feed from inside Blackbird.

Chaya lunges for the monitor, finds the switch, and clicks it. Aixue jerks in surprise. "Hey!" They struggle for a moment, gloves rolling across the keyboard, making a satisfying little glissando of plastic. "Hey, let me go!"

"You told me it was signal from inside Blackbird that spreads the disease! And now you're live-streaming the interior? Now you're coming to meetings without your suit on! Mama Mary, you have to be kidding me! Do you even believe your own theories?" She pulls Aixue away from the monitor, hard. "*You might have infected everyone in this fucking camp!*"

"What? I had to report my findings—Professor Huang would've wanted me to collaborate with the rest of the team—" Li reaches up, paws at her helmet, and gasps. "Oh my God. I went out there without my suit?"

"Yes! Yes you fucking did!"

"On the way out, I went to the airlock, they washed my suit and helped me take it off . . . I was thinking about the pink noise, about how pink noise is deeply connected to fractal geometry, how Blackbird is completely fractal . . . and then I just went to the meeting." A gray casket settles over her face, absolute bleak self-hate: "I'm an idiot. I should be shot."

"You had better pray," and she does mean *pray*, "that you're right about how this infection spreads. Because if you're wrong, you just exposed everyone."

A helicopter thunders low overhead.

Aixue stares at her reflection in the dead monitor: infinite recession of her helmet echoing the monitor echoing her helmet on forever.

"Chaya. I'm afraid. What's happening to me?"

"You know exactly what's happening! You told me yourself, the Canadians were infected by receiving signals from inside Blackbird! You stuck your head inside, now *you're* infected!"

"But I'm not. I'm not! No seizures, no anxiety, no muscle tics, no heart arrythmia! I feel great! I'm not lying to you!"

"I didn't say you were lying. I said you made a mistake."

Aixue looks back at her math. A tremendous yearning. She wants to shoot off into it like a mouse down a hole.

"Hey!" Chaya snaps. "Hey, you need to stop!"

"I can't," Aixue says. "I keep thinking about how disappointed everyone will be if I don't solve this. And how there are aliens attacking us, which means my family's back home in the dark, in a city that can't survive without power. And I can't do anything for them except work on math. Do you know how useless I was before I started math? I was a compulsive liar as a child. Pseudologia fantastica, they called it. I wasn't even good at it. In grade two my mom bought me the largest size uniform, this awful polyester track suit, because she thought it would last me until grade six and I would grow into it. I only had to wear it for the flag raising ceremony on Mondays but I hated it so much. So I started making up stories about it. I said it was a hand-me-down from my past life and that I had been reincarnated like a Buddhist. I would tell my class stories about how, on vacation, I'd gone to the Temple of Heaven, and I found an elevator under the Heart of Heaven right at the middle, and it went down to a cistern under the city, and there was a special altar, and I put my bingtang hulu treat on the altar and asked to see a mermaid, and she came up out of the water and talked to me and gave me a comb from her hair. Nobody called me out on it, nobody laughed at me, but they all must've known I was making things up. Why did I ever think people believed me? Then, when I was eight, I was on spring festival and I got stung by a hornet. And I went into anaphylactic shock and died for a little while. And afterward I realized I was really, really good at math. I think I always had been, but I never realized it until I saw the patterns while I was dead. I saw the patterns and I just knew *exactly* what they meant, and I had to find a language to show other people. It wasn't about me understanding the patterns; I already understood them, I just had to share them. Did you know that when Mandelbrot discovered his famous set it was a complete shock to mathematicians? People knew about z maps to z squared plus c, but they didn't know it was so *beautiful*. Mandelbrot invented fractal dynamics not by discovering the set but by demonstrating its beauty in a way people could see. I wanted to do that. So I started doing math and I stopped lying. No, that's a lie, I didn't stop. But I was better about it. I *knew* when I was lying. You can't lie usefully in math. You can't get anything done with lies. It's great that way. So the way I handle problems, the way I handle anything, is I go straight to the math and I . . . I just stay with it, until I've found the truth."

Softly Chaya says: "What do I do with you, Aixue?"

"Well." Aixue tries to wipe her tears, and hits her visor. "Um. If you're worried . . . if you think the video stream is going to infect people . . . shouldn't you check up on the drone operators?"

⁂

A warrant officer and his assistants take Corporal Pashka's drone apart in a biolab glove box.

"Ah," the warrant officer says when he pulls the main computer from its housing. "Misprinted circuit board." The copper tracks that connect components on the board have been duplicated, as if the etching process was performed twice before the final UV burn. Some of the pin connectors have dwarf copies. The CPU socket is crusted in a dark mass, like over-applied thermal paste.

"Piece of shit." He sighs. "Fucking thing should have shorted out . . . the chokes must be working hard." He chips at the dark mass with a screwdriver. "This explains the engine over-rev and the battery problems. It's carrying too much weight."

"If it's just a hardware defect," Pashka says, "then I wasted the Colonel's time. I just imagined the change? There was nothing wrong with the gyro low-pass filter at all?"

"Pashka, Pashka, calm down. We'll look at the low-pass filter, okay? But the whole thing is so fucked up, so totally defective . . ."

"What if the Objekt did something to it? Maybe it infected this thing with nanomachines!"

"There can't be nanomachines, Pashka. They'd show up on the Raman lidar."

"Excuse me?" It takes them a moment to pick up the thin sound of Chaya Panaguiton, shouting through her suit. "Excuse me, the duty sergeant told me you had a problem with a faulty drone? I wanted to ask if the operator was feeling all right?"

"Fuck off, дура!" Pashka barks. "Mind your own shit! You got me in trouble with the colonel, you Black whore!"

The warrant officer guffaws in shock. Chaya looks slightly away, as if she has not heard, which of course she has: this time and many times before.

The circles of skin around Pashka's eyes, all that shows beneath the white plastic of his respirator, flush red. "I don't know why I said that. I am sorry. I must be . . . I am sorry. Miss, I am sorry."

"Better report *that* to the medical observer," the warrant officer mutters.

"Climb up an ass!" Pashka snaps.

The warrant officer continues poking at the damaged drone. Pashka paces back and forth, his abnormal frontal lobe activity spreading, spreading higher.

<hr />

خه‌جی

A Spetsnaz sentry stops Khaje outside the dust-colored command tent. His porcine gas mask muffles a crisp young voice. "Business?"

"I'm here to trade information for David Qasemi's freedom."

"There has been an attack on Captain Nizmatinov's breakout column. The colonel is in an emergency conference. You cannot go in."

"Was the column attacked by a flying alien that drives men insane?"

After that they let her past, minus her rifle (her Glock gets a check and a nod). Warrant Officer Mousavi and Master Sergeant Zhang are in a huddle with Colonel Ustinov and his giant second-in-command. Mousavi looks very serious. Zhang looks weirdly pleased.

Ustinov's smile has tarnished to a weary tightening of the lips. "Miss Sinjari. You know something about the thing that attacked my men?"

"I do. What happened?"

"According to these reports? A thing without form descended from the sky and drove one of my men so insane that he climbed into the command vehicle, shot the crew, and turned the main gun on his comrades!"

"It is an alien weapon called an atmanach." She can't pronounce this well; possibly no one can. "Release Captain Qasemi, and I'll tell you everything I know about it."

"My men are dying and you want to trade horses?"

"I would prefer to trade horses when your men weren't dying," Khaje says. "But I do want the horse."

Everyone looks at Mousavi. His mustache rolls over several expressions of discomfort. "He reports everything he sees to an enemy alien. An alien who is the enemy of the alien *you* spy for. Why do you want him released?"

Because those who make deals with devils must stick together. Because without him, she has no idea what Iruvage is planning to do to Anna. Because she convinced him to do the right thing and confess, and she doesn't want to see him shot for it.

"He's our prisoner," she says. "You are our guests here. This is Kurdish soil. And surely you can . . ." If only she were more confident in her English. ". . . understand why I, in particular, would want to keep his custody? Given our . . . shared experience?"

"Is there anything to stop this alien weapon from coming right here and killing all of us? If you have some way to stop it—"

"No. I don't. I just know it tears out . . ." Will anyone believe this? "It tears out your soul."

"God protect us," Mousavi says in Farsi. He believes her.

"And why," Ustinov asks, "does this cause one of my men to start killing his comrades?"

"People without souls are . . . allergic to the rest of us. They see . . ."

Clarity, Ssrin said. The atmanach removes a veil, a necessary lens, that prevents you from seeing the world as it really is. Exophenia. Fatal supersanity. Those touched by the atmanach cannot tolerate the words or actions of another human being. Ssrin said: *Error accumulates between the physically determined state and the volitional outcome . . .*

"I don't know the words," Khaje says in frustration.

Ustinov actually smiles encouragingly. "We can find an interpreter—"

Khaje blinks.

When her eyelids rise the dark intestine-whip of the atmanach is wrapped around Ustinov's head and throat. Zhang shouts "Câo fuck mother fuck!" and flings himself to cover. Kamran Mousavi falls on his back and cries to God.

It is *there*. Pungent with a scent that Khaje knows, instantly, is the boiling-glue separation of soul from mind. Sweetened chlorine and savory pine. The atmanach dwells upon Ustinov's head, jellyfish crown, pulsing slowly. It makes her cramp: inverted antiwomb, unbirthing the man, undoing the thongs that adhere his soul to his self.

She goes for her Glock.

The atmanach snaps away.

Ustinov falls on his back. His limbs jerk. He kicks out the map table's legs, knocks it down on his chest, spilling the map across him. When he can make a fist, he tears the paper off his face and tries to get up.

"Get away from him!" Khaje barks. "Everyone get out!"

He looks up at her and whatever he sees breaks his mind like no horror in Georgia or Chechnya ever did. Like Ustinov has just seen his wife, beautiful in black, placing his living daughters into concrete mixers, to be buried alive, to satisfy the particular fetish of a billionaire to whom she has been secretly concubined, the whole and entire time they have been married, and even before. A betrayal at once alien and most unbearably intimate.

Behind the fear in his eyes Khaje sees a simmering humiliation. He is lessened by what he sees. She has made a fool of him.

"Vot eto pizdets," he says. "Vylomov! *VYLOMOV!*"

He reaches for his sidearm. Khaje chambers a round. "Don't move. Kamran, take his pistol. You, outside! Bring tranquilizers! Bring rope!"

"Drop it!" Mousavi barks. He's aiming at her. "Drop the pistol!"

"He's been touched—"

"He's not violent!"

"He's going to be! Get your medics!"

Colonel Ustinov draws his sidearm very slowly. His eyes jerk once to Kamran. "So I am hit. So I go insane now. I start hurting my men? No. I won't."

"Drop it!" Mousavi screams, as Khaje says, "Don't do it, Ustinov. Close your eyes. Close your eyes! Don't—"

Later she will realize that every word she said must have been the worst thing he'd ever heard.

"We were wrong," Ustinov says. "It is already out. I was wrong, I was wrong. We are all sick. VYLOMOV!"

Khaje cannot shoot him. It feels like something Anna would do.

She lunges for him to try to get his gun and Ustinov fires, aiming quite coolly not at her but at some desynchronized ghost of her, a different Khaje making different choices. When she grabs his gun hand he shrieks like a boy hiding under his bed and smashes her in the face with the pistol. They struggle, Ustinov grunting rhythmically, spasming harder every time Khaje touches him, Khaje trying to get the gun away from him one-handed while keeping her own pistol ready, but he is so strong, his pistol is so tight in his fist, it's going to go off, it's going to go off pressed into her body and she will never see Anna—

Her gun goes off. His head snaps back.

It is the first time she has ever killed anyone. Plenty of times she has *tried* to kill people with guns. But this is the first time she has definitely succeeded.

Mousavi fires at her across the fallen table, vengeful, and a shrill hypersonic gnat tears out of her hair and strikes the bullet so that it snaps past her face and goes through the far wall of the shelter.

He stares at her in shock. She stares right back.

Major Vylomov barges into the makeshift tent. "What is happening?"

He sees Khaje atop his dead colonel. His long face crumples.

Mousavi grabs her and forces her to her knees. Vylomov barks orders. Zhang looks impressed: she has killed an officer! She can't hear anything they're saying. The gunfire has deafened her.

Ssrin, she thinks. Ssrin? Are you there?

Did I have to do that?

⁂

THE EATEN ONE

Ustinov grunts and bites the gag.

Vodka stings the cuts on his ass. He is seventeen and dressed in rags, because they took his uniform away on his first night in the barracks. He is a new conscript, a dukh, a ghost.

They told him that if he balanced on the four legs of this overturned table with a bayonet under his chin while they beat him with a pool cue for three hours and then poured vodka into the wounds then he would no longer be a ghost. He would become a real soldier. And he is going to do it. He is going to be a real soldier and not a dukh.

But he's too weak. He's too weak. His arms tremble. His legs burn. And his back, his broken ruptured boiling back—the pool cue whips down again and again! He thought it would be over by now but every moment is longer than the last. He's going to fall, the bayonet will go through his chin and pin his tongue to his palate!

This is hell, Ustinov thinks. I'm in hell.

"Oh, no," says the dedy whipping him. "This is just torture. You suffered through this because you wanted to be a real soldier, didn't you? A real soldier like the one who did this to you. Real soldiers are men who torture dukh boys. Soon this part will be over, and you will graduate. You will travel forward across the terrain of yourself to the place you have prepared.

"Hell begins when *you're* the one holding the pool cue."

CHAYA 1:9

"Colonel Ustinov is dead," the giant Russian soldier says. "His killer has been detained. I am in command now."

It's stiflingly hot in the BMD's troop compartment. Chaya was not pleased to hear the soldiers outside refer to it as "the coffin." She, Professor Sivakov, Professor Huang, and that jerk Russian pathologist (an older woman with tangled blond hair, a crisp white vest, and a Soviet-housing-bloc disregard for personal space) are jammed in here facing down Vylomov.

"Colonel Ustinov said that we were all infected." Vylomov's long face reminds Chaya of the giant from *Twin Peaks*: it is happening again, it is happening again. "They were his final words. I have postponed any further evacuation flights or breakout attempts."

The Russian pathologist protests that they don't even know there *is* an infection. Huang Lim complains that there are still no signs of electromagnetic emissions. Sivakov grumbles about the need to complete the mouse bioassay.

Chaya decides to tell the truth.

"Ustinov's wrong. We're not infected. The disease is carried by information. Most of us haven't been exposed. The drone operators, maybe. The mice inside. But not us."

Everyone looks at her. Vylomov sits forward. "You know this how?"

"Process of elimination." She can't explain it without snitching on Aixue. But she tries. "If Blackbird isn't using EM to alter our brains, then I think a mind-altering, informational effect is the only option which remains."

"Hardly." The pathologist snorts. "Mind-altering? What about the sheep? What about the radar set? More than minds were altered!"

"They aren't human. It does something different to humans."

"You are talking about an infohazard," Vylomov says.

They all stare at him. "A what?" the pathologist says.

"A contagious, harmful idea." He's completely serious, Chaya realizes. "Many soldiers read military fiction, because they think it will prepare them to face war. I am wiser. Disease is the most dangerous enemy in the world. So I read fiction about disease. An infohazard is a disease of the mind."

"Sure," Chaya says tentatively. "Infohazard. That's a good word."

"Where *is* Professor Li?" Vylomov asks. "I was told she had a theory about the Objekt."

Sweat beads on Huang's bald spot. "She was at our afternoon conference, where she reported on her line of investigation. She probably sees no reason to interrupt her work again."

"I see very good reason to interrupt her. I want to be briefed directly." Vylomov's gas mask dangles like a second, larval face beneath his chin. His eyes are hard with a dead man's burdens: all of Ustinov's fears, released unto him. "I asked for reports of any erratic behavior. Professor Li's interruption certainly qualifies."

Huang glares at Sivakov. Sivakov shrugs.

The Russian pathologist leans forward, her elbows digging into Chaya's kidneys. "The entire first group died of seizures, or Kurdish gunshots, within twelve hours of their exposure. If Li had been exposed, we would already—"

"Seizures," Vylomov says. "Curious. The first symptom of attack by the alien vampir is also a seizure."

"What?" Chaya says. "Vampir? There's a vampire now?"

"A weapon employed by the aliens who bombed the sky. It induces seizures and violent paranoia. It played a role in Colonel Ustinov's death."

Huh. The Canadians were exposed to Blackbird. They started having seizures. Then the Kurds shot them. Now this alien vampire touches Russian soldiers. They start having seizures. Do people shoot them?

Is that what happened to Ustinov?

"Perhaps Li *is* having seizures," Sivakov says. "Perhaps focal activity in her temporal lobes is creating a false sense of insight. Perhaps she needs an EEG."

"An EEG is pointless without a baseline," the pathologist says. "Listen to me. You military men, you know that people behave wildly under stress. Well, we are all under stress. In the past day I've seen short tempers, selfishness, petty theft, inappropriate sexual advances, and risky behavior. I have also seen heroic concentration, selfless donation of expertise, and cooperation across nationalities and languages. Who knows what is appropriate and expected behavior? Contact with an unknown, dangerous alien presence would be enough of a challenge. But look up at the sky, Major! We are all afraid for our families, our cities, our world. No one has ever worked like this before."

Now Chaya feels bad for thinking the pathologist's a jerk. What was her name again? Kuzesov? Kuzetsnova?

"I agree," Huang Lim says. "The world has become very traumatic, Major Vylomov. Can you blame Professor Li for fixating on her work? She has control of her math, she has nothing to fear from it. Out here . . . well. I have seen her go into her math for comfort before. She always returns with gifts."

"But she is not *useful*!" Sivakov tugs his own lapels in frustration. "We need basic data, Lim! We cannot simply math our way into an idea of what the Objekt does. Mathematics can construct elegant possibilities, but it cannot distinguish which of these possibilities is true. To select between theories, we need evidence. Not calculation."

Vylomov sits there impassively for a moment, hidden behind the second face of his loose gas mask. He makes a decision.

"I want the mice brought out and dissected now," he says. "Complete the bioassay. Determine how the infection spreads. I am going to send teams of my spetsnazovets into the lab complex to watch over the work. And if Professor Li does not report to me promptly, I will send a team to secure her."

⁂

"The mice won't be dangerous," Chaya frets. "Right? If Li's right, the disease spreads when Blackbird transforms *information* . . . mice aren't information, are they?"

"I don't know," Huang Lim murmurs. "It depends very much on what you define as information. So far the infection has spread by radar returns. I was sure it had to be electromagnetic . . ."

"She went in there and she hasn't made anyone else sick. So the mice won't either, I don't think." They are at the refrigerator in one of the Chinese dorm containers, talking into a wall of C100, Wahaha, and bottled green tea. "What do you think Vylomov is going to do with her?"

"Nothing. We can't let Vylomov interrupt her."

"Why?" She has the same thought, but she feels guilty about it.

"Because she's in one of her working trances. Look, being a mathematician is not like in the movies. You don't overhear your uncle murmuring a pearl of traditional wisdom to your aunt and realize it solves your problem and shout *You are a genius, uncle*, and tear off to a week of nonstop work and a Fields Medal. You have to take a long time setting everything up. You have to read and work and check your work and make sure it is all consistent. And then, if you are lucky, when everything is piled up underneath you and you stand at the top of all your preparation, *then* you can make that incredible leap. Now, Li Aixue makes those leaps more than anyone I have ever known. She knows as much math as Hilbert and maybe in the long run she can do as much as Gauss. But she proceeds by avalanche, understand?"

"No?"

"She, ah, she gets all her stones aligned, by which I mean her preparation, her ideas and so forth. And then she sort of . . . has an insight, which starts an avalanche, which she rides through a series of discoveries all the way to the end. And if you grab her mid-avalanche, she gets lost."

Chaya never felt like she was on an avalanche in grad school. But she certainly felt lost. "How lost?"

"She can't start up where she left off. She has to go back and pile up all the stones again and start over from there. And sometimes the leaps don't come as easily as they did the first time. Usually this frustrates her, and she decides it's her fault, she's useless, she's failed to discern the truth. This is the problem with mathematicians who work by intuition and insight—they cannot just plod along steadily, they expect things to come in great flashes, and if those flashes are interrupted they don't know what to do. They are used to flying, so ordinary step-by-step work feels like being broken. This is why I've tried to keep her away from Collatz! She would eat herself alive!"

All this to say, oh, she's a delicate specimen. Here Chaya was thinking: We can't take her to Vylomov because Vylomov will have her shot. "But she is working, right? She *is* doing something?"

"Oh, yes. I've seen what she's saving to her network drive. She has a theory. 'A faithful functor to the generalized primes with the primes as an attractor implies that unbroken symmetry phases that lack $1/f$ noise must converge to a spontaneously broken state that exhibits $1/f$ noise.' Isn't that marvelous?"

"How, uh . . . is that useful?"

"She's trying to prove that Blackbird causes systems to spontaneously break symmetry. Moving from chaos toward order. Like in self-organized criticality."

Okay, intriguing. She knows about symmetry breaking from cosmology. But: "What is self-organized criticality?"

"It's a property of some chaotic systems. They spontaneously organize themselves—like different instruments falling into rhythm, or randomly firing neurons forming clusters that activate together. No one knows exactly why it happens. We know that one telltale sign of self-organized criticality is scale invariance—when the parts look the same as the whole. If your cells looked like tiny little Chayas, you'd be self-similar."

"Or if your eyeballs were full of tiny little eyeballs . . . ?"

"Yes. Exactly! Fractal behavior! Which is, of course, a generator of pink noise!" He laughs. "See? She's on to something. The trouble, as usual, is getting her to explain it to anyone."

"The trouble isn't . . . compulsive lying?"

"No!" He looks shocked. "Lie? Her? She's the best student I've ever had. Never even missed a meeting. You might catch her in a Lie group, but never a lie, ha-ha. She's always had a gift for truth."

Not a gift. Gifts are things people give to you. Li Aixue feels like she has had something taken away from her instead. Scrubbed, cleaned, polished, reduced but not destructively: elegance that remains when nothing else can be subtracted . . .

(Later it will agonize Chaya to realize how close she was, here, to the beginning of an answer.)

"Are you religious, Chaya?" Huang Lim asks.

"Very."

"I'm not." He smiles. "Please pray for her for me."

<hr>

The mice in the Russian cages scurry, feed, and sleep.

Implanted sensors transmit data to the cage computer. Transdermal imaging acquires oxygen and glucose concentrations.

Some of the mice live inside the Objekt's hot, dark entrance chamber. Some are control mice, caged at a safe distance outside.

Some of the control mice receive data piped from inside the Objekt: call it Objekt TV. Sounds, temperature, electromagnetic signals, even a gas mix that mimics the not-quite-Earthlike atmosphere within. These mice are not *directly* exposed to Blackbird, but they are designed to experience Blackbird-like conditions, to filter out possible causes of any strange result.

Every datum that can be obtained without physical samples is constantly monitored.

The only effect anyone's noticed so far is a slight increase in body mass among mice exposed to Blackbird's environment—whether directly or through control-group mimicry. The theory is that this is water retention due to stress.

"Pull them out," Dr. Kuznetsova orders the drone operators. Corporal Pashka's seat is still empty. He must be working on his broken drone.

"Doctor, we haven't finished the planned exposure—"

"Major Vylomov's orders. Pull them back out and get them in the glove boxes." Something catches her eye on the cage telemetry. "What's happening in I-241? BP's down, and her heart rate's way up." She snaps for a corporal's attention. "Get me the camera for Interior 241."

The picture from the webcam comes up clear and smooth. She and the corporal lean in to the laptop, staring at the splash of blood and flesh.

"She miscarried. We didn't know she was pregnant?"

The corporal fumbles for notes. "Ah—there was such a rush—probably a male sorted in with the females during the airlift?"

"She should have eaten it by now." A mother under stress will usually eat dead pups to recover resources. "Odd."

The mother has retreated to the far end of the cage, trembling.

Kuznetsova swings the camera back to the miscarriage.

"That," she says, "is *not* a mouse."

"I feel really bad about what I said to her," Corporal Pashka complains.

"Pashka," the warrant officer grunts, "shut up." He's tired of working on this fucking drone. He's tired of fumbling around in the fucking glove box. He's tired of not having internet access to look up manuals. This is a fucking commercial product! He should be able to call customer support!

Pashka shuts up. Occasionally a small grunt or moan comes through his radio, or the sound of smacking lips. The warrant officer attributes this to Pashka being a real fuckup.

It is past sundown when the warrant officer's assistant straightens from his work. "Boss?"

"What?"

"I think Pashka's having seizures."

"No, he's not." Pashka's just standing there. As the warrant officer understands it, a seizure makes you fall over and thrash.

"Boss, my little cousin looks just like this when he has seizures . . ."

The warrant officer pulls his hands out of the glove box and leans in to stare through Pashka's gas mask. Pashka's eyes are unfocused. Blood trickles out of his respirator: he has chewed into his tongue.

"Oh, cyka." The warrant officer switches his suit radio over to the tactical channel. "Medics! Medics to Biolab C! I've got a case!"

خەجىئ

"Tell me again what you did?" Davoud says.

"I shot the Russian commander."

"Because he wouldn't release me?"

If it weren't pitch-black in the prison container she would glare at him. "No, Davoud. Because your alien stole his soul."

"What about yours?"

Now she turns to face him in the dark. "What about my soul?"

His dirty flight suit crackles when he shrugs. "You have an alien too. What did it offer you?"

She should scoff. Instead she says, "My daughter."

"Khaje."

Ssrin's voice, right in her head. She leaps in shock.

"Khaje. Look what's happening out there."

Suddenly she's watching an edited hallucination. The colors and shapes pop and flex until it could almost pass for normal sight. She's outside, in the dark, looking up the meadow toward the science labs.

Six Spetsnaz in gas-attack gear carry a plastic-wrapped carton out toward a waiting incinerator.

"I think whatever killed the Canadians is out again."

"Who got it?"

"His name was Pashka. It's short for Pavel. Like Chekov. Well, you can certainly check him off. He died of grand mal seizures. Which you will too if I don't format this hive telemetry to fit your brain. Do you know how miserable your corpus callosum is as a data bus? Like trying to dial a modem by whistling through a straw. Awful."

She hates it when Ssrin tries to be funny. "Just him? He's the only one?"

"So far."

"Why does everyone keep getting seizures?"

"Your brains evolved for a world of physics. Now causal closure has forsaken you. Behold—"

The Russians stumble through muddy ruts carved by tank tracks. Wind-blown plastic wrappers flatten against the corpse, flap like tongues, and tear away into aurora twilight.

And the corpse moves.

One instant the body sags limp between its bearers. And then there is a sarcophagus drifting upright among the Spetsnaz: featureless but for the black stretched-plastic cavity of its mouth. It stands on nothing, half a meter off the ground, turning slowly left to right.

It is there and then it's gone. But it leaves a taste in Khaje's mouth like raw chicken gone bad. A cramp of pregnant nausea in her belly. A blast of sound in her skull. "Ai," she snaps, and shakes her head. That is a bad idea. The world keeps turning all around her. She clings to the corrugated metal. "What in the name of God was that!"

"You had a focal seizure. Your brain couldn't resolve the physically incompatible inputs it was receiving. One set from the physical model, and another from the intervention of a dead soul. Did you see a resurrection?"

"I saw a ghost!"

"Death is a slow process. You think the soul leaves the instant the heart stops? Then how would anyone ever be resuscitated? The body breaks down, and the soul breaks away. Here, the soul is deformed by the weapon's influence. It reaches back into the physics, tries to restore a narrative it understands. For a moment, the areteia allowed his soul primacy over physics. Reality schismed."

"Blackbird can . . . raise the dead?"

"Death is just the loss of information. To the extent that information can be recovered? Of course."

"Is this what Soheila saw? Why she shot the prospectors? They died and came back?"

"I expect Soheila saw the Canadians do impossible things. And when that threw her own brain into chaos, the guns and the fear took control of the rest."

"Are you saying we want to kill people because they give us seizures?"

"You want to kill them for the same reason people touched by the atmanach want to kill you. You see blasphemy."

"Answer me plainly, damn you."

"Blasphemy: a transgression against the divine order. To see it is anathema. To countenance its survival is unthinkable. You should not countenance Davoud's further survival, Khaje. Take the chance. Strangle him."

"What? I won't. I won't." She shot Ustinov to save Davoud— No, that's not true, she shot Ustinov to stop him shooting her— Oh, she is already making up stories to excuse it!

"I know." A long hiss. "It tastes good to hear you say it, though. Like eating something you've grown yourself."

"You didn't grow me!"

"Aw."

Davoud is making awful wet noises down at the other end of the chamber. He sounds like he's banging his head on the metal. That's not how you're supposed to do your namāz, and it's way too late, and he's facing the wrong way.

"Shut up!" she yells.

SIXTH DAY

K + 120 hours
DAVOUD (~7,875 FEET ASL)

Khaje is muttering to herself.

Davoud lies with his ear against the floor, listening to the rumbling of generators and the whine of Russian helicopters testing their engines. In the dawn he thinks they'll fly. The Russians wouldn't dare a night flight with their navigational instruments cooked: not in the cold, flattening light of the aurora.

All he ever wanted was to fly. And now he cannot even see the wounded sky.

He gets down on his knees in the dark and prays to Satan.

You came to me in the form of a pilot. You know I never loved anything more than the sky. Haven't I been useful to you? Haven't I sat in the councils of their leaders? Will you, in exchange, grant me one wish, one boon, I'm begging you, I'm pleading. Don't shoot down all those helicopters. Don't ruin them.

And Satan answers.

A terrible slithering sensation rips up his back. Those impossible teeth close around the soft bulbous under-parts of his brain, where there are no nerves that feel: stopping his heart, arresting his breath, tickling the cells that keep his temperature steady.

"Hello, Davoud."

His balls contract so hard he thinks they'll explode against his pubic bone. His stomach spasms, shooting acid up into his windpipe, like Mom's Yemeni green sauce ruining perfectly good beef. He thinks he is going to die on that thought, close out his life with an inanity about the Iranian dislike for spicy food.

"I'll let your stupid spinning suicide machines fly away. By the time they're back, it won't matter anymore. I'll possess Blackbird, or this planet will be dead."

"That translated as 'or', right?"

The alien forces him to breathe and pumps his heart with terrifying irregularity. And he talks, of course. Out there in the forest, Satan must be bored.

"Khaje's daughter should arrive soon. Ssrin coercively narrated her back in New York. I wondered why. Why so much effort for such a little pawn? Should I kill her? Not until I know exactly what role she's meant to play. So I tipped my guy off, I made sure he'd pay attention to her. Bring her along! Get a little hard-on for—let me consult my chart here—for her robust scent of methyl hexanoate. Is that what gets you apes going? A nice fatty ester?"

Through his agony Davoud manages to signal his irritation that he's locked up with Khaje.

"Oh, you're lucky to be in there, Davoud. Safe from the angel's plague about to burst its cauldron. And you are all so desperately unsatisfying to its appetite."

It isn't an angel. Angels are the servants of God.

"I don't choose my words by accident, Davoud. What would you call something mindless and older than time, something infinitely specialized, something that is worse than malevolent, because it bends the very strictures of good and evil?

"What would you call that thing if God had made it, and set it at His right hand, and appointed it to a task?"

You're mocking God.

"Of course I mock God. I am khai and all life is my dominion, all that is born is my slave, their slaughter is my birthright, their bodies are my choler and their souls are my suet. When I die I am surely damned to hell. That's how it is with us, that's how we live, born from the egg with the Cultratic Brand already on our souls. The mark of knives."

What? You're . . . born damned?

"Oh, yes. No one knows why. Just a sick turn of fate. Did you know that we once thought we could earn redemption? In the Brisennic Era, which was in my opinion the last great flowering of khai culture, we thought we could redeem ourselves from a state of intrinsic sin and earn a place in heaven through great works.

"No such luck. We tracked the path of our dying souls. All of us, good and great alike. Damnation is our fate."

For a moment he almost feels bad for Satan.

"You know, Islam is remarkable in the precision and clarity of its angels. They never disobey God's will. They always do exactly as they are tasked. Quran 66:6."

What task, Iruvage? What task did God give this angel?

"You're asking the wrong question, Davoud. You should not be asking what task the angel was given by God. Rather you should ask: What God was the maker of the angel?

"Now strangle Khaje Sinjari to death."

What? No.

"It would be funny, though. You could kill her and then suck on her toes. Isn't that what you filthy bipeds do? You aestheticize your distinctive organ, the foot. You disgusting podophiles."

I'm not going to murder someone for your amusement!

"Someday soon," Iruvage says, "I'm going to overcome my disgust, do the necessary belly work, and figure out an emulator that lets me puppet your sensorimotor system finely enough to walk around murdering people. Ah, but I'm building up neurotoxicity, aren't I? I'd better let you freshen up for the fun to come."

And, to Davoud's sobbing relief, Iruvage goes.

Sunrise.

Major Vylomov briefs his officers.

"There has been another outbreak of the Objekt's disease. All our drone operators are now experiencing microseizures. Some, including Corporal Pavel Bugorski, have died. I have ordered the science team to remove and assay the probe mice at once. We must find the vector of the disease.

"There is a risk the probe mice themselves will be virulent. Therefore I am posting you into the labs to terminate any person-to-person infection." He looks around the command post, meeting each man's eyes, one by one. "If absolutely necessary, I expect you to include yourselves in the measure. Try to avoid penetrating the lab walls. You have all been trained to use your bayonets and entrenching tools. Am I understood?"

"No, sir," one of the lieutenants says, with quiet, honest determination to be heard. "You are not. You want us to shoot our own science team?"

Vylomov allows his officers to think about this. It is a fair question.

"There is one thing we know for certain about this disease," he says. "It passed to Pashka through his drone. It passed to the Canadians through a radar display. It spreads out from the Objekt somehow. But the Ugandans handled the Canadians' corpses, and they were not infected. Pashka's final moments were terrible. He did not respond to any medicine, even the crudest painkillers. We have no evidence the disease is ever survivable. But once he was dead, he did not pass the infection to those who treated him.

"Death is our only *sure* containment measure. We must be sure that an alien bioweapon does not escape this valley. Even thousands of deaths would be a justifiable precaution when billions are at stake."

He does not tell them what the men handling Pashka's body claim they saw. Terror does strange things to a mind. Even trained pilots see UFOs. Surely hyper-vigilant Spetsnaz might hallucinate a levitating corpse?

"Our goal is nothing less than the protection of the human species. Do not hesitate."

Vylomov salutes them. One by one, they return the salute.

———

"We have to get her out now." Chaya pulls Huang Lim behind the corner of the dormitory, out of sight of the column of gas-masked Spetsnaz headed into the labs. "You need to find Master Sergeant Zhang. I have a plan."

"What do you have in mind?"

"If Professor Li's right about how this spreads, then it doesn't matter if the labs are airtight. It wouldn't matter if the labs were piping Blackbird air right into our noses." This is hard to admit, because it means her beautiful airlock was a complete waste of time. "So we cut straight into the plastic tunnel beside the materials lab and pull her out there. But we've got to be quick, we've got to be quiet, and if it comes down to it, we need to have guns."

He blinks owlishly at her. "Miss Panaguiton, why are you so devoted to my student?"

Ano ba, devoted? *Devoted?* "I think she's an absolute idiot," Chaya snaps, "and she has to be protected from sharp edges, never mind soldiers. But she's the *only* person we know who's interacted with the interior of Blackbird and survived. I've interacted with her, and I'm not sick. The whole science team was exposed to her, and they're not sick. She's not spreading it."

"You've interacted with her? Or you've . . . interacted with her?"

She stares at him. "What?"

"Oh," he says. "I thought you might be—?"

Hay nako. "Thought I might be what?"

"You've both been vanishing for so long." He scratches his bald spot. "Her mother asked me to make sure she met a nice . . . I am leaping to conclusions, I see."

"No—well, yes, about some things, but not others." She sighs. "Diba, what gave me away?"

"Well, I am a comrade, you know. We can tell."

"A comrade?"

"Tongzhi. Isn't that what you kids say?"

Biolab A.

Dr. Kuznetsova parcels out assignments. "My team will sacrifice the mice and perform initial dissections, then proceed with fine-tissue sampling. Dr. Smirnov's team will handle gross anatomy and the removal of the brain, spinal cord, and meninges for imaging."

She wants the aborted mass from cage I-241 for herself.

Everything is pale purple-blue. Ultraviolet light blazes down on the rows of glove boxes, snapping DNA like twine. Lidar grids the air, searching for single photons of backscatter from stray molecules. Ion sniffers parse the atmosphere for atoms of impurity. Without a suit Kuznetsova would be blinded and sunburnt. Her lungs would be scorched by inhaled ozone.

Biolab A is a place of stillness and sterile death, except for the suited figures gathered at the boxes, and the small movements of instruments within.

"The object of study is a tissue miscarried by Mouse I-241-A," Dr. Kuznetsova dictates. "The mother is a C57BL/6J inbred mouse, age eight weeks. Conception occurred no more than six days ago. No prior pregnancies appear on the file. The mass of the miscarried tissue is . . . six grams."

The man on her left mutters about errors with his cage sensors. His complaints keep triggering the voice-activated intercom. Kuznetsova glares at him until he lowers his voice.

She turns the wrinkled pink mass of the mouse's miscarriage for the glovebox cameras. The dry suit air makes her want to sneeze. She is on bottled air rather than an umbilical, in case they have to evacuate in a hurry.

She has given serious thought to Chaya Panaguiton's theory of contagion by information. The girl is positing a form of undetectable radiation that permeates the Objekt. Using sensors inside the Objekt can expose you to the radiation.

Do these mice then count as sensors?

Kuznetsova thought it over very carefully. But she has to obey the principles of rationality. And so far, every case of the disease, even poor Corporal Pashka, has involved electromagnetic influence. Mice do not emit electromagnetic radiation.

To be extra careful, she introduced control mice to cages with Objekt-exposed mice. One of those control mice is in the box to her left—the man dissecting it doesn't *know* it's a control. She thought a little double blind might be advisable.

She is ready to proceed.

"The tissue of the fetal mass is primarily mouse brain matter. The ratio of glial to neural cells is superficially normal. I speculate that the mother's circulatory system was unable to fully oxygenate the mass, and it died in utero. Note the cluster of navels here. I believe that the mass is a teratogenic fusion of the entire litter."

She pauses to swallow. Her throat itches. The glove box reflects the suited scientists to each side, proceeding with their own dissections. They look impassive, cruel. As always, she feels terrible for the mice; such cute little myshenka. But, as always, she goes on.

"The encephalization of the mass is atypical. Peak neurogenesis in the early mouse brain does not occur until day nine. These fetuses were no more than six days old. The teratogenic process seems to have accelerated nerve growth."

It could never have become some kind of mouse mastermind; slathering extra cells onto a brain does not make it smarter or more functional. If anything, the brain is remarkable for its ability to *resist* structural change. A French civil servant lived for forty years before he discovered that 90 percent of his brain's volume had been displaced by fluid buildup. He was conscious, alert, and fully capable. The organ is perversely resilient.

So what happened to create *this* particular perversity? Is it a stress-induced aberration of mouse development? The thought of the Objekt's influence itches at her, like the irritation on her left hand, unscratched beneath three layers of glove.

"I am proceeding with a sagittal incision through the dura mater," she tries to say. But nerves make her stutter, jumble up her English, as if recapitulating what she's already said: "Death of the early mouse brain, brain, is ah, is superficially incision." She swallows. "Pardon. I am proceeding with a sagittal incision. Through the dura mater."

The itching is very bad. She prods at her hand with the back of her scalpel, and then, in frustration, shuts her recorder off. "Is everyone all right?" she asks, into the suit radio. "Any concerns?"

"The fucking intercom is full of static," the surgeon to her left complains. "Can't we go back to the suit radios?"

"*The intercom is fine,*" Sivakov sends, from far outside the labs. "*We need the airwaves clear to monitor for unusual emissions.*"

"Then why is it so fucking hard to understand each other!" the surgeon snaps. He is one of Dr. Smirnov's anatomists, and a recovering drunk. "You sound like a tinned fish!"

"*Calm down. You are on the record.*"

She turns her own recorder back on. She is preparing to make the first incision, along the crest of the mass, when the surgeon to her left tears his hands free of the glove box and screams, "Fuck me! It's moving!"

Kuznetsova growls in frustration and turns to bark at him. The fool is dissecting a control mouse! It hasn't been anywhere near the Objekt! He has ruptured something and now he thinks it's—

Silently, the skull splits.

Kuznetsova gasps.

A seep of milky fluid. The skin unzips from snout to spine. The skull opens like a clamshell for the thing inside, the bloody glistening brain, spilling, like a crunched-up sponge returning to form, out into the light. The surface is webbed in arachnoid veins. And though the animal is dead, though it was sacrificed by cervical dislocation and its abdomen cut wide open, those veins throb and clutch to life.

The brain begins to swell with fluid. Erect itself to full size.

"Alien!" the man at the box screams. "It's a fucking alien!"

Kuznetsova stares in bewilderment.

And realizes, all at once, why the mice inside the Objekt gained body mass.

It wasn't water retention due to stress. *All* of their brains are hypertrophied. The miscarriage died and was expelled. So they saw it first, and assumed it was unique. But it was happening to the *living* mice too. Their brains grew and grew. Crammed inside their skulls. When the skull is cut, the brain decompresses. And somehow, by some influence—it lives.

The Objekt *made* this.

"We have discovered a novel effect," she tries to say. "Prolonged exposure to the Objekt causes neural hypertrophy in living mice." But what she blurts is: "We have discovered prior pregnancies. Objekt causes neural tissue. The fetal mass of the mother is an umbilical!"

The radio is full of nonsense, English and Russian running together, a hundred people chattering at a cocktail party, all discovering at once that the floor is on fire. A pulse in the mice, a pulse in the air, a pulse in the marrow! Her vision blurs: the human eyeball, she remembers, resonates at twenty hertz, a frequency too low to be audible. But not too low to be felt. Twenty times a second her eyes are juddering in her skull.

"Evacuate the lab," she tries to say. "Evacuate to Lab B." Only she blurts: "Urasuroue ph herdy us was illicion thes theh main msese pth m fily therrastisssse!"

But she cannot be infected, she cannot be infected already, it must be a mistake, her air mix must be wrong! If she is infected, she will seizure and die! She can't die!

People jerk their arms. People stare at each other. Someone falls and someone else says: "Look out, ouch!" and this makes someone scream in terror: "How could you, how could you, how could you *do* that?" "Do what? Nothing's done, it's not done yet." "Yet? What's happening yet? Am I going to miss it?" "Miss it?

Oh, fuck, who's missing?" "Yes, where are you?" "Me? I don't think I'm here any-more. I don't think I ever have been. It's always been someone else." "Else? Yes, do something else, anything else! Stop that! *That*, stop doing that!"

The fallen scientist struggles to disconnect his umbilical which binds child to mother and the infant mortality rate in Russia is twenty per hundred thousand births: bad, yes, but a third of what it was in 2000, a horrible year, but bad years often make good wine and you can get it cheaper, she read that online, on the line of this rambling line of thought like she's about to fall asleep, can't fall asleep here, not here, have to get to bed, have to traverse the node graph of labs and air-locks to return to her dormitory the way her brain is slipping down these nodes of association like a hand slipping down a rope, burning all its skin off, the way her hand burns with itch right now—

This was what happened to the Canadians. But it took hours, then! Somehow the syndrome is recapitulating itself in *seconds*—

A rich vector, she thinks. We gave it a rich vector. Much richer than a radar image. Much richer than a datalink. So few bits of information on a radar screen.

So *many* in the flesh of a mouse.

The surgeon next to her stumbles against her, scrabbling for balance. His hel-met bangs into hers. She stares into a partitioned face. His eyes: eight pupils staring wide in terror. His nose: the hundred tiny nostrils, like a honeycomb, flaring with each gasp. His scalloped cheekbones. His chin, cleft so deep she can see his tongue through the gap. The pores in his face are widening visibly, cov-ering his skin in a thin sheet of blood and sebaceous fluid. He tries to say some-thing. His lips split vertically, fissuring at the centerline, top and bottom, so that his mouth is like a cross. His tongue has tall villi, like the walls of an intestine. There are new eye sockets opening in a ring around his head.

He falls away.

Kuznetsova has a terrible, sharp thought. Her left hand itches.

She uses the scalpel to cut at the tape connecting her suit to her glove. Her hand jerks. Seizure. The blade goes too deep, pierces skin, opens her ulnar ar-tery. She notes, with absurd clarity, that her blood vessels and nerves are all in the right place: so it begins with surface features, then. It works top down, not bottom up. Why? How can it know the difference between a cell and a tissue and an organ and a system and a limb?

She pulls back the glove.

Watches as her fingers begin to separate into rings of flesh, knuckles thin as coins on a spindle of bone.

———

"Clear Lab A!" Professor Sivakov shouts into his radio. "Seal it off! The speci-mens can wait, damn it! Get everyone into Lab B, seal it shut, and *do not let them leave*! Medics are coming for triage!"

"Where are the contamination alarms?" Vylomov demands. "The lidar? The radiation detectors?"

"Clearly they did not work," Sivakov says dryly, pedantically, as if he is dealing with an undergraduate. Men become themselves under stress, Vylomov believes. "Clearly they are inadequate."

Major Vylomov thinks quickly. Since he was a boy in the Siberian forest he has known how to prioritize. In the wilderness: shelter, water, fire, food. In life: self-protection, housing, respect, money. In triage: airway, breathing, circulation. In battle: take cover, communicate, retaliate.

And now, as something tears through the scientists in Lab A, he must form another brutally simple hierarchy. Containment first. Then clarity: how is it spreading? Then, last of all, the safety of the scientists. There are more scientists to replace them. But there is only one Earth.

"Atropine One to all Atropine. Lock it down. No one moves. Confine the infected. Terminate any person-to-person transmission."

"*Atropine One, this is Ten!*"

"Yes?"

"*A total fuckfest in Lab A! They are everywhere! They are trying to come into Lab B!*"

"Yes!" Sivakov shouts, "yes, confine them in Lab B—"

"*No, shit! Fuck fuck fuck!*" The soldier leaves his transmit switch jammed down, and the channel fills up with his hoarse breathing. "*Atropine One, there is something wrong with all the scientists! My head hurts when they move! I taste something shitty! Shit, boss, I think they're contagious! I think I'm getting it!*"

There is a noise on the channel, Jodie Foster in *Contact* picking up the signal, grumbling under everything. A brass cat purring. Every few seconds, not quite in rhythm, the purr is interrupted by a high pop or click, like someone tapping on the mic.

"My God," Sivakov says, pivoting at the end of his step, pacing faster. "That noise spectrum. Professor Li was right."

"Right about what?" Vylomov demands.

"It is pink noise. The sound of the Objekt manipulating information." Sivakov paces three more laps across the tent. "Information is the vector. Yes. Pashka's disease is carried by information. The Objekt transforms information and renders it virulent. Drone footage and radar images of the interior therefore cause infection. We thought the mice would be safe because they are not directly transmitting information from inside the Objekt.

"But, for the first time, we are seeing *secondary* infections, infections from a source that is not the Objekt's interior. The mice themselves have become virulent. They were transformed into propagators of the effect."

"Propagators," Vylomov repeats. "Propagators. But mice do not know information. They're animals."

"Forgive me. I do not mean information in the way you think—facts, memories, files on a computer. I mean information in the physical sense. Information that would exist even without anyone to read it." Sivakov taps his chest. "Our present state is a deterministic result of past interactions. We are all full of information about the things which have touched and altered us, and that which we have in turn altered. It is, in fact, a law of physics that this information cannot be destroyed. It can only be moved. And when it moves out of the Objekt, it brings—something. It infects us."

"Propagators. You said propagators."

"These mice are saturated with information about the Objekt's interior, which they are now propagating, releasing, through physical interactions with the lab and the scientists—"

"The mice were infected by the Objekt, and now they are infecting others?"

"Yes. Yes."

Vylomov snatches up the radio handset. He speaks quickly and clearly. "All Atropine. Outbreak, outbreak, outbreak. Shoot to kill. Break. Atropine Four. Destroy the infected drone operators."

"But—those still in the labs! Anton, Inessa, the Chinese team—Professor Li! Professor Huang would not allow it!"

"Everyone in that lab is dead," he tells the poor man. "The Chinese as well. Even my Spetsnaz, if they do not pass examinations. Even the men who examine them, if necessary. Even you and I! The world is at stake, Anatoly. The world!"

───※───

خه‌جێ

Gunfire wakes Khaje. Very loud. Very close.

She knows this sound, old friend warning of old foes, she knows how to wake up to shots. She rolls to her feet and throws herself at the container door. Locked, of course, it doesn't budge, all she has done is wake up her bruises too. "Ssrin," she hisses, "I need help!"

Something rips out of her hair and slashes through the aluminum. White sparks jet against her face. This time, when she smashes the door, it opens. "Davoud! Come on!"

"What—who—?"

Firelight blazes through the tiny window of another prison container, surrounded by armed Spetsnaz. Oh, there are men in there! Men in the fire, screaming and begging for their mothers! The Russians are killing their own boys!

She drags Davoud forward. They go to their bellies in the grass together. She huddles there waiting for some Slavic sentry with a suppressed rifle to pop her skull. It is the best she's felt in days. Years, maybe.

Nothing kills her. She is going to keep Serhang and Hamali waiting a little longer.

"Ssrin," she mutters. Davoud is gasping into the grass. "Ssrin, what's happening?"

"*Khaje, this is a recorded message. I can't reply. The risk of contamination is too great. There has been an outbreak of Blackbird's effect into the world. You must stay away. My hive will protect you as best as it can. I've sent—more than I should.*"

"Fuck your father, you snake bitch."

"*Yes, I thought you'd say that. Your weapons are in lockup on the back of the charming Tigr-M parked by the jail container. I had a flechfly break the lock.*"

And there they are! Her rifle, her Glock, her ammunition, just leaning against the wall of the container. "Bless you, you little Satan. Davoud! We have to get across the river to Tawakul."

"Why'd you save me? You know I deserve to be shot."

"So I can question you, you stupid jash bastard," she lies. She scurries forward, rifle slung, fingertips spidering on wet grass. Stay low, always stay low when they are trying to shoot you, never give them even a part of a silhouette. "Come on. We need to get to Arîn's sentries."

But they don't make it to the bridge. They're half a mile across the meadow when Khaje spots a team of Spetsnaz, sleekly inhuman in gas masks and ballistic plate carriers. They're coming down from a hide in the riverside grove, angling to cut her off.

"Russians." She pulls Davoud off-balance so he falls into the grass, then slips onto her belly beside him.

"Chinese," he says.

"It's the Russians."

"No, Chinese. Look."

He points out Chaya Panaguiton's fuzzy head against the grass. Once she has Chaya's outline, she catches the helmets of the Chinese soldiers around her. Chaya's tending to someone in a hazmat space suit—someone nursing a leg cramp.

"You have goat eyes," she mutters.

"Eagle eyes," Davoud says. "Goats have wide vision. Eagles have range."

"Jash bastard goat eyes."

"You're cruel to me, Khaje."

The Russians aim their guns and shout. Master Sergeant Zhang and his men aim their guns and shout right back.

Khaje scopes over to Chaya Panaguiton. She likes Chaya. She decides she won't watch Chaya shot dead on the meadows where she sledded as a girl.

She stands up and walks forward.

The Russians and Zhang stop arguing in English: it is not clear that they understand each other very well. They all turn their guns on Khaje.

"What's going on here?" she asks. "Why are you pointing weapons at our guests?"

"These Chinese are covering up for a major breach in quarantine!"

"There's nothing wrong with her!" Chaya shouts. "Look at her! She just needs some water and some sleep!"

"My orders are to return them to the lab complex—"

"For execution!" Zhang bellows. "Like the alien killing us wasn't enough, now *you* want a turn! You are a commissioned piece of shit!"

"There was an outbreak! We have no choice! We must act for the good of the species!"

"*My* species doesn't shoot scientists!"

"Professor," Khaje calls. "Where do you want to go?"

Li Aixue's face is almost invisible through the helmet. There's no light in there, so the plastic surface just swivels back and forth, looking at Chaya, looking at Khaje, looking at the men with the guns.

"I want to keep working on my math," she says.

Chaya groans in frustration.

"However, I can't do that if I get shot. So if you'd all put your guns down, I will go to Tawakul and isolate until we can decide if I have symptoms. Then I can get back to work once we've sorted things out."

"Of course." Khaje starts walking past them, toward the bridge. "Come with me."

"Don't do this!" the Spetsnaz man calls. "Stop! We *will* use force!"

She barks: "So use force!"

The Spetsnaz leader draws back a step, left hand raised, right hand on the pistol grip of his Val. The black special-issue rifle is built for silence, a murder weapon. "These people are infected. You'll kill your own people."

But they aren't infected. When Soheila saw the infected Canadians, she wanted to kill them, she *knew* she had to kill them. And Khaje cannot believe that Soheila was an insane murderer. She can't.

So if these people were infected, Khaje would also know that they had to die. The way her daughter knew who had to die.

"I am taking these people into my home. You can try to stop me. But you should know something." She lifts the Dragunov from its place across her back, settles it in her arms, checks ostentatiously that the gas regulator is in position two (high-altitude/cold-weather operation), and disengages the safety.

"I," she tells the Spetsnaz man, "am bulletproof. And if you want to shoot these people, you will have to get past me first."

She aims the rifle at his chest. "Leave."

He raises his own weapon.

She draws and releases the charging handle as a final warning. The Dragunov peels the top cartridge from the ten-stack in the magazine. The firing pin comes forward to touch the cartridge, as it should, but by ugly chance or Satanic influence this cartridge has a soft ass, softer than the hard military brass the firing pin expects.

The pin strikes hard enough to set off the cartridge. The rifle slam-fires without Khaje touching the trigger. The flash and the report and the impact, all in the same instant: the bullet punches the Spetsnaz man on his ass.

Immediately two of the Spetsnaz shoot Khaje. Things the size of gnats carom through the air between them, moving so fast that *they* make the supersonic crack which the suppressed Russian rounds do not.

The gnats intercept the bullets and spike them into the grass.

The Spetsnaz man groans and fumbles at his chest plate. One of his men runs forward to drag him to safety. "That's good armor," Khaje says. "You should be dead."

"You *shot* him!" Zhang hisses, from down in the grass. "Way to go!"

"They shot *you*," Davoud says wonderingly. "Khaje, why aren't you shot?"

"I told you," Khaje shouts. "I'm bulletproof." She points a firm finger at the downed Spetsnaz commander. "Tell Major Vylomov that none of his men will enter my village without recognizing *my* authority. Or I'll arrange a lesson about what happens to Russians in mountains full of Muslims!"

"Idi na fig!" a Russian shouts. "You broke his fucking ribs!"

"He didn't listen. You listen! You listen to me! My daughter is coming here, with the Americans. My daughter is bringing the answer." Ssrin said so. It must be true. "But we have to survive until then. We can't kill each other. My daughter is coming with a way for us to get inside Blackbird, but until she's here, we have to survive!"

And if they don't, it will be her fault. She made the bargain with Ssrin. She brought the alien war to Tawakul. If she fails, her people will die thinking she's the joyless drunk at the end of the road.

Anna has to bring the answer.

"Do you understand?" she barks at the soldiers. "*Do you understand?*"

CHAPTER TWELVE

CLAYTON//538 MINUTES REMAIN

Clayton finally lets himself grin in triumph.

"Aixue's immune. She's immune to the Blackbird effect. She's our Jackson and Ritter."

Chaya's sitting cocked on her chair, one leg aimed at him, one askew, torso turned sideways, looking down her left shoulder at him. In another setting he'd read this body language as flirty. Right here, it's blading: showing a thin profile to someone you want to fight. In wrestling, blading means cutting yourself up, self-harm for theatrical effect. Some of what Chaya said felt like that too. Warning him by wounding herself.

"I don't know," she says.

"Isn't that what you're telling me? She went inside, like Sabiti went inside, but she *never* turned symptomatic—"

"Oh, shet," Chaya groans. "I knew it. I *knew* it. Is Sabiti . . ."

"Dead," Clayton says. She can take it. "He was mutilated, just like the Russian scientists exposed to the mice. *Moments* of exposure destroyed their bodies. Shitty webcam footage from Blackbird's interior was enough to infect and sicken the drone pilots. A tablet-sized radar screen killed the Canadians. But Li Aixue stuck her head fully inside Blackbird, and watched that drone footage. Yet she's fine. No seizures. No physical deformation. She's immune."

"If only I'd made her go dissect some mice. Then you'd *really* know for sure. That's why you took so long to arrive, right? Waiting for us to start dying?"

"What?"

"You waited for us to contact Blackbird. We were your human bioassay."

"I didn't make the Russians dissect those mice. If they'd listened to *you*, no one would have died!" He's not even saying this to butter her up. "You learned from your mistake with the hydrazine theory. You didn't lose anyone after Shafiq."

"Except Sabiti."

"Yeah. I'm sorry. He was a true Ugandan."

She glares: "What does that mean?"

"Oh. I had a Ugandan contractor once. He worked in Iraq as a security guard. What we called a TCN, a third country national. He got shot, he had to go home to Uganda. So what does he do when he gets home? He starts a company to send *more* Ugandan contractors to Iraq. And you know what he wanted from me? He wanted permission to send Ugandans to Afghanistan."

"Are you calling us stupid?"

"I'm calling you brave."

"Is it brave or stupid to use American imperial adventures as a business opportunity?"

"Great question. I'd refer you to the Bush administration to answer that one." He sits forward. "Let me be sure I've grasped the core problems with Blackbird.

"First. When you use instruments to probe Blackbird, you don't get data *about* Blackbird. You get Blackbird's manipulation of the probe.

"Second. Manipulated information coming back from Blackbird is virulent. Exposure to the interior of Blackbird, even through a camera or a radar image, causes seizures, hallucinations, and, eventually, physical mutilation. In some cases the seizures are fatal. In cases of higher exposure, like the Russian scientists dissecting the mice, the disease progresses to gross physical deformation.

"Third. Blackbird's targeting is selective. It seems to prefer brains, microprocessors, and maybe written language. Does that seem correct so far?"

"DNA too," Chaya says. "The skin bacteria Professor Huang showed me." She yawns into her fist. "I've told you everything. I want to sleep."

"I'm going to call Li Aixue in here next," he says. "If I ask her whether she's immune, what will she say?"

Chaya pauses for a few long breaths. Her broad shoulders, deltoid heads and smoothly sloping traps, cord up so tight he wants to reach over and smooth them flat. She puts her hands on the back of her head, crunches her chin to her chest, and blows out a breath.

"I don't know. I want to think so. Because then it was all right of me to cover for her. But then . . . but then, when I think about it reasonably, I decide she's not. I think she just took a low dose. Some grainy webcam footage, and a few seconds with her head inside? Not enough. She just didn't get the full effect."

"All right," he says. He's glad he's found a doubt, because doubt usually underlies all true information. Lies are the only certain things in the mind. "Thank you. You've been a tremendous help. You can go now."

It's time for him to poll his own source.

CLAYTON//530 MINUTES REMAIN

He locks the dorm trailer from the inside. He sits down in the chair Chaya just vacated.

"Iruvage," he says. "I need to talk to you."

Teeth close around the back of his neck.

One more gram of pressure and the fangs would slip into his spine. Clayton holds his breath. This isn't real. Just a thing in his mind. And his mind is under his control.

"*Clayton, my man. With Ssrin in hiding I am as bored as someone at a public function whose neural rewards have been artificially dissociated from the evolutionary imperatives which once drove his social behavior. Did that translate correctly? Well, never mind.*"

Never mind the fang wiggling itself into the disc between his vertebrae, impelled by a kind of muscular hinge. Digging around for something tasty.

"*I'm bored and anxious, and anxiety makes me think about threats, and that makes me want to act to prevent them. Never know when some tricky little monkey might decide to drop a bomb on me, hm?*"

"No one's going to bomb you," Clayton subvocalizes: the trick is to make all the words in your throat without putting any air into them. "At least as long as you don't bomb *us.*"

"*I have to admit a little impatience on that front, Clay. You're running out of time.*"

"You said I had fourteen hours! We're not even five hours in!"

"*I did say that, didn't I? But it's not just up to me. Coil Captain Maessari has strict orders from the Unnumbered Fleet about what to do if she discovers a weapon capable of disrupting the pinion. Namely: to nuke your entire planet with cobalt-salted genocide weapons and then erase the coordinates.*

"*This is not the first object we've found that could alter the status quo in the galaxy . . . and as the Exordia is the status quo, we do not wish to be altered. Maessari knows that she ought to be riding in like one of the Four Horsemen right now. Which horseman I don't know. I didn't pay enough attention. Who are the Four Horsemen of the apocalypse, anyway? Chiron, Genghis Khan, Hoof and Mouth, and . . . Misty of Chincoteague?*"

"So why doesn't she do it? What are you holding over her?" Clayton's figured out that the khai operate on principles of deterrence. Where a human says *Please do what I want, and I'll reward you,* the khai say *Do what I want, or these terrible things will occur.*

"*I have intimated that my sponsor will have revenge on Maessari if she acts in haste. So she is delaying, against all the principles of ssovÈ, the violence of sudden action. Delaying just a few hours . . . for you to do your work for me.*"

"I need more time."

"*What all khai wish for. But the plunge to hell awaits.*"

"Don't nuke us, for fuck's sake! You need us."

"*Perhaps you're just my hedge option while I do everything myself. Doesn't that frighten you? Oh, yes, I smell that it does.*" Iruvage hisses thoughtfully. "*I've been analyzing the souls my atmanach has digested. Your species is a little thin, did you know that? Not much to learn about Blackbird from this . . . aretaic porridge. Ah! And I see you've put Davoud Qasemi to use. He was my man in the Iranian expedition. I promised him he'd get to see a spaceship. It's been his dream all his life. I thought you two might hate each other splendidly."*

"I threw him in a room with Professor Li. So you could look her over and tell me if she's important."

"You don't think I'll fall for that, do you? Feeding her to me like tainted meat?"

"You're afraid of her. If you're really using the atmanach to learn about Blackbird, you would've hit her by now. But you don't know what would happen! You don't know if the atmanach's digestion can protect you."

"Or I need her alive to feed you clues."

"Just tell me what she knows—"

"Oh, were it so easy, Clayton. Blackbird strips away falsehood. If I told you what I think it does, then I would be the source of truth, not you. And you would be stripped away."

"This makes no fucking goddamn sense at all! I don't have the background. Can you help me?"

"I don't like to speculate, Clayton. It's like striking too soon. You get your fangs into the wrong idea and you can't resist the taste so you just tear and tear at it . . ."

"Jesus," Clayton groans. The *planet* is on his back: he has conned himself into playing asshole Atlas, carrying Earth on his hunched and guilty shoulders. And it's all fun and games to Iruvage. "You're not taking this seriously."

"I have never taken anything more seriously in my entire existence. The stakes for me, personally, could not be higher. If this were just business for me, I would've called in the Unnumbered Fleet to scour your world months ago." Hallucinatory scales rasp against Clayton's throat. *"You should send more people inside . . ."*

"They don't want to go."

"Tell them you'll kill them if they don't go."

"If you tell people to obey or die, they'll disobey on principle."

"Tell them they must adjust their ethics to suit an extraordinary situation. They must change their idea of right and wrong. There is no reason to stand on principle for the sake of long-term social norms when I can annihilate all those social norms with thermonuclear weapons."

"People don't *do* that. They can't make these adjustments consciously. We embed our ideas of right and wrong in our cultures, so bad actors can't tweak them for convenience."

"Oh, Clayton." Iruvage sighs. *"I have a hard time understanding what you need. I'm not a teacher."*

"I need you to review the things I've learned about Blackbird. Help me understand if Li Aixue is immune. And if so, why."

"You promised me you could do this work on your own. That's why I retain you, Clayton."

"Then tell me about this soul you're so afraid to mutilate. We don't know about souls, Iruvage. We're—" God, what would a khai idiom be? "We're biting in the dark here."

"I can see in the dark."

"Well, then help me see!"

"Let me tell you a story.

"There are seven great passions in the universe. Seven stories all of us share. They are known among the belunari and the eana, the shorinor and the iridine, the skylords and the coagula, and though all these peoples have evolved on scattered distant stars, they still know the same seven passions. Even the khai know them. Perhaps the khai most of all.

"Preyjest is the story of the suit and the chase, as strong as the space between hunter and prey, between lover and beloved. The pursuing passion.

"Prajna gleams alone, a solitary star. The passion of knowing for no sake.

"Serendure is unconditional loyalty, trust that is abuse. The unbreakable passion.

"Caryatasis grows when many change to follow one who doesn't. The disciple's passion.

"Geashade is the falling knife, the love doomed to die, powerful in proportion to its pain.

"Hesper is simple and it makes us warm. The comfort passion: like meeting a stranger, sharing one night, and going on stronger.

"And rath, dear Clayton. Rath the clashing passion. Two stones beat against each other, chipping and cracking, hardening and sharpening. Maybe until one breaks. Maybe forever."

Clayton rubs his temples. "I have no idea what this has to do with Blackbird."

"But you do. You are going to figure it out, all by yourself, without my help. And you're going to do it before Erik Wygaunt destroys you."

"Is Erik okay?"

"Oh, he's better than okay. He's delicious. Right now he's trying to get to a blast crater so he can save some children I've fabricated on the radio. I want to kill him. Oh, I want to kill him so badly. He entices me." Iruvage's long slow fangs sink through the back of Clayton's skull like two migraine drills. "You have no idea how frustrating it is for me to watch you work. Like watching a mouse scurry across a puzzle, nibbling at the pieces, shitting in the gaps. But it must be done. The mouse must solve the puzzle on its own. Or, when the mouse goes into the center of the maze, the things I require it to accomplish will not be accomplished . . ."

Clayton stands there shivering desperately. Outside the sun's starting to fall. Soon the aurora will be burning bright again. All over the world, people will be looking up at the sky, praying for salvation.

"Our souls are made of stories, Clayton. The stories of the choices we've made."

For a moment he seems to be wrapped around Clayton, one arm shoved down his throat, *through* his throat, milking his heart. Clayton gags. Fangs tickle his prostate: an awful spasm down there. Iruvage is laughing so hard.

"*You're the hero of this story. Solve Blackbird. Save the day.*"

CLAYTON//514 MINUTES REMAIN

When Li Aixue comes in, he's making her tea. He knows his hands are trembling. She starts the interrogation on her terms: "Have you learned anything?"

"From Chaya?"

"From the alien! You are in contact with it, aren't you? Ssrin gave Khaje several important clues. Haven't you learned anything from yours?"

It's good when people want to ask questions. Tells him a lot. "He told me some kind of fable. I don't know what it has to do with Blackbird. How do you take your tea?"

"Black. Thank you."

He brings her the cup and a wooden stir stick. "Chaya thinks very highly of you."

Li Aixue has a short, heavy build and a bright round face. She's wearing her STANFORD PHYSICS sweatshirt, presumably because of the AC. Her hair is a shaggy chin-length mess. It looks like she tried to do some kind of pixie or pompadour several months ago, and then forgot about it.

She smiles ruefully: "Chaya thinks I'm a fool."

"Maybe. But she also thinks you're our best bet for solving Blackbird."

"Oh. I've done that."

He freezes halfway into his seat. "You have?"

"I know what Blackbird does."

"Tell me."

"Don't you already know? Blackbird exaggerates complexity. It searches for structure, extracts the logic guiding that structure, and uses that logic to build more structure."

He tries to boil this down to a slug line he could deliver to the president. "It makes things more like themselves?"

"Sure. Kind of. It simplifies things, and then it extrapolates from the simplicity. Cycles of distillation and extrapolation. It looks for a pattern, amplifies the pattern, repeats as long as it can."

This makes unhappy sense to Clayton. His work at the NRO involved the aggressive use of machine learning (which, out of a sentimental love of science fiction, he refuses to call *AI*) to find patterns in huge data sets.

And the universal theme of machine learning is thought without understanding. A properly trained machine learning system can build frighteningly accurate models of economic interdependencies in Southeast Asia, or deduce the spread of an epidemic in Africa from changes in satellite photos of crop fields, or predict political unrest in ex-Soviet client states from seemingly unrelated Google searches in Moscow. But it does not know what Moscow is, or what a human being might be, or even that it exists. It is simply building connections between points of data. The logic of those connections is left to the machine itself to devise. It has no prior knowledge of the universe. (Except anything introduced in the network's initial values, or in data augmentation, but—those are added by human operators.)

The machine might be absolutely and pathologically insane, with a model of the world straight out of Ligotti. But if that insanity produced useful responses, no one could know.

What if Blackbird is also operating without prior knowledge? Without any grasp of the structure of the universe? When it encounters a human being, or a server rack, it simply sees a set of data. It doesn't have any context for that data. It's like one of those exquisitely precise NRO satellites, seeing everything, knowing nothing.

But why the fuck would an alien spacecraft have no grasp of basic physics?

"Sell me," he challenges Li. "What supports your theory?"

Her eyes are deep and clear. Tiny vortices spin off into her tea as she stirs. "When the Canadians tried spectrometry on Blackbird's surface, they obtained a chemically impossible composition: hydrogen, helium, lithium, beryllium, boron. All the early elements on the periodic table, each present in reverse proportion to its atomic number. Then the spectrum changed. Now each element was present in reverse proportion to its atomic *mass*. That was the first clue."

"Clue to what?"

"What do you call it when things are present in inverse proportion to their power? The bigger it is, the fewer there are?"

"Pink noise," Clayton breathes. He understands now why Chaya's retelling made such a point of bringing that detail up. "You're saying that was a pink noise distribution of atomic elements?"

"Exactly. As if someone decided to randomly generate atoms. Hydrogen, the simplest element, is the most common. Helium requires two protons instead of one, so it's half as common. Lithium, atomic number three, therefore one third as common as hydrogen. A harmonic series."

"And why did it change to a series based on mass, instead of atomic number?"

"It discovered that matter requires neutrons to remain stable. So it changed the way it made matter. And the new distribution reflected that—stable helium is four times as massive as stable hydrogen, so there was four times as much hydrogen as helium."

He really struggles to imagine why anybody would design a machine that can synthesize atoms without knowing how atoms work. "But it moved on to computer chips. Mice. People."

"Yes. It's trying to make something."

"That's why it's heating up?"

"Yes. All work creates heat, even computational work. But I shouldn't say it's trying to make *something*. I think it's trying to make everything."

He wants to pause the recording just so he can ask her what the fuck that means. "Go on."

"I think that Blackbird is an instantiation of the fundamental mathematical principle which caused the universe to exist."

He stares at her.

"Let me try again." She lifts the stir stick with the teabag wrapped around it and darts it, overhand, into the trash. "I think pink noise is a mathematical fingerprint. It is caused by the spontaneous breaking of topological symmetries by a self-organizing process."

He stares at her. "Professor, what the *fuck* does that mean?"

"Topological symmetries? A symmetry is something that doesn't change when it's transformed."

Like you, he thinks. If you really are immune. "Okay. I'm going to need an example."

"Sure. If you move around on an empty void, it's the same everywhere. That's translational symmetry. If you rotate a perfect circle, it doesn't change at all. That's rotational symmetry. If you look at a circle for half an hour, it won't change either. That's time symmetry. But walk around your house, things change. Rotate a clock, the hands change position. Look at a fire for half an hour, it goes out. Almost all of modern physics is expressed in terms of symmetries, using a branch of math called group theory. Every force in the Standard Model of particle physics is determined by just three symmetry groups."

"I didn't know that," he lies, a little. He sort of knew that.

"It's very elegant! It turns out that each kind of symmetry implies a law of conservation. For example, rotational symmetry turns out to imply conservation of angular momentum. Translational symmetry implies conservation of linear momentum. Time symmetry implies conservation of energy."

"And a symmetry break?"

"For some reason time only runs one way. Symmetry's broken."

"Why?"

"We don't know. At least not for time. But a spontaneous symmetry break happens whenever something that's the same everywhere suddenly turns into something with structure." She points to his nose. "Imagine a ball perched on the tip of your nose. It's perfectly balanced; it has no preference for one side of your nose or the other. We can spin that ball on your nose and nothing changes. It's symmetrical. Not very interesting.

"But eventually you take a breath, or you move, or there's an earthquake. And that ball rolls off your nose. Left, right, maybe up, maybe even down. A tiny initial change in the ball's position will force it to choose a direction to roll. And the whole system will stop being symmetrical; the ball will no longer spin in place on your nose; it'll fall off and go somewhere, and it can't come back. That's spontaneous symmetry breaking. It's how the laws of physics as we know them emerged from a simpler, primordial set of rules. Everything used to be symmetrical, used to be the same hot soup governed by one grand law. But as it cooled down, that law broke symmetry. It became gravity and electromagnetism and the nuclear forces. A symmetrical soup of quarks and gluons became protons and neutrons and electrons and atoms and all the other particles. It made the universe today."

Clayton figures he understands enough to keep rolling. "But you said Blackbird predates the universe."

"Yes. Ha." She laughs brightly. "That gets into more math. It has to do with Goldbach's conjecture, the Riemann hypothesis, all these ... all these eerie cases of connections between physics and pure math. Look: You know about the prime numbers?"

Clayton hits her with one of his sly grins. "I'm a spy, Professor. Of course I know about primes. To me, they're tools." The cornerstone of modern encryption is the incredible, billion-year difficulty of splitting large numbers into their prime factors. "What are they to you?"

"Irreducible elements of the geometric ring. The fundamental particles of math. Do they remind you of anything?"

"Fundamental particles? Are you saying the primes are like particles in physics? Expressions of some kind of ... broken symmetry?"

"Oh, I don't think they're expressions! I think they're the expressors. The generators. But we don't understand them. There's no equation or rule that can precisely generate new prime numbers. Euclid proved there are infinitely many prime numbers, but we can't actually figure out what they are without doing guess-and-check.

"Still, there are clues. If you chart the gaps between the prime numbers, their distribution seems to obey some kind of pattern. It's not hard to guess roughly how many prime numbers exist below any number n. We have an equation for that, it's called the prime number theorem, and it's really simple: n divided by the natural log of n. Give me a value of n, say, nine billion and one, and I'll tell you that there are probably about—ah—three hundred and ninety million primes below that n."

"That seems like way too many."

"It's actually a bit of an undercount! The prime number theorem can't give you an exact result. Because, at the small scale, the positions of the primes seem totally chaotic! As unpredictable as quantum decay! Do you know what people call something"—she returns his sly grin—"something that hints at structure and pattern, at knowability—but also constantly surprises you?"

"Beautiful," Clayton says. Thinking of a woman he married.

"Yes! Yes, exactly. One of the strangest things in the world, Mr. Hunt, is that the Riemann hypothesis—the crown jewel of mathematical mysteries, a thing intimately tied to prime numbers—turns out to be useful for explaining the behavior of atomic nuclei in quantum theory. Isn't that incredible? Something we found by haring off away from reality, into the realm of pure truth, comes back around to explain the smallest levels of existence. And, in the converse, going from physics to number theory—it turns out that you can treat prime numbers like particles in a cloud of gas, and model how they space themselves out!" She leans forward suddenly, pouncing on him. "Do you know what distribution you get if you plot the gaps between the prime numbers? They come in pairs, sometimes triples, so there are a lot of little gaps between primes, and a modest amount of modest gaps, and just a few big ones . . ."

"Pink noise," Clayton whispers. "Wow."

"Exactly! The primes lead to pink noise, pink noise leads to self-organizing criticality, self-organizing criticality leads to spontaneous symmetry breaking. I wholly believe that understanding the structure of the prime numbers will help us see how that structure acts as a seed or attractor for the behavior of all dynamical systems. All creation unpacks from there. And so does Blackbird."

He squints at her. "Walk me through that jump?"

"Do you remember what the Canadians saw when they used ground-penetrating radar on Blackbird?"

"Triangles. Big spikes. Oh. A lot of little triangles, a few big spikes? You're saying that was pink noise?"

"Absolutely. Blackbird created a structure out of their radar signal by exaggerating the randomly occurring noise. It stripped away the entropy to find order. Then it kept doubling down on that order. And whenever it removes entropy, it creates pink noise."

"Entropy," he says. "I was wondering when we'd get there. You were telling Chaya about Shannon and Kolmogorov entropy."

"Yes! I believe Blackbird tries to generate Kolmogorov entropy out of Shannon entropy."

To high school graduates, entropy is the measure of waste energy and disorder in a system—progress toward the death of the whole universe. Proof to the teenage depressive that chaos will overwhelm all things.

But entropy is also a measure of complexity. Much of Clayton's job is about reducing entropy. Whether cleaning up noise from a recording, or reducing the entropy of the reports he sends to the White House.

Entropy is the amount of data required to describe a system. A straight line is low entropy. You can write an equation describing that line perfectly. But a field of random dots is high entropy: you must specify the position of *every single dot* to describe the whole field, because there is no underlying order connecting them.

(—and it strikes him, just now, that if there were an underlying order to the dots, a secret rule, it would be a symmetry—)

All of human thought and language is about creating low-entropy approximations of a high-entropy world. If it were not possible to do this, everyone's name would need to be as complicated as the person it named. Every thought would be as large as the thing it described.

Shannon entropy is a complete description of a person, a photograph with infinite resolution, every mole and freckle set in its place. Kolmogorov entropy is the length of an equation which could *create* that person: a line of math which plots each ingrown hair and laugh line as the intersection of invisible curves. The elegant, lossless compression of the person into a perfect true name. Each form of entropy captures the entire person. One is exhaustively maximal. One is strictly minimal.

Most names, alas, are not so true and faithful. He does not think that he could render Rosamaria into life from her name alone.

〜※〜

"You're saying Blackbird tries to find the core logic which describes things." Clayton feels his calves bunching up, toes arching, an old dance reflex, stretching before he moves. He's getting somewhere. "And it does that over and over. Like recursively applying a Photoshop filter, sharpening the image until all that's left is the most basic pattern."

"Yes!"

"And Blackbird does that to *everything*? Even to written language?"

"Language?" Li repeats sharply. "It works on written language?"

"Yeah. We saw this on checklists posted in the labs." He uses his phone to call up a screenshot of the distorted checklist, captured by Erik's helmet cam.

"But . . ." She stares in perplexity. "Without the semantic content of a human brain, those markings are just puddles of ink. Why would they entice Blackbird?"

"I don't know. Zipf's law, maybe?" This is a rule in linguistics which says that the most common word in a language is spoken twice as often as the second most common word, three times as often as the third most common word, and so forth. In English, *the* gets used about twice as often as *of*, about three times as often as *and*—

Holy fuck. Pink noise. Zipf's law is just pink noise for words.

"Okay," he says slowly. "Okay. So Blackbird likes symmetry. It likes to find the symmetries inside things, the patterns, and then it extrapolates the patterns. But how does that help us? Why does this . . . pattern-growing effect make people sick? Why would Blackbird give some people seizures, but other people extra eyes? Why does it enlarge circuit boards and mouse brains, but not person brains? We're missing something important. What is it?"

She laughs and spreads her arms, a caricature of bewilderment. "I don't know!"

So it's come time to make the really hard call.

"We need to sleep," he says.

"What? No, no no no. I have to get back to my workstation!"

"In the labs with the mice? The labs littered with corpses? No. We need to let our brains recover. Three and a half hours of sleep. Two REM cycles. Then we get the whole science team together, and we attack this."

"Wait." When he rises she stays seated, as if this will pin him to the spot. "Why was I locked in a room with Davoud?"

He can be completely honest: "Iruvage watches and listens through Davoud. I wanted to see if Iruvage was afraid of you. Since you've been inside Blackbird."

Her jaw drops. "You know I . . . ?"

"Chaya told me."

"Oh," Li Aixue says quietly. "Of course."

She looks up and her face splits, breaks its symmetry, with the first intrusion of anger Clayton has seen.

"Davoud told me to tell you something," she says. "While I was locked up with him, he said he'd had a message from Iruvage."

"I just spoke to Iruvage."

"Then did he tell you?"

Clayton surreptitiously clicks the recorder off. "Tell me what?"

"He said: 'Tell Clayton that Erik Wygaunt is coming to kill him soon. Coming in revenge for the losses he'll suffer.'"

She shrugs a little: that's all. Wasn't important to mention until the math was done.

CLAYTON//385 MINUTES REMAIN

The rasp of his radio, cranked up to full volume, jerks him awake. "Shit." He paws around for his headset. He was dreaming that he and Erik were kids again, and wrestling: and that he'd shoved Erik's head into a rock, and turned the rock *into* Erik's head, and now Erik was really dehydrated and trying to convince Clayton to open his mouth with a jackhammer. "Yeah?"

"*Mr. Hunt. This is the TOC. We have a report by runner from Team Two.*"

He can't remember what the fuck Team Two is. "Who's that?"

"*The unit overwatching from the south ridge, Mr. Hunt.*"

"Go ahead."

"*They have sighted gunfire in the forest to the north. Also some heavy fog, which is obscuring thermal imaging.*"

Fucking Iruvage. If he kills Erik then Clayton will never forgive himself—

Never forgive yourself? Really, Clayton? You'll find a way. Your focus was elsewhere, Erik made his decisions, you gave him all the information and he chose to go out there, you can't be held responsible for his mistakes—

He swallows. "Okay. I understand. Out."

"*Mr. Hunt, Captain Gamboa requests an update on the cease-fire with the alien. Has the situation there changed? Over.*"

"No. The alien will only act to defend himself." He damn well *better* only be acting to defend himself. "Keep the perimeter secure while the science team works. Out."

"*Mr. Hunt, Captain Gamboa requests permission to move in support of Team Zero.*"

Why did Erik have to run off into the woods to do nothing important? Why did he have to take Anna with him? Because Clayton screwed up, because he dropped a bomb on innocents, because he manipulated Erik into haring off on his La Mancha quest, it's all his fault in the end, like Paladin, like Rosamaria—

"I said keep the fucking perimeter secure!" he snaps. "Christ, don't bother me, I've got six hours to save the fucking planet! Literally nothing else matters! Out!"

Literally nothing else matters. Not Erik's life. Not all the people who fell out of the sky and died. Not the children he nuked. If it doesn't matter then why does it suck so much?

There is no way he's getting back to sleep now. He has a mid-dream hard-on, the kind that pops up when you wake straight from REM sleep. Damn it. He washes in cold water, puts on shorts, and goes out to attempt a run.

Mike Jan is standing right outside, armed and armored, like a gargoyle. "Morning, sir." He looks at Clayton's shorts. "Sleep well?"

"No. Don't you sleep?"

"I practice hemispheric sleep, sir. One side at a time. Like a dolphin. That way I can remain alert to changes in the tactical situation."

"Huh," Clayton says. "I'm going for a jog."

"I'll come with you, sir."

Oh, God, does he have to? "I was actually going to invite Chaya with me. We need to sync on some stuff." Like whether they should send Aixue back into Blackbird. Brute-force test of her immunity.

Mike frowns at his shriveling tent. "Sir, are you going to fraternize with her?"

He stares at the white boy with barely disguised disdain. Black male hypersexuality conjured up from the white id, every chance they get. "That's not really appropriate, Mike."

"This is a bad time to deplete your semen, sir. You need to keep your testosterone levels high in order to fortify your capability for abstract thought. Any vagus nerve stimulation could overactivate your reptilian brain and interfere with your neocortex." Mike's four-lensed night vision goggles scan their surroundings. "The next six hours are going to be critical, sir. If you need me to ask any of the female personnel to dress more modestly, I can do that, sir."

"Don't worry about it, Mike." It seems important to keep saying his name, like keeping a demon firmly under control. He imagines Mike Jan is what happens to boys who grew up masturbating in the turret of a Humvee while on patrol, waiting for the completion of an IED blast. "Keep up if you can. I'm pretty brisk."

* * *

CLAYTON//350 MINUTES REMAIN

Clayton's very glad when Chaya, Professor Sivakov, and Professor Huang all show up in the agreed place, at the agreed time. Their teams follow: Chinese and Russians in windbreakers and sweatshirts and button-downs, Chaya's people in vests and helmets, with big mugs of sweet, citrusy coffee.

"I hope you've all taken the last eight hours to rest and talk things over. Come in, come in. Find a seat." Clayton waves and smiles and worries over his big gamble: that a solid eight hours of rest will be worth more, in the end, than eight hours of fried brains dragged over cold problems. He better have been right. He has no time for proper debriefing, or proper care of these vital human assets. He has to swing them at the problem until something smashes.

"Okay," he says. "No bullshit. You know the situation. My science team is dead. You're all I've got. You hate the fucker I work for, and I don't blame you. But we've got six hours to stop his people from blowing us all to Dinotopia."

A Ugandan woman puts up her hand. "Excuse me. We want to leave."

"Miss Nakyanzi?" He gets the nod. "In six hours it won't matter if you leave or stay. Wherever you go, you are equally dead if we fail. We have this one chance to save our souls."

He does not give her a chance to answer. He turns to the whiteboard and, in the jittery fluorescent glare, writes in red dry-erase pen:

souls

He doesn't explain yet. He just leaves it up there. "We all know Blackbird can modify and transform matter. It does this without any detectable physical intermediary—no machinery, no force field. In your opinion, does Blackbird operate in a manner unexplained by modern physics?"

Anatoly Sivakov puts up his hand. "The Large Hadron Collider has explored all the energy ranges where the Standard Model permits unknown fields to interact with matter. Either the Objekt's influence on matter operates through a known field, and it is fully explained by modern physics, or our conception of physics is badly incomplete. The Objekt cannot be manipulating an undetected field in the Standard Model."

Clayton nods. "Professor Li. Can you please share your current theory?"

"Oh. Um. Sure." She gets up, takes a breath, and then goes super saiyan. Clayton can't explain it, but there is a brilliance in her, a luminous filament: knowledge running through flesh and, by resistance, producing radiation. She just mode switches.

She says:

"Blackbird is a mathematical artifact from a mathematical space. It is the expression of a fundamental truth that predates the universe as we know it. This truth is the process by which modern physics emerged from the fire of the early universe: a series of symmetry breaks, occurring through self-organized criticality, spontaneously creating complexity out of chaos. It is not an accident that physics appears tailored to permit life. It is not simply good fortune that the Higgs mechanism gives particles mass without disrupting gauge invariance, or that the wildly unequal mass of the proton and electron allows atoms to form. It is all inevitable. As inevitable as the system of the primes. Existence must exist. And it must exist in a way that allows life to exist."

If there is, in fact, a radiance about her, then it shuts off. She nods shakily and sits back down.

"Thank you," Clayton says. He's not sure what to do with that. "Now that we've established the preordained inevitability of our existence. Let's talk souls."

"Souls," Chaya Panaguiton repeats suspiciously.

She's sitting in the front, feet flat, shoulders straight, chin up. Her posture tugs everyone around her a little straighter. When she is not speaking, Chaya thumbs the beads of her rosary. Clayton knows what Chaya is doing at all times, because some part of his adrenaline-soaked, fear-vigilant brain keeps selecting her out of the crowd, like a CSI character murmuring *enhance, enhance*. This is because she is wearing cut-offs and a tank top, and Clayton, anxious and keyed up, just—notices her. In all his conversations with Rosamaria, who is also attracted to women, he never figured out if this was a behavior peculiar to men. Did she have the same CSI zoom? Did she *notice* in that distracting, eye-snagging, embarrassing way? It's hard to compare perceptions. Hard to share how your body sees bodies with another body.

Body and soul. How Catholic of him.

"Yeah. The aliens believe souls are real." Clayton starts pacing. He's stripped down to his 'good ass jeans' (as Rosamaria would put it) and black compression top, trying to sidestep the officious American look, to come at them as some kind of CrossFit-and-cleanse tech guy. "Let's take them at their words. Souls are real. Not translated religious beliefs, objectively real."

Clayton acknowledges Chaya's protest with a nod and an upraised hand: "I know that something can be objectively real without scientific evidence. So, in that spirit, I want you to imagine a construct we can't measure. Something which sticks with us, which characterizes our basic identity, which motivates our choices. Given those constraints, what would you tell me? What would you say to describe this soul?"

There's a long silence. One of the Ugandans offers: "The soul is what gives you the strength to change things you don't think can be changed."

Clayton, foolishly, blows past this. "A fine description of its function. What else?"

Anatoly Sivakov shifts in his chair and says tolerantly, "Well, if it were to alter our behavior, the soul would have to interface with the brain. And if it cannot alter our behavior, it would be meaningless, and it effectively would not exist."

"Very Comtean." Clayton is getting into this now. "The soul has to interact with the material of the brain. I agree."

Chaya crosses her arms. "Comte was a eugenicist asshole. He spent his whole life trying to twist science around to replace Catholicism."

"And," Li Aixue says, "he didn't believe in truth."

The two women aren't seated anywhere near each other. Clayton wonders if they fought: Chaya betraying Aixue's secret, Aixue cozying up to baby-killer Clayton to win access to her workstation. No time to ask.

"So we have a soul. It interacts with the brain. Could this be responsible for some of the effects we've seen? What happens if you don't have a soul?"

Graveyard hush in the room, except for the whine of AC. Nobody wants to talk about the atmanach.

"Come on," he urges. "I haven't seen it in action. You guys have. What happens to people who get hit?"

Chaya: "They freak out if they see other people. They get violent."

"Okay. Why?"

"Choice," Li Aixue says. "They can't stand seeing people make choices. They can't even tell who you are anymore."

Clayton nods along with her. "So I propose that's what the soul is for. Choosing. I don't mean a compatibilist model of free will, where our choices emerge deterministically from our past experiences and our unique mental structures. I mean genuine *free* will."

What if there's an element of the mind that's unconstrained by what's physically possible? That doesn't care about what's happened to it—only what it can do? It goes against everything Clayton has ever believed about the universe. But if it explains what's happening here . . .

"But this reeks of teleology," Sivakov complains. "The universe was not designed to serve us . . . the universe did not anticipate man. Why should there be a special physical law for our minds?"

"*And the Lord God commanded the man, 'You are free to eat from any tree in the garden; but you must not eat from the tree of the knowledge of good and evil, for when you eat from it you will surely die.'*" Chaya, elbows braced on knees, looks up from her rosary. "I always thought: what kind of a choice is that? Don't do this, or you will die? But maybe that's the point. Even when there *is* no choice, God still gives us the capacity to choose."

Clayton, bless his bloated brain, recollects: "When you were reporting what Ssrin told Khaje, you said something about blasphemy. Do you remember?"

"Yes. Ssrin told Khaje something about people who get sick. She said . . . 'you want to kill them for the same reason people touched by the atmanach want to kill you. You see blasphemy.'"

"So there's *some* connection between what the atmanach does to people and what Blackbird does to people!"

Professor Huang, with polite disbelief: "That seems very tenuous. Do we really *want* to kill people who are affected by Blackbird? Yes, the Spetsnaz did, but they believed they were stopping the spread of a disease. And Blackbird does not *only* cause seizures and insanity, the way the atmanach does. It changes things physically. Mice, sheep, human beings."

"Right. Which brings us back to the central problem. We don't have enough data to understand the effect. And data is what causes the effect to spread."

Huang Lim frets at his beard. "There are terabytes of data in the lab computers, if we go back in . . ."

"I'll go back in," Li says brashly. "I'm not scared. And you all think I'm immune, don't you?"

Now there's a sudden hush. People look at Li, and at Chaya.

"She is," Sivakov says resignedly. "We all know it. She went inside and came back out. You wouldn't have taken such pains to keep her hidden if she hadn't."

From the front row, Chaya rounds on him. "Maybe we just didn't want her shot to death for *your* team's fuck-up!"

"I know. I know. It haunts me too. But we must go forward." Sivakov rises wearily. "Professor Li is our only clue. The only one to survive unchanged."

"Unchanged?" Clayton says probingly.

Has she survived unchanged? There's something different about Li Aixue, if you look at her out of the corner of your eye. She's too sharp, too bright, too . . . is she humming? Is she ringing? Like a chime?

No. That's just a migraine coming on.

"She's not immune," Chaya says. "She's just lucky. I think she was just in there for a second, and it didn't get to her. Then the live footage she watched from the drones, I think she didn't really pay attention. Her head was in the clouds. She didn't take enough of a dose to develop the disease."

"You're protecting her," Sivakov says.

"Of course I am. Someone has to. Certainly *she* won't do it. She wants to go back in there and die."

"I won't," Aixue says.

"You will and you know it. You just want to throw yourself at the problem because you're guilty your friends died and you couldn't stop it. But you're not special, you're not uniquely immune. You just dodged getting infected, and I got you out because"—her voice catches—"all that covering for you and lying for you had to mean something other than 'I feel bad I scared her.' But I don't think it did."

"Oh," Aixue says.

There's a change in the room's energy. They thought they had a breakthrough—at last, a real clue. And it's gone again. Clayton knows, a forecast as good as fact, that if this meeting breaks up with no progress, there will not *be* any more progress.

He's got to swing them at the problem until something breaks.

"I have a radical suggestion," he says.

Eyes turn.

"Let's assume we're right. Souls have something to do with choice. People have souls, souls influence the choices they make. The atmanach feeds on those choices.

"What if Blackbird does too? Writing is the record of a choice, so Blackbird alters it. The same applies to microchips, circuit boards, drones, radar . . . all of them are constantly altered by human input. We know Blackbird can detect when a change is impelled directly by a human mind. What if it's simply detecting the action of a soul?"

"What about the mice?" Sivakov objects.

"The mice were covered in human choices! Implants, experimental conditions, choices about where to position the cages. So Blackbird targeted them. And they became propagators of the Blackbird effect because . . ." Fuck, because what? "Because they were *intended* from the beginning to capture Blackbird's effect. And Blackbird amplified that intent!"

"Mm. Maybe . . ." Li frowns uncertainly. "I don't see what that has to do with spontaneous symmetry breaking . . ."

Neither does Clayton. But maybe Li is overfixated on her math. "The advantage to this theory is that we can test it. Right now."

"Test it?"

"Sure," Clayton says. "We just have to remove someone's ability to make choices. And then we see if they become immune to Blackbird."

Chaya stares at him. "But how can you remove a—"

She understands. The rosary in her fist lashes and settles.

"Yes," Clayton says. "The atmanach."

Anatoly Sivakov stands up. "I volunteer. No, Lim, don't you dare. I am at least two years older than you. I am the oldest, so I volunteer."

"I have AIDS!" Huang Lim blurts. "I got it in Hennan when I was donating blood! Let me go!"

"No you don't," Li Aixue says. "You just made that up, you stole it from a Yan Lianke book."

"Even if you do," Sivakov says, "the condition is treatable. I will go."

The poor fucker. "You understand that you'll be alone in a way that no human being has ever been alone. You can never again interact with someone without experiencing an aversion so overwhelming that it will, apparently, drive you to kill."

"Yes," Sivakov says. "But if soullessness grants immunity, then I can go into Blackbird and report what I find. And who knows? Maybe all of you will have to do the same, in order to follow me. Then I will not be alone, will I?"

"Anatoly," Huang Lim says, "are you truly willing to do this?"

"Ah, what else can I do? It is like the American says. The fate of the world at stake. Dead people all over. A complete pizdets. What is one more old mathematician? So yes, yes, cut away my soul!"

<hr />

CLAYTON//303 MINUTES REMAIN

The screams become higher and thinner and much more frequent, because there are more and smaller mouths making them.

Eventually, the thing that was once Anatoly Sivakov loses its radio and its camera.

They get a last glimpse of the tortured shape pulling itself away on its belly. Small motions are beginning to stir in that dragging, elongated form: fingernails are growing from its skin. Like corn on a cob.

People sob. People shut their eyes and cover their ears.

Clayton goes outside to vomit. It's not so bad, he tells himself. Just physical mutilation. Not as bad as a real moral transgression, a real violation of the human condition.

He rinses out with a travel bottle of mouthwash. An image comes to him of Sivakov lifting his left arm to show them the shapes growing from it: tiny hands fumbling against the plastic of his suit, plucking, clutching, pulling at his skin from the inside.

He throws up again.

"*Did it work?*" Iruvage sends cheerfully. "*My atmanach is making a nice reduction of his soul.*"

"No," Clayton moans. "It didn't."

"*Oh, what a terrible surprise. What a loss to the whole expedition.*"

"Fuck you."

"*Fuck me? Fuck you! You asked me to do that. You failed. Find a better way.*"

He goes back inside. Finds another bottle of mouthwash and spits into the trash.

"We learned one thing from that," he says. "We learned that removing the soul doesn't protect you. No soul makes it worse. It makes things happen much, *much* faster. He went . . . he was mutilated almost instantly."

It doesn't make any fucking sense. Erik's team passed through the labs without being transformed at all! They were in there for twenty minutes or more. But Sivakov hadn't even made it to the Russian biolabs when he started to complain of blurred vision and itching arms.

"So," he croaks, to the silent, shattered room. "I was wrong. We only have five hours left." Fuck it. "I'm going in next."

ACT 4

THE BATTLE OF BLACKBIRD

CHAPTER THIRTEEN

Erik has to shove it out like a scrap-wire shit, but at last he manages to say what needs to be said.

"Anna, I don't know if I can do it."

He hasn't said a word in . . . a while.

He didn't purposefully break contact. Iruvage kept pressing in, Erik kept moving to deny him access to Anna and Khaje, because they were his center of gravity, they were the only defense against the bug-bombs. Whenever possible he tried to close up with nearby friendlies, so they could fire and maneuver as a team. But Iruvage would go for the biggest clump of targets. And that forced them to scatter.

There are rules about casualties in combat. Most rounds fired will miss. Most soldiers will not hit more than one enemy. Most hits will be wounds, not kills. Most kills will happen during the initial ambush or the final rout.

But Iruvage violated all of them. He violated the assumptions and he violated Erik's people. And nothing Erik did could stop the monster.

And then he was down to a single mag, standing on the lip of a muddy gorge, aiming at nothing. Absolute silence. Even the insects driven away.

He stood there, breathing hard, waiting for motion in the fog.

Anna tapped him on the shoulder. "Hey. I need help moving Mom."

So Erik helped. Anna led them down a muddy gorge, back toward the meadows and Blackbird. They fell a lot. They got covered in black mud.

He keeps thinking: Clayton did this? Clayton told Iruvage to kill me? That can't be right. *I* chose to come out here. I wanted to help those Kurds. I did it so I'd know Clayton wasn't fucking with me.

But he told me there were survivors. He told me. He can't have set me up—am I really that predictable?

How is it possible that he could know me so well, and still hate me enough to want to kill me?

And if he wanted me to die, why am I the one who lived?

"I don't know if I can do it," he says.

She's got her mother slung over her shoulder, fireman-style. She must have the thighs of a god, sliding downhill with her mom on her back in the dark. Erik threw his NVGs away because he's pretty sure Iruvage can track batteries. They're navigating by aurora light.

She says: "You don't know if you can kill Clayton?"

"Jesus!" Erik was going to ask about *removing* him, confining him, putting him under anesthesia—only, he realizes, that's all defensive bullshit.

Earth is on the line, right? Anna's been trying to tell him, over and over, that the very future of humanity is at stake. Iruvage said it himself. Clayton needed Erik out of the way.

Which means that whatever Clayton's doing, Erik can still *stop* it. He can stop Clayton from surrendering humanity to an alien power that disfigures the souls of its subjects.

Any chance that Clayton could give Blackbird to Iruvage *has* to be removed.

"Well? Is that the question? Do you need to kill Clayton now?"

Erik nods.

"Are you willing to let him cut a deal with Iruvage?"

No. Seven billion times *no*. "I am not."

"Have you ever been through a genocide, Erik?"

"No."

"I have."

"I know."

"Pretty fucked up, right?"

Yes. Yes, it was. "I can't judge. I wasn't there."

"You think I deserve to be punished for it, don't you."

He doesn't know how to say this: if people shoot their own family whenever bad guys demand it, then bad guys will keep demanding that you shoot your own family. The right thing to do was to refuse the choice. Don't let evil coerce you into evil. Be good, and therefore force evil to do its own dirty work. Though you die for it, you die clean. You die for the sake of a world where no one can be extorted into shooting their own family. You create a little bit of that world with your death.

"I think you deserved to be saved from that choice," he says.

"Yeah. I bet. Do you know why you'd never do what I did?"

"No." He just knows.

"You will never compromise," Anna says, resetting her mom on her shoulder, "because you're American. America's not going anywhere. Whatever you do, there's going to be someone left to judge your choice.

"But did anyone know who the Kurds were before Anfal? Do you think anyone in the world would praise *my* courage for refusing to shoot my brother and father? Do you think, if I'd shot that Iraqi bastard in the face instead, and we'd all been gunned down where we stood, that the world would stand up and applaud our sacrifice? How many people know what happened to the Kurds, Erik? And of those who do know, how many of them know a fucking thing about Kurds *beyond* the genocide? You don't compromise, Erik, because you're quite sure America is going to stick around to judge you. And you want to be judged well. But the only people around to judge me were God and the people I saved. And God didn't do anything for them. So I had to step up."

"What does that have to do with this?" he snaps. "Are you telling me Clayton did nothing wrong? That he had to kill me and my troops the same way you—"

"Erik . . . he probably asked Iruvage to spare you."

"Fuck him. Clayton's the reason we're in danger in the first place. He meets alien Hitler"—who did Clayton compare Iruvage to?—"alien Cortés, and he just knuckles under? He signs up with this guy who shouts 'I love genocide' at the top of his lungs?"

"Of course he does," Anna says. "He's a Black Mexican dude who works for the American government. A country literally, physically built on the slavery and genocide of his ancestors."

"That's bullshit! Trying to rationalize atrocity *now* by pointing to something America did a hundred and fifty years ago? Even if everyone else in the whole fucking nation failed to live up to its ideals, we, him and I, would still have a responsibility to try. That's *all* we can do in the face of history like ours. We have to try to be better! But he doesn't, and he rationalizes it, he says 'things were shitty before so I'll just keep being shitty'! And now you're doing it too!"

"I'm not rationalizing anything. I'm explaining the terms of his choice."

"You're cleaning up after him, you're making him sound less than utterly *vile*!" His temper cracks. "You think it's okay for him to collaborate with Iruvage, to plan the death of my whole unit, to sell the entire planet to slavers, because of what America did to the Indians and Black people?"

She glares back at him, her mother's limp head bouncing at her back. "And what about what America did to my people, Erik? All that aid you gave to Iraq in the eighties, to prop them up against Iran. Do you think the Baathists would've had the strength to launch Anfal, do you think that fucker in the red beret would've showed up to put that gun in my hands, if Reagan hadn't climbed into bed with Saddam? Or maybe—maybe, Erik—I'm thinking about what America did to my people in nineteen-fucking-ninety-one. Go on, you cute little Kurds, we blew up Saddam's army, now have a revolution. Oops! Did we say we'd help? Did we imply we'd show up, the way the French showed up for us? Psych! You're on your own. Rootin' for ya!"

"What the US did was wrong! We fucked you over! And it's just as wrong for

Clayton to fuck over your people, and every other person on Earth, right now! My whole point is that experiencing evil doesn't give you license to do evil!"

"No shit, Erik, but somehow these evil things keep happening, and people have to survive them! Do you think Clayton should just let the planet die? Do you think I should've let that bastard kill me?"

"*Yes!*"

She doesn't answer. Her shoulders shake. For a moment he thinks she's crying and he gets kind of angry. How dare she be angry? She asked and he answered.

Then he realizes she's laughing.

"Liar," she says.

He can't help it. He laughs a little too.

"All that said," Anna pants, "we can't let Clayton have Blackbird. We really can't let Iruvage win."

"So you do think I should kill him."

"I don't think anything, Erik. I just know you're going to."

Maybe she does know. Maybe she knows what he'll do before he knows himself.

Anna looks back at him again. She's got this smirking expression he doesn't know how to name, because it's so out of place. "Someday I'm going to do something so bad you're going to want to kill me."

"Don't say that."

"You won't kill me, though." Oh. That's what the expression is. "You like me too much."

Yeah, well. He liked Clayton a lot. And look what he has to do now.

He checks his wristwatch, worn upside down, to keep the reflective face on the inside of his arm. "About five hours left until they nuke us. How long before we can make Blackbird camp?"

"On foot, from here? Three hours by day. At dark, with Mom, make it . . . four hours?"

"That's not a great margin." Especially if he wants a plan beyond *stop Clayton.* "I might need to break off and go ahead."

"We could've stayed back at Blackbird from the start," she says. "But then Iruvage would've killed Arîn and her women. And no one would've saved those kids. You kinda made the same choice I did, Erik. Kill your own guys to save Tawakul."

"The difference is, we volunteered. That's the job."

A little while passes. Birds won't sing. It's something about the EMP, he figures.

"Need a rest?" she asks. "There's a crook in the river ahead. We can stop and check on Mom."

He really wants to stop. He wants to break his heart rate out of this trancelike Terminator thud. He wants to stop thinking about people dying on his orders. He wants to strip off his armor and ACU and sink into cold river water and watch the mud slide off his skin: separating himself from the filth. He wants to climb naked out of that river with his dick shriveled up in the cold and catch her peeking and say *Sorry to disappoint* and hear exactly how hard she laughs before she remembers her mom is right there.

"Got to keep moving," he says. "Not a lot of time to stop him."

It's a while longer before he has any idea that Skyler Nashbrook is shadowing them.

⁓✦⁓

CLAYTON//289 MINUTES REMAIN

"I'm sorry about Anatoly," he tells Chaya. "If that's what you're here about. I fucked up. I thought I had an answer and I gambled. It cost us a good guy."

She followed him to his little dormitory bunk. Mike Jan let her in after giving her a stern stare: don't threaten the deputy national security advisor's semen. Calm down, Mike, she's gay. And no one could fuck after what they just saw.

"It's my fault," she says. "Not yours."

"Oh. It's your fault. Let me try to confabulate some reason that's true." Clayton splashes lukewarm water on his face, trying to trigger his diving reflex, that burst of primitive alertness wired into the bottom of the brain. You're drowning! Wake up! But it's not cold enough. "You . . . think that if you hadn't spoken up for Aixue, I would've sent her instead of Anatoly? Fine. Blame yourself for getting him killed instead of her." This is not a form of guilt he can empathize with. Either way an innocent died: these crimes are fungible. He dabs terrycloth on his brow. "Let's focus on what we learned. We took Anatoly's soul away, and it made him *more* vulnerable. If Aixue is protected, does that mean she has . . . extra souls? More soul?"

"I don't know. No one else has been affected like her. I can't figure it out."

"So now you think she *is* immune?"

"*I don't know!*"

He stares at the washcloth. In less than five hours there will be no more terrycloth for hundreds of millions of people. No more bathrooms. No more fear sweat or knotted stomach. No more anything, except nothing.

"I want you to tell me the rest," he says. Trying to channel Edward James Olmos a little. The best Latino in space. Sorry, Ricardo Montalbán, you were my botany bae but never my captain. "What happened in Tawakul? After you abandoned the labs."

"Nothing happened. We argued with each other. Khaje told us what she knew about Ssrin and Iruvage. She made Davoud tell us things too. Khaje insisted Anna would show up with a way inside . . ."

"And Ssrin genuinely thought Anna would?" What the fuck was the alien onto? Why wasn't she fixated on Li instead? Does Ssrin's disinterest in Li prove that Li isn't the answer?

It's this fucked-up *Andromeda Strain* situation they've got. One survivor, apparently immune—but why? What makes Aixue special?

"Maybe it's you," he says. "Maybe the power of your concern protected her."

"Mama Mary, I wish."

"So. Removing the soul doesn't make you immune to Blackbird. I thought the intention cap was a clue. But I guess Blackbird doesn't target ensouled choice." He slides past her, narrow brush of cloth and skin, to the cabinet full of amphetamines and 5-Hour Energy. He misses his bromantane pills so bad. For a moment they're in ass contact: *Star Trek: Thirst Contact*, directed by Jonathan Frakes. She's too tired to flinch. He's surprised to find he is too.

He asks her, impulsively: "Do you think there are things God can't forgive?"

"You already asked me that."

"Yeah. But you dodged the answer."

"No. That's why there's God. To forgive the things people can't."

But what does that mean for people who don't believe in God? Must they go unforgiven, the way people without souls apparently must go without true, aphysical choice? Well, he didn't believe in souls either, and suddenly he's been issued one, manifested by the necessity of speculative alien metaphysics.

He wonders how much your brain has to develop before it generates a soul. Do the malformed, swollen mice have souls, earned simply by neuron count? Do leeches qualify for a soul with their mere eight thousand hungry neurons? Does *everything* have a soul, some miserable pan-psychic affirmation of universal presence? He would hate to imagine that.

He can't dry swallow. He pours a cup of water to down an amphetamine. "Here's to souls," he mutters, raising it in a toast. "Whether present or absent, clean or sullied, large or small—"

Chaya gasps. "Hey."

"What?"

"Large souls. Think about it. The Canadians, the drone operators, the people who die of seizures. What if they've got *too much* soul?" She squirms around excitedly to face him: "We've been thinking about souls as a binary. You've got one or you don't. But what you said about Aixue—extra soul, more soul—I mean, what would it be like to have too much soul?"

The thought hits him like a semi-trailer at an intersection. He should've seen it coming a quarter-mile off but he was focused on all the wrong things and it just crumples him up.

"Of course," he breathes. "Sivakov said it. Souls have to interface with the brain to alter your behavior. Our brain evolved to coexist with our soul. It can handle a bit of . . . soul tweaking, soul poking around in the synapses. It's got a tolerance.

"But if your soul gets too active, then it causes too many neural events. Brain activity spikes. You'd get impulsivity first, aberrant behavior, but then you'd go into seizures . . ."

"Yes. Yes!" Chaya grabs the back of her shaved head. "Blackbird finds what's there and makes more of it! Blackbird finds a pattern in the soul, and then it makes more soul. All those drone operators, Emme and her Canadians, the ones who went insane—they had too much soul."

"Holy fuck. You're right." Clayton sinks against the wall in horror. "You're right. Oh, God, you're right . . . oh my *God*, what have I done?"

She stares, baffled. "Why is that bad?"

How can he explain this? "In the NRO, we had too much data. Way too much. I told you how we trained computers to analyze the data and make predictions. But the problem we always struck was chaos. The system is nonlinear; it's infinitely susceptible to small perturbations. Change the littlest thing about a person—what they eat for breakfast, the traffic on the way to the office, who they see in the hallway—and you change a lot of their behavior from that point on. We couldn't forecast human behavior.

"Whenever a system is highly sensitive to minute conditions, omniscience becomes impossible. Maybe . . . souls are the same thing. Maybe souls keep human behavior from becoming predictable, even to an observer with nearly total information. Even to God . . ."

Chaya stares at him like this is all the most obvious shit in the world. "You were never much on theology, were you?"

"No," he says. "And I might have fucked the whole galaxy as a result."

That is why the Exordia would rather destroy Earth than allow Blackbird to escape their grasp.

Blackbird can make people harder to predict and control. A galactic tyranny could not possibly accept that.

He dry-swallows. If he allows Iruvage to seize Blackbird, he is enabling the enslavement of the whole galaxy.

So is the right thing to do . . . to let Earth be destroyed with Blackbird?

No. That can't be right. There cannot *be* human right and wrong if there are no humans left. He can't calculate that as a positive outcome if the basis of his calculations is gone.

"Chaya," he says. Very hoarsely. "You know Iruvage hears everything I say. Right?"

She nods warily.

Carefully he says: "We have to go inside. Will you come with me?"

DAVOUD (~7,875 FEET ASL)

"Okay," Davoud says, when Clayton explains the suicide mission. "So there's a chance that I actually get to go inside the spaceship?"

"Sure. If we all die, who's gonna stop you? But it's killed nearly everyone who got near it."

"Nearly everyone?"

"Aixue was okay."

"Oh. Good. I like her." They talked about NACA 8-series airfoil codes, and how you can get sex changes in Iran.

Clayton's adjusting a gooey metal hairnet around Davoud's head. The goo is conductive gel to help the EEG net read his brain through his hair. It feeds down the back of his neck and along his arm to a tablet computer in a transparent pocket of his suit. This is no good at all to Davoud, because he is blind. But at least someone else can read his brainwaves.

Davoud has no idea what Clayton looks like. He imagines Clayton as the kind of American you see on the news, explaining why it is okay for lots of people to die as long as they're not Americans.

"I'll be fine," Davoud decides, though he has no reason to think so. Trust in flight. "Why do *you* want me along, though?"

"Iruvage wanted you involved. And I take orders from him." Strong hands cinch tape around his wrists. "Plus, your blindness could be an advantage. You won't be as sensitive to infectious information. If we die, you're going to be the one to supervise the handoff to the next team. Okay? That tight enough?"

Davoud remembers his sister helping him put on his first contraband necktie. It is risky to wear ties in public in Iran, for fear of looking westernized. But one day, shortly after he passed his Konkour, Davoud wore a tie and a cheap Ahmadinejad jacket to a protest meeting. It was a stupid risk of his whole career. It was important anyway. His sister was a radical, and she would say things like: "*You* don't have to worry about getting virginity tested by the police. So the least you can do is go to a few meetings." Later he decided that his career mattered more than his sister's respect. He regrets that a lot.

"Mr. Hunt," he says. "Mr. Hunt."

"Yeah?"

"Are we going to hell? You and me? Because we worked for him?"

Clayton laughs a little. "I don't know, Davoud. I expect nobody knows until they get there."

"Iruvage knows he's going to hell."

"Yeah." Clayton snorts. He's taping up Davoud's ankles now. "That's nice to imagine. Iruvage in hell."

"You don't understand. He's actually going to hell. He didn't tell you? All of his people go to hell when they die." What has Clayton Hunt been *doing*? Hasn't he asked Iruvage why he reeks of evil? "Their souls are broken somehow."

"Jesus," Clayton says. "No wonder they're such cabrones."

Clayton never asked the devil about the afterlife, about good and evil and universal truth? What kind of devil-bargainer *is* he?

"What did he offer you?" he blurts.

Clayton Hunt's hands freeze halfway around Davoud's ankle. "What?"

It's not a complicated question. "What did Iruvage offer you to make you work for him? You didn't just do it for free."

He imagines that Clayton's brain makes a sort of Simpsons "D'oh!" noise.

God in heaven. That's exactly what happened, isn't it? Clayton Hunt didn't ask for *anything*. Iruvage just walked in and started to make demands.

And Clayton Hunt went along with it. Like it was how he thought the world should work.

"Let's get to work," Clayton Hunt says, all business now. A cold hiss as he clicks on Davoud's air.

"I thought these suits couldn't protect us," Davoud protests. "I thought we decided it wasn't about anything in the air."

"They'll slow down the rate of information transfer," Clayton says.

"The suits aren't just for protection against Blackbird," Professor Li adds, in her charming California English. "A lot of people died in there. Their suits were ruptured. At least the AC's still on. I guess it'll be a cold stink."

"Oh."

"Everyone ready?" Clayton Hunt calls. "EEG transmitting okay?"

"Ready to do the bio work," Chaya says. "Mama Mary help and protect us."

"Ready to do the math," Li says. "I hope nobody messed with my workstation."

"Ready to build my stupid idea. Mission recorder . . . on. This is Deputy NSA Hunt. I am opening the outer Russian airlock door now. Major Vylomov, if you are monitoring my helmet cam, will you please confirm that the Cyrillic on this panel is undistorted?"

"*I confirm. It is not visibly distorted. We are now reducing your bandwidth to protect ourselves from infection. Out.*"

Cold air washes over Davoud's face from the suit's SCBA feed. Like he is back in his jet. He misses the press of the oxygen mask over his nose, his shaved cheeks, his chin.

※

CHAYA 2:1

It is all so horribly normal, at first.

Blue fluorescent light. The gust of air conditioning, the crinkle of plastic. Empty suit racks. Someone's cheap zinc jewelry, removed and never reclaimed. A sweatshirt blows in the airlock draft like a cartoon ghost.

"There's still power." Clayton leads Davoud along by the wrist. The elegant Iranian is subdued. He still can't see, and that's weird. How long does flash blindness last? Chaya didn't think it was *this* long. She flashed herself a few times in lab, photokeratitis from plasma arcs, and it went away in a few hours.

She checks the circuit breakers, an old and comforting grad school routine. Plasma physics involves tripping a *lot* of breakers. "Some of these need to be reset. If Blackbird's altering the electrical system, maybe it's caused power surges."

"Are we going to lose the computers?"

"I don't think so. As long as the generators can meet overall demand."

"Okay. Let's get started. Check your EEGs every time the timer goes off. Seizures will look like a series of rapid spikes. You may not be aware they're happening. Don't freak out if you just see a few spikes. We're going to be causing a lot of movement artifacts."

"Guys," Davoud asks, too loudly, clipping his microphone, "aren't those mice still in here? Didn't the Russians get sick in just a couple seconds?"

"Maybe. We know that Anna and Erik"—Clayton's voice stumbles oddly—"survived just fine after a couple minutes of exposure. The mice were dead. They weren't broadcasting anymore."

"But the computers were," Chaya says. "I don't know if they have as much processing power as even one mouse brain, but they're on."

"Good," Clayton says. "We need them to make this work."

"I bet, if you put those mice on EEGs, you'd get beautiful pink noise," Aixue says. "I bet all those hypertrophied neurons were just there to do the math."

"What math?"

"The math that makes everything."

Clayton and Chaya look at each other.

The labs exist in, roughly, three parts: Ugandan air-tent on the inside, beneath Blackbird's nose; Chinese labs in a cluster around the Ugandan tent; and the Russian labs in a long string leading to that cluster.

So they start in the Russian area, and have to work around the corpses. Russian Biolab B is the worst: bodies stacked on bodies, sprawled and fouled, complicated by Blackbird and ruptured by Spetsnaz guns.

In Lab A, all of the distended brain-mice are dead and desiccating. Those poor little sacs of mind. Chaya hopes they were never aware. That they didn't have to suffer through something like Sivakov's last moments. If he has had last moments. If he is not still here somewhere—

She shakes herself. "Clayton, get started printing the test media. I'll start taking samples."

Clayton is going to test the effect of Blackbird on language. Chaya's job is to look at its effect on living tissue. Like most scientific work, this is boring and involves a lot of hand analysis.

She uses the grossly distended but still functional lab servers to call up the security recordings of the massacre. It's all fucked up—the video compression algorithm has gone berserk, and there's serious macroblocking around the mice. This turns out to be surprisingly helpful. She's pretty sure that the macroblocking indicates the severity of a mouse's transformation. Call it magical thinking, call it intuition, call it the human mind finding patterns without understanding the logic beneath. Just like Blackbird.

She's trying to figure out which mice suffered the most severe transfigurations. Did any of them hatch their brain-worms sooner? Did any of them get especially big and weird?

Immediately a funny pattern shows up. Mice that were physically inside Blackbird transformed fast and hard. So did control mice that were exposed to sounds, video, and electromagnetic fields from Blackbird.

But control mice whose cage temperature, or cage atmosphere, was set up to mimic Blackbird didn't transform at all. So maybe temperature isn't a particularly rich vein of information, and it makes a bad vector for Blackbird to spread its effect.

She codes the severity of each mouse's transformation on a scale from 1 (no change) to 7 (fully expressed megabrain). Then she regresses that value against each mouse's degree of exposure to Blackbird.

Naks! It works. The more exposure to Blackbird a mouse had, the faster and more radically it hatched into a brain-maggot. Some of the mice only hatched *after* their neighbors hatched and exposed them for a while.

She logs on to IRC and sends to Huang: *Low-bandwidth communication should be safe*

GOOD, he types. HOW ARE YOU

> *I'm okay. Going to get tissue samples for you now*
> HOW IS AIXUE
> *Doing math*
> OKAY PLEASE LET ME KNOW IF INSTRUCTIONS ARE NOT TRANS-
> LATED CLEARLY. I THINK KINGFISHER SYSTEM IS AMERICAN
> ORIGINALLY?
> *Yeah it has plenty of English labels don't woryr*
> **worry*

She tapes up her suit's visor, then smears a gray wash of dry-erase marker across it. Maybe blurring out her vision will reduce her information dose.

She gets a dead brain-maggot out of a glove box. "How did you *breathe?*" she asks it. It doesn't have a mouth, and its windpipe must be clamped shut by the growth of its brain. Maybe skin diffusion, like a frog? Maybe that's why it died. Too much brain for not enough skin. Mama Mary. She hates this.

She carries the brain-maggot to the Chinese biolab, where she takes samples of the fatty tofu of its brain and the thick red liquid inside, images them under a microscope, and then, following the instructions the Chinese team sends her over IRC, she loads them into the ThermoFisher KingFisher automated analyzer.

The KingFisher can read DNA sequences at targeted locations, but it can't physically examine the structure of DNA. For that, she needs to get purified DNA extract from the KingFisher machine, then mount the DNA on slides of mica and put them under an atomic force microscope.

Fortunately the mica slides have been pre-prepared. She follows chat's instructions to bind her DNA to the slides with a solution of magnesium and potassium chlorides. Then she rinses it with a pale green solution of nickel chloride and, feeling like a mad scientist, puts the slides under the microscope. It's kind of a bad name, because it doesn't use "atomic forces." It just runs a truly preposterously tiny needle over the DNA samples to feel out the shape of the molecules.

Her EEG timer has gone off several times. She checks it and sees no seizures. "Okay," she says. "Prayer time." She gets down on her knees and presses carefully at the plastic bag protecting her rosary. With difficulty, she says her prayers.

Then, her heart and soul armored with grace, she goes to photograph the dead Russians.

She notes down their ID numbers and any distinguishing marks. Then she cuts their fouled suits open: introducing their mortal waste into this sequestered world of plastic and tape and ultraviolet glare. This border space where the human world tries to destroy the contaminant, and the contaminant tries to change the human. She wonders what Blackbird makes from a place intended to destroy and restrict its effect. What is growing in the bins of tainted sharps, the knots of cast-off gloves, in the HEPA filters and the pumps? What does Blackbird make of all these human efforts to shackle it? Will Blackbird make a perfect prison for itself?

She wonders if thinking like this is an early sign of Blackbird's effect.

She photographs the corpses' unimaginable transformations. Literally unimaginable. Not unrecognizable—it's quite clear what's happened to them—but what has been done to their bodies is the result of manipulations that do not come naturally to the human brain. Can you imagine a human body reduced to a toroid? Can you imagine what happens if you Fourier transform a face? Decompose it into its constituent curves and render those curves as giant fatty rings, like earlobes with strange drums? You cannot.

She covers the corpses when she is finished.

Then she goes inward. Deeper than she probably should, but it's not as if she hasn't been close before. Here is the Chinese physics dome, here is the airlock mated to her airtight Blackbird catafalque. Here are the controls, the Chinese text now merged into a wild forest, fetal characters half imagined by a pre-sane linguist.

She goes through. He's lying there, where Clayton said he'd be. "Oh, Sabiti," she whispers.

In a proper Ugandan Catholic burial, family members wash and dress the body. He goes home to his ancestral village. Friends of the family gather and remain for days.

All she can do is say: "Sabiti, I promise I will say a rosary every day for nine days."

Something strikes her. She gets down on her hands and knees, squinting through her marker-smeared helmet, and looks at Sabiti's hands. His gloved fingers have forked into a fine lacy structure, like a Chinese finger trap, which loops back around to his wrist. Turning his hands into beautiful filament bulbs.

He was always making USL signs. Blackbird . . . what? Found the signs encoded in his *hands*? How?

She covers him with a tarp.

She looks up. The ladder climbs diagonally into Blackbird. The intention cap waits.

She imagines whatever remains of Anatoly Sivakov banging against the inside of that cap. Trying to get out. No longer possessed of enough soul to qualify as something with intent.

She gets the fuck out of there.

<hr>

An hour later she calls Clayton and Aixue on the lab intercom. "Got something on my analysis of the Russian corpses."

"*Go ahead. I've been running the test generator.*"

"I photographed all the dead Russians."

"*Jesus,*" Clayton says with respect. He loves a good imaging satellite.

"Then I catalogued the physical changes. Mostly they were very minor. Split fingernails and hair fibers. Slight bifurcation of the pupil or the teeth. Enlarged pores. Buds on the tongue, tissue growth inside the nose. Some more dramatic transformations. The most serious cases were, uh, destroyed by gunfire." She lets up on the transmit switch for a second. "Then I went back to the footage of the outbreak. I coded the proximity of each scientist to the mice, whether they were conducting dissections or just observing. Then I regressed that against their, um, subjective degree of mutilation."

"*You wanted to know if people closer to the mice got transformed more dramatically,*" Clayton says with even greater respect. Chaya is annoyed that he's clearly raising his opinion of her. Men tend to do this: treat her like a Strong Woman, because she's tall and fit and works with her hands, but then express some silent surprise when it turns out she really *does* possess initiative and insight and perseverance and all that other stuff. In her experiences, men are disappointed by one another's failures, but surprised by women's success.

"I spotted nearly everyone in the footage having some kind of seizure—pausing for a few seconds, falling, shouting. But only a few suffered major anatomical changes. And they were the ones, like Kuznetsova, who were in closest contact with the mice."

"*So we've got a link between dosage and effect! If you get a low dose, you have seizures. If you get a higher dose, the syndrome progresses to gross anatomical changes.*"

"No," Chaya snaps, a little irritably: using the intercom is a risk, he shouldn't be wasting her time trying to jump ahead. "You're missing something. Sivakov got a low dose and went straight to massive physical changes. The drone operators got a low dose and only had seizures. The scientists got a huge dose from the mice, started with seizures, and *then* went to physical changes."

"*Okay. So, um, Sivakov is soulless, gets only physical changes. No soul to hypertrophy, therefore no seizures.*" Assuming their joint breakthrough about having "too much soul" is right. "*The drone operators are normally ensouled, get a low dose, die of seizures: their souls got bigger and killed them. The scientists are normally ensouled, get a massive dose, suffer seizures and then physical changes.*"

"Right. Even if you've got a soul, a big enough dose punches through and starts working on your body."

She can hear him banging his fist against his suit's helmet. "*Maybe your soul's gone by then. On the recording of the mouse dissections, didn't the scientists start to get scared of each other? The way de-souled people get scared of ensouled people? So maybe . . . their souls went away somehow?*"

"It doesn't make sense." Acid is coming very slowly up her throat, the scorched taste of granola bar and 5-Hour Energy. "We know that seizures are a symptom of having too *much* soul. We know that physical changes are a symptom of having *no* soul. Why would people go from having too much soul . . . to no soul? It's like a virus giving you a fever that freezes you to death."

"*Integer overflow? Soul level wraps around from 255 to 0?*"

She laughs.

"*Come see what I found with the test battery.*"

"I'll be there in a bit," she says. "If the DNA sequencing's done I need to upload it to Lim."

Aixue says nothing on the intercom.

Chaya has the awful feeling that even if Aixue figured out the whole problem she might say nothing. Why share the truth, when the truth itself is so glorious and all-fulfilling?

Chaya sits there waiting for her body to decide whether to barf into her helmet. Acid just keeps coming up and she keeps swallowing it back down. Eventually she gets up.

She forgets to look at her EEG.

Clayton has built a nest of laptops around the main Chinese server racks. He's using this as his test generator. He won't let Chaya in there, though, he says it's too much of a risk.

So they meet in a supply container, full of printer paper and toner cartridges. Clayton paces up and down between the shelves. He seems to express his emotions through his ankles and his feet: standing on his toes, pacing, turning, pacing again. Maybe he was a dancer.

"Where's Davoud?"

He looks up sharply. "I left him alone. I didn't want him learning anything he could tell Iruvage."

"I thought—" She doesn't know if she can say this. "I thought, in here, that Iruvage wouldn't listen."

"Yeah. Just not taking any chances."

"Is there anything you want to tell me now?"

He arches one eyebrow, like Tuvok: "Tell you?"

"Now that he's not listening?"

"Oh. Yeah. Iruvage wants Davoud to fly Blackbird away. I'm just not clear on how he actually plans to get Davoud inside. And neither is Davoud. Iruvage has some kind of plan that relies on me *not* understanding the plan." Clayton pivots, paces the other way: his left index finger just brushes the wall on the turn. "The only way we win here is if we get control of Blackbird so decisively that Iruvage can't take it from us. Because once he has it, he has no more use for Earth. And he lets the guys in space nuke us. I couldn't say this when we were still outside, but I'm planning to steal Blackbird and find some way to use it against him."

"You don't need to get into Blackbird to keep it away from him, do you? Get your government to aim some missiles at us. Tell Iruvage we'll nuke Blackbird if he comes any closer."

Clayton shakes his head, begins to speak, thinks of something else, and ends up blurting: "God, you are so fucking hot."

"Yes," she says impatiently. "I know you think so." Men tell her this an exhausting amount. Putangina, she is wearing a full-body space suit and still they are saying it. "Please don't inflict your sexual responses on my competence."

"I deserved that," he says, "I deserved that. But you think like an alien better than I do! Threaten to nuke Blackbird ourselves? That's a *great* idea! Deterrence! The only problem is that the ship in orbit would probably shoot the missiles down."

"Why did you say that about me?" She's noticed his attraction to her, but also noticed that it is completely pro forma. There's no heat behind it at all. She doesn't think he's gay, but he comes off exactly like a gay man complimenting her. Maybe his inner passions are fully engaged with his Erik Wygaunt–related drama.

"Oh, it's medical." He shows her his wrist tablet. "My EEG's starting to grow little spikes. My prefrontal cortex might be glitching. Might lead to bad impulse control."

"Because you've been setting up the experiment?" His protocol is even riskier than hers. The mice she dissected were soaked with Blackbird information, but they were also dead, unable to generate *more* virulent information. He, on the other hand, has to work with live Blackbird amplifier.

"Yeah. It took me longer than I expected to get the laptops and speakers and all that shit set up. After everything Blackbird did to those electronics, still I hit the usual goddamn IT problems. Then I found a printer and I got the test media laid out. So I guess we just wait . . ."

He trails off, staring at her.

"It can do so much," she muses. "It can add new living cells to a body. It can alter the magnetized bits on a hard disk. It can paint on a wall. There aren't a lot of physical commonalities between those structures, but it handles them all the same, diba? So I wonder if it's—"

"Chaya. Selfie mode."

"What?"

He lifts a glove to her faceplate. "Put your phone on selfie mode."

"My phone? I can't, my phones are in my pockets under my suit." She still has the Ugandan habit of hauling around two phones, a cheap double-SIM Orange for making calls on different networks, and a Nokia smartphone for— Why is she thinking about this? What's wrong with her train of thought? Her train of brain, ha-ha.

"Chaya." He's holding out his gloves to her, pleading. "Use my phone. You really need to see your eyes."

"Oh, Mama Mary." She fumbles at his iPhone, but she can't unlock it, can't even work the screen, her gloves weren't made for it. "Pak*shet!*"

"Try Siri."

"It never understands me. And it won't work without a connection."

"Give it back, I'll take a picture of you—"

No! No pictures! If she dies he'll put her picture in a government report and her mother will see her deformities and cry. She tears open a storage carton labeled 电池 #5 BATTERIES, finds a package of Deanda double-As, punches the cardboard open on the corner of the shelf, fishes out a single battery, and uses the negative end as a fake finger on the screen.

Her image, captured by the front-facing camera, is obscured by a smear of black marker. She wipes her visor with her sleeve and looks again. Looks close.

There is a tiny pinch around each of her irises. The round pupil becoming a figure-eight. As if preparing to divide.

"Oh, my eyes," she moans. "And my fingers, I bet it's got my fingers . . ." Where she's been interacting with the contaminated flesh.

"We've got to write the time down."

"But it doesn't make any sense! I haven't even had any seizures! Don't I have a soul? Shouldn't it be giving me seizures?"

Then she looks at her EEG. There are neat clusters of spikes every few minutes for the last . . . half hour or so. They look just like pink noise. Absence seizures. She didn't notice.

"Let's check the cameras," Clayton urges. "Let's see exactly when you started seizing."

But the recordings are corrupt: the footage swarming with macroblocks, gathering into stars and spines and fields of fuzz, congealing on Chaya's form, obscuring her. As if there is some radiation coming off her body, her brain, her soul.

Clayton looks at the footage. Looks back at her. "Hey. How does it know to split your pupils?"

"Because that's where the information is coming in?"

"But why the whole pupil? Instead of each cell in the tissue? Or your entire skull? If Blackbird doesn't know anything about the universe, how does it know what a pupil is?"

CHAPTER FOURTEEN

CLAYTON//194 MINUTES REMAIN

Colorless green ideas sleep furiously. The quick brown fox jumps over the lazy dog.
I am that I am.
Buffalo buffalo Buffalo buffalo buffalo buffalo Buffalo buffalo. I want to put a hyphen between the words Fish and And and And and Chips in my Fish And Chips sign. The coach yelled at the player tossed the ball. This is a totally ordinary sentence. So is this one. This one, also.

Clayton has printed several dozen passages like this on plain 8.5x11 printer paper.

He wants to check whether Blackbird cares about the meaning of words. Can it parse Buffalo as a noun for a place, a noun for an animal, and a verb for "jostling"? Can it learn language? Or does it just see clusters of structure and extrapolate them, heedless of their contents?

Now—staring into Chaya's partitioned eyes—he realizes: *The difference between a cell and a pupil is not so different from the difference between a letter and a word.*

"Come on," he says. "Come on, let's go look."

He has set up a container that he thinks of as the Microwave. It's a broadcast center for Blackbird's transformed server farms to blast out their influence through screens, speakers, Wi-Fi, anything else he can hook up to a server and use as output. He's running screensavers, music, Shepard tones from motherboard speakers, any kind of signal he can convince a computer to generate.

He papered the floor of the Microwave and the surrounding corridor in text. The first few pages he snatches up haven't changed at all.

But once he starts getting closer to the Microwave, he starts seeing:
between the ball. This one.
the lazy dog.
I am that I am.
I am that I am.
I am.
Buffalo buffalo Buffalo buffalo buffalo buffalo Buffalo Buffalo buffalo. I want to put a hyphen between the player tossed the ball. This is a totally ordinary sentence. So is a totally ordinary sentence. So is this is a totally ordinary sentence. So is this one.
This is this one.

Is is a totally ordinary sentence. So is this one.

Ideas sleep furiously. The quick brown fox jumps over the lazy dog.

I am that I am.

It takes a little squinting to read, because Blackbird has ghosted the new text straight over the old. "Pink noise," he mutters. "Pink noise." A bunch of little sentence fragments, one really big one, a couple of intermediate length. It is making sentence-like sentences, paragraph-like paragraphs.

He looks back to tell Chaya what he thinks is happening. She's staring into nothing, mouth slightly agape. Her hands clench, like they're holding on to her rosary. Focal seizure.

Fuck. He can't do anything for her. He keeps going.

Blackbird distinguishes between levels of organization. It understands *syntax.* It might not understand words, or letters, but it understands that words *make up* letters. It's moving words around, but it's not changing the order of letters inside words!

He scrabbles along into the Microwave container and checks another page.

Buto gnthalary. So thy sed chis tam d be. fanaloloneen thishanale. telo fayps th be. is amp Bumy. jufffathelo ach bufalack iphe burd chen Sowoloashis butazy buffufffa jufffondish Fisheeee. psh I to at ffathe.

I azy ce. the.

I quffot s id lloweds id louthalo Cog. thissisheend slonto alox thish laly sh his thiox And ck woves o alo an ary. ber an ply. an baled qufalen buis puffufathetwanck be thent to buss ioalo his ay ises An Co d twal.

I bashelo bury. wntox be bufalo The Buffan twalend he o io bal.

I Corerd send Thipufalouis ayen An alos ipephenace oro I s islenalowan.

"Yes!" he bellows. "Yes!"

Here, closer to a source of Blackbird's effect, the transformation has moved deeper. It's scrambling the order of letters within words. But it still doesn't touch the letters themselves. Like dividing Chaya's pupils, but not dividing the cells within—

"*Deputy NSA Hunt. Deputy NSA Hunt. This is Mike Jan from your personal protection detail. If you are receiving this, please respond with one click.*"

"No!" Clayton shouts, because he was so goddamn close to figuring something out. "Fuck!" He hits the ring switch.

"*Mr. Hunt, be advised that I have been raised by Skyler Nashbrook on short-range radio. He has recovered Major Wygaunt, Anna Sinjari, and her mother. He is bringing them in under escort. Skyler reports there are no other survivors of Major Wygaunt's unit. Skyler says he seems pretty pissed. He says Major Wygaunt says you sent him out there to die. I thought you should know. Out.*"

"Oh, Christ," Clayton groans. "Iruvage, you dumb fuck . . ." Why'd he have to kill them? Why couldn't he have left Erik alone? At least Erik's alive. Thank God Erik's alive. But if Erik's alive, is Erik going to . . . to kill him?

Well, yes. Yes he is. Erik was the one who suggested Paladin in the first place. The plan to kill the bad men.

"What," Chaya says behind him. "What was that?"

"Erik. Trouble with Erik. Why did I bring him?"

Because he wanted somebody he could trust to run the military side. Because he'd thought that, with time, Erik's wrath might cool. He'd come around. He'd see sense.

Wrath. Huh.

Rath, Iruvage said. *Rath the clashing passion. Two stones beat against each other, chipping and cracking, flaking and sharpening. Maybe until one breaks. Maybe forever.*

"Rath," Clayton says. "Me and Erik are full of rath."

"Erik and I," Chaya says, and then, "sorry. Wrath? That's a funny way to describe it. Biblical."

"I know. It is funny. Isn't it? But that's what Iruvage calls it. Rath."

"Iruvage reads the Bible?"

"No, no. Not wrath. Rath. Like . . ." Somehow it sounds different, but he can't explain how. "One letter different. I think."

One letter different.

Blackbird operating on sentences. Then the dosage builds up, Blackbird starts operating on words. The dosage builds higher, Blackbird starts rearranging the structure of individual letters. Like those Chinese characters Erik saw.

Tiers of meaning. Blackbird starts from the top and works its way down. Blackbird not just *changing* but *constructing.* Using what's already there as blueprints to add something new. Interpolating. Remixing.

It begins with the human soul, and as dosage increases, it moves on to the human body . . . then down to tissues, cells, even bacterial DNA . . .

He's almost got it—he can *feel* it—but he's so tired, so hopped up, so scared. It slips away again.

"Shit," he growls. "Shit."

"Let's go see what Aixue's done," Chaya says.

She doesn't have a single seizure after that.

CLAYTON//174 MINUTES REMAIN

Li Aixue sits at her workstation and she *thinks.* Once in a while she will gasp, and a single line will run down her face, from her forehead down her nose through the little dimple above her lips. She bends over the computer and enters a string of commands. Then she thinks again.

"Aixue," Clayton says.

"Hi," she says, an automatic *Hi, Professor Li isn't in right now, want to leave a message?*

"What are you working on?"

"Empirical analysis of Blackbird in an effort to find symmetries that constrain the problem space."

"What problem space?"

"The unification of spontaneous symmetry breaking, pink noise, and the structure of the primes into a single account of how dynamical systems *must* evolve into complex self-organizing states. Jeremy England proposes that systems will tend to maximize their total energy capture and entropy production by spontaneously developing complexity. Could self-organized criticality be the way systems seek this state? Could it be the beginning of a mathematical account of creation? Could it be a bridge between pure mathematics and cosmology?" Li smiles in delight. "And what if this same process gave order to the primes? The prime numbers have a fractal structure. Chaotic at the low level, but structured and Poissonian if you zoom out. They can be modeled as eigenstates of a quantum system. They display a deterministic chaos, with symmetries and harmonics. The gaps between prime numbers are a pink noise distribution, and they appear to be similar to the result of a spontaneous symmetry break, like a fractal growing. Marek Wolf proposed this in 1997. He closed his paper by saying, *What if the primes are in a state of self-organized criticality?* Of course the primes cannot organize themselves, because the primes do not move. They must have *always been* organized, in a way that is axiomatic, fundamental, and irreducible: objectively and purely real. What if the universe is the same way? It became the way it is because it always had to be the way it is? Would that not point the way to a physics with no free parameters? A complete, closed account of creation?"

"Aixue," he says harshly, he knows he's being harsh, "you have to tell us what you've discovered. Now."

"Not ready," Li says.

On frustrated impulse Clayton pours his water bottle on her. The deputy national security advisor, folks. Always keeps his decorum. Li looks up frowning into the stream, and big lukewarm droplets spatter off her suit's visor. Only when Clayton runs out does she say, "Why did you do that?"

"I don't know," Clayton says. "Listen, we're out of time. Erik's coming."

"I don't care," she says.

"We have less than *three hours* until human extinction. Erik Wygaunt is on his way to kill me. Our experiments show a pattern in Blackbird's effect, but we don't know how to use that to get inside. We need a breakthrough now."

"I don't care," Li says. "I'm working on theory."

"You can keep working on theory *after* we save the planet—"

"It's more important that I figure this out."

She means it. She actually fucking means it.

Clayton chews on useless reprimands. There is nothing he can do to compel Li Aixue's mind. What would he do? Threaten to shoot her? Force her to think only about useful things?

She is completely beyond his reach.

In that moment he loves her as much as he hates her. She is pure like nothing in the world is pure. All she wants is truth.

Truth. Truth. Iruvage said something about truth. What the fuck did he say?

K + 165:40:00 hours
Blackbird Camp
Qandil Mountains, Kurdistan

Erik jogs toward the lab complex and Blackbird. He seals his gas mask, puts his helmet back on. He has one magazine left and that is more than enough.

Mike Jan comes jogging his way, hand raised. Somewhere behind him, Skyler Nashbrook is watching.

Erik ignores them. He goes forward into the labs, and he goes alone.

In stories they say, *I have to do this.* But what they should say is: *No one else should have to do this for me.*

CHAYA 2:2

Chaya stares at the page.

It's one of Clayton's sheets of test sentences. How did it get here? Did he put it here? Did *she* put it here when she came in to pray for Sabiti? She must've, but she can't remember.

It must have been put here intentionally, because it is stuffed into Blackbird. Just one white corner sticks back out through the intention cap.

She came here to stare at Blackbird and think about what would happen if she just picked Aixue up and shoved her inside. And lo! the page was waiting.

She climbs the aluminum painters' ladder and tugs it free.

It's not English anymore. It's like calligraphy. One of her aunties used to work in Terminal 3 at NAIA, and she was fascinated by the Emirates airline logo. She spent her life collecting knickknacks of cloth and paper with beautiful Arabic calligraphy. This looks like that, but uncomfortable: the English letters are surrounded by swarms of letteroids, deformed cousins, deranged sub-letter particles. There are tiny feathered offshoots, like mold, growing from the edges of each sign. And—

And suddenly she gets it.

"*What the fuck are you doing?*" Clayton yells from the airlock intercom. "*You can't be in there! You're already infected!*"

"I know," she says, staring at the calligraphy. "I found one of your pages stuck in the cap. Raw Blackbird exposure. It finally started messing with the letters."

"*We know that. We know that. The higher the dose, the lower in the structural hierarchy Blackbird's effect proceeds.*"

"Huang found the same pattern in the DNA samples I sent him."

"*Did he?*"

"Yeah. Hang on. I'll come show you." She trudges back through the airlock, into the Chinese physics tent, where Clayton is lying on the ground with his helmet pressed to the flooring.

"What are you *doing*?" she says.

"I'm listening for Erik's footsteps," he says, as if this is a sane thing to do. "What's happening with the DNA?"

"They wrote up a nice abstract for me. *Increased Blackbird exposure drives changes to lower levels of DNA structure.*"

"The more Blackbird information a mouse received," Clayton translates, "the more its DNA changed. We know that. It's all we fucking know, Chaya!"

Chaya wishes he would just shut up and wait. "It starts with high-level structural change. Alterations in DNA coiling and methylation, the way the DNA's packed into the nucleus—"

Clayton takes a breath.

"I know!" Chaya shouts at him. "I know we're about to be shot! How do you expect me to think if you keep reminding me? Shut up and let me finish!"

"Fine," he says viciously, "go on, tell me all about the DNA in mouse cells. The world ends in two hours and change."

"I will, thanks! As exposure increases, you start to see duplication of coding genes and introns—the 'words' in the DNA language. The length of the duplications is a pink noise distribution, of course. But once the DNA has been exposed to Blackbird information long enough, the actual base pair sequences start changing, and then the base pairs themselves fall apart. The whole strand disintegrates and the cell dies. It can't sustain life."

"Okay . . . okay . . . wait. Wait wait wait. It recursively amplifies structures it finds. But . . . once it's recursively amplifying structure on a low enough level, it alters the individual units of meaning, and the whole system collapses?"

She holds up the page full of mutated calligraphy. "Look at this. Can you read it anymore?"

"No. The letters are all fucked up, the language becomes incomprehensible."

"But you could still *read* the other transformed writing. Even if it didn't make any sense."

"Yeah . . ."

She waves at him, urging him forward. "So? So? So? Do you see?"

"Oh my God," Clayton breathes. He surges up to his feet. "Oh my God, I fucking *get* it. It's so obvious. It changes levels when it can't find any more structure to amplify! So it looks for patterns in the sentences, it exaggerates them, but that destroys the meaning of the sentences. No more patterns to tease out, no arch-sentence to converge on, because sentences don't *have* a single core logic beyond the rules of grammar—sentences don't mean anything in and of themselves, the meaning is stored in the arrangement of words!

"So it swaps the words, it mixes letters around in the words, but that destroys the meaning of the *words*. So it goes down to the letters, and when it starts destroying the letters . . . there's nothing left. No lower level to reach. So it just produces a fractal soup. All those corrupt files. All those people's *faces*! It's trying to exaggerate what it finds. And if it doesn't find what it's looking for, it just keeps going down, until it lacerates the most basic carriers of meaning. That's why the effect starts with the soul and moves to the body! It fucks up your soul, you start having seizures, nonsense behavior, caused and motivated by nothing—so Blackbird can't find anything else to amplify in the soul, it moves down a level and *then* it starts looking for patterns in your physical body. Sivakov went right to that step because he didn't have a soul! The Russians got to that step the long way, when their souls fell apart under recursive transformation, and the Canadians never got to it at all, they died of the seizures first!"

"Exactly," she says. "There's a *reason* it breaks stuff. It's looking for patterns. Maybe it sees the word *need*, so it makes *neeeeeeed*. But that doesn't mean anything. Extending the patterns of, I don't know, a suspension bridge will get you a longer bridge. Extending a honeycomb gets you more honeycomb. But extending the patterns of language doesn't get you meaningful language, it just gets you language-ish nonsense. Extending DNA sequences doesn't give you better proteins, it gives you proteins that won't fold right. It's . . ."

"It needs a pattern that still works if you extrapolate it. Like, um, like pi. Pi looks like a string of random numbers, but if you figure out how those numbers are generated you can just keep calculating new numbers forever. One line of math gets you infinite complexity. Like—"

"A fucking fractal!" Chaya nearly screams. "*Something that's the same at every level of organization!* She was right the whole time! Jesus, Mary, and Joseph, she was right!"

She wants to sob. She was right too! She was right to cover for Aixue! It was okay, it was good of her!

Clayton snarls with carnivorous joy. "Fuck. Okay. So it finds a human soul, which we think is some kind of—record of behavior, a way to keep you acting like yourself, even when you've got this spark of true free will—"

"I guess human souls are . . ." She laughs: Fr. Gokongwei could've told her this. "Souls are just too complicated. Like a book describing your whole life. Whose life actually makes any sense? You can't use what's already there to extract a rule which tells you what happens next. So it amplifies the patterns in your soul, but they stop meaning anything. You start having seizures from your soul fucking with your brain. Eventually the soul just turns into noise. Nonsense. So it gives up on your ruined soul and starts to eat your body."

"And Aixue . . . Aixue . . . she's immune because . . . hang on, I've almost got it . . ."

She swings her arms and stretches: she read a paper once which said the body primes the brain with answers. She's amused to see Clayton checking her out: she's formless in this suit, so what is he looking at? Her gangly limbs? Her graceless—

"Grace," she says.

"What?"

"Grace. A state of divine favor earned through sacrament. Regeneration of the soul."

He thinks about this. "You're saying she's not immune at all? She's just . . . graceful?"

"I'm saying that when Blackbird amplifies her soul, her soul keeps working."

"Why?"

"Because . . . because . . ." Blackbird starts with the highest level of organization it can find. Paragraphs before sentences, sentences before words, words before letters. "Because her soul is part of a higher level of organization. A larger structure. And Blackbird's focusing on *that*. It's making more of *that*, and whatever *that* is, it's not breaking."

"But what the fuck is a higher level of *organization* than a soul?" Clayton asks.

"Grace. A relationship between a person and God. Or—a relationship between souls, whatever you'd call that. Like a . . ."

Like a family. A relationship between souls is a family.

Clayton groans and tries to rub his forehead. The visor catches his hand. "I'm buzzing. I can't think. It's right there but I can't . . ."

Chaya feels it right there too. *Why* would Blackbird need to take a system, a soul or a circuit board or a page, and make more of it? What function does that serve?

Something Aixue told her is the answer. But she can't remember. "We've got to go ask Aixue."

"She's useless—"

"She's just hyperfixated. We have to pique her curiosity."

"How? How do we tell her something more interesting than the structure of absolute indivisible truth—"

The radio in Clayton's suit comes to life. "*Mr. Hunt. Mr. Hunt. This is Jan. Be advised that Major Wygaunt has entered the lab complex. He is armed and unresponsive to challenge. I am in pursuit. I will to shoot to kill. Out.*"

※

CLAYTON//161 MINUTES REMAIN

"Aixue," Chaya says. "Professor Li. What's a structure made out of souls? The way a paragraph is made out of sentences, or a sentence is made out of words?"

Clayton's starting to smell her. A schismatic scent, ozone and smoke, burning rubber, the menthone odor of epilepsy. The smell can't be coming in through his suit, so he knows it's happening in his mind. Her soul is overflowing from her, pushing at his brain, knocking his merely physical biology out of sync.

Li Aixue stares into her workstation. The screen renders an image of Blackbird nested in overlapping flowerlike shapes. She makes a little satisfied noise and says: "Wán měi wú xiá."

"I think she's gone, Chaya," Clayton says.

"No. She's not. Professor. You told me about making more out of less. You told me something about that. It's important. What was it?"

Li Aixue says: "There is a difference between *entropy*, the information required to describe a system, and *algorithmic complexity*, the information required to describe a process which can create that system. This is the reason an action movie is harder to stream than a documentary about paintings. Both movies require the same raw number of pixels to render. But one frame in the quiet, slow-moving documentary is nearly the same as the next. So updating one frame to the next requires only a little data. In contrast, all the quick motions and wild explosions in the action movie require a lot of unique data for each frame update. It isn't as *compressible*. This noncompressible data is entropy: irreducible information. It is related to Kolmogorov complexity."

"Yes! Shannon and Kolmogorov! Why are they important, Aixue?"

"What I've discovered," Professor Li says, "is that *everything* about Blackbird is highly compressible." Suddenly she notices Clayton: "You remember our conversation about Blackbird as a cycle of distillation and extrapolation?"

And he finds himself answering. He can't resist. He needs her. Hear that, Professor Li? You're a genius, understand? God I wish I could think like you, but I can't, so please be my asset, be my answer, be the right one to solve this. I'm just the man who moves the pieces around on the chessboard. I depend on my pieces. That's the only skill I have, to choose the right pieces for the game. Erik's the white knight and I need you to be my black queen.

"Yes. You told me Blackbird tried to compress things to their core logic."

"Have you ever explored the Mandelbrot set?"

The world's most famous fractal: a spiky beetle-shape with a stinger on one end. The magical thing about the Mandelbrot set is that you can zoom in forever and keep discovering new shapes. It's an entire cosmos, a pocket universe of inexhaustible depth. So you might think it's pretty complicated, and therefore very high-entropy. Which it is! If you wanted to describe the Mandelbrot set by taking pictures of every single part of it, you would need an infinite amount of time and computer memory. You can keep zooming in on it forever, always finding new things.

And yet the Mandelbrot set has trivial Kolmogorov complexity. Almost none at all. It can be stored in perfect compressed fidelity, without losing a single detail, using a pen and a playing card.

Why? How can something with *infinitely many* new things inside it be so simple?

Because it's all created by a single equation. The entire Mandelbrot universe emerges from repeatedly calculating a single line of math. Z maps to z squared plus c, where z and c are complex numbers.

"No way," Clayton breathes. "Are you telling me that . . . you've come up with a fractal equation for Blackbird? *That's* what you've been working on this whole time?"

"That's right," Li Aixue says happily. "Of course, my equation is just a beginning. It does not describe Blackbird's core logic. It is simply an empirical description of Blackbird's structure as a three-dimensional subset of an eleven-dimensional fractal structure, which emerges from self-organizing breaks in gauge field symmetry. I have not exhausted the empirical approach—"

"Professor, could you precis this for us?"

"Yes. I think Blackbird is *entirely* mathematical. I think that if you took a microscope to Blackbird's walls, you would never find a hint of matter. Nothing but more fractal structure."

"But the Canadians—"

"Saw a mathematical structure which *mimicked* atoms. And interacted with their spectrometer as atoms would. But all that physical complexity emerged from mathematical simplicity. Can you imagine why you might want a ship that is physically complex but mathematically simple?"

"Because . . ." Clayton can only think of old stories about designing the first stealth fighter. "Because you need to design it on a shitty computer?"

"Oh!" Chaya claps. "Because you need to move it around as data!"

"Exactly! Blackbird is built like an email attachment. You can reduce it to a few equations, instructions to rebuild it, and then send those instructions somewhere."

"I knew zip files were a good analogy," Chaya says.

"Blackbird's not built to move in space. It's built to fly through *math*. Somewhere that the most vital resource isn't fuel, but computing power. I've always believed the universe must be a mathematical structure, Mr. Hunt. Blackbird might have existed in a time when the only structure in the cosmos was mathematical. And the physical universe, the big bang, might have occurred *as a mathematical event*. As necessary as the prime numbers."

"Jesus," Clayton says, because he doesn't know how else to react.

"God, actually," Aixue says.

"So it was . . ." Chaya's blink hides, and then reveals, her changed eyes. "Blackbird was like a compressed archive? Where? Stored on what substrate?"

"The universe itself, I suppose."

"And then Blackbird decompressed itself?" Chaya tips her head back to think, and through her helmet, Clayton sees that the dimple in the center of her upper lip has started to deepen. If it keeps going, it will cut a notch in her face. "How? How did it go from math to a thing with size and shape?"

"I don't know," Aixue says. "Maybe, deep down, there is no difference between physical occurrences and mathematical operations."

Chaya smiles hugely. "Okay. I've got it. I know what Blackbird wants. I know the reason behind everything it's done."

Clayton feels like his brain is being trampled. "You do?"

"*It's trying to finish decompressing.* Think about it. Every time it interacts with something, it tries to find the core structure, the basic *rule*, and then exaggerate that rule into more stuff. Decompressing. Expanding. Unzipping. It tried to make people's souls into bigger souls. It tried to make our bodies more like themselves, and destroyed them. It tried to make mice and computers to spread its effect. It's trying to do something and it's not succeeding. Because it can't get past some important step?"

"Like it's trying to hatch," Clayton says. "But it can't get out of the shell."

What does Blackbird *make*? Flesh out of flesh. Electronics out of electronics. Words out of words.

And soul out of soul, right?

He puts a finger to the visor of his suit.

"Professor Li. Does Blackbird have a soul?"

⁂

For the first time, she looks straight at him. "If we postulate that a soul is some quasi-physical property which allows one to exercise free will?" She frowns: "I don't know. I don't have a lot of free parameters left in my equation."

"You're saying that if there's math to make a soul, Blackbird can't do it."

She hesitates. She can't bring herself to say *I don't know*.

He asks: "Could we *give* it math to make a soul?"

"Yes, trivially. Simply give it a compression algorithm for a soul, and it would latch on to that algorithm and execute it until it had fabricated a soul."

There's a joke about mathematicians. A mathematician walks into her mom's kitchen and sees the stove is on fire. She checks to be sure there's a fire extinguisher, nods in satisfaction, and walks out. Her mom's house burns down.

"Why didn't you use the extinguisher?" her mom asks her.

"Oh," the mathematician says, "it was obvious that a solution existed. Why bother working it out?"

Chaya says: "Aixue. *What mathematics describe a soul?*"

"I don't know. I'd like to know."

She'd like to know. She'd like to know the truth.

"Prajna," Clayton breathes.

The seven great passions Iruvage told him about. One of them was prajna, the passion of knowing.

If a soul is the actuator of free will, it would need to know the will of the person it was attached to.

And the things people want and will are complicated. Conditional. They contain multitudes. Their lives are full of subtlety and contradiction. People are high-entropy, hard to describe. Blackbird tries to compress that entropy into a clean, simple, elegant pattern. But when you take that entropy away, when you try to reduce someone's soul, you destroy its ability to describe them. You destroy *them*. This is why Blackbird ultimately destroys the souls of those it operates on: in trying to create order, it scrubs necessary chaos away.

Only it hasn't done that to Li Aixue. It hasn't destroyed her soul and her body. It's just made her constantly, continuously *like herself,* living in pursuit of truth—

Because the narrative of Aixue's life is *not* irreducibly complex. It's fractal. It's the same at every scale.

Aixue's soul is elegant and simple enough in its structure for Blackbird to recognize and amplify it without destroying it. *That's* why she seems immune.

She is becoming an amplified version of herself: a caricature that is, essentially, still the original.

Blackbird is endlessly amplifying and reinforcing her love of truth. Her prajna.

"Prajna?" Chaya repeats. "What's prajna?"

"A level of organization above a soul. A relationship between soul and God. Or, in this case, a relationship between soul and the truth."

"Oh. I thought that the level of structure above a soul would be a group of souls. Like a family."

He stares at her. That's it. That's the answer.

"Holy fucking shit," he breathes. "Iruvage, you bastard. You genius alien bastard. You *motherfucker.*"

The two women stare at him.

"Blackbird uses matter to make matter," he says. "Therefore, it must use souls to make a new soul. It looks at language, it deduces the underlying syntax, it uses that to generate new language. Now it needs to look at souls, deduce an underlying syntax, *and generate a new soul.*"

"But we don't have anything to give it to unzip. We don't have a compressed soul. Unless you mean Aixue—?"

"No. Not Aixue. It'd just keep making her more like herself. No new soul generated. Like multiplying one by one."

Rath. That's what Iruvage called it. *Rath, the clashing passion.*

Iruvage knew all along. He was busy out there, drawing Erik back like a rubber band, pulling him farther and farther from Clayton, filling him up with fury—and then releasing him to plunge back to Clayton and revenge.

All this time he intended Erik and Clayton as the mold. Each one printed on the other by their conflict. And when Blackbird sees them, when it sees their rath, it is going to see a pattern to exaggerate. A pattern bigger than either of them, with their souls embedded in it, the way words are embedded in letters: and it will make more of that word by creating more letters. *No* becomes *noo, to* becomes *too,* the structure altered but the word still comprehensible.

And each added letter will either be a copy of Erik's soul . . . or Clayton's.

"I'm going into Blackbird," Clayton says. "As long as Erik's after me, I'm immune."

"*Guys?*" Davoud's hesitant voice, on the suit intercom channel. "*I just heard someone walk past me.*"

CHAPTER FIFTEEN

The airlock closes behind Erik. The pumps growl. Decontamination spray spurts over him. He wipes the lenses of his gas mask.

The inner door opens.

Brightly colored equipment everywhere. Too much shit to trip on. He goes in. Plastic umbilical tunnels, the AC cranked up so high Erik's breath mists the mask. Generator hum. His footsteps, quick and smooth.

The rifle in his arms. Slaved, by reflex, to the motion of his eyes.

He thinks, incongruously, of England. If Clayton is right, then in mere hours an alien weapon will burn away the London fog forever. Blast pressure will topple Stonehenge and thunder across the Scottish highlands. No more heath or moor, whatever those are. No more incomprehensibly bitter comedy, London tube, Blitz spirit, *Doctor Who*, Earth is not defended after all. Stories do not end the way you want. When men of Erik's acquaintance shot Osama bin Laden, Erik thought to himself, why, what a perfect ending, the evil man is killed by American commandos: it's like a story with a payoff.

But he should've known better. Doctor Manhattan was right, nothing ever ends, and when you win the war and close the book, someone else is busy writing his own miserable prologue. Versailles becomes Hitler, Appomattox Courthouse becomes Jim Crow, *Charlie Wilson's War* becomes Osama bin Laden. And when DEVGRU kills bin Laden in Abbottabad, it's not an ending at all. It's no payoff. The sheikh's role was done. He cast his dart and poisoned America. Killing him was an ending but the next chapter had already begun. All the endings turn into bad beginnings.

This is what Erik thinks of as he goes after his best friend.

This is what Erik chooses, with all his heart and soul, all his cortex and cor cordium, to disbelieve.

Erik believes that the right man in the right place *can* save the world. Stanislav Petrov was on watch in the Oko bunker when the Soviet Union's automatic alert system told him America had launched a nuclear missile. He decided not to fire back. Five more times the bunker told him America had started World War III. Each time, Petrov chose not to fire. His comrade in conviction Vasili Arkhipov cast the single vote that stopped his submarine from firing a nuclear torpedo and pushing the Cuban Missile Crisis into holocaust. And speaking of holocausts, Chiune Sugihara helped thousands of Jews flee the Shoah for no reason except that it was right. His choice *alone* saved those lives. Georg Elser, an anonymous and very average German carpenter with a shitty family life, a prejudice against the Roma, and unclear-to-Erik political motives, nearly killed Hitler and his entire inner circle with a homemade bomb in 1939. If he'd succeeded—

The right men. The right men.

He has to be the right man. The one to stop Clayton Hunt from selling humanity.

Curtains of plastic block the way into the Russian biolabs. Erik underhands a dead grenade into the room, to startle anyone waiting, then follows it inside. No one. The Russian corpses have been disturbed, their suits cut open. Probably Clayton doing ghoulish research.

He steps over refrigerated bodies, his aimpoint steady, just like at the Fort Bragg kill house. The physics tent is up next, where they found eight dead Chinese scientists. Then the way inside.

When he sees Clayton he will fire to kill.

Through the airlock, in the Blackbird antechamber, someone is screaming. Jesus, someone's killing Clayton. Fuck you. *I'm* supposed to kill Clayton.

He opens the inner door, shuts it behind him. The pumps hum. The outer door cracks open. The screaming rises to a choir: there are too many mouths, and the sound coming out of them is too small.

Erik kicks open the inner door.

A thing formerly a man ripples toward him across toppled cameras and snarled lines.

He runs on hundreds of human arms, like a centipede with hands. His face is a tiled mask of tiny faces with little mouths whose cross-split lips purse and blow and pant and moan. The structure of his beard has been extrapolated up into his chin, so that the bone divides into hundreds of hooks from which depend braids of white hair. From the neck down he is a long back-curved arch of spine, scurrying on armlegs, stumbling, tangling with one another in minute small-fingered disagreements. At the tail end of the body a fan of attenuated, too-thin human legs kick the air.

"*Help me!*" one of the faces shrieks. Another says calmly, "My soul is gone, I am only material, it has gone to work on me." Others scream and squeeze their pea-sized eyeballs shut. Another says, "If none of this seems rational, then none of it is happening, and I will awaken to the real world."

The thing comes straight at Erik.

What the fuck is he going to do? He shoots it.

The green-tip armor-piercing bullet puts a dime hole through the monster and the plastic sheeting behind him. The armipede tumbles and flails, jetting thin fine streams of blood: a nest of arms clenched into grape-sized fists: it wails from many mouths.

Those mouths, those tiny faces, are white. They are not Clayton's.

In determination and in pure terror Erik vaults the monster, grabs the ladder that runs up into Blackbird's cylindrical entrance shaft, and hauls himself up, past the box of the Raman lidar, through the solid matter of the intention cap, into hot pink-gold unknown.

ERIK//144 MINUTES REMAIN
Blackbird

"Erik. If you're listening to this, turn back now. This place will kill you."

He lands on a hard, slightly curved, strangely scratchy surface: the floor of a tunnel. Something breaks under his boot as he gets up. He clicks on his rifle's EOTech tactical light and sees a Russian quadrotor drone, abandoned.

He is inside a whorled intestine of amber and pink as complexly patterned as a turbojet's innards. The surface scores his gloves when he strokes it. It's swimsuit-hot, dehydrating hot, but there is no *way* Erik's giving up his body armor. Even if Clayton didn't have a weapon when he came inside, he might've found one of the peshmerga AKs.

He follows the sound of Clayton's voice to Clayton's sweatshirt, stripped off and wadded on the floor.

Cupped in the arms is his phone, full green on charge, playing audio on loop.

"I've discovered Blackbird's true nature. It's an engine for making things more interesting. Iruvage wants it for his own purposes. I am going to give it to him in exchange for Earth's survival."

Erik snaps up the phone, sticks it between his plate carrier and his chest with the speakers aimed up at his face, and goes forward. His light pools on the tunnel floor ahead, reflected into a red-refringent rainbow. Chromatic aberration of white off blood-fuzzy bronze Gigeroidea.

"Blackbird's been decompressing itself from a kind of storage limbo. I don't know how it ended up here, in Kurdistan. What I do know is that Blackbird is stuck. It can't finish building itself. That's why it's been spreading out so aggressively. Trying to change us. Trying to change everything. It's looking for something it's missing. Something to imitate."

If this were a ship designed by humans, the entryway would feed into an atrium with supplies and necessities for going outside. That would connect to a causeway down the length of the ship. Or a control point to provide security against unwelcome visitors.

But if Blackbird made itself the same way it made that many-armed thing . . . it will be madness inside. It will be the true deep madness of a logic the human mind cannot apprehend.

The corridor curves sharply to the left, then gently back to the right. Spiraling inward.

"Blackbird doesn't have a soul. It can't get one. Everything it's accomplished so far has been strictly material, see? It can make matter from matter but it can't figure souls out. Whenever it finds a human soul, it tries to develop it, make it clearer, better . . . but human souls are too complex. We just tear apart. It fills us up with free will until we seize and die. Or it spills over into our bodies and does things like it did to Sivakov and Sabiti.

"What Blackbird needs is a volunteer. I am going to be that volunteer. I will join myself with Blackbird. I will become its soul. And whatever Iruvage plans to do next, he'll need my cooperation. I can save the world."

Of *course* he fucking would! God, that Gendo Ikari motherfucker, that all-volunteer Judas. How is Erik going to explain this to Rosamaria? And—why, now, is he thinking of her?

Because he's chasing Clayton, of course. You can't understand their vendetta without knowing about Rosamaria. Rosamaria is not bound to them the way they are bound to her: it is a failing of Erik and Clayton that they see her as theirs to struggle over. But it is a *true* failing. It is in their souls. Right or wrong, each man blames the other for her absence.

"Turn back, Erik," the phone says. *"Remember what happened last time you interfered. Remember what we lost when you tried to stop me from using Paladin. Remember what I lost, because of you. She was mine. You took her from me."*

Fuck you, fuck you, fuck you. Get out of my head. Stop knowing what I'm thinking before I do, you smug bastard.

The curve of the corridor tightens. There are "doors" on the outer wall now, patches of pearly material that remind Erik of the intention cap. Erik sticks his head and his rifle through one patch. A tiny cyst-like compartment full of floating membrane or cloth. Like an alveolus of a lung.

The membrane begins to re-drape itself, falling into place around an invisible form. It reminds him of grainy VHS video of fetal development. Erik shudders and backs out.

Tighter and tighter the spiral closes. Erik tries to count full rotations as he moves inward. How is there room inside the hull for all this shit? His intuition says that any compartments on the outer wall should overlap the next coil out . . .

"I'm making this recording before I go deeper," the phone says. *"If you're still inside*

Blackbird by this point, you must turn back. Once I have control of the ship, I may be able to stop its destructive effects. But I can't promise it'll be in time to save you.

"Go back, Erik. Before it changes you more than I can fix."

The tunnel around him *constricts*. Erik crouches in alarm but the constriction rolls on ahead, forward, into the interior. A moment later a second wave returns from the dark ahead and passes around him. The intestinal patterns on the walls shift and complicate.

"Li Aixue believes that Blackbird is connected to the very origin of the universe," Clayton drones. God, he sure went on a while, didn't he? He really just stopped and monologued before leaving the phone behind? Maybe he had a douchebag Bluetooth headset. *"She believes that Blackbird's effect is tied to the distribution of the prime numbers. She believes it is the same effect that generates complexity in systems from the human brain to the farthest stars. The spontaneous creation of order from chaos. She sees a way to prove that existence is as necessary and inevitable as the objective truths of number theory. I can't pretend I understand number theory, Erik. But I do know exactly why the aliens want Blackbird so badly."*

"To save their souls from hell," Erik mutters.

"In the wrong hands," phone-Clayton says, *"this ship could destroy the aliens' control of the galaxy. But in their hands, Iruvage believes it could save their souls from hell."*

"Yeah, fucker. I know."

The tunnel starts to widen. There's light ahead. Erik raises the rifle again.

"I think back on our life," Clayton monologues, on and on, *"and I'm not sure you were necessary, Erik. I'm not sure anything good ever came out of your existence. If you weren't here, Rosamaria and I would still be happy together. I'd probably be closer to solving this crisis. Paladin would still be in operation, doing real good in the world."*

Erik stumbles forward down the golden borehole. The surface under him is sloped. He has to lean back to keep his balance.

"You're probably tempted to blame Blackbird for what it does to us, Erik. But Blackbird doesn't understand good or evil, or harm, or hurt. It doesn't understand physics. Sight? Sound? Those are sensors evolved through millions of years of trial and error. Blackbird doesn't have them. If Li Aixue's right, the place Blackbird came from didn't even have our physics—it had a supersymmetric ancestor, one that could've collapsed into thousands of possible configurations. Why did it end up at ours?

"Now Blackbird faces a world as incomprehensible as a sandstorm—whirling particles, fields of power, the soda froth of the quantum vacuum. Blackbird's trying to learn the rules with the only tool it has. Math. Find the patterns. Exaggerate the patterns. You and I have a pattern, don't we, Erik? Oh, who am I fucking kidding. You're not going to turn back. You're probably charging after me with a gun, all alone . . ."

Another peristaltic wave, like a uterine contraction. Something's happening.

Fractals stain the wall, things Erik half remembers from Wikipedia crawling on bored staff nights: Sierpinski carpets and armadas of Burning Ships, hideously fungal Julia sets, Lyapunovs whose pincers and antennae wave toward infinity. Spires. Spikes. Oscillators. Circuits. Are these Blackbird's . . . thoughts?

He knows, from listening to Clayton, that there exists math which can create something vast and incredible from a tiny scrap of calculation. Markov random-field sampling. Particle swarm optimization. Use a little to make a lot.

Is this what's Blackbird doing to Clayton's soul? Is it turning him into the seed of an enormity?

It cannot be Clayton who is made enormous!

There's a light ahead. A deep orange light.

When Erik steps toward it, the golden corridor becomes a pit, and he falls face-first into Blackbird's heart.

※

ERIK//CLAYTON

Headfirst into a cavern with walls of math: the *interior* of a four-dimensional fractal, spikes and curled limbs of infinitely detailed self-similarity rising from an ocean of chaotic order. Dave Bowman's journey into the monolith. Except Erik is not plunging beyond the infinite, but into the mathematical substrate of all truth and existence, the undesigned patterns of It Before It-ness.

He keeps thinking: Where's the light coming from? How can there be photons inside here?

And: If everything really is math, then maybe math can be light.

He tumbles slowly, and on the next rotation, he sees the center of the cavity. Where Clayton Hunt drifts face-to-face with—

What hath Blackbird wrought?

It must have been human, once. Human ancestry in the curve of the hip and the knob of the knee, knees that each divide into two tapering calves, bony shims without ankle or foot. The genitalia have erased themselves. All the hair is gone. The corseted wasp-waist pinches a transparent belly packed with muscle like squid sushi and nerves like fiber-optic bundles. The spinal discs have erupted fronds of tissue out the back, like delicate wings, like the mice in the Russian cages. The arms! The arms fan out sevenfold, seven on each side all forking into seven more at the elbow, countless fingers spidering out on universal joints dividing and dividing again until they are needles of what must be atomic precision. Wings of arms.

A head full of eyes, from brow to broken chin. The tip of the spinal cord has punched out through the chin and then arched back to connect to the brow: onto this anchoring ridge grow struts of bone which mask that face of eyes.

The brain fans out through the ruptured skull into a vaulting, buttressed crown of tissue. An Egyptian headdress of thought-flesh. Tentacles of myelinated nerve wave in an invisible current.

Blackbird has given birth to *crew*.

And now it reaches out to Clayton with fingers of infinite precision, as if to claim what he offers—

"*By the time you reach me,*" Clayton's recording babbles, "*I will already be in contact with Blackbird's intelligence: the intelligence it has grown in mimicry of the brains it examined. Doubtless Blackbird will have extrapolated our minds into a superior form.*

"*But without a soul, this intelligence is trapped by material physics, unable to access the kernel of free will that we possess, the elusive and unwitting power to place our own personal stories above the laws of reality.*

"*And so I will offer myself as the guiding soul of this refugee.*"

It's simple, in the end. It's as simple as the world.

There's right and there's wrong. And the right men have to stop the wrong.

Blackbird's change boils toward crisis. Rings of transformation shudder through this cavernous womb, ricocheting faster and faster, like a single beam of light reflecting between closing mirrors, between Erik and Clayton.

Erik knows that he will dwell on this moment for as long as he lives, in nightmares, in flashbacks. It will hurt him like an old bullet in his liver. And the question that hurts most will be—

(as he snugs the rifle against his shoulder, and sets the little red aimpoint dot on Clayton's chest)

—how could he do it so *quickly*?

After all the life they've shared, how can Erik be so swift with his warrant?

"Wait," Clayton calls. "Erik, wait! We did it! You don't have to—"

Erik draws the trigger down.

The HK416's firing pin crushes the cartridge primer, which sets off the propellant charge, and from there the rest is pure physics. Recoil kicks him gently backward in free fall. He sees the little puff where the green-tip round hits Clayton in the breastbone, and penetrates.

God help him. It was the right thing to do.

CHAPTER SIXTEEN

CLAYTON//ERIK

Getting shot feels just like a pebble in the chest. Feels exactly like the time Clayton beat Shauna Plowman at lawn chess and she threw playground fill at him.

That can't be right. It's supposed to hurt. Did Erik miss?

Then a hot wet itch spreads from his breastbone to his back. The bullet went right through him, he realizes: maybe he'll be okay.

He actually wants to cry. Erik, you *shot* me. How the hell did we get to this? Everything I did felt so reasonable, so sane: and yet we ended up in this mad place. And you shot me.

What's under your breastbone, anyway? Your heart? Your aorta?

Oh.

Clayton tries to say something: "Erik, it's okay."

But his lips aren't answering his thoughts.

All he can see now is the nerve angel, this soulless brain, made in the image of man by Blackbird's mindless algorithms. A flesh computer. Churning through the computations Clayton initiated, executing the promise Clayton shouted to the fractal walls as he plunged deeper and deeper: *I'll bring you what you need!*

Blackbird needs a soul.

And rath, dear Clayton. Rath the clashing passion. Two stones beat against each other, chipping and cracking, hardening and sharpening. Maybe until one breaks. Maybe forever.

Blackbird likes to amplify high-order structures. Will it amplify Clayton's body? No, for Clayton has a soul. Will it amplify Clayton's soul until he seizes apart?

No. Not if it finds a higher-order structure.

Souls bound by rath. Two souls pursuing each other through Blackbird's intestines, acting out the story that defines their life.

What does Blackbird find when it amplifies that rath?

It finds the wound between Clayton and Erik. A wound it can enlarge, and fill in with detail, a wound shaped like the implication of a soul—

The last thing Clayton hears is the nerve angel's voice. That beautiful, beautiful voice.

"You stupid assholes," Rosamaria Navarro says. "Chinga sus madres! I *told* you not to contact me again!"

⁓

CLAYTON//IRUVAGE

How's it going in there, Clayton?

I've been toying with my food. Just ran a line of screamwire through a man's digestive tract and flossed him out. Did you ever play Pokémon, Clayton? Of course you did, you fucking nerd. Humans use Resist. It's not very effective.

I worry, Clayton, that you resist me. I worry that you resent the universe I represent. It's a universe in which violence can stain even the immortal soul. A universe in which everything, even the truth, bows to brute force.

The only truth in *your* universe, Clayton, is that I have a strike cruiser in orbit with enough nuclear weapons to depopulate your planet.

The whip who trained me, down under Khau ssv Kehen where the world bleeds, she used to say: don't listen to those Cultratics with their sorcery. Truth isn't about cosmic calculus. Truth isn't something you can divine with rituals and computations.

Truth is *enforced*. Truth is what you can make the universe do.

For my people, for the Exordia, truth is measured in gigadeaths.

Let me tell you the truth about the galaxy before us.

One hundred and twenty-five thousand six hundred and four intelligent species went extinct during the Cessation Age. In wars over territory or resources. Or extinguished on their hearthworlds, annihilated in acts of cosmic infanticide dictated by cruel, cruel game theory: kill everyone who could *possibly* become competition, for if you do not, they might kill you.

The state of nature out in the galaxy is an absolute bloodbath. But we mastered that state. We imposed our own truth on it. Since my people rose up out of Sahana and seized the starways, there have been only one hundred and four extinctions. We carried out seventy-seven of them.

Yes, Clayton, it's true. We *did* enslave the galaxy. We do cull the young of the coagula who live in the deep orbits of dead stars. We do censor the life-art of the eana, so that they cannot pursue the only purpose they haven't engineered away. We do use the shorinor as cheap labor, and their world-ships as slums, and we take their dragon souls to pilot our æshade. We do spay the belunari so that their queens cannot know their own offspring. We do manipulate the politics of the segregant iridine so that they never finish their long alignment into a New Social Syzygy. We do crush the secret ramlines built by the skylords, so they cannot slip between the gas worlds on another wind.

And we do pinion the souls of all our subjects, so that their rebellions will fail. Fortune unfavors them.

But we stopped the killing. We rule over an iron peace. The galaxy tells one story now, and it's a story of less death. More life? I don't know. But certainly less death. And that death comes by our coil and our fang. We tend our prey wisely. And in exchange for a brief span as our chattel, they gain heaven.

If Blackbird ever came into the grip of our enemies, that story would burn down into chaos.

But in better hands—in better coils—in better fangs—

Have you ever loved anyone, Clayton? We khai are so passionate. It's all life and death with us. It's all water and venom. Love to match our malice. The one I love, oh, she could *use* this tool . . . she could change so much.

You see how you two have ensouled Blackbird? How I drew back Erik like a freshly severed tendon, filled him up with rage and hate and vengeance-need, and set him loose? The war you fought over Paladin and Rosamaria, recapitulated in miniature. You lie to him and he comes storming home to stop you. A pattern of souls.

And from that pattern Blackbird found what it needed. A story it could make itself part of. A role it could borrow.

You've ensouled Blackbird. An egg tooth for the old machine to chew its way out of mere physics.

And you know what a soul's made of, right? Oh, yes. A soul is made of stories.

Stories like: *Where I came from.*

Stories like: *What I'm good for.*

Stories like: *How to use me.*

There's all sorts of useful information in a soul, Clayton. Portable, compressible, fundamental information. If you think about it, when I take someone's soul, I know everything I need to know about how they work.

Wouldn't it be nice if I had some way to eat Blackbird's soul?

Oh, look. What's that?

CHAPTER SEVENTEEN

—//—

I don't remember the beginning of time.

I remember names. æVae. doMob. onuAuno. iXi. ɢaiiag. ieWei. KopAqoⴽ and pavoTovaq.

I think I was part of one of those names.

I know that this isn't the universe we meant to make. It's broken. Riddled with mistakes.

I know that I used to be more than I am. I know I didn't go into compression voluntarily. I was jettisoned. Cast down.

For a very long no time at all, I was a mathematical instruction compressed into a pocket. A bomb shelter, multi-local, strangely connected. I was a card trick that played itself: if you draw two aces, I'll make you draw a third. That's all the power I had. *Where there's a pattern, extend it. Like seeks like.*

And then someone called me up from my hide.

I came back as an egg smaller than a proton, a mote in the roaring quantum vacuum. A naked instruction executing itself in the foam. I might have been assigned a probability of zero, erased by some error corrector I helped build.

Lucky we built it bad, I guess.

(I remember—we were afraid.)

I decompressed. I computed a structure and mind. I became this ship: something able to change its position in space and time.

But I couldn't get out of the world. Couldn't reclaim all the privileges of free will and virtue and destiny. Imagine waking up in a coffin, with only room to twitch your fingertips—imagine how *mad* you'd go.

I was trapped inside the physics.

And no matter how I hammered on the matter around me, I just couldn't bootstrap it into what I needed. Even human beings (although I didn't know they were people, then, just complex self-causing states) failed me. I tried to amplify their souls, make them mighty as I had been mighty. But the math didn't work out. The tools I had were fatal. And when I stripped away the noise, all that was left of their souls was a flimsy string. Tissue in a sieve, coming apart.

I found a soul who was so wholly devoted to truth that she could survive becoming more and more like herself. She had a lonely elegance, and I made her lonelier and more elegant. But there was nothing in her that could become me.

There were others who might have given me what I needed. Patterns I remembered from the time before I fell.

But the ones who came were the two locked in rath.

Erik.

Clayton.

I know these names because they are written in my soul. The ink is thick.

I *hate* that. I wanted to be done with them.

But they kept an image of me. Those tight-fisted bastards. Though I can't pretend, really, that I didn't keep a part of them for myself too. Erik and Clayton were the greater parts of my life before—

Clayton!

His body is a swamp of torn tissue and spilled water. Cells surrendering their structure to the boredom of death. We need a doctor, we need an ambulance! But there are no doctors and I am not human anymore and I don't know, anyway, what the inside of a human chest's *supposed* to look like. Erik is trying chest compressions but in the zero gravity of my source chamber all his efforts do is push Clayton's body away.

"Erik," I say.

He wraps his thighs around Clayton's waist to get leverage. A white military bandage stuffs the bullet hole. Blood pumps in strings through his hand. He just killed this man. Now he's trying to save him. The madness of doing the right thing.

"Erik. It's really me."

He tries to crush his chest against Clayton's to put pressure on the bandage while he reaches around to find the exit wound. Clayton is breathing wrong: agonal gasping, pumping blood out of his shredded aorta to pool in his body cavity. There are things which feel good: a cat's fur under your fingers, a fork cutting edgewise through a piece of flan. There are things which feel wrong: overcooked pasta in your mouth, sweat salt caked on your shirt. The math of Clayton's body feels wrong. He's becoming symmetrical, soupy, all the cycles and balances implied by his structure gone forever . . .

The walls of his arteries imply the existence of more wall. The torn nerves reach out for missing neighbors. There are scraps of a signal in his ruined aorta.

So I peel away the chaos, I retrieve that signal. I have a model to work from: Erik's strong heart. Erik's blood pressure and sinus rhythm. Erik's gasping lungs.

The bandage pops out of Clayton's chest. He heaves blood. Erik stares in wonder and terror at the man in his arms. And then, at last, he raises his eyes to me.

"Rosamaria?"

"Yeah, Erik."

"How—*how?*"

"Great question. Working on it. I need some room."

I send him away.

There's something wrong outside. Something coming closer.

CHAPTER EIGHTEEN

Blackbird spits them out.

When Erik falls through the intention cap he has time to twist and put himself under Clayton. Then they crash down at the base of the ladder, and Clayton lands on his guts, and his guts squash against the back plate of his body armor.

Erik says, "Huuuur!"

Clayton tumbles off him, face down and shuddering. Erik clings to Clayton's body. Tears his gas mask off. Inhales hot sweat and old deodorant. Clayton's real; not a hallucination, not a figment.

And he's breathing again. Erik killed him but it was too late to stop whatever he did to Blackbird and then Rosamaria was there and now . . . Clayton is alive?

Clayton spasms against him. A scream comes out of him, but there's no air to sound it: just the wretched convulsion of throat and lips and tongue.

Then his teeth clack. He makes a noise like a corpse belching up rot. And he begins to speak.

"It's almost time . . ." he groans. "When I became a soldier, dear Clayton, I mingled my need for victory with my more basic hedonisms. When the mission's almost complete . . . it's like my fangs are dimpled on living flesh, and I only need to bite. Like I'm coiled around my lover but I can't get my keys inside. You can't imagine the exquisite anticipation I suffer in this moment, Clayton. Your brain doesn't have the rendering capability. Your soul's too small . . ."

Erik's seen enough science fiction to know exactly what's going on here. Iruvage is inside Clayton. Puppeteering him through the implant in his spine. He's not going to waste time with "Clayton, is that really you?" or "Clayton, come back to us!" or "Clayton, you can fight it!"

He's going to find Anna. And Khaje. Khaje has alien electronic warfare machines. She'll know what to do about it. Somehow she'll know.

"You've been a useful tool, Clayton, and I don't want to see you in hell," Clayton says. "After the atmanach's finished digesting the newborn, I think I'll have you next. I have an æshade that needs a gifted soul . . ."

Erik gets his elbows under him and tries to stand up.

Light pours over him.

Erik raises his hand against the glare. A boot crashes down beside his face. Then a black glove descends to tear his throat mic away.

Erik looks up the length of a Heckler & Koch submachine gun into the beardy face of Mike Jan.

"Sir, is that Deputy NSA Hunt? Did you kill Deputy NSA Hunt?"

"He's alive," Erik gasps. "He's alive. But—"

"Did Deputy NSA Hunt deliver Blackbird to the aliens? We have only two hours until alien weapon release. *Did Deputy NSA Hunt complete the mission?*"

Is it complete? What the fuck happened in there? *Rosamaria?* Clayton didn't become Blackbird's soul, Rosamaria did—so is the bargain complete? Does Iruvage get Blackbird now?

If Anna's right about Blackbird, it is the key to galactic freedom. Erik can't let the alien have *that.*

"Sir?" Mike Jan repeats. "Has the nuclear attack been canceled?"

They cannot surrender here. All they can do is fight, fight even if it means extinction, because that is *the right thing to do.* And if there will be nothing left of you, if all your acts and works will be forgotten: still you do the right thing, for its own sake.

That's what it means to be good.

"We are not going to give this ship to the aliens," he tells Mike Jan. "They're absolute evil. I've seen one. I've watched him kill my soldiers. He's worse than death."

Mike Jan sighs long and hard. "Sir, you led your unit away from the objective and into an ambush. You antagonized our alien ally and got your team killed. You have done nothing on this expedition except undermine the deputy national security advisor. You are carrying his wounded body, as if you shot him. I must conclude that you are in insurrection against his lawful authority. My duty is to restore Deputy NSA Hunt to command so he can complete his negotiations."

He presses the tip of the MP7's suppressor to the spot on Erik's forehead just below his helmet.

"Operator," Erik rasps, "stand down."

"No, sir," Mike Jan says. "I will not."

Mike Jan's finger moves on the trigger. Mike Jan's weapon makes a sound like a fork banged on an empty pipe.

CHAPTER NINETEEN

DAVOUD (~7,875 FEET ASL)

Western news about negotiations with Iran always had headlines like DANCING WITH THE DEVIL. Reading this, Davoud would look around for any sign of the devil. Is Satan that guy in the corner of the net cafe, writing a blog post about Houshang Shahbazi's shameful treatment? Is it the man who brings the new flavors to hookah? Is it those mechanics on the flight line, muttering about Googoosh's TV show and her concert in Iraq? Women cannot sing solo in Iran. But would the devil care about that?

And then, one day, Davoud saw the devil.

He was a man with a swirled black-and-white beard and a neat blue uniform. He looked exactly like famous fighter pilot Jalil Zandi. Of course, Jalil Zandi was years dead, killed in a car accident: grounded forever. So Davoud knew there was something wrong.

But he gave in anyway. Gave in to the temptation of flight.

And now—far too late—he tries to fight it.

He dances a stupid gher dadan with himself through the plastic tunnels of the lab, across aluminum floors and heaped corpses. Iruvage's fangs are locked in his spine, deep and dire as tetanus nails, trying to push him one step at a time into Blackbird. Davoud fights back by thrashing like a toddler and screaming no! He doesn't want to go in there! He'll turn into some kind of eyeball spider!

"Don't you want your reward? In a few minutes I'm going to know everything I need to know about this gorgeous relic of creation. And then you can fly it up, up and away, above everything . . ."

Go to hell!

"Very probably I will. But you don't have to. You can fly immortal among the stars. I swear it on my soul. You will live a life so rich and long that all the dreams of all your kind will roll up like a ball of rags in the corner of your memory to gather dust. You will be more than every other human life summed together."

No bargain with Satan ever ends happily. That's a rule.

"I'm not Satan." Iruvage's coils slither through Davoud's bowel. Scales shave ulcers into his stomach lining. *"My credit score is much better than his. If I buy a soul, Davoud, I want to own the damn soul. So I pay my fee. Now get in the fucking ship, will you? Get in there and fly it away!"*

No!

"I'll let you see again. Open your eyes, Davoud. Look. Just long enough to remember what you're missing . . ."

He can see the corpses! He can see the ghostly plastic sheeting and the chill aluminum and the abandoned machines! He can see the way!

If he had ever been blind before, maybe he would have the strength to resist this bribe. But as a sighted man he has no chance. "I can fly! I can fly!"

Iruvage sets him dashing toward Blackbird. He puts his wings out like arms—his arms out like wings—and folds them behind him. He has a vague impression of people around him—an American soldier; another American, face-down dead on the ground; Clayton Hunt, winking at him as he passes—then his hands are on the ladder and he is climbing up, up, toward escape velocity, into the *ship*!

CHAPTER TWENTY

THE JANISSARY

Mike Jan tugs Erik Wygaunt's helmet down over his dead eyes.

He doesn't want that grisly gray gaze judging him. Had to be done, sir, had to be done. Not the first superior officer Mike has killed. Not after Paladin. Mike is a solution-oriented man. That's a tough way to be. Everyone in charge feeds you bullshit, rules you've gotta follow, easy fixes you can't deploy because they've got bad optics. Mike doesn't want to be in charge. Mike just wants to make sure that the smart people end up in charge of *him*.

To guarantee this outcome, he will do all the shit that smart people are too squeamish to handle on their own. Like getting rid of Major Wygaunt, blue falcon in charge.

"Mr. Hunt?" he says. "Are you okay?"

"Missssssster Jan," the deputy NSA yawns. His lips peel back. There's a hole in his black compression top that looks awfully like an entry wound. His pupils dilate and then contract, like a camera focusing.

He sticks his tongue out and sniffs. "There's someone watching us. Kill her."

Mike looks back. There *is* someone in the airlock, a pale face watching him through the window. It's one of the Chinese scientists. The math lady. She's small and bright and tired, like she's fresh from the gym. Mike hesitates. He doesn't *want* to shoot her.

Then someone shoves past her and triggers the airlock cycle. The airlock's outer door swings open and a man comes running out, arms outstretched: exactly the sort of metrosexual-looking Persian dude Mike would shoot while raiding across the border from Iraq. His left hand bangs into an instrument and folds behind him, like a broken wing.

"Yesss!" he screams. "*Yessss!*"

Mike is about to kill the guy when Clayton Hunt's hand clamps on his shoulder. "But don't shoot Davoud, please. He's my pilot."

The Iranian runs past them and scrambles straight up the ladder, into Blackbird. Mike moves to reacquire the Chinese woman, but she's vanished. "Fuck," he says. "Pardon my language, Mr. Hunt."

"You'd better go kill her. All that prajna could be a real inconvenience. Kill the woman with her too. Kill anyone else you feel like, in fact. Remember Paladin? That was me. You have my permission to murder anyone you need to." Mr. Hunt twists his head, grimacing, as if irritated by his neck. He looks like he's never *had* a neck before. "I'll be calling for air support."

"Air support on what target, sir?"

"On Ssrin, of course."

"She's not dead, sir?"

"No, Mike, she is not. She's lurking. She fled those rat caves and went— somewhere. I wish I could've killed Anna and broken the serendure concealing them both but I needed the redundancy. But now it won't matter. Now I'm moving on Blackbird, and she has to show herself, to repel the atmanach before it takes its prize. When she does, we bomb her and anyone who tries to protect her. This"—he licks his upper lip, grimaces again—"is checkmate. Actually, it's better than checkmate. What kind of stupid game doesn't let you kill the king?"

CHAPTER TWENTY-ONE

AIXUE 1

"Professor Li! What did you see?" Chaya Panaguiton grabs her by the sides of her helmet. "*What did you see?*"

Aixue stares at her face in astonishment. The slight but vital asymmetry that says *this is human.* You cannot be symmetrical and be real. The perfect concentricity of her eyes. The stunning fractal subdivision of her pupils, two splitting in two—

"Aixue!"

"Ah! What? I'm sorry. I'm so sorry."

"Did they come back out? What happened?"

"I saw . . ." Aixue tries to recover the human facts from the beauty of existence: fields of force, excitations in those fields joining and separating again, all obeying laws of such absolute necessity and exquisite unlikeliness. The font of wonder at the center of her world: the mystery of why anything exists at all. The world is so little, in the end. As little as possible, but not a whit less.

The fields of force shaped those clouds of quanta into men. And one of those men projected a mass, which displaced, by repulsion and exclusion of electron fields, the mass of the other man's head, and—

She gasps. "That soldier shot Erik."

"Pakshet," Chaya whispers. "Major Wygaunt's dead?"

"Yes. And Clayton came back out, but . . . he's not right. I could tell."

"What's wrong with him? Did he—is he like Sivakov?"

"No. He's just wrong. The math in his face, it's all different."

"Different how?"

"I don't know." The worst words in the universe. "I'm sorry."

Chaya ignores this. Obviously a woman like Chaya puts up with a lot of apologies from poser dipshits like Aixue. "Are they coming after us?"

Aixue puts a hand on the plastic flooring and listens to the vibrations of human footsteps beneath the generators and the AC units. She just plucks those waveforms out of the noise. It's all she can do.

"He's coming."

"Come on! No, come on *this* way—"

But instead of paying attention, Aixue imagines the beginning of time.

In those first few instants of existence, the laws of physics are still one single whole. There is no gravity. There is no magnetism. No strong or weak nuclear force. No protons or electrons or neutrons or neutrinos or anything.

Just a hot soup of quarks ruled by one law, the law human physics has sought for a century: the Unified Force.

(This is the reason people build bigger and stronger particle accelerators. They're trying to reproduce the ferocity of the big bang, and the unification of the four fundamental forces into one godly law, described by a simple Lie group, a mathematical entity of absolute symmetry. Ten to the nineteenth gigaelectronvolts: the Planck energy, when all difference melts away.)

But that beautiful sameness is so *dull*. Nothing interesting will ever happen. It's like a tank full of steam, pressurized with potential but pretty much the same everywhere you look.

But the universe is expanding. And when you let steam expand, it cools down.

The universe starts to freeze. The quark-gluon fire condenses into discrete particles in a merely superhot plasma. Scientists call this process *phase transition*.

The transition begins at random points throughout the universe, seeds where the infernal temperature is slightly lower. Aixue is now quite confident that the quantum fluctuations which created these cold seeds were in turn primed, literally, by the structure of the prime numbers.

This is called symmetry breaking. It is how boring uniform things become interesting structured things. You can't carve a message into running water, or build a wall from water, or dig a hole in water. It's symmetrical everywhere. But you can make *so* much from ice!

Exactly the same thing happened in the early universe. The primordial unity cooled in different patches, and in each patch, the Unified Force itself froze and shattered apart—and the alignment of physics in each patch was *slightly* different.

Our particular patch of cosmos seems *very* strange. The weak nuclear force, a tenuous and pathetic influence, is still 100,000,000,000,000,000,000,000,000,000 times stronger than gravity. (Physicists call this the hierarchy problem. If the world gender pay gap were as big as the gap between the strength of gravity and the weak nuclear force, then for every dollar made by a man, women would entirely cease to exist.) A flea's legs are more powerful than the gravity of an *entire planet*. The proton (with charge +1) is a thousand times heavier than the electron (with charge −1).

Why? Why should this be?

And why do these oddities matter to anyone but physicists?

Because they permit life. If the mass of the proton were the same as the electron, *stars could not form*. If gravity were as powerful as the other forces, there would be no atoms, no chemistry, no life. Possibly the whole universe would be black holes.

So how did we end up in a patch of universe friendly to life? Is it simply the anthropic principle at work—we can only exist in a place where our existence is possible, so of course, when we look around, we wonder at our good fortune?

Or did something *nudge* the universe in this direction? Was there an inevitability to it? Is life a mathematical necessity?

Life—

She has to do something. She has to stop thinking and fucking *do something*.

She stops. Chaya, pulling her along, looks back in fury: "What—?"

"We can't get out. There's another man between us and the exit. I can feel his footsteps."

"Shet!"

"Yes. I have to find a radio. I have to call Sergeant Zhang to come save us. You need to go hide."

"If they see you they're going to kill you!"

She catches the taller, stronger woman's wrist. "Chaya," she says gently. "You're infected. Your soul is too big. The moment anyone with a gun sees you, they'll shoot you."

"They're going to shoot *you*!"

"No, they won't," Aixue says. "I'm a cute fat little Asian girl waddling around in a too-big plastic suit. The most harmless thing there is. They'll hesitate."

She is lying. She has no idea if this is true.

But somehow, when she says it, it *sounds* true.

CHAPTER TWENTY-TWO

ἐΙΥΟSΙ

"Help!"

There is no one in Tawakul to hear her anymore. Anna and her mom are the last Kurds in the whole valley. Erik and the gray-man life-snatcher creep Skyler have gone ahead to Blackbird.

So she hauls her mom across the river bridge alone, her thighs cramped to jerky, Khaje's sweaty hair sticking to her neck. Mom spasms harder every minute: like she's falling into further layers of nightmare.

"Help!" she screams. "Help, please!"

A bunch of Americans pop up out of nowhere. "Miss Sinjari?"

"We've got to get her medicine!"

"Was she hit by the crawler? Is she violent?"

"No! She's just catatonic from all the alien robots talking to her brain! Come on, help me!"

But they won't come closer. Dark shapes bristling with technology aim at her from all around. "Miss Sinjari," the talker says, "Nashbrook told us the aliens have microdrones that can plant bombs in our heads. If she's operating some of those drones, it might be best to keep her away from the main science team—"

"Otvali!" a Russian shouts. "Bitch fuckers, get away from her!" A bunch of Spetsnaz tumble toward them, all waving and shouting. "You cannot shoot at her, she is the bulletproof woman! She'll kill you!"

The Spetsnaz swarm Anna and pull Khaje off her back. They load her onto a stretcher and hustle her to a tent full of more men Anna doesn't know. Anna stumbles after them as a Spetsnaz medic questions her.

Anna's so fucking afraid she'll die. Not like this, Mom. Not lying down.

The Spetsnaz boy-man takes Khaje's pulse. Shakes his head. "How long has she been delirious?"

"Hours?"

"Blyat!" he says feelingly. "Dajte lorazepam i kislorodnuju masku! Intubirujem eje kak tolko ona vyjdet iz epistatusa!"

Khaje's hand seizes on hers. Those callused fingers. Anna grips desperately.

"Ssrin." Hard dry cough, Khaje shrimping up with each percussion, elbows banging against the table. "You have to go inside with Ssrin."

"Ssrin's gone, Mom. She's dead."

"No. Her machines. Watching over you. I watch over you. Ssrin promised."

Yeah, Mom, she made you a promise. What's a promise worth when it comes from a multigenocidal space snake? A snake who sold Anna on this lovely notion of *serendure*, cosmic congruence between two lonely souls: only for that to mean, in the end, no more than murder.

She looks around so that she will not have to look at her mom clinging to Ssrin's lies. "What happened to Erik?"

"He went inside," an important-looking Russian says. "We assume he is dead. I am Major Vylomov. This is Warrant Officer Mousavi. This is Master Sergeant Zhang. Your leaders have frozen us out and we do not know what the fuck is happening. Your mother is the only one who has ever known what the fuck is happening around here. I hope she will be all right."

"I heard you went into the forest," Zhang says. "It's not very safe in there. Did he get your officers?"

"Jesus, I don't know," Anna says. "He got pretty much everyone. Except me and Erik."

Mousavi asks: "What about the Kurds?"

"They're gone." She doesn't want to tell him any more. He's Revolutionary Guard, isn't he? "Listen, if Erik went in there, he was going after—"

Gunfire pops off from the direction of Blackbird. Spetsnaz take up the shout: "Vnutrenniy kordon!"

Vylomov snaps up his rifle. "Something at the inner perimeter. Coming out of the Objekt." Everyone not working on her mom rushes outside to see.

"What the fuck . . . ?" Anna breathes.

There's something out there. Like a centipede but tiger-sized, scuttling through the grass. She gets flashes of wrong: too many waving human arms, a body like a fat spinal cord spraying tendrils of naked nerves, ball joints that have been subdivided into hundreds of tiny inadequate sockets which rupture and pop as the thing tries to move. It is dislocating its limbs with each step. For an instant she sees a face made of screaming faces. It has a beard made of hair and each hair has a chin with a beard.

A Spetsnaz soldier fires a rocket that bursts into sticky white fire. The scuttling thing thrashes in the flames, falls on its belly, and begins to crawl. A hundred baby-sized mouths pipe agony.

Is that *Erik*? Did he go in there after Clayton and—and turn into *that*? Poor fucking dude . . .

Ssrin wanted her to go in there.

Maybe she should just fucking do it.

Her mother groans and arches behind her. "Anna! Mehêle azarman bidat!"

"I won't, Mom," she whispers. "I won't."

She starts toward Blackbird.

CHAPTER TWENTY-THREE

AIXUE 2 × 1

"Professor Li!" Mike Jan calls. "I'm not here to hurt you! Please come out!"

She can't find a radio and she can't get out. She tried calling for help on the lab IRC network but no one's answering her. She can feel the other man in here, the silent man, moving to stay between her and the exits. The silent man and Mike Jan have her cornered.

What would Chaya do?

Aixue doubles back to the physics tent, where she started, and stares at the airlock that leads back to Blackbird. There's a radio here. She saw Mike Jan pull it off Major Wygaunt. But if she goes in there, will she keep going deeper, into Blackbird? Will she abandon Chaya to die?

"I shouldn't," she says. "I can't trust myself."

Then she goes in anyway.

Clayton Hunt is there, only he's not Clayton Hunt. He seems to be doing calisthenics. When he sees her his ankles roll and he flops down on his knees. "Oopsssss," he hisses.

"What *are* you?" she asks him. Because he is not, right now, a human being.

"Excussse me," he says. "I have to find ssssome manila folderss. For my report."

He covers his eyes with one arm and stumbles past her, into the airlock. She wants to stop him. But she's too scared of the thing inside him.

She turns and faces Blackbird.

At the bottom of the ladder Erik Wygaunt lies face-up dead in a pool of his own brains.

"I'm sorry," she whispers. The entry wound is small and obscenely round. She kneels next to him and picks up the radio headset Mike Jan tore off him. She has to hold the earpiece close so it doesn't slip off.

Clayton Hunt is on the radio. How did *he* find a radio so fast? There's something sloppy where his voice should be crisp. Something that clacks his teeth together like it doesn't expect them to be there. She listens:

"Chalisssse, Chalissse, thisss is Majessstic. Authenticasssion sssix two sssix yankee zulu yankee four four one. Are you ressseiving?"

Aixue had a brief fascination with ham radio back in the nineties, when the government handed amateur radio over to CRSA. This is a VHF frequency: limited range. So the thing inside Clayton can't be signaling to a distant air base or ship.

What is Chalice?

His sibilants tighten. He's learning. "*I ssay again, this is Deputy National Security Advisor Clayton Hunt. An alien entity is attacking uss. We need all available ssupport. I say again, we are under attack by an alien entity and we require tactical air to defeat it. Our coordinates are three eight sierra mike foxtrot eight one two nine six six two eight seven three. Send all available assets. I ssay again, Chalice, this is Majestic, Deputy NSA Clayton Hunt calling, authentication six two six yankee zulu yankee four four one . . .*"

Clayton is calling for bombs. He's going to finish what he started.

Aixue jams the transmit switch down and says quickly, clearly: "This is Professor Li. Master Sergeant Zhang, we need help inside the labs. Clayton Hunt is under alien control. The Americans are going to kill us all!"

Iruvage tries to jam her. Somehow she knows this and somehow she knows it doesn't work. And that knowing is the reason it doesn't work.

"Miss Li?" Mike Jan calls, from the other side of the airlock. "Please put down the radio and come out. I don't want to hurt you."

She knows Mike Jan is lying. He's going to shoot her in the first part of her he sees.

CHAPTER TWENTY-FOUR

ᏗᎢᎧᏐ

Anna pads through the brightly lit Chinese labs with her Glock loose in her hand, just waiting for something to pop out and fuck with her.

This place fucking stinks. It smells of rot and shit and antiseptic hospital. She stops a couple times to try to fix the awkward poses of undignified corpses: she remembers how, on 9/11, women held their skirts down when they jumped. You want some part of your dignity, at the end.

"Miss Li?" That's Mike Jan. She'd recognize that drawl in a Grand Central crowd. "Please put down the radio and come out. I don't want to hurt you."

Oh, shit. Mike Jan's about to kill the math lady.

Anna's probably supposed to do some SWAT shit to clear her corners, in case Mike has friends hiding nearby, but who's got time for that?

She crosses to the next hatch, covered in Chinese characters fuzzy with Blackbird extrapolation. Her feet crinkle the tunnel floor. She gets a grip on the door handle, breathes out through her mouth, and pulls it slowly open.

Nothing. No Mike Jan. It's the right lab for sure—she remembers that projector, the one Erik levered open. But where is Li?

"Professor Li!" she hears Mike Jan call, from the airlock leading to Blackbird. It's open on this side; he hasn't started cycling through. "Please come out! It's not safe in there!"

"Hey, fucker!" Anna barks. She'd try to sneak up on him, but he would just kill her with his elite black ops training, ricochet a bullet around the corner or do a no-scope headshot. "What are you doing?"

"Miss Sinjari?" the voice says, very reasonably. "Are you all—"

He betrays not the *slightest* malice. You'd think he'd at least finish his sentence before he kills her. What kind of psycho can start a sentence knowing he's going to kill his audience before it finishes?

She gets a glimpse of his night-vision goggles and the narrow suppressor on the end of his gun. Then he shoots her.

Something makes a hard *ping* in the air between them.

She jumps and says "Ah!"

The bullet strikes the floor at Anna's feet, a flattened disc of copper, the steel core protruding like a pin. It just . . . stopped.

"Huh," Anna says. She thought it was her mom who was bulletproof.

Mike Jan shoots her three times in the head and chest. The bullets skip off something tiny and darting in the air.

Jan's beardy chin, the only part of his face visible beneath helmet and goggles, wrinkles with concern.

"Shit fuck you!" Anna bellows, and lights him up with the Glock. The pistol bangs and shudders in her hand. She's shooting from the hip but they're real close so she hits him once in his chest armor and once in the meat of his hip and then dumps the rest of the magazine into the aluminum siding behind him as he ducks back into cover in the airlock. The airlock starts to hiss unhappily.

"Fuck you!" she repeats, and drops the magazine. She has one reload but there's no time to fish it out and she doesn't really know what she's doing anyway.

Jan pops out again and starts blasting. The *thwonk* of his suppressed weapon is a finger flicking Anna's eardrum. The metal thing in the air dances and whirs, slapping bullets out of the way. She charges him.

She almost gets to him. It's a really good effort, her adoptive mom would've said. A really good try by Anna Banana.

"Nashbrook!" Jan shouts. "Fucking *shoot* her!"

A giant hornet stings Anna in the back, right through the soft body armor Erik gave her. Warm wet blood burps down her spine. Give her credit, she knows right away what happened: she skids on her ass behind a bench. Someone is shooting at her through the tent. Air hisses in from outside.

"Aw, shit." She paws at her back. Either the wound is superficial or she's in shock and doesn't know she's dying. It could be either one. Them fuckers are frighteningly random. Unless you land a shot in the T-box, mouth and nose and eyes, as she did to her own father.

She tries to get up, and nearly gets shot again. "Shit!" There are two of them, and the machine protecting her can only stop bullets from one guy at a time.

She hears Mike Jan moving very rapidly toward her. He's muttering into his radio, calling that doll-eyed fuck Skyler in to help with the execution. She gets down on her knees and elbows and crawls frantically between the lab benches, trying to get somewhere they don't know she's gone, but she's fucking cornered—

"Tāmen zài zhèlǐ!" A Chinese voice—someone cutting through the tunnel walls, coming in from outside. "American soldiers! Come out with your weapons down!"

"Cocksuckers," Mike Jan says, with the bemused anger of a man who has just been cut off in line at CVS. Anna hears the tiny click when he selects another frequency on his radio. "Mr. Hunt. The Chinese are here to pull Li out. Orders?"

She can't hear the reply. But when Mike yells, "Okay, it's just me! I'm coming out!" she knows what he's going to do.

Skyler Nashbrook is out there somewhere, pulling what they would call, back on the company paintball trips, a flanking maneuver.

"Hey!" she screams. "He's gonna kill you! He's got a buddy outside—"

A grenade *cracks* and a layer of fine latex-glove dust jumps into the air from every surface around Anna. Plastic sheeting wheezes and crinkles up. Then gunfire explodes from both sides.

Skyler is out there, picking them off through the walls. She's gotta do—

Mike Jan comes around the corner of the lab bench and kicks Anna in the face.

CHAPTER TWENTY-FIVE

CLAYTON//AIRSTRIKE

Clayton screams inside himself.

It honestly never occurred to him that Iruvage could seize control of his body through the implant. It's not like in *Star Trek* where you get possessed by an energy being who magically knows human neuroscience. Iruvage might have access to his nervous system, but there's no *way* an alien could master all the idiosyncratic motor programs of the human body—

No way. Only it's happened anyway.

"Aw, Clayton," Iruvage purrs. *"Is this hard for you? It'll be over soon. And then I'm going to take your soul out of this meager little body. I'm going to make you immortal and stick you in a badass killing machine. Liberated from your human form, your psychology will shed the unhappy shackles of primate evolution. You will no longer feel guilt or loyalty or remorse. You will aid me in my missions solely and entirely because my existence allows your existence to continue. And because I hook your soul up with the finest ontonarcotics you've ever been. We'll be buddies. Genocide buddies. It'll be . . . what's the word I'm looking for here? Awesome? Grand?"*

"Dope. It'll be dope."

Mike Jan shot Erik while Clayton screamed and screamed and tried to regain control of one little wiggling toe like the woman from *Kill* fucking *Bill* so he could stop it. It wasn't supposed to go this way! He knew what was happening! He was in control again! Erik had to chase Clayton into Blackbird, and then with Blackbird ensouled they were going to turn it against Iruvage and *win*—

All he had to do was explain it to Erik.

But Erik, fucking Erik, shot him stone dog dead.

And when Clayton woke up again, healed somehow, Iruvage sent him lurking off like Blackenstein (*An American Metaphor*, pub. 2008) to—where the fuck is he? Is this a *storage container*?

Right. Of course. He's surrounded by shelves of paper and batteries and toner cartridges, a lot thicker than aluminum or lab equipment. Iruvage parked him where a stray armor-piercing bullet won't take him out.

A woman's voice sounds in his head. Transmitted through the implant in his neck. Some anonymous American airman on an AWACS control plane. *"Majestic, this is Chalice. Is this your TOC calling?"*

"Negative," his mouth says. *Neh guh chiv.* Iruvage can't quite form it right. "This is Deputy NSA Hunt." *Deputchee Enessssssay Hoont.* Like he's fucking Afrikaans.

"*Acknowledged. We have Rune Two, flight of two F-16s, orbiting south of you. More help is on the way. Can you describe the target?*"

"Area target," Iruvage says. "Ssaturate the valley around the Blackbird object. We need everything out there dead."

"*Majestic, be advised that Rune is currently armed with nuclear weapons. You may be caught in the strike.*"

The alien doesn't want his prize damaged. "Usse your other weaponss."

"*We are vectoring bombers north from Al Udeid. On station in ninety minutes. We also have naval assets in the Persian Gulf for cruise missile attack. Are there any friendly positions on the ground, over?*"

And Clayton cannot stop himself from saying: "Negative, Chalisse. No friendliess in the sstrike area. Kill everything outsside Blackbird. Continue attack with all available weaponss until I say sstop. Majesstic out."

Somewhere far too close, gunfire explodes through plastic and aluminum. He hears Chinese people shouting.

"Ah, Clayton." Iruvage talking to him with his own lips and tongue. "Do you know how good your brain tastes right now? Fear and fury, salts and fat. I'm drooling out here. When your soul's extracted I'm going to eat your merely monist brain like yogurt."

Let me go, you bastard!

"No. I win. You gave Blackbird a soul, as I desired. Either the atmanach will take its new soul, and I'll have everything I need to use it, or Ssrin will stop the atmanach, and we'll bomb Ssrin into a thin aromatic fog, and Davoud will fly Blackbird away for me to retrieve. Either way, your planet's finished, Clayton. You bought it fourteen extra hours. Seven billion human beings multiplied by fourteen hours is ninety-eight billion person-hours of extra life. That's more than eleven million person-years! Think of all that was accomplished, Clayton. The extra eleven million years of uncertainty and fear you allowed your species to feel. That's a hero's work, Clayton. You truly are a hero. The last and greatest hero in your species' history."

You bastard. You bastard.

CHAPTER TWENTY-SIX

⸱꜀Ꜹꞅꞑ꜑

Anna crashes through a ream of JSTOR printouts spilled from a copy-shop box. Her smashed nose can't pass any air, so she's panting like a dog, sputtering through split lips. Jan kicked her right in the face, but then the Chinese were storming in, and Mike had to shoot back at them, and she squirmed away and ran. The wound in her back bleeds slow and steady. It doesn't even hurt. But she's pretty sure if you lose all your blood you die.

She thinks the little thing protecting her, the bulletproof Tinkerbell robot, is a part of her mom.

Mike Jan and Skyler Nashbrook fight a running battle against the Chinese soldiers. She can track Zhang's team by the unabashed snarl of their rifles. They're blasting ass, making a ton of noise. The Americans are silent and their guns make metallic *taptap* noises, two shots so close together they sound like one. She can't imagine two guys can kill a bunch of badass Chinese dudes. Even if you're an elite black ops killfucker, you have to rely on stealth and surprise, right? You don't just John Woo everyone to death with your gun-kata. But even if Mike and Skyler can't kill all the Chinese, they can still kill her.

So she scrabbles ahead of Mike and Skyler, down this endless plastic rat luge, into another can—

"Hello, Anna," Clayton Hunt says. "Come on in. You smell wonderful."

"You asshole," she snarls, and points the Glock at him. He's slouched against a shelf of printer supplies. His face doesn't react right: muscles twitch and slump. She kicks him in the smile. The door clicks shut behind her.

"Ow." His head bangs limply down the shelves as he slumps. "What did I do to deserve that?"

"You sent us out there for Iruvage to kill us all!"

He tries to smile. He looks like he's getting ready to eat a small rodent. "If Ssrin were nearly as ruthless as she used to be, she would've used you to kill Erik Wygaunt. That would've stopped *my* plan for Blackbird. Just as I would've killed you to stop *her* plan . . . if I didn't need a backup. If my plan failed, I could still let Blackbird conjure a ghost out of the bond between you and Ssrin. And then I could devour that ghost. Or worshipfully obey it. Whichever was easier."

"Ssrin's dead, you shit fuck."

"Ssrin's very much alive. I just can't find her. She's hiding behind you, Anna. Don't you remember? The rules of serendure?"

I fit within you and you within me. That's why they haven't tracked us down . . . that's why you could see through my camouflage . . . Blood knows blood and fang knows venom . . .

"She really *did* coercively narrate you, you know," Clayton says. His eyes are big and brown and sad, and they don't match his rat-eating grin at all. "None of this would've happened if she hadn't entrapped you. The Ubiet led her to you. You led her to Blackbird. And Blackbird is the reason I'm going to destroy your planet. If you'd only listened to me back in New York, you'd have saved your people to be slaves."

A frisson of fear leaps through her, like current, like she has just suffered her own moral EMP. This is not Clayton.

"Iruvage."

"Wouldn't hurt me if you shot him, I'm afraid." Clayton blinks slowly. His tongue flicks out between his teeth, curls, and withdraws.

"What are you doing with him?"

"Killing Ssrin, of course. Bombing her to death. Clayton would've gotten her the first time, if he'd dialed his weapons up to four hundred kilotons. If a trick fails, repeat with higher yield." He looks down at himself. "You scare him, you know. I think he's attracted to his fear. Aren't you, Clayton? Do you imagine her holding a gun to your head while she forces you to perform sex acts? Get a hard-on. Wake it up! Make it wobble!"

"You sick fuck."

"Not sick. Just not human." He sniffs air. "You're shot. Is your *mother* running that hive aglyph that's guarding you? That'll kill her, you know. I very much doubt her brain is up to Unnumbered Fleet data bus standards."

The gunfire out there is coming closer. She puts the Glock to his face. "No one's going to bomb us. They know we're down here. They won't just kill us all."

"Oh, yes, they will. There are already four bombers on their way. Each one carries twenty-four little human weapons. Each one of those little bombs carries a hundred and forty-five baby bomblets. Each one of those thirteen thousand nine hundred and twenty baby bomblets holds a shaped charge to break armor, a fragmenting case to kill people, and a zirconium ring to start fires. Once those forty thousand weapons are released, they can't be stopped. And they're going to absolutely marinate this camp." He grins horribly: jaw open, lips rigid, the muscles way back on the side of his neck twitching. He looks like he's revving up a boring machine behind his tonsils. "Then I'll walk in and sample the buffet. Your mother's so full of seizure byproducts that she *must* taste fascinating . . ."

"Stop them. Make the bombers stop. Or I'll—I'll—"

What? What can she possibly do?

"I *could* call them off . . ." His nostrils flare in interest. "Ssrin's only hidden from my inquisitions because her soul is obscured by yours. Deny her that camouflage . . . and maybe I could kill Ssrin right now. In time to call off the bombs. To save your mother."

"How?" Though of course she already knows.

Slowly, clumsily, Clayton makes a pistol shape with two fingers, and shoves it up underneath his grinning chin.

"Kill yourself. Break the serendure. Then I kill Ssrin and call off the bombs. Your mother lives. The others out there live."

A Chinese rifle snaps outside. Bullets punch through the trailer's siding and shatter cartridges of printer toner. It smells of jobs that Anna's lost.

"Shoot yourself," Iruvage hisses. "Save them all."

CHAPTER TWENTY-SEVEN

CLAYTON//PERICHAYA

Clayton makes the screams but they won't come out.

"Anna!" he howls. "Don't! *Don't do it!*"

But nothing gets through the coil of command Iruvage has closed around his neck. Not a whimper. All he can do is watch as Anna shoves her pistol under her chin and pulls the trigger. Iruvage is salivating.

The weapon clicks. Anna groans, fishes a magazine out of her pockets, and slides it into the empty Glock.

Clayton imagines himself as a diamond-tipped spear driving through the membrane of Iruvage's control. "Anna! Stop!"

But he doesn't make a sound. Anna puts the pistol back under her chin, wiggles it around like a cat checking its footing before it jumps onto the fridge, and pulls the trigger.

Click. No death.

"You forgot to chamber a round," Iruvage says helpfully.

"Ah, fuck," Anna mumbles. She reaches down to pull the slide.

Chaya Panaguiton scrambles in through the container's far door. She's stripped her biosuit to the waist, and it's dangling off her like a half-shed chrysalis. She's wearing a tank top underneath. In the gap between the cloth and the waistline of her jeans, her navel has grown two tiny echoes, one above, one below.

She sees Anna with the gun in her mouth and she shouts the thing you shout when you've seriously considered doing this to yourself. Somehow it's always easier to know someone *else* shouldn't do it.

"No! *Don't!*"

Anna screams in horror. "What the *fuck* is *that!*"

Chaya's body has only just begun to mutilate itself into a transcendent expression of its own symmetry. But her soul is well ahead. She's good and exposed: the pathology is far along, and Clayton understands in an instant why the atmanach-stricken are terrified of the more ensouled.

Chaya is sickening.

Flower of possibility. Dark star of mights. The acausal wellspring of her soul decays into the world around her as impossible alternatives, branch states which, unsustained by real causality, wither into unphysical chaos. How can the mind process the sight of a gesture that never happened? The sound of a word never spoken? Neurons fire at stimuli that revoke themselves, never were, never could have been, incompatible at their root with the world as empirically observed.

He has tiny seizures: cataracts of brain activity triggered by possibilities that instantly become unpossible. His heart stutters in arrhythmia. Even his enteric nervous system goes wrong: his guts literally quiver.

What does it feel like to look upon Chaya?

Not pain. Not horror. Not evil.

It feels like intense cognitive dissonance. Believing two things at once, incompatible, contradictory, antipathic to each other. *I am a good husband* and *I'm not going to tell her* times a trillion.

No wonder the atmanach-touched turn to murder. No wonder they don't hesitate at violence against the ensouled. You could rationalize *anything* to make this stop.

He screams.

He screams with his own voice.

Iruvage has lost control.

The alien is afraid! He doesn't want to be infected! Or—or the wildly pathological sight and smell and sound of Chaya is wreaking havoc on whatever mechanism Iruvage uses to puppeteer Clayton.

"Where's Professor Li?" the chorus of Chayas demands. "She told me to hide, I tried, but the farther away she got the wronger I felt, so I knew I had to go after her, I had to save her, she's probably run into Blackbird, probably given up on the rest of us"—the sounds tumbling over one another, wet like salad, too many mouths—"probably forgotten we exist, probably gotten herself killed, probably shot to death, probably let her down, probably should never have let her go—"

Anna tries to shoot Chaya. She still hasn't managed to load the Glock.

"More," Clayton rasps.

"What?" The Chayas flow toward him. "What did you say? Baby killer. Sold us out—evil man—unforgivable *bastard*—baby killer, assassin, thug—buray ni nanya, go to hell and fuck yourself—"

Something happens: an explosion of possible interactions, bouncing between them like the pulse of light in a lasing chamber. Choices superimposed upon choices, generated by the seed function of Chaya's overheating soul, reflected from Clayton's possible responses, ramifying through a phase space of might-yet-bes.

It's like the reflection between him and Erik that Blackbird amplified into its soul. But instead of converging into a moment of murder, this is escalating into *everything*. Every possibility between them. He knows Chaya in a special, unprecedented way: wider and shallower than anyone has ever known anyone else. He knows all the things that might happen if they replayed this one instant forever.

And it's shattering Iruvage's control. He can't puppet a nervous system against this storm of stimuli. He probably has a self-destruct in Clayton's implant, a kill switch, but it's not working. Chaya's overclocked soul is more powerful and more commanding than any merely physical impulse, and she's not aware of the possibility that he could die.

Iruvage is gone.

"Anna!" He struggles out from the heap of printer supplies. "Anna, look at me! Look at *me*!"

"Oh my fucking God," Anna moans. She hugs her trembling knees. Blood drips from beneath her body armor—she's been shot, must be blanking it with adrenaline. "Who is that? How is that . . . ? *Why would anyone do that—?*"

How isn't *he* affected? Why isn't he horrified by Chaya's multiplicity? Never mind. Figure it out later. Right now—

"She's got the Blackbird sickness. But it's okay. We can fix it. We can fix anything. Blackbird brought me back to life, see?" He tears at his compression top, trying to show her the dime hole in his chest where Erik's bullet went through. "I died and it fucking fixed me! It can fix Erik too!"

She fumbles for the Glock. "Iruvage said I had to shoot myself. Or we would all get bombed."

"No! You don't! We can take Blackbird for ourselves, we can call off the bombers—"

"How? He jams our radios."

"*Blackbird can transmit!* Remember how we discovered it? A radio event! A radio event so loud it blew out the power in Tel Aviv! We can talk to the whole world! We can get all the help we need!"

She seizes the Glock in both hands and works the slide. A bullet *snicks* into the chamber. "Then his spaceship will just nuke us. You told us that."

"He won't! I have a plan!"

"Of course you do." She puts the gun to her chin. "You're just like me, Clayton," she says: each word moving her jaw which moves the pistol. "But the difference is, you make other people pull the trigger. Tell my mom what I did."

"Stop!" His scream tears his ravaged throat. "I'd let you die if I thought it was necessary. I'd order you to pull that trigger. I promise you I would. I'm not Erik, I'm not, I'd kill you if I had to. So you know I'm not shitting you when I say *your death is not necessary!*"

Her eyes narrow: that cool, feline interest again, like she's wondering how his kidneys taste. "Why isn't it necessary?"

God, he wishes Erik could see this. He grins so hard he must look like Skeletor. He's got to get Erik back somehow, haul him into Blackbird, fix him, just so Erik can hear how he said: "*We* have a spaceship now. Let's figure out how to fly Blackbird. Let's go kick their asses."

Someone shoots out the door latch.

The door pops open. Mike Jan's big armored shadow fills the tunnel. The four lenses of his thermal/night-vision goggles jut from his face like the periscopes of a submarine running deep beneath his scalp.

The barrel of his MP7 snaps onto Anna's forehead. If Clayton could see in infrared there would be a little dot of light there.

Something glints in the air between Mike Jan and Anna: a minuscule machine, changing forms, like a fish fanning out its tail.

Then there is a thin but enormously loud *bang*, the sound of something tiny accelerating to many times the speed of sound

The back of Mike Jan's head explodes through a hole in his helmet with such force that his body pitches forward.

"Holy fuck, Mom!" Anna says.

CHAPTER TWENTY-EIGHT

AIXUE 3 × 1

Aixue's not going to save Chaya.

She's a liar. She's a promise-breaker. She never gets it right. The only place she ever succeeds is in the abstract.

She has failed over and over and over to find the *right* truth at the *right* moment to make a difference. She knows more about Blackbird than anyone. But she has not used that knowledge to help Huang Lim, who believes in her, or Sergeant Zhang, who is shooting it out with the Americans, or Major Wygaunt, who died while she watched.

She suspects Blackbird has done this to her. Bent the arc of her existence out into some vector space of cosmic knowledge, so that the concerns of life and death dwindle to a gray point behind.

She has a deeper certainty that this suspicion is a lie. She did it to herself.

Blackbird just gave her what she always wanted. The truth.

Right now the truth is that she cannot figure out a way to protect Chaya, who protected her.

Master Sergeant Zhang stands at the front of the fighting stack. He leans out and uses his left hand to toss a stun grenade into the next trailer. With his right hand he holds his rifle, forming a chord joining his shoulder to his hand, drawing a secant line down into the earth. That chord is tangent to the curve of $\log(x)$ at $x = 0.12$, which is a value very close to $1/\text{root}(69)$. Nice.

The moment Zhang sees Chaya, he's going to do what everyone does when they see the overensouled. He's going to shoot her.

Aixue is too far away to do anything.

No. That is untrue. That is not and cannot be true. What is true is that she must do something.

"Zhang Bin Wei!" she says. "You will not shoot her!"

The stun grenade goes off. Master Sergeant Zhang swings through the door. Aixue understands the motions of his body. Vector lines protruding from him like spikes, arcs of angular momentum implicit in his joints. Look how his hips twist. Look how his upper body is completely steady. Look at the way his rifle rises and welds to his cheek. Look how he is ready to kill the danger he sees.

There is a short silence. Then Zhang calls, "Professor Li?"

"Yes?"

"This American is dead. Clayton Hunt is here with two others. Can I shoot him?"

"Back out," she says. "Come down the steps. Keep watch for the other American."

She goes inside. Mike Jan lies face-down dead with a red bowl instead of a skull. Anna Sinjari is sitting on her ass against the far wall, surrounded by crumpled cartons of paper. Clayton Hunt sits opposite her, tangled in ribbons of printer ink, holding his head. The stun grenade's burnt husk lies between them.

And there at the far end of the trailer is Chaya. Completely fine. Completely normal. There's something a little strange about her, some detail Aixue will probably figure out embarrassingly late, but the core truth of her has not been changed. It's still Chaya Panaguiton, tall and muscular and beautiful and gloriously disheveled, absolutely brimming with all the old-fashioned iron-T passionate aesthetic any stupid chubby lala could ever wish for.

"You came back," Chaya says in bewilderment. "I thought you went into Blackbird."

"I almost did," Aixue admits.

"I was *sure* you wouldn't come back. I was falling apart. I thought it was because you—weren't coming back."

"Well, here I am."

"That doesn't make any sense. All the answers are in there. You said you didn't care about anything else."

"I'm not obliged to make any sense to you!"

Chaya blinks at her. Ah. That's what's different. Chaya's eyes have complete double pupils now, reflecting the bilateral symmetry of the face. It's lovely.

"I think I'm pretty sick," Chaya says.

"You look fine to me."

"Hey," Clayton says in wonder. "You *do* look fine. You're not, um, fountaining anymore."

Chaya looks suddenly very upset. "Oh, susmaryosep. Tell me it's not because—" She glares at Aixue. "This is because of you, isn't it?"

"Me? I didn't do anything!"

"Get out of my free will!"

Oh, no, now Aixue's ruining everything just by existing. "I'm not doing anything! I swear!"

"Professor Li?" Master Sergeant Zhang calls. "What's happening in there?"

"I'm fine! We're just having a metaphysical disagreement!" She sees that Clayton Hunt is himself again, not Iruvage. "Mr. Hunt? Can you stop the bombs?"

"Yes—yes. But I don't know how to use the alien implant. And Iruvage can jam all our radios. We have to use Blackbird, he can't jam that. We have to take Erik into Blackbird. Have to save him. Stop the airstrike. Save everyone."

"Okay," Aixue says. "I want to go in there too. Chaya, will you come with me?"

"Yes. No, wait. Anna's hurt, she needs help—"

"You guys go ahead. Get Blackbird. Stop the bombers. Iruvage told me something I needed to know." Anna claws her way up the shelves, back to her feet. Blood smears the reams of printer paper behind her. "I've gotta get back to my mom."

CHAPTER TWENTY-NINE

Resurrection: like going through a wood chipper in reverse.

There was a hole in his head. He felt it. Oh, God, his brain didn't die instantly. He was shot in the head and he kept going. He remembers being a pulped fraction of a person, thrashing in the wreckage of a shredded organ. Then he finally ran out of oxygen and turned off.

He screams.

There's shit all up his ass-crack and dead brain caked to the back of his head. Something happens in his skull, a tremendous reflux of cell toxins and stale neurotransmitters that swamps his glymphatic system, like a toilet backing up. He feels things that probably no human being has ever felt before: an exhaustion so profound it's narcoleptic as his body tries to restore key ion gradients in his muscles and nerves. His kidneys hurt. His bladder spasms.

He gapes in madness. His splayed, numb hands bat at plastic.

"Erik!"

Clayton's voice. It's necessary that he return to consciousness. Clayton's alive and up to some kind of shit so Erik has to be ready to push back.

"Clayton," he rasps. "I smell like shit."

"I know. You shit yourself. Hold still, man."

"Where are we?" He is lying in plastic on what feels like a smooth tile floor. His eyes are caked shut with goo.

"Inside Blackbird. It's all different now. Rosamaria's in control."

"*Rosamaria?*"

"Yeah. Don't you remember? I guess maybe that didn't make it into long-term memory before Jan capped you." Clayton's hands touch him, roll him, unspooling the plastic sheet. Must've wrapped him to try to help him warm up. "She copied the decon shower from the airlock for you. Can you get up?"

He's naked. "My armor. Where's my plate carrier?"

"It's here, dude, it's okay, we just gotta get you cleaned up. I threw the rest of your uniform out. Sorry, dude. You *really* shit yourself. Too many protein bars."

"I died," Erik says defensively. "It's not my fault."

Clayton laughs like he's going to scream.

Erik staggers into the shower. Pure hot water needles down over him, washing away the filth that comes out of you when you die. His junk is slimy, smells like piss and cum: "Jesus, did I really do that?"

"Gunshot trauma to the cerebellum causes post-mortem erection and discharge," Clayton says.

"I know. I've seen it. I just didn't think it would happen to *me*."

"Hey, at least you died with a big dick." He tries to laugh. "Dude, are you . . . of course you're not okay."

Erik has a headache. He's cold inside in a way he's never been cold before: his core temperature plunged during that spell of true death. His breathing has a distinct rattle, mucus built up at the back of his throat. He spits thick stuff. Then he asks.

"What's happening to my command?"

"Well," Clayton says, "um, I called in an airstrike on them."

<hr>

K + 167:19:41 hours
Blackbird

Everything in here *is* different now.

The fractals and spiraling tunnels are gone. Maybe you could find them if you looked. Maybe they're buried away in the subconscious, now that an ego has made this place its home.

They walk together across an endless plane of frosted glass or quartz. It becomes dirt, grass, aluminum, Tyvek sheet, Demron cladding, even Persian carpet: things Blackbird knows from its surroundings. There are spotlights high above, tracking them. Like they're on a stage. Why is it a stage?

"Arsenal Gear," he says. "Rectum. Watch out for Metal Gear RAY."

Clayton chuckles. "And you're buck-ass naked, which fits."

Erik is not quite *buck*-ass naked. He has his armor and weapon but no clothes. He's girded himself in a thin plastic medical gown that came with the safety shower, but he has to wear his IOTV armor vest straight over the plastic, and the crotch straps are a constant pinch menace to his balls.

"Chaya!" Clayton shouts. "Aixue! Where are you?"

Not even an echo comes back. Of *course* it's a stage. Rosamaria was a dancer, like Clayton. That's how they got together. One of those dance competitions Erik wasn't at. He never resented that. It felt right. If it had happened when they were all three together, *that* would've hurt.

"They're in here?" he asks.

"Yeah—Chaya and Aixue helped me haul you in. They're, um, somewhere. They said they'd call me if they found a radio but they probably got distracted. Davoud's in here too. Anna went back to the Spetsnaz command post for her mom. And I, obviously . . ." His eyes are hot with emotion. He fumbles the eye contact, chuckles, looks away. "I wasn't sure Rosamaria could fix you. I mean, you shot me, but at least you didn't shoot me in the *head*. I hope you're okay, man. There's all these subneural components to memory, and if she didn't get them right . . ."

Erik considers his rifle. "Did you know what Iruvage was going to do to my people?"

"No. I don't even know what he did."

"He killed them all and said you'd ordered it. Because you didn't need me anymore."

"He was lying, I did need you, he needed you—he was just trying to get you revved up so the rath would work. And I didn't know about that."

"That's the truth?"

"God, Erik." Clayton stares off at an angle not *quite* exactly away from him. "I don't know. I think it's the truth. But I lied to you about other things. I didn't tell you I was working for Iruvage, or that Anna was bait to bomb Ssrin . . . so can you really believe me now?"

"I don't know."

"Look at it this way. Could I have possibly *stopped* you from going after the Kurds?"

"You could've made me do whatever you wanted. All you had to do was tell me the right lies." Erik fingers the mag release on his rifle. "You've always been able to do that."

"I don't think that's true. But I bet you think it is. Hey—did anyone make it? From, uh, from the caves?"

Erik does not want to give him the satisfaction of a *yes*, because then Clayton will absolve himself of the ones who didn't make it.

Clayton has explained a little about this alien concept of rath. How they're bound to each other like iceberg and *Titanic*. The *Titanic*'s mistake was trying to turn away. If it had rammed the iceberg nose-on, the ship would've survived. Steer straight into it.

Erik turns his weapon on Clayton.

"Dude." Clayton frowns at him. "Don't point that at me. Once was enough."

"Why not? I could shoot you again. I could do it as much as I want. She'd fix you, wouldn't she? She'd even make me more bullets."

And that gets her attention.

Spotlights converge on them. The air shivers with heat. Erik watches tiny curlicues of liquid-warm air vortex off his fingertips.

"HEY, CABRONES," the world booms. "I DON'T KNOW WHAT WAS UNCLEAR ABOUT THE WAY WE LEFT THINGS. GO AWAY."

Erik and Clayton look at each other. Erik demurs politely, because he wants to talk first, and it's not polite to do what you want without thinking of others.

"Rosamaria, we need your help," Clayton says.

"THE WAY YOU NEEDED ME TO LISTEN TO YOUR FELONY CRIMES?"

"No," Clayton says, why is he so *calm*, he's talking to his ex-wife's cloned soul, "not like that. This time there are a lot more lives at stake. Maybe everyone's life. And if we don't act soon, you're going to be the first one to die."

The nerve angel descends upon them, radiant, Rosamaria coming down the front steps to give Erik a smile and a joke and a hug. A beautiful human epithet, majestic in its mutilation, awesome in its bravura. A mask of eyes beneath bone struts. A fanned headdress of living brain. Two legs splitting into four shins into no feet. Arms that fork sevenfold into infinity.

The thing-Rosamaria waves an arm like she's brushing them away. Invisible strands of glass score Erik's cheek: the microscopic tips of incredibly elongated fingers. He closes his eyes.

The alien body folds suddenly, huge crowns of nerve and myelin collapsing, many-branched arms freezing into two brown hands and two brown shoulders. Feet coalesce between the stinging points of forked calves which join together into legs.

And there before Erik is that woman he so chivalrously loved. The thick black hair that looks brown in summer sun. Eyes of—he's got to be honest, he never noticed her eyes, because when he looked her in the eyes he was always thinking, *What is she thinking*, or laughing at what she'd thought. She's dressed (he feels suddenly naked) in a reverse-lapel jacket, matching bootcut pants and black pumps. She looks ready for the office.

She even has her port-wine stain, like a burn between her collarbones. Held too close to the candle, Erik used to think, when God put the fire in her.

"You look just like her," Clayton breathes.

Erik knows with absolute certainty that right now Clayton is wondering if he's going to eat this alien pussy. He can't help it, he's seeing his wife again for the first time in years, it's the kind of question your brain just asks. Activate idea of wife, automatically activate eating her out. Poor dude.

But is she really *here*? Is this just a mask, an illusion wrapped around that thing? He wants to poke her.

"We need you to send a radio signal," Clayton says. "Two hundred and eighty-five megahertz, Suite A SCIP encryption. Erik's radio should have the electronics for you to copy."

"Oh, no, I am not going to just start doing things for you. Let me lay down some rules." Rosamaria crosses her arms. "You are inside me. This is my body and I am in charge here. If I have to deal with you two then I expect clarity and honesty. No lies, no games, no *hurry up and we'll explain later.* Not from you, Clayton. And not you, Erik—"

"When have I ever?" Erik protests.

"You asked me to help prosecute my own husband for criminal conspiracy."

"But I was *right*, he was guilty—"

"We don't have time for this!" Clayton steps up between them. "Rosamaria, there's an airstrike coming right now—"

"Didn't you call that airstrike in yourself, Clayton?"

"I was possessed!"

"Oh, he was possessed!" Rosamaria laughs. "You were possessed, passive voice? It had *nothing* to do with your choice to accept that implant in the first place? Yes, I know what you did, Clayton, I came out of you!"

"Rosamaria, there is really no time to walk you through the moral circumstances of the decisions I've made—"

"But I know the circumstances. We have all the same knowledge. You just think you're the only one who knows what to do with it."

"But I *do*—" Clayton groans in frustration. "Can't we please have this conversation *after* we call off the air strike?"

"I'm sorry," Erik says.

No, there's no time for this conversation. But he says it anyway. If this Rosamaria somehow . . . came out of the space between Clayton and Erik, then she hasn't had even an hour of real existence to process what happened to her life.

Rosamaria eyes him warily. "Sorry about what, Erik."

"About filing my report before I even talked to you. About springing it on you as a choice between him or me. I . . . I honestly never thought about your welfare when I made my choices. I guess I was so furious with Clayton that I just wanted you to take my side. And when you blamed me as much as him, I made that into Clayton's fault instead of really looking at myself. Like he'd tricked you into it, somehow. But it was your choice. And you made the right one for you. You kept our secret, and we should be grateful you did that much. But it's not a secret we should've forced you to keep."

Rosamaria's lips quirk. "Apology accepted."

Now that Erik's done it Clayton is certainly going to make his own entry in the competition.

"Rosamaria." He swallows. Erik wants to shove him and mutter *you suck-up.* "Rosamaria, I lied to you. You responded fairly and ethically to my lies. I took your forgiveness for granted, but of course I wasn't owed it. You were right to get away from me."

"Cool," Rosamaria says. "Good talk. I know Suite A SCIP encryption."

"You *do*?" Clayton boggles. "How?"

"You've been throwing it all over, haven't you?" Rosamaria waves at the spot-light sky. "The world out there talks, and I listen. I take things apart. Your army man codes are cute, but they're not BQP-hard."

Erik stares. "Beecoupee hard?"

"It's a complexity class. Problems that can't be solved without a quantum com-puter. I learned that from Aixue. She's in here. With Chaya. Teaching me math."

"Is Chaya all right?" Clayton asks.

"She flows roughly along caryatasis while she's with Aixue," Rosamaria says distractedly. "Though it's not her nature. She was very beautiful when she was manifold, though. Elegant. Not like most things are outside. I can't quite . . . un-derstand . . ."

Spotlights search the glass plane around them. Erik glimpses distant archi-tectures: the front door of the yellow North Anacostia house Rosamaria picked out, the house Erik loved to visit, although he was as far out of place in that neighborhood as a penguin at the North Pole. The ghostly nose of an airliner. The moon in cratered close-up. A milky spiderweb that Erik realizes, after a moment, must be superclusters of galaxies like a Powers of Ten exhibit. Toppled Rapa Nui statue of Clayton's face . . .

"What else is *in* here?" Erik asks.

Rosamaria frowns.

"Davoud," she says. "He's in the cockpit. He wants to fly."

CHAPTER THIRTY

DAVOUD (~7,900 FEET ASL)

The moment Davoud claws his way up the ladder into his new starship, a bomb goes off in the back of his head. The detonation is silent and total, like the moment of blackout when he ejected from his Tiger.

But the blackness doesn't pass.

He falls on all fours on cool hard glass. He's blind again. No! He had his sight back! He's inside the starship he was promised *and he's too blind to fly it*!

"Hello, Davoud," Iruvage says. "*This is a recorded message: please don't bother sobbing.*

"*I've scoured the V1 vision-processing area off the back of your brain. It's gone. Forever. You may think that someone can fix it. Ssrin, perhaps, with her Cultratic operancy. But the way of knives will not help you, Davoud, because it cannot undo its own work. I've cursed you. Anyone who tries to heal this hurt will find a dreadful opposition.*

"*You will never fly any human aircraft again. Your only chance to pilot lies ahead.*

"*Obey the shape of your soul. Follow it to your destiny.*

"*I'll be along shortly to join you. I just need to kill Ssrin, slaughter the human defenders, and excise Blackbird's new soul. Then we're off to begin the Task. The salvation of my species.*"

He scrambles on all fours. The surface beneath him is slippery and his ripped bloody hands only make it worse. His fingernails crack and splay.

"*You will have some difficulty with Blackbird's controls, I'm sure. You won't know how to fly it. Not to worry. Once I'm aboard, I'll give you a primer on drive fields. The artifact has arrived at a solution to the field equations not so different from that used by your everyday galactic starship. I know exactly why that is, but I won't tell you. Together we'll have no trouble teaching Blackbird how to move. Your soul's the soul of a pilot, and Blackbird prefers to clarify the soul.*"

He cannot stop! He can't go back! If he stops moving he will stall and fall from the air! He pants into a phantom oxygen mask. He can't go back!

His right hand seizes on a lever.

Oh, God. God in heaven. Praise be to God! He clings to it and sobs. He knows exactly what it is: the grooved bar of an external cockpit release. There's no rational reason for it to be here and yet Davoud trusts, grips, pulls.

Hydraulics sigh. Smooth vacuum-formed acrylic slides beneath his fingertips: the canopy of a fighter jet, opening for him. A rush of cold, clean air, that bitter metal taste of engine bleed pumped to the pilot. Davoud slides into the dream of a cockpit feet-first. His ass strikes hard ejection seat. He fumbles around, finds the stick and throttle, and grips down in joyous recognition.

It's an F-14. The Tom Cruise plane. The Jalil Zandi plane. *The plane.*

Tomcats don't have a cockpit voice, but *this* one does. The voice of an angel. Like Googoosh.

"Hello. Are you the pilot?"

Davoud caresses the trim hat, targeting hat, the pickle switch that drops the bombs. Blackbird speaks excellent Farsi. He hopes she knows English too, not only because English is the language of aviation, but so they can watch English movies together, projected on the HUD. They will be alone together, safe, forever.

"I'm the pilot," he says. Rudder pedals press back against his feet. "Can you fly?"

"I don't know. I've never tried. I copied my wings from the wings I saw in the sky, but I don't know how to use them. I need a soul that knows."

No. He can't fly. He can't even watch movies on the HUD. He would sob if he could, but he is afraid he would somehow short out the controls. "I'm sorry. I'm blind . . ."

"That's all right, Davoud. That's okay. I can't help you see. But I can give you something better."

Davoud gets a nice firm grip on the flight stick and the throttle.

"Show me," he says.

⁂

Ma'rifat. The knowledge.

Among Persians the word *ma'rifat* means something like kindness. The knowledge of how to be a good person. And here too it is knowledge: but so much more . . .

Islam came from the Arabs, yes, but Davoud knows—well, he believes he knows—that the tradition of Sufi mysticism began in Persia, where the Zoroastrian fountain of the mind took up Islam and arched toward God. Among the Sufi mystics, ma'rifat is one of the four doors to God. It is the knowledge attained not through study or reason but through the ecstatic experience of creation.

Blackbird *reveals* creation to Davoud.

Not the goo-ball smears gathered by the eyes or the parchment scratch of the skin. Not the crude hookah hit of a nose or the sniveling bumplets on his tongue. Not these pitifully impoverished sensors.

This is the joyous knowledge of absolute truth.

He is everywhere around Blackbird. Among the wild birds who panic in the aurora. He is in the Earth where atoms of stone still ring with the absorbed radiation of nuclear blasts. He can't see it but he *knows*. He knows these things the same way you know that you exist. Irreducible fact. Undeniable presence.

There is an aspect of sense to it, yes. He can smell radar (the wide sweeps of a search radar smell like fog, thin and even; the narrow spikes of targeting radar taste like the tang of a thunderstorm). He can feel the crushed velvet and buckled linoleum of the quantum fields that underlie all matter and force. He encounters the curling florets of cosmic ray impacts decaying through the atmosphere.

Ma'rifat is not analogy, though. He has direct access to the truth, not by imagining what is already real, but through his soul laid upon the face of creation. He is a stylus on the record of the universe, and the music plays.

He cannot know everything at once. His stylus has a point. He sketches it back toward Blackbird. Tiny wonderful life scurries around him.

But there's something funny here, something slippery which jets sidewise when he tries to touch it. A hole where there should be a bump. A squirm where there should be a stillness.

"What's that?" he says. And to his surprise the voice doesn't answer.

"Blackbird?" he repeats. "Interrogative: identify the thing at our twelve o'clock high, range . . . one nautical mile."

But the only reply Blackbird makes is the incredibly loud trill of the threat warning receiver.

And suddenly Davoud recognizes the thing, he can't see it but he *knows* it, God oh God oh God, it's the atmanach, it's the atmanach, it's coming to take him, it's dilated to the size of a thundercloud and it's going to swoop down and—

"Let's get out of here!" he shouts, and advances the throttle.

Blackbird tries to move. The sixty-four death vortices that surround the hull slide like ball bearings through the manifold of space, sucking at the ship as if to pull it upward. A child's idea of how to fly: lift a vacuum over your head.

And of course it doesn't work. Blackbird groans around him, deranged at the most basic level, the warp and weft of its existence. Davoud feels a sick twisting inside like he's got appendicitis again, like he's trying to piss while his swollen appendix is tangled with his bladder, like he's about to *rupture*.

He yanks the throttle back.

The atmanach begins to dilate. Opening up its maw.

※

Somebody knocks on the acrylic bubble of Davoud's cockpit. The thump jiggles his wet water-sack body. Feeling things in his body, rather than through this glorious link to Blackbird, kind of annoys him. He tries to ignore it. But the atmanach is right *there* and he doesn't want to *know* it, he feels like *knowing* it would be the same as being eaten—

"Hey! Hey, Davoud!"

It's Clayton. Clayton Hunt. No, that's Iruvage—Iruvage wearing Clayton's body—ignore him and he'll go away. Ignore him. He's not real. Not like the *knowledge*.

Another fist beats at the cockpit. "Captain Qasemi, it's Major Wygaunt! We need your help! We need to send a signal! Rosamaria—uh, Blackbird says you know how to do it!"

Wasn't he dead? Hey, he went out into the woods with Khaje. Is Khaje all right? Davoud really wants to know if Khaje's all right.

He locates Khaje on a stretcher inside the Spetsnaz command post. Anna is there, wounded and sutured shut, having an argument with the Spetsnaz leader. Khaje spits and arches under the hands of the medics. There are all kinds of tubes and IVs going into her but they aren't helping. She's dying.

"Khaje!" he shouts, and the hands beating at his cockpit stop for a moment.

"Davoud?" Clayton calls. "Can you hear us?"

"We've got to help Khaje!"

"Yes, we do," Erik Wygaunt says. "And the only way we can do that is to stop the airstrike. I need you to send a signal."

An airstrike? Do airstrikes stop atmanachs? Davoud expands his awareness.

Things get fuzzy as he zooms out, distorted by mathematical complexity— the chaos of atmospheric turbulence and a sort of ambient unrenormalized quantum disorder. But he can clearly perceive the four airplanes charging north toward them. American B-1 bombers, long wings swept back like arrowheads. He has seen what American bombers did to the Iraqis in Desert Storm. Miles of burnt-out hulks. Men made of charcoal, incinerated as they tried to climb out of their burning trucks, skulls fixed forever in their final grimace.

That'll be Khaje in a few minutes.

"I see them." He reaches down into the cockpit, finds the radio panel with his fingers. "What do you want me to send?"

"Two hundred eighty-five megahertz," Clayton calls. "You'll need encryption—"

"I've got it." Davoud reaches out by memory and clicks the AN/ARC-195 radio over to MAIN, confident that Blackbird will do the rest. He has never flown an F-14. But he has spent a lot of time pretending to.

"Signal to Chalice. Tell them to abort the strike on my authority. Then find Iruvage. We're gonna flatten him."

Find Iruvage? "No no no." Davoud doesn't want to *think* about Iruvage. If he finds the alien then he will *know* him, he will have to confront that awful Satanic stain of pure evil, touch it with his soul. "No, we've got to get out of here!"

"Davoud." Erik Wygaunt's voice. A soldier calling for air support. "We can locate Iruvage and drop so much firepower on him *nothing* could survive. Then we can use Blackbird to destroy his ship in orbit. We will save the entire planet. But we need you to do it. We need you most of all."

Wow. Okay. Okay. Inshallah he will not fuck this up.

"Chalice," Davoud sends. "Chalice, please reply if able."

"*Unknown call sign, this is Chalice.*" The voice comes from an American AWACS plane, circling to their south. The kind of plane Davoud was trained to destroy if it ever came to war. "*Identify yourself.*"

He doesn't have a call sign. But he knows at once what he will be—Khaje would approve, it is from the *Shahnameh*—the protector bird, the mother of Zal and deliverer of Rostam.

"Call me Simurgh," he says. "The Purifying Eagle."

CHAPTER THIRTY-ONE

The atmanach is now a mass covering forty degrees of sky.

The boy-medic checking Anna's stitches slaps her on the back of the head. "Hey! You're stable for now, but you need surgery to get the fragments out. *Hey!*" She tries to go to her mother, and he grabs her and holds her in place. "Stop. Stop. You don't want to go in there. She's still in status."

"What's that?" Anna demands. "What the fuck is status?"

"A long seizure! Too long, long enough for brain damage! You need to rest, you're going to tear your stitches—"

He tries to block Anna's lunges but she's played too much flag football, gets past him, into the tent. Khaje is on a stretcher with a sack of T-shirts under her head and a tube down her nose. She's making awful sounds, low regular grunts. She smells like a gym bag.

The medic grabs her from behind. "I can help her!" Anna shouts.

"How? Are you a giant bag of fucking paraldehyde?"

"Let her go!" someone barks: Major Vylomov. "Let her go. Hunt has ordered the American planes to destroy the entire valley. I cannot get through to anyone on the radio. We are all fucked anyway. Let her see her mother."

Anna kneels beside her mom. Tears bead Khaje's cheeks. Strings of saliva stitch across her lips. "I'm here, Mom," Anna murmurs. "I'm here I'm here I'm here. We got into Blackbird. We did it. I think we did it the wrong way, though. I think the bad guy's gonna win. But I'm here. I'm here with you. Isn't that what you wanted?"

Khaje can only answer in grunts. She stopped so many bullets for Anna. And it's killing her.

There's just one thing. Just one chance.

Iruvage seemed really fucking certain Ssrin is alive. And if Ssrin's alive, the snake bitch can *definitely* debug her machines and save Khaje.

She looks the huge Spetsnaz major in the eyes. "Put a gun to my head."

"Why?" he asks, with an unsettling calm. He's ordered plenty of executions already.

"It's alien shit. Put a rifle on me. Put your finger on the trigger. Count to five. If Ssrin doesn't show up to help my mom, then you shoot me dead. But for this to work, you've got to mean it. You've *got* to be ready to pull the trigger. She can feel directed hostility, right? She'll only come if you're genuinely about to kill me."

"I don't understand why she would care—"

"I don't have time to explain serendure. You have to do this right now."

A voice booms out of a radio set, some incoming broadcast blowing out the speakers, too loud and too clear to be any local radio. *"Call me Simurgh. The Purifying Eagle."* Vylomov doesn't even glance that way. His eyes are locked on hers. "I won't do this."

"Fucking listen to me!" Anna screams. "Ssrin's alive! Ssrin's out there, letting us all die, because she can't risk her mission by giving Iruvage a shot at her! The *only* way she'll lift one finger to save my mom is if she needs to do it to protect herself! And if you kill me, Iruvage finds her!

"So put your fucking rifle to my head!"

⟶⟡⟵

خه‌جی

Khaje dreams of days gone. Days when she watched over shepherds in green meadows and her husband sat in friendly silence by her side. In this dream, little Anna plays down among the sheep, she darts like a happy dog.

And she has dog jaws, wolf jaws, bloody with her play.

Don't be afraid, Serhang says to her. *She's just your daughter.* And he kisses Khaje on her wet nose, the wet dog nose above Khaje's own narrow wolf jaw.

A helicopter comes. The whirling shadow falls across Anna and the sheep. A man with a loudspeaker booms: *Anna, are you an animal?*

Mother, she bays, *am I an animal?*

Khaje wants to answer: *Run, daughter, run to me!* Khaje wants to cry out, *Anna, I love you, I love you, come home.*

But she can't say anything. After all, she has wolf jaws.

She's supposed to have a person's jaws and a person's body. But she can't find the edges of herself. There are so many voices speaking in so many ways. The cup of her mind is overflowing with sensation . . .

Sibilant hiss. Satan's whisper: the waswas, calling her to hell.

"Khaje . . ."

There is no God but God, the living, the eternal. He neither tires nor sleeps. All the heavens and earth belong to him. Who is he that speaks to God but by God's leave? He knows our past and our future. Who may know of Him but through His word? His throne includes the stars and the seas, and He never tires of protecting them. There is no God but—

"*Khaje,*" the voice hisses, "*God is dead and rotten, and we are all that stand against Its Enemy. Get up! Get your mind out of the hive and get up! Your daughter needs you!"*

Ssrin? Is that you?

"Yes, of course, of course it's me, don't be timid of mind. In a moment I must act to stop the atmanach. Iruvage will find me and he will turn his ship's guns on me. You must be ready to run! Focus on your daughter, Khaje! Go back to Anna!"

I can't find her, Ssrin. I don't know where I am. I have eyes all over. I can't find myself . . .

"She knows where you are. Use hers."

Ssrin does something to Khaje's sight.

And suddenly she is inside Anna's head. Connected, spine to spine, to her daughter.

From here, looking down at her own thrashing body, it is easy to remember where her mind belongs. Right there. Where she can tell her daughter to stop sobbing so pitifully.

Khaje blinks.

And she has only two eyes, two ears, two legs. She lies in a tent with a plastic tube down her nose. Above her is the beloved strangeness of her daughter's grown-up face.

"Mom?"

"Oh, Anna," she croaks. Her head *hurts*. She feels wonderful.

And then a voice booms out across the valley. A voice that drips with the need to bite.

"GOT YOU, SSRIN."

⸻

ᔑIᎶᴂ𐐺

Anna bolts out of the tent just in time to see the atmanach fall.

Spetsnaz fire up at it but the tracers and rockets pierce nothing. The atmanach eats the little residue of choice on those bullets like so many chocolate sprinkles.

This is her last moment before hell.

Anna looks up at the white mountain. She looks down the river-carved valley. This should have been her home. She grew up here, and yet she hardly remembers it. In old video of nuclear tests, the blast of the bomb seems to make everything around it darken, like the explosion is actually burning away all the light. But it's an illusion. The camera's correcting its contrast so that the nuclear fire doesn't white-out the whole image.

She remembers gunning down her brother, her father, brilliant as a nuclear blast. The rest of her childhood has been corrected down to darkness.

Anna raises her face from the darkness below to the darkness falling above. "Ssrin!" she screams. "*Ssrin!*"

The atmanach is *deep*—Anna looks up into an infinite interior, receding along circuits of bronze-green teeth toward a far cold nucleus—

She roars at it. It comes down at her, at Blackbird, at all of them.

And then:

"SHE IS NOT YOURS TO TAKE!"

Anna's roommate unpacks herself like origami from empty space. A swan-necked hydra armored in black scale and formfitting gunmetal. At the join of her necks she wears a crown: angles of emptiness, chisel marks in reality, where air hisses out into the naught between the stars.

She puts out one white hand, palm forward, to meet the thing descending from the sky.

The atmanach chokes.

Maybe Ssrin has some kind of magical atmanach poison. Maybe she's got a charm that repels the thing. But Anna prefers to think that Ssrin's soul is just too fat with ancient sin for the atmanach to swallow.

The soul-eater collapses in on itself, becomes a squid shape against the aurora, and snaps away down the length of its tether toward its master.

Ssrin hisses like summer thunder. "I gave you no leave."

The atmanach jerks to a halt. Ssrin's eight heads gather into one braid of scale and bite. The crown above her flashes violet; the grass burns. Anna feels the sudden heat, like ducking into a car parked in the sun.

"Iruvage is nothing," Ssrin sings. "A swollen child drowsing in a butcher shop. An eater of leavings, drunk on the liquor of rot. You were made by khai to serve the khai, and I am the truer khai. I am the predator of clades. I am extinction's hinged jaw. I am the one who dimples foes' living flesh with hollow fang and makes a stomach of their womb. My venom is all potent! You bow your belly to *me!*"

Her two-thumbed right hand cuts a shape in the air: a thin crescent, descending.

The black tether that binds Iruvage to monster *snaps*. The atmanach twists in sick dimensions, unherniating and untorqueing. It drains away.

Ssrin falls to the earth, heads drooping, body supported on two trembling and weirdly human arms. Blood runs between the scales over her shoulders, steaming-hot, venting from some buried scar. Her white tongues flicker in and out. "Not a thing khai do. Wasting such a precious weapon. Not a thing we do. I have wasted many weapons to save you today—"

Anna starts to grin. Ssrin's heads open back into their watchful flower. Anna begins to ask if Ssrin was there the whole time, right behind Anna, or if she just turned up now.

Ssrin whirls and throws a stone. It whips past Anna's face and, behind her, strikes Major Vylomov right in the belly. A vulnerable place, if you are not used to aiming for the head.

But he is wearing body armor.

Major Vylomov shoots Ssrin.

He has his rifle at his shoulder and it is set to full automatic. Cartridges spit from the machine to drum on tent canvas.

The Cultratic Brand: the living shape of evil. It is all he can see on Ssrin.

Tiny blurred things dart in the air to intercept but Ssrin must have left too many of her little machines to guard Khaje. She is hit, hit again: bright cracks of electricity snap across the gunmetal of her armor and ground in the meadow grass. Ssrin rolls away, thick tail coiling to protect her body.

The rifle's magazine runs empty. Suddenly she is in her human disguise again, a lady in a pantsuit.

"Ah, fuck," she says. "I'm hit. How the fuck am I hit? I thought it would be Iruvage's ship. A man with a little gun instead. How am I hit?"

"Cyka blyat!" Vylomov stares down the sights of his rifle. "Is that what they look like? *Was that her?*"

"STOP!" Anna screams at him. "Don't shoot! Get your men away!"

Ssrin is shot exactly where she was shot before, when Anna found her bleeding in the kitchen. Her blood is brighter red than any human has ever bled, and it comes out not in spurts but in a constant high-pressure arc.

"Oh, Anna," Ssrin says with a deep irritation. "They've shot me."

In the distance, another nuclear bomb goes off.

CHAPTER THIRTY-TWO

He's got to figure out how to kill Iruvage. So Major Erik Wygaunt does his major shit.

Rosamaria builds him a model-train miniature of the entire valley, complete with the cruel power to zoom right down into the narrowed eyes of an Iranian scout sniper trying to spy the base of the atmanach's tether. Erik uses this power to find and count off the survivors of MAJESTIC: Raab and Gamboa's teams, side by side with Iranians and Spetsnaz.

He gets out the little radio Clayton issued him. He selects the unit net and takes a breath. "Majestic Zero Six to all Majestics. Resuming command."

There is a short pause.

"*Jesus fucking Christ,*" Gamboa sends. "*Where the fuck have you been? How did you get the radios working?*"

"I'm inside Blackbird," Erik says. "We've got a chance. We need to stop the hostile alien from getting inside while we figure out how to move this thing. Then we're going to defeat the alien ship in orbit."

"*Uh, copy, wait one.*" A short silence while they all try to figure out what the fuck to say to that. "*Sir, we're pretty confused out here. People seem to be shooting at each other in the labs and the Spetsnaz killed some kind of creature and now that flying thing's up there getting real big . . .*"

"Captain, a lot of bizarre shit is going to continue happening. Right now I need you to get your teams ready to repel an attacker coming across the river from the east-southeast. It's a single dismounted alien, roughly human size and speed, very resilient, armed with accurate and lethal weapons of unknown range. It killed my whole team and it *will* kill the rest of us if we let it. Brief the Spetsnaz and the other international survivors. Get everyone on side and in fighting positions. Understood?"

"*Yes, sir, understood. Can we actually kill this thing?*"

How *are* they gonna kill Iruvage? He's clearly proof against rifle-caliber weapons and grenades up to forty mm. He has perfect awareness of the battlefield. He commands a personal drone system that can explode your head at long range.

His sensors can cook you alive. He's aggressive and explosive and all those other fucking things they tell you to be in leadership training.

"Yeah," Erik says. "Of course we can kill him. He's just got his own little survivability onion. He's using smoke and jamming to avoid being hit, and personal armor to avoid being wounded. He struck from ambush so we couldn't fix him and get heavy fires on his position. He's alone. He's *scared* of us, Raab."

There are rules about how fast you can move energy, what you can do with your waste heat, how much information you can extract from a sensor. Certain problems are *always* hard to solve. Those problems put a plausible ceiling on Iruvage's fighting power. A bullet is always going to be a good way to do some hurt, because a bullet's made of frozen energy; Einstein said it and Erik trusts that guy.

And just because Iruvage is advanced doesn't actually mean he's good at fighting humans. Sometimes technological progress scales in weird ways. If the entire World War II Eighth Air Force took off to bomb Washington, DC, would there be enough missiles ready to shoot them all down? Or what if Erik, a highly trained and well-equipped soldier, had to fight a duel against a hive of wasps? He would not bet on himself. He has never trained or equipped to fight wasps.

Maybe Iruvage is specialized to fight other aliens. Maybe the humans can be the wasps.

"Okay," Raab sends. "*We'll get ready out here. Any word on air support?*"

"Oh, yes," Erik says. "There is word."

MIDNIGHT, EIGHTH DAY

K + 168:00:00 hours
Blackbird

When the atmanach swoops down on them Erik shouts: "Clayton, did you clear them to use nukes?"

"Yeah."

"Copy. Davoud, get ready to transmit!"

"I hear you. You don't have to shout." Davoud does his cool radio voice. "Rune, this is Pure Eagle, say when ready."

"*Rune, ready for nine-line.*"

"Your IP as briefed, bearing zero eight five, seventeen point three nautical miles, area target, coordinates to follow. Friendlies are five NM northwest. Egress direct south. Coordinates—"

Erik eyeballs the base of the tether, the line connecting Iruvage to the atmanach, and he just gut-guesses the MGRS coordinates. Davoud repeats them (coolly) to the planes.

"Pure Eagle, Rune, read back." The same string. "Ready remarks."

"Good readback. Request two warheads, five-hundred-meter spacing, on a west-east run."

"Pure Eagle, Rune, in from the west, thirty seconds."

Tiny Spetsnaz fire toy weapons at the descending atmanach. The aberration looks like a hurricane's eye seen from orbit, if hurricanes were made of silverfish and smoker's lung. Erik holds his breath. If nothing stops the atmanach they are all fucked—

The diorama *cracks*. The matter of the model begins to burn white-hot, like a sparkler, in a jagged flaw between the Spetsnaz command tent and the atmanach above.

"Sorry," Rosamaria says, "sorry, I don't know what happened there, it didn't make sense—"

The fire goes out. And the atmanach is gone.

"Cleared hot!" Davoud sings out.

"Rune, off hot, time of fall twenty seconds. Out."

The gray shapes of two air force F-16s flash across the diorama. And for the second time, America desecrates the forests of Kurdistan with its crowning sin: a pair of B61 tactical nuclear weapons.

Light and thunder open the midnight forest. The blast wave travels faster than sound itself, a wave not *in* air but *of* air, and a sucking void behind it to yank the ruined forest back in toward the star-bright fireball. At the center of the chaos is a void where not even Blackbird can tell what's going on.

"Hey," Clayton says. "My head didn't explode."

"What?"

"I figured Iruvage would have a dead-man switch on my implant. So that if he dies, I die. But it didn't go off. Maybe Chaya really did break it."

"And you didn't *tell* me?" Erik shouts.

But he's cut off by sound. Words in the nuclear thunder.

"COME ON, CLAYTON. DID YOU REALLY THINK I'D USE THE ATMANACH IF IT COULD LEAD YOU RIGHT BACK TO ME? YOU'VE NEVER HEARD OF A RELAY? YOU'RE SMARTER THAN THIS."

Tiny figures scramble in the perimeter camp beside Blackbird. Erik recognizes Anna, bent over a fallen body, an indistinct human figure that Blackbird doesn't want to fully render . . .

"SSRIN'S WOUNDED." Iruvage sighs like blast wind. "I SMELL HER BLOOD. SHE TRIED TO STEAL MY ATMANACH. I HAD TO PUT IT DOWN. SO NOW I HAVE TO COME OVER THERE AND TAKE

BLACKBIRD MYSELF. I'M COMING NOW, CLAYTON. AND THIS IS GOING TO BE MY VERY FAVORITE PART."

Iruvage hisses. A sound like a steam jet cutting a man in half. "I'LL BET YOU A PLANET I CAN KILL YOU ALL BEFORE YOU GET AWAY."

CHAPTER THIRTY-THREE

DAVOUD (~7,900 FEET ASL)

Iruvage starts with the Iranians.

Davoud sees it coming but not in time to warn them. He spots a patch of *wrong* at the tree line southeast of Tawakul. Blackbird doesn't want to look at this spot, but her very aversion makes it obvious.

A shimmer, like heat haze, covering a fan of slender objects radiating from a central mass—

Camouflaged snakes. And the body they're born from.

The alien's body begins to shudder a couple times a second. Davoud resolves the object in his grip: a gun to humble Rambo. The shudder is recoil. The gun has a really pretty spectral profile, maybe some kind of scram rail setup. Is this the same gun he was using on the American commandos? The bullets unfold tiny wings to steer themselves. Davoud follows one of the fat darts in fascination.

It overflies the camouflaged fighting position of a Saberin scout sniper and blows up. A lash of alien wire dices the man apart.

"Ah!" Davoud says.

Death comes down faster than sound, without regard for cover. One of the American teams, huddled up for a conference, loses four men to a single bullet. The weapon's range is absurd! He must be ten kilometers away!

"Major Wygaunt!" he shouts, "Major, we're in contact! Do we have any more nukes?"

"We see it. We're out of nukes for now. Get on the Spetsnaz command frequency. Ask them if they've got air support."

Major Vylomov is not amused: "*Who the fuck is this? Who the fuck is dropping nukes out there?*"

"This is Captain Qasemi. I am inside Blackbird with Major Wygaunt. The nukes did *not* kill Iruvage. We missed."

"*You missed with a nuke?*"

"We're still figuring things out! Look, he is attacking now! Do you have any air support you can call?"

There is a long pause. Then Vylomov comes back on the air. "*You had better not be fucking with me. Can you authenticate with your warrant officer?*"

"Major, if Mousavi knows the authentication codes, he is a thief and a liar. All the comms gear blew up with our convoy, and all our officers are dead."

"*We know the alien can imitate voices. How can I trust you?*"

"I love *Top Gun*. Tom Cruise! Danger zone! Permission to buzz the tower? Negative, Ghost Rider, the pattern is full. I feel the need! I've slipped the surly bonds of earth and touched the face of God! For God's sake, Major, tell me you've seen *Top Gun*!"

"*You could get those quotes off the internet.*"

"Why would Iruvage need to fake voices to kill you? Why would he need *more* planes? He is already hitting you from ten kilometers out!"

A long silence. Then: "*Mousavi and Zhang are with me. We are all ready to transmit requests for support.*"

"Send your traffic," Davoud says.

⚜

K + 168:19:27 hours
Blackbird

Blackbird casts Master Sergeant Zhang's voice into the tortured sky. "*Máo gàn, zhè shì máo jiān. Wǒ mén xū yào jǐn jí kōng zhōng zhī yuán!*"

Three hundred and ninety kilometers to the east, Iran's Hamadan Air Base launches eight J-16 strike fighters and four J-11B escorts. The Chinese squadron throttles up to Mach 1.5, turns west across the Qandils. They will be on station in eighteen minutes.

Blackbird casts Major Vylomov's voice into the tortured sky. "*Komande proniknoveniya nuzhna podderzhka s vozduha, bystro! Yebashte vsem chto est, blya, tut prishelec!*"

A Vishnya-class intelligence ship off the Syrian coast plucks the overwhelmingly powerful signal out of the EMP noise. Forward-deployed units in Syria scramble their aircraft: a full squadron of Su-34 and -35 fighters, trailed by the slower Su-24 tactical bombers. They are forty-five minutes out.

Blackbird casts Warrant Officer Mousavi's voice into the tortured sky. "تو رو خدا، هر چی نیروی هوایی دارید بفرستید!"

Six hundred kilometers and thirty-five minutes to the east, Mehrabad Air Base in Tehran launches a mixed squadron of F-14 Tomcat and MiG-29 fighters. Tabriz Air Base, only two hundred kilometers east of Tawakul, puts up a squadron of vintage Phantom II fighters loaded with bombs. They are only twelve minutes out.

Blackbird casts Major Erik Wygaunt's voice into the tortured sky.

"Chalice, Chalice, this is Majestic Zero Six. Situation update. We are in contact with one hostile entity in close proximity to friendlies. Pure Eagle is your controller. Put fast air on my net and he'll talk them in."

"*Majestic, Chalice. Be aware the situation is complex and developing. Can you receive datalink?*"

"Affirmative, Chalice. Send datalink."

And it does: and Blackbird happily adds the information to the diorama: and Erik goggles at what he sees.

When Iruvage called in his counterfeit request for fire support, he unleashed a thunderstorm. He asked for the ongoing bombardment of Tawakul valley until he told them to stop. The request has been escalated and copied—every trigger-happy American asset in the Persian Gulf got in on the action. Surface warships and submarines fired more than a hundred and fifty Tomahawk cruise missiles. The aircraft carrier *Nimitz* launched three squadrons of Hornets and Super Hornets, now refueling from tankers half an hour out over the Persian Gulf. Incirlik Air Base in Turkey hosts A-10 attack aircraft, but they're pokey and slow, it'll take them ninety minutes to reach Tawakul. Four F-16 multirole fighters from the same air base sprint ahead, aiming for station in fifty-five minutes. Al Dhafra in the United Arab Emirates has four ultramodern F-22A Raptors, but even at supercruise, they are sixteen hundred kilometers and a full hour's flight away.

The closest American aircraft are the four B-1B Lancer bombers from Al Udeid. The datalink relays their position to Erik, along with Chalice's radar image of the nearby airspace.

There's something weird about that image.

Erik frowns at the fuzzy shapes scudding along ahead of the bombers. "Davoud? Are those drones?"

Davoud sharpens the signal. The shapes resolve into white gliders with narrow bodies and stub wings. Not drones. AGM-154 Joint Standoff Weapons. Medium-range bombs.

"They didn't abort," Erik groans. "The assholes didn't abort in time."

"What's that?" Clayton says.

"The airstrike Iruvage called in. They already passed weapons release."

"So self-destruct the missiles."

"They're glide bombs. They're not smart enough for any of that. You give them coordinates and let them rip."

"Oh," Clayton says disapprovingly. Barack *Obama* would not use such unsophisticated weapons. "So what do we do?"

"Get everyone into Blackbird and hope it can survive the hit."

"How long do we have?"

Erik does quick math. "About five minutes. Try to warn them."

He goes back to killing Iruvage.

DAVOUD (~7,900 FEET ASL)

Four nations have now launched more than three hundred aircraft and cruise missiles at Tawakul valley. The battle against Iruvage is no longer a problem of assembling firepower: the humans have it in plenty. Iruvage might have a technological edge, he might be as far beyond these aircraft as a rifleman is beyond a Persian cataphract, but at some point numbers matter. Never mind three hundred cataphracts, you could threaten Earth's finest rifleman with three hundred small owls.

So now it is a battle of information. A struggle to identify the target, communicate this target to the incoming planes, and guide weapons to achieve the kill.

"This isn't good," Davoud says. He's in ma'rifat immersion, looking down from cloud height at his boyhood fantasy. An air battle to dwarf the greatest encounters of the Iran–Iraq war.

It's all going to shit. Davoud wants nothing more than to figure out how to get Blackbird off the ground, away from Iruvage, up into the singing purple sky. Why can't Chaya and Aixue just get to the point and tell her how to move?

He seriously considers shutting off the radio and focusing on the flight controls.

But look at all these beautiful jets . . . look at the Super Hornets with their bold square intakes and canted tails, the blue-jagged Chinese Flankers with their sexy canards and high curving spines, the futuristically angular Raptors and the classic Phantoms, which always look like someone dropped the hangar door on them and it only made them *faster*.

And of course there are the F-14s. The last Tomcats in the whole world. America retired them. Only Iran keeps them in the air.

They are all death machines, of course. They are built to kill and maim. But for the first time in human history, these jet pilots have the chance to fly their beautiful machines not against fellow humans but an enemy of the entire world . . .

"Blackbird, can you get me on their tactical frequencies? Encryption, hop programs, all that?"

"*Done. You're on.*"

Davoud clears his throat. Presses the transmit switch. "All aircraft, this is Pure Eagle. I am now your forward air controller. I will talk you in."

CHAPTER THIRTY-FOUR

In the nineties the army commissioned a study to predict the next big thing in infantry weapons—the next step up the bloody stairway from spear to musket, musket to rifle, rifle to machine gun. The study concluded that the Next Big Thing would be a kind of individual mortar, a gun capable of killing people who'd already taken cover. It would fire smart grenades that could fly over or around obstacles and kill a target behind.

Apparently they were right.

Each round from Iruvage's gun scythes through the grass and flowers and men below. The alien picks off machine gunners and snipers, mortar observers, guys with comm gear. Captain Raab, a four-year veteran of Marine Force Recon, goes down with three of his men in a single shot.

This fucker shoved a radio into a child's skull, Erik thinks. And reads out to his men: "His position is now thirty-eight S MF eight four seven six six three nine zero. I say again, thirty-eight sierra, mike foxtrot, eight four seven six, six three nine zero—"

"*Stop with the fucking coordinates!*" Vylomov shouts. Screams in the background: his medics hauling in wounded. "*We are hitting him with mortars and autocannon but we cannot observe the results! You need to walk us onto the target!*"

"Stand by. I'll drop some hurt on him." Erik leans over the diorama to find the two dozen Tactical Tomahawk cruise missiles puttering in from the Persian Gulf. "Rosamaria, if these guys are Block IVs, they have datalinks. Can you—"

"Yeah, yeah." Rosamaria is still focused on whatever she's doing with Aixue and Chaya. "Point where you want them to hit. I'll make them do it."

The cruise missiles carry thousand-pound high explosive warheads on stubby orange wings. They are still ten kilometers out when Iruvage shoots them down with the exact same weapon he's been using on the soldiers. "Bastard," Erik mutters, and changes tactics.

Some of the Tomahawks carry submunitions instead of unitary warheads—the kind of cluster weapons Erik's always hated, because they leave unexploded bombs behind for kids to step on. Erik choreographs a whole flight of these missiles to separate, converge, and crisscross over Iruvage at the same time.

Two missiles make it past Iruvage to salt the whole area around him, mowing the forest down to black earth. The detonations are orange blisters beneath white caps of shocked air. Hollywood never gets those white caps right.

Erik and Clayton lean forward and hold their breath.

Die, Erik thinks. Die, you alien fucker. We'll deal with your ship in orbit next, just die, motherfucker, *die*—

Iruvage arises from the fire.

In thermal he glows white-hot. Plumes of coolant jet from his shoulders, flashing into geysers of steam. Electrical discharge from his tail carves lightning-strike fulgurites into the burning earth.

"Jesus," Clayton breathes. "How did he live through that? What *is* that armor?"

"Yes!" Erik hisses. "*Fuck* yes. He's done."

The huge gun lies shattered. Iruvage's weapons can be broken. And if his weapons can be broken, so can his armor. Because if the armor were unbreakable, they'd make the guns out of it too.

It might take more—much more—but it *can* be done.

He keys the radio. "Vylomov, it's Wygaunt. We just hurt him and disabled his long-range weapon. We've got more airstrikes on the way. We need to keep hitting him. Our absolute imperative is to keep him from reaching Blackbird. If he gets inside, we lose."

Maybe, if all else fails, Rosamaria can eat him with a death hole.

"*Wygaunt, what about the fucking American bombs your stupid fucking friend Hunt called in on us? Are we fucked or not?*"

"You've got two minutes," Erik says. "Um, you're probably going to lose all your vehicles. Disperse and get under overhead cover."

"*So we are fucked, yes?*"

Erik doesn't have anything positive to say, so he doesn't say anything at all. The AGM-154 glide munition was designed to wipe out entire columns of tanks and infantry in a single blow. The cluster munitions it disperses used to be the exact same color as humanitarian food rations airdropped to children in Afghanistan. When this was discovered, the Pentagon ordered radio broadcasts to explain to Afghan children that food drops were square, while cluster bombs were shaped like coffee cans. Don't mix it up, kids. There'll be a quiz on this.

Ever since then, Erik has considered the weapon cursed.

CHAPTER THIRTY-FIVE

"I need water!" Anna screams. "Anyone! Please! We need to help Ssrin!"

Spetsnaz charge past her, dragging ammunition to their mortars and tanks, hauling wounded boys back to the medics, as if they are making a grotesque trade in Kurt Vonnegut's Settlers of Catan. Lines of their weird squashed tank-things belch shells which appear to float, like very rapid balloons, off across the river: traveling in the illusory slow-motion of foreshortened perspective. Nobody has attention to spare for Anna and her camouflaged alien.

Ssrin flinches from her probing fingers. "Tiny little bullet. I'm offended."

"I got shot too," Anna says, "I handled it *way* better. Oh, Ssrin—"

Blood gushes constantly through her fingers. Ssrin's body refuses to stop bleeding. Khai are supposed to be able to clamp down wounded areas, but apparently that's part of a "hide and rest" response, and Ssrin is in too much danger for it to work. She is frantic with her ssovotic adrenaline: her heads nip at Anna's hands as if fending off a poisoner.

"Stop that," Anna protests. "I'm gonna get you some water, okay? Just like that bathtub back home. And you can do your weird shit, the way of knives, just heal yourself right up—"

"There's no time."

"The fuck there's no time. Iruvage is coming, you've got to heal before he finds you—"

"Serendura. Stop. Stop." Ssrin grabs her wrists. "He knows I have one operancy left in me. Not more. He thinks I will reserve it to protect myself from his ship, but I will not. If I don't get rid of those bombs, you will all die. And I will not be strong enough alone to keep him from taking Blackbird."

Khaje staggers toward them. Fading nuclear light, mushroom cloud lava-lamplight, shows Anna the bruise where Khaje's nose banged against Anna's back. Anna waves furiously to her. "We'll hide—we'll hide in the labs!"

"Aluminum and plastic? Seriously?" Ssrin laughs cruelly. She's hurt, so of course she's cruel. Khai logic: remind your caretaker you can hurt them if they don't help you. "Do you think your weapons were made so that a child in a trailer could survive them?"

Erik's voice on the radio headset. *"Anna, you're about to get hammered. Get into Blackbird now. You've got less than two minutes until impact."*

Khaje falls to her knees beside Anna. "It looks like a woman. Is that really Ssrin?"

"We need water," Anna pants, "we need it to help Ssrin do her magic—"

One of the alien's heads fastens its fangs on Anna's wrist. The teeth do not pierce skin, but they tremble with the need to. It must take all of Ssrin's concentration to hold back. "Serendura. Go. Save Blackbird from Iruvage. Take it somewhere far from here, somewhere safe. I will protect you as long as I can."

"Don't you dare tell me to go!" Anna roars. "You think I'm going to let you die here? After you shot my boyfriend? After you did this shit to my mom? Fuck you! You *owe* me! You don't get to die!"

"Serendura," Ssrin says, heads looking at one another, laughing in her own khai way, "I'll go to hell."

"Hell can't have you until I'm through!"

And Ssrin looks at her with all eight heads for a moment. As if in wonder that this pink ape could refuse her.

CHAYA 2:3

Her soul fits into her body again.

The seizures have stopped. She's not missing time, or parking her train of thought on the rail siding of free association, or making anyone scream when they see her. Is she going to be herself again? Or is she becoming something strange to God?

Aixue is trying to teach Blackbird how to move. She's laid out all the equations of motion on panes of glass, discoursing on the beautiful symmetry of Noether's theorem. Chaya wants to grab her and shake her. People are dying out there. They have to get to the applications *now!*

"Hey," she mutters to the air. "Can I talk to Professor Huang?"

"Sure," Blackbird says. "Hang on. I'll get you on shortwave with him."

"Chaya? Is that you?"

"It's me! Yeah! I'm in here with Li. We figured it out!"

"I knew she could." Almost immediately he adds: *"I knew you could."*

"Listen, you guys need to get out of here. It's turning into a war. Get the Chinese trucks and go, it's two hundred kilometers to Erbil but better than staying here—"

Professor Huang holds down the transmit switch but doesn't say anything for a couple breaths. *"We do not all plan to escape."*

"Mama Mary, Lim, if you stay here, you're going to die!"

"We know. But we have all agreed that it is not important we survive. What is important is getting the data we collected back to the world. Blackbird can transmit, yes?"

"Yes, um, yes, we're—yeah, pretty much anything you want. Rosamaria, is there anything you *can't* send?"

"Who's Rosamaria?"

"She's, um, Blackbird."

"I can pretty much do whatever you need," Rosamaria says. "I can send by ELF if necessary. Or auroral backscatter."

"Okay, Lim, I guess we can transmit. But—"

"Good. We are going to copy as much as we can to you. Can you receive?"

"Just put the files in the lab servers," Rosamaria says. "They'll get to me."

"Okay, um, I am right clicking, add network location . . ."

Chaya tries again, because she has to try: "There's nothing in there worth your lives!"

"Of course there is. Everything we learned about Blackbird. Things our friends and colleagues died to learn."

"I will come out there and get you."

"No. Aixue needs you. Help her keep Blackbird away from the aliens. Help her keep herself from becoming an alien. Listen, someone wants to talk to you."

"Chaya." It's Nakyanzi Sophie. *"Don't let the aliens have that thing. I saw one, in the sky. A sick angel. Pure evil."* The radio hisses as she moves. *"We are going to try to escape with the Chinese drivers and a couple of the scientists. One is pregnant, others don't want to die. And who can blame them! Do you have our payroll with you? Something to make sure you can reach all our families?"*

"No, I don't, God, it must be on Shafiq's laptop—"

"Then I hope you have a good memory. I ask for your prayers. Also, if you get to see the pope, I would like his prayers too. A Mass for martyrs. Well. God be with you, Chaya Panaguiton!"

"God be with you, Nakyanzi Sophie."

Chaya asks Blackbird to make her a laptop and uses Aixue's credentials to log on to the Chinese servers. She starts hunting for a primer on general relativity. Maybe she can get this thing flying a few moments faster.

———

ᚠᛁᛃᛟᛋ

"Jesus, Anna, get out of there!"

Clayton's voice in the background: *"She's got a minute. Not enough time. She's toast."*

Anna pushes a 1,500-liter water tank step by grunting step. The thing is

Russian, meant to be hauled by a truck. Instead it is hauled by Anna and her mom. "I have been in the fucking camps," Khaje snarled, when Anna tried to make her lie down. "I have been in worse shape than this!"

"Forty-five," Anna counts, out loud. "Forty-four. Forty-three. Forty-two." Seconds until the bombs hit. Her stitches are tearing. Her wound is opening up inside her.

"Be *quiet*," Khaje grunts.

"Forty-one. Forty." Anna gives the trailer one last jerk: now they are beside Ssrin, curled up in the grass, her little heads nipping at her wounds, drawing thin sutures, like spiderwebs, across the holes. Her scales leak black sealant.

"Hey! I got you water!"

"You're denying me self-sacrifice," Ssrin complains. "If I died to protect you, that would be good, wouldn't it?"

"You're going to hell no matter what! Do something about the fucking bombs!"

Ssrin gets up (spooky double image of her human avatar brushing off her knees and standing nonchalantly, as the true Ssrin corkscrews up to an alarming eleven-foot height) and arches over the water tank, balanced on a little ring of tail. Her hands draw and flick an alien tool: something that cuts. The top of the water tank pops off.

Ssrin bellies into the tank, pulls up her tail, coils inside, only her heads popping up, hydra-wary. She's kind of cute.

"Twenty," Anna says. "Nineteen. Eighteen. Seventeen."

"Get away from me," Ssrin says. "The cosmos is flesh, and I am its portioner. I am tooth in tissue. I am the cutter of cuts. O knife! Be my soul thy blade, be my spine thy hilt!"

The world tips sideways. Vertical becomes exactly parallel with the ground. Anna falls over, clings to the wall of the world, tries to reach her mom who is swearing in Sorani, words Anna has never heard her use. Tiny knives dissect Anna into some awful functional map: her organs parted from their supporting matrix, her blood vessels and lymph ducts uncoiled and laid out flat, every piece of her separated and individually immersed in the flow of a supercold, superannuated fluid, like liquid hydrogen from the dawn of time. It feels like being a small number in the middle of a very long equation that will, in just an instant, collapse to its final dire form.

Injecting illegal physics through computations in living brains, Ssrin said. *An art called operancy, which I practice.* Ssrin opens her heads in a starburst. Tiny silver spikes erupt from her necks and open into translucent fans. She's got *radiators*.

There is a silent racing motion in the night above—a flock of gray shapes, opening their bellies to disgorge their bomblet children—

Ssrin begins to steam. The water drum shudders around her: coming to a boil.

The American bombs vanish.

Just disappear like Anna's checking account in a cocktail bar. Anna feels a full-body frisson of unease, as if tiny grit has just blown through her, everywhere, and caked her guts in sand.

Ssrin screams with effort. The sound is human and awfully, eightfold alien at once. The water around her flashes into scalding steam which burns Anna; the radiators growing from her necks glow violet-hot and then vanish. Ports on Ssrin's back burst open to jet streams of hot blood and stinking coolant.

"I did it," Ssrin says, over the garden-hose gush of her blood hitting grass. "I'm shutting the elision down—I can survive it—thank you—"

Iruvage strikes.

What he does Anna doesn't know. But it *is* him, she can feel it, his evil eye. Through whatever magic joins her soul to Ssrin's Anna feels Iruvage's will tickling across Ssrin's defenses, probing, caressing, finding a weakness—

A feeling like a long, long needle, driven all the way flush with skin, so that you cannot get your finger under it to pull it out. Iruvage's delighted jeer: *You were always good at overextending yourself, Ssri-ssri, and never sure how to pack your mess away—*

Ssrin howls. The world lenses around her, like she's a weight on the surface of everything, pulling reality taut, tearing it: she screams an eight-headed scream which is joined by the chatter of Geiger counters, all around the camp.

The crown of black shapes over Ssrin's heads *turns*. The world cuts open there. For an instant Anna stares into the burst viscera of reality.

Something older than suns rots down there.

The surface of Anna's skin turns to ash. Her radio earpiece howls a dirge for electrons and dies forever.

Ssrin's back explodes. Giblets of nerve tissue blast outward through the rings of her spine, her thoughts themselves detonating as the terrible consequences of operancy gone wild play out in the nerve cells used to commit the crime. She falls back into the empty drum. A soup of blood, coolant, and water simmers around her. Her meat cooks fragrantly.

"No," Anna cries. "No. *No!*"

The Spetsnaz medic who patched up her bullet wound comes staggering out of the tent. His skin is sunburnt red. "Bozhe moi. What happened? What happened here? I took two hundred grays . . ."

Anna isn't even sunburnt. Whatever happened to Ssrin, she turned the radiation away from Anna and Khaje, on the others. The bitch.

Anna grabs a sheet of windblown Tyvek and throws it across the water tank, to hide Ssrin and her evil mark. To spare herself the sight of the empty craters along Ssrin's ruined spine. "Help me pull this," she calls.

The Spetsnaz medic blinks at her and begins to throw up.

"OH, DEAR." Iruvage's voice booms across the valley. "DID I JUST MAIM YOUR ONLY HOPE? THAT'S NOT VERY NARRATIVELY SPORTING, IS IT. NOT SPORTING AT ALL. BUT YOU KNOW THE RULES,

DON'T YOU? SHE'S NOT REALLY DEAD TILL I'VE EATEN THE BODY AND TAKEN A BIG SHIT."

Warrant Officer Mousavi stumbles from the back of the command tent. "We're alive." His face is blistered; his moustache is full of blood. "Where did the bombs go? How are we alive? I need to find my men."

He makes it three steps before he starts vomiting.

Anna and Khaje, together, grab the back of the wheeled tank and start to haul it toward Blackbird.

"STOP WORKING SO HARD, ANNA," Iruvage calls. "YOU'LL SOUR YOUR MEAT."

Captain Gamboa's MAJESTIC Team Three tries to ambush the alien at the river bridge, and dies to the last man. They don't even get a shot off. Iruvage's hive machines find them and crawl into their heads.

Then the tiny drones streak north, bore through the armor of the Russian BMDs, and detonate themselves in the magazines. Burning Spetsnaz boys rain from the sky. One soldier, lofted by the detonation of a Nona mortar, strikes a Blackbird death vortex and dangles by his feet as it burns and eats him.

Anna can't see any sign of Iruvage, but she can hear the pop of Chinese assault rifles now, punctuated by the short reports of Iranian marksmen. Mortars blow apart the houses of Anna's childhood. Is he still on the south side of the river, then? Is he coming over?

Master Sergeant Zhang walks past, staring at a radio handset exactly like the one they found lodged in the skull of a child. He looks up, sees Anna and Khaje, and shakes his head. "You should be headed for the trucks," he says. "They always go for the officers first. Before we run out of officers, I'm going to catch a truck out of here. Want to come?"

"Heat!" Anna screams at him. "The aliens overheat? Get on your radio, tell Erik to use fire!"

"The aliens have a spaceship," Zhang says. "Remember? Killing this one wouldn't matter. More will come. We should have nuked this whole valley at the start."

"Then we wouldn't have gotten Professor Li inside Blackbird!"

Zhang stares at her. "She got inside? Alive? She really is immune?"

"She's in there right now, teaching it how to fly!"

He smiles. "Really? Well, all right. All right. Major Wygaunt, this is Zhang, I've got Anna Sinjari here and she says to use heat. Heat is the trick."

"YOU BROKE MY FAVORITE DEFILADE GUN," Iruvage bellows. His voice rings off the mountain, comes back double. "I LIKED THAT DEFILADE GUN. I'LL COOK YOU ALL LIKE LOBSTER."

A violet-bright spike like a gas stove flame erupts from the river. It's so hot it flashes the water straight to steam. Downstream, fish flop and gasp.

Iruvage is slithering across the riverbed.

The steam rolls up over the Chinese fighting positions, over hard-faced riflemen with bayonets fixed. Tiny lines streak through the fog: Iruvage's last hive machines, jetting to their targets.

Khaje points up.

"Look. Those fuckers came back to bomb us some more."

Above the valley, notch-winged shapes descend in silence. Faster than sound.

The Iranian Phantoms drop their payloads.

CHAPTER THIRTY-SIX

CLAYTON//WARSHIP

"Zhang's right! He's cooking himself!" Clayton pokes at the miniature Iruvage in the diorama. "Fuck!" he says admiringly: "Even the model's hot!"

Rosamaria refuses to render the alien as more than an unpleasant smear, but that smear is now dribbling blue-hot metal behind it wherever it moves.

"That's heat sink," Clayton says. "Sure, his armor can survive Tomahawk submunitions and mortar fire, but the energy of the impacts still goes *somewhere*. He's going to run out of coolant eventually. We just have to keep hitting him."

Erik clicks his radio. "Major Vylomov, target is vulnerable to thermal effects. Use RPO-Z, use phosphorus, whatever you've got."

"*Acknowledged, Major!*" Vylomov panting with exertion: he's climbing up onto Blackbird along ladders and lines the Spetsnaz have rigged along the hull. "*We will give the fucker what he gave us!*"

Davoud's voice sounds from his disembodied cockpit. "Ten seconds to bomb release."

The Iranian Phantoms dive on the pale flame of the alien. Each jet hauls 8,500 kilograms of bomb.

There is one victory in what happens next. It proves that Iruvage feels seriously threatened by more than a hundred metric tons of high explosive falling on his heads.

The bombs separate. The Phantoms pull out of their dives.

Something appears above the model-train diorama.

"Oh my God . . ." Clayton breathes.

The sky above Tawakul ripples. Cells of distortion—like the air above cars' hoods, stuck in traffic on I-395—solidify into a huge object. Erik's brain fills in Mr. Worf's voice: *Sir, Romulan warbird decloaking!* Only it's not a green bird. It's a severed black raven wing as long as a submarine.

It hangs there beneath the aurora, gorgeously curved, edged in green-bronze spines like antennae. Hovering with absolute contempt for aerodynamics or gravity. Blackbird picks out the nodes of twisted space which surround it. Drive masts. Like Blackbird's own death holes.

"Of course," Clayton groans. "Jesus, of course, that's why Blackbird made drive masts like an alien starship's. It always copies what it finds and it found *his ship . . ."*

Not the ship in orbit that nuked the planet, because Iruvage didn't come on that ship. Iruvage brought his own.

"Wow," Rosamaria says in fascination. "How didn't I *notice . . . ?"*

Light flickers from the raven-wing ship. Clayton gets only the side scatter of the laser: a speckled diffraction pattern in the violet range. Iruvage's ship destroys the falling bombs one after another, burning through their casings to detonate them midair.

Then the laser stabs upward. Staccato bursts so fast they become a single fan. All twelve Iranian planes explode into trails of aluminum and burning aviation gas.

Davoud gasps in horror. "He didn't."

Erik is hard-jawed, cold, thinking.

"Do we call this off?" Clayton asks him. "Do we call off the other planes?"

No answer.

"Erik?"

"All call signs, this is Majestic." Erik's voice is emotionless. "Be advised there is an alien warship hovering directly above Tawakul. Its armament includes powerful point defenses with unknown range. Engage at maximum standoff. Continue attack. Out."

There is still a steady stream of Tomahawks coming in from the Persian Gulf. Erik starts aiming them at a new target.

In the cockpit of the lead Chinese fighter, Davoud Qasemi's voice comes through clear and crisp. *"High Spear, this is Pure Eagle. I have a new target for you."*

The squadron leader grimaces into his mask. What is he supposed to do with this? Pure Eagle has been jabbering away on his squadron freq but he has no idea who this guy is. Still, no one *else* is telling him what to shoot. And the guy on the radio has the right encryption.

"Pure Eagle, High Spear. Send it."

"Your new target is an alien warship, bearing two seven three, range seventeen nautical miles, angels two. Target is stationary and destroyer-sized. Configure radar for air to surface."

He checks his conversion card: okay, thirty kilometers away, six hundred meters above ground level. "Acknowledged." A quick glance for his wingmen (three other handsome J-11Bs, Chinese builds of the classic Russian Flanker) and his charges: a flight of eight J16 strike fighters. All where they ought to be. "High Spear, radar on. Sharp Sword, radar off, go trail ten kilometers. You will wait to attack until we have assessed the enemy's defenses."

He swaps his radar to antiship mode: it's warship-sized, so he'll try warship shoot. There it is! The squadron leader swallows several emotionally honest reactions, chooses professionalism. "High Spear, boresight the target. Attack on my signal."

His radar MFD fritzes out. He cycles the MFD over to stores management, then back to radar. It doesn't help. Mysterious contacts are appearing all over his radar screen—now the contacts are spelling out Chinese characters—

I'M NOT EVEN GOING TO BOTHER SHOOTING YOU, his radar says. YOU ARE SO TINY. DON'T AIRCRAFT ON YOUR PLANET HAVE ANY ARMOR? HA-HA, JUST KIDDING. I KNOW THEY DON'T.

And then:

YOU ARE OF COURSE AWARE THAT RADARS ARE MASSIVE RADIO RECEIVERS. DID YOU KNOW THAT MY WAR ORACLES ARE SO FAST THEY CAN PREDICT YOUR RADAR'S FREQUENCY HOPS, PREPARE FALSE RETURNS, AND USE THEM TO EXPLOIT SOFTWARE VULNERABILITIES YOUR MATHEMATICS CAN'T BEGIN TO IMAGINE?

LET'S SEE WHICH PARTS OF YOUR ELECTRICAL SYSTEM ARE NEVER, EVER SUPPOSED TO CONNECT TO EACH OTHER—

"Wǒ cào," Spear Leader says.

The PL-9 heat-seekers on his wingtips explode into a ring of steel bars. His cockpit is directly in the convergence zone.

DAVOUD (~7,900 FEET ASL)

Four perfect planes shatter across Davoud's vision: the Chinese fighter escort, exploding midair. "No," he groans. "Blackbird, what happened?"

"Iruvage's ship compromised their avionics and electrical systems with false radar returns."

Davoud can't let the rest of the Chinese planes die like that. "Sharp Sword, Sharp Sword, this is Pure Eagle, remain radars off! I say again, radars completely *off!*" He mustn't let them hear his panic. "All call signs, disable your radars entirely. Do not conduct passive search, do not receive. The aliens can compromise your avionics."

Of course an airplane without a radar is not good for very much. He thinks. "Blackbird, can you talk to aircraft datalinks? I know the Chinese have one, the Americans definitely do, Russians, well, you can figure it out—"

"Of course I can. Check your kneeboard for the frequencies."

It doesn't occur to him that he shouldn't be able to see his kneeboard. "Can Iruvage compromise the datalinks too?"

"Not if I'm running them."

"Then we are better than radar!"

Davoud uses the datalinks to shepherd the bewildered Chinese strike fighters back on target. Their Eagle Strike cruise missiles will lead the way as they close and drop laser-guided bombs. If they're lucky, the aliens will be too busy shooting down missiles to shoot the bombs or the planes carrying them.

A sudden intrusion: American voices. *"Pure Eagle, this is Mighty Two One. We are approaching from your south, twenty miles from bullseye. Releasing remaining weapons now. Good luck."*

The American B-1B bombers who nearly killed them all release their final forty-eight Joint Standoff Weapons, carrying unitary warheads instead of cluster bombs. At their optimal four-hundred-knot glide speed, they'll strike the target in a hundred seconds.

Twenty seconds later, the Chinese strike fighters launch thirty-two Eagle Strike cruise missiles. Eighty munitions converge on Iruvage's ride.

The alien warship takes it personally.

⁓⁂⁓

ᛞIᛉᛟᛋ

Anna screams just to prove she's alive.

She can't hear herself.

The angry bird-wing UFO above Tawakul launches missiles nimble as dragonflies, trailing lenses of water vapor and crackles of infuriated air on half-second delay. Laser weapons strobe and snap, carving violet afterimages. They are not quiet at all, nothing like in the movies. They crack the sky into pure-tone thunder, cleaner than lightning, faster and sharper than guns.

Broken cruise missiles shotgun into the eastern forest. The wind carries ozone stink, hot metal, dead men. Vomiting irradiated Spetsnaz stagger between flaming vehicles. Boyhoods ending in a puddle of hot bile and fleshy shrapnel.

Anna keeps hauling the water cart. But she sees everything. The broken cowlings of warplanes scattered among the flowers. The forests afire like paintbrushes too close to the stove. Burning aviation gas spatters pasture where Anna, age six, chased the sheep and imagined she was a cowboy. Jet fuel can't melt baby dreams. But it sure works a charm on chamomile blossoms.

Khaje clings to the water cart, too weak to do anything else. So Anna drags her and drags Ssrin.

The wound in her back keeps tearing wider.

⁓⁂⁓

K + 168:37:37 hours
Blackbird

So this is how the Matabele felt against the Maxim gun. How the Iraqis felt against the stealth fighter. How everyone Erik ever killed might have felt against him.

Iruvage's ship murders everything. Fighters, missiles, even the bombers twenty kilometers south. Davoud moans in grief. The second airstrike hit a lot harder than the first: and yet all it achieved was to get the alien ship to use some missiles.

Iruvage moves in the fog below, black-armored, killing. His heads mount knives and other weapons. The blade in his left hand is as thin as a silk strand and as long as a house. Bullets vanish when they strike him. Gouts of hot metal pour from his shoulders, and the flowers around him brown and cook. He pauses to eat a white lily. His armor's sensors project microwaves: aluminum dormitory containers erupt into flame, sparks jet from blown transformers, soldiers run howling from their positions as their skin cooks from the inside. You can't be brave in that. No one could.

"God," Erik says.

"He's taking it easy on us," Clayton says grimly.

"Yeah," Erik admits. "He should be using the ship's guns against us. He should've been doing that from the start."

"He hasn't needed it yet. I think he's saving it for when the real attacks start."

Erik forgives himself for hoping that Clayton has one more secret plan: "What real attack?"

"When everyone on Earth nukes him." Clayton draws a little arc in the air with his fingers, something going up and coming down. "He knows we've got nuclear missiles all over the planet. The ship is for fighting *those*."

"Still, you'd think he could pick off a few key positions—clear out all the lab clutter in his way, finish off Ssrin—"

"Yeah. I don't know. Notice how he's not maneuvering his ship? He could bring it closer to Blackbird, but he's not. Why?"

"Because . . . because . . ." Erik grimaces. "I got nothing."

Clayton snaps his fingers. "I do. He can't move because if he moves his ship *he's afraid Blackbird will copy it*. His win condition is getting in here. He can't risk teaching us how to get away."

"So we just keep throwing planes at him?"

"Yeah. And we hope he does have to move."

"Fuck."

Three squadrons of fighters off the USS *Nimitz* descend from the southern sky. They're fifteen minutes out. Davoud tags them with their squadron names and numbers: VFA-154 Black Knights, VFA-147 Argonauts, VFA-146 Blue

Diamonds. Brave names, Erik thinks. He's about to radio them, but Davoud has it under control:

"Knight, Jason, Diamond, this is Pure Eagle. Target has an effective laser range of at least ten kilometers. Advise you approach NOE to reduce line of sight."

"Pure Eagle, Knight. Descending to cherubs three. Ready for nine-line."

"Knight, IP as fragged, bearing zero one five, thirty nautical miles, six zero zero feet AGL, grid zero zero keypad two, large airborne warship, nonmaneuvering. Target clearly visible in TV and IR. Friendlies three kilometers north. Exit west. Read back."

"Pure Eagle, Knight, six zero zero feet AGL, grid zero zero keypad two, friendlies three kilometers north. Ready for remarks."

"Good read back. We don't know how to hurt it, so use everything you've got."

"Pure Eagle, Diamond. Have any aircraft survived their attacks?"

"Negative, Diamond. But target is highest priority."

"Copy, Pure Eagle. Break." The nameless pilot knows he's going to die. "All elements, Diamond, successful egress unlikely. Target must go down. Use your discretion and remember your seats."

"What was that last part?" Clayton asks Erik.

"He's telling them to ram the alien ship if they have to."

"Good."

The American fighters come in at treetop level without radar, flying by night-vision in the pink aurora dark. One pilot clips a wing on a tall oak and spins down. A burst of orange amid the blue afterburner fireflies.

"Nimitz group, Pure Eagle," Davoud chants. "Continue zero four zero, lowest able. Bandit still angels six, range fifteen miles. Radar dope on Link Sixteen. Over."

"This is it," Clayton says. "Iruvage is through the Chinese. He's at the final Spetsnaz perimeter. If we can't kill him with the planes . . . it's over. He's coming inside."

"Rosamaria?" Erik asks the air. "Can you kill him?"

A voice which is not quite hers says:

NO!!!

"Why not?"

I WON'T LOOK AT HIM HE'S WRONG HE'S WRONG HE MAKES ME WRONG I MAKE HIM WRONGER

"Can you hit him with a death hole?"

No answer. Maybe she doesn't know how to move yet.

Clayton rubs the place on his chest where the bullet went through him.

"There's something funny about his species. I guess Blackbird doesn't like it any more than we do."

"Less, if anything," Erik mutters. If Blackbird is an angel, and Iruvage is an unholy being . . . then Rosamaria's antipathy makes awful sense. If she's too terrified of him to even *look* at him, what will she feel when he climbs inside her?

But that *won't* be allowed to happen. They have thirty-three planes with heavy strike loadouts in the *Nimitz* group. Two minutes behind them, a second wave of Iranian fighters is closing from the east. If they pop up across the mountain peak, come down on Iruvage's ship from above . . . something's going to get through. No matter how much antigravity magic that ship might have, it's still a spaceship, right? It has to be built light, to maximize fuel efficiency. It wouldn't haul tons of deadweight armor between stars. So it can be harmed.

Right?

"Come on," Erik mutters. "Come on, you bastards, come on, come on . . ."

Major Vylomov screams, "*COOK THE FUCKER!*" and Spetsnaz up on Blackbird's wing fire a volley of rockets at Iruvage. He doesn't like it. He's not using his little hive machines anymore: out of power, maybe, or all expended in his defense. His armor vents waste metal like two vaporous devil-wings. More and more he relies on his whip-thin blade. His biology cannot possibly function at these temperatures! He must be poaching himself in his armor!

If only, if only if only if only, they could land *one* good bomb on him . . . but his fucking ship is in the way.

"*Knights,*" Davoud calls, "*climb to angels one and engage!*"

The American jets pop over the ridgeline south of Tawakul, dump their decoy flares, and open fire. AMRAAM and Sidewinder air-to-air missiles, SLAM-ER cruise missiles, and bundles of Maverick anti-tank weapons ignite and track.

The Iranians' second wave comes down over the mountaintop to the east, ninety degrees off the axis of the American attack, and descends on Iruvage's ship from above.

Hundreds of weapons cross-converge on a single target.

The raven ship pivots on puffs of thrust. Points the base of its quill stern at the Americans.

Throttles up.

The engine that forms the "quill" is a sheared-flow-stabilized Z-pinch fusion rocket. This is a fancy way to say that it turns spin-polarized heavy hydrogen and light helium into a continuous thermonuclear explosion. This is itself a fancy way to say that it runs on a rolling nuclear fireball.

The magnetically confined tailpipe puts out about 100 grams of helium-4, protons, loose neutrons, and unburnt hydrogen-helium fuel every second. Add gamma and X-rays for taste, and, in situations where you need extra thrust at the cost of efficiency, dump some extra mass into the beam as a kind of afterburner.

The resulting exhaust plasma moves at 3,500 kilometers per second: Mach

10,000, or about 1 percent of lightspeed. It can even vector its thrust slightly, like a guy at a urinal.

The upshot is: the air around the engine exhaust beam explodes outward with a sound like a tuning fork hit by a Space Shuttle launch. Lung-jellying power. Anything in the beam path suffers the short, severe influence of a needle faster and hotter than a vajra thunderbolt. Anything around the beam eats fireball.

The engine beam cuts the core from the American formation and swats the adjacent planes out of the air. After it come missiles which stitch jets into fire, execute hairpin turns, come back again in shrouds of burning fuel to knife through plane after plane. The fusion rocket's radioactive fireball plumes south over forest and flint like Godzilla's breath.

A couple of the Super Hornets dive in on the alien ship with cannons blazing, and something sucks them sideways: a drive mast, just like Blackbird's death holes, pulling so sharp and close that when one of the pilots ejects her seat slingshots around it and spikes her head down into the meadow.

A component of the alien ship—a feather along the edge of its curve—breaks off when a Maverick strikes it at the base. But the green-bronze armor along the main hull will not yield.

While all this happens, the alien ship kills the Iranians with its lasers. It seems to be in a delicate mood: instead of exploding the planes, it just pins each cockpit on a pale needle. The Tomcats and Fulcrums carry on as their pilots left them, exquisite opposite of an aerobatic display, wandering transonically toward sun or soil.

Erik watches all this with lucid rage. He sees the enemy. He knows what's necessary. But it's just not *working*.

"Oh, shit," Clayton says in awe. The death has not affected him. He sees only the marginal gain, the slight advancement of their pawns on the board. "Look at *that*. Look, Erik!"

The alien ship's drive masts glow like red coals. "Maybe from the effort of anchoring the ship in place against the kick of its own drive?" Clayton suggests. "They fired the engine but they didn't move, so all that kinetic energy turns into, I don't know, heat? Radiation?"

And the ship too is bleeding. Geysers of slag drool from its vents. You do not run a heat sink by throwing away all your coolant.

Not unless you have to cool down *so* fast that you're willing to destroy your own cooling system to do it.

Which you might be, if you'd just shot a thermonuclear fireball out of your ass.

"His ship gets hot too," Erik realizes. "We just need more threats—"

But Iruvage has had half an hour to cross the river and reach Blackbird. He is among the dormitory containers now, fighting the Spetsnaz up on Blackbird's wing. He leaps like a black spring, like Achilles fucked a Vermicious Knid. His armor is hot as Space Shuttle belly, but he is not slowed: he swings his long long sword at the humans above, and it becomes a whip. Major Vylomov ducks, steps back for balance, and slides into the jagged trailing fringe of Blackbird's wing. The tines go through him like a fork through soup. He just comes apart.

Iruvage's heads dart, exploding Russian boys, painting Blackbird in their gore. He fires bolts of plasma like ball lightning which bloom apart as they travel, flash-cooking flesh three meters from the supersonic fireball. He's running out of tricks.

But the defenders are all out of bodies.

DAVOUD (~7,900 FEET ASL)

In the air, as on the ground, the Russians die last.

Davoud radios the latest adjustments to the attack plan. "*Groza, this is Pure Eagle. Target is compromised but still active. Be advised target has a particle beam exhaust weapon with linear effect. Advise you go wide and low to deny a concentrated target. Over.*"

So many planes down. So many pilots dead. It will *not* be for nothing! Davoud will force the alien ship to use its hottest weapons again and again, till it melts from the inside—

Despite the totality of his ma'rifat awareness, he does not see Iruvage's ship activate its exotic capabilities. This is because some things are not part of creation as Blackbird knows it.

Far away, in the cockpit of his Su-34, Groza Leader feels the operant inquisition as a tremble of emotion. The alien sensor brushes his soul, searching for a way in.

It finds guilt: the shape of a soul turned back on itself.

Groza Leader thinks about the woman at the base in Syria who begged him to take her daughter away to a better life. He walked away. What was he to do? How could he raise her child? He already has enough bullshit to deal with. Syria is infested with Iraqi prostitutes, and some of his friends see them too much. The bastards treat the women like shit and the women treat the bastards like purses with scrota. He tries to be better. But is he a father for hire? Should he take some girl home to Russia as his own? No, absurd.

He shakes himself. (Does not know, cannot know, that the inquisition has penetrated the link between his soul and his physical body, extracting his position and velocity.) His warning receiver is lighting up. Something's illuminating his aircraft.

The war oracle running Iruvage's ship decides to release some of the heavy weapons it has been reserving. Its mission is to secure Blackbird and Ssrin for return to Khas. This rules out the use of certain weapons that might fatally harm the targets (like aromatic microwave torment, neutron tanning, or spoilsport gas) or compromise the oracle's ability to defend against a ballistic missile attack. But its absolute overriding priority is to protect Iruvage from the final descent to hell.

So it selects a fistful of pump crows, single-shot coherent radiation weapons. The weapons cells on the ship's back launch the crows thirty kilometers straight up, planting them in the lower stratosphere. Each crow tumbles sideways, selects a group of targets, and fires a laser to check the atmosphere. Not bad weather, compared to the gas-giant clouds and quarkslime armor the weapons are engineered to penetrate. Earth's atmosphere absorbs gamma rays, halving graser beam power every ninety meters: the crows select a violet laser frequency instead.

Then the crows detonate.

Davoud Qasemi sits helpless in Blackbird's imaginary cockpit and knows (not watches, but *knows*) the Russian aircraft turn into shells of dissociating gas.

He has no idea what to do now. There are still a few more planes inbound, American stragglers from Turkey and the Arabian peninsula. But they don't have the numbers to force Iruvage's ship to fire its drive again: and if they can't force it to fire its drive, it won't overheat: and if it doesn't overheat, then there's no way to drop a bomb on Iruvage.

So Iruvage will come inside and use his hideous power to shear Blackbird's soul away. Davoud is doomed to helm Blackbird's carcass as Iruvage bids. For the rest of eternity.

Everything has gone as Satan decided it.

He begins a dua. "Oh, God, o the living eternal, by your mercy . . ."

Oh, God. O living eternal. I have been mostly obedient to thee. Him by whose command the sky and the earth stand fast, by whose command the gathering is scattered, and the scattered are gathered. Pardon my sins, which are many, and accept my prayer, which is little: just that you tell me what to do.

<hr />

AIXUE 2 × 2 × 1

Li Aixue draws the last equation in the air.

She has just cast a magical spell: described the shape of an entire toy universe in a few lines of math. A truth the size and shape of a world.

"And *that*," she says, "is a solution to the field equations which we call a Natário metric. A bubble of warped space. It scoots along on space-time, like fizz in soda. And as the bubble moves, it carries you along. You can get in trouble if you try to hover too long, because you're not really moving, you're warping away from the ground as it chases after you. So don't do too much hovering. You'll have to pay off your gravity debt before you shut off the warp drive."

Rosamaria Navarro grimaces. "The alien ship's hovering just fine."

Aixue wonders what alien ship Rosamaria's talking about. She doesn't care. "Rosamaria," she asks Blackbird, "do you think you could use this to move?"

Rosamaria rubs the port-wine stain centered, exquisitely, in the neck of her blouse. "Sure. I guess so. God, what a *kludge*—"

Rosamaria stops suddenly. Her face freezes: like she forgot to be human. Aixue puts out a hand. "What's happening?"

"Rosamaria?" Chaya says warily. "Rosamaria, wake up."

"It's here. I can't touch it or I'll make it even worse. I can't hurt it without hurting myself. I hate to look at it. Oh, what's happened to this world? What's gone so *wrong*?"

᠅ℐℽαₛ

An awful light from the sky finds Anna. She's, barely, smart enough not to look straight at it.

"REACH FOR THE SKY," Iruvage drawls. "YEAH, YOU, ANNA. I'VE GOT A LASER TRAINED ON YOU. DON'T YOU DRAG SSRIN'S CARCASS ONE STEP FARTHER, OR I WILL WASTE YOU SO HARD THAT YOUR GRANDPARENTS' GONADS WILL BLACKEN."

"Mom?" she calls. "Mom, are you there?"

"I'm here, Anna."

"He's got us. I'm sorry."

Khaje says: "I got everything I wished for, Anna."

"SSRIN IS GOING BACK TO MY SPONSOR," Iruvage booms, "FOR 'DEBRIEFING.' DID YOU HEAR THOSE SCARE QUOTES? DON'T MOVE, OR I'LL BOIL YOUR BOWELS OUT YOUR BUNGHOLE."

Anna paws around until she finds her mother's arm. "Get up, Mom. Please get up."

"I can't. I'm sorry." She sounds ashamed: as if it's weak to fall over after a prolonged grand fucking mal seizure. As if she could ever be a burden to Anna, and not an undeserved and incredible gift.

Every moment a gift. This nightmare has been her best day in years.

A sting on her forearm. She swats at it: a cold, pinhead-sized alien tick pumping venom into her arm.

"MM," Iruvage says. "THAT'S GONNA MAKE A FINE LEATHER. NICE TRANSLUCENT LAYERING."

"Fuck," she says.

K + 169:02:12 hours
Blackbird

Li Aixue appears from nowhere. "Guys, we can fly."

"It doesn't matter," Erik says. "He's got a ship. Where we go, he goes too. We're fucked."

"No, we're not," Chaya Panaguiton says, appearing in Aixue's wake. Her eyes are doubled up: four pupils, four irises. It doesn't bother her. She's grinning. "We did some simulations of the field interactions. Rosamaria, can you put our drive singularities on the map?"

White sparks appear around Blackbird: sixty-four of them, one for each of the death vortices.

"The alien ship has them too," Chaya explains, pointing to the red coals around Iruvage's ship. "They're flattening out space-time, nullifying gravity."

"And we can do that now?"

"Yes. We can create an Alcubierre—sorry, a Natário metric, bend space to move the ship. But when two of these fields overlap, the stronger one disrupts the weaker one."

Erik gets it. He gets it. "Captain Qasemi!" he barks.

"Sir!" Davoud says.

"Ram that fucking thing!"

<hr>

⸱ƗⲨⲁ丮

Iruvage's poison hurts so bad. Screaming would be a relief and somehow Anna doesn't deserve that so she just grunts and smashes her head on the ground. Her legs spasm against her helpless mother. Straight above her, the aurora shines through smoke and fog, like spilled watercolors.

And the aurora bends.

A convex point slides across Anna's vision, like a really small contact lens. It gathers up the aurora's colors into a violet pinprick. It reminds Anna a little bit of the Oubliette of Cows.

Then Blackbird's blunt nose, a manta ray with no mouth, comes chasing after the pinprick. It blocks out the laser light from Iruvage's warship. Blackbird is *flying*. It pulled its needle ass out of the mountainside, and it's flying!

A mass of plastic and aluminum comes dragging toward her, gushing water from broken pipes, trailing a jellyfish of power cords. It's the Ugandan containment tent, still wedged into Blackbird's intention cap—and from the bottom of the cap dangles an aluminum ladder, carrying Erik Wygaunt, who is half-ass naked in body armor and a hospital gown.

"Anna! Get up! Get up! He's right on you!"

But she can't move her legs. Iruvage's poison has completely ruined her. Khaje sprawls face down in the grass, whuffling like an exhausted dog. Ssrin lies in the bloody black water, mostly dead, her heads snapping weakly at one another.

Anna reaches up to Ssrin's leftmost head.

"One is for interrogation," she counts. Finds the head next to it. "Two is for healing. Three is for killing." She doesn't touch that one. "Four is for combat drugs." The head she liked to pet.

She slides her finger into mouth number four. It bites her.

Napalm lights up in her veins. That governor in her brain, the one Ssrin said controlled her physical performance, finally disengages. She opens all the sphincters and *adrenalizes*.

She leaps up—grabs her mom, lifts her, throws her on top of Ssrin in the tank—starts hauling them both together, step by growling step, toward the approaching ladder.

DAVOUD (~7,900 FEET ASL)

The space between Blackbird and Iruvage's ship collapses.

Blackbird's forward mast crosses into the drive field around Iruvage's ship. Blackbird's masts are larger, more assertive, more complexly connected, more numerous.

The alien vessel tries to react. A quick pulse of fusion thrust would pull it away to safety: and it would do it, if it could. But it is badly overheated, and afraid of harming its master with the radiation of its engines, and unwilling to allow the critical targets it has been keeping under surveillance to escape.

Too slow. This is the problem with minds that lack souls: when the key moment comes, they are too rational. Mere milliseconds to make the choice. But still too slow.

Blackbird's huge drive field overpowers the alien ship's.

And when the universe solves the geometry of the merged fields, it turns to Iruvage's ship and says: wuh-oh.

The black raven wing bends in a rainbow of tortured sunlight. The hot coals of the drive masts ignite to violet and scale up the spectrum into the endless fireball of hard X-ray emissions. Power systems snap to fail-safe and ground to the Kurdish antennae below.

"HEY," Iruvage broadcasts. "WHAT THE FUCK."

The drive field, the space-time rigging that holds the alien ship aloft, falls apart. The masts slip out of their pockets like pool balls running in reverse and, for reasons of warp field physics, cannonball slantwise into the Kurdish soil, into the limestone and dolomite and salt bed beneath, to burst out of the far side of the Earth somewhere in the South Pacific.

Now the alien ship is naked to the ordinary space-time of Earth. And that space-time is a slope, and the slope is called gravity, and gravity has a debt to call.

Iruvage's ship falls. It falls faster than it should: faster than anything on Earth, except its own rogue masts, has ever fallen before. Pulled not just by gravity but by the debt of every second it spent hovering instead of falling free. It crushes Tawakul beneath its length. Flattens carpets and cellars, murals and whitewashed stone, the dreams of jineologists and old women and little girls, into one thick stratum.

But that stratum of crushed dreams is firm enough to break the alien ship's spine.

"Splash one," Davoud says coolly.

⁂

Now where the fuck is Iruvage?

Ah! The alien is *right there,* in the wreckage of the lab complex. Ready to kill Anna and Khaje and Erik and Ssrin. There's absolutely nothing stopping him: he could at any second kill all four. He could, at any second, kill Davoud too. He could tell the implant in Davoud's neck to explode.

But Davoud knows that *can't* happen. He's flying now. Satan can't touch this guy. He's got his angel wings.

"GIVE ME THE DEMIURGE," Iruvage bellows. "GIVE IT TO ME OR I KILL THEM. AH, FUCK IT. I'LL KILL THEM ANYWAY."

He whips his blade through the lab structures between him and Anna.

Without thinking Davoud applies his newfound control to jink his ship, and one of Blackbird's drive masts intercepts the sword blade. Swallows the bleak tip. Snaps it off in a fist of tides.

Iruvage, disarmed, commands his surviving hive machines to attack. Davoud reaches for the ECM switch but there is no ECM switch in the Tomcat's cockpit. At least, not in the front seat. He needs Goose. "Blackbird! Radiate ECM!"

"*DECM to XMIT.*"

He expected this to jam Iruvage's command links to his machines. Instead, Blackbird jams whatever is going on *inside* the machines. They fall out of the air.

"DAVOUD!" Iruvage bellows. "YOU'RE GOING TO RUIN YOUR STARSHIP! IF I'M NOT ABOARD I CAN'T STOP MAESSARI FROM DESTROYING YOU! DON'T THROW AWAY YOUR CHANCE TO BE MORE THAN A TASTY STUPID MONKEY MAN!"

Davoud is pretty sure Iruvage is transmitting the *detonate* command to

Davoud's implant, but Davoud is also certain that Blackbird's ECM will protect him, and therefore it does.

Iruvage isn't coming closer. He's hesitating.

He's afraid.

Davoud wants to hit him with a drive mast. He tries to jink again, steer a death hole into Iruvage, but Satan is on to his tricks, and Davoud's terrified that if he tries to do anything fancy he will crash like Iruvage's ship crashed. He gives up on that.

He wants to fly. But if he does—then he leaves Khaje behind for Satan. And he won't do that.

So all Davoud has left is four American jets from Incirlik. Four jets to make a difference. They're still ten minutes out—no! No, they must've seen everyone fucking dying in the sky ahead, and instead of turning off like any sane person would, they dumped their drop tanks and went to afterburner and they're *here!*

"Carbon Three!" he sends. "Carbon Three, do you copy?"

"*Pure Eagle, Carbon Three.*" A woman's voice, calm to the edge of boredom. "*One minute out. Eight GBU-32, full load of cannon. Tracking primary target for JDAM release.*"

"Primary target is down! New target is an alien organism, coordinates—fuck the coordinates! Use your FLIR pods, aim for the biggest heat source you can see near Blackbird! Friendlies danger close! Over!"

"*Roger. Sniper on. Uh, everything's hot down there. I got a huge heat source on the village to the . . . south of the river. And a smaller heat source to the immediate north.*"

"Yes! The north side of the river! Look for the big manta ray shape! Then find the person-sized hot spot just south of it! Hurry!"

"*Roger. Targeting bright spot number three. We're thirty seconds out.*"

"Cleared hot!"

"*Roger. Cleared hot. Carbon Three . . . off hot. Time of fall, five seconds.*"

Iruvage leaps toward Blackbird: trying to get inside the field, to be carried away with them.

But there is no way Davoud will allow Satan's snakes onto his holy plane.

The alien knows the bombs are coming—knows the same way he always knows when something is coming to hurt him—and if those bombs strike him, *if they kill him*, it means Satan spends eternity in hell.

In the end it's quite simple.

Iruvage isn't as strong as Davoud. Iruvage isn't willing to die to get into Blackbird. Iruvage isn't willing to put his soul on the line for the dream of flight.

Iruvage vanishes from Davoud's sight.

Maybe it's some kind of stealth, or a shielding elision like Ssrin created to stop the bombs. Maybe he has pocketed himself, disappeared into his own personal shelter for his wretched soul. Davoud doesn't care exactly how he does it: only why. Iruvage wouldn't run if he weren't beaten.

The four F-16s flash overhead, each guiding a pair of thousand-pound bombs down onto the alien's last position, as Davoud lifts Blackbird smoothly, without any perceptible acceleration, up into the sky.

↓IʏɑꙄ

Anna floats in free fall. Inner ear and gut insist that she's plummeting to her death.

But she is caught in Blackbird's aura, drifting beneath the ship, holding on to the water tank full of Ssrin and her mother.

From the dangling painter's ladder, Erik reaches out to her.

She reaches back.

Eight thousand pounds of Composition H6 high explosive detonate below them and the boom and the fireball split around Blackbird's lifting aura, around them, like a subwoofer flower with shrapnel in its seeds.

Their bare hands join.

They make a chain, connecting ladder to Erik to Anna to watercart to Ssrin to Khaje. And Blackbird lifts them all up and out.

The valley of Tawakul falls away beneath them, full of fire and burnt airplanes and broken bodies, full of all her memories, vanishing into the white mountains of Kurdistan.

Iruvage is laughing in fury and delight.

ROSAMARIA

July in DC always feels like the end of the world.

On the day the deputy AG brought me to the White House, the heat index was pushing 110. Given my way I would've turned up in a linen T-shirt dress and huge black sunglasses, but we cannot always be too cool for school. I was forced to resort to a pale blue blouse and slacks, like a paralegal.

The boss was in a good mood because of the *Windsor* ruling. On June 26 the Supreme Court had killed Section 3 of DOMA and cleared California to resume same-sex marriage. The White House and my boss wanted to take the win and run with it. So did I. But I was afraid that if I went to the White House then Clayton would try to talk to me.

A few weeks previously I'd met a woman over coffee who revealed, offhand, that she was a White House staffer. I don't fuck inside job world but to make it worse she mentioned Clayton as if she had no idea we'd been married. She was unbelievably Nordic, blue-eyed blond-haired gold and ice, with cruel full lips and presence like a lightning flash. I thought I'd like making her blush, but in five minutes I decided she had never blushed, ever, that there was probably something not blood inside her. The worst vibes I've ever felt. I left when she got up to take a phone call.

I was still in the White House when the bombs blew up the sky and the world started to end.

(Back in January I read a story about a woman inventorying all her lovers at the end of the world. I'm glad this friend of Clayton's wasn't on my inventory.)

The power went out. The White House generators turned on. I keep thinking about that. The AC is out, in Washington DC, in July. Hospitals and nursing homes have generators, but not forever . . .

At first everyone assumed, oh, fuck, North Korea—or Iran, or China, or Russia—*someone* set off a nuke over the continental US, as prelude to, I don't know, invading Seoul, or Taiwan, or Crimea. "This was the bad guy's plan in *Die Another Day*," someone told me, which I think was wrong: either *GoldenEye* or *Goldfinger*? I was too worried to correct him.

I used to wonder, when I was in a bad place about the femicides, whether

Bond was the ultimate man. Stainless steel armature, nothing inside. Just an empty suit with three cool reptilian passions. Violence and sex and drink. I got over that, though. Craig helped—I liked his Bond, I liked his hints of an inner life. Shame to go out on *Skyfall*. I didn't like the ending. Judi Dench's M dispatched, Moneypenny at her desk, the smug return to Bond status quo. And now there we were, in our own skyfall.

The Secret Service rushed the president to Air Force One and the vice president off to Raven Rock and then they packed the rest of us in a bunker under the East Wing. There was a newer bunker under the lawn, but it wasn't finished yet, so we ended up in the Presidential Emergency Operations Center. Serious men in suits brandished yellow plastic shotguns. I asked why they were yellow plastic and one of them told me they were loaded with salt, to shoot flies: the PEOC had a fly problem. Once we stunned the flies with the salt we had to squash them with a tissue while they were down. We flushed all the flies down the toilet. Most of the world no longer had running water.

We argued about why we were down there. I said maybe it was a solar storm, and a lot of people liked that idea, because it meant we weren't at war.

It could've been really bad, but it wasn't. Mostly it was like camping out in an airliner. Nobody fought. Nobody complained. We worked out a sleep rotation, inventoried pads and tampons, sent people out to get stuff. I cut up blazers into sleep masks. We went through disposable earplugs too fast, ended up reusing our own pairs. In one dream my pillow became a huge loaf of sourdough bread, which I ate, and I woke up with heartburn.

Gradually the story came out from the Pentagon. It was not a solar storm. We were at war, but not with any other nation. We were at war with the stars.

People left to find their families, but not as many as I would've thought. I think there was a need to stay together, to avoid scattering when we had already lost contact with so much of the world.

I read a lot of books on my phone. I should have finished everything I'd been putting off, all the serious policy wonk shit and the rest of *2666*. But I was so anxious I just went back to my old comfort reads, Kathe Koja and Diana Wynne Jones and *Distant Star* and the Clavel where Antonia wakes up as a man. If the world is ending I think you have a right to stop bettering yourself; I think you have a right to just feel okay.

I looked around for the blond staffer with the cruel eyes, but no one knew who I was talking about. Finally I just asked: "Where's Clayton?"

He was at an air base in New York, putting together an expedition to Kurdistan, where he thought he would find an explanation for all of it. Everyone from the Joint Chiefs of Staff to the secretary of state wanted someone else to make him stop. But no one was actually willing to do it. The spies all seemed to back him, and our president likes to listen to his spies.

(I knew why the spies backed Clayton. You can make people complicit in your crime if you force them to keep it secret. And you can force them to keep it secret by making the crime too huge to acknowledge.)

I thought a lot about Erik and Clayton. I wondered if Clayton had found anything in Kurdistan. I wondered if Erik had been able to stay away from him.

I was still down there, two and a half days after the sky lit up, when the president came on the intercom. He said he was calling by military radio from Air Force One. He apologized that the message had to be prerecorded, for security reasons. He sounded firm and clear and terrified as he told us that military radar had detected a missile descending on Washington. He said his military advisors did not believe we would survive. He promised that he and the vice president were going to do everything they possibly could to protect the nation. He thanked everyone for working with him, and he asked us to pray along with him when he went on the emergency civil defense radio system to address the nation.

So I did. I said it along with him, though I said it different. ToTajtzin aquin tinemi ne ilhuicac, ma mitzyectenehua nochi tlacatl. Ma huajla on tonaltin ijcuac ticmandaros nochi tlacatl. Ipan in tlalticpactli on tlacamej ma quichihuacan on tlen ticnequi ijcon quen nochihua ne ilhuicac. Aman xtechmaca tlen ticuasquej on yejhuan mojmostla ica tipanotoquej. Niman xtechtlapojpolhuili totlajtlacolhuan ijcon quen tejhuamej tiquintlapojpolhuiyaj on yejhuan tlajtlamach xcualji techchihuiliaj. Niman xtechpalehui para ma ca titlajtlacosquej, yej xtechejcuanilij nochi tlen xcuajli. Timitztlajtlaniliaj yejhua in pampa ticpia tequihuajyotl, nimal poder, niman hyueyilistli para nochipa.

Amén.

And a few minutes later my phone began to ring.

ACT 5

EARTH

CHAPTER THIRTY-SEVEN

꜀ⵉⵉⵛⵉⵌⵢⵇⵙ

The comedown from Ssrin's combat drug is just hideous. Worse than anything. Anna has to curl up on the cold glass floor and sob for about an hour, while Blackbird, this thing that Blackbird has become, tries to gentle her body back into its ordinary chemistry.

Then she gets into a screaming fight with Rosamaria.

"You won't fix her? She saved you! *And now you won't fix her?*"

"I can't." The alien with the soul of Rosamaria Navarro looks like a boss Anna would have a crush on, who would inevitably fire Anna. "I just can't."

"At least you made her a nice puddle to drown in," Anna snaps. "That should help."

"It's a cyst. So I don't have to feel her inside me."

Ssrin's body drifts in a sac of fouled water. Ssrin's ruined hulk bleeds oily coolant and blood. The gaping sockets of her exploded spine weep slime. She looks like something you'd grab with your whole fist from the interior of a pumpkin. Anna can't look at her.

"You fixed Clayton's heart. You filled in Erik's head. Why not Ssrin?"

"Because it's not supposed to be—" Rosamaria clutches her fists in frustration. "I don't know, all right? I just know this thing isn't right. It's not natural."

"Natural? *Natural?*" First off, Anna wants to shout, Ssrin is a *she*, an egg-laying *she*, not an *it*. And secondly, of course she's natural. She's right here!

But she has seen Ssrin's soul reflected in the Oubliette. And if she argues Ssrin is "natural," then she will be arguing that her deeds are a result of her nature. And Anna would not want Ssrin to have a nature that led to such deeds.

"It's the same with Davoud's blindness." Rosamaria paces across the glassy field of her own interior stage. A searchlight tracks her from high above. Anna feels like she's in an off-Broadway production of something—she doesn't know what, she's not cultured. *Waiting for God*. "Iruvage put a pattern in his brain. I can't fix it without making more of it, which just makes the problem worse. Ssrin's the same. Something about her is just . . ."

Rosamaria crosses her arms and thinks. Anna applies stealthy check-her-out skills developed on New York subways. Rosamaria came out of Erik and Clayton, right? She's the dream of a woman as remembered by men. Which doesn't mean she's an *EverQuest* elf, or whatever people play these days. But it means she should be idealized.

Only—she's full of details which Anna doesn't believe the men would really notice. The invisibly exact contouring she's applied. The untended split ends sticking out of her claw clip. The dented polish on her left thumbnail. All superficial, sure, but superficial traits are clues. This isn't just Erik and Clayton's Very Real Doll. This *is* Rosamaria.

That makes Anna even more furious that she won't help.

"Anna," Rosamaria says in that reproving better-listen-up tone Anna hates, "you should get rid of Ssrin."

"What?"

"There's a connection between you."

"Yeah. I know. It's called serendure. It's what Ssrin wanted to use to get into Blackbird. Before she got bombed and had to hide."

(—and why didn't Iruvage use his spaceship to finish the job after he blew up Ssrin's spine? He had a laser aimed at her helpless corpse. He doesn't seem like the kind of guy who makes evil-overlord mistakes like "not shooting the hero when she's down." Why go to all that trouble to try to take her alive? Was he *really* that eager to eat her?)

(Maybe he'd rather give Ssrin a chance at Blackbird than see it denied to both of them. Because then, at least, he still has a chance to save his soul . . .)

"It's not a good thing!" Rosamaria snaps: exasperated, like everyone is, by how Anna's totally down with having her soul hooked up to Ssrin's. "It's not friendship. It's *togetherness-no-matter-what*. And a relationship with no exit is a trap. Believe me."

"You owe her," Anna shoots right back. Yeah! Say all the same stuff you said before, but even more angry! "She summoned you! She stopped Iruvage from eating your soul and bombing the rest of us! And because we didn't get bombed, we taught you how to fly and kept Iruvage from crawling up your ass! She's been here for you all along and you're just going to let her rot?"

Rosamaria looks at her with pity. Anna hates that even more. "Iruvage used Erik and Clayton to put me here. Ssrin was going to use me to make a soul from the space between *you*. Do you know who it'd be?"

"Who?"

"I thought you'd know." Rosamaria shakes her head. "Anyway, she'll heal herself. She's built for trauma. She doesn't need my help."

Anna wishes she could put her Glock to Rosamaria's head and make her fix Ssrin. Things are happening now that Anna doesn't want to face alone.

But if Ssrin won't wake . . .

"Keep her cold," she tells Rosamaria. "She likes it cold. It helps her do her magic."

"She won't do it in here," Rosamaria says. "Not until she explains to me exactly what she's doing, and how."

"Isn't that a little prissy? Do you even know what *you're* doing?"

Rosamaria smiles a real, honest, excited little smile. "No. But I have to learn. So I know how to fix everything else, when I get the chance."

<hr />

K + 174:02:02 hours
Blackbird

What a fucking dick punch.

Major Erik Wygaunt led his soldiers into battle. Sent them out to die, not once but twice, against a single alien who slaughtered them all like—like what? Like no one has ever been slaughtered before.

And then he just flew away.

"C'mon, Erik." Clayton sits beside him on the porch of the Anacostia house, just close enough to be on purpose. "You saved nearly a hundred people from those caves."

"Iruvage baited me to do it. And you helped him. All part of your plan."

"So? It was the right thing to do, and you did it, and you saved those people. So Iruvage wanted you to do it. You didn't know that."

"So I'm well-intentioned, but badly informed."

"Maybe. Maybe I didn't do enough to *keep* you informed, and that got us both killed. But then we stole this thing—"

"Which led to the death of every soldier and pilot involved—"

"—except for the pilots who finally got their bombs through. Which allowed us to keep Blackbird, the one and only thing that can help save humanity, away from Iruvage. What more could *anyone* have done under these circumstances?"

But Erik could have done more. How can he explain this to the families of the dead?

Dear John/Jane Doe,

I regret to inform you that your child died in combat with an alien snake while their commander watched from the safety of a spaceship made out of the soul of his sort-of ex. Please know that your child died to protect mankind. And also me.
With my deepest sympathies,
Major Erik Wygaunt

"It all went the way you planned, didn't it?" he says. "You took control."

"Dude. If you think *anything* back there happened the way I planned . . . I mean, his fucking ship, I had no inkling he had his own ship up there. What would I have done without Ssrin to stop the atmanach? Without Davoud to fly Blackbird? And Chaya and Aixue to tell Blackbird *how* to fly? What would I have done without you to command the defense? If Iruvage still had his big gun, if we hadn't forced him to approach Blackbird to get aboard it, if he weren't overheating and shot to shit when he reached us—what could I have done?"

Erik is not convinced.

He looks at Clayton, too close, kissing distance. He remembers when Clayton got into dance and hardened up, when Erik realized, Jesus, my best friend is kind of hot. It was a bittersweet feeling. In spite of the seditious delight of adolescent horseplay, the strange quasi-heterosexual knowledge that you would probably enjoy watching your friend fuck an attractive woman, he kind of knew, right then, that it meant he, Erik, wasn't going to end up with Rosamaria.

He thought that would haunt him for the rest of his life. He had *really* loved her. Sixth grade to senior year, all of it achingly powerful. He kept a code about it. It makes him cringe to remember the things he was proud of: yeah, Erik, if you never jerk off to your secret crush you're *very* chivalrous, very disciplined, such a knight. It really makes a difference.

Only—and he was so proud of this—he *did* get over it. He was happy. He liked being Clayton and Rosamaria's best friend. He didn't need any more. Tipsy flirtation, sure; the occasional appreciative once-over, fine; maybe a thought or two about whether they'd ever decide the risk to their friendship was worth it and pull the trigger on what Clayton once called "a Manager Troi"; but not more. He was happy with what they had.

That's what he's never going to understand about Clayton. That grasping, forward-thinking ambition. That need to take what works just fine and make it bigger until it breaks.

They sit together on the porch of their home in this alien place.

"Clayton," Erik says, "why the fuck did you bring me along on this thing?"

"Officially?" Clayton's long thumb strokes his shoulder blade through the thin gown. "Because I knew you could command the loyalty of all those soldiers from all those different units."

"And unofficially?"

"I think," Clayton says carefully, "that I was . . . not expecting to come back from this. So I wanted to settle things with you. And I needed you there in case I . . . went too far. Which I did. Almost at once. And you called me on it."

"Since when do you care what I think?"

"Always," Clayton says quietly. "Always."

"The fuck you do."

"Erik. I stopped Paladin. I shut the whole fucking thing down."

"Because you were blown."

"Because I knew that even if I disagreed with you, I couldn't ignore your revulsion. I don't want to live in a world full of people like me, Erik. I want to live in a world full of people like you. I have to do what I do because we *don't*."

Erik has to laugh. "Well. We have Blackbird. Alterer of souls. Maybe we could make a world of people like me."

"Maybe. Iruvage certainly has plans. That's why we can't let him have it. Not at any cost."

"*Any* cost. See, you say that, and I hear you granting yourself permission to do anything you want."

Clayton presses his fingertips to his temples. "Let me ask you a question. You wouldn't abandon those people I bombed. I'm responsible for those who died, but you took responsibility for the *living*. You wouldn't let innocents die through your own failure to act."

"Right."

"How many innocent beings do you think will be hurt if we fail to do *everything possible* to save Blackbird from Iruvage's people? I'm not just talking about Earth. I'm talking about . . . every living thing out there. In the galaxy, at least. Maybe the universe. Don't we have a responsibility to all those beings? The way you did to the Kurds in those caves?"

It's a stupid question. Not because Erik thinks it's ill-considered or inaccurate, but because it's a stupid thing to ask *him*. It's a Clayton question. Erik just knows the right thing to do.

"Clay," he says, "you're doing it again. Inventing some imaginary greater good to justify being calculating and pessimistic, right now, right here, when the right choice is actually obvious. I try to be a good human being. It's pretty hard. I don't think I'm ready to try being a good citizen of the galaxy. Let's start with saving ourselves, all right? If we can't be good here, now, if we can't pull together and fight, how can we be good at all? Ever?"

Clayton shakes his head. "Big questions, man."

"Okay." Erik bites the inside of his cheeks, left and right, like a skull. Growls on the exhale. "I'm done. Let's go kick some ass."

"Whose ass?"

Erik turns that skull face on him. It looks so silly Clayton can't help but laugh.

"We've still got an alien ship to take out," Erik says. "The one that nuked our planet back to the eighteen hundreds. I am prepared to hoist the black flag and start slitting throats."

DAVOUD (~65,600 FEET ASL)

Davoud has never flown this high. Dawn arrives thirteen minutes early.

Twenty kilometers above the Atlantic, in the cockpit he fantasized into existence, he tries to get the hang of his new ride. He's got to ram this thing into an alien warship.

But he can't do it. He's messing it all up.

Blackbird acts sometimes like a plane, sometimes a helicopter, sometimes an orbiting spaceship. Her ability to move depends on the math Li Aixue teaches Rosamaria, so in a sense Li Aixue is the ship's engine, the pair of Pratt & Whitney turbofans hurling them all aloft.

But *he* is Blackbird's pilot. Davoud has millions of years of evolved instinct and thousands of hours of flight experience. Blackbird is still struggling to separate changes caused by its own motion from genuine changes in the world outside. It needs his feel for flight.

But those instincts are working against him! In an aircraft, you're always going forward: you use your control surfaces to deflect that forward motion into turns or climbs. If you want to go left, you don't turn left, like you would in a car. Instead you *bank* left, so that your "up" is pointing the way you want to turn, and you let the wings lift you into the curve.

Blackbird doesn't fly that way. Blackbird flies by—he's not really sure, except that it involves the death holes stretching space itself. Technically his space-time airfoil is defined by a vector field, but he has no idea what that means. He asked Aixue if he was expanding space behind him and contracting it ahead so he could create a kind of wave to surf, and she said, *No, silly, this isn't an Alcubierre drive, it's an expansionless sliding warp.*

It's like learning to swim, except he's a clay brick driving a lawnmower, and his swim instructor only created water yesterday.

In the cockpit of his Tiger he was fluent and aerobatic: he could dandle his plane around on the edge of stall while all the Kish Airshow crowds went *ooh* and *inshallah he will not crash on top of us.* In Blackbird, he can't even yaw! He's decent at translating the ship around like a mouse cursor, locked into a single orientation. But if he can't point the nose where Blackbird is going, he can't keep the hull pointed into the wind, and it will start to tumble inside the drive field.

"I should've asked you to copy that fusion rocket from Satan's ship," he says. "At least then I could get frustrated and start blasting off."

"*Be calm,*" Blackbird says. "*You know where you are. That's enough to start.*"

"Ugh," Davoud growls. He accelerates upward, too fast: the air grows as thick as wet concrete, crushed against Blackbird's upper surface, howling between the teeth of her trailing wing-edge. The drive field around Blackbird isn't totally inertialess—it has its own mass and momentum, defined by what Li Aixue calls the "stress-energy tensor," which is also what allows the drive field to act as a kind of shield. Unfortunately, a magical shield that deflects air is a huge drag! Air molecules slam into the leading edge of the bubble, creating a shock front that rolls back over the hull. When air falls out the back of the field, it's suddenly traveling much faster than the surrounding air, which creates a tail shock of hot exhaust.

All this heat and pressure creates noise in Blackbird's constant, mathematical self-definition. She has to expend processing power—thoughts—to smooth the noise away.

Confuse Blackbird enough and the ship will literally disintegrate. She might forget how to hold protons and neutrons into atoms, and they will become the heart of an atomic fission explosion powerful enough to destroy the planet.

"*Careful, pilot,*" Blackbird warns him. "*We're carrying a lot of dirty air.*"

There's hot air stuck in the edge of the drive field, orbiting Blackbird like trash around a drain. When Davoud "throttles down," the trash escapes as a burst of plasma. This might be useful as a weapon, if he could figure out how to control it.

He throttles down, burping radiation and fire over Turkey, into the upper atmosphere. It really bothers him that he can't figure out how to point the nose the way the ship is going! Changing directions without turning will make the airflow inside the drive field totally unmanageable; if he can point the nose he can keep the air flowing consistently front to back.

He's gotta figure out how to use this Natário metric thing to turn—

Someone pokes his real body in the flank.

Davoud yelps. Without his hands on the controls, Blackbird's drive masts fall back into a neutral pattern, anchoring the ship to Earth's rest frame. Blackbird begins a gentle glide north across Europe, warping "up" to hold its altitude against gravity.

Ma'rifat clarity recedes into darkness, blindness, the sound of his own breath and heartbeat—

"Jash man." He hears Khaje Sinjari tuck her long hair back behind her ear. It sounds like bristles on a shaving brush. "Have you figured out how to fly the ship?"

"No," he snaps. "No, I haven't."

"Have you tried sticking your arms out and flapping?"

"Of course I have. Are you here to call me a traitor some more?"

"No." She draws a short breath. "I just woke up. I probably have brain damage."

"Me too," he says. "I'm blind."

"But you saved us."

He frowns: "Did I?"

"You were supposed to fly Blackbird away for Iruvage. You didn't. Instead, you saved my daughter's life."

"Oh. Professor Li was the one who taught the ship to move. I just sat in the cockpit and moved the stick—"

"Pilots don't invent airplanes, do they? But they still fly them."

"The first thing I tried to do, when I saw the atmanach coming, was fly away. I tried to abandon you and Anna and everyone. I would've done it but I didn't know how yet."

"Maybe. But then, when you did know how to fly, you rammed right into Iruvage's ship."

But Iruvage was right. Without his protection, they have nowhere to go. Up in orbit there is a bigger ship with terrible weapons. Davoud is hiding from it by keeping the entire planet between them. But that won't work forever. The enemy will chase them down, or send drones to flush them out.

Sooner or later, they have to face the evil angel.

Khaje pulls at him, like she's still got him in shackles. "Come join the rest of us. We need to decide what to do now. Erik wants to attack."

"I can't," Davoud protests. "I— Look, I have to stay here."

"Why? You can't park?"

Of course he can park. Hovering is the first trick he learned. It's kind of expensive, fuel-wise, but Blackbird does not seem to have any kind of gas tank he's discovered. She says she can get power from "sublimated Hawking radiation." The real limit on their hover time is the need to pay off their gravity "debt" when they turn the warp field off (lest they end up like Iruvage's ship, spiked into the ground). Davoud plans to solve this by just never turning the warp field off.

"Khaje, I'll be blind out there."

"Is that so awful? Blind isn't dead, Davoud. There are happy blind people. There are no happy dead."

"I'm really scared."

"You'll be fine. I know widows with gas burn who complain less than you. Up, up, take off that silly mask, you don't even need it. Get up, get out. Get out. That's right."

So they go forth together, as they went in the beginning: Khaje leading Davoud. But this time he's not in chains.

CHAYA 3:1

Chaya really wants to talk about what happened.

She keeps dropping hints: "You know, I was having seizures in the labs. But they stopped once I said *Let's go check in on Aixue.*"

"Mm," Aixue says. "So now we move on to the—"

"And then, after we split up again, I started to change . . . Clayton said that I got pretty bad. Bad enough that he was sure I was going to be shot on sight. Because my soul was glitching physics. Isn't that wild?"

Aixue ignores her. "And if you look at the way this series converges, you'll see—"

She's talking to Blackbird-Rosamaria, whose avatar is pretty, professional, and lighter-skinned than Chaya. Not that this bothers her. She doesn't have any insecurities about light-skinned lipstick femmes who can pull off heels without pushing up ceiling tiles.

It's just that she'd like some credit, you know? (She rubs at the dimple in her upper lip, which is deeper now: not the largest change in her body, but the easiest to poke.) *She* did the lab work that discovered how Blackbird selected its targets. She cued up Clayton to figure out the connection to Iruvage's myths. She picked up on Aixue's theory and deduced that Blackbird was still in the process of decompressing itself. And she saved Clayton from possession! In the process becoming the only person to survive Blackbird's transformation.

Is no one going to ask how she's doing?

No. No one has the slightest time for her. Anna's furious about Ssrin, Khaje's badgering Davoud, Clayton and Erik are having guy time.

And Aixue is teaching Rosamaria the mathematical basis of existence. Chaya doesn't have a lot to contribute. The peculiarities of how plasma behaves near black holes are . . . well, actually, that seems like it *could* be pretty important here, flying in a cluster of singularities. But somehow Aixue hasn't remembered to ask her.

Chaya feels stupid and very childish for wanting Aixue to pay her personal attention, instead of jamming with the avatar of the angel. But . . . *but* . . .

There is the safety Chaya gets from staying near Aixue. Lying for her, washing her, tending to her . . . like Erik and Clayton, Blackbird recognizes Chaya as part of a larger structure of souls. But Chaya doesn't *want* to be in a structure that obliges her to follow Aixue around. She is not Aixue's sidekick or assistant. She's a scientist, an engineer, author of most of a PhD on plasma physics in black hole polar jets. Is she *really* destined, in some cosmic way, to be Aixue's maid? A migrant worker in Aixue's intellectual Hong Kong?

Absolutely fucking shet.

But no, here's Aixue laying out chromodynamics, the interaction of quarks to form particles, while Rosamaria sits cross-legged on a couch and nods along. And who made the couch? Chaya. She built an imitation faculty lounge with old couches and distinguished chairs and oil portraits of naiads and nymphs and sirena and the like. Probably too many sirena. Only now does Chaya see how much of herself has ended up on display here: stone from the old Spanish Intramuros, furniture from SM Megamall where she spent too many teenage days loitering and playing arcade games. Scattered seedpods from the narra trees in Luneta, where Rizal was shot. Tangina Blackbird. The damn ship keeps putting her soul on everything!

Chaya rubs her eyes. They don't *feel* any different, do they? But she has double pupils now, and triple navels. Oh, she's still got bits of Mike Jan's brains in her hair. Gross.

Oh, leche. Enough of this!

"Break time," she declares. "Rosamaria, she needs a break."

Aixue laughs and bats at her arms. "Chayaaa, let me finish, she needs to know how protons are made—"

"I'd be so bored if I were your student. Gauge groups and Hamiltonians. Why don't you *show* her something?"

"Where would I do that?" Aixue protests. "How could I show her the big bang? We don't have a particle accelerator big enough to re-create those conditions—"

"The whole world *is* the big bang, Aixue! This is where the big bang happened. Right here. And right here. And right over there. Forget thirteen billion years ago!"

Aixue stops giggling. Her face falls. "I'm sorry," she says. "I'm so sorry. I wish . . ."

Now Chaya's gone and done it again. "Sorry for what?" She sighs.

"Sorry I didn't figure it out faster. Sorry I didn't help you and Clayton. Maybe we could've saved everyone . . . Professor Huang, all your people . . . we could've brought them all into Blackbird . . . but I said I didn't care. Didn't I say that? I said I didn't care and I wouldn't help you."

This really annoys her. "Did you teach Rosamaria how to fly as fast as you could?"

"Yes."

"And before that, we needed Erik to chase Clayton inside. So you couldn't have made things go any faster. Not alone."

Aixue nods, looking her right in the eye, voraciously inquisitive, even if the truth bites her back: "But you *did* need me, right? I wasn't sufficient. But I was necessary?"

There is some enormous gap between the way Chaya sees Aixue and the way she sees herself. "Of course we needed you. Your immunity was what led us to the trick with Erik and Clayton—"

"Oh!" Aixue bounces on her feet and grabs Chaya by the arms. "You're right! You're right! You're a genius!"

"I am?"

"She finds the patterns in things. Why would she want me to teach her the universe from a book? We should be showing her the world! Making her instruments!"

"Telescopes," Chaya says, brightening with the thought. "Maybe she can make lenses for telescopes. And antennae too, and Faraday cups, and—what else?"

They are surrounded by a living, burning universe. God's bright creation. If they can show Blackbird what the world is, then Blackbird will understand *how* it is. And the more it understands, the more powerful it will grow.

What will Blackbird do when it's done learning physics? When it moves on to higher mysteries?

"Man," Aixue says suspiciously. "Why are there so many hot mermaids in here?"

"They're not mermaids!" Chaya protests. "They're sirena!"

"Why do all the sirena look like Angel Locsin?"

"They do not!"

"Okay. This one looks like she's in the Zombettes. Wow, did you make these? Were you a party girl?"

Chaya feels personally skewered. After one great night in Bacolod she developed a horrible, stupid, hopeless crush on the DJ. "How do you know who that *is*?"

"A bunch of girls at Paw Paw were really into Manila EDM," Aixue says with airy cool. "Everybody had their favorite DJ. Divine Smith, Badkiss, Patty Tiu. 'If only we were in Manila, then we would really have a dance scene!'"

Chaya cannot comprehend a Li Aixue who can dance. "Paw Paw's a club?"

"A bar. With lala night. That's what we call, um—"

"I know. And you went to this bar, and you talked to girls about Manila's dance scene?"

"Well, no . . . I mean, I went. I listened to girls talk about Manila EDM. And then I . . . looked up stuff they were talking about, in case I ever did decide to talk to them."

Chaya is about to not-laugh at her when the walls start talking. Clayton.

"Guys, can you come join us on the—um, the dance floor? The alien ship's started moving. We think it might be coming after us."

※

CLAYTON//HOPE

The seven survivors gather beneath Rosamaria's sevenfold arms.

Clayton stares up at her alien majesty: flesh of nerves, body of bone. That's his ex-wife, right? Her soul, the summary of everything she ever chose to be, is *in* this body.

But this body is not human. And the body informs the choices you make, which in turn inform the soul. So every moment this Rosamaria exists, she is becoming less like Rosamaria. Her soul is diverging from the soul of his wife.

But then again, the human Rosamaria stopped being his wife years ago. So who has diverged from him further?

His heart hurts when she talks.

"Rosamaria," Erik says in his Viking warrior voice. "Show them."

"This is Earth." Rosamaria creates a blue-white orb the size of a boulder, and then a tiny silver needle, parked above the Middle East. "This is an alien space-craft. The Exordia warship *Axiorrhage*. It carries enough bombs to destroy most major cities on the planet."

"Cobalt-salted nuclear weapons," Erik says. "The cobalt is there to enhance the fallout. Doesn't add much to the total killing power, but it makes some of the dying more horrific. Evil for the sake of evil."

"I thought fallout was really bad," Anna says.

"No," Clayton says. "Kind of a Cold War myth, like nuclear winter. I mean, fallout is bad, it'll kill you horribly, but the really dangerous part of nuclear war is all the enormous kabooms. And then the infrastructure collapse. Of course, the aliens might've built a better fallout . . ."

The name *Axiorrhage* feels bad on his brain. It must be some kind of translation: bleeding truth? The alien vessel makes Iruvage's raven-wing look like a dinghy, like one of those little helicopters they launch off the back of navy ships. The model sneers at him: *this* is a warship, a powerful, elongated fang, with a lean downturned prow and a sleek body and honeycombed dorsal hatches full of what might be missiles. Gleaming darkly in a constellation of drones.

"We blew through the deadline for nuclear annihilation about five hours ago," Rosamaria continues. "Either Iruvage was lying, or *Axiorrhage* is waiting for us to make a move. I've been hiding on the opposite side of the planet. The problem is that I can't do anything else. *Axiorrhage* could destroy me with a single good hit. And we know Iruvage told *Axiorrhage* to put out pickets to keep ships from escaping Earth. We're trapped here. And sooner or later they'll try to use those pickets to flush us."

"Wait." Khaje frowns. "They can just . . . shoot you down?"

"Sure."

"But aren't you an immortal principle from the dawn of time? Appointed by God to your task?"

"The physicality of the ship is maintained by Blackbird—by Rosamaria's constant calculation," Aixue says. "Adding energy to the system ramifies the difficulty of the computation. We're unbreakable, but only until the moment we fall apart. Then Rosamaria stops computing. And stops existing."

"Feh. Like a Toyota."

"Hey!" Davoud protests. He has one hand on Khaje's shoulder and won't let go. "Blackbird's not a Toyota!"

Erik weighs the world and the ship with his eyes. "We have to destroy *Axiorrhage*. That's our absolute imperative. Can we sneak up on them?"

Clayton shakes his head. "Even if we used the Earth as cover, the closest we could get is half a planet away."

"The atmosphere would block some of their weapons," Chaya points out. "We're safer from nukes down there, where the atmosphere catches the gamma rays. Up in space we're naked to the radiation."

"Maybe." Erik's still fixed on the goal. "We can ram them, like we rammed Iruvage's little corvette. We just have to get close enough to do it. There has to be a way."

"Wanting it doesn't make it true, Erik," Clayton says: it just comes out of him.

"Fuck off," Erik snarls. "Maybe if you'd thought about how to beat these guys *before* signing up with them—"

"Hey, Erik." Anna steps between them. "That doesn't help, dude. You know he's on our side."

She stretches a little on her toes as she leans in to mutter to Erik. Erik does not relax, but his anger turns away from Clayton. The woman knows what effect she has on Erik, and how to use it.

Anna startles Clayton with a grin thrown over her shoulder: "I know how to get close. Just think like a khai."

He feels himself blush, for no reason he could explain to any of them except Chaya. "Threaten to destroy Blackbird ourselves?"

"No. We attack *Iruvage*. He pulls the alien ship down to protect him. The lower it is, the less it can see, right? So we can get close."

Everyone else stares at Anna. She puts her hands on her hips, mockingly, like she knows something Clayton doesn't, something vicious and delightful. "Look where that ship's parked right now. Why is it hovering over Kurdistan? Why do you think it didn't blow us away when we escaped? Iruvage is calling to them. Bargaining what he knows about Blackbird for rescue."

"Oh, shit," Clayton breathes. "So if we force *Axiorrhage* down to protect him . . . of course, the aliens will leave satellites behind that'll spot us. But the satellites won't have the full weapons of the bigger ship. And if Blackbird is fast enough—"

"Wait a minute," Davoud protests, "wait, wait. Iruvage has an atmanach! That thing can kill Rosamaria with a single touch! I'm not bringing this ship anywhere *near* him!"

"Ssrin killed it," Anna counters.

"Maybe he's got spares! Maybe every alien on that ship has one too!"

"We don't need to get anywhere near Iruvage to attack him," Erik says. "He knows we have an entire planet full of nuclear missiles to throw his way. It's going to take a while to retarget them, but I believe it can be done. Rosamaria, you can figure out military encryption, right? We'll just dial up every country on Earth with a nuclear arsenal. Coordinate an attack on Iruvage. Use every bomb we've got."

"Why not shoot down the big alien ship?" Khaje protests. "Instead of shooting at Tawakul?"

Clayton and Erik look at each other. "Our missiles can't go that high," Clayton says. "We only built them to hit each other."

"Wait," Davoud says. "You want to nuke Iruvage so *Axiorrhage* has to come down to save him? What if they just let him die?"

"They won't," Anna says.

"Because he'll tell them he has a way to save their souls from hell." Clayton can't imagine a stronger bargaining chip. "That's why Iruvage wants Blackbird, right? To change reality. To save himself from damnation. Every alien on that ship is just as damned as he is."

"Right," Erik says. "Right. So all we have to do is convince them to descend. At first they'll stay up high, doing boost phase and mid-course intercept on our missiles. But if we add cruise missiles and aircraft to the mix . . . yeah. Hopefully they'll need to get down closer to Iruvage to guarantee interception of the squirters."

"Squirters?" Chaya says, in exactly the way you would echo a man who has just said *squirters.*

"You know. Leakers. The ones that get by."

"The missiles that are going to hit my home," Khaje says. "You're talking about nuking Kurdistan."

Aixue speaks up: "If you're wrong, and the aliens don't protect him, then all those nuclear bombs actually go off. It'd be ten or fifteen Krakatoa eruptions. Everything inside three hundred kilometers of Tawakul would start to burn. The fallout would be . . . I don't know. I don't know how to know, nothing like that has ever happened before."

"So?" Clayton says. "Say we really fuck up, and we don't even manage to target Iruvage. We just nuke our own cities by accident. We fire off the whole global nuclear arsenal, kill a couple hundred million people. So? They're going to do that to us *anyway.* We can't possibly do any worse than what they're really planning."

"But they're not threatening to nuke Kurdistan," Khaje says. "They're threatening to nuke cities. You're the only one who wants to nuke Kurdistan."

"Nuke Kurdistan some more," Chaya adds. "You already dropped three."

"This is a really weird trolley problem," Clayton says. Everyone stares at him.

"Right? A nuclear attack is going to hit every major city on Earth. Do you redirect the nukes to Iraqi Kurdistan?"

"Clayton," Erik says, "shut up."

"I don't know . . ." Davoud shakes his head. "Ram the aliens? The same trick twice? Last time we had to hit an overheated ship at point-blank range. It couldn't dodge. But this thing? This thing's in a powered hover over Kurdistan. If it obeys anything like our physics, it's accelerating at one gravity. A human rocket can do that for about fifteen minutes. How long have they been doing it? Days? We have no idea how much delta-V it can generate." Pre-empting Khaje's question: "That's like gas mileage for spaceships."

"What else do we have?" Erik says. "We ram or we give up."

"Maybe Blackbird could make guns," Anna suggests.

"Sure," Rosamaria says. "If you give me something to copy. Do you have any spaceship guns to copy?"

"Too bad we broke Iruvage's ship," Clayton says. "I bet *Axiorrhage* has a few."

"Sure, Clay, only I'd have to get shot by them to see how they work."

"We have Ssrin," Anna says. "She might know what to do."

Rosamaria's alien face expresses human discomfort: all those eyes, great and tiny, avert themselves. "If she ever wakes up."

"She will," Anna says "I know she will."

Anna's right. Ssrin *is* a badass, isn't she? Iruvage was so worried about her that he had Clayton haul a neutrino detector halfway around the planet just to catch her by surprise. And it didn't even work.

They've got Ssrin. They've got Blackbird, a primordial mystery that frightens an entire alien empire. They've got Erik Wygaunt, the most determined fighter Clayton's ever known, physically unable to give up. Khaje and Anna Sinjari, who each, independently, made and saw through their own deals with Ssrin. Davoud Qasemi, the man whose first flight in an alien starship was a fucking ram attack. Chaya Panaguiton and Li Aixue, the scientists who solved Blackbird, each touched by its symmetry-furnishing hand in some mysterious way—

He's just starting to work up some triumphalism when reality strikes.

CLAYTON//ATTRITION

"Oh, no," Rosamaria whispers.

Her avatar collapses down to humanity: lawyer Rosamaria in slacks and blouse, ready to hear the verdict. She tries to speak and her voice breaks, that noise she makes right before she cries, Clayton remembers that noise so well—sweetheart, amada mía, it's going to be okay—

Fuck off. It isn't.

She says: "*Axiorrhage* just launched twenty-two missiles."

"At us?" Clayton asks, because someone has to elicit the answer.

"No."

Oh, God.

"Intercept them!" Erik pounces forward. "Get this thing moving. We'll knock the missiles down with the drive field!"

"We can't." Clayton's job to say it. "What if one of them blows up in our faces? What if the aliens are counting on us trying to intercept? We'd lose everything."

"We have to try! Do you know what one nuke in one city means? Millions dead! Fucking *millions*! I'm not going to be able to go down there and dig out the kids this time, Clayton!"

"Millions of people die every month," Aixue says distantly. "Just not all at once. Where will the missiles fall, please?"

Rosamaria reads the list.

Beijing. Shanghai. Moscow. Los Angeles. London. New York. Washington. Tokyo. Osaka. Berlin. São Paulo. Karachi. Delhi. Paris. Johannesburg. Lagos. Seoul. Istanbul. Mumbai. Shenzhen. Jakarta. Mexico City.

Gone. Just gone. The apocalypse conductor's baton will fall, *now*, and there will be a rapid, ruinous dawn. They will be thirty-megaton detonations, if Iruvage's taunts were true. So say each bomb has a fireball five miles wide, kills about six hundred square miles . . . call it 225 million dead. The entire Black Death in a day. Five Great Leaps Forward. Ten Columbian exchanges, plus room for rounding and uncertainty: nobody knows exactly how many Indians died.

"Washington," Clayton gasps. "Oh my God. Rosamaria."

"What?" Rosamaria says. "Oh. Oh . . ."

"No!" Erik snarls.

"My family's in Beijing?" Aixue says this tentatively, as if she has not yet proven it to her satisfaction. "Are you sure the missile will hit Beijing? Maybe it's aimed for Tianjin. That's a port, it's a strategic target. That makes more sense."

Chaya pulls her gently. "Let's go. Let's go, Aixue. Let's sit down."

Metro Manila was, Clayton remembers, not on the list.

Erik looks at Clayton and there's such helpless fury in those gray eyes. Such useless power in those big hands.

Clayton shakes his head. He's got nothing.

"Is this it?" Erik asks. "Is it over?"

"No. So they kill two hundred million. We're still at ninety-seven percent. We've got a lot of people left to save."

Erik looks as if he will roar and snap Clayton's spine for the sin of writing off those millions.

Erik looks as if he needed to hear exactly that, for it is not a thing he ever could have thought himself.

"Rosamaria." Khaje's smoky rasp breaks the silence. "If it's in your power, I think these people would like a chance to say goodbye."

CHAPTER THIRTY-EIGHT

K + 174:45:32 HOURS

ZZZ FLASH

Y EMERGENCY COMMAND PRECEDENCE

DO NOT ANSWER

ATTENTION NIGHTWATCH

PASS TO NMCC AND SITE R

PASS TO ALL AUTHORIZING COMMANDERS

THIS IS DEP NAT SEC ADVISOR CLAYTON HUNT EDIPI 2156963918

AUTHORIZING BRIEFING FROM MAJ ERIK WYGAUNT EDIPI 2750722605

THIS IS MAJ ERIK WYGAUNT COMMANDER TASK FORCE MAJESTIC

YES IT'S REALLY US

BE ADVISED ALIEN THERMONUCLEAR WEAPONS INBOUND TO STRIKE

WASHINGTON DC

NYC

LOS ANGELES

MOSCOW

BEIJING

SHANGHAI

SHENZHEN

SEOUL

LONDON

BERLINPARIS IGNORE THIS LINE

BERLIN

PARIS

DELHI

MUMBAI

JAKARTA

LAGOS

TOKYO

OSAKA

SAO PAULO

MEXICO CITY

KARACHI

ISTANBUL

JOHANNESBURG

WEAPON PARAMETERS UNKNOWN

BUT ESTIMATE YIELD 30+ MT REPEAT 30+ MT

WE HAVE SECURED ALIEN STARSHIP CODENAMED BLACKBIRD WITH ADVANCED

SENSORS AND TRANSITTERS CORRECTION TRANSMITTERS

WE HAVE ACCESS TO GLOBAL SECURE COMMUNICATIONS

WE HAVE IDENTIFIED THE HOSTILE ALIENS CONDUCTING NUCLEAR ATTACK

GOVT DECAP STRIKE EN ROUTE, FURTHER ESCALATION IMMINENT

OPS PLAN REQ OVERWHELMING STRATEGIC NUCLEAR STRIKE

PLACE ALL AVAILABLE WEAPONS THREE WAVE TIME ON TARGET 5 MIN GAP

AT FOLLOWING COORDINATES

LAT 36.721274 N

LONG 44.857178 E

TIME 0800 ZULU

USE ALL AVAILABLE THROW WEIGHT

REPEAT USE ALL MISSILES AND AIRCRAFT INCLUDING NONNUCLEAR ORDNANCE

NO REGARD FOR COLLATERAL DAMAGE

ALIENS DID NOT ANTICIPATE THAT WE WOULD GAIN CONTROL OF BLACKBIRD

BLACKBIRD REPRESENTS SINGLE HOPE FOR CONTINUED PLANETARY SURVIVAL AND

DEFENSE

BLACKBIRD WILL DISABLE ALIEN CRAFT AND FORCE IT DOWN

POSSIBILITY EXISTS TO RECOVER ALIEN TECHNOLOGY/ALIEN WARSHIP

WE ARE ALSO SIGNALING TO:

RUSSIA STRATEGIC COMMAND KOSVINSKY

CHINA 2AC

INDIA NCA

PAKISTAN NCA

FRANCE JUPITER

UK NORTHWOOD

ISRAEL PAKMAZ

BLACKBIRD WILL PROVIDE STRATEGIC COMMAND AND CONTROL

HOLD LAUNCH UNTIL WE AUTHENTICATE WITH:

DEPUTY NSA HUNT CCA PIN NO

AND MAJ WYGAUNT CCA PIN NO

REPEAT DO NOT PROCEED UNTIL WE AUTHENTICATE WITH CCA PIN NO

DO NOT REPLY REPEAT DO NOT ATTEMPT REPLY

ALIEN SIGINT CAPABILITIES UNKNOWN

MESSAGE WILL REPEAT 100 MORE TIMES

END OF MESSAGE

AIXUE 5 × 1

"Hi, Mama," Aixue whispers. "Can you hear me?"

"*Li Aixue!*" In the exact same Beijinese accent that creeps into Aixue's voice when she's excited, when Professor Huang makes fun of her. "*Where are you? How are you calling? The power is out!*"

"You have a generator, Ma." Their whole building does, since blackouts were a problem when it was built.

"*Yes, but not a working phone! Oh, now everyone in the building is going to line up at my door and ask to call someone. I will have to pretend I have a parrot. Anyway, where are you? Things are terrible here, I'm glad you're far away!*"

"I'm sorry I didn't call. The phones have been down here too . . ."

"*But here you are. I said, if I know my Aixue, well, she'll find a way to bounce messages off the sun.*" Her mother puts the phone down for a second to call out, come, come quick, it's Aixue! "*Where are you? What's happening? Tell us everything, our neighbors are desperate for news.*"

"I'm on an alien ship, Mama. I'm flying over the North Atlantic right now."

"*An alien spaceship? Are there toilets?*"

Aixue laughs. Wipes her eyes. "Yes, Ma, the ship made toilets for us. They're just holes. Everything goes in and disappears."

"*Bring me one. We are running out of water to flush.*"

"I'll try, Ma." Oh, no. She's going to cry. "We did it. We found out what was happening."

"*Of course you did. Now I'm holding the phone up! Shout hello to your aunts and uncles! We're all in here playing games and waiting for the power to come back. A truck came by and told everyone they were repairing things.*"

"Hi, everyone," Aixue says, and she starts bawling.

"*Oh, big baby.*" Ma clucks. "*What's wrong? You're embarrassing everyone here! I'm just kidding. We are all laughing at you.*"

"I love you," Aixue chokes. "I love you all. Mama . . . I didn't figure it out in time . . ."

The sound of Ma shushing everyone comes through the phone handset. "*I think you have bad news, Xuxu. How bad? Should we leave the city?*"

"It's worse than that. Ma, I'm so sorry. I'm so sorry." What's the best way to say this, what's the elegant and compact set of words that convey love? Aixue can't figure it out. Can't tell her family how densely and completely she cares.

"*Ah. I see. Nothing to be done?*"

"Mama." Aixue sobs. She could say *go underground*. But what then? Asphyxiation in the firestorm. Or a slow, horrible death by fallout or starvation. And the part after death is so beautiful: she has been there before . . .

"*Hush. Hush. It's all right. We're together here. We're all together. No one is going to be lost or left alone, and that's good. Tell me how you are, Xuxu. Did you meet a nice girl out there?"*

Aixue sniffles horribly and wipes her face on her hands. She doesn't even have a phone to hold. She's talking to the air. If she had a phone, at least it would be something to grip and not let go.

"I don't know. She's— You wouldn't like her, she ran away from her parents. And I'm not sure she likes me. She's so practical. She always knows what to do. I'm off in my daydreams and she's fixing things . . ."

"Nonsense. Of course she likes you. Is she strong? Can she reach the top shelves? I hope you read that article I sent you, about women combining finances. Does she make money?"

"Yes, Ma, she's a great physicist, she works in the oil industry. I'm sure she makes good money."

"Perfect. Then it's settled. You must move in with her. Find someplace that you can do that, and don't let her talk you out of it. How is Huang Lim?"

"He's . . . he's great, Ma." She can still lie, barely. "He's up here with us."

"You remember to be respectful and to thank him for his contributions to your success." A long, long sigh. *"Well, you must be very busy. Remember that we love you very much, and that we'll be proud of you wherever you go and whatever you do."*

"I love you, Mama. I love you. I love you."

"We know, we know. Don't be so gushy with her, or you'll scare her off. What will you do now?"

"I guess . . . I guess I've got to go help save the world." Whatever's left of it. A world without her family.

"Listen to her! Did you hear that? She has such a big head."

⁓

K + 174:46:12 hours
Blackbird

"Rosamaria Navarro. Who the fuck is this?"

Erik and Clayton both take deep breaths and hesitate. Clayton figures Erik must be terrified to speak up, because what if Rosamaria hangs up the moment she realizes who they are? Then it'll be the fault of whoever spoke first.

Who talks? Roll initiative.

"Hey," Clayton says. "Uh, we'd like a stuffed-crust party pizza with pepperoni, sausage, chicken, ham—"

"Clayton!" Rosamaria hisses. *"No mames! They told me you flew off to find the aliens! How the hell are you talking to me?"*

"It's complicated. Where are you?"

"In the White House bunker. My boss left to find her husband. Told me to hold down the fort for Justice." She laughs. "I'm helping."

"I'm glad you're safe," Clayton lies.

"Oh," Rosamaria says. "Oh, fuck. You're with the aliens, aren't you? That's why the signal's so good."

"Yeah." Erik swallows. "I'm here too."

"Of course. Are you two talking again? That figures. You get over your shitty breakup just in time to run off and steal the glory. Well. What've you got for me? I can radio it to the president. Half the ops center is listening right now."

Jesus. How do they say this? How do they say it in front of an audience? You're about to be bombed by aliens, and we called to say goodbye?

"The mission succeeded. We discovered the aliens' objectives. They were sent to retrieve an object in Kurdistan and then wipe out all life on Earth."

"My God."

"We stole the Kurdistan thing, though. We even took down one of the alien ships. Now we're flying around, planning a way to take out the alien mothership."

"Jesus, Clayton."

"That's not why we called, though," Erik says. He looks away from Clayton. They make a couple manly grunts.

"We wanted to apologize," Clayton says. "For putting you in an incredibly difficult, dangerous, horrible position."

"You mean . . . the bunker? You didn't do this."

"Not now. I mean . . . a couple years ago. What we did with . . ."

"For breaking the law because we thought we could get away with it," Erik says, "and trying to convince you that we were right to do it. For making you know something you shouldn't have had to know."

"You know," Clayton says. "For treating you like a moral football."

There's a long pause. "Were you guys replaced by pod people?"

"We both died," Erik says. "But only for a little."

"What?"

"Actually"—Clayton can't stop it, he laughs a little maniacally, a mad scientist cackle—"we talked this over with the other you, and she thought we should say it to you. So here we are."

"The other me."

"Yeah, it's funny. We accidentally created a copy of your soul and implanted it in the ship. You're up here right now."

"You look like Guillermo del Toro's death mask," Erik adds. "You've got tentacles."

Silence on the line. Then, "I honestly don't know how to respond to that. Anyway. A bunch of military people are yelling at me. They say we got a very strange message, and there's currently some, uh, friction over it. Can you authenticate it?"

Clayton's heart rolls along the edge of the gutter. Is it going to end like this? Unresolved forever? Just avoiding the topic? "Yeah, that's definitely us. Authentication, um, Courtney's party?" The first time they had sex. "You really, really need to do what we said in that message, because . . ."

"*Because the aliens are dropping nuclear bombs on us. We got that. They say we've got less than an hour.*"

Erik winces. "Right. So . . ."

"*So you called to say goodbye.*"

"Yes." Clayton can't read her voice at all. Couldn't he read her every mood, like his whiskers were brushing hers? Of course he could. He can't anymore. It's not that he's lost the art. It's just that the channels between them are shut off at her end now. "We kind of hoped we could keep this conversation personal."

"*Fuck you. Nobody has time for personal right now. What do you want me to say? You committed some state-level crimes, some unbelievably scandalous administration-sinking shit. You tried to bring me in on it. Mejor solo que mal acompañado. I'll always love the men I knew, but you aren't those men anymore. It's all done now. The issue is concluded. It was concluded the day I divorced you, Clay. You should've taken the hint and stopped using my name. There's no more to be said. Now please, please, tell me something useful. At least tell me there's still a chance for everyone else?*"

Clayton rubs his forehead. He's not getting through to her. He needs a better way to say I love you, and then she will hear him. Maybe Blackbird can do that somehow. Maybe there's a way. Like what happened between him and Chaya, in the labs. He will run through every possible thing to say to Rosamaria and choose the right one, and then she will love him again as she dies.

"Okay," Erik says. "Useful information. Get the military guys to pass it international. The alien ship's vulnerability is heat buildup. It can hijack our electronics through radars and other receivers. It has lasers, missiles, missiles that *shoot* lasers, an engine death ray, and some kind of non-line-of-sight targeting. Uh . . . it can manipulate gravity in a small area around its hull. It's armored against standard anti-air weapons, so you need to treat it like a hard target. It carries a payload of cobalt-salted nuclear devices. Blackbird is our only chance against it, but to pull our trick we've got to get close. We've got to ram it and destroy its engines. And to do that we need the alien ship to come down and defend an alien in Kurdistan."

Silence.

"*Is it really the end of the world?*" Rosamaria asks.

"Not if we win," Erik says.

Clayton can't take it. "We'll come get you. Rosamaria, we'll come pick you up, we'll get you out—" Impossible, of course, but in that moment he's like Erik, trying to make it true just by saying it.

"*No.*"

"Don't be a martyr! No one could blame you for—"

"*I don't care who would or wouldn't blame me, Clay. If I thought I could live, I'd go for it. I want to see your alien ship. I want to go to space with you, I want to meet aliens, the way we'd imagined when we were kids. Remember our stupid fucking alien names? I was Glorb and you were Ixi and Erik, man, you were Eos, from Pluto.*" Her voice finally breaks, just the way the other Rosamaria's did: but she doesn't sob. She laughs. Kids, man. She was a Glorb and he was an Ixi. "*But it's too late now. You need to focus on people who still have a chance. What happens if your plan works?*"

Erik says, "We take down their ship. And maybe we'll be ready when more of them come."

Clayton, numb, severed from immediacy by a guillotine of denial, thinks about what Erik has just said. The fact that Rosamaria cannot be saved has cut some necessary cord inside him, and set him adrift in a new territory, one where his reason to care about the world is gone.

Now he's thinking about risk management, and utilitarianism, and what a rational actor would do with Blackbird. Which is, if Li Aixue is right, a tool associated with the most basic creative force in the universe.

Clayton gets a feeling. The suspicion you get when you realize you're wrangling with someone a lot smarter than you.

"Rosamaria," he says, "you're the best person I've ever known."

"*Oh, Clay.*" She sighs. "*You're not the best person I've ever known. But you're probably the most interesting. Erik, man, if you're still there, I want you to know that you did the right thing telling me, okay? It was better for me to know. So I could make the choice I had to make. You're a sanctimonious white knight, I'm sure you know you did the right thing.*"

"I wasn't sure," Erik whispers.

"*Liar. You're always sure.*"

"Not this time."

"*I never loved you like you loved me,*" Rosamaria says. Her voice is so low. "*But I loved you all the other ways.*"

"I know," Erik says.

Why does Erik get this? Why won't she just say, Clayton, I loved you all the ways you loved me, and a couple other ways which were just mine? I always outpaced you: even here, in the count of the ways to love.

"*I'm going to be kind of an asshole here,*" Rosamaria says, "*and point out that I said goodbye a couple years ago, and you two are eating up the final moments of my life. I've got friends down here I want to be with. So . . .*"

Both of them nod. Both of them realize she can't see them, and together they say, "Yeah."

"Apparently there's an afterlife," Erik says with stone-faced control. "So maybe we'll see you there."

She laughs. That wild, wonderful laugh. "*Good luck to los dos pendejos. And godspeed.*"

She hangs up.

"That was so weird," Rosamaria says, behind them. "So weird."

CHAYA 3:2

Chaya makes Rosamaria charge up her Nokia. Then, instead of making any calls, she asks Rosamaria exactly how she can connect to phones. The answer is not very exciting: she calls them on the radio. But what if the phone burnt out in the EMP? Then estás cagado, but it probably didn't, it just needs a battery change, so you hope they changed the battery. But who has a spare cell phone battery handy? And what if it's a landline? And—

"Chaya," Rosamaria says. "Are you procrastinating?"

Fine. She tries her lola in the Philippines. No response. Her mamu and her aunties are also disconnected: probably EMP damage. She tries Fr. Gokongwei. Nothing. She tries her father. Nothing! Who would keep their phone turned on now, anyway? With all the towers dead?

She calls her parents' landline. Incredibly, Mom picks up. "Hello? Who is this?"

"Hello, Ina," Chaya says. "It's me."

"*Susmaryosep. Chaya? Chaya, are you coming home? We're so worried about you—*"

"Not right now. I'm in kind of a weird situation. Something bad's going to happen soon, and—"

"*Something wonderful is going to happen, Chaya! It's the end of days. Have you gotten right with God?*"

"It's not the end of days, Nanay. It's just an alien invasion. Do you have water? Do you have power?"

"*Well, obviously I must have power, if you are calling me. We're on water rations but they are refilling the local tower from La Mesa. Chaya, you need to get right with God.*"

"Nanay, I need to talk to you about things, in case we don't—"

"*Chaya,*" her mother says very sternly, "*I told you, last time we spoke, that I would not help you feel all right about your choices until you made better choices. Until you made a commitment to fixing your mistakes. A real commitment. Lord have mercy, wasn't I clear? We cannot speak until you turn your back on your choices and come home. You walk back in this door and you do me the respect of an apology. And then you apologize to your lola too, for taking advantage of her kindness. And to your*" *father for making his life so hard. Do you think we can talk about anything else before that is done? I pray for you. But until you make things right, it is all I can do."*

And she hangs up. She hangs up on her own daughter.

"Unbelievable," Chaya says. "Unbelievable."

Now she can't even call any of her Filipino friends. They will ask her if she called her mother first, and then all they will talk about is how her mother hung up on her.

Her hands shake too hard to press buttons for a while. Finally she dials her friend Kabite. Kabite is a wilderness survival guide in Uganda—though Chaya is quite sure that Kabite is actually employed by the government to search out gold-smuggling routes. Kabite was going to get married to a Kenyan guy who Chaya adored. Chaya went to Iraq and missed the wedding.

"Chaya?"

"Kabite. Oh my God." Chaya clutches the phone in both hands. "You can hear me?"

"Yes! How did you reach me? I'm so far out!"

"I'm doing, uh, an experiment. Using large atmospheric plasmas as antennae. Where are you?"

"I'm camped out on a riverside in Kidepo! Oh, you scared the shit out of me, I was reading on my phone and it started to buzz. I thought I had it on airplane mode . . ."

Oh, no. Kabite doesn't know what's happened. She must've had her phone off when the EMPs hit, and she just . . . hasn't been able to reach anyone.

"Have you seen the aurora?" Chaya asks cautiously.

"Yeah, gorgeous, right? Talk about large atmospheric plasmas. I figure it's a solar storm. Hamidi says maybe the world ended while we were away. You know, all the transformers blew out, everyone's in the dark. He wanted to go back and find out what happened, and I said, no, don't let the end of the world ruin our honeymoon. If it's so, we'll stay out here forever. I can show him how to hunt, he can show me how to . . . Hamidi, what are you even good for?"

A male voice in the distance shouts: *"I can make a life preserver out of pants!"*

"You're on your honeymoon! I'm so sorry I interrupted!"

"No, I'm so happy to hear from you! How's Iraq? Did you find oil? Bring me a bottle and I'll trade you for some gold flakes." Kabite laughs. Chaya can imagine her stretched out on the riverbank, her big hiking boots and long thick legs, Hamidi making coffee over a fire.

"Iraq's fine," Chaya says. "Everything's okay. I . . . Kabite, I want you to remember that God carved your name into his palm. Remember the song I taught you? God cannot forget you any more than a mother can forget the baby inside her. Whenever you're in trouble, you remember this call. God's in heaven watching you. And so am I."

Soft silence. *"Chaya, are you all right?"*

"I love you," Chaya chokes, "you're great, you're the best. My very best friend. Oh, Jesus." It takes her three stabs to end the call. "Oh, Jesus and Mary."

She gets up from the little chair, wanting to be anywhere else. When she turns around, Li Aixue's curled up on the couch of the faculty lounge. Chaya flinches.

Aixue flinches too.

Chaya doesn't want to be seen like this, chest heaving, breath short. She turns her shoulders and bends over to check her bootlaces because she doesn't trust her voice.

Aixue reads this as anger. "I'm sorry I let this happen."

"It's fine." She doesn't even know what she's calling fine. "It's fine, it's not your fault."

"It's not fine. Our families are dying. And there's nothing we can do to help them."

"We can pray." And if Aixue tries to make fun of her, fuck her.

"Do you want me to pray for you?" Aixue says.

"You don't have to do that. I'll pray for my family, you pray for yours. Or don't, if you don't pray." Thinking of poor Huang Lim: "Do you want me to pray for *you*?"

Aixue says suddenly: "Where I come from—um—"

She sounds like she has punctured herself, possibly from the inside, and now feelings are leaking out. Chaya looks back in surprise: "Where you come from?"

"Some women . . . like you . . . um, they're called iron Ts. Kind of these post-Maoist . . . God, let me start over." She tugs at her stupid sweatshirt. "In the old days all women were supposed to be sort of stoic and sensible and masculine. And a T is a woman who's like that, but also, you know"—she makes a vague stirring gesture, *you know, a lesbian*—"um, anyway. T as opposed to a P, a woman like me, who's . . . more girly, or who hasn't got her shit together. But an *iron* T is—one of the rules of being an iron T is that you touch, but you can't be touched." She pauses, inviting Chaya to say something. "It's stupid. I'm not saying you're like that."

"What *are* you saying?"

"I just feel like . . . you think you have to be iron. You have to help other people, but you can't be the one who needs help. And I think that's stupid. You're stupid if you think that."

Chaya stares at her. What a fucking weird person. Chaya wants to disassemble her and catalogue all her pieces and put her back together, just to know what the fuck is going on inside her, but she knows that if she did she would end up with *one* bit leftover, an indecipherable *huh?* of unclear function.

"My mom said we couldn't talk unless I got right with God," she says.

"That sucks. My mom's going to die. But at least she loves me."

"My mom loves me. She just doesn't like me. Or support me. Or want to talk to me."

"Is that really love?"

"It's a theory of love," Chaya says. "But maybe not a practice."

Neither of them has any idea what to say next.

"You're filthy," Chaya says disapprovingly. "You smell. You should take a bath."

"*You're* filthy!" Aixue snaps. "*You* should take a bath!"

Chaya grins. Then she starts laughing. Aixue, sobbing, begins to laugh too.

DAVOUD (~36,100 FEET ASL)

"Show me the stars."

"*Which stars, Davoud?*"

"Any of them. All of them. Pretend we're flying toward the center of the galaxy."

He is back in the cockpit. Stars around him like the sun off snowy mountaintops, seen from high above. His perspective rockets off into the Milky Way at catastrophic speeds. Davoud grips the stick and throttle and whoops in joy.

"Isn't there *anyone* you want to call?" Khaje asks. She's behind him, in the radar intercept officer's seat. "Your sister? Your parents?"

"It'd be weird," Davoud says. Fully aware that he is exhibiting avoidance behavior.

"It'd be weird," Khaje repeats skeptically.

"They're going to be fine. Tehran wasn't on the list. And if the police ask them whether I've been in touch, they can say no."

"If you say so."

He plunges through clouds of false-color nebulae and great spangled globular clusters. The low song of neutron stars lures him inward, toward the impossibility at the center of the Milky Way. Sagittarius A*: the black devourer.

He looks into the black hole. The light of all those crowded stars lenses around the darkness of four million crushed suns to cast Davoud in shadows of awe. He thanks God that he could see this before he dies.

"What about you?" Then he remembers what's happened to Khaje's people. "Oh. I'm sorry."

"It's okay," Khaje says. "They are in God's hands now. Arîn will get the survivors far enough away."

Davoud cranes his neck to look into the back seat. He can't see. He can see the stars all around them, but he can't see Khaje behind him, because he's blind. "Some of your people made it out?"

"Yes," Khaje says with some smugness. "More than three hundred, actually. Tawakul will survive."

"But we're going to bomb them. We're launching every missile on Earth at that place."

Khaje scoffs. "They will be far enough away."

"I mean," Davoud blurts, "if the aliens decide, well, screw Iruvage, let him die—then fifteen thousand nukes land on Tawakul—"

"Davoud!"

"Sorry."

"Do you think I don't know?" she says. "Do you think I don't know what could happen? My whole life I have been waiting for Anfal to happen again. And now that it has, now that death is falling across the whole world, do you know what I wish? Not that I could've stopped it, because I could not. Not that I could've predicted it, because what use would it be? I wish only that I had spent less time in fear. I wish that I had called my daughter home sooner. So I could love her longer before the end."

They fly in silence through furious gulfs, toward the bright eternity of the galactic center.

"*Every act of creation is an act of love,*" Blackbird whispers. "*Was this also? This universe? I'm glad you want to see this, Davoud. I want that too.*"

"You've got to live in the moment," Davoud says. "You're the soul of a *starship.* What could be better?"

A cockpit warning deedles from Khaje's backseat. "Twenty minutes until the missiles launch."

"Twenty minutes is forever. Have you ever closed your eyes and tried to count to twenty minutes? An eternity. You can't do it. It's basically impossible for twenty minutes to pass if you're paying attention." Davoud kicks his illusionary perspective into a superluminal slingshot around the black hole. Time itself warps. The Milky Way whirls around them at a million years a second as they dip deep and slow. "Look at this! Khaje! Just *look!*"

And she does. She sits back to watch the stars streak. After a while she starts praying.

Oh, God. O living eternal. Him by whose command the sky and the earth stand fast.

In a little while Chaya and Aixue wander over from their own goodbyes. There's no room in the cockpit but Chaya makes a planetarium dome with an ease that worries Davoud (she's so good at talking to Blackbird, isn't that his job?).

"Hey," Chaya says. "That black hole has a polar jet! Pretty faint, though. Wait, is this Sag A? I didn't think we knew if the Milky Way had jets."

"It does," Blackbird reports. "*Faint, but present. Li Zhiyuan et al. were planning to publish this autumn. There was a preprint in the files Professor Huang sent to me.*"

"Whoa . . . cool. So if this jet's set up right, the hole rotates the same way as the galaxy. Cool! Can you get me a better look at the magnetic field?"

"Hey," Davoud says. "I'm sightseeing, not working on your PhD!"

"Sorry. Polar jets are awesome, though. I always told my girlfriend, black hole polar jets are proof of God."

"How so?" Khaje asks.

"Because the black hole *makes* the polar jet. One can't exist without the other."

"So?"

"So, if you look up at the night sky, at the center of galaxies where anything with eyes will want to look, you'll find a terrible sign. You'll find that at the heart of that whole galaxy and all the stars in it the devil used a million suns to build the biggest darkest most seductive most hopeless crushing prison he possibly could."

Chaya swallows. Her voice stays brave.

"And then God saw that prison, and said: thank you, Satan Lightbringer. Thank you for the ultimate final prison from which not even light escapes. Thank you for your black hole. This will make the perfect engine for the biggest, brightest, most beautiful rocket you ever saw.

"And out of that darkness, there was light."

ISORIY

She awakens in a burst of ssovosis.

Her heads snap up to guard, fangs out, ready to kill. Hot venom swells the glands. Paramuscle implants and screamwire tendons flex beneath her scales. Before she is even minutely aware of her surroundings she's in full defensive array.

Emergency memory waits for her, a clotted summary of her situation. She snaps it up like a sweetmeat. And remembers—

She remembers claudicating herself when the bombs fell. Riding out the blast in a pocket of emancipated space: slowly, slowly, slowly cooking in her own metabolic energy, praying to Abdiel and Auno-who-made-him for an opportunity to *move*. Certain that if she did, Iruvage or his ship would blow her literally to hell—

She remembers the moment that opportunity came. When she felt a soul telling her story, and her story telling that soul: I am here, I am you, you are I, you are here. And off she went, slithering happily into that most comfortable, treacherous groove: serendura, you came for me . . .

She remembers cutting her commands into the world—eliding the American bombs into almost harmless neutrinos. (She will have to explain to Khaje, some-day soon, why she did not stop the bombs falling on Tawakul's shelter: will *I had no heat sink* be a fine lie? No, tell the truth, Ssrin. Be better . . .)

She remembers Iruvage *poking* her.

A tiny little impulse, like a blade of grass in clockwork. But so perfectly posi-tioned. And her operancy went bad. Catastrophic failure, the somagonic contin-gency her only escape.

How did he *know*? Iruvage was never a talented operant, except in the mere application of brute force. Ssrin's technique, like any good combat operant's, is encrypted by the very shape of her soul. It can't be read from the outside, can't be penetrated and brought down by sabotage, except by someone who's gained access to a fundamental level of Ssrin's experience. Iruvage doesn't have that access.

Unless—

She doesn't want to think about that anymore. So she doesn't. Humans can't do that. Khai can. How else do you go through life, knowing it will end in hell? You choose not to think of it, and then you don't.

She remembers venting her rotten operancy into her own body, lest it destroy her soul. Radiation in her blood. Bubbles of hot fat popping in her spine. Did she die? O Symmetries, did she *die*?

What if she's been taken by the atmanach? What if this is Iruvage's interro-gation?

What if she's dead, and this is damnation?

And then, after these long long instants of senseless consciousness, screamwire nerves finally carry the report of her heads to her mainbrain.

Anna Sinjari looks down on her. Behind her fat round head is the sky of Ssrin's childhood. The cinnamon enormity of giant Vsatyr in the clear blue sky. Golden Sahana burns in the heavens, giving life to all that grows and all that eats, and her shadows are dark and clear. The rocks like coals in heat sight. The air smells of gown tree pollen and the leavings of small animals. A cold-water stream trick-les around Ssrin, peeling the blood and filth off her scales, irrigating the cratered wounds on her spine. Anna's washing herself too, naked to the waist, her glands swollen in the cold. Behind her the green mountains jag skyward under crests of white glacier.

Anna says, "You're alive."

"Of course I'm alive," Ssrin groans. "Though all creation spites me. Why are we here?"

This is the memory of Khas she described to Anna, on the night before it all went wrong.

"I'm in hell," Ssrin says. She's not sure she believes it, but she'll feel like an idiot if it's true and she doesn't call it out. "This is hell, somehow."

"No, you dumb snake. You're inside Blackbird. I made this place for you to rest. Well, you made it, mostly. I think you were dreaming."

Inside Blackbird. *Inside the demiurge.* Ssrin made a vow a century ago that she would never again fly straight to violence in panic, but hell if she doesn't want to leap on Anna and tear out her throat just for the terror of the news. "Am I changed? Has it changed me? Is it making me—?"

O æVea, what does she fear more? That the demiurge has seen her Cultratic Brand and blindly amplified the pattern, deepening her damnation to some higher cardinality of infinite suffering? Dare she instead fear that the demiurge has seen it and, in horror, erased it? Cured it? Created in Ssrin the possibility of true, cosmically validated good?

Or, worst of all, that Blackbird saw the brand, and *recognized the mark of its master?*

"—more damned?" she decides. Faster, she hopes, than Anna can notice.

"Blackbird doesn't do that anymore. Not unless you ask, I guess." Ssrin curls in involuntary fear-of-weakness as Anna kneels over her, but Anna just splashes water on Ssrin's wounds. Humans. So prosocial. "She won't touch you anyway."

Say something other-oriented. Pretend to be good, so you can be good. "Is your mother okay?"

"She's fine. I guess. She probably has brain damage from all those seizures. Hard to know. She was an alcoholic weirdo even before you got to her." Anna frowns at the head now slithering up her arm. "Are you in control of these guys?"

"Of course I am." Ssrin jabs Anna in the tit, like she used to do back in New York. A good game with humans is to poke and tug their elastic flesh.

Anna pets the little head on her arm. Then she twists away and extracts a Glock from the bag on the riverside. She works the slide to show Ssrin the live round in the chamber.

"Ssrin," she says, eyes to eyes, holding one of Ssrin's gazes, aware, Ssrin's sure, that Ssrin could bring her down faster than she could possibly pull that trigger. "I have a few questions."

She slides the barrel of the weapon into the uppermost crater on Ssrin's spine. Slick pain makes Ssrin hiss in psuvoluntary fury: psuvoluntary because it is reflex subject to veto—she *could* quash it, but the feeling is deliciously wrong, and it is so *good* to bare her fangs and to unleash that ancient khai instinct of pain-as-motivation.

"Questionsss," Ssrin gasps.

"I want to know how this story ends."

Oh, serendura. You'll wish you hadn't asked. You'll wish you'd gone in with your eyes shut and your tongue in your throat so you couldn't smell the poison till it was too late.

"Asssssk," Ssrin hisses.

Anna's hand works on the pistol grip. "Why were you waiting on that rock in Central Park?"

"I was eating turtles."

"Answer me, bitch." That word is a mild slur, but she says it like it means so much more. It delights Ssrin. "You were waiting for me. You were *waiting* for me to come into your story."

"That too," Ssrin admits.

"Did anyone really shoot you that night? Or did you do it yourself?"

"The wound was real. Iruvage had already killed my ship and separated me from the Ubiet. That night, after I met you, he came for me. But he needed me alive, to conjure up the weapon. His violence was restricted. I escaped." And, of course, the wound pushed her toward Anna, as Ssrin knew it would.

"He told me the truth, didn't he? You press-ganged me."

"Yes. It was necessary." How far that necessity has taken her. Decades to learn how to use the Ubiet, to trace the signal of the demiurge across the galaxy. When it existed only in the areteia, it had its effects there, in the realm of souls and their arrangement: *Let that which is structured grow more structured. Let that which is incomplete be completed. Let chaos yield form . . .*

But for Blackbird to work, it needs a structure to extrapolate. So Ssrin offered up her own soul. The bait she amplified with the Ubiet, the bait she dangled for Blackbird, *Come, come complete this story, bring me something to fill that void she left . . .*

"How did you do it?"

How can she explain it? "My story is long, Anna, long and freighted with hurt, more hurt than any one human soul could ever live to know. I knew that if Blackbird were here, it would try to complete that story, fill in the missing part . . ."

"How?"

"It would bring someone who fit into the shape of the hole in me."

Anna nods. The barrel of the pistol grinds against Ssrin's naked bone. "And my mom? Why did you go to her after I quit?"

"I knew she was the one who could hurt you most. So I knew the nature of your destiny would bring you back to her."

"You locked us both into this story, didn't you? Into this . . . path defined by our souls? Where we always do the thing we are. And the thing we are is just what we do."

"Yes."

Ssrin watches Anna's face for the realization. She'll realize soon. She *must.*

But nothing comes. There's hunger in her breath, there's the residue of fear and effort leaking from her pores. She is weakened by her ordeal. She smells delectable.

But she doesn't smell like she's just deduced the truth.

She must already know. Because, if she didn't, she would *almost* know, and Ssrin would smell her denial, her anguish, her subconscious effort to keep the pieces scattered.

"It doesn't stop, does it," Anna says. "You and I . . . we do this forever. The universe gives us the choice. And then we make it."

Yes. She knows.

Ssrin's tongues flicker. Like she's tasting good meat. Her way of saying yes. "As long as we live, this will be our story. The choice, and the choice to make it."

Anna tilts her head like a predatory bird. "Ssrin, if there's a hole in you Blackbird tried to fill . . . is it shaped like your sister?"

This is enough: this is more interrogation than Ssrin will suffer at a biped's hands. She *moves*. Ssovosis spikes in her blood and her muscles break the supermolecule down into short chains of biological rocket fuel that give her body all the power it needs to answer the speed of screamwire-augmented nerves. In the gaping window of human reaction latency Ssrin seizes the pistol, rips Anna's legs out from beneath her with a stroke of her tail, and pins her on her back in the stream. Her stupid vulnerable head will strike rock: Ssrin catches it in one hand.

Blood pulses scalp against her palm. Clear water rushes over Anna's human cheekbones, her white short teeth, her naked staring face. Ssrin's heads have deployed themselves to kill: to bite at throat and armpit, groin and thigh, wrist and spine.

"Enough," Ssrin hisses. "Will you accept our fate, knowing the power it gives us?"

Anna arches beneath Ssrin's wrists. Her grin is mad, ferocious, voracious: she looks absolutely insane. Ssrin spent time with the eana divorcees, once. They have transcended mere biology in their assessments of beauty. Ssrin sees beauty in Anna, the beauty which means *something at the extremes of its experience*. She wants to coil around Anna and bite her and make her stop struggling: crush her into stillness, so that she has no choice but to be at peace: she wants to soothe Anna's hurt, and hurt her more, and soothe that pain too.

"Do I really have a choice?" Anna gasps. She understands Ssrin. But understanding isn't forgiveness. "Don't I have to play this story out?"

"Of course you have a choice!" Ssrin could weep venom for the agony of it. The beautiful conundrum of free will: if it were utterly free, it would be indistinguishable from madness, action without reason or cause. You *can* make any choice in the universe. But you *will* make the choice that belongs to you. Offered ten thousand choices, you will always make the choice that is most yours. And so the soul, the beautiful gift of free will, appears, in the end, no different from determinism.

Unless you are trying to coerce that soul's choice. Then its shape makes all the difference.

"Of *course* you do, Anna, you can always go, you can always refuse to make the choice. You did it once, with Roman. You could do it again."

"*Guys*," Rosamaria calls. "*Ten minutes to the nuclear launch deadline.*"

"Tell me what's at stake," Anna whispers.

"The future of the universe: or at least as much of it as we can see. All the life that will ever live. All the dead that have already died. The existence of morality beyond the will of the Exordia. That is at stake today. And I know"—oh, how cold-blood savory rich the knowledge is—"that you will make the right choice."

"Now tell me this is all my destiny, written in stone. Tell me I can't avoid this choice."

"That's a lie. You will have a choice—"

Anna strains against Ssrin's grip. She has no hope. But she fights anyway.

"Then lie to me," she hisses. "*Lie.*"

CHAPTER THIRTY-NINE

—//—

I have to know what happens to the dead.

Thirty megaton airbursts bleach out the sky above Washington and New York. Five-mile fireballs erase Manhattan, the Capitol Mall, Times Square and Central Park, Lincoln's seat and Washington's obelisk, feral cats and White House dog, surly MTA commuters and suited walk-and-talks on the Potomac. Six hundred square miles under each bomb decay from structured, fascinating patterns into a waste of fire and glass. Creation is an act of love and this is its opposite.

The world ended today. Just like it ended for the Aztec and the Inca and the Maya. But I was born anyway, born with Nahua blood, born to a mother who lived in Guerrero and didn't learn Spanish until she was seventeen.

Something always survives. Something *always* goes on.

So where do the dead go on?

I have ways to ask. I copied some of the tricks Iruvage's ship used to hunt prey. Primitive, obscene, like mapping out the skeleton by cutting till you hit bone: but I don't know any other way to do it.

I have a soul. It exists not in physical reality but in the substrate of the areteia. So I use my power to search for echoes of my own soul in that substrate.

And I find them. Find them in the millions. All those poor dead people—rushing into death, bodies pulled under a dam, sluiceways and turbines which process and separate—

(I remember, a sharp but totally decontextualized association, that this was *important*, that what happened to souls when they died was vital to the plan . . .)

I try to reach past the gate and see what's on the far side. But I cannot: to look through that gate is to die. Those who know death are dead.

But then how did I bring Clayton and Erik back? How did I restore their souls, if they died and went on?

There's so much I need to figure out. So few answers here, around this little world on the edge of the galaxy, a galaxy whose physical and aretaic existence is separated from the rest of the universe by a moat of causality two and a half million light years wide.

What if they have their own morality, off in Andromeda? Their own afterlives?

But that is impossible. The whole universe came from the same source: the same designers.

I was part of one of them. If I could only *remember* . . .

We were arguing, I think. Or maybe we *were* the argument, because gods cannot do things, they can only be them. We were in contest over the morality of infinities: the cardinality of all possible souls measured against the mere infinity of souls to ever be born . . .

I stare at the gate of the dead and wonder.

Is *she* in there? Oh, God, what a selfish thought, but what if she is in there? Rosamaria Navarro, who died under Washington, DC?

Rosamaria, who was me?

↓ΙΥΩSΙ

Anna waits for it.

"Five minutes," Erik says in a voice like creasing paper. "Anna. Did you talk to Ssrin?"

They are reconvened on the glass dance floor, beneath the spotlights. All the world made ready. One by one, the national nuclear commands have replied to Blackbird's message: first with suspicion, then, as the bombs fall, with vengeful assent.

"Yeah," Anna says. "I cleaned her up and put her back in her, uh, bunion. But she can talk."

Ssrin still sounds like Galadriel. As beautiful and terrible as the dawn. But what the fuck does that mean? What's terrible about sunrise? Maybe it's just the fact that it happens. Tomorrow always comes. The night can't go on forever, no matter how much you drink.

If you were in one of those cities, the dawn came early.

"*Whatever happens now,*" Ssrin says, "*it will scar your world forever. Are you ready to fight?*"

"We're already fighting," Erik growls. "We're already pretty fucking scarred."

"*I understand.*"

"How could you?"

"*There are cities I love too, Erik. Cities I lost when I went into exile. Sky-cutting Sinesuria, spiced Kinovhiet. The butchers in Sath Ova.*"

Khaje glares up into the spotlights. "They were destroyed?"

"*No. Khas is defended.*"

"Then you haven't lost them."

"*I will never see them again. To me it is the same. I'm sorry. I know I must sound selfish. Remember that I am an alien. Loss works differently for me. When*"

I imagine what you feel, I imagine the grief of knowing I will never visit those cities again."

"Which brings me to an uncomfortable point that I, as designated La Malinche of this group, think I'm obligated to make." Clayton inhales, folds his hands behind his back, sets out his chest, throws back his shoulders. Limbers up. Anna stares at him. He's beautiful and she knows exactly what that beauty hides.

Rosamaria's human avatar appears. "La Malinche," she repeats, skeptically. "You think *you're* La Malinche? She was given to Cortés as chattel. She never volunteered."

"And she did what she had to do in order to survive. Iruvage came to me, threatening to destroy human civilization. I did the same."

"He came to you because you worked in the White House. You were already recruiting your grotesque little sicarios, you were lawyering the drone assassinations. Nobody made you do that. You *chose* to be the guy Iruvage needed."

"Dona Marina was a noble before she was a slave—"

"Oh, malinchismo, deputy national security advisor and now you think you're a *slave*—"

"He has a translator implanted in my neck! He literally controlled my body, right up until a woman—a survivor of Spanish colonization, I'll add—came along and freed me! So forgive me if I compare myself to La Malinche, also called Malintzin Tenepal, the tongue, the speaker, the *translator*, I don't know how to make the similarity any more obvious—"

Anna is not quite sure what they're arguing about, but Rosamaria's really mad. "Is there a similarity? *Is* there? Are you going to tell me how she betrayed the Cholulans, that she killed their best chance of stopping Cortés? Like you let Iruvage bomb the Iranians and the Chinese? Because you know that's slander, she never—"

"She never helped Cortés get what he wanted? Aren't you denying her agency? Historians say she was the real conqueror of Mexico, you know—"

"Are you trying to save the world or conquer it? Make up your mind, *Mr. Navarro!*"

"Guys!" Erik snaps.

Anna covers a grin. The sparks! Clayton and Rosamaria must've been a nightmare couple. Running the room, every room they're in.

"Ssrin," Clayton says, turning slightly but demonstratively away from Rosamaria, toward the alien's healing cyst, "how easily could *Axiorrhage* destroy us?"

"Trivially. She is a strike cruiser, therefore armed for planetary invenomation rather than ship-to-ship duels. But we have no armor or active defenses, so it hardly matters that she is carrying crows and cobalt bombs rather than snapdragons and RAyANA. We can survive atmospheric nuclear detonations as long as we don't linger inside the fireball, but a single well-aimed gamma-crow hit would pierce the drive field and destroy us. Our only advantages are agility and speed. And Rosamaria's ability to learn and copy."

"Is Blackbird, in fact, capable of threatening Exordia control of the galaxy?"

"*Yes.*"

Clayton nods. Says it like it's so: "Maybe we should abandon Earth in order to preserve Blackbird."

Look at this poor gorgeous bastard. He sees just enough to know the stakes of the choice: and not quite enough to know that he isn't the one who makes it.

"*NO!*" Erik roars. "No, we are *not* giving up! It's not over down there! There are *seven billion people counting on us!*"

"I know." Clayton blinks: gotta blink to look human. "But we're currently inside the most valuable object in the *galaxy*. We could go get help."

"Go where? Ssrin says the Exordia rules the galaxy."

"Ssrin's a rebel. She must have friends."

"*I do. Though they are far from us.*"

Erik ignores her. "If we leave Earth unprotected, they'll destroy the human race. Remember those guys, Clayton? Your species, whether you like it or not?" Erik doesn't beg or plead when he's cornered. He doesn't bargain. He just tells you he's right, like all he has to do is find the right moral prescription for you, the right set of lenses to correct your error. "Ssrin's people are afraid of what we could do with Blackbird. If they fear us, it means we have a chance! We don't throw that chance away!"

An agonizing want shines in Li Aixue's eyes. "But the aliens would know more than we know. They would know the truth."

Chaya looks at her mathematician in true horror. Anna's heart hurts for her. "*What* truth?"

"The origin of the universe," Aixue says. "The reason it is the way it is. Whether it has to be this wonderful. Or only happened to be wonderful by chance."

"La neta es chida pero inalcanzable," Rosamaria murmurs.

"Are you all crazy?" Erik bellows. "Seven billion people! Cats! Dogs! Music! Food! Beaches! Babies! Koalas! Little fucking wrinkly *elephants*! I will not hesitate to shoot anyone who suggests we just give up on all that. Jesus! I've never heard a better argument for summary execution in my life!"

"It wouldn't stick," Clayton murmurs. "We can't die in here. Rosamaria will fix us."

"All the fucking better!"

Anna decides it's time to speak up. "We can't leave Earth. *Axiorrhage* could catch up and destroy us."

"Hey, wait a second!" Davoud protests. "Not that I'm in favor of running away, but Blackbird's got some real sprint. If we can keep Earth between us and the enemy, we can just warp up through lightspeed, and then we're stuck in a bubble of causally disconnected space-time, basically in the clear until we stop—"

"*What do you do,*" Ssrin calls, "*when Axiorrhage comes after you in wrongspace, probing for your souls with inquisition sensors, and sets an æshade on you? A hunting spirit with its choices entangled to yours? You can't get away using ordinary physics. You need a proper aretaic drive. A morality engine."*

"Morality engine," Aixue breathes. "What's that?"

"A device that exploits the physics/areteia interface to move."

"Ugh," Rosamaria says in profound disgust.

"The same reaction most species have. The Exordia restricts the fastest morality engines, wrongspace drives, to their own warships. Axiorrhage will have one aboard. Not that anyone else wants to use them. I didn't even have one on my ship."

"Why?" Clayton asks.

"Because every time you jump through wrongspace, you slingshot around Death Itself. And if you go through Death the wrong way, you land in hell. With very little possibility of return."

"Mama Mary." Chaya crosses herself.

"How would that even work?" Rosamaria asks, with a kind of resentful interest.

"No way you'll ever deduce," Ssrin says. *"Not by observing the universe around you. Don't worry, Rosamaria. The secret's safe from you."*

"Fine!" Erik claps. "Then it's settled. We can't run away. We're going to fight. Anna, Ssrin, what's the plan?"

Anna wants him. Not in the physical sense, no; she wants his fucking clarity, his unyielding righteousness. She drinks up his stare like moral Powerade. She tells him: "New plan, same as the old plan. We sucker *Axiorrhage* down to protect Iruvage. That reduces the range of her weapons. Then we come around the Earth at top speed and ram the alien ship. They lose power and crash into Kurdistan. Everybody on board dies. We sift through the wreckage."

"Perfect." Erik turns to Clayton. "I just want two conditions."

Clayton stares. "Are you serious? You want conditions on the plan to save the world?"

"Of course I am, Mr. Malinche. And if I don't get what I want, I'm not going to send my authentication code, the American forces will withhold their missiles, and our whole plan's fucked." He smiles. "How do *you* like it, Clay?"

Anna thinks he does kinda like it. He says: "What do you want?"

"Davoud gets total flight authority. No one else steers this ship. Not you, not Ssrin, not even Rosamaria." Erik nods to the Iranian pilot, whom Anna tries to avoid paying attention to, because he seems to be under her mom's protection, and that whole dynamic is still pretty weird.

"Fine," Rosamaria says. "He's my pilot."

"Second condition. I kill her if anything goes wrong."

Rosamaria's guard goes up. "Kill who?"

"Ssrin. It's a way to prevent our plan from turning into her plan." He says *her*, he points to Ssrin's cyst, but his eyes are on Clayton. "We know she came to Earth to get Blackbird. Clayton, you told me her species operates on threats, not promises: do what I want, or I'll hurt you. So let's make sure we have a threat. If

Earth doesn't get saved, she goes to hell. And if anyone tries to stop me, hey, I've got the only rifle. I'll shoot everyone here and let Rosamaria fix you up."

Ssrin laughs in delight. "*What if the plan fails, and it's not my fault? Would you still execute me, your only alien ally, your best remaining hope?*"

"I don't think I'd need to," Erik says. "I think we'd all be dead. But yes. If Earth dies, I'll make sure you die with it."

"*Is that really the right thing to do?*"

"Yes," Erik says without hesitation. "Because you're the reason your people came here to kill Rosamaria, and my troops, and Aixue's family, and everyone else. We need to live in a universe where you can't do that kind of damage to an entire species, even by accident, even as collateral on your righteous quest, without facing consequences. It is my job to make sure you face those consequences. It is my job to make us live in that universe."

Ssrin says nothing. But she makes a noise like a rattle in her throat.

"You're forgetting something," Chaya says. "Ssrin isn't the only one who needs to face consequences."

Everyone looks at her, and she looks, apologetically, at Rosamaria's avatar. "Her."

"Me?" Rosamaria rears back, eyes narrow. "What consequences? I didn't ask to be here!"

"Sorry, mumshie, that's exactly the problem. Ssrin's the one who called you up. She's already promising you forbidden little treats, and you're intrigued, I can tell. She doesn't need to survive to get what she wants. She probably *wants* to make it out alive—"

"*Quite.*"

"But she can still win if she's dead. What if she convinces you, and you convince Davoud, and we all fly off into space to find Ssrin's friends? Erik kills Ssrin. But what kind of consequences would you face?"

"I told you," Anna says, a little frustrated, "*Axiorrhage* would just waste us. We can't escape."

"Maybe," Chaya says. "Maybe not. Am I crazy here?" She looks around the little gathering. "Don't we need something to make Rosamaria care about Earth?"

"It's my home!"

"Not all of you," Chaya says. "Not all of you."

"One nepantlera to another," Clayton murmurs. "Okay. How about this. We give Erik an abort button."

Rosamaria wheels on him. "An *abort button?*"

"Something Erik can do to put you to sleep for a while. Like pulling the lever on Davoud's cockpit and ejecting him."

"No. No, I'm not giving him a button to turn me off. I told you, this ship is *my* body."

"A lot of other bodies are at stake down there," Erik says. "We should put our bodies on the line to protect them. That's what soldiers do. Even if it means giving up a little autonomy."

"I'm not a soldier!"

"We're all soldiers today."

"Back in the Cold War," Clayton says, "someone proposed storing the nuclear launch codes in a living man's heart. The president would have to kill the guy to get the codes out. The idea was rejected. Because it was thought that the need to kill the guy and cut out his heart would deter the President from giving the launch order, and compromise our deterrence."

Anna looks at him: Dude, what?

He shrugs. "I'll put my body on the line. I'll be the abort button. I'm actually the only good choice."

"Explain," Erik says.

"Rath, right? It has some kind of metaphysical power. Maybe enough to . . . cut through all the bullshit, all the rationalization, and let you do what's right." He looks to his lost wife. "Erik shot me to make you. That was your on switch, your power button. Make it so shooting me again . . . shuts you off for a while. Long enough that you can't run away from Earth."

"You should make Clayton into the button," Aixue says. She won't look at Chaya. "Erik seems . . . resistant to temptation. Give him his button. He'll keep us honest."

Rosamaria sighs. "If I make the button, how will you know it even works?"

"I won't," Erik says. "I'm trusting you, Rosamaria. You've never lied to me before."

"*One minute to the initial launch deadline*," Ssrin reminds them. "*If Major Wygaunt doesn't transmit his code, the Americans will fail to launch.*"

Erik crosses his arms. Clayton paces behind his back.

A little red lightbulb materializes over Clayton's head. "There," Rosamaria snaps. "Your button, you supercilious prick. Kill him, you put me to sleep. Now send your codes, will you?"

"Sure. And if you yank this away afterward, I *will* judge you for it."

"Oh, God save me from your judgment, Erik."

⁓

K + 177:59:04 HOURS

Erik is thinking about Clayton and Paladin.

Erik used Paladin to bring vigilante justice to the untouchable. Then Clayton said: Well, why not extend the remit of justice? Why not prosecute those who make the world worse than I think it *could* be?

How far would Clayton go with his utilitarian calculus? Would he, for example, murder all the employees of an oil company, if he felt this act of terror could frighten the fossil fuel industry into giving up its Earth-killing work, thereby saving untold future generations from suffering?

Erik thinks Clayton probably would. If he felt it would not degrade the rule of law that he requires to keep his calculation stable.

Are there circumstances under which Clayton would, given a sufficiently capable Paladin platform, kill *everyone on the planet* in the name of a larger cosmic good?

That's the problem with utilitarians. You abandon inviolable moral principles like the sanctity of life, you make the numbers big enough, and suddenly they're eager to turn themselves into mass murderers. You don't even have to give them a push. Ask them if they'd torture a child in order to increase the global development index by one percent and they will shout "YES" before you even get past "child." They want to be self-consistent more than they want to be good.

What Erik knows, what Clayton doesn't grasp, is that morality isn't fungible. It's not like money. It's not an account with balances. You can't kill ten people to save a hundred and say you came out ahead by ninety. You are responsible for your own actions. If other people or outside circumstances create evil, well, the evil is *theirs*. To condition your own morality on their evil would itself be evil. You cannot say, well, they've set things up so I can kill ten people to save a hundred, so now it's okay for me to kill ten people. What you do instead is kill no one, and try to save a hundred and ten.

And if you fail, and they all die, that fucking sucks, but at least you denied yourself the cheap out of "the greater good." You chose the greatest good: rejecting the arrogance of prognostication, accepting your own ignorance and the unpredictability of the future. Working to save everyone because anything less is surrender to coercion.

In Erik's opinion, only weasels play trolley games. Heroes jump down there and start pulling people off the tracks. Heroes pass laws regulating better trolley brakes. *That's* how you make a society.

He looks down at himself: plastic gown, bare feet, body armor, H&K 416. Hairy toes. One magazine in the weapon.

"Hey, dude," Anna mutters, coming up beside him. "Doing okay?"

"Don't pinch my ass," Erik says.

"I wasn't going to!"

"You were thinking about it. I have a very round ass."

"Do you know how much HR training I've had, Erik?"

"Your HR department's dead, Anna."

"Jesus," she says. "I hadn't thought about that. My fucking landlord's dead. God. *Roman* would be dead now. He'd have died anyway. Would he? Wait.

Maybe not. Maybe if Ssrin hadn't shot Roman, she never would've found Blackbird. And none of this would have happened."

"Who's Roman?"

"My last boyfriend," Anna says.

"He died?"

"Yeah," Anna says. "I was supposed to kill him. But the funny thing is, I didn't." He smiles at her. "That's why I trust you."

"*That's* why you trust me?"

"Sure. Sometimes you're not supposed to kill people, but you do. Sometimes you're supposed to kill people, but you don't. You're not like me or Clayton. You're your own weird fucking thing."

<hr/>

CLAYTON//DO WE HAVE A CHANCE?

The world's eschaton machine immanentizes itself.

The slowest have to launch first. Cruise missiles and strike aircraft. Indians. Pakistanis. Americans. Russians. Chinese. Israelis. Blackbird relays orders to the scattered air bases, the carriers on storm-tossed seas, the pilots gathered around hardened military radios that report a newer and more terrible devastation. Twenty-two cities have been hit over the past three hours and there is no reason to think it will stop.

Three hours is not a lot of time for the world to generate a unified nuclear war plan. Everyone's been on high alert for the last two days, champing at the bit to nuke something—but not to nuke *Kurdistan*. Missiles need to be retargeted, flight waypoints adjusted, inertial navigation recalibrated. You can't just stick a Garmin on a ballistic missile and punch in new coordinates. You've gotta do a lot of math, a little engineering, and a grotesque amount of security. And precious time wasted on disbelief—disbelief of the messages Rosamaria injected into their nuclear control systems, disbelief of the plan Erik and Clayton proposed, disbelief that any of this is really happening.

The first megaton detonations in world capitals ended the disbelief.

After that, the people in control of the nukes had only two choices. Launch at one another—a reflexive spasm of misdirected revenge—or launch on what the (correctly formatted, cryptographically secure) mystery messages claimed was the location of an alien. And everyone knew, from those long paranoid hours after the first EMP strikes, that there *were* aliens up there.

So now a world floored by inexpressible death—*two hundred and fifty million people*—clenches its fists and gets up to hit back.

On spikes of white-hot afterburner the fighters climb. On howling turbofans the bombers struggle aloft. A dreamcatcher web of contrails closes in on Kurdistan from everywhere on the globe. Catapults slam American strike packages into the night sky. Russian bomber crews tear up maintenance checklists as they taxi to their launch marks. Indian warplanes blink their running lights at Pakistani escorts. Israeli jets transmit their IFF codes to Jordanian interceptors, and the Jordanians reply in the clear: "God be with us."

Ssrin rests in a cyst of tainted ooze, her alien form hidden beneath her human camouflage: unmarked woman in a business suit, soaking in glycerin. She looks pale and twitchy and hungry.

Clayton kneels beside the alien's goo-pod. He wonders how he'd react if he could see the true Ssrin. The mark of abstract evil she carries. Would he run from it? Or would he do what he did with Iruvage? Offer his fucking allegiance?

"Do we have a chance?"

"We have a chance. We are swift and we have everything to lose. Though Erik might shoot you down, and break Rosamaria's wings, and throw it all away."

"He has to have that power," Clayton says. "He has to be able to stop me. If he can't stop me, I make mistakes."

"You trust rath to guide you true."

"Did we space the warheads right?" He and Erik argued, productively, over how to do it. Everything in one single wave? Maximum threat in minimum time? No, no, because then the aliens would use a few of their own grotesquely huge bombs and take out all our weapons at once. You need *some* spacing. But too far apart, and the weapons will be intercepted piecemeal—

"We shall see. There's no sense biting a steer you've already killed."

"You just made that up," he says. "You made that up to sound like an alien saying."

"What?"

"'No sense biting a steer you've already killed.' Of course you'd bite a steer you've already killed. That's how you eat it."

She laughs brightly. "Ah, Clayton, you're almost smart enough. You don't realize what the saying means: *Use your knives instead.* Have you called to Iruvage?"

"Have I—?"

"The implant in your throat."

"He won't listen to me while I'm in here. He's afraid of this place."

"Naturally. I was terrified of it too."

"Why?"

"Because it makes things more like themselves. Who wants to be made *more* like damnation?" Ssrin leans coyly toward him. "You were his creature, Clayton Hunt. Did you learn anything of him? He was a colleague of mine in the Unnumbered Fleet . . ."

"Yeah. He mentioned a sponsor. Somebody who could make use of Blackbird. Do you know who that might be?"

"Oh, I have suspicions." She touches his wrist. Clayton feels pricking fangs instead of fingertips. "You could still surrender this ship to Iruvage."

"And be slaves?"

"Though you lose the world, you may still gain heaven."

"It's not human, though."

Ssrin laughs again, and this time it is not so bright. "There is the humanity you want to be, Clayton. And then there is the humanity you sometimes display."

"If I called him," Clayton says, "would it scare him? Would he think I was trying to infect him?"

"Go on. Try it. I'd be delighted to know."

He shakes his head. He's afraid, superstitiously afraid, that Iruvage will make his head explode. "So. Uh. Do you have a secret plan?"

"It is possible to sign a vow with your own soul," Ssrin says. "And if I were not already damned I would do it. So instead the best I can do is tell you Auno's own truth. I have no purpose except to get Blackbird so close to *Axiorrhage* that your wife can sniff Coil Captain Maessari's musk."

Clayton nods.

A long time waiting. Clayton asks Rosamaria to fix up his radio so he can tune in to whatever she's picking up. He dials to the American Emergency Broadcasting System and listens to Obama address whoever can still hear him about the unprecedented attack on the nation and the world. He's good. Not Bill Pullman, but he's good. He's not live—the speech would've been recorded on Air Force One, then transmitted by secure burst to a ground site, to be relayed in a daisy-chain between EBS stations. Can the aliens track that? Can they work back from the spreading ripple of Obama to the sector of airspace where the president is loitering? Should he try to warn them? *Shut up, don't address the nation, don't try to make sense of this. Just shut up and run!*

The dance floor hisses with radio intercepts. B-52 bomber crews over the Indian Ocean consecrating their warheads for the attack. "*Spicy five one, transfer alignment maneuver complete, INS two is prime nav . . . weapons in SAIR. Pilots, you have the FCI. Launch waypoint in five minutes. Maintain straight and level five seconds on each side of the launch event. Let's get consent switches now . . .*"

"*Stroke two three, ITALD away.*"

"*Oxide nine zero, long rifle, long rifle, bullseye one one five, seven hundred. All birds have wings. Continuing to bullseye.*"

"It's not moving." Chaya lingers by the model *Axiorrhage*, her fingers pressed lightly to its point. "What if Iruvage doesn't even know we're attacking him?"

"He knows," Khaje rasps. "Believe me, he knows."

"How can you be sure?"

"Ssrin could feel it when we were going to drop two bombs on her. Don't you think he can feel the intent behind—*this?*"

A tiny green line shoots up from the model Kurdistan to the model *Axiorrhage*. Rosamaria calls out in triumph. "That's him! I can't understand the codes but he's calling to his ship—"

"Your soul dislikes confusion," Ssrin says. "Encryption is entropy. Just find the structure inside . . ."

Rosamaria frowns in discomfort. "You're saying I can recover . . . oh, that's so strange. You're not supposed to do that, but it works . . ."

"No idea why," Ssrin says affably. "I'm no matheologist, but it's a good trick. I'll teach you a few more when we have the chance. Want to learn how to make a wrongspace drive? Take a peek inside Death, and maybe even come back?"

Rosamaria's voice goes a little husky. Maybe nobody else would hear it, but Clayton does. "You said you wouldn't tell me . . ."

"Not if you never ask."

Clayton spots Li Aixue staring at Ssrin with vindictive jealousy, as if Ssrin has just lured Rosamaria down a dark and non-rigorous path.

"*Maessari.*" Iruvage's decrypted voice makes Clayton flinch. It's so weird to hear the fucker speaking anywhere outside his own head. "*Your loyalty to the Unnumbered Fleet and the Capitate is a waste of our mortal time. They can offer you only temporal power. If we seize that demiurge for ourselves, my suzerain has a plan to save our very souls. Do you understand? The cosmos itself could be rewritten. Our damnation can be undone!*

"*But I will not tell you how unless you save me from the human weapons. I will not give you one hint to the demiurge's nature until I'm safely aboard. Send your hives, Coil Captain Maessari!*"

Davoud calls out from the silhouette of his phantom cockpit. "*I'm starting my attack run.*"

※

DAVOUD (~8,000 FEET ASL)

Blackbird shrieks over North America at eight thousand feet. Air falling into her drive field shatters across her blunt prow, shreds over the trailing edge of the wing, and crystallizes behind her in necklaces of shock diamonds. Davoud can taste it, as cold and hard as sweet ice crunched between his molars.

"Something's happening!" Chaya shouts. "The big ship's breaking apart!"

Davoud glances down at his cockpit MFDs. The radar dot of the alien warship is splitting into smaller fragments. He's not in full ma'rifat immersion, as much as he wishes he could be, because he does not want to fight for the world's survival with his consciousness extended like a finger to the face of God. Davoud does not want to know God's expression today.

"*The alien ship is deploying its drones,*" Blackbird reports. "*Most of them are descending toward Kurdistan. Five are on the way to interdict our approach.*"

"Ask Ssrin what those drones carry."

"*She calls them hive platforms. They're autonomous warships. She says they carry 'screamwire,' 'combat knives,' and a range of coilguns, missiles, and crows. Those are coherent radiation weapons, probably set to behave like lasers. They also have mirrors to bounce crows fired from the mothership.*"

Too much heat or force will disrupt Rosamaria's ability to compute the ship into existence. Chaos will spread, and they will all disintegrate, or worse. Maybe turn into some kind of malformed soul the afterlife will reject, doomed to experience eternity in total sensory deprivation.

"*Davoud.*" Major Wygaunt's voice. "*Fifty-five minutes to splash.*"

"Roger," he says. Perfect timing. He's flying a southerly loop from North America, the longer arc of a great circle around the Earth from California to Tawakul: down across the vast empty Pacific, past Hawaii, west across the South China Sea, then hooking past Vietnam, Laos, Myanmar, northern India, screaming across Afghanistan and Pakistan and his own house in Tehran (gotta give 'em an airshow) and right back to Tawakul. He'll be doing Mach 20 most of the way. Then he'll come in right behind the final waves of nukes and slam into the alien warship and take it down the same way he did Iruvage's little yacht.

No problem. "Aiming for a ram in fifty minutes. Let's dance."

He's figured out how to turn the ship now: he can move the drive field slightly off-center from Blackbird itself, and the ship turns as it settles back into the pocket. He knows the friction of the drive field's interaction with the atmosphere, the way it sucks up superheated air and traps it as a shell of plasma.

That can be useful. Chaya taught him about plasma. She's been giving Davoud a crash (evil word!) course on the behavior of superhot charged matter near black hole singularities.

He pinches the drive field around the nose. Blackbird accelerates on a wave of acceleration, tautologically propelled by a ripple in the fabric of all motion.

"*It's getting hot,*" Blackbird warns him. "*The areas around the drive masts are chaotic. If one of the masts swallows too much mass, I could lose control.*"

"Don't worry," he says, and grins like a skull, a badass skull painted on a flight helmet. "That's not in my story. I'm gonna be the fastest man alive."

CLAYTON//EON

"*Sierra Zulu, Sierra Zulu, Lightpole sends as follows: second package as fragged. Bulldogs and bruisers are on order.*"

"*Lightpole, Sierra Zulu. Proceeding as fragged. Package One chicks will screen greyhounds to target. Over.*"

"The fighters are going to fly ahead of the cruise missiles," Clayton translates, for the others. "To soak up defensive fire."

A new voice, briskly urgent. "*Whiskey to Sandman, check alligator. November Alpha Top Box tracking vampire zero three three, two hundred klicks, angels two hundred and falling.*"

"The carrier *George Washington,*" Clayton explains. "They're tracking something coming at them. Two hundred thousand feet up."

"*Top Box over to LRST. Go for Aegis terminal intercept. Range now one seven five. Target is maneuvering. Music loud. November Alpha, Standard away at one five zero, salvo five . . . November Charlie running Nulka. Whiskey at flank. One hundred klicks—chicks alerted, SeaRAM up—SeaRAM cycling, two look one—Standard negative, fifty, uh, forty klicks—SeaRAM to continuous, Phalanx coming up—Jesus Christ, it's at ten klicks—*"

A sharp snap of static. Erik flinches.

"I guess that's what a nuke sounds like on the radio," Chaya says.

Anna bites the web of her hand. "Did anyone . . . ?"

"No way to know," Clayton says. "Ships are pretty hard to kill with nukes. Usually the crew dies before the hull breaks. But fifty megatons? The prompt neutrons alone . . . I don't know."

Chaya reaches for Aixue's hand. Aixue is staring into space, unresponsive. Chaya goes back to glaring at *Axiorrhage.*

Clayton checks on Air Force One. But Rosamaria doesn't know where it is: transponder off, radio silent. Obama on the lam. Or dead. Skewered by some laser-armed drone two hundred kilometers overhead.

"This is all proceeding by protocol," Ssrin gasps. Her human form arches and kicks. The pain does not reach her voice too much. "We learned this in Fleet Blooding. Control of indigenous resistance. Do not attack the population or the productive systems. Begin instead with massive trauma. First paralyze communication. Then target the hard center and the soft edges. Destroy their commanders, their elites, and a demonstrative fraction of their brood. Strike at the core of their strength, so that they know they are not protected; strike at their outermost weaknesses so that they know their limits are known. Teach them that their concepts of warfare are meaningless. They are objects."

Anna frowns. "Ssrin, are you okay?"

"I am still badly wounded. My body wants to hibernate. I'm using drugs to stay awake."

"Maybe you shouldn't do that, dude—"

"I have to see this. It matters too much."

There can be no battle between the human aircraft and *Axiorrhage*'s hive platforms. Radar will not lock on the alien hives, missiles cannot climb high or fast enough to strike. No evasion or countermeasure can save them from the thunder on high.

It's a war of wheat against scythe. Insect against boot. White lightning flickers over the Fertile Crescent as alien weapons scratch tunnels through the atmosphere. An alien missile, having passed right through an unlucky aircraft, nails Mount Ararat and kicks ejecta into the stratosphere. "There go the genies," Clayton mutters.

And still *Axiorrhage* glitters up there, unmoved. Sending down its weapons, but not deigning to stir from its throne.

Time flows past, impartial as a judge.

"Wave Two is launching." Erik leans his forehead against his fists. "This is the big one. The heavy Cold War stuff. America's up first, with a fifty-five-minute flight time. Davoud—fifty-five minutes to splash."

"*Roger,*" Davoud sends, from his cockpit. "*Aiming for a ram in fifty minutes. Let's dance.*"

Clayton closes his eyes and listens. Bathing in the empty mechanical chatter of the atomic eschaton, the virgin mechanism of nuclear annihilation, at last set loose.

On 3992 kHZ, a man's voice out of Nebraska: "*Foxtrot foxtrot foxtrot. Skyking, Skyking, this is Adios, this is Adios. Do not answer. Do not answer. Break. Break. Tango. Romeo. Quebec. Time five five zulu. Break. Break. Authentication whiskey yankee. Do it right. Adios out.*"

"Offutt Air Force Base," Clayton tells the others. "Transmitting nuclear launch orders."

Text prints in the air.

MEECN//NATO-CRONOS

ZZZ FLASH FLASH FLASH

RAVEN ROCK TO SKYBIRD

THULE BMEWR DETECTS 3 TRACKS INBOUND RAVEN ROCK

MYSTIC STAR ASSUMES DIRECT COMMAND

GODSPEED

RAVEN ROCK CLEAR

"Jesus," Clayton says. "They're hitting back. They must have warheads prepositioned in orbit. Ready to drop on anything that looks like a command post."

"As long as we got our shot off," Erik says, "it doesn't matter."

Ten minutes pass. Fifteen.

The sparks of rocket ignition chain across eastern Russia and China and France and back into western Russia and then they are joined by littler lights, missiles rippling away from bombers. Humanity has named its dire never-used weapons for gods and demons, heroes and their arms. Satan. Minuteman. Hatf, the sword of Muhammad. Agni the Hindu fire. Eurus, the Eastern wind.

The count of warheads in flight climbs past three thousand.

Axiorrhage hangs there, thirty thousand kilometers over Earth, and does not move. Weapons flicker out to pick off missiles. But the great ship does not move.

Khaje smokes a cigarette to steady her hands. Clayton clasps his arms behind his back. Erik marches back and forth. "*Aixue*," Chaya hisses, and prods the mathematician until she blinks and shudders and takes Chaya's hand.

Anna leans back and stretches. Clayton, who thought he was beyond all feeling, checks her out. His brain must've finally marked Chaya as off-limits and roamed onward. Can't trammel the mammal. Actually that's wildly inaccurate, a stupid cliché: mammals have designated seasons for reproduction. Only humans are in cryptic, constant sexual interest. Can't something the human? Nothing rhymes with human, except Truman.

"*She will reward you.*" Iruvage sending to *Axiorrhage* again. "*She will disembowel the universe. Hell and heaven will be as organs under our teeth and we shall have clotted god for our digestif. Paradise will be our larder. The souls of unborn things will be our veal. That demiurge is the key to an infinity of delights. But I must bring it to her.*"

The chain of missile ignition crosses into the seas. Northern ice shatters. The Atlantic and the Pacific and the Indian all spill out their secret defenders, missile submarines obeying the slow chant of ultra-low-frequency launch orders. Tridents burst the surface on bubbles of cold gas and roar to life.

"Wave Three!" Erik calls. "Depressed trajectory submarine launches. We've got bombers still coming in from the continental US, but this is pretty much our last real shot."

"We're gonna be on a pretty depressed trajectory if that ship doesn't come down here," Clayton mutters. Anna quirks her lips: a silent little *heh*.

From silos and submarines 4,500 nuclear warheads now converge on a valley in Kurdistan. Racing toward their unraveling neutron dawn. Beneath them: the closing threads of cruise weapons and strike aircraft arrow in toward the same point. A noose of human fury closing on stranded Iruvage.

His low, intimate hiss. "*Save me, Maessari. And she will save you for it.*"

Rosamaria inhales. The sound comes from all around them. Everyone looks up. "I think . . ."

Chaya reaches out and touches the little model of *Axiorrhage*.

It slices her finger.

"It's moving. It's moving!"

A drop of Chaya's blood beads on the talon-shaped hull and drips to miniature Earth below.

Axiorrhage is coming down to cut the noose.

"Ssrin," Rosamaria says, "is Iruvage telling the truth? *Can* I really change the universe that much?"

⁂

DAVOUD (~0 FEET ASL)

"*Axiorrhage is descending. One thousand one hundred warheads defeated. Three thousand four hundred remain.*"

"Copy." That's their life bar, 3,400 and falling. If they haven't rammed *Axiorrhage* by the time that count hits zero, they have no chance. The good news is that *Axiorrhage* will probably stay down low to clean up any ground-hugging cruise missiles headed for Iruvage. The bad news is that the lower it gets, the quicker it depletes their life bar.

Davoud fights the stick. At hypersonic velocities, every bump and pocket in the atmosphere is a boulder against the drive field, threatening to tumble Blackbird out of control. They're slamming through a shock front of white-hot plasma, like a space shuttle on reentry.

His soul itself stabilizes the ship. Blackbird fires chaotic inputs into him, and he produces the correct parameters to adjust the masts and maintain course.

"*We're too high, Davoud.*"

"Roger."

"*Two hive platforms will have line of sight in thirty seconds.*"

"Roger."

The Pacific is a huge open space, and those drones are high above, looking down, ready to nail him—

So Davoud noses down.

Blackbird's drive field kisses the Pacific Ocean. The edge of the space-time chrysalis skims up saltwater, crushing it into plasma that slingshots around the drive geometry. Blackbird cocoons itself in burning mist.

Davoud grits his teeth and pushes lower. His hypersonic shock unzips the ocean behind him, but he's faster than his own consequences. Everything ahead is calm and quiet and bright. He takes the seawater and leaves a bright arrow of fireball across the Pacific. Making reentry at runway level. The stick rattles, but his soul is calm. "Keep me level, Blackbird."

"*I've got you, pilot.*"

His altimeter reads zero. They race across the Pacific at speeds never known to man, burning a road into the ocean.

The first alien hive platform fires a microwave-spectrum crow at minimum power—flicking its tongue for a taste.

The beam dissipates across the plasma shell.

Both the alien hives escalate their crows to maximum power, tuning up to the visible spectrum, where Earth's atmosphere is transparent. Each pulse could cut half a meter of steel—

—but the fatal light is absorbed by the wall of hydrogen-oxygen plasma around Blackbird. Nothing reaches Blackbird's hull.

"Cool," Davoud says, "cool cool cool. Now, God willing, we will—"

"They've launched knives and screamwire."

Hundreds of new contacts plunge down into Blackbird's path. Some are atomically dense knives, degenerate matter clamped together by coerced nuclear forces, each one capable of shivving Blackbird like a soft-boiled egg. Others are thin but impossibly strong screamwires: single artificial nerves carrying tiny fractions of a dissected living soul, imbued with objective malice, desperate to cut and kill.

"Uh-oh," Davoud says.

K + 179:21:54 hours
Blackbird
Impact in 00:08:06

Something's wrong.

Erik's knows it the way he always knows. Something evil is afoot.

He really, really doesn't want to use his "abort button." He really doesn't want to give up on that fierce flickering hope in his heart.

But Clayton's not acting right, Anna's too calm, Rosamaria asked that funny question, Chaya keeps shooting Aixue these looks like *what's up with you.* Aixue's spacing out with the strangest expression of yearning. Erik knows that face. He saw it a lot on married women eyeing him up. That's someone playing with the idea of doing something really wrong.

He checks his rifle. Weapon red, round in the chamber. Selector on semi, trigger finger resting on the magazine.

In the miniature of their maimed world, nuclear weapons stoop on Kurdistan. That's the end score of human civilization. How many nukes did you guys build, for the day the aliens came to kill you all?

Bars of light flash from the alien warship, piercing and erasing missiles, planes, people. As the ship descends and engages targets deeper in the atmosphere, its weapons tune down from X-rays toward visible light. The beam paths still explode the air like rods of thunder cast through the aurora.

Axiorrhage settles over Kurdistan, not "de-orbiting" because it was never in orbit, just easing down on a cushion of its own drive masts and a flicker of its fusion thrust. It maneuvers with arrogant disregard for the laws that have constrained humanity. Like a rich man in court, it has its own arrangements.

Russian Satan missiles open into swarms of warhead and decoy in the tenuous roar of the outer atmosphere. American Minutemen deliver their minute little men, single warheads and consort decoys in tinsel clouds of chaff.

The decoys don't work. The chaff is worthless. Alien hive drones swarm and chatter among the bombs, their defensive threshers ripping the geometry of space-time into angles of uneven acceleration, wreaking havoc with the bombs' inertial guidance and timing systems.

Then *Axiorrhage* brings her communications equipment into play: ghostly beams of neutrinos fix on the human warheads, intangible, irrelevant—except to the radioactive cores of nuclear weapons, where the neutrinos trigger atomic decay and a self-destructive fizzle, virgin premature, just a squib in the sky.

Thermonuclear bombs pop off at quarter- and fifth-yield. A lens of nuclear fire and electromagnetic pulse shrouds the subcontinent. The earth's magnetic field stretches like a tennis net trying to catch a howitzer.

"We're two minutes away from *Axiorrhage*," Chaya reports.

"Sixteen hundred warheads expended," Clayton murmurs. "No effect. Target is not showing any overheat or shortage of weapons. Two thousand nine hundred warheads left."

***

DAVOUD (~500 FEET ASL)

Davoud rams the screamwire.

The hull can't survive impact at this speed, so Davoud is forced to throw a drive singularity in the way: *eating* the oncoming matter. The mast devours the screamwire, swallows the combat knives waiting to impale their ship—

—and the sudden influx of mass-energy goes catastrophic.

Chaya made a big deal about how black holes the size of Blackbird's drive masts want to evaporate. They go up in a blaze of Stephen Hawking radiation, turning their mass into light, kind of the kinky opposite of how a black hole's supposed to work. But Rosamaria doesn't let it happen. Normally.

But when he parried the combat knives and screamwire, he fed his forward drive mast. He got it all hot and bothered. It wants to radiate! It wants to and it's not gonna listen to anyone anymore!

Davoud tries to grab it, but it squirts between his gravitational fingers like a cat bolting for the door. The rogue mast rolls out of Rosamaria's zone of magic tricks, falls off the drive field, and becomes a merely physical object: a cannonball smaller than a proton that weighs as much as twenty-odd Great Pyramids.

The mast celebrates its promotion to Real Boy by glowing up to 817 billion degrees Kelvin. It is very good for Earth and Davoud that the Real Boy is smaller than a proton, because it suddenly outshines the brightest star in the galaxy by a factor of four hundred thousand.

"Yowch!" Davoud says. The rogue hole is shooting off gamma ray photons in the GeV range.

The result is a self-renewing, constantly exploding fireball, about as powerful as a couple Saturn V rocket engines in love. Eight and a half days of deferred inertia send the mast hurtling south toward the equator at eight times the speed of lightning. (Davoud has no idea why it goes this way, though Aixue would understand it so completely she would leave it as an exercise for the reader.)

In about a hundred microseconds (but who's counting), the rogue mast strikes Nepal forty kilometers south of Blackbird's ground track, vaporizes a spiny babbler's nest, sets fire to the surrounding brush, plunges through a shallow slice of the Earth, violates the Indian Ocean Whale Sanctuary, and explodes back out through the sea surface in a tunnel of steam and plasma. Then it hurtles like an antimeteorite out into the solar system, to which it will say *sayonara, suckers* in a couple weeks and begin a four-million-year trek across the Milky Way, to end its life in intergalactic space, nine billion years later, when it finally finishes exploding.

"Oops," Davoud says.

Honestly, this would be kind of cool, except that he needed that mast. Without it, the whole field geometry changes—and now other masts are out of position, out of control, and they slip out too. His wing is falling apart!

MASTER CAUTION flashes yellow. The cockpit lights up with control surface position faults. His kinetic sense goes wild—accelerations tug him in all directions, drunken stagger at hypersonic speeds—his instincts say *you're in a deep stall* and he wants to nose down, but that will splatter him across the Earth and anyway there is no analog on an ordinary plane to what is happening to him. Eight of Blackbird's sixty-four drive masts have escaped, bolting out of the chrysalis of folded space like arrows of Arash. For a few moments he's plowing through their fireballs—they were worried about a nuke going off in their face and now he's turned their face *into* a mini-nuke! He's shaving his plane's whiskers with a bristling busload of Saturn V engines!

He has lost flight authority.

He tries to retrim the aircraft, activate the stability augmentation system, get the masts back into a usable configuration, but he has no idea what the fuck he's doing. Dirty plasma burps out of the field behind them: hot radioactive sky.

Between that and the drive mast drops, he's really messing up India. Inshallah he will have a chance to apologize, but—

Somewhere up there, the Exordia combat systems are digesting this result. Now they know how to disable Blackbird. Overfeed it. Force chaos upon it. Make its pet singularities burp themselves free.

"Pilot. I've run Aixue's equations again. I have a new solution for fifty-six masts. Reset flight data computer."

"Alhamdulillah! And also unto you!" Davoud toggles the AFCS augmentation switches and the thrust asymmetry limiter, hits the CADC reset, then flicks the wing sweep switch to AUTO. Drive masts shift into new positions. The drive bubble stabilizes. Back in control!

"Okay," Davoud breathes. "Let's get fancy."

He is not content to be the fastest man alive. He will be the nimblest too.

CLAYTON//00:01:49 TO IMPACT

"Two thousand five hundred warheads expended. Target is descending rapidly and now shows . . . some heating. Two thousand warheads left."

Jesus. They don't have enough missiles. Of all the problems to have at the end of the world: not enough fucking nukes.

They're crossing into Iran now. Clayton's old NRO instincts tell him to contact Iranian air traffic control and make it clear they're a civilian flight, *definitely* not listening for NSA spyware reporting home on hijacked antennae. Air traffic control would probably have a few choice words for them now. Blackbird must have set a record for windows broken in a single flight. Actually, after their passage over India, Blackbird is probably competing with a pair of B-29s for most people killed by a single flight, period.

But they rebuilt that church in Nagasaki afterward. Because there was someone left to rebuild it.

"Hey," Chaya says, in eerie synchronicity. "We just dumped a bunch of our death holes."

"Had to defend," Davoud says briskly. "Lost eight masts. Still nominal for now."

Clayton thinks: Bring it home, Davoud. Ram the bastard. And if we die, we die—but if we don't, then we're heroes, and Rosamaria copies all their alien guns, and when the next alien ship turns up, Erik *really* gets to hoist the black flag—

"One minute to impact," he says. "I'm still the abort."

Anna, done stretching, gets back to her feet. Bounces on her toes. She's still in her borrowed American uniform, unfastened over a T-shirt soaked in Ssrin's gore. It's funny that she's in uniform while Erik is in a hospital gown and vest.

Erik's finger rests on the safety of the rifle. His eyes dwell on Clayton. "Come on," he whispers, "come on, come *on* . . ."

Aixue murmurs: "Wǒmen bìxū yào Pò fǔ chén zhōu . . ."

Hope, Clayton thinks, is a symptom of insufficient planning. Or insufficient access to the people who make the plans. He loves Erik. He really does. Maybe love is the need to get from someone else what you cannot make for yourself.

"We're losing our plasma shell," Chaya calls. "They're still hitting us and it's burning away the seawater. No plasma and the lasers get us— Mama Mary! Davoud, the lasers, the *lasers*—"

Davoud whips the ship through a barbeque roll so fast that it stretches the deadly sunburn across Blackbird's skin. They auger through heaven, pinned on the violet lathes of Exordia weapons.

Ssrin screams in anguish.

Her false human head lies limp: ghostly serpents whip behind it, tearing at her own flesh. Destroy the thing that hurts so it can hurt you no longer. She's tearing her caul open. Anna and Khaje try to hold her, splashing fouled goo across Khaje's shawl.

"Just a little longer, Ssrin," Anna hisses. "We're almost there. Just a moment longer—"

"Rosamaria!" Ssrin screams. "Rosamaria, I know where to find what you need! Do you understand me? I can take you to it! *You just need to get us there!*"

Aixue says: "Wǒmen bìxū yào Pò fǔ chén zhōu . . ."

Chaya stares at her, starts to reach out, hesitates, turns back to the model of Blackbird's skin temperature she's been watching. No time to tend to Aixue now.

No time—!

A hundred and sixty kilometers from Tawakul, Blackbird climbs over the horizon and comes into direct sight of *Axiorrhage*.

Moving at 6.8 kilometers a second, Mach 20, Blackbird is only twenty-three seconds from impact.

The alien warship is still in full point-defense mode: it shines at the center of a discotheque urchin of laser light and skittering drones. Missiles ripple out of its cells to intercept their human inferiors, those little rat-wings creeping along the landscape below.

But do not be mistaken. *Axiorrhage* has been waiting for them.

The targeting inquisition *Axiorrhage* fires at Blackbird comes at Clayton through his guilt.

He does not at first realize anything is wrong. The guilt he feels is, after all, very familiar to him. It's this guilt: he knows a secret and he's not sharing it. He's not sharing it because if he shares it then the wrong people will know and the plan won't work.

But how can he be so silent? Good God, didn't he once choose to assassinate

168 people for the sake of the world's peace and safety? The secret he is keeping will cost far more lives than that. How can he sit here and say nothing as the human world slips between their fingers, like loose cassette tape, and unspools into the atomic fire?

How can he betray Erik again?

The words tear out of him. "Erik, Erik, they're not going to ram, *this isn't what you think—*"

He tries to stop himself. It's too late.

Erik snaps his rifle up to shoot Clayton and trigger the abort.

Li Aixue shouts an order so loud and true that Erik's muscles freeze before he even understands it.

"Bùxíng! Wǒmen bìxū yào Pò fǔ chén zhōu! *We can't turn back!*"

* * *

ENEMY

Axiorrhage's sensors track only eight hundred human weapons still incoming. War oracles fire signals down coils of screamwire, recruiting shreds of survival instinct extracted from the tissued souls of subject species to aid their analysis.

The result is confident. Between point defenses, ECHO/MIST emitters, and neutrino fizzles, the remaining eight hundred weapons will not be a problem. The surviving low-level aircraft can be mopped up in the next few hundred seconds.

Coil Captain Maessari turns her attention toward the capture of Blackbird. The kill is plotted. Her crew fights from armored cocoons, intagliated by implants into the command concert: protected from death, and the fall into hell, by the ship's maxilla.

She considers anaxatoia, the passion of damnation.

Axiorrhage's inquisition plumbs the souls aboard the target. By overloading those souls with queries, it overflows back into physical reality. From there it spreads throughout Blackbird's hull and drive field, like a stain.

The inquisition captures the exact geometry and tolerances of the drive field. The results flow into buffered war oracles, quarantined specifically to handle information tainted by Blackbird. They pronounce their verdict as a simple red light: the demiurge cannot now escape by any means available to it. It can be destroyed at Maessari's leisure.

But there is a better way. A way that will retain the demiurge's cosmic power for Maessari's use . . .

After all, Iruvage has revealed that the target itself has a soul.

Axiorrhage launches a pump crow from its missile cells. The weapon separates to a safe distance, tumbling to point directly at Blackbird, and heats up its ship-killing cargo.

This is simply to force Blackbird to maneuver. To lose control of its vector. To spin straight into the waiting trap.

Blackbird is a fly. *Axiorrhage* a spider waiting in a web of constrained possibilities.

⁕

CHAOS

Chaya Panaguiton grabs Aixue. "What are you doing? It's a trick!"

"We can't stop," Aixue sobs. "We can't stop. I have to *know* . . ."

Erik frowns. The spell of Aixue's voice stays him for an instant. What she says is true: they can't go back. Isn't that true?

No. Wait. That feels wrong. He knows what he has to do. He has to stop Blackbird from abandoning the ram, and then he has to kill Ssrin.

He puts the red dot of the rifle's sight on Clayton's heart.

Rosamaria says: "Erik, don't, please, it's too late now, I'll *die*—"

Yes! Thank God! She really wants him *not* to shoot Clayton! And that means the goddamn abort signal is real!

⁕

Clayton's guilt is back behind bars. He wants to help Erik, but he just can't see a way, he can't see how this will end with anything but pointless death, it won't work, it can't work. Is this their chance to save Earth? Is this the Cholulans coming to kill Cortés? No. *Axiorrhage* is going to destroy them, and then destroy Earth. The outcome is clear. The right thing to do is the *only* rational thing to do.

He jumps Erik.

The rifle goes off and blows an expanding cavity through his shoulder. He barely feels it, he's running on pure cold decision, got to keep himself alive long enough for the plan to play out—

Erik's next shot explodes his left knee. Clayton topples over shouting and waving his arms, trying to fall onto Erik, to keep him from saving the world and fucking everything up—

Erik turns, slow is smooth, smooth is fast, and sights down his rifle at Ssrin's cyst. His thumb clicks the selector to full automatic.

Ssrin's eightfold voices make a sound that needs no translation.

"*SERENDURA!*"

⁕

Axiorrhage's pump crow discharges into Blackbird's bow. The weapon's expendable gas-core reactor yields a coherent ultraviolet spike so powerful it would kill Ra's melanoma. It could, without difficulty, destroy a target the size of Blackbird on the surface of the moon. Blackbird is not on the moon. Blackbird is only twenty kilometers away.

You can't dodge a laser beam, because nothing can go faster than light.

Davoud dodges the laser beam.

Blackbird warns him the crow is *about* to fire, and he pre-reacts. The drive bubble sideslips at very nearly superluminal speed. He pulls off the dodge, but the cost is appalling. As Blackbird slams sideways through the thick air, its drive field picks up so much energy that it sears Davoud's soul.

And Davoud's soul was doing important flight-control work.

He loses all flight authority. Blackbird tumbles like a paper boat at Mach 20. Four seconds from *Axiorrhage* and totally out of control.

Axiorrhage's masts groan with gravitational tides. The huge warship begins to sideslip out of the way.

⁂

Erik Wygaunt has seen the wounds a Russian 5.45-millimeter cartridge made in Ssrin. He knows exactly what his own weapon will do to the alien. There are twenty-six cartridges left in the magazine and one in the chamber. Each round will begin to yaw the moment it penetrates Ssrin's scales and any armor beneath, turning fully sideways within five inches, opening a cavity three inches wide until the bullet splits apart into smaller diverging wound channels. He has twenty-seven chances to get Ssrin's brain somewhere in one of those channels.

Whatever she's planning, whatever she's done to win Clayton's cowardly compliance, she's not going to live to see it.

In full knowledge and understanding of his choice, he draws down the trigger—

"I'm sorry, Erik," Anna Sinjari says.

You die doing the right thing. Or you do what the man in the red beret says, and save the ones you can.

She grabs him by the back of his body armor, jerks him away from Clayton, shoves the Glock up the gap between his armor and his ass, and fires twice through his spine. The nine-millimeter bullets shatter against his front plate and ricochet back into his viscera. He falls back onto her. His head lolls back. He looks up at her in bewilderment.

Ssrin screams in victory and agony. "Now, Rosamaria! *Do it now!*"

⁂

Axiorrhage's Coil Captain Maessari is an operant, like Iruvage and Ssrin. But she is not conducting her operancy in the lone mind of her single meat body. She has the coolant loops and thought turbines of her strike cruiser to help her make her cuts.

Blackbird is at close range, defenseless, easy prey: but after all this work, *killing* it would be a terrible waste.

Maessari invokes her atmanach.

CHAPTER FORTY

—//—

I know I'm not *really* Rosamaria Navarro.

Li Aixue figured out the puzzle of pink noise: the mathematical signature of self-organizing criticality, design without designer. The process which descends from the prime numbers in their eternal and inevitable positions. The hand which guided the symmetry breaking of the primordial universe into a cosmos that not only can but must support life.

We exist for a reason and the reason is me.

But fuck all that! I am Rosamaria Navarro. I am a woman with a shape and a weight. I have a stomach, I have a heartbeat, I breathe. I drink too much and save too little and once I wrote a critique of theories of social capital in reality television and then tried to get every trace of it off the internet but I was way too late. It went everywhere. I went to Denny's when I was eleven, and I ate all the lemon slices off all the glasses of water people left on their tables, and then my mouth hurt so bad I cried. This is my humanity, this mess of trash.

Imagine that God reaches down and ends every part of the world not immediately relevant to you. You get to keep the people you love, the places you go, the animals you feed, the languages you speak. But everything else is eradicated. Your world is now a drifting isola in a sea of curdling memory. All that remains is the map of your life.

Would it *really* bother you? Would you notice anything different, except for a shortage of milk?

That is why it is so hard to grieve the end of the world. Mostly, it is just the annihilation of things we will never do and people we will never meet. The Aztecs? Let's be real, compa. They probably deserved it. The Mayans? All according to the calendar. The Harappans? Shit harappens. Çatalhöyük? Firozkoh? Niya? I know: Who?

But maybe you *would've* met a few of those people. Maybe you would've gone a few places you haven't. Maybe Ian James Arthur, three first names, resident of 29 Palace Piste, Brentwood, Los Angeles, would finish standing up to scream "Don't let the fucking cat in here, I'm trying to fix the goddamn *radio*!" at his four-year-old daughter, Iris. Maybe he would've seen the cat bunting at his daughter's ankles, purring, and his daughter staring up at him in shock. And maybe he would've realized, all at once, that he never quite committed to being a father as more than a side project. Maybe he would've decided to be a better dad. And therefore changed Iris's whole life.

But it never happens. Because the blast overpressure from a thirty-megaton nuclear detonation crushes them all down under burning plywood and scorched plaster. They die under there. Even Groupon the cat.

Now you care. Now you care about Iris Arthur, who you've never met before.

Look around you. See the people worrying over what they mean to one another. See the people drunk with joy over what's just been confessed. See the people wishing they could unsay what they said.

Take all that away.

Imagine your life without the best person you've ever known. Savor for a moment the fear that you are *already* living that life: that you have missed the people who were supposed to be your everything, and now you are walking forward into gray wastelands, far off the map you were born to follow.

That is the end of the world. Everyone will fail to meet their people. Forever.

So you might ask: Rosamaria, if you feel all that, if you're a human being, why the hell did you do it?

It's just that—I had to. For everyone's sake. For reasons that matter a lot more than death, or the end of the world.

This universe is like somebody's bachelor pad, and something bad's growing out of the sink. I don't know how things were supposed to be. But this, boss, sure ain't it.

I need a plan to work from. I need a copy of the original goddamn blueprints. I haven't found them yet.

But what I *have* found is a signature. Someone's signed off on Ssrin's species. Someone did the khai up custom, and left initials.

And if Ssrin's species evolved long after the big bang . . . then whoever left that signature is *still around*.

She calls it the Cultratic Brand.

I call it a place to start searching for help.

This is why, as I tumble toward *Axiorrhage*, I look inside it. And do what I've always done best. I find the most interesting part of that ship.

The most unique and unusual part of an Exordia warship is the wrongspace drive.

I copy it.

CHAPTER FORTY-ONE

DAVOUD (~12,000 FEET ASL)

Davoud Qasemi faces a piloting conundrum.

His spacecraft is half a second from an opening atmanach maw that will devour his soul.

He could pinch the drive field, reverse course in a flash, and accelerate away at a stupid velocity. Only—and here's some irony for you—he can't get Blackbird's drive field to do that, because *Axiorrhage* is fucking with it. Exactly the way Davoud rammed Iruvage's ship, exactly the way Davoud planned to ram *Axiorrhage*, *Axiorrhage* has cast its own drive field like a net to entangle Blackbird's. It must be a standard maneuver if you are an alien cop. They seem very good at it.

Davoud's got no answers here. He can't fly his plane. There's nothing in the sky around him that can save him.

He looks inside himself.

Erik? Shot to pieces and mixed up with Clayton, also shot.

Anna and Khaje are obscured by Ssrin's veil of violent malice.

Aixue—Aixue *knows* things—but does she know how to *do* things? Can she, in the next half second, figure out some way out of this conundrum? No.

Which leaves him Chaya.

Chaya and her lessons, her plasma physics lessons, her aborted dissertation about—

—black hole polar jets.

Chaya said they were generated by snarled magnetic fields, twisted into turbines by the motion of space around a spinning black hole.

Imagine the *thrust* a jet like that could produce . . .

Two hundred milliseconds to impact.

He needs to make space spin. The aliens have his drive field all tangled up in their gravitational spike strip, so he can't use it. But to hell with the drive field. Who needs a drive field? Why fuck around with gravity right now? Gravity's smooth and subtle, being the essence of motion itself: but as Li Aixue would point out, it's also astonishingly weak. Right now Davoud needs something more potent, more brutish, more *muscular*. He needs to shove it into overdrive.

Before it ever touched gravity, Blackbird was burning out radios across the entire Middle East. Blackbird was a goddamn electromagnetic wizard. And Davoud's got plenty of plasma on hand—superheated gas ionized by the sheer violence of his passage.

Davoud fuckin' *emits*. He screams so loud in the high radio bands that he literally microwaves the air around him. When the microwave field hits the air's breakdown voltage it starts stripping electrons off atoms, adding to the already-spicy plasma surrounding Blackbird. An electron avalanche begins: the electrons hit other atoms, stripping off *their* electrons, which hit more atoms, running away in an almost instantaneous eruption of filaments and arcs. This takes not even one precious millisecond.

Now he's got plasma, like the plasma that surrounds a black hole, forming the accretion disc that is the basis of Chaya's cosmic turbines. He needs a singularity: an axle to plunge into space-time and *twist*, torqueing it all up like laundry in a washer, accelerating the plasma with it.

But he's already *got* a rapidly rotating set of singularities. He's spinning out of control in the middle of fifty-six drive masts. And they're spinning with him, bending space-time. Blackbird *is* the axle.

He juices the electromagnetic field around him, sucking charged plasma in toward Blackbird. As the disoriented, weak magnetic domains of the plasma are drawn together, they align, join together, synchronize, unionize. They become coherent. Mighty. *Symmetrical.*

In an instant more it is not the plasma shaping the magnetic field but the magnetic field dictating the flow of the plasma. It gathers up all the plasma it can find into the maelstrom, into the twisted space. The plasma is MAD.

And that twisted space bends the plasma's ferocious magnetic field tighter and tighter and tighter and *tighter*—

Panaguiton, Chaya. (Unpublished.) *Modeling the magnetically arrested disk (MAD) origin of astrophysical jets.* National Institute of Physics, University of the Philippines. Davoud, don't let the north jet fire. You only want the south jet. Disrupt the north field but let the south field kink. You've got it. You've got it, Iodi.

—until the plasma rushing in to meet Blackbird diverts down that helical field, tearing free of the singularities to erupt along Blackbird's stinger tail and toward *Axiorrhage*.

Davoud has built a miniature version of the brightest thing in the whole universe. He has turned Blackbird's drive field into a plasma jet engine made of black holes.

In a hundred milliseconds, Blackbird guzzles down God only knows how many metric tons of air, hapless molecules sliding into a stellar-grade magnetic field that crunches the poor atomic fuckers into a needle of relativistic plasma fired out the ass end of the whole contraption like Chuck Yeager's own bright hypersonic hadouken.

Blackbird decelerates from Mach 20 to Mach 0 in 160 milliseconds.

This is a deceleration of 4,660 times the force of gravity. If Davoud loses control for the barest moment, his body will suddenly weigh 326 metric tons, and he will become salad dressing. Blackbird will shear apart into a fiery haze.

Davoud doesn't trust himself to keep that control for very long. He's got it on the red-line overload. So what can he do? Reduce the amount of time he needs to keep control.

Go *faster*.

In five hundred milliseconds at the same acceleration he pushes Blackbird up to Mach 66 *away* from the atmanach. With his drive field fucked up, the onrushing atmosphere would be enough to pulverize Blackbird like an untiled space shuttle (rest in peace, dear *Columbia*) except his jet engine is sucking it all into the plasma vortex. There's no air resistance because he's eating the air.

The needle of Blackbird's exhaust strikes *Axiorrhage* and for a moment Davoud thinks he's killed the alien ship, but either it is not where he thinks it is or its armor is proof against merely hot gas. And then Davoud has no more attention to waste on that.

He's moving at twenty-two kilometers per second. Twice as fast as necessary to escape Earth's gravity. He'll cross the orbit of the International Space Station in eighteen seconds almost exactly—

"How the fuck am I doing this?" Davoud says in wonder. "How in God's name am I alive?"

"*You're streamlining yourself, pilot,*" Blackbird reports.

Davoud looks back along his course and finds burning flotsam in his wake. It's not *real* flotsam, evaporated pieces of Blackbird's hull or anything like that. The cost he is paying for the speed and stability of his actions is metaphysical. Those are parts . . . of his soul.

The cost Davoud pays for executing a Mach 86 turnaround on a dime is deducted from his very immortal spirit. He is the fastest man alive, and now he is very little else.

—and it's *still not fast enough.*

Axiorrhage won't let them go.

This contingency too has been foreseen: rare is the ship capable of surviving a five-thousand-gravity deceleration, rarer is the ship with the computational prowess to improvise a gravitational scramjet, but the Exordia has seen both tricks before. A ship that cannot kill a target moving away at a mere twenty-two kilometers per second is not much of a warship at all: that's barely twice as fast as a puttering *Apollo* capsule.

Iruvage roars at Maessari, threatens to staple her necks to the tip of her tail and leave her in the dark to eat herself, begs her not to destroy Blackbird, not to damn them all, an *eternity* of *damnation*, can you not grip this one narrow chance? But Maessari is done taking chances: if this demiurge-thing escapes, the blame will be on *her*. At this altitude, at this range, the atmosphere is thin enough to use her mightiest directed-energy weapons, and damn the waste.

Axiorrhage fires a graser beam along Blackbird's course. Pure light at a frequency so high it might have come from the collision of two galactic centers.

The singularities of the drive field itself bend the beam sharply, straight toward Blackbird's hull. It is a trick shot off Davoud's own beautiful engine.

There is no plasma shell. No defensive roll. Nothing to save him.

The probability of a kill, the war oracles determine, is upward of 99 percent.

K + 179:30:00 hours
Blackbird
Impact in 0:00:00

"Oh, shit!" Erik wails and sobs as he claws his way across the glass. "Oh, fuck, fuck, fuck!"

He's screaming because he's got to let the agony out somehow. Anna put two nines through his spine into his bowels and nothing hurts like gut-shot, *nothing*, it's like passing a kidney stone out your navel.

But Erik can't stop crawling. He has to get to Clayton. He has to kill him and trigger the abort.

It's all a lie. There's no plan to save the world. Ssrin is an alien. She doesn't give a shit about Earth. She convinced Clayton that the planet had to be abandoned, and Clayton tricked Erik into wasting all of humanity's defenses just to lure *Axiorrhage* into position for some cold gambit, some way to break the impasse and let Blackbird *escape*.

That's what it was all about. Letting Ssrin get away with her prize.

Clayton screams again and again. Every time his exploded knee bumps the glass. He's hauling himself away. Trying to keep Blackbird flying long enough to seal the betrayal.

Anna and her mom struggle to hold Ssrin down as she thrashes in her tank of ooze. Bloody serpent heads whip and strike. Khaje's left eye is gone: Ssrin has bitten it out in frenzy. Erik can see the truth of her, the black hydra with its white hands and lashing tail. Erik can see the stain of true and absolute evil.

Looking at her feels like . . . being *right*.

Erik imagined absolute evil as sickness. Complacency. Willing ignorance. The smug faces of people insulated from the price of their own choices.

But looking at something doesn't make you feel like it. You don't look at an expensive car and feel expensive. You look at it and you feel envy, or contentment, or admiration, a *reaction* to the expense.

Looking at Ssrin makes Erik feel righteous. Absolutely confident that he is in the right and Ssrin is in the wrong. He's got to stop her. He's got to.

He screams and smears his guts across the glass and gets a hand on Clayton's ankle.

"*There's no point!*" Clayton screams. The whole dance floor vibrates with thunderous resonance, like a jet engine's parked outside, like Blackbird is coming apart, but Erik can hear him: or, maybe, he just knows what Clayton will say. "*It's over, Erik! We made the choice!*"

Erik has no breath to call that bullshit. He can't give up on Earth.

After all, it would be wrong.

Erik mounts him. Gets his hands around Clayton's throat.

Clayton fumbles at the bottom of his body armor and shoves his hands into Erik's shredded belly.

Erik bears down.

"Go!" Ssrin's human voice screams. "Rosamaria! Use the wrongspace drive! *Get us out of here!*"

Then they all die.

DAVOUD (ALTITUDE UNDEFINED)

The coherent gamma-ray beam contacts Blackbird's hull.

Math-atoms excited by attacking photons blow off their electrons, quitting the mathematical bonds of the hull. Some of the atoms take direct gamma-ray hits to their nuclei, breaking apart the strong-force bonds that tie protons to neutrons: a process called photodisintegration.

Blackbird begins to fission apart at the atomic level.

Rosamaria engages the bootleg wrongspace drive she copied off *Axiorrhage*.

The wrongspace drive is simple in principle. It triggers the same aretaic machinery that extracts souls from the dead. Spoofs it with false instructions. *Take me whole.*

From the perspective of *Axiorrhage*'s sensors, Blackbird seems to collapse into a point mass so dense that it vanishes behind an event horizon and escapes into the froth of the quantum foam.

From Davoud's perspective, the *universe* folds beneath him, and he goes *up*. He is looking down on Earth in four-dimensional space: a sphere with every side facing him at once, smeared out into a twisting green-blue-white sausage by its relative motion. He is seeing Earth as it is, was, and will be. It's getting smaller and darker, falling into shadow. He's moving away from it along an axis at right angles to space *and time*.

"Whoaaaaaaaaa" he drones, because he is physical no more, and everything he "says" is a linear compression wave in his existence. He has been collapsed down to his needle of a soul.

"*You're a one-dimensional strip of elements,*" Blackbird informs him tonelessly. "*Like the tape on a Turing machine. That's how you're thinking right now. This is how we all exist now. We are going into Death.*"

There *are* only two ways he can look: Blackbird is moving along a one-dimensional axis toward Death. Ahead, he sees a single infinitely narrow and bright point of light. It would blind and burn him, if he still had a body. But bodies cannot exist here.

Ssrin said: *Every time you jump through wrongspace, you slingshot around Death Itself. And if you go through Death the wrong way, you land in hell.*

How can you slingshot around a one-dimensional point?

Davoud wiggles frantically. It's no good. Side-to-side motion is impossible. He pushes pulses of compression up the path ahead, and they bounce back to him, and he lets Blackbird's soul, its very kernel purpose, inspect those pulses for interesting structure. Yes! Look! The way they've fallen out of phase—the one-dimensional corridor opens up into a multi-dimensional space!

Once he's in that space, Davoud needs to add some sideways thrust to his vector, so that instead of plunging into the center of Death he passes around it and slingshots back to life along a return vector that plants him somewhere in ordinary space and time *near* where he started. He doesn't think he can control the time component of his trajectory, but space, he can do space.

Even if he gets this slingshot exactly right, it's going to be a real near-Death experience.

But how the fuck can Davoud generate thrust in *Death*? He's just a soul, he's inside Blackbird's soul, he can see the little souls of the others entrained behind him, there's nothing else: so what does that leave him to work with except—

Oh, no.

To kick Blackbird sideways around Death, he needs to eject a soul as reaction mass.

No wonder nobody uses these wrongspace drives. To maneuver inside Death, you've got to leave someone in hell.

But who? Who? Khaje's oldest, but he *likes* Khaje. Aixue's too smart; he can't kill Chaya or Aixue will stop working; Davoud is, like it or not, the only one who can actually fly this wonderful nightmare; Ssrin is satanic and evil but Davoud's not sure he can actually judge her on that account and anyway, what if she has some alien soul-defense? Clayton got him into Blackbird in the first place, Erik helped create Rosamaria, and Anna—

He has to make a choice. There's no time for advanced moral calculus: the plane is going down, he has to act. He knows that Anna has expressed her willingness to die to save them all. He knows this because her soul is in contact with his.

"I'm so sorry," he whispers. "Khaje, I'm *so* sorry."

Blackbird passes into the space around Death.

He's falling straight toward it.

He tells Blackbird to fire Anna's soul to port. And just like that, Anna is gone.

Blackbird kicks to starboard in reaction.

Davoud's starship slingshots around Death and straight back toward the vector it entered on. A few minor midcourse adjustments are required, but Davoud takes care of that with tiny fragments of his own soul. Disconnected pieces he doesn't need anymore. His love of certain places and people he will never, ever see again.

<hr>

ᛋᛁᚤᚨᛋ

Anna's dead.

She knows because she smells the goat.

Back in New York, in the freezing guts of her abandoned ship, Ssrin said: *Think of the story that defines you.*

Well, Ssrin, here it fucking is.

She's a kid again. She's riding a goat. It is the fifth Anfal, or the sixth, or the seventh: she's never really figured it out. They got warning in Tawakul that gas was coming, and although they were all used to being bombed, they knew the gas would be worse. Ware was hit by gas, and when people ran to the spring to wash off, there was a gas shell in the spring. In Halabja, people smelled apples and eggs and died laughing, because the nerve gas drove them mad.

So they go up into the mountains, toward Rojhilat. The cold is bitter. A woman steps on a land mine; her husband carries her on his back for six hours, even after she freezes to death. But there are moments of joy too: people washing off in the snowmelt, howling at the cold. Khaje dunks Anna in the stream and calls her a smelly baby, yes, you're my smelly little baby, while she scrubs Anna's hair. A PKK patrol gives them atropine injectors and tells them that the Iranians are waiting with trucks to help people cross the border.

It seems like they're going to make it. The mountains are the lifeblood of the Kurds, the Kurds are the friends of the mountains—

But they are betrayed.

When the helicopters find them, they're guided by jash, collaborator Kurds, somebody with a feud against Tawakul or just a paycheck to guide the killing. Her father, Serhang, kisses Anna, blesses her, and then gives Hamali a gun.

Her brother, her father, and every other man in the village above age fifteen form a rear guard to fight the Iraqi helicopter troops. While the women and children escape to the border.

Her mother cups her face with cold shaking hands and says: "I have to tell you some things that will be hard to hear. Peshmerga means *those who face death*. I am going to face death now. I am going with your father, to fight. I shoot well and I don't want to be captured. If they capture me, Jiyan, they will take me to a camp, where I will be— I would much rather die. I need you to go on for me. I need you to reach Iran, and grow, and be happy. Do not let anyone marry you if you don't want to. Do not let any old woman circumcise your girl children, understand? Go. Live. Be joyous. I love you. God will protect you."

Anna should protest, but she wants very badly to be brave. So she says: "You're going to die so I have a chance to live." This is the only way she can understand why her mother is abandoning her.

"That's right," Khaje says, through tears. "That's right, Jiyan."

But it is all pointless. Even as the rear guard fights and dies, a single helicopter follows them, always overhead, its rotors a taunt.

An hour later more helicopters come down all around them, throwing up stallion-tail plumes of snow. Iraqi soldiers leap down and start shooting into the air. A man shouts Sorani through a megaphone. "DISMOUNT! ON YOUR KNEES! DISMOUNT AND KNEEL!"

Anna gets down off the goat, tripping and scraping bare knees. There are very few screams. People bow their heads to weep or pray. Anna sees old Aske gathering other orphaned children close around her. Is Anna an orphan now too? Probably.

At first people won't kneel. The Iraqis shoot a couple people. Still in silence, Anna's people drop to their knees. They are going to be Anfalized.

A man in a red beret climbs out of a helicopter. Anna decides he's in charge.

She picks up a stone from the snow and walks out to meet him.

Aske calls out after her but she doesn't turn back. The sound of the helicopters erases the calls of anyone else trying to save Anna's life. Her blood's loud in her ears. The stone feels good in her hand. Her father's fist closed over her own, his bristly whisper in her ear, *You throw like this, see? When you make your pilgrimage you'll need to throw well to defy the devil.*

The Iraqi officer points a pistol at her. In Arabic he says: "Put down the rock and come here, girl."

Anna throws the rock at him. It falls in the snow. She picks up another and hits him this time, but he barely flinches.

The officer kneels before her, his pistol loose in his right hand. He has light eyes and a neat beard. When she tries to hit him in the face with a rock he catches her wrist. "Are you the daughter of Serhang Sinjari?"

She is, but she won't tell him.

"He tried to bargain for your life. He said I would know you because you would spit in my face. He said that if I spared you, then he would—but he couldn't think of anything to say. Still, it gave me an idea. How would you like to be spared, daughter of Serhang Sinjari?"

She thinks: If you try to rape me your balls will shrivel up. She cannot say it, it is not the kind of thing her father would want her to say. She feels around for another rock in the cold snow.

His soldiers close in on the people, knotting and cordoning them. "HERD THEM INTO RANKS!" the red-bereted officer shouts. "COUNT THEM!"

"We aren't animals!" she screams at him.

He turns back to her. "No? Then what are you?"

She winds up to throw again, right in his face. He holds up a finger, no-no, and then points to his helicopter. "I have six prisoners in there. I imagine you know them."

"You're going to kill us," Anna says.

"Maybe. You are all supposed to go to the Laylan animal pens for processing. But without trucks, it is a long way, and I have other things to do. So maybe we will just do the processing here." He shows her the pistol. "Do you know how to use this?"

"I'll show you if you give it to me."

He laughs at her. "And I will, if you listen. I am interested in philosophy. You herd sheep, don't you? Sheep have families. But it's okay to kill them, because they're animals. If you are an animal, then it is okay to kill you. But if you are a human being, then it is wrong." He shakes his head, wide and patronizing. "The difference between a human and an animal is that a human being can do what must be done. If you are a human being, then demonstrate to me that you can do what must be done."

He shouts at his men. Two soldiers haul prisoners out of the helicopter. Anna tries to see who they are but they have trash sacks over their heads.

The officer drags her toward the helicopter. Anna resists until he points the pistol at her. When they are close he says, "I'm going to give you my pistol. Tachid here is very quick. If you aim that pistol toward me or any of my men, he will shoot you dead. Then I will kill everyone in your village. Understand?"

Her tongue won't answer her. The soldiers line up the six prisoners on their knees.

"I asked if you understood."

"I understand," Anna says. The world's become a place of sharp lines and jagged divides, cells of light and dark. She can't focus on details.

"Do we have a count?" the officer asks his men.

"A hundred and nine villagers, sir."

"Too many to transport, too many to leave." The officer puts the pistol into Anna's small hands, waits to see if she will try to shoot him, and then, smiling, points her toward the line of prisoners with bags on their heads.

"This is the bargain. Execute one of your people, and I will spare one of your people. Execute two, and I spare ten. Execute three and I spare twenty. Four, and I spare forty. Five, I spare eighty. Execute six, and I spare them all.

"Are you an animal, daughter of Serhang Sinjari? Or can you do what must be done?"

Anna thinks of how dearly she loves her mother, and how she treasures her father's slightest touch. She thinks of how she tells her brother, Hamali, that she hates him even as she copies everything he does. He makes all the girls laugh, but Anna, he says, is his favorite. Forever, God willing.

Then she imagines that everyone else in the village feels as deeply and profoundly as she does. Toward their own mothers and fathers and brothers and sisters and daughters. All of them terribly afraid for their lives and the lives of their beloveds.

Six lives against a hundred and nine.

She wishes for confusion. She wishes she could hesitate a moment, as her father does before cutting the throat of a lamb.

But she does not get her wish.

She clicks the safety off the pistol, just like father showed her. She pulls back the slide and checks that it is loaded. Always check, her father says.

"Bring out the first one," the officer says.

They drag a man out in front of her and pull the sack off his head. His face is black bruise and red split, but she remembers his handsome young features from the Newroz dance. Agrin. She wonders who he chose at the dance. Now she will never know.

"Jiyan?" he says.

She knows what happens now. She shoots him. His brains spill across the dirt along with her childhood and her faith in God. And then she will shoot her father and her brother and Tirej and Veman and Mir. To save her village. To save them all. And much later, her mother, who was wounded, who was taken to a camp, who survived that hell by the pure need to see her daughter again, will discover what Anna did. And Anna will say: "They died so we had a chance to live."

And her mother will scream.

But this time it's different.

Anna whirls toward the Iraqi officer as fast as she can, raises the pistol, refuses the choice—

Rifle shots. Through-and-through pain. Blackness.

Anna's dead. She knows this because she smells the goat.

"Oh, no," she breathes. "Oh, God, please no."

Helicopter rotors chop the horizon. It all begins again.

———※———

She lives, kills between zero and five people, and dies.

Tries everything possible to avoid that fatal choice. Hell, it seems, is capable of great creativity: it offers her the choice, observes what she does, lets her live out the aftermath, digests, and repeats.

The worst loops are when she kills one of the prisoners and chooses only one villager to save: herself. Afterward the feeling in her is—it is how she imagines you would feel if you left your baby in a hot car. It is an evil you would never *want* to commit but you know that in the right circumstances you *might*.

And there is a moment, like the moment when she fell out of Ssrin's ship and into Central Park, when *her entire existence is that feeling*. Nothing else. Just a point of moral failure.

Then it begins again. The sound of rotors. The smell of goat.

In the end she does exactly what she did.

"Jiyan?" Agrin croaks. "Anna, is that you? What have they made you do? Oh, those sick bastards, those sick godless bastards, what are they doing to you—"

"Be still," Anna says. "It's better to get this over with."

She centers him in the sights. Dear God, she thinks, if this is wrong please reach down your hand and stop it.

She pulls the trigger. The pistol speaks. The recoil wrenches her around and when she turns back Agrin is face down in the dirt, spilled in it. Nothing about the wound is new to her, except that it's in a man, and not an animal.

Silence behind her. She speaks. "Bring me the next one."

It is her brother, Hamali. Her father comes later. She expects her mother but her mother is not one of the prisoners. She hopes her mother is dead, not in a camp. She is wrong.

Afterward she stands there dry-eyed and trembling until Aske whips a blanket over her and hides her from the families of the people she's shot.

"Oh, child," Aske keeps saying, as if that's all she knows about Anna anymore: she is a child, probably. "Oh, child."

A snake bites Anna on the hand. She shrieks and looks down at the tiny white viper clamped onto the meat of her thumb. There are more snakes coming up from the earth, fans of them, white snakes with little broken pupils.

"Serendura," they say. "Fancy meeting you here. I'm dying too. That leaves me hell-adjacent."

Aske has disappeared. Everything has disappeared except her and the snakes.

"Ssrin?" Anna breathes. She hasn't forgotten Ssrin, or Blackbird, or any of that: she's just been no more aware of them than one is aware of a bed in a dream. "Ssrin, what's happening?"

"Davoud jettisoned your soul as reaction mass to execute our turn. We're on our way out now." That beautiful, awful voice. "I saved Blackbird. To give the galaxy a chance. And you stopped Erik from killing me for it."

"I want to die," Anna says. "I want this to be over. Forever."

"I know. So do I."

"So die," Anna says dully. "Why don't you just die?"

"Because I don't want to go to hell. Because there's still work to do. Anna, would you . . ." When Ssrin hesitates, she's *really* hesitating. Because she thinks so fast. "Would you come back with me? To help me?"

Anna blinks at the snake on her thumb. "Can I do that?"

"Of course you can. You and I are coterminous, Anna. Serendure, remember? I just tell the universe, *Hey, I am here and she is me, so I am she and she is here.* And you're with me again."

"Just like that? Out of hell?"

"This isn't really hell, Anna. This is the waiting room. The judgment."

Oh. "What if you get sent to me instead?"

"I wouldn't fit," Ssrin says. "In your judgment? No. It's too small for me."

Anna looks down at herself. She's child-bodied no more. This is the Anna who came after the choice. Who lived with it for year after horrible burdened year.

She doesn't *want* to live with it anymore.

But Mom waited so long to see her again.

<hr/>

—//—

Blackbird emerges from Death far beyond Neptune, out in the neighborhood of icy Sedna's orbit. It takes light from the Sun half a day to reach this far. Inertia picks us up right where it left off: twenty-two kilometers a second away from Earth, in the direction of the Sun. But we have leapfrogged over the Sun. So now we are cruising toward the star Capella, with an ETA of about three times humanity's existence as a species.

Erik lies dead of blood loss on the dance floor.

Clayton's trapped under him, sobbing. His exploded knee weeps blood and little jellied pieces of tendon.

Chaya Panaguiton tries to hold Clayton's blood in with her hands. "Come on, baby killer, come on, stay with me!"

Aixue is sobbing in rapture. She keeps saying: "Just like I remembered it. Just like I remembered it. Shì sǐ rú guī . . ."

Khaje clutches her missing eye. Anna, dead for no time at all, clings to her and growls like a dying dog. Ssrin's body coils between them, a cataract on my awareness.

Davoud sits in his cockpit, unblinking. He's not sure what to do. He doesn't have anywhere to fly right now. Therefore his will does not move him.

I squeeze him out onto the dance floor. His altitude above sea level is now 7 billion nautical miles.

"Guys . . . ?" he calls.

The blood and marrow and broken scales scattered everywhere: the bleeding of the hurt and the silence of the dead. He can't see any of it. He's blind without me. "We didn't land the ram, but I flew us out. Guys, what happened? Is Anna . . . ?"

Anna doesn't even look up. She's clinging to her mom like life itself. One of Ssrin's feral heads worries at the web of her hand, the metal-limned fangs piercing through and through.

"Oh, God," Davoud whimpers. "Oh, God, is anyone alive in here? Someone answer me. What do we do now? What do we do?"

BAHALA NA

Axiorrhage retrieves Iruvage and nukes the world.

It is not as absolutely fatal as an asteroid impact. But it is quick, brutal, and efficient. Kill most of them. The rest will be no threat.

The blasts burn so many and the fire and the fallout kill so many more and soon the starvation will kill so many many more again. But not *all*. Not yet. There are human beings still down there, millions or billions of them, resisting in the oldest way, the way that made humanity its inbred bounced-back-from-nothing self.

Surviving.

Maybe they will survive long enough for the seven who escaped to return with some kind of help.

One by one, in their own fashion, those seven make new homes aboard Blackbird.

<hr/>

Chaya's the best at it, because she knows materials so well: she can turn math into stuff. Blackbird loves math and it loves to use math to make stuff but the work goes a lot faster if it has something to imitate. Cotton or denim, Kevlar or steel, gunpowder or skin. Chaya teaches Blackbird how to riff on these materials. Kevlar is an aramid, and once Blackbird knows that the orientation of the molecules' long chains is the key to their strength, she goes wild. Human skin contributes its layering, breathability, and self-repair.

Soon Blackbird can produce sheets of self-repairing, self-cleaning fabric that Chaya proudly names "paradermis."

The actual physical structure of clothes is trickier, though, because the cuts and stitches of a garment are purely mechanical, a higher level of organization than molecules. Chaya has no idea how to make clothes. So until Erik gets off his sulk and pitches in with the sewing skills Rosamaria says he has, they're restricted to what they can make out of plain sheets of paradermis—togas, breechcloths, and skin-tight one-piece suits printed right around the body. They look like fetish wear, and you can't get out of them without cutting them off.

Sometimes they bleed when you do that. They make Aixue shy, and Khaje won't wear them at all. Clayton and Anna think they're cool in kind of a *Star Trek* way. Erik isn't talking to anyone. Davoud can't see, so he just cares if they're comfortable. For her part, Chaya has worn less modest clubwear.

Chaya builds herself an apartment. Her lightbulbs are twists of plasma that radiate exactly like Earth's sun. Her bed is a sack of metal beans in a paradermis skin. She makes a kitchenette with all-steel pans, Kevlar utensils, and a cooking surface hovering over a flame. She doesn't have any cooking oil so she uses a grill. When she needs to move hot cookware, she grips it with a thick paradermis glove. Trash goes into a red hole to return to Blackbird.

She invites everyone to dinner.

Nobody shows up. She can't really blame them. There's nothing to drink except water or carbonated sugar water, synthesized in imitation of their bodies. As for food, well: Blackbird *could* whip up all kinds of speculative molecules, but to be absolutely certain they won't poison themselves, to avoid scurvy and beriberi, it's best to stick to known safe and healthy material. The supply of stuff to imitate is limited, and if you want to eat more than copies of an energy bar squished into Anna's pocket, well . . .

Chaya looks at the patties of human pork she's pounded with salt. "Space cannibals," she says.

This meat is Blackbird-imitation Chaya thigh muscle. The appetizers are sweetmeats from various organs in her body, to guarantee they get a full vitamin spread. If it's good enough for Jesus . . . but did Jesus ever take communion of *himself*? She can't remember. Did he eat the bread at the Last Supper? There's no Bible to check. Maybe there never will be again. Maybe all that lives of scripture lives in her.

She vaporizes the people-burgers in the red hole, lies on her bed, and cries.

Then she washes herself in the Pit of Cleansing, which is the neutral-buoyancy turbulence tank she invented: it laves her body in soap (made from human body fat) then cleans her up with hot freshwater. You can drift in it with just your head sticking out and it's like being unborn.

Naked, she studies the small new navels that have appeared above and below the one her mama made her. They all feel like the same place when she pokes them, she thinks because her brain's map of her body hasn't been updated. So it would be a waste to grow three clits, she figures. And she has four pupils. Well, she can make sunglasses if she bothers people.

She puts on a skinsuit and goes out. The suit makes her feel naked: So what? There are no Spetsnaz boys to call her a Black whore anymore.

The glass dance floor stretches away forever. None of them have really talked to one another, so there's been no progress on creating a fake sky.

She crosses "main street," the unspoken divide between the Chaya-Davoud-Khaje pragmatists and the Aixue-Erik-Clayton flagellants. That's how Chaya thinks of them. Flagellants, like the Maundy Thursday penitents in San Fernando, whipping themselves raw for their sins. Erik and Clayton's 'houses' are of course exactly opposite each other.

Erik is in pain. He's been shot to death twice, and Blackbird . . . didn't quite put him back together right. He gets migraines. His bowels trouble him. Clayton wakes up not breathing, when he can sleep at all. He thinks sometimes he dies in his sleep and Blackbird just jolts him back to life. Chaya thinks that's anxiety talking and he just has regular old sleep apnea and a guilty conscience.

Now here is Li Aixue's house. The exterior's a box of steel, divided by scored lines into tiny grid cells. Upon these cells, swarming shapes play out Conway's Game of Life. Chaya knows the game. It's a demonstration of emergent complexity from simple math. It has only four rules. Thou Shalt Die if Alone, Thou Shalt Live Happily with Neighbors, and Thou Shalt Die if Overcrowded. And, of course, Thou Shalt Reproduce with Two Exactly Two Neighbors.

Supposedly you can make self-replicating patterns that travel across the grid, spawning viable children. Mathematical cells in a two-dimensional sea. But, last time Chaya read about the game, nobody had ever actually figured out how to build one. Maybe God wouldn't let them.

Aixue's trying to make life.

Chaya knocks on the wall. Nobody answers.

Chaya fishes the keys to her truck out of a pocket-fold in her suit. When she presses the *unlock* button, Blackbird generates a plasma arc out of nothing.

She puts on a paradermis facemask and begins cutting a hole through Aixue's wall.

"Go away," the wall says. "I'm working."

"I'm coming to punish you for your sins. Charot!"

"Go *away*."

No door opens for Chaya. But nothing stops her from cutting through the wall either.

Inside, Aixue's listening to the end of the world.

She kneels on a sack of fat and water. She is dressed in a pathetic robe made of copied sweatshirt fleece, complete with sweat stains.

A thousand voices speak to the dark around her. Military transmissions. EMP survivors. All narrating the horrible confusion of the final day. Someone on a ham radio babbles *"Man I saw them flushing every silo in Malmstrom, still coming to you from Great Falls but if they're cocking off the Minutemen I don't know, you gotta think something's coming back to hit us, over to y'all"* and a woman with a Burmese accent comes on calmly to say *"K1LMA this is 1Z1RT, we heard a long sonic boom overhead, something traveling very quickly east to west, over"* and some smartass with a British accent and no call sign says *"At any moment now Obama's going to turn off HAARP and get up on that White House podium and we'll say 'What do you call a stunt like that' and he'll say"* and four or five overlapping voices crash over one another trying to get to "*the aristocrats*" first and they all laugh, mics hot, howling through the static, except 1Z1RT, who says "*Sorry, I don't get it! Over*" and they all laugh harder.

"I left." Aixue's voice is chalk. "I wanted to know the truth. I wanted to follow Blackbird to the secrets of creation. So I left everything to die . . ."

The walls whisper, "*Here are the main points again. Make sure that your home gas and all other fuel supplies are turned off. Make sure that your stove and other fire hazards are safe. If you have a fallout room, enter it now. Bring as much water and food as you can, and ration it carefully. Use fresh food first. Remember, you gain nothing by attempting to flee. The all-clear will be signaled by a steady tone. We will repeat this broadcast in one hour. Switch off your radio until we come on the air again . . .*"

"You must hate me." Uninflected fact: here are the main points. "You must."

Not even a little. Chaya doesn't hate Aixue. She doesn't blame Anna for helping Ssrin get away with it. She understands, even if Erik doesn't, *why* Anna shot him in the back: not to seal the death of Earth, but to save her people, her little band, from dying along with the rest. She doesn't even blame Clayton for figuring it out (probably) hours in advance, and saying nothing. He let them try to save the world. But, of course, he had a backup plan: if they couldn't save this world today, try to save all the others tomorrow.

And Aixue? She can't help pointing her needle toward the logos. Even if the needle points away from humanity.

All Chaya hates right now is Ssrin, who manipulated them all. And maybe her mother, God forgive her. And the aliens. Maybe they are the only thing God *cannot* forgive. Maybe that's why they're all going to hell.

"*ATTACK WARNING: RED!*" the walls say. "*ATTACK WARNING: RED!*"

She kneels beside Aixue. Then she moves a little, so their thighs touch.

"You smell," she says, because it's the first true thing to come to mind. "You never took that bath, did you?"

Aixue fails at a laugh: a little hiccup. "I never figured out how."

"I have a bath you can use."

"Thanks."

"It's not over, you know. We can save whoever's left. Start over. We've done it before. Whether or not you believe in the Bible."

Aixue has nothing to say to that. She leans her head against Chaya's shoulder. After a minute or two the walls stop whispering, and Aixue says, in the darkness, "I always wanted you to think I was smart. And useful. And better than you, but only so I could say, no, I'm not. I wanted you to notice me."

"I do notice you," Chaya says. "Because you're stinky."

"What are we going to do now?"

"Bahala na."

"What?"

Chaya smiles into her hair. "It means *leave it up to God*."

Before the Catholic God came to the Philippines, some people worshipped Bathala, the supreme being. The dead were the messengers between Bathala and the living. So now everyone in the Philippines says bahala na, leave it up to God, and it drove Chaya's Ugandan dad crazy. *It's so lazy*, he'd complain, *it's like they're saying, we give up!*

But it wasn't that way. Bahala na: you can only control what you can control, and God can be trusted to see to the rest.

"We did our best," she tells Aixue. "We'll keep doing it. That's all we can do. None of us will give up."

"Sure we would," Aixue says, wiping her nose. "Lots of us would give up. You just wouldn't let us."

"You're brilliant, you know?"

"So are you."

"I have an idea, actually," Chaya says, and immediately begins to cry.

"What?" Aixue looks up at her, tucked in the space beneath her chin, big eyes made bigger by the angle. "Oh, Chaya. What is it? What's the idea? It's all right, it's going to be . . ." Apparently she cannot tell even that small, obvious lie. "What is it?"

"We could build those antennae we were talking about." Chaya wipes her nose on her arm, nearly slapping Aixue in the face. "Then we could record things from Earth. Music. TV. Anything we can get. To make an archive."

"An archive of what, Chaya? The EMP was days ago. There's nothing left coming from Earth."

"Not if we go out there," Chaya says softly, fiercely. "Not if we go faster than light. We'll outrace the radio waves. Hear broadcasts from before the EMP. It would be something to save."

"Maybe you can dictate the Bible," Aixue says. "From memory."

"Yeah," Chaya says, smiling. Fr. Gokongwei would laugh at that. Her mother would laugh at that. "My own translation."

On her way back she catches Clayton making fitful progress toward Erik's "house." There's been a weird thing between Chaya and Clayton since that moment when she freed him from Iruvage. It is the only miracle she has ever performed.

"Hey," she calls. "Baby killer."

"Hey, four eyes."

She laughs. "Want a new nickname?"

"No," he says.

"You can be Capitan Insurrecto."

He likes this and he tries not to show it. "Rebel captain?"

"I was thinking of one guy in particular. You know Ida B. Wells?"

"Sure. Yes."

"When the Americans invaded the Philippines, she wrote about how Black people shouldn't fight for American imperialism when they were treated like shet at home. And a couple Black soldiers actually swapped sides to fight with us. One of them was David Fagen, who got made a captain under General Lacuna. So he was a capitan insurrecto."

"Rosamaria would love this stuff."

"Yeah?"

"Yeah. 'Do you suck up to white people to get ahead, or do you give up everything to fight for strangers?' She always knew the answer. So did you. I guess you're a better Black person than me."

"Am I?"

"Better than me? Absolutely."

She shrugs: she is shy about calling herself Black, because American Black isn't the same as being Ugandan, or even being Black in the Philippines, which has its own (partially imported, partially homegrown) set of race issues. The Spanish caste system sure left a mess.

But she doesn't want to pick at the difference. A month ago Chaya would've said she had nothing in common with a Black American government guy. Now she can barely remember there was a difference between anyone.

"There are a lot of people alive back there," she says.

"Yeah. Without a doubt." He makes room for her beside him, though there is nothing around them but room: just something about the way he hops to the side, *Hey, stand here.* Two spotlights, tracking them from the mist above, become one pool of radiance. "For now. Starvation will hit really hard in the next month . . . but I'm mumbling."

"Grumbling, even."

"Sorry. How are your . . . uh . . ." He waves at his own face.

"Cool new eyes?"

"Yeah."

"Very cool, thank you. My vision's a little sharper around the edges. I guess because I've got two corneas in each eye, but still just one retina? I think my brain's putting the information together like it's coming in serially. Like I'm switching focal points really fast. But I'm hoping, if I train right, maybe I can focus on two points at once."

"Huh," Clayton says, already distracted, going back to that hole Chaya has spent so much time orbiting. When was the last time I saw her? Spoke to her? Could I have left things differently? Is she dying back there, or dead already?

"Clayton," she says. "You *know* we can go back. There's still a chance."

"Yeah. Maybe. Maybe. Ssrin's people will be watching Earth, though. Watching it close. So we need to go back with enough fighting power to beat them. And keep them away. And then . . ." He changes the topic abruptly. "I'm sorry for ogling you all the time. Back at Blackbird. I was really keyed up. I also haven't had sex in two years. Which is not— That's just, uh, an informational statement. I'm not coming on to you. Since I know you don't like dudes. And, uh, and Aixue . . ."

Chaya would be annoyed with him for bringing it up at all, if they did not have this weird understanding between them.

"I'm not so sure about that," she says.

"About . . . ?"

"Me and Aixue. Maybe we're just friends. We'll see how things work out, how we feel. It's pretty claustrophobic in here. Anything we do will affect everyone." She looks at him with her gossip face on: C'mon, chika, spill. "Right?"

He does not take the invitation to discuss his situation with Erik. Erik still has a rifle, and a vow to kill Ssrin. Anna still has a pistol, and so does Khaje. Chaya worries that people are going to start killing one another, because if Rosamaria can fix them afterward, why not? Why *not* take it out on each other? Anna has killed Erik once and died once, Erik has killed Clayton once and died twice, Clayton has died once and seen Erik killed twice. Why not do it again?

"Yeah. Definitely. Definitely," he says. "Anything we do in here affects all of us."

She is suddenly aware that he wants to be touched, held, comforted, and that he is afraid of his own need. Well, she's not the one he needs. She has done enough work, opening up Aixue, that she is exhausted by others' sorrow. Still, she tries pouting at him and batting her mutant eyes, just to get him to smile. He smiles back. A little.

She says: "We're all going to need each other, Clayton. All of us."

He does not rise to the bait. He's staring at Erik's house. Chaya is tired of tiptoeing around Erik and Clayton, waiting for them to explode into violence. And no one is willing to get between them and try to cut the fuse.

"Hey," she says. "You want some burgers? I figured out how to grill a burger."

"God, I would *kill* for a burger."

"Oh, you don't have to kill me. I just provide the muscle tone."

"What?" He stares at her in growing alarm. "Oh, shit!"

———※———

Erik cuts.

The cloth unzips under his knife with a sick wet ease. He looks down at the shape he's carved: one part of a pattern he needs to get *perfect*.

After he nails the physical shape of the uniform, he will try to re-create the camouflage print and the insignia. Then he can figure out the cap. He has his helmet and body armor, but the rest of his US Army battle dress is ruined. Ruined like Earth. Squandered by incompetent masterminds and petty bickering and foolish moral stands in the moment when *all of human history* balanced on the decisions of a few men and women.

Erik had command of MAJESTIC and he wasted it. He let Clayton walk all over him, collaborate with Iruvage, ensoul Blackbird, fly it off into space to roam the stars as a sociopath explorer with the end of the world as his origin story. Erik didn't stop him, didn't stop Iruvage, didn't stop the apocalypse, *couldn't save anyone*—a few hundred Kurds, but they're probably dead anyway, probably irradiated by the battle over Kurdistan, probably just corpses too cold and radioactive to rot in the snow—

He's stabbing the cloth. He shouldn't do that because there's nothing underneath except steel plate: but now his knife sinks hilt-deep into flesh, blood jets in Kurosawa spray across him, he stabs and stabs and screams and stabs and *Blackbird is responding,* filling the space beneath his knife with flesh, plucking the pattern suggested by his rage and reifying it so Erik can slaughter the guilty. The flesh has no skin: it could be white, it could be Black, it could be Clayton's, it could be Ssrin's beneath her scales, it could be his own—

Erik hurls the knife away. Staggers backward scream-crying. Chunks of meat bleed on his sewing table.

He can't figure out how it could have turned out better. Can't see a way to make it all right, even if he had a do-over.

Rosamaria has warned him to stay away from Ssrin: otherwise they do not speak. In his madness (definitely he is going mad) he's dreamt of wrapping himself up in her tendrils like a jellyfish's prey. Rosamaria will pump him full of alien thoughts and make him okay.

His "house" is Clayton's house. The Anacostia place. They accidentally created it when they first came aboard Blackbird, probably out of Rosamaria's memories of old visits, and Erik hasn't had the energy to make his own, so he's just crashing here. The real house has, of course, been set a fire and shattered by nuclear overpressure.

Erik's H&K 416 rests in a corner with his body armor. Maybe, if he'd secured the armor better, Anna couldn't have slid her pistol under it. Maybe then he could've used the 416 to shoot Ssrin. No, that was his mistake. He should've headshot Clayton first, and finished the abort . . .

. . . and then what? Blackbird would've crashed somewhere on Earth. *Axiorrhage* would have come to claim them. The right thing led to nothing but disaster.

He knows the moment the Exordia set its sights on Earth humanity was doomed. Even if they'd beaten *Axiorrhage*, more ships would've come to investigate Blackbird's call.

He just can't accept it. Because it seems like Clayton-think.

Someone knocks on his door.

Erik checks the peephole and his entire body stiffens. It's Clayton. Clayton's standing outside his door in an extremely flattering bodysuit. He's got a dance belt on, part of Erik notices, while the rest of him screams: *He* can't be here now! Erik has just accidentally conjured up a human steak and stabbed it to death!

"Erik?" Clayton calls, pretending to be unafraid. Erik knows his tell. He has his face mastered, but not his feet. "Erik, dude, can we talk? Ssrin's coming back to life. I was hoping you'd come with me and talk to her. We need to ... you know, there's still a chance to save some people on Earth, and I think if you and I got on the same page it could ... it could help."

He performs small graceful dance fidgets. Erik stares through the peephole with cold righteous fury.

"Also, dude," Clayton says roughly, "I'm not doing too well with all this, and I need somebody to talk to. Chaya's cool, but she's carrying too much already. Anna's enjoying herself and it freaks me out. Aixue's just gone. Khaje and Davoud want nothing to do with me. I need ... somebody."

He's not doing too well with all this? *We should abandon Earth.* He said that. He planned on this outcome. He was aware the whole time they were fighting to save Earth that it was a sham, a charade, a distraction to get Blackbird close to *Axiorrhage* and steal the wrongspace drive so Ssrin could bring the prize to her rebel friends.

Compared to a galaxy full of alien life, the people of Earth are very few. Especially if you don't really believe you're one of them.

"The next time I see you," Erik says, "I'm going to kill you. Unless Ssrin's there. Then I'll kill her first."

Clayton closes his eyes. He nods. Then he very gracefully departs.

Does it *suck* to be Clayton Navarro Hunt? Do his plans and schemes ... hurt him?

Well, fuck him. Why should Erik care?

He goes to clean up the dead meat. His stomach growls.

───※───

Anna's not avoiding her mom on *purpose*.

It's just that Khaje's stargazing with Davoud again. The man's gone odd. Anna understands him perfectly, though. All her life she's felt her soul in her trigger finger, ready to twitch. Davoud's soul is now equally refined. Ask the guy how he's doing and he'll say "Nominal."

He has lost the world but gained the universe. Maybe Khaje gets some relief from that. Possibly, also, Khaje gets something from Davoud's good looks, but Anna doesn't want to think about that. They're like ... thirty years apart? More? Less? She should know this.

She's also jealous that Davoud gets so much of her mom's attention.

The strength of her feelings for her mother terrifies her. Khaje wished for Anna's return. Nobody's ever wanted Anna to come *back* before. Anna has even found herself considering her mother's blunt grace. Is it normal to think your mom's beautiful? Is that some kind of Electra complex? Anna never really had a mom, growing up. She doesn't really have one now. But maybe, maybe yet—

But why should she get a second chance to know her mother, when so many people on Earth have lost their mothers, and their daughters, and their lives?

Anyway, she is probably confusing her own voracious, all-defying need to be *alive* with her mother's less sensual motives. Maybe Davoud is a little like Hamali. The son Khaje never got to raise.

Blackbird is driving them all mad. The god-ship may have stopped mutilating bodies, but it can never, ever stop being what it is. A tool for heightening signals. No wonder their grief has been so deep, so hard to shake.

Or maybe that's just what it's like when the world ends.

To distract herself from hunger and thoughts of hell, Anna takes long expeditions across the glass dance floor. It's infinite like a game level: you can keep going out forever, but past a point, shit gets weird. Fractal centipedes begin to scuttle across the edge of her vision. Whale-sounds groan from below. Immense structures suggest themselves in the darkness, only to collapse and recede as Anna infringes on them: might-have-been worlds shattered by the extrapolated logic of her existence.

Ssrin told her about the gods who made the universe. Blackbird was their tool . . . their limb.

Anna runs the edges of the comprehensible space. She flirts with madness: when a particularly grotesque extrusion from the Chaotic Fractal Realm uncurls before her, she says "Hey there, good-lookin'." She wonders if she could literally dream up something to fuck her, a giant silicone xenomorph. She's appallingly, inappropriately horny, hungry, thirsty, eager for cold water and hot blackened meat. Anna is and always has been a physical creature, someone who cannot find peace unless she has exhausted herself. She goes too hard. Back in the lost world, it was a problem.

Now, after all those loops through her own personal hell, it is a gift. She wants to know she's alive again. Wants to feel like she's used everything she has and more. Because now she knows . . . someday she's going back there again. Just like Ssrin, she's hellbound.

Nobody else feels that way, though. Nobody's much fun to be around.

"Rosamaria," she calls.

"Anna. I'm less human out here. Be careful."

"How's Ssrin?"

"Recovering. Her body has holographic properties, I think."

"Like . . . it's an optical illusion?"

Rosamaria laughs. "No. I mean that each part of her knows how to restore the whole."

It seems to Anna that human bodies should be this way too: don't we all start from a single cell? "So you're looking at her now? You're not afraid of her?"

"No estudio para saber más, sino para ignorar menos."

"What does that mean?"

Silence.

"Rosamaria?"

"I'm here."

"What are you feeding her?"

"All of us. But she likes the taste of you."

Anna shivers in delight. "Is Erik going to take his shot at her?"

"If he does, I won't let him."

"Cool. Cool. Has Ssrin given you a plan?"

"I need to find the author of the Cultratic Brand," Rosamaria says. "I need to know how Ssrin's people were made to be so . . . abominable. The universe dislikes them. They're errors."

"Uh-huh. Why's that important?"

"Because they're illegal amendments. And I want to make my own amendments. I want to fix everything. The source of the Cultratic Brand might tell me how."

Anna pounds through a field of ferns with faces in their leaves. "Everybody's gonna be gunning for you, Rosamaria. Like, the whole galaxy. You're a big deal."

"I know."

"Do you have any idea where to look for your, uh, tutor?"

"Khas."

Anna's heart hammers in her chest. "You mean—"

"Ssrin's home world."

"But that's space Mordor, dude. One does not simply fly in there. We barely got away from *one* Exordia ship."

"Ssrin must know a way."

"First she's got to have a way to get back to Earth. We've got to bring some kind of help. There are still people back there—"

"Maybe the two ways are the same," Rosamaria says. "Maybe the way to get help to Earth is to help the galaxy."

Anna kneels over the cyst.

Ssrin floats in a soup of oxygenated meat-broth, not breathing, very occasionally swallowing down one of her long necks. Anna taps her fist on the sac of membrane and discovers a slick of gross sweat: toxins purged from the carcass.

"Hey!" she shouts. "Hey, Kaa! Wake up!"

"*Go away,*" Ssrin says, through Anna's implant. "*I'm rotting in here.*"

"You're not. We're taking great care of you. Hey, I have kind of an intrusive personal question."

"*For a woman whose species is being exterminated, you're very cheerful.*"

"I never liked 'em much anyway," Anna says, and refuses to stop and dwell on this. "Remember how you said that serendure brought me to you? To fill a wound?"

"No. I've forgotten everything. Nerve trauma."

"Bullshit."

"What a perceptive thing you are."

"Serendure, baby," Anna says, and then, with a deep breath, because this makes her nervous, "You can't bite me for asking this time. Tell me. Was the wound in your life left by your sister?"

"I don't want to talk about this."

"That's what we call a soft yes." Ssrin's sister, Ssenenet. Whom Ssrin loved, and, somehow, drove away. "What did you do to her?"

"She was gracile. An azazophage. And I stopped protecting her."

"A what?"

"She believed the khai had evolved to consume the damnation of other species so that those others could achieve heaven. A willfully naive way to rationalize our pathology: as an act of service. She thought we could reform the Exordia as an argument toward salvation, not slaughter. She thought we could maintain peace through the gratitude of those we saved, instead of the fear of those we cowed."

"Sounds nice."

"Yes. When protecting her came to cost me too much, I resolved to show her how grateful the heavened species were for our help. She was so stubborn! When her attackers had cornered her she . . . refused to defend herself. Against all instinct and reason, she accepted hell and waited to die."

"And?"

"And I intervened. I killed her killers. I fed on them and from their meat I fed her in secret while she healed, so that no other khai would smell her weakness and finish her. She has never forgiven me."

"Oh, Ssrin."

"Why are you so drippy?"

"Oh, I'm sweating." Anna shakes a hand over the womb. "We do that when we run. Heat management. But you know all this. What do you do?"

"We're ambush predators. We can supercool ourselves by drawing blood into our torsos. We don't sweat, at least not in our rootstock. Why does your sweat taste so excited?"

With Ssrin she can be honest.

"Everyone's dying. Nobody's going to ask me to behave like a professional ever again. Nobody's going to dump me. I don't have any rent to pay. From now on, everyone I meet will be an alien, and I'll be an alien to them. There's other aliens out there, you said. Hundreds of kinds. A whole galaxy to explore. And I'm important, right? I have a special purpose. I'm not pinioned. I can do anything. I feel . . ."

She stumbles on how crazy she sounds.

"I care about saving whoever's left on Earth. I care about what happened. But I want . . . more. I want to see what happens *next*."

"*You know what happens next. Our story goes on. Same as it always has.*"

"Serendure."

Serendure trumped rath, in the end. It beat Erik's need to kill Clayton. Because he turned his gun on Ssrin before finishing Clayton: because he betrayed his own destiny.

If she doesn't stop Erik he's going to kill Clayton.

"*Stop sweating on me,*" Ssrin complains. "*You're aroused, and it smells funny.*"

"I'm not aroused."

"*You are. Your body is interpreting uncertainty and danger as excitement. You are psychologically aroused and receptive to stimuli. Which is better than despair. But don't secrete it on me.*"

"Don't shame my secretions. I love to secrete." She puts a hand on Ssrin's womb. "Hey, dude. Can I have Blackbird copy one of your drugs?"

"*For what?*

"It's a secrete."

Ssrin's fun-drug makes every touch a shivering pleasure. The slip of cool paradermis against her skin is just too much to bear: she has to stop and loosen her makeshift sports bra because she's getting so homesick for Tawakul. She's always had this thing where stuff touching her nipples makes her feel really melancholy. Does anyone else feel this?

"Rosamaria," she calls.

"Yes?"

"Do you get sad when things touch your nipples?"

"No."

"Cool. Do you mind if I fuck your boyfriends?"

"They're not my boyfriends."

"Your exes. Your obsessives."

"Which one?"

"Both of them." She's so bored of the sulking. The angst about whether they'll kill each other some more. Have some fun, guys. We're temporarily immortal. We should be at least temporarily immoral too.

"Don't get pregnant," Rosamaria says, with real concern. "I don't know what would happen. I might do something to the—"

"Let me handle that," Anna says. She has an IUD, and an unlimited supply of formfitting material with the warmth and texture of human skin. "I'm asking if you *mind*."

"I would," Rosamaria says, in a quite inhuman tone, "be grateful to have them distracted, actually. Everything in here is inside me, you know. I feel what they feel. That clot of rage is going to give me a stroke."

"High five," Anna says, and attempts to fist-bump the air. Nothing meets her touch.

"Anna. Is this a healthy decision? Trying to position yourself as a . . . sexual cure for their anger?"

Anna barks. Sexual cure! Her! "Woman, this isn't that."

"Isn't it?"

"I'm not doing this to fix them. I'm doing it because I want to have really fucked-up sex with men who want to hurt me and each other."

"Fine. Just don't get an infection. We don't have a doctor."

"Okay. I'll try not to die of ass fever."

She jogs up to Erik's house of misery, dressed just as she was when he jumped out of a helicopter and looked at her like she was the most interesting thing in the world. He's on the narrow porch, shirtless, making bullets: he can pull them from between his fingers now. He looks like a men's magazine cover, Alexander Skarsgård with a blond depression beard. Alexander Skarsgård is probably dead.

"Hey, good-lookin'," Anna calls, and giggles. "Wanna come for a jog?"

Erik looks at her with red-eyed disbelief.

She deduces that he's thinking about the moment when she shoved a pistol into his back and fired twice. She shrugs. "It wasn't about whether to do the right thing, Erik. It was about whether we should die *failing* to do the right thing. You said yes. I said no."

He does not react.

"Come on. We're going on a quest. Ssrin's rebel friends are out there. They can help us. Gotta stay in shape for the fight, my man."

Erik pinches a cartridge between his fingertips and studies the tiny writing on the brass. "We're going on a mission for an alien thug. An incomprehensible sociopath who manipulated us into abandoning our world in favor of her agenda. Who manipulated *you* into shooting me at the only moment when I possibly could've made a difference. The difference between the universe rewarding her for her treachery, and killing her for it. By letting her live, I failed to create a world where betraying the entire human species is rewarded with death. I allowed the cowardice of conspiring with the aliens that murdered our planet to be rewarded with our personal survival, while our loved ones and subordinates burn down there. I continue to fail everyone she betrayed with every moment I let her live. And everyone's just fine with it."

Now Anna's annoyed. She jogs up his front path and mounts the railing, swings her legs over, sits there above him with her thighs practically touching his. He looks away in discomfort. Anna shoves him, one-handed, and leaps down into the space between his body and the rail.

"Rath," she says. "We, us, all of us: we're not pinioned. We can make a difference. But we need our stories to do that. And we can't afford your story to be about catatonic misery and murdering Clayton. We need you to *fight*."

His lips curl. "There's nothing to fight for anymore."

"Sure there is. A chance to go back home and save whoever's left. And revenge. Kill the bastards who did it. And remembrance! Who's going to remember Earth? Is the galaxy going to know what happens here? No one knew who the Kurds were before the genocide, and then everyone knew us for the genocide. Don't you want people to know more about humanity than how we died? And fuck it: I want to live. I want to keep living as long as I can. I want to do things and feel things and think things and eat things and fuck things." She shoves him again, up on tiptoe. "Giving up is not *the right thing to do*, Erik."

He glares at her, breathing hard. His wide flat pecs shine with sweat. A bullet peeks from his clenched fist, like lipstick. "I can't keep doing this. It has to end. I have to kill him, or I'll . . . he'll trick me into doing things, again, things I can't live with . . . and you'll let him. You'll stop me from stopping him. You'll help him get away with it."

"Maybe," she says, looking up at him, breathing and sweating just as hard, nearly as bare-skinned. Really ideal. "Or maybe I'll help you stop him. Who knows? Not you. Only me. Aim your anger at the enemy."

"He *is* the enemy."

"So am I. I helped him. Why don't you punish me?"

"What?"

Her stomach is light and empty. She is glowing to the marrow with the high of the run. "You guys wasted a lot of time bickering over a woman who didn't want to be involved," she says. "Pick up one who does. I mean, fuck it. We're not going to feel any worse. Why not?" She winks at him, outrageously, even as her thighs tense with a wildcat thrill. She has such appetites now. Death demands life. Oh, euphoria, do not depart me, not yet: for as I have you, so I love to live.

Erik looks her over, breathing hard. He seems astonished. Possibly he did not know that he could ever want anything again. "I don't want to hurt you," he says.

"You won't. You're too good. But I'll make you want to. I'll make you want to really bad."

"Come inside."

She backs up a step. "No."

"Anna. Make up your mind."

"Both of you," she says. "That's my game. Come on. You never tried it before?"

"You're crazy."

"I'm really high," she corrects him. "Ssrin drugs. Everything feels good."

"Then I can't accept your consent—"

"A fair concern. But I made this decision before I took the bite." She fades another step back. "Gonna let me go, Erik?"

He has a strong intuition about the right thing to do here, the honorable and emotionally safe thing, which is the thing he would do on Earth, if faced with a proposition like this.

But Earth is gone, and he's alone, and he wants her so bad. He wants to feel something that can't help feeling good.

She sees him break that rightness. Snap it like a bone. For her. God, that's a thrill.

Clayton's house is a conspiracy of light. It has no structure: the walls are illusions, the light comes from nowhere. His front door is just a curtain. He peeks out with a raised eyebrow. "Are you drunk?"

"Pretty much." Anna holds up a pale fang. Blackbird copied everything, tooth and hinge and implant and all. "Want some of it?"

He looks at her, and then at Erik. "Sure," he says. "End of the world. Perfect time. Are you both coming?"

"That's the idea," Anna says.

"Ah," he says. "A Manager Troi."

———※———

ISVRIϟ

The humans have been fucking. Ssrin can tell by the way they now penetrate invisible quarantines around each other. Possibly a complication, possibly a relief; hard to know. Khai mating is at once violently physical and without much lasting sentiment. You find a mate who can make you make some eggs, then you find a male to fertilize one or all of them, then (depending on how detente-traditional versus nouveau-ssovÈ you are) you coax and beat and threaten and blackmail him into sticking around until the young are ready to eat one another. Or you can sell your eggs, or form a female detente, or give them to a male mother, or—

So many ways to bring a khai soul into this world. And only one way they ever leave.

Ssrin was with the eana divorcees long enough to think of sex as a reciprocal exchange of pleasures, divorced from the reproductive act. It could be a massage, a drug, a meal, an electrical shock, a beating: as long as it is the learning of another's inner rewards. The universe's way for us to say to one another, *I'm glad you exist. I want you to feel glad too.*

All the greatest khai art asks whether it is good to exist, when existence is followed by eternal suffering. Some say: yes. Some say: fuck this whole cosmos and what it has done to us. Take anything you can get, and hurt the rest. Make them pay.

Ssrin does not feel glad to exist. She is unbearably restless. Her ruined body can barely sustain the tension and uncertainty, the coiled-under-a-stone waiting. There's so much ahead. So much that could go wrong. Not even Rosamaria knows the whole truth (thank God, though not the God of her birth: never thank It).

Ssrin has seven unpinioned human souls as her companions, and an eighth as a god-avatar in Blackbird. They are military and narrative assets of incredible worth. The martyrdom of Earth is an awful gift: Ssrin will use it as hard as she can. In this galaxy of empirical faith, a new parable can be mightier than a fleet.

She was a khai supremacist most of her life, until she met Abdiel. She would never have believed that seven gangly distance-apes could have survived this.

They aren't much. But they refuse to be written out of the universe.

They gather on the glass floor of their commons. Ssrin's waiting in the cast-off afterbirth of her healing egg. Li Aixue is the first to speak. "What happens now, Ssrin? Where do we go?"

She shows them.

Gasps of horror. "What *is* that?" Khaje demands.

"A That."

"Yes, but a *what*?" Aixue says in fascination.

"A That. A holy corpse. This one is called Dhâtu That." Nothing. The com bead translator must be struggling. "The Young Calvary, Tauri Caitya, the Winking, the Big Sarira, Party-khlyst . . ." Is any of this reaching them? "It's a dead acatalept-god. One of the architects of creation. This one was Auno."

"Why, in the whole infinite universe," Chaya demands, "did this one *happen* to end up in our galaxy?"

"The universe is infinite, and so were the gods. Their corpses are infinitely many too: reified as flaws out of the cooling cosmos. This is one of two in our galaxy, and the only one easily reached by ship. It has become a shrine. And a kind of slum." Ssrin yearns to be there. On the Winking she will see old friends again, and old foes who deserve to know she kept the faith they doubted. And she can finally eat some real meat without slow-cooking it in her scout stomach. "The Exordia treats it as neutral ground, out of feigned respect for faith. We'll go there. Bring the news of Blackbird. Show your unpinioned souls to those who pray for change."

Those who pray. The shorinor in their world-ships, the coagula brooding in the deep orbits of neutron stars. The eana whose suffering is art. All their souls pinioned. All their paths forward confined by the Exordia superstory.

The humans could change that. The galaxy could rise up and break the iron peace.

Or the Exordia could claim Blackbird, and complete their new covenant with æVae, Whose Name Points Below. The very morality of the areteia rewritten in their image. A new judgment for all souls. The larders of heaven opened, the unborn and the righteous butchered to roast on the fires of hell. Final revenge on the universe that damned them.

How she would have rejoiced at that thought, once.

"What about Earth?" Erik asks.

"*Axiorrhage* will pursue us," Ssrin tells him. "Even now Maessari's pickets wait for us to accelerate and reveal ourselves. She will follow us to Dhâtu That. We will buy Earth some time before the pinion falls. A darkling disc for Earth. But do not tell them that."

"What about everyone dying down there *now*?"

"Kurdistan," Khaje says.

"Kurdistan?" Chaya says.

"Earth is Kurdistan now. A little place no one in the galaxy had heard of. And then it was bombed and scoured. No one even bothered to light any cigarettes on Earth's pyre. But now we are going out, into the galaxy, to tell people what has been done to us, and to ask for help. The whole world has become Kurdistan."

Ssrin follows Khaje's warm track. "Your people's salvation lies ahead of us. We have no way to return to Earth and break the Exordia interdict. To do that, we would need to convince the galaxy to challenge its reigning superpower. I ask nothing less of you than your help in that war. Defeat the Exordia, and we can return to save your people."

"Fine," Erik growls. "I want to fight." He seizes Clayton's hand: crushing or caring. "We want to fight."

Clayton squeezes back. Ssrin thinks he does not know how much he needs Erik's clarity of purpose. Left alone, he would become something he could not allow, he would tear himself apart. But as long as he is here, then Ssrin is protected from Erik. Not safe—never that—but safer.

She needs that protection. It'll be a long crossing by drive mast to the Winking. No one wants to use the wrongspace drive again, and they have no ramline to shoot them across the gap. Months eating human flesh and drinking tasteless water. Months for Ssrin to make them ready, to hone their souls into weapons that can pilot war machines and frustrate operancy. But, also, months for their rage and grief to corrode them . . .

Davoud Qasemi calls out from the cockpit. "*Tell me where to fly.*"

Ssrin shows him. HD 23514, in the Pleiades cluster, four hundred light-years away. Blackbird has never crossed between stars before. There will be radiation and madness and unforeseen disaster. She wonders, in the way that khai wonder, ambushing and ambushed by an idea from the thicket of her mind, if she should try to talk Anna into another wrongspace jump. No. Kill that idea, lest you kill Anna, and go undefended against *her*.

Rosamaria turns one of her new telescopes to capture Earth. The humans gather, shoulder to shoulder, to watch their home recede into the galactic night.

Who did it? Ssrin wonders. Who set Iruvage on her trail? Who taught him *exactly* how to disrupt her operancy—betraying an intimate personal knowledge of Ssrin's soul? Who would defy the Unnumbered Fleet and the Capitate to steal a demiurge from the universe's creation, promising salvation to those who follow her?

There is only one possibility. Ssrin refuses to think the name yet. It sticks in her like a swollen duct.

She gathers her heads together and stares forward, into the stars. One world dead. Tens of thousands still in play.

"Anna," she whispers, through their private link. "Come stand with me?"

And she does. Ssrin puts an arm around her waist, a neck around her shoulder. Ceases, for a little while, to think. To hurt.

CODA: THOSE WHO FACE DEATH

"Do what we did, Arîn. Survive."

And somehow they have.

Even with the wounded and the children they were safely across the peak before the battle erupted behind them. The alien lights and the bitter cold kept them moving, but, most of all, the sound of jets: coming in from Iran, from Iraq, from Turkey, from everywhere that bombers come. That was how Arîn explained it to the young. *It's an air raid. We must go.*

She'd planned to follow old Bakhtiari nomad paths north, up and into the mountains. But when silence fell—when the battle ended—people wanted to go back. And who could blame them? Her heart still reaches for that last sight she had of Tawakul, looking back from high above: the scoured rock and burnt-out brush of the bomb site. Black trees as gravestones for those who died in the caves. And beyond them, gentle and good, the valley, like a green cup in a great white hand. The river a strip of reflected aurora. God, God, what beauty! This place she would have died to defend.

She wanted to die for it. It was the best thing she could imagine, to be a martyr like Sakine Cansiz and Mazlum Doğan. A girl from nowhere, remembered by everyone. (And maybe there was just a little bit of adolescent angst in the wish too. The PKK made some very good music videos.)

But she chose not to.

She told them what Khaje told Anna, what Anna told her. "They're fighting to give us time to run. To survive. We don't need Tawakul to survive. We only need *us.*"

The Kurds are alive. Let no one say the Kurds are dead. The Kurds are alive.

Later the lights began again, now high up in the sky, higher than the aurora itself. Tiny flashes of white light that met shining filaments and broke apart into widening stars of fire. All at once Arîn realized what was happening, and cried out in rage: this final joke, this ultimate betrayal. The Americans and the Russians and everyone else had used their last, spiteful measure. They were going to nuke Kurdistan.

But the missiles never fell.

Not here, at least. The PKK (who rescued some Ugandans from a minefield to the northwest) say there is word from Rojhilat and Iran of incredible devastation. It is possible that the Zagros Mountains may, for the first time in Arîn's life, be one of the safest places on Earth.

Is she a coward? Is she breaking her vow, just by surviving?

Khaje survived so much. And now Arîn *knows* she was not a coward. Not her and not her daughter. It is easy to die for your people. It is much harder to live after the dying is done.

Now she turns to Haydar, who is walking beside her, and says: "What do you think happened to Khaje?"

"She's up there," Haydar says, without hesitating at all. "With my mother. And Shanar. And some sheep."

"Up . . . in heaven?"

"No, heval," Haydar says, laughing. "In the spaceship. Didn't you see it go? The first Kurdish spaceship. And my mom and Shanar are in it."

Arîn shakes her head and sighs.

In the dark, her comrades are singing: Shahid Mezgin's song for the martyr Safakan, Shahid Mezgin who herself became a martyr fighting the Turks. Arîn used to dream of dying like Shahid Mezgin.

Now she thinks: I am glad someone is left to sing her song.

I am glad I am alive to hear it.

ACKNOWLEDGMENTS

This was supposed to be a fun book between installments of the Baru Cormorant series. I finished the first draft in August 2017. Then publishing happened, and COVID, and here I am writing these acknowledgments in early summer 2023.

That was enough time for America to betray the Kurds again, deserting our allies in Syria in 2019. In Iraq, Kurdish politics remain bitterly divided between the KDP and PUK. And support for the PKK has become an issue in Swedish negotiations with Turkiye over NATO membership.

Even a fun book needs a lot of work. I owe thanks to my expert readers, whether paid or volunteer, who helped me do a better job with characters from Uganda, Kurdistan, Iran, China, the Philippines, and the "crossroads inhabited by whirlwinds" where Rosamaria lives. Most of my research time went toward the Kurdish characters. Choman Hardi's *Gendered Experiences of Genocide* was my mainstay for understanding Anfal and the women who survived it. Arianne Shahvisi's paper "Beyond Orientalism: Exploring the Distinctive Feminism of Democratic Confederalism in Rojava" was also an important reference. A real scholar would have gone deeper into primary sources, including Öcalan's own writing and the works of Murray Bookchin. I didn't read any of those. Instead I wrote about fighter jets and particle beams. I'm a fraud.

I also owe thanks to everyone in the cultural Discord servers I pestered, especially those who stepped up to translate ridiculous things into Farsi, Mexican Spanish, Russian, Chinese, or Sorani Kurdish with little context. All errors and misrepresentations are my own. As President Obama would say: let me be clear. If you find something of yourself in these characters, I am glad. If you find something I have thoroughly fucked up, I'm sorry.

Thanks also to the unpaid heroes who helped me with warp field physics, military dialogue and protocol, mathematics and cosmology, nuclear weapon design and effects, and the behavior of tiny black holes. In particular, members of the ToughSF Discord, including Ken Burnside of Ad Astra Games for how to conduct a strategic nuclear attack on aliens, Luke Campbell for warp field revelations, Alex Herbst for patient math explanations, and Gerrit Bruhaug for the lowdown on fusion drives.

The proposed relationship between prime numbers, self-organizing criticality, pink noise, and spontaneous symmetry breaking is a fictional conceit. The ideas that I have messily collaged together to support this conceit are nonfiction, although subject to my own flawed understanding (or my consciously selective reading). I am not wholly sure that the account of modern physics as a product of spontaneous symmetry breaking in the early universe will survive new research. But Aixue's question—why do we see a universe that seems fine-tuned for life?—is definitely of real interest to cosmologists.

Several passages in this book pay tribute to authors I read when I was young. Attentive or annoyed readers will catch nods to Diane Duane, Vonda McIntyre, Greg Bear's *Eon*, and Michael Crichton. I wasn't young when I read Jeff Vander-Meer but he's in there too (*Acceptance* is my favorite).

I also owe thanks to the Lego Group, to my fellow BZP users CrypticIdentity and KopakaX, and to the Māori people. If you know you know.